IVAN
GONCHAROV

OBLOMOV

The sly, subversive side of the nineteenth-century Russian literary character – the one which represents such a contrast to the titanic exertions of Tolstoy and Dostoevsky – was most fully realized in Ivan Goncharov's 1859 masterpiece, OBLOMOV. This magnificent farce about a gentleman who spends the better part of his life in bed is a reminder of the extent to which humor, in the hands of a comic genius, can be used to explore the absurdities and injustices of a social order.

EVERYMAN,
I WILL GO WITH THEE,
AND BE THY GUIDE,
IN THY MOST NEED
TO GO BY THY SIDE

IVAN GONCHAROV

Oblomov

Translated from the Russian by Natalie Duddington
with an Introduction by Richard Freeborn

E V E R Y M A N ' S   L I B R A R Y

Alfred A. Knopf   New York   London   Toronto

124

THIS IS A BORZOI BOOK
PUBLISHED BY ALFRED A. KNOPF

First included in Everyman's Library, 1932
Introduction, Bibliography and Chronology Copyright © 1992 by
Everyman's Library
Typography by Peter B. Willberg
Third printing (US)

US website: www.randomhouse.com/everymans

ISBN: 0-679-41729-X (US)
1-85715-124-0 (UK)

A CIP catalogue reference for this book is available from the
British Library

Library of Congress Cataloging-in-Publication data
Goncharov. Ivan Aleksandrovich, 1812–1891.
[Oblomov. English]
Oblomov / Ivan Goncharov.
p. cm.—(Everyman's library)
Includes bibliographical references.
ISBN 0-679-41729-X
PG3337.G601213 1992 92-52923
891.73'3–dc20 CIP

Book design by Barbara de Wilde and Carol Devine Carson

Printed and bound in Germany by GGP Media GmbH, Pössneck

CONTENTS

v

INTRODUCTION

'In each of us,' wrote the radical critic Dobrolyubov on the first appearance of Goncharov's masterpiece, 'there resides a significant part of Oblomov ...' In 1859, when these words were written, they did not mean exactly what they may be taken to mean nowadays, yet they acknowledged the simple fact that Oblomov as a type had features with which every reader could easily identify. Archetypally characteristic of an ultimate, not to say pathological, lethargy, a laziness raised to the level of an ideal Arcadian existence, a total slothfulness of such majestic dimensions it has something in common with religious zealotry or political fanaticism, Oblomov has acquired an appeal far transcending the historical circumstances in which he originated or the national characteristics of which he was thought so typical.

Everyone is lazy. No human being can ever deny the impulse to do nothing. On the other hand, laziness as an idyll, as a vision of earthly paradise justified in Oblomov's case by his own philosophy of 'Oblomovism', flies so splendidly in the face of all conventional ideas about the purpose of life it has the unsettling, seditious glamour one associates with Hamlet's self-doubting vengefulness or the comically exaggerated altruism of a Don Quixote. Should human beings be like this? The image of Oblomov naturally invites such a question. It is one that many people asked on first reading the novel, but none put the question as artfully or as tendentiously as did Dobrolyubov in his famous review of the work, 'What is Oblomovism?'

The appearance of Goncharov's novel in 1859 was fortuitous. Nineteenth-century Russian history was dominated in the middle decades by the defeat suffered in the Crimean War of 1854–5. The repressive, militaristic policies of Nicholas I were so discredited by the defeat that his successor, Alexander II, felt obliged to embark on far-reaching internal reforms. The intention was to give the country institutions which were common in Europe but so far largely unknown in

Russia – some viable form of local government, an independent judiciary, an updated army and expanded higher education. In this way Russia could be modernized.

The single most essential reform was the abolition of serfdom. Semi-feudal Russia, with a vast peasant population mostly enserfed to a numerically small landowning class, had suffered defeat at the hands of France and England in the Crimean War chiefly because it was economically and socially backward. The abolition of serfdom could therefore be justified on socio-economic grounds, but the moral grounds for such radical change were far stronger. As soon as the need for reforms became officially recognized, demands for something far more sweeping began to be heard. Under conditions of secret police oppression and government censorship such demands were expressed not in street demonstrations, nor in any form of overt protest, but in journalistic polemic couched often in an Aesopian or oblique language. The most outspoken journal in this respect was *The Contemporary*. Under the guidance of the leading 'progressive' of the day, N. G. Chernyshevsky (1828–89), the journal became the mouthpiece for a dissident, younger generation of the Russian intelligentsia who contemplated wholesale reforms amounting virtually to revolution. The consequence was a bitter journalistic polemic in which battle lines were clearly drawn between liberal and radical views, between hidebound concern to preserve landowners' privileges and the need to liberate the Russian peasantry from centuries of servitude.

At the height of this polemic, just as the reform process was beginning, Goncharov published his masterpiece, *Oblomov*. All the manifold viewpoints seemed to converge like rays in the focus of this novel. For Nikolay Dobrolyubov (1836–61), Chernyshevsky's young protégé on *The Contemporary* and the journal's leading literary critic, the novel's principal merit was the way it implied that the serf-owning nobility had become morally corrupted by its privileges. In a brilliant, but sweeping, interpretation Dobrolyubov suggested that all the major heroes in Russian literature prior to the appearance of Oblomov showed his traits of indecisiveness, weakness of will and emotional immaturity to a greater or lesser degree. The reason for this was that they were all rendered ineffectual by belonging to the serf-owning nobility. The master–serf relationship could be seen to be morally corrupting to both parties. In Goncharov's novel the servility of the serf Zahar could be seen to be so closely interwoven with Oblomov's role as his master, the two appeared so mutually dependent on each other, it was virtually impossible to make a distinction between them. Oblomov consequently exhibited a 'moral servitude' which was to all intents and purposes the single most interesting aspect of his personality.

Dobrolyubov's review of the novel helped to ensure its popularity. His was a judgement on the novel and its hero which admirably served the polemical need to show how corrupt and retrograde was the Russian nobility. He implicitly posed the question: How could the nobility, supposedly the leading class in Russian society, possibly play a leading role in the moral revolution needed if a society based for so long on serfdom were to be transformed into one based on justice and freedom? His implicit answer, symptomatic of the Aesopian way in which issues had to be raised in the circumstances of the time, was that the serf-owning nobility was morally disqualified from playing such a role. Leadership should therefore pass to the younger, radical intelligentsia. The younger intelligentsia understood only too well that it was the progressive types such as Stolz, the positive hero in the novel, who were to inherit the future and become the instruments of moral change.

In representing Goncharov's novel as an important item in the polemic over Russia's future, Dobrolyubov was clearly enhancing its reputation as a masterpiece of Russian realism. Simultaneously he committed the injustice of forcing upon it the straitjacket of a tendentious interpretation. Most Russian critical interpretations have been coloured by Dobrolyubov's approach. Non-Russian, predominantly Western, interpretations have stressed the universally typical features of *Oblomov*. It is a novel which, like so many other great works of nineteenth-century Russian literature, drew sustenance from the pressure for change in Russian society while offering portraiture of such scale and psychological depth it can be read and appreciated without the need to know too much about its provenance. However, in the case of *Oblomov*, the issue of whether or not it is an objective portrait of a type, or a subjective one deriving chiefly from the character of the author, naturally comes to the fore.

Ivan Alexandrovich Goncharov (1812–91) was not born into the nobility. He was the son of a prosperous grain merchant in Simbirsk on the Volga, birthplace also of Lenin (after whom the city was renamed Ulyanovsk), and he received his early education at a boarding school in the locality. So much of his writer's experience derived from this Simbirsk world it would be hard to exaggerate its influence. Nostalgia transformed it into a paradise of quietude and contentment that is mirrored for us in the long prose poem 'Oblomov's Dream', the source of the eventual novel. If Goncharov romanticized the semi-feudal, landowners' world of Oblomovka, the cradle from which his hero, Oblomov, never seemed to escape, there was also in his attitude a subversively critical tone. Goncharov himself was not of that world. He could understand the temptation to indolence which such a condition offered, but the realities of his own life enforced a more workaday approach. He liked to think of his own literary achievement as one that showed the struggle between romanticism and realism in Russian social life. About his own life, though, as about his prose style, there was always a leisureliness and expansiveness, a surface laziness containing depths of meaning often unnoticed by the casual eye and bearing a resemblance to the unceasing flow of the Volga by which he spent his childhood. Such ingredients as the romantic and the realistic merge in his work, seeming often indistinguishable as separate attitudes, liquefying in the sense of flux which dominated Goncharov's view of the world. So, though he may have been born outside the landowning nobility and not destined to enjoy its privileges, he knew it so nearly and had the sensibility to observe it so sympathetically he could be said to have chronicled it from the inside more truthfully than such famous contemporaries of his as Turgenev or Tolstoy who were hereditary members of that class.

Periods of study at the Moscow School of Commerce and

INTRODUCTION

Moscow University during the 1820s took him away from Simbirsk, but the most important transition in his life occurred when he finally left his place of birth in 1835 to embark on a career in government service in St Petersburg. The greater part of his life was to be spent in the imperial capital where he always remained on the fringes rather than at the centre of the literary world. After his fashion he was 'a man of the forties', meaning a member of the first generation of the Russian intelligentsia whose ideas and aspirations were so profoundly moulded by the critic V. G. Belinsky (1811–48). Apart from his seminal role in encouraging literature to be realistic – that is to say, socially committed and unsparing in the exposure of social injustices – Belinsky also upheld a Westernist approach to Russia's problems. This meant that it should follow the example set by Peter the Great and strive to become more Western, as opposed to the conservative, Slavophile approach which emphasized the importance of past religious and social values in securing a specific non-European path of development. Goncharov became heir to both these attitudes and both are equally traceable in his work. His first novel of 1847, *An Ordinary Story*, presented the issues chiefly in terms of a contrast between rural and urban life, between the romantic notions of a young man nurtured in the country and the hard realities of urban pragmatism as personified in the young man's uncle, a St Petersburg bureaucrat. The myths of the nephew's romantic idealism are gradually stripped from him when confronted by the uncle's hardheaded arguments. Ironically the nephew learns his lesson all too well and makes the profitable if loveless marriage to which his uncle may have guided him, only for the uncle to regret how all fresh, romantic spontaneity seems to have gone from his own life in the souring of his own marriage.

Goncharov did not marry, though he studied the ways of love with the same appreciative sensibility he brought to his observation of the nobility. A marginalized, spectator's view, interested but uninvolved, dominated his attitude to the human scene, but ironically enough, for someone who seemed so content to remain on the sidelines of life, he saw more of the world than any of his illustrious contemporaries. In 1852, to his friends' astonishment, he joined the voyage of a Russian ship, the frigate *Pallas*, on a diplomatic and trading mission to Japan and the Far East and spent nearly three years in circumnavigating the globe. The result was a brilliant travelogue, *The Frigate Pallas* (1858), which described various colourful ports of call from a Russian provincial point of view, dispelling all illusions of romance in faraway places in its realistic appraisal of foreign reality while paying respectful, often appreciative, attention to the beauties of Japan, the ultimate destination of the voyage. The Crimean War curtailed it. Goncharov returned home and for some years was employed as a censor in the Ministry of the Interior, an employment which he apparently found neither demeaning nor incongruous. Meanwhile, the experience of the round-the-world voyage had entered his writer's soul. It was to have a transforming effect upon the masterpiece which he had been slowly gestating throughout the period 1848–59.

In 1849 he published 'Oblomov's Dream' as a separate work. It described with an abundance of poetic detail, in a prose as epic and slow-moving as the Volga, the virtually static world of Oblomovka, Oblomov's country estate where he was born and grew up. Positioned in the eventual novel as a kind of climax to Part I, it is the culminating moment in the elaborate, moment-by-moment picture of Oblomov's static, dressing-gown existence, the longest single scene in the whole of Russian literature. The debt owed by Russian realism to the theatre is clear enough in this opening scene of Goncharov's novel. We tend to witness Oblomov as if he were offered to us in the stage setting of his run-down St Petersburg apartment. Depth, or a degree of biographical reference, is given to his portrayal by the gradual unfolding of his childhood experience in the sleep-dominated world of Oblomovka in his 'Dream'. As a result, Part I of the novel, including the 'Dream', and the early chapters of Part II describing the arrival of Stolz, comprise an elaborately sustained static, single-scene portrait of Oblomov, the consequence, perhaps, of a view of the novel as a genre devoted principally to portraiture which was the view prevailing in Russian literature during the 1840s.

INTRODUCTION

It seems that Goncharov took his unfinished novel with him on his voyage round the world. Even if this were not so, we do know that it was not until he visited Marienbad in the summer of 1857 that he managed to complete it. In an inspired seven weeks of writing, a burst of creative energy he was never able to repeat, he wrote most of the remaining three Parts. They tell the story of Oblomov's love for Olga, the end of their relationship and the gradual return of Oblomov to the chrysalis-like existence of his Oblomovism in the company of Agafya Matveyevna, the woman whom he marries and who has his son, Andryusha. The novel in these sections has a constant, if slow-flowing, movement to it. It tells of the fluctuating relationship between hero and heroine, the hero's fluctuating fortunes and his eventual surrender to a placid decline. It is as if something of the fluidity associated with the sea has overtaken what originated as a landlocked, immobile study of a dressing-gown existence. It is as if a novel characteristic of the 1840s in its preoccupation with static portraiture has acquired the dimensions of a near-epic. The resulting work not only explores the experience of its hero in minute, cumulative detail over the course of a single day, it also gives a virtually complete picture of his life from birth to death. In doing so, it established new norms of portraiture in the Russian realistic novel and acquired a stature that has since earned it a place among the masterpieces of nineteenth-century Russian literature.

Whether the picture of Russian life which we find in *Oblomov*, particularly in its hero, can be said to be grounded in reality, or whether it derives chiefly from Goncharov's own experience, is a question that has been actively debated by commentators ever since the novel first appeared. One must, of course, respect Goncharov's own view that he did not write one great novel but a triptych of novels, starting with *An Ordinary Story* in 1847, followed by *Oblomov* in 1859 and *The Precipice* (a manifestly less successful work) in 1869. He liked to claim in retrospect that these were three galleries which showed the passage of Russian social consciousness from romanticism to realism. The central frame in this triptych – *Oblomov* – was devoted to the 'sleep' of Russian life, while the third 'gallery' was devoted to the 'awakening'. Such claims for his work seem unduly grandiose. More apposite is the claim at the end of his 'Better Late Than Never', a statement of his aims as a writer written in somewhat aggrieved terms ten years after his last novel appeared:

That which did not grow and bear fruit within me, what I have not seen, have not observed, have not experienced in my life is inaccessible to my pen! I have (or had) my own field, my own basis, just as I have my own homeland, my native air, my friends and enemies, my own world of observations, impressions and recollections – and I wrote only *what I experienced, what I thought and felt, what I loved, what I saw closely and knew* – in a word, I wrote *both my own life and whatever accrued to it.**

The accretion of experience to his own life was doubtless as slow and cumulative a process as the gradual, multifaceted accumulation of details which contribute to the 'lazy image' of his hero Ilya Ilyitch Oblomov. First revealed as he is to the reader lying in bed one morning in his flat in Gorohovy Street, his most striking initial characteristic is a strange indefiniteness, as if he is hardly distinguishable from his dressing-gown. Vagueness characterizes his age – thirty-two or -three – his medium height (unverifiable by normal standards since he is only seen on his feet on one occasion during the day) and his pleasant appearance. Significant is the qualifying sentence in the opening paragraph: 'His attitude and the very folds of his dressing-gown expressed the same untroubled ease as his face.' The indefiniteness points to a principle owing something to Gogolian techniques of characterization in which the comic exaggeration of one feature only achieves full meaning when it is 'placed', as Oblomov is 'placed' in his realistically detailed, down-at-heel setting. Accompanying the process, and emerging as a kind of *alter ego* to the hero, the second partner in a comic double act, is that living embodiment of seediness, prevarication and endearing indolence, his serf manservant Zahar.

The day, incidentally, is 1 May (probably in 1843), the

*The emphases are Goncharov's.

beginning of spring, and the nearest thing to a crisi[s] overtaken Oblomov's life. It transpires that he is being obliged to find somewhere else to live. If that were not bad enough, he has also received a most unpleasant letter from his estate warning of poor harvests and serious lack of income. To confound him still further, he finds himself besieged, in the manner of a French farce, by a succession of visitors.

There is the first visitor, Volkov, for example, who comes 'straight from the cold' of a St Petersburg social whirl into which Oblomov refuses to be drawn. Then there is Sudbinsky who enthuses about a successful career in government service which Oblomov finds far too exacting and demanding. Penkin, the journalist, who turns up next, provides the first occasion on which Oblomov jumps to his feet. Then comes the totally indeterminate visitor Alexeyev, 'an incomplete, impersonal shadow of the human crowd, its dull echo, its dim reflection', a sinisterly characterless portent of the final visitor that morning, the Mihey Andreyevich Tarantyev who is eventually to prey on Oblomov and almost ruin him. All these visitors in their largely caricature, one-dimensional fashion provide contrasts to the predominantly static image of Oblomov. In so doing they ironically illuminate the superiority of his refusal to 'play the game', as it were, to be a socialite, to be successful in a career, to be an intellectual devoted to what could be considered 'politically correct'; and this last rejection of conformity is by far the most instructive and revealing.

The conversation between Oblomov and Penkin becomes heated over the question – close, evidently, to Goncharov's own heart – of the need for a writer to show greater concern for the human qualities of those he portrays:

'Give me man,' Oblomov said; 'love him....'

'Love usurers, sanctimonious prigs, stupid officials – do you hear that? What are you talking about? One can see you don't go in for literature!' Penkin protested warmly. 'No, they must be denounced, cast out from citizenship, from society....'

'Cast out from society!' Oblomov began with sudden inspiration, jumping to his feet. 'That's forgetting that there is a higher element in this unworthy vessel; that, however corrupt, he is a man – the same as yourself. Cast him out! And how will you cast him out from humanity, from nature, from the mercy of God?' he almost shouted, with blazing eyes.

'That's going a bit too far!' Penkin said in his turn with surprise.

Oblomov saw that he also had gone too far. He subsided, stood still for a moment, yawned, and slowly lay down again.

Not, admittedly, a very cogent defence of individualism, but at least, for Oblomov, a statement of principle that can also embrace his fallen condition and justify his right not to be cast out of humanity and nature and the mercy of God. For the whole of this opening scene of the novel fairly obviously presents Oblomov in a censorious light, as a type perhaps to be denounced and cast out of society, since the critical attitudes epitomized by his visitors tend to take priority over any other estimates of his human and social worth. His own self-deluding vision of himself as an invincible conqueror like Napoleon, the compensatory ideal which he erects in his imagination, can seem both touching and pathetic. It has an arrogance about it that is expressed openly in his refusal to consider himself the same as *other people*. *Other people* are, as he puts it, 'God-forsaken wretches, rough, uncultured people who live in some attic in dirt and poverty ... What are "other people?" ... They are people who clean their own boots, dress themselves, and though they sometimes look like gentlemen, it's mere pretence, they have never had a servant; if they have no one to send on an errand they run themselves; they think nothing of stirring the wood in the stove or of dusting ...'

Zahar, who remarks, gloomily and pejoratively, that lots of Germans are like that, connives in his master's self-delusion, and hardly surprisingly: they are both products of the same background, that nursery idyll of Oblomovka to which Oblomov himself is heir, which cocooned him in childhood and produced a kind of romantic infantilism in him as an adult. The dream of a cosy, summer idyll which is at the heart of Oblomov's ideal, at the heart of his 'Oblomovism', necessarily repudiates adult responsibility. To disregard the ideal, though, to cast it out, would be unjust. It may turn conventional values on their head, it may not be what 'other people' want, but society, in Oblomov's view (as he expresses it to Stolz), has no centre, no depth, nothing vital to it: 'All these society people are dead men, men fast asleep, they are worse than I am! What is their aim in life? They do not lie in bed like me, they dash backwards and forwards every day like flies, but what is the good?' No, he concludes, theirs is an abnormal life. 'No, it is not life but a violation of the norm, of the ideal which nature has put before man ...'

Oblomov, then, epitomizes an ideal. Compared with the assertive, business-like practicality of the novel's positive hero, Oblomov's boyhood friend, Stolz, it is not a successful ideal in conventional terms. But in endeavouring to depict such a positive hero, Goncharov cannot wholly escape the charge of producing a caricature figure almost as thin and one-dimensional as Oblomov's other visitors. Stolz 'was all bone, muscle, and nerve', we are told, 'like an English race-horse. He was lean: he could hardly be said to have cheeks, for though there was bone and muscle there was no sign of fat or roundness; his skin was smooth and dark with no touch of red in it ...' Teutonically efficient, and perhaps arrogant with it as his name implies, a go-getter, he seems to lack as a character precisely the rootedness and Russianness which are Oblomov's birthright. His role is rather to be a commentator on the hero's life than an exemplary contrast to it. If he finds it easy enough to criticize his friend, the subject of his criticism deftly turns the tables on him when it comes to defining 'Oblomovism' as an ideal:

'Ob-lo-movism!' Ilya Ilyitch pronounced slowly, marvelling at the strange word and dividing it into syllables, 'Ob-lo-movism!'

He looked at Stolz with a strange fixity.

'What, then, is the ideal life, you think? What is not Oblomovism?' he asked timidly and without enthusiasm. 'Doesn't everyone strive for the very same things that I dream of? Why,' he added more confidently, 'isn't it the purpose of all your running about, your passions, wars, trade, politics – to secure rest, to attain this ideal of a lost paradise?'

The exchanges between Oblomov and Stolz naturally shed light on their shared memories and reveal the supposed change that has overtaken Oblomov in the previous ten years.

They speak, as it were, almost in the same tone of voice, like twin consciences confronting each other, and, in this sense, Oblomov's ideal of a lost paradise can seem merely a salve to his own bad conscience at backsliding from the image of himself projected by his friend. Proof of the validity of such a will-o'-the-wisp dream may only be demonstrated by the failure of other ideals. What other ideal can possibly match or challenge the ideal of his Oblomovism? The answer lies with Olga.

The courtship of Olga is the central episode of the novel. Aroused from the hibernation of his dressing-gown existence by the coming of spring, he courts Olga throughout the months of summer until winter again approaches. The experience is mutually agonizing. Love is talked about, scrutinized, allowed to lapse and then revived in an often slightly hysterical and sometimes rather cruel fashion. Oblomov's own streak of cruelty, vented on insects in his childhood, expresses itself in the cruel letter he writes to Olga. Virtually incapable, it seems, of overcoming prevarication in writing to his estate bailiff, he can write eloquently and at length to the woman he supposedly loves, accusing her of being unable to love him and diagnosing the emotion itself as a disease, 'a gangrene of the soul'. Love as a smiling vision, the sound of the *Casta diva* or the fragrance of lilac, soon begins to lose its rainbow hues in the course of the courtship and when marriage becomes a practical possibility Oblomov retreats from the implied responsibility in gradual, hardly perceptible stages until the novelty of the relationship fades and boredom, however carefully concealed, begins to take its place.

The last thing Oblomov wants is to live in a hurry. A reader may justifiably feel that a courtship undertaken at such a snail's pace hardly involves a rush to marriage. Still, the consistency of Oblomov's character, that refusal to change or be changed which is at the heart of his Oblomovism, comes into its own at the end, however sad the final acknowledgement may be. Olga recognizes that what she had loved in him was 'what I wanted to find in you, what Stolz had pointed out to me, what we had both invented. I loved the Oblomov that was to be!' The end, therefore, was unavoidable:

'Why has it all been wrecked?' she asked suddenly, raising her head. 'Who laid a curse on you, Ilya? What have you done? You are kind, intelligent, affectionate, noble ... and ... you are ... doomed! What has ruined you? There is no name for that evil....'

'Yes, there is,' he whispered, almost inaudibly.

She looked at him questioningly, with her eyes full of tears.

'Oblomovism!' he whispered; then he took her hand, wanted to kiss it and could not; he merely pressed it close to his lips and hot tears fell on her fingers. Without raising his head or showing her his face, he turned and walked out of the room.

Oblomov slips back instinctively into his dressing-gown existence and by the beginning of Part IV of the novel he is as solidly ensconced in Agafya Matveyevna's house as he was in his apartment at the beginning of Part I. Time, as Goncharov now emphasizes in recurrent metaphors and analogies, becomes his hero's closest companion. By gradual degrees he sinks into a paradisial cocoon of inactivity woven for him so assiduously by the twinkling elbows of his landlady, socially far beneath the level of Oblomovka and his noble status. The botanical analogy seems magically appropriate here: 'It was as though some unseen hand had placed him as a precious plant in a spot where he was sheltered from the heat and the rain and nurtured him tenderly.' Stolz may glibly castigate Oblomov's indolence by claiming that 'it began with you not knowing how to put on your stockings and ended by you not knowing how to live', but his own marriage to Olga, however conventionally happy, faces him with the same question of how to live, especially how to create the redeeming magic in life which appears to be Oblomov's abiding secret.

In an uncannily fairy-tale manner he eventually comes to Oblomov's rescue and saves him from the machinations of Tarantyev. To him, too, falls the task of pronouncing the epitaph on what is most appealing and enduring about his friend's character. In fact, by the end of the novel the critical emphases in Goncharov's portrayal of his hero seem largely irrelevant. To Stolz, as perhaps to the author himself, what stood out above all else was Oblomov's

'... honest, faithful heart! It is like pure gold in him from nature; he has preserved it throughout his life unharmed ... His heart has never struck a single false note and nothing has sullied it. The most alluring sham cannot deceive him and nothing will make him go wrong; a regular ocean of evil and meanness may be storming around him, the whole world may be poisoned and turned upside down – Oblomov will never worship false idols and his soul will always be pure, honest, good.... His soul is clear as crystal; there aren't many men like him, they are rare; they are like pearls among the crowd.'

In virtually changeless circumstances, then, Oblomov lived out the idyll of his life. He exemplified 'the ideally restful aspect of human existence' and died after a stroke 'like a clock that stops because it hasn't been wound up'. He left a grief-stricken widow in Agafya Matveyevna, a small son named after his best friend and a serf Zahar, reduced to beggary. He was indolent and lived his life in idleness because others worked to ensure his contentment. He could afford to be Oblomov, otherwise he might simply have ended up like his manservant.

The indictment contained in Dobrolyubov's masterly review of the novel has much to justify it. Oblomov can be seen as parasitic. Yet whether this is evil or merely symptomatic of a natural human proneness to lethargy depends on many things. Goncharov does not seem to invite judgement on his hero so much as understanding, a readiness to acknowledge, as Oblomov himself claimed in debating the matter with Penkin, that no one, however socially unworthy, deserves to be cast out from humanity, from nature, from the mercy of God. His is a world, it should be noted, unlike Dostoevsky's or Tolstoy's, in which no divinity is immanent, let alone present. Oblomov lives his life unaffected by religious influences. His search for God appears as earthbound as his idyll.

An ultimate appraisal of Oblomov can be said to demand such a balance between pity and censure, such an awareness of the tragi-comic elements in his personality and his situation, that Goncharov has to all intents and purposes obliged the reader to suspend judgement in conventional terms. In so doing, he has tacitly posed to the reader a much profounder puzzle about the nature of human idealism, about the purpose of life and its choices. Oblomov, of course, is no Hamlet, no Don Quixote, no Faust, but in an insidious fashion his example touches on moral choices of the same magnitude and meaning as those confronted by these heroes. He may scarcely be exercised by whether to be or not to be, whether to engage in an absurd knight-errantry or – heaven forbid! – sell his soul, but somehow, at a much deeper level in the human psyche, the fact that, as a boy, he was never allowed to play snowballs left him forever wondering why adulthood should not be as cocooned and pleasing as the lost paradise of a happy childhood. The challenge Oblomov makes to the guiltiness of human beings about not being mature is, in all its rich detail, as comic a commentary on human ambition as it is a tragic reminder of human smallness.

*

Natalie Duddington, whose translation is used here, was born Natalie Ertel and first came to England in 1906 at the age of twenty. After winning a scholarship to London University, she obtained a first-class degree in Philosophy in 1909. An interest in Theosophy brought her into contact with the Rev. John ('Jack') Nightingale Duddington, then Rector of Ayot St Lawrence, and she went to stay with him at the rectory. This house was later let to Bernard Shaw and has now become Shaw's Corner. The rector and the young Russian girl fell in love. He left his wife and daughter to live with her. She was intelligent and strong-minded and, though they were hardly ideally suited, Jack Duddington proved invaluable to Natalie in her translation work. She also became an assistant to Constance Garnett and one of her closest friends.

Evidence of Constance Garnett's influence is to be felt in this vivacious translation of Goncharov's masterpiece. It shows a special awareness of the nuances of the Russian and a native sense of the natural rhythms of the language. Here and there one may discern traces of an un-English accent, and the occasional old-fashioned usage may betray its age. It is based on Goncharov's revised version of his novel (of 1862, rather than the first version of 1859) which is now recognized as definitive (see the authoritative edition of the novel by L. S. Geiro, Leningrad, 'Nauka', 1987). Natalie Duddington's, therefore, is a translation that not only deserves republication,

OBLOMOV

it is also a translation of what must be assumed to be the authorized text. In its particular sensitivity to the subtlety of Goncharov's Russian, in its liveliness and its elegance, it has about it a freshness of manner that admirably matches the same enduring quality in the original.

Richard Freeborn

RICHARD FREEBORN is Emeritus Professor of English Literature at the University of London. He has translated and edited many novels by Turgenev, and is the author of *Turgenev, the Novelist's Novelist*, *The Rise of the Russian Novel* and *The Russian Revolutionary Novel*.

SELECT BIBLIOGRAPHY

This is a bibliography of the principal works in English.

Milton Ehre's *Oblomov and His Creator: The Life and Art of Ivan Goncharov*, Princeton University Press, New Jersey, 1973, and Vsevolod Setchkarev's *Ivan Goncharov: His Life and Works,* Jal-verlag, Wuerzburg, 1974, are two works of solid scholarship which deserve special consideration by anyone wishing to know more about *Oblomov* and its author. The first, as the title indicates, concentrates on *Oblomov*, the rhythm and pattern of the novel's relationships and structure, the Oblomovian dream and the many delightful intricacies inherent in the work's detailed realism. It also deals with Goncharov's other novels and writings in the context of an informative study of his life. Vsevolod Setchkarev's is less sparkling as an interpretation, but more solidly exegetical as a study of the writer's life and main works. More space is given to the third of Goncharov's novels and emphasis is placed on what is described as the 'existential boredom' (*pace* W. Rehm) which Goncharov identified as one of the main forces behind the life and culture of his times.

Less detailed, and deliberately intended to be introductory in character, is Janko Lavrin's *Goncharov*, Bowes and Bowes, Cambridge, 1954. A straightforward assessment, it neatly combines information and general comment. *Ivan Goncharov* by Alexandra Lyngstad and Sverre Lyngstad, Twayne Publishers Inc., New York, 1971, is an extremely valuable introductory study, particularly useful for *Oblomov* and for insights into Goncharov's art. Richard Peace's *Oblomov: A Critical Examination of Goncharov's Novel*, Birmingham Slavonic Monographs No. 20, 1991, is the most detailed and probing of studies available in English, dealing with a range of issues from the question of Oblomov's relationship with 'the other' to the novel's structure, imagery and style. A doctoral thesis of a specialist kind is offered, as the title indicates, in Natalie Baratoff's *Oblomov, A Jungian Approach: A Literary Image of the Mother Complex*, Peter Lang, Bern – Frankfurt-am-Main – New York – Paris, 1990.

More general contributions of some note, especially in regard to the place of Goncharov in the history of the Russian novel, are to be found in Henry Gifford's *The Novel in Russia: From Pushkin to Pasternak*, Hutchinson University Library, 1964, and in Richard Freeborn's *The*

OBLOMOV

Rise of the Russian Novel, Cambridge University Press, 1973, as in the same author's chapter on 'The nineteenth century: the age of realism, 1855–80' in *The Cambridge History of Russian Literature*, 1989.

The single most important pioneering work on Goncharov to appear in the West was André Mazon's *Un Maître du roman russe: Ivan Goncharov*, Paris, 1914, of particular value for the documents relating to Goncharov's work as a censor. N. Dobrolyubov's famous review of the novel 'What is Oblomovism?' is available in an English translation by J. Fineberg in N. A. Dobrolyubov, *Selected Philosophical Essays*, Foreign Language Publishing House, Moscow, 1956, under the title 'What is Oblomovschina?'

CHRONOLOGY

DATE	AUTHOR'S LIFE	LITERARY CONTEXT
1812	Ivan Alexandrovich Goncharov born (18 June) in Simbirsk (now Ulyanovsk) on the Volga, into a wealthy merchant family. He is one of four children.	Birth of Herzen. Byron: *Childe Harold* (to 1818).
1814–15		Birth of Lermontov (1814). Scott: *Waverley*. Jane Austen: *Mansfield Park*.
1820–22	Following the death of his father (1819), his mother takes over the family business. Ivan is sent to a local boarding school for the sons of the landed gentry, where he begins to learn French and English.	Pushkin: *Ruslan and Lyudmila*. De Quincey: *Confessions of an English Opium Eater*. Birth of Dostoevsky and Flaubert (1821).
1822	Joins his elder brother in Moscow at the School of Commerce, where he distinguishes himself in languages rather than in business studies.	Griboedov writes *Woe from Wit* (to 1824). Mickiewicz: 'On Romantic Poetry'.
1825		Pushkin writes *Boris Godunov* (published 1830).
1826		Scott: *Woodstock*.
1828		Birth of Tolstoy. Mickiewicz: *Konrad Wallenrod*.
1830		Stendhal: *Le Rouge et le Noir*.
1831	Enrols in the philological faculty at Moscow University. Mixes with neither of the famous student groups of this era (the Moscow Hegelians led by Bakunin and Stankovich, and the political circle of Herzen).	Gogol's first collection of stories: *Evenings on a Farm near Dikanka*. Pushkin: *The Tales of Belkin*.

Napoleon's invasion of Russia and retreat from Moscow.

Congress of Vienna. Exile of Napoleon and restoration of the monarchy in France. As part of postwar settlement, Russia gains control of central Poland. Russia, Prussia and Austria form Holy Alliance to preserve European status quo. The hated reactionary Count Arakcheyev in charge of Russia's internal affairs (to 1826).

Purging of the universities by Golitsyn and Magnitsky begins. Foundation of Northern and Southern Societies, secret associations of noblemen and officers supporting political and social reform (1820). Russian expedition led by Thaddeus Bellingshausen discovers the Antarctic continent.

Outbreak of Greek War of Independence (1821).

Death of Alexander I. Accession of Nicholas I. Decembrist conspiracy: plot by reformers to replace Nicholas by his brother Constantine and to obtain a constitution. Attempt fails and leaders are hanged.

Nicholas founds notorious 'Third Section' under Count Benckendorf to act against subversion and revolution. It controls censorship and operates a widespread network of spies. War between Russia and Persia.

War between Russia and Turkey (to 1829). Russo-Persian treaty of Turkmanchay gives Russia Erivan. Start of peasants' revolts in Russia, averaging 23 per year until 1854.

Major Russian cholera epidemic reaches Moscow (and St Petersburg the following year). July Revolution in Paris; accession of Louis Philippe.

Failure of Polish uprising against Russian rule: Poles lose their constitution and most of the autonomy granted them in 1815.

DATE	AUTHOR'S LIFE	LITERARY CONTEXT
1832	Goncharov's first appearance in print as the translator of a novel by Eugène Sue, published in a Moscow periodical.	Lermontov: 'The Sail', 'No, I am not Byron'. Death of Goethe and Scott.
1833		Pushkin: complete version of *Evgeny Onegin*. Balzac: *Eugénie Grandet*.
1834	After graduation, returns to Simbirsk where he obtains a civil service post as private secretary to the provincial governor which he gives up after only a few months.	Belinsky: *Literary Reveries*. Pushkin: 'The Queen of Spades'. Mickiewicz: *Pan Tadeusz*. Arrest and internal exile of Herzen and his circle.
1835	Moves to St Petersburg where he enters the Ministry of Finance as a translator, later becoming head of a small department – the beginning of an unremarkable thirty-year career in the civil service.	Gogol: *Mirgorod*; *Arabesques*. Balzac: *Le Père Goriot*.
1836	During his early years in St Petersburg Goncharov becomes friendly with the painter Nicholas Maykov and coaches his sons Apollon (the future poet) and Valerian (the future critic) in Latin and Russian literature. He meets many leading literary figures at the Maykovs' salon.	Gogol: *The Government Inspector*. Pushkin: *The Captain's Daughter*. First of Chaadaev's *Lettres Philosophiques* published in Russia. Pushkin founds *The Contemporary*.
1837		Pushkin killed in a duel. Dickens: *Pickwick Papers*.
1839	First story, 'A Lucky Error', appears in a private miscellany.	Stendhal: *La Chartreuse de Parme*. Dickens: *Nicholas Nickleby*.
1840		Lermontov: *A Hero of Our Time*.
1841		Lermontov: *The Demon*. Death of Lermontov in a duel.

CHRONOLOGY

Doctrine of 'Official Nationality' – Orthodoxy, autocracy and nationality – proclaimed by Count Uvarov. Promoted to Minister of Education (1833–49), he presides over the modernization of the education system, at the same time declaring his aim to build a 'dam' to hold up the flow of new ideas into Russia. First Parliamentary Reform Act in Britain.

Treaty of Unkiar-Skelessi between Russia and Turkey: Russia given the right to request closure of the Straits (Dardanelles) to foreign warships.

Speransky's codification of the law completed: the new code replaces that of 1649 and lasts until 1917.

Abolition of slavery throughout British Empire.

Michael Pogodin becomes first professor of Russian History at Moscow University.

As Supreme Procurator of the Holy Synod (to 1855) Count Pratasov brings the church more thoroughly under government control.

Count Kieslev begins reorganization of state peasants. His reforms include shifting of taxation from persons to land. First public railway in Russia, between St Petersburg and Tsarkoe Selo.

Accession of Queen Victoria in Britain.

After two years of severe fighting in the Caucasus, rebel leader Shamil is largely successful in driving the Russian line back.

Straits Convention between Turkey and the five European Powers: Russia loses special rights obtained in Treaty of Unkiar-Skelessi.

DATE	AUTHOR'S LIFE	LITERARY CONTEXT
1842	Writes 'Ivan Savich Podzhabrin' (published 1848), a story set in the civil service milieu of St Petersburg.	Gogol: *Dead Souls*; 'The Overcoat'. Sue: *Les Mystères de Paris*.
1846	Meets Belinsky.	Dostoevsky: *Poor Folk*.
1847	*An Ordinary Story* published in *The Contemporary* (first translated into English by Constance Garnett in 1894). This first novel is enthusiastically greeted by Belinsky and brings Goncharov immediate recognition.	Thackeray: *Vanity Fair* (to 1848). C. Brontë: *Jane Eyre*. E. Brontë: *Wuthering Heights*. Balzac: *Le Cousin Pons*. Herzen: *Who is to Blame?* Herzen leaves Russia.
1848		Death of Belinsky.
1849	'Oblomov's Dream' published in *The Contemporary*. For ten years it stands on its own as an independent work until it is incorporated into *Oblomov*.	Dostoevsky arrested and sent into Siberian exile.
1850		Turgenev: *A Month in the Country*. Herzen: *From the Other Shore*.
1851		Melville: *Moby-Dick*.
1852	In October, embarks on a round-the-world voyage on the Russian frigate *Pallas* as private secretary to the vice-admiral in charge of the expedition – a diplomatic/trading mission to Japan and the Far East.	Death of Gogol. Turgenev: *A Sportsman's Sketches* (1st volume edition). Tolstoy: *Childhood*. Harriet Beecher Stowe: *Uncle Tom's Cabin*.
1854		First volume edition of Tyutchev's poems published.
1855	Returns to St Petersburg overland via Siberia (February). Begins to publish a series of travel sketches about his experiences in the Far East.	Tolstoy: *Sevastopol Sketches*. Trollope: *The Warden*.
1856	Appointed literary censor in the Ministry of the Interior.	Turgenev: *Rudin*. Aksakov: *A Family Chonicle*.

CHRONOLOGY

DATE	AUTHOR'S LIFE	LITERARY CONTEXT
1857	Completes the writing of *Oblomov* while staying at his favourite foreign spa of Marienbad during the summer.	Flaubert: *Madame Bovary*. Herzen and Ogarev's radical journal *Kolokol* (*The Bell*) published in London (to 1867).
1858	Publishes *The Frigate Pallas*, a two-volume account of his voyage. It includes a detailed description of London, English life and English colonialism. *Oblomov* serialized in the St Petersburg periodical *Home Annals*.	Aksakov: *Years of Childhood*. Pisemsky: *A Thousand Souls*.
1859	*Oblomov* published in book form. (It is first translated into English in 1915.) The critic Dobrolyubov's favourable review in *The Contemporary* ('What is Oblomovism?') helps to spark controversy over the novel, and to secure its popularity.	Ostrovsky: *The Storm*. Turgenev: *A Nest of Gentlefolk*. George Eliot: *Adam Bede*.
1860	Goncharov already beginning to suffer from the mental illness which later turns him into a recluse. He accuses Turgenev of stealing his plots, and over the years becomes convinced that his more successful contemporary is the ringleader of a conspiracy against him.	Birth of Chekhov. Turgenev: *On the Eve*; 'First Love'. Dostoevsky: *The House of the Dead* (to 1862). Eliot: *The Mill on the Floss*.
1861		Herzen publishes *My Past and Thoughts* (to 1867). Dickens: *Great Expectations*.
1862	Revised edition of *Oblomov* published.	Turgenev: *Fathers and Children*. Hugo: *Les Misérables*. Chernyshevsky exiled to Siberia (to 1889).
1863	Appointed a member of a committee of review of Russian censorship groups.	Tolstoy: *The Cossacks*. Chernyshevsky: *What is to be Done?* Nekrasov: *Red-Nosed Frost*.
1864		Dostoevsky: *Notes from Underground*. Nekrasov: *Who Can Be Happy and Free in Russia?* (to 1876).

Russians finally capture Shamil and gain control of the Caucasus. Russian colonial expansion in South-East Asia begins.

Port of Vladivostock founded to serve Russia's recent annexations from China. Garibaldi and 'The Thousand' conquer Sicily.
1860s and '70s: 'Nihilism' – rationalist philosophy sceptical of all forms of established authority – becomes widespsread among young radical intellectuals in Russia.

Emancipation of the serfs (February), the climax of Alexander II's programme of reform. While his achievement had great moral and symbolic significance, many peasants felt themselves cheated by the complex terms of the emancipation statute.
Outbreak of the American Civil War. Victor Emmanuel first King of Italy. Bismarck becomes chief minister of Prussia.

Polish rebellion. Poland incorporated into Russian Empire.

The First International. Establishment of the Zemstva, organs of rural self-government and a significant liberal influence in Tsarist Russia. Reform of the judiciary: trial by jury instituted and a Russian bar established.

DATE	AUTHOR'S LIFE	LITERARY CONTEXT
1865		Tolstoy: *War and Peace* (to 1869). Leskov: 'Lady Macbeth of the Mtensk District'.
1866		Dostoevsky: *Crime and Punishment*. *The Contemporary* suppressed.
1867	Retires from civil service.	Turgenev: *Smoke*. Trollope: *The Last Chronicle of Barset*. Zola: *Thérèse Raquin*. Marx: *Das Kapital*, vol. 1.
1868		Dostoevsky: *The Idiot*. Lavrov: *Historical Letters*.
1869	Publication of the last novel of his 'triptych', *The Precipice* (translated into English in 1915). Popular and critical response is negative. Goncharov writes little more during the last two decades of his life.	Flaubert: *L'Education sentimentale*.
1870		Death of Herzen and Dickens.
1871		Dostoevsky: *Demons* (to 1872). Ostrovsky: *The Forest*. Eliot: *Middlemarch* (to 1872). Zola publishes the Rougon-Macquart series of novels (to 1893).
1872	Publishes 'A Million Torments', an essay on Griboedov's *Woe from Wit*.	Leskov: *Cathedral Folk*.
1875–8	Writes *An Uncommon Story*, accusing Turgenev of plagiarism (not published until 1924).	Saltykov-Shchedrin: *The Golovlyov Family* (1875–80). Tolstoy: *Anna Karenina* (1875–7). Turgenev: *Virgin Soil* (1877). Hardy: *The Return of the Native* (1878).
1879	'Better Late than Never' (essay).	Dostoevsky: *The Brothers Karamazov* (to 1880). Ibsen: *A Doll's House*. Strindberg: *The Red Room*.
1880	'A Literary Soirée'.	Chekhov publishes his first stories, in the periodical *The Dragonfly*. Death of Flaubert and George Eliot. Birth of Blok and Bely.

CHRONOLOGY

HISTORICAL EVENTS

Russian colonial expansion in Central Asia (to 1881).
Slavery formally abolished in the USA.

Prusso-Austrian War.

Gladstone becomes British Prime Minister.

Late 1860s–'70s: *Narodnik* (Populist) campaign gathers momentum. Young intellectuals incite the peasantry to revolt against autocracy.

Birth of Lenin. Franco-Prussian War.
Paris Commune set up and suppressed. Fall of Paris ends war.
Wilhelm I of Prussia becomes Emperor of a united Germany.

Meeting of the three emperors in Berlin leads to an *entente* between Russia, Germany and Austria-Hungary.

'Bulgarian Atrocities': Bulgarians massacred by Turks. Founding of Land and Freedom, first Russian political party openly to advocate revolution. Death of Bakunin (1876). War between Russia and Turkey (1877); at the Treaty of Berlin other European Powers compel Russia to give up many of her conquests; partition of Bulgaria between Russia and Turkey. Mass trial of Populist agitators in Russia (1878).
Stalin born. Land and Freedom divides into terrorist organization The People's Will, responsible for numerous political assassinations including that of the Tsar in 1881, and Black Repartition, which continues campaign among the peasantry and later the urban proletariat.

DATE	AUTHOR'S LIFE	LITERARY CONTEXT
1881	Essay on Belinsky published.	Death of Dostoevsky. Henry James: *The Portrait of a Lady*. Flaubert: *Bouvard et Péchuchet*.
1883		Death of Turgenev. Fet: *Evening Lights* (4 vols, to 1891). Garshin: 'The Red Flower'. Maupassant: *Une Vie*; *Clair de Lune*.
1886		Tolstoy: *The Death of Ivan Ilych*. Chekhov: *Motley Stories*. James: *The Bostonians*; *The Princess Casamassima*.
1887–8	Publishes reminiscences of his childhood and university days in *The Messenger of Europe*.	Chekhov: 'The Kiss', 'The Steppe'.
1891	Death of Goncharov (27 September).	Birth of Bulgakov.

CHRONOLOGY

PART I

I

ILYA ILYITCH OBLOMOV was lying in bed one morning in his flat in Gorohovy Street, in one of the big houses that had almost as many inhabitants as a whole country town. He was a man of thirty-two or -three, of medium height and pleasant appearance, with dark-grey eyes that strayed idly from the walls to the ceiling with a vague dreaminess which showed that nothing troubled or occupied him. His attitude and the very folds of his dressing-gown expressed the same untroubled ease as his face. At times his eyes were dimmed by something like weariness or boredom; but neither weariness nor boredom could banish for a moment the softness which was the dominant and permanent expression not merely of his face but of his whole being. A serene, open, candid mind was reflected in his eyes, his smile, in every movement of his head and his hands. A cold and superficial observer would glance at Oblomov and say: 'A good-hearted, simple fellow, I should think.' A kinder and more thoughtful man would gaze into his face for some time and walk off smiling in pleasant uncertainty.

Ilya Ilyitch's complexion was neither rosy nor dark nor pale, but indefinite, or perhaps it seemed so because there was a certain slackness about the muscles of his face, unusual at his age; this may have been due to lack of fresh air or exercise, or to some other reason. The smooth and excessively white skin of his neck, his small soft hands and plump shoulders, suggested a certain physical effeminacy. His movements were restrained and gentle; there was a certain lazy gracefulness about them even if he were alarmed. If his mind was troubled, his eyes were clouded, his forehead wrinkled, and an interplay of hesitation, sadness, and fear was reflected in his face; but the disturbance seldom took the form of a definite idea and still more seldom reached the point of a decision. It merely found expression in a sigh and died down in apathy or drowsiness.

How well Oblomov's dress suited his calm features and soft body! He wore a dressing-gown of Persian material, a regular Eastern dressing-gown without anything European about it – no tassels, no velvet, no waist, and so roomy that he could wrap it round him twice. The sleeves, in true Asiatic fashion, gradually widened from the wrists to the shoulders. Although the dressing-gown had lost its original freshness and was shiny in places with an acquired and not a natural lustre, it still preserved its brilliant Eastern colouring, and the stuff was as strong as ever.

The dressing-gown had a number of invaluable qualities in Oblomov's eyes: it was soft and pliable; it did not get in his way; it obeyed the least movement of his body, like a docile slave.

Oblomov never wore a tie or a waistcoat at home because he liked comfort and freedom. He wore long, soft, wide slippers; when he got up from bed he put his feet straight into them without looking.

Lying down was not for Ilya Ilyitch either a necessity as it is for a sick or a sleepy man, or an occasional need as it is for a person who is tired, or a pleasure as it is for a sluggard: it was his normal state. When he was at home – and he was almost always at home – he was lying down, and invariably in the same room, the one in which we have found him and which served him as bedroom, study, and reception-room. He had three more rooms, but he seldom looked into them, only, perhaps, in the morning when his servant swept his study – which did not happen every day. In those other rooms the furniture was covered and the curtains were drawn.

The room in which Ilya Ilyitch was lying at the first glance seemed splendid. It had a mahogany bureau, two silk-upholstered sofas, a handsome screen embroidered with fruit and flowers never to be seen in nature. It had silk curtains, carpets, several pictures, bronze, and china, and a number of pretty knick-knacks. But the experienced eye of a person of good taste would detect at once that all these things were put there merely to comply with unavoidable conventions. This was all Oblomov had in mind when he furnished his study. A refined taste could not have been content with these heavy, clumsy mahogany chairs and shaky chiffoniers. The back of one of the sofas had sunk in, the inlaid wood had come unstuck in places.

The pictures, the vases, and the knick-knacks were no better.

The owner himself, however, looked at the furniture of his study coldly and unconcernedly, as though wondering who could have brought all this stuff there. It was because of Oblomov's indifference towards his property, and perhaps because of the still greater indifference of his servant, Zahar, that the study struck one, at a more careful inspection, by its neglected and untidy condition. Dusty cobwebs hung in festoons round the pictures on the walls; mirrors, instead of reflecting objects, might have served as tablets for writing memoranda in the dust; there were stains on the carpets; a towel had been left on the sofa. Almost every morning a dirty plate, with a salt-cellar and a bone from the previous night's supper, was to be seen on the crumb-covered table.

If it had not been for this plate and for a freshly smoked pipe by the bed, and for the owner himself lying in it, one might have thought that the room was uninhabited – everything was so dusty and faded and devoid of all traces of human presence. It is true there were two or three open books and a newspaper on the chiffoniers, an inkstand and pens on the bureau; but the open pages had turned yellow and were covered with dust – evidently they had been left so for weeks; the newspaper dated from last year, and if one dipped a pen into the inkstand a startled fly might perhaps come buzzing out of it.

Ilya Ilyitch had, contrary to his habit, woken up very early – about eight o'clock. He was much perturbed. His expression kept changing from one of alarm to that of distress and vexation. He was obviously suffering from an inward conflict and his intellect had not yet come to his aid.

The fact was that the evening before Oblomov had received a disagreeable letter from the bailiff of his estate. Everyone knows what kind of disagreeable news a bailiff can write: bad harvest, debts, smaller income, etc. Although the bailiff had written exactly the same letter the year before and the year before that, his last letter had the effect of an unpleasant surprise.

It was no joke! One had to think of taking some measures. In justice to Ilya Ilyitch it must be said that, after receiving the bailiff's first unpleasant letter several years before, he had begun to think of various changes and improvements in the management of his estate. He proposed introducing fresh economic, administrative, and other measures. But the plan was not yet thoroughly thought out, and the bailiff's unpleasant letters came every year inciting him to action and disturbing his peace of mind. Oblomov knew it was necessary to do something decisive.

As soon as he woke he made up his mind to get up and wash, and, after drinking tea, to think matters over, taking various things into consideration and writing them down, and altogether to go into the subject thoroughly. He lay for half an hour tormented by his decision; but afterwards he reflected that he would have time to think after breakfast, which he could have in bed as usual, especially since one can think just as well lying down.

This was what he did. After his morning tea he sat up and very nearly got out of bed; looking at his slippers, he began lowering one foot down towards them, but at once drew it back again.

It struck half-past nine. Ilya Ilyitch roused himself. 'What am I thinking of?' he said aloud with vexation. 'It's disgraceful: I must set to work! If I let myself go, I'll never . . . .'

'Zahar!' he shouted.

Something like a dog's growl followed by the sound of jumping feet came from the room divided by a narrow passage from Ilya Ilyitch's study. It was Zahar jumping off the stove, where he generally sat dozing.

An elderly man, wearing a grey waistcoat with brass buttons and a grey coat torn under the arm and showing his shirt, came into the room; his skull was perfectly bare, but each of his big side-whiskers, light brown streaked with grey, was thick enough to make three beards.

Zahar made no attempt to change either the appearance, which Providence had bestowed upon him, or the costume he had worn in the country. His clothes were made after the pattern he had brought from Oblomov's estate. He liked the grey coat and waistcoat because they vaguely reminded him of the livery he had worn in the old days when he accompanied his late master and mistress to church or on a visit to friends; and the livery was the only thing in his memories that expressed the dignity of the Oblomov family. There was nothing else to remind the old man of the peace and plenty of his master's house in the depths of the country. The old master and mistress were dead; the family portraits had been left behind and were probably lying somewhere in the attic; tales of the old way of living and the family grandeur were being forgotten and only lived in the memory of a few old people who had remained on the estate. This was the reason why Zahar loved his grey coat: he saw in it a dim reflection of bygone greatness, of which he was reminded, too, by something in Oblomov's face and manner that recalled his parents, and by his whims, at which Zahar grumbled both to himself and aloud, but which he inwardly respected as expressions of a master's will, a master's rights. Were it not for these whims he would not have felt he had a master over him; nothing would then have brought back to him his youth, the country they had left years ago, and the legends of the old house. Oblomov's family had once been rich and famous in the province, but gradually,

Heaven knows why, it had grown poorer and meaner, and at last was lost among the newer families of the country gentry. Only the grey-haired servants of the family preserved and handed down to one another faithful memories of the past, treasuring them as something holy. This was why Zahar loved his grey coat. Perhaps he valued his whiskers, too, because he had seen in his childhood many old servants who wore this old-fashioned and aristocratic adornment.

It was some minutes before Ilya Ilyitch, absorbed with his thoughts, noticed Zahar. Zahar stood before him in silence. At last he coughed.

'What is it?' asked Ilya Ilyitch.

'You called me, didn't you?'

'Called, did I? What could I have called you for – I don't remember!' he answered, stretching himself. 'Go now and I will try and remember.'

Zahar left the room and Ilya Ilyitch went on lying and thinking of the accursed letter.

Another quarter of an hour passed.

'There, that's enough lying in bed!' he said. 'I must get up. . . . Though I had better first read the bailiff's letter carefully once more and get up afterwards. Zahar!'

Again the same jump was heard and a growling louder than before. Zahar came in and Oblomov sank into thought once more. Zahar stood for a couple of minutes looking at his master sideways disapprovingly, and at last walked towards the door.

'Where are you off to?' Oblomov asked suddenly.

'You don't speak, so why should I stand here for nothing?' Zahar said in a hoarse whisper; he used to declare that he had lost his voice riding to hounds with the old master, when a strong gust of wind had blown into his throat. He was standing in the middle of the room half turned away from Oblomov, still looking sideways at him.

'Have you lost the use of your legs that you can't stand? You see I am worried – so you must wait! Haven't you been lying down long enough? Find the letter I received from the bailiff yesterday. Where have you put it?'

'Which letter? I haven't seen any letter,' said Zahar.

'You took it from the postman, such a dirty letter!'

'Well, where did you put it – how should I know?' said Zahar, slapping the papers and various articles on the table.

'You never know anything. Look in the waste-paper basket! Or perhaps it has fallen behind the sofa. Here, the back of the sofa has not been mended yet; why don't you send for the carpenter? It was you who broke it.'

'I didn't break it,' Zahar answered, 'it broke of itself; it can't last for ever – it is bound to break some day.'

Ilya Ilyitch did not think it necessary to argue the point.

'Have you found it?' he merely asked.

'Here are some letters.'

'No, that's not it.'

'Well, there aren't any more,' Zahar said.

'Very well, go,' Ilya Ilyitch said impatiently. 'I will look for it myself when I get up.'

Zahar went to his room, but he had no sooner leaned his hands on the stove in order to jump on to it than he heard a hurried call: 'Zahar, Zahar!'

'Oh my goodness! What an infliction!' Zahar grumbled as he went into the study again. 'I wish I were dead and done for.

'What is it?' he asked, holding with one hand to the door and, in token of disapproval, turning so that he could only see his master out of the corner of his eye, and Oblomov could see nothing but an enormous side-whisker out of which, it seemed, two or three birds might fly any moment.

'A handkerchief, quick! You might have thought of it yourself; can't you see?' Ilya Ilyitch said sternly.

Zahar showed no sign of being more than usually annoyed or surprised by his master's command and reproach, probably finding both quite natural.

'How am I to know where the handkerchief is?' he

grumbled, as he walked round the room, touching every chair, although one could see there was nothing lying there.

'You lose everything!' he remarked, opening the door into the drawing-room to see if the handkerchief was there.

'Where are you going? Look for it here: I haven't been there for two days. Do be quick!' Ilya Ilyitch said.

'Where can it be? It isn't anywhere about,' said Zahar, throwing up his hands and looking round the room. 'Why, there it is!' he hissed angrily all at once. 'It is under you! There's an end of it sticking out. You lie on it and then you ask for a handkerchief!'

Without waiting for an answer Zahar walked towards the door. Oblomov was somewhat abashed by his own mistake. He hastened to find another reason for putting Zahar in the wrong.

'You do keep the place tidy! The dust, the dirt, my goodness! Why, look in the corners – you don't do anything!'

'Don't do anything, indeed. . . .' Zahar protested in an injured voice. 'I do my utmost; I wear myself out; I dust and sweep nearly every day. . . .'

He pointed to the middle of the floor and the table at which Oblomov had dinner.

'There,' he said, 'everything is swept and tidied as for a wedding. . . . What more do you want?'

'And what's this?' Ilya Ilyitch interrupted him, pointing to the walls and the ceiling, 'and this? and this?' He pointed to the towel left on the sofa since the day before, and to a plate, with a piece of bread on it, forgotten on the table.

'Well, I might take this away,' Zahar answered condescendingly, taking the plate.

'Only this! And what about the dust on the walls, the cobwebs?' said Oblomov, pointing to the walls.

'I sweep the walls before Easter; I clean the ikons then and take off the cobwebs. . . .'

'And when do you dust the books and the pictures?'

'I do the books and the pictures before Christmas; Anissya and I turn out all the bookcases then. But now, when am I to clean the place? You sit at home all day.'

'I sometimes go to the theatre or to see friends; you might do it then. . . .'

'Why, what can I do at night?'

Oblomov looked at him reproachfully, shook his head and sighed, and Zahar looked indifferently out of the window and sighed also. The master seemed to think: 'Well, my dear, you are more of an Oblomov than I am,' and Zahar very likely had it in his mind to say: 'I know you! You are good at using high-flown words that upset one, but you don't care a hang about the dust and the cobwebs.'

'Don't you understand,' Ilya Ilyitch said, 'that dust is a breeding-ground for clothes-moth? And sometimes I see a bug on the wall too.'

'I have fleas as well,' Zahar responded indifferently.

'It's nothing to boast of. It's disgusting!'

Zahar smiled all over his face so that his eyebrows and whiskers moved and a red flush spread to his forehead.

'It's not my fault that there are bugs in the world,' he said with naïve surprise. 'I didn't invent them.'

'It's because of the dirt,' Oblomov interrupted him. 'What nonsense you do talk!'

'I didn't invent dirt either.'

'You have mice running about in your room at night – I can hear them.'

'I didn't make the mice either. There are plenty of these creatures everywhere – mice and moths, and bugs.'

'How is it other people have neither moths nor bugs?'

Zahar's face expressed incredulity or rather a calm certainty that this never happened.

'I have plenty of all sorts,' he said obstinately. 'One can't see to every bug and get into the crack after it.'

He seemed to be thinking, 'And what would sleep be without bugs?'

'You must sweep and clean the dirt out of the corners, then there won't be any,' Oblomov instructed him.

'If I do clean it, to-morrow there will be plenty of dirt again,' said Zahar.

'No there won't,' his master interrupted him; 'there shouldn't be.'

'I know there will,' the servant insisted.

'Well, if there is you must sweep it again.'

'What? Clean all the corners every day?' Zahar asked. 'Why, life wouldn't be worth living! I'd sooner be dead.'

'Why is it other people's rooms are clean?' Oblomov retorted. 'Look at the tuner's opposite – it's a pleasure to see his place, and he has only one maid.'

'And how should the Germans have any dirt?' Zahar objected suddenly. 'Just see how they live! The whole family gnaw one bone all the week. A coat passes from the father to the son and from the son back again to the father. The wife and the daughters wear wretched short frocks and keep putting their legs under them like geese. . . . How should they have any dirt? They never have stacks of worn-out clothes lying in chests for years as we do, or get a whole corner-full of crusts of bread during the winter. . . . They never waste a crust; they make it into rusks and have it with their beer!'

Zahar spat through his teeth at the thought of such niggardly ways.

'It's no good your talking!' Ilya Ilyitch remarked. 'You had much better set to work.'

'Sometimes I'm ready enough, but you don't let me,' Zahar said.

'He is at it again! It's I who hinder him, it seems.'

'Of course you do; you sit at home always. How can I work with you here? Go out for a whole day and I will tidy the place.'

'Anything else? Go out, indeed! You had better go to your room.'

'But really you ought to,' Zahar insisted. 'Go out to-day, and Anissya and I will set everything to rights, though we could not manage, just the two of us: we should have to hire charwomen to scrub and wash.'

'What an idea – charwomen! You had better go,' said Ilya Ilyitch.

He was sorry to have provoked the conversation. He always forgot that as soon as he touched upon this delicate subject he was involved in endless trouble. Oblomov would have liked to have his rooms clean, only he wanted this to happen somehow of itself, unobtrusively; but if Zahar was asked to dust, scrub floors, etc., he always made a fuss. He invariably began proving that a tremendous disturbance was necessary, knowing very well that the mere thought of it terrified his master.

Zahar went away and Oblomov sank into thought. A few minutes later the clock struck another half-hour.

'What's that?' Ilya Ilyitch said almost in terror. 'It will soon be eleven o'clock and I haven't yet got up and washed! Zahar, Zahar!'

'Oh my goodness! I never! . . .' was heard from the next room, and then came the familiar sound of a jump.

'Is my water ready?' Oblomov asked.

'Ages ago,' Zahar answered. 'Why don't you get up?'

'Why don't you tell me it's ready? I would have got up long ago. Go now, I will follow you in a minute. I must work, I will sit down to write.'

Zahar went out, but returned a minute later with a greasy notebook covered with writing and bits of paper.

'If you are going to write, you might check these accounts too – they must be paid.'

'What accounts? Who must be paid?'

'The butcher, the greengrocer, the baker, the laundress – they are all asking for money.'

'Money is all they care about!' Oblomov grumbled. 'And why don't you give me the bills one by one instead of producing them all together?'

'But you don't let me – you always say to-morrow will do. . . .'

'Won't it do now?'

'No, they keep pestering us; they won't give us any more credit. This is the first of the month.'

'Oh dear!' said Oblomov miserably. 'A fresh worry! Well, why do you stand there? Put the bills on the table. I will get up, wash, and have a look at them. My water is ready, you say?'

'Yes, it is.'

'Well, now. . . .'

He sat up, sighing with the effort, preparing to get out of bed.

'I forgot to tell you,' Zahar began, 'this morning, while you were still asleep, the landlord's agent sent the porter to say we must move . . . they want the flat.'

'Well, what of it? If they want it, of course we'll move. Why do you bother me? It's the third time you've told me.'

'But they keep bothering me.'

'Tell them we will move.'

'They say you have been promising that for a whole month, but you don't go; they'll tell the police.'

'Let them!' Oblomov said decisively. 'We'll move without their asking as soon as the weather is warmer, in another three weeks or so.'

'Three weeks, indeed! The agent says the workmen are coming in a fortnight's time to break the place down. . . . You must move to-morrow or the day after. . . .'

'Oh, they are in too much of a hurry! To-morrow! What next! Perhaps they'd like us to move this minute? And don't you dare to mention the flat to me. I have forbidden you once and you are at it again. Take care!'

'But what am I to do?' Zahar answered.

'What is he to do! That's how he treats me!' said Ilya Ilyitch. 'He is asking me that! What business is it of mine? So long as you don't bother me, you can make what arrangements you like to save us going; but you won't put yourself out for your master!'

'But what arrangements can I make, Ilya Ilyitch, sir?' Zahar began with gentle huskiness. 'The house is not

mine, you know. How can we refuse to leave if the landlord drives us out? Had it been my house I would have
been only too glad. . . .'

'Can't you persuade them somehow? Point out to them
that we have lived here for years, have always paid the
rent. . . .'

'I did tell them,' Zahar said.

'And what did they say?'

'Oh, they just keep on saying we must move because
they have to do up the flat. They want to knock this flat
and the doctor's into one before the landlord's son is married.'

'Good Lord,' Oblomov said with vexation, 'to think
that there are men asses enough to get married!'

He turned over on his back.

'You might write to the landlord, sir,' Zahar said. 'Perhaps he would not disturb you then, and have that flat
over there broken down first.'

Zahar pointed vaguely to the right.

'Very well, I will write when I get up. . . . You go to
your room and I'll think. You can never do anything,' he
added, 'I have to look after every little trifle myself.'

Zahar went out and Oblomov began thinking; but he
had difficulty in deciding what he was to think of: of the
bailiff's letter, or of moving to new lodgings, or of checking the accounts? He was lost in the torrent of worldly
cares and lay in bed turning over from side to side. At
times abrupt exclamations were heard in the room: 'Oh
dear, life doesn't leave one alone, it gets at one everywhere!'

One cannot tell how long he would have remained in
this state of indecision, but there was a ring at the front
door.

'A visitor already!' said Oblomov, wrapping his dressing-gown round him. 'And I haven't got up yet – it is a
disgrace! Who can it be so early?'

And as he lay in bed he looked curiously at the door.

II

A YOUNG man of twenty-five, radiant with health, with laughing lips and eyes, came into the room. It made one envious to look at him.

He was irreproachably groomed and dressed, and his complexion, linen, gloves, and frock-coat were dazzlingly fresh. An elegant chain with a number of tiny trinkets stretched across his waistcoat. He pulled out a handkerchief of finest cambric, breathed in its Eastern perfume and then lightly touched his face and his shiny hat and flicked his patent boots with it.

'Ah, Volkov, how do you do?' Ilya Ilyitch greeted him.

'How do you do, Oblomov?' the dazzling gentleman said, walking up to him.

'Don't come near me, don't come near me, you are straight from the cold air!' Oblomov exclaimed.

'Oh, you spoiled sybarite!' said Volkov, looking round for a place to put down his hat, but seeing dust everywhere he kept it in his hands; he parted the skirts of his coat to sit down, but after a careful look at the arm-chair remained standing.

'You haven't got up yet? What sort of a wrapper have you on? This style hasn't been worn for ages,' he reproved Oblomov.

'It isn't a wrapper, it's a dressing-gown,' Oblomov answered lovingly, wrapping the wide folds of the dressing-gown round him.

'Are you well?' Volkov asked.

'No, indeed,' said Oblomov, yawning, 'far from it: I keep having giddy attacks. And how are you?'

'I? I am well, very well – and having a jolly time,' the young man added with feeling.

'Where do you come from so early?' Oblomov asked.

'From my tailor's. Look, isn't it a fine coat?' he said, turning round before Oblomov.

'Excellent! in very good taste,' said Ilya Ilyitch. 'Only why is it so wide at the back?'

'It's a riding-coat, for riding on horseback.'

'Why, do you ride?'

'Of course! I had the coat specially made for to-day. It is the first of May to-day; the Goryunovs and I are going to Ekaterinhof. Oh, you don't know: Misha Goryunov has received his commission, so we are celebrating the occasion to-day!' Volkov added enthusiastically.

'I see,' said Oblomov.

'He has a bay horse,' Volkov went on; 'they all have bays in their regiment and I have a black one. How will you go – will you walk or drive?'

'Oh . . . neither.'

'Not go to Ekaterinhof on the first of May! What are you thinking of, Ilya Ilyitch! Why, everyone will be there!'

'Oh no, not everyone,' Oblomov remarked lazily.

'Come, Ilya Ilyitch, there's a dear! Sofya Nikolaevna and Lydia will be alone in the carriage and you could have the front seat. . . .'

'No, there wouldn't be room for me on the front seat. And what should I do there?'

'Well, then, would you like Misha to hire another horse for you?'

'What will he be saying next!' Oblomov said, almost to himself. 'Why are you so keen on the Goryunovs?'

'Oh!' cried Volkov, flushing. 'Shall I tell you?'

'Do!'

'You won't tell anyone, on your honour?' Volkov continued, sitting down beside him.

'Very well.'

'I – I am in love with Lydia,' he whispered.

'Bravo! Since when? She is very charming, I believe.'

'I've been in love for the last three weeks!' Volkov said with a deep sigh. 'And Misha is in love with Dashenka.'

'Who is Dashenka?'

'Where have you lived, Oblomov? You don't know Dashenka? Why, the whole town is raving about her! How she dances! To-night he and I are going to the ballet; he will throw a bouquet. I must introduce him. He is shy, still new to it all. Oh, by the way, I have to go and buy some camellias. . . .'

'Where are you off to? Don't bother, come and dine with me instead; we could have a talk. I have had two misfortunes. . . .'

'I can't, I am dining at Prince Tyumenev's; the Goryunovs will be there and she . . . Lydinka,' he added in a whisper. 'Why have you given up the prince? Such a gay house! Such style! And his summer villa! It is simply buried in flowers! He has added a balcony to it – *gothique*. In the summer, I hear, he is going to have dances and living pictures. Will you be coming?'

'No, I don't think I will.'

'Oh, what a house it is! Last winter there were never fewer than fifty people there on Wednesdays, and some-times as many as a hundred. . . .'

'My goodness! It must have been frightfully boring.'

'How could it? Boring! Why, the more the merrier. Lydia used to come, I did not notice her at at first and then suddenly . . .

> "In vain I try to think of her no more
> And let my reason overcome my passion,"'

he sang, and without thinking sat down in the arm-chair, but jumped up suddenly and started dusting his clothes. 'How dusty your room is!' he said.

'It's Zahar,' Oblomov complained.

'Well, it's time I was going,' said Volkov. 'I must get those camellias for Misha's bouquet. *Au revoir*.'

'Come and have tea with me in the evening after the ballet, and tell me all about it,' Oblomov invited him.

'I can't, I promised to go to the Mussinskys': it's their *jour fixe*. You come too. Would you like me to introduce you?'

'No, whatever should I do there?'

'At the Mussinskys'? Why, half the town goes there! Do there? It's a house where they talk about everything.'

'That's just what's dull – talking about everything,' Oblomov said.

'Well, then, visit the Mezdrovs,' Volkov interrupted him. 'There they talk about one thing only – art; all one hears is the Venetian school, Beethoven, Bach, Leonardo da Vinci. . . .'

'Always the same thing – how boring! They must be pedants,' Oblomov said, yawning.

'There's no pleasing you. But there are plenty of houses where you can go. Everyone has fixed days now: the Savinovs have dinners on Thursdays, the Maklashins on Fridays, the Vyaznikovs on Sundays, Prince Tyumenev on Wednesdays. I am engaged every day of the week!' Volkov concluded with shining eyes.

'Isn't it a bore to go gadding about day after day?'

'A bore? Not a bit of it! It's great fun,' Volkov said lightly. 'In the morning I read – one must be *au courant* of everything and know the news. I have a post that doesn't oblige me to go to the office, thank goodness; I only go twice a week to see the general and have dinner with him. Then I go to call on somebody I haven't seen for a time; well, then . . . there's some new actress either in the Russian or in the French theatre. . . . When the opera season begins I shall book seats for every week. . . . And now I am in love. . . . Summer is coming; Misha has been promised leave; we'll go for a month to their estate for a change. We can go hunting there. They have splendid neighbours who give *bals champêtres*. Lydia and I will go for walks in the woods, pick flowers, go boating. . . . Ach!' he turned round with sheer delight. 'But it's time I went. . . . Good-bye,' he said, trying in vain to have a look at himself in the dusty mirror.

'Stay,' Oblomov detained him, 'I wanted to talk business with you.'

'I am sorry, I haven't time,' Volkov was in a hurry;

'another day! Won't you come with me and have some oysters, then you can tell me? Come, Misha is treating us.'

'No, thank you!' said Oblomov.

'Good-bye then.'

He walked to the door and came back.

'Have you seen this?' he asked, showing his hand in a beautifully fitting glove.

'What's this?' Oblomov asked in perplexity.

'Why, the new *lacets*! You see how beautifully it pulls the glove together: one needn't struggle over a button for two hours. You just pull the lace and it's done. It's fresh from Paris. Shall I bring you a pair just to try?'

'Very well, do!'

'And look at this, isn't it charming?' he said, picking out one of his trinkets. 'It's a visiting-card with a corner turned down.'

'I can't read what's on it.'

'Pr. – prince, M. – Michel, but there wasn't room for Tyumenev's name; he gave me this at Easter instead of an egg. But good-bye, *au revoir*. I have another ten calls to make. By Jove, how jolly life is!'

And he disappeared.

'Ten calls in one day – unfortunate man!' thought Oblomov. 'And this is life!' he shrugged his shoulders. 'What is left of a man, frittered and split up like that? Of course it isn't bad to look in at the theatre and to fall in love with Lydia . . . she is charming! To pick flowers and go driving with her in the country is quite good; but ten calls in one day – unfortunate man!' he concluded, turning over on his back and rejoicing that he had no such empty thoughts and desires and that he did not rush about, but lay where he was, preserving his peace and human dignity.

A fresh ring at the bell interrupted his reflections.

Another visitor came in.

It was a man in a dark-green coat with brass stamped buttons; dark whiskers evenly framed his worn-out, clean-shaven face, with tired but calm and thoughtful eyes and a dreamy smile.

'How do you do, Sudbinsky?' Oblomov greeted him cheerfully. 'You've looked up your old colleague at last! Don't come near me, you bring the cold air in!'

'How do you do, Ilya Ilyitch? I have long been meaning to call,' said the visitor, 'but you know what a devilish lot of work I have. Here you see I am taking a whole case full of papers to report on; I have told the courier to gallop straight here if I am asked for. I can't call my soul my own.'

'You are going to the office? So late?' Oblomov asked. 'You used to be there at ten o'clock. . . .'

'I used to, yes, but now it's different; I drive there at twelve.' He emphasized the word 'drive.'

'Ah, I guess!' said Oblomov. 'You are head of the Department! Since when?'

Sudbinsky nodded significantly.

'Since Easter,' he said. 'But the amount of work – it's simply dreadful! From eight to twelve I work at home, from twelve till five at the office, and then again in the evening. I have grown quite unsociable!'

'Hm, head of the Department, indeed!' said Oblomov. 'Congratulations! That's fine. And we used to be office clerks together! I should think you will be made a State Councillor next year.'

'Oh no, no chance of that! I must first get an Order of Merit; I thought I was to have it last year, but now that I have received my new post I can't expect a fresh promotion just yet.'

'Come and have dinner with me, let's drink to your promotion,' Oblomov said.

'No, I am dining with the vice-director to-day. I must prepare the report for Thursday – an awful business! There is no relying on the provincial reports. I have to check the lists; Foma Fomitch is so particular, he wants to see to everything himself, so we shall sit down to it together after dinner.'

'After dinner, really?' Oblomov asked incredulously.

'And what did you think? I shall be lucky if we finish early and I have time to drive to Ekaterinhof. By the way,

I came to ask won't you come with me? I would call for you. . . .'

'I can't, I don't feel very well,' said Oblomov, frowning. 'And I have a lot to do. . . .'

'That's a pity,' said Sudbinsky. 'It's a fine day. This is my only chance to have an outing.'

'Well, what news at the office?' Oblomov asked.

'Oh, a good many changes: in letters you no longer write "your humble servant," but "rest assured of"; it's not necessary now to send in two copies of one's official record. Three more sections are being opened and two special officials will be appointed extra. Our Committee has been closed. . . . Many changes!'

'And what is happening to our former colleagues?'

'Nothing, so far; Svinkin has mislaid a set of papers!'

'Really? What did the directors do?' Oblomov asked in a trembling voice. He felt frightened as in the old days at the office.

'He has withheld Svinkin's promotion until the papers are found. It's an important case, concerning fines. The director thinks,' Sudbinsky added almost in a whisper, 'that he has mislaid them . . . deliberately.'

'And so you are always busy,' said Oblomov, 'working!'

'Fearfully busy! But, of course, it's very pleasant working with a man like Foma Fomitch; he never fails to encourage one; he doesn't forget even those who do nothing. Those who have served long enough he recommends for promotion and those who haven't – for a bonus or an order of merit.'

'What do you earn?'

'Oh, nothing to speak of: 1,200 roubles salary, 750 for food, 600 for lodging, 900 subsidy, 500 travelling expenses, and up to 1,000 in bonuses.'

'I say!' cried Oblomov, jumping off the bed. 'Have you a fine voice or what? You are paid like an Italian singer!'

'Why, that's nothing! Peresvetov has additional moneys as well, and he does less work than I and doesn't know his business. But, of course, he hasn't the same reputation. They think very highly of me,' he added modestly, casting his eyes down; 'the minister said the other day that I was a credit to the Department.'

'Well done!' said Oblomov. 'But fancy working from eight till twelve and from twelve till five and then at home again – oïe-oïe-oïe!'

He shook his head.

'But what should I do if I weren't at the office?' Sudbinsky asked.

'Oh, lots of things! You could read, write. . . .'

'Why, I do nothing but read and write now.'

'That's not it; you might write for the Press. . . .'

'Everyone can't be a writer. You don't write yourself.'

'But I have an estate on my hands,' Oblomov said with a sigh. 'I am thinking out a new plan of management, introducing all sorts of improvements. It's no end of trouble. . . . But you are doing other people's work, not your own.'

'Well, there is nothing for it! One must work if one is paid. I shall have a rest in the summer: Foma Fomitch has promised to think of some special commission for me, then I shall receive travelling money to hire five horses, three roubles a day for my keep, and a bonus afterwards. . . .'

'They've money to throw away!' Oblomov said enviously, then he sighed and grew thoughtful.

'I need money: I am getting married in the autumn,' Sudbinsky added.

'What! Indeed, to whom?' Oblomov asked sympathetically.

'Yes, really – Miss Murashin. Do you remember, they were staying next to me in the summer holidays? You had tea with me and I believe you met her.'

'No, I don't remember. Is she pretty?'

'Yes, she is nice looking. Let us go to dinner with them, if you like.'

Oblomov hesitated.

'Yes . . . very well, only. . . .'

'Next week,' Sudbinsky suggested.

'Yes, yes, next week,' Oblomov was relieved, 'my clothes aren't ready yet. Well, is it a good match?'

'Yes, her father is a general; he is giving her ten thousand roubles, and has free Government quarters; he has given us half the twelve rooms; furniture, lighting and heating is provided; it won't be so bad. . . .'

'I should think not, indeed! You lucky fellow!' Oblomov added, not without envy.

'You must be my best man, Oblomov, remember!'

'Certainly, by all means. And how are Kuznetsov, Vassilyev, Mahov?'

'Kuznetsov has been married for some time, Mahov is now in my place, and Vassilyev has been transferred to Poland. Ivan Petrovitch has received the Order of St. Vladimir, Oleshkin is now "His Excellency." '

'He is a good sort,' said Oblomov.

'Yes, quite; he deserves it.'

'So good-natured, kind, and even-tempered.'

'So obliging,' Sudbinsky added, 'and never trying, you know, to put himself forward, to make mischief, to trip one up or outshine one . . . he does all he can for one.'

'An excellent man! I remember if I made a muddle of some report, omitted something, made a wrong summary, or quoted the wrong law, he never made any trouble, but merely told somebody else to do the work over again. A splendid man!' Oblomov concluded.

'And our Semyon Semyonitch is incorrigible,' Sudbinsky said; 'he is only good at showing off. You know what he did the other day? – We were asked to have kennels for watch-dogs next to our Department buildings in the provinces, to guard Government property; our architect, a practical and honest man who knows his business, drew up a very moderate estimate, but it struck Semyon Semyonitch as too high; he began making inquiries how much the building of a dog-kennel may cost, found a contractor who would do it for thirty copecks less, and at once wrote an official report about it. . . .'

There was a ring at the bell.

'Good-bye,' Sudbinsky said. 'I've stayed chattering too long. I may be wanted at the office. . . .'

'Don't go yet,' Oblomov detained him. 'I want to ask your advice, by the way: I have had two misfortunes. . . .'

'No, no, I would rather call again one day soon,' said the visitor, leaving the room.

'You are stuck in it, my friend; in it up to your ears,' thought Oblomov, watching him go. 'He is blind, and deaf, and dumb to everything in the world but his office. But he will get on, he will be somebody to be reckoned with one day, hold a high rank in the service. . . . It's called making a career! But it's wasting a man: intelligence, will, feeling are not wanted; a mere luxury! He will go through life and a great deal in him will never be awakened. . . . And he works from twelve till five at his office, from eight till twelve at home . . . unfortunate man!' He felt a peaceful joy at the thought that he could stay in bed from nine till three, from eight till nine, and was proud that he need not go and make reports or write papers, but could give free play to his feelings and imagination.

Oblomov was so occupied with his reflections that he failed to notice a very thin dark man standing by the bed; his features could hardly be seen for whiskers, moustache, and an imperial, and he was dressed with intentional carelessness.

'How do you do, Ilya Ilyitch?'

'How do you do, Penkin? Don't come near me, you come in from the cold!' Oblomov said.

'Oh, you queer man! The same incorrigible idler, with no care in the world!'

'No care in the world, indeed!' Oblomov said. 'I'll show you a letter from my bailiff; I keep puzzling my head over it, and you say I have no cares! Where do you come from?'

'From a booksellers', I went to ask whether the magazines are out. Have you read my article?'

'No.'

'I will send it you, read it.'

'What is it about?' Oblomov asked, yawning violently.

'About trade, about the emancipation of women, about the lovely April weather we have been having, and about a new fire-extinguisher. How is it you don't read the papers? They reflect our everyday life. And above all, I am a champion of realism in literature.'

'Have you much work?'

'Yes, a good deal. I write two articles for the paper every week, review novels, and have just written a story....'

'What about?'

'Of how the mayor of a little town boxes the shopkeepers' ears....'

'Yes, that is indeed realism in literature,' said Oblomov.

'Isn't it?' – the literary gentleman was pleased. 'The idea I want to express is this – and I know it's a new and bold one: a traveller passing through the town saw the beating and complained about it to the Governor. The Governor ordered an official who was going to the town on legal business to inquire into the matter incidentally, and to find out all he could about the mayor's character and conduct. The official called the tradespeople together as though to ask about their trade, and began questioning them about that too. And what do you think? They bowed and laughed and praised the mayor up to the skies. The official made inquiries elsewhere and was told that the shopkeepers were fearful rascals, sold rotten goods, gave short measure, cheated the Government, were immoral, so that the beating was a righteous judgment upon them....'

'So the mayor's fists play the part of Fate in the ancient tragedies?' Oblomov asked.

'Precisely,' Penkin acquiesced. 'You have much subtlety, Ilya Ilyitch, you ought to be a writer! And I have

succeeded at the same time in showing up both the
mayor's tyranny and the people's depravity; the bad
methods adopted by the subordinate officials and the need
for stern but just measures. Don't you think it's a rather
– new idea?'

'Yes, especially to me,' Oblomov said. 'I read so little.'

'That's true, one doesn't see many books in your
room!' Penkin said. 'But I implore you, read one thing, a
magnificent poem is going to be published, a denunciatory
poem, if one may say so: *The Love of a Bribe-taker for a
Fallen Woman*. I can't tell you who the author is, it is still
a secret.'

'What's in it?'

'The whole mechanism of our social life is shown up,
and it is all done poetically. All the springs are touched,
all the rungs of the social ladder are commented on. The
author calls up, as though before a judgment-seat, a weak
and vicious statesman and a swarm of corrupt officials
who deceive him; all the varieties of fallen women are
considered . . . Frenchwomen, German, Finnish, and
everything is so wonderfully, so incredibly true to life. . . .
I have heard parts of it – the author is great! He reminds
one of Dante and of Shakespeare. . . .'

'That's going a bit far!' said Oblomov, sitting up in
surprise.

Penkin stopped, seeing that he really had gone too far.

'Read it, you will see for yourself,' he added, this time
without enthusiasm.

'No, Penkin, I will not read it.'

'Why not? It is creating a sensation, people are talking
about it. . . .'

'Oh, let them! Some people have nothing to do but
talk. It's their vocation.'

'You might read it just out of curiosity.'

'What is there to be curious about?' Oblomov asked.
'Why do they write? – merely to amuse themselves.'

'How do you mean? It is so true to life! Laughably so.
Like living portraits. Whomever they take – a merchant, a

Government clerk, an officer, a policeman – it's just like the real thing.'

'Is it for sport they do it, then – just to show they can take anyone they please and make a true likeness of him? But there is no life in anything they do, no understanding, no sympathy, no human feeling. It's mere vanity. They describe thieves or fallen women exactly as though they had caught them in the street and taken them to prison. One feels in their story not the "invisible tears," but only the visible, coarse, malicious laughter. . . .'

'What more do you want? It's excellent, you have said it yourself: this burning malice, bitter denunciation of vice, contemptuous laughter at fallen humanity . . . that's everything!'

'No, it isn't everything!' cried Oblomov, suddenly firing up. 'Depict a thief, a fallen woman, a stuck-up fool, but don't forget they are human beings. Where is your human feeling? You think you can write from the head only,' Oblomov almost hissed. 'You imagine thought does not need the heart? Yes, thought is made fruitful by love. Stretch a helping hand to the fallen man or weep over him, but don't jeer! Love him, try to see yourself in him, and heal him as you would yourself – then I will read you and bow down before you . . .' he said, lying down comfortably once more. 'They describe a thief or a fallen woman, but forget to bring out the human being in them or perhaps don't know how to do it. What art, what poetry do you see in that? Denounce depravity and filth, only please don't pretend to be poets.'

'I suppose you would have us describe nature – roses, nightingales, or frosty mornings, while everything around us is in movement and turmoil? We want the bare physiology of society, that's all; we have no time for songs nowadays. . . .'

'Give me man,' Oblomov said; 'love him. . . .'

'Love usurers, sanctimonious prigs, stupid officials – do you hear that? What are you talking about? One can see you don't go in for literature!' Penkin protested warmly. 'No, they must be denounced, cast out from citizenship, from society. . . .'

'Cast out from society!' Oblomov began with sudden inspiration, jumping to his feet. 'That's forgetting that there is a higher element in this unworthy vessel; that, however corrupt, he is a man – the same as yourself. Cast him out! And how will you cast him out from humanity, from nature, from the mercy of God?' he almost shouted, with blazing eyes.

'That's going a bit too far!' Penkin said in his turn with surprise.

Oblomov saw that he also had gone too far. He subsided, stood still for a moment, yawned, and slowly lay down again.

Both were silent.

'What do you read, then?' Penkin asked.

'I – well, mostly books of travel.'

Another silence.

'You will read the poem when it comes out, won't you? I would bring it you . . .' Penkin asked.

Oblomov shook his head.

'Well, shall I send you my story?'

Oblomov nodded.

'It's time I was going to the printers',' Penkin said. 'Do you know why I have called? I came to ask you to go to Ekaterinhof with me; I have a carriage. I must write an article to-morrow about May Day festivities; we would look round together, you might point out to me what I don't observe; it would be more amusing. Do come!'

'No, I don't feel well,' said Oblomov, frowning and covering himself with the blanket. 'I am afraid of the damp, the ground isn't dry yet. But you might come to dinner with me to-day; we could have a talk. . . . I have had two misfortunes. . . .'

'No, the whole of our staff dine at St. George's to-day, and we go to Ekaterinhof from there. And in the night I must write and send the stuff to the printers before the morning. Good-bye.'

'Good-bye, Penkin.'

'To write at night,' thought Oblomov; 'when does he sleep? I expect, though, he earns about five thousand a year – that's something! But to keep writing, to spend one's mind and soul on trifles, to change one's convictions, to sell one's intelligence and imagination, to do violence to one's nature, to be perpetually astir with excitement, to know no rest and be always constantly on the go! . . . And to write and write, like a wheel or a machine, to-morrow, the day after, on holidays; summer will come – and he must still be writing! When is he to stop and rest? Unfortunate man!'

He turned his head towards the table where all was smooth and bare, the ink dry, and no pen to be seen, and rejoiced that he lay as free of care as a new-born babe, without dissipating his energies or selling anything. . . . 'And the bailiff's letter and the flat?' he remembered suddenly, and fell to musing again.

But there was another ring at the bell.

'I seem to be having a regular reception to-day,' thought Oblomov, wondering who the visitor was.

There was nothing definite about either the age or the appearance of the man who came into the room; he was at a time of life when it is difficult to guess a man's years. He was neither plain nor handsome, neither tall nor short, neither dark nor fair. Nature had not bestowed upon him a single striking, noticeable characteristic, good or bad. Many people called him Ivan Ivanitch, some thought he was Ivan Vassilyitch, and others Ivan Mihailitch. There were several versions of his surname too: some said he was Ivanov, some called him Vassilyev or Andreyev, and others thought he was Alexeyev. If a person seeing him for the first time was told his name he invariably forgot it at once as well as his face, and never noticed what the man said. His presence added nothing to society and his absence took nothing away from it. His mind was as lacking in wit, originality, and other peculiarities as his body in any special marks. He might have been able to relate what he had seen or heard and to entertain other people at least in that way, but he never went anywhere; he was born in Petersburg and never left it, consequently he saw and heard what others knew already. Is such a man attractive? Does he love, does he hate, does he suffer? One would think he, too, can suffer and love or not love – for no one is exempt from that – but he somehow manages to love everyone. There are people in whom one cannot at any cost rouse the spirit of hostility, vengeance, etc. Whatever one does to them, they go on being affectionate. Although it is usually said of them that they love everyone and therefore are good-hearted, in truth they don't love anyone, and are said to be kind simply because they are not ill-natured. If such a man sees others giving alms to a beggar, he, too, will give him a penny; but if others abuse the man or laugh at him and drive him away, he will join in the abuse and the laughter. He cannot be called wealthy because he is rather poor than rich, but he cannot be called poor either, because there are many people poorer than he. He has a private income of some three hundred roubles a year; he has, besides, a small post of some sort and receives a small salary; he does not suffer privations and does not borrow money, and it certainly never occurs to anyone to borrow from him. He has no special job at his office because his colleagues and superiors can never discover if there is any one thing he does better or worse than other things, and cannot decide what precisely he is fitted for.

It is not likely that anyone except his mother notices his appearance in the world; very few notice him while he lives, and certainly no one will miss him when he is gone; no one will ask after him, will regret his death or rejoice at it. He has no friends and no enemies, but plenty of acquaintances. Perhaps only his funeral procession will attract the attention of a passer-by, who will for the first time honour this colourless personality by a profound bow; and maybe some inquisitive man will run in front of the procession to ask the dead man's name, and immediately forget it.

This Alexeyev, Vassilyev, Andreyev, or whatever you like to call him, was simply an incomplete, impersonal shadow of the human crowd, its dull echo, its dim reflection.

Even Zahar, who in his candid talks during the social gatherings by the gate or in the shop gave keen character-sketches of all his master's visitors, always felt puzzled when it came to – let us call him Alexeyev. He pondered, trying to catch some outstanding feature in the face, the figure, the manners, or the character of the man, and at last said with a wave of his hand: 'And this one is nothing to look at and has nothing to say for himself.'

'Ah,' Oblomov greeted him, 'it's you, Alexeyev? How do you do? Where do you come from? Don't come near me, I won't shake hands: you come straight from the cold air!'

'Why, it isn't cold! I hadn't meant to call on you to-day,' Alexeyev said, 'but I met Ovchinin and he carried me off. I have come to fetch you, Ilya Ilyitch.'

'What for?'

'Let us go to Ovchinin's. Alyanov, Pkaïlo, and Koly-myagin are there.'

'What are they doing there, and what do they want with me?'

'Ovchinin invites you to dinner.'

'Hm! to dinner . . .' Oblomov repeated without expression.

'And then they are all going to Ekaterinhof; they ask you to hire a carriage.'

'And what are we going to do there?'

'Do there? Why, everybody goes there to-day! Don't you know it's the first of May?'

'Sit down; we'll think about it,' Oblomov said.

'Do get up! It's time to dress.'

'Wait a little, it is still early.'

'Early, indeed! They asked you to come at twelve; we'll have dinner early, about two o'clock, and go to Ekaterin-hof. Make haste and come! Shall I tell Zahar to help you to dress?'

'I can't dress, I haven't washed yet!'

'Well, wash then.'

Alexeyev walked about the room, stopped before a picture which he had seen a thousand times already, glanced
out of the window, picked up some knick-knack off the
chiffonier, turned it about, looked at it from all sides, put
it back and began pacing up and down the room again,
whistling, so as not to disturb Oblomov getting up and
washing. Some ten minutes passed in this way.

'Well!' Alexeyev asked suddenly.

'What?'

'You are still lying down?'

'But need I get up?'

'Of course, they are waiting for us. You wanted to
go. . . .'

'Go where? I didn't want to go anywhere.'

'Why, Ilya Ilyitch, we have just been saying we
were going to dine at Ovchinin's and then go to Ekaterinhof. . . .'

'To think of my going there in the damp! And what's
the attraction? It looks like rain, too, it's dull outside,'
Oblomov said lazily.

'Not a cloud in the sky and you talk of rain! It seems
dull because your windows haven't been washed for
months! The dirt on them! You can't see the light of day,
and one curtain is almost down.'

'Yes, and if you try to mention it to Zahar he will at
once suggest hiring charwomen and driving me out of the
house for the whole day!'

Oblomov fell to musing and Alexeyev sat by the table
drumming his fingers on it and looking absentmindedly at
the walls and the ceiling.

'Well then, what shall we do? Will you dress or remain
as you are?' he asked after a few minutes.

'Where do you want me to go?'

'Why, to Ekaterinhof.'

'How you do keep on!' Oblomov answered with vexation. 'Why can't you stay here? Is the room cold or is
there a bad smell that you are so anxious to dash away?'

'No, I always like being with you; I am quite content,' Alexeyev said.

'And if you are happy here, why want to go elsewhere? You had better spend the day with me and have dinner, and then in the evening you may do as you like. Oh, I have forgotten, I can't possibly go! Tarantyev is coming to dinner: it's Saturday.'

'If that's how it is . . . very well . . . I'll do as you wish,' said Alexeyev.

'Have I said anything to you about my affairs?' Oblomov asked quickly.

'What affairs? I don't know,' Alexeyev answered, looking at him open-eyed.

'Why do you suppose I haven't got up all this time? I've been lying here thinking how I can get out of trouble.'

'What is it?' Alexeyev asked, trying to look alarmed.

'Two misfortunes! I don't know what to do.'

'What misfortunes?'

'They are driving me out of my flat; just imagine – I have to move! The fuss, the breakages . . . dreadful to think of it! I have lived here for eight years, you know. My landlord has played me a nasty trick, "Make haste and move," he says.'

'Make haste! So I suppose he needs the flat. Moving is a fearful nuisance; such a lot to see to . . .' Alexeyev said, 'Things get broken and lost – very annoying. And you have such a nice flat. . . . What rent do you pay?'

'Where can I find another such, and in a hurry too?' Oblomov went on. 'The rooms are warm and dry, and it is a respectable house: we've only been burgled once! You may think the ceiling is unsafe – the plaster has almost come off – but yet it doesn't come down.'

'Just fancy!' Alexeyev said, shaking his head.

'What could I do, I wonder, so that I need not – move?' Oblomov argued with himself thoughtfully.

'Have you a contract for the flat?' Alexeyev asked, looking the room up and down.

'Yes, but the time is up; I've been paying the rent
monthly for some time. . . . I don't remember for how
long.'

Both were thoughtful.

'What, then, do you intend to do?' Alexeyev asked after
a pause. 'Will you move or stay?'

'I don't intend anything,' Oblomov answered. 'I don't
want even to think of it. Let Zahar think of something.'

'And some people, you know, like moving,' Alexeyev
said, 'that's their one pleasure – changing lodgings.'

'Well, let people like that move! As for me, I can't
stand changes of any kind. But this about the flat isn't the
worst! See what my bailiff writes me. I will show you the
letter . . . where is it? Zahar, Zahar!'

'Oh, Queen of Heaven!' Zahar hissed, jumping off his
stove-shelf. 'When will God put an end to my troubles?'

He came in and looked dully at his master.

'Have you found the letter?'

'Where am I to find it? How do I know which letter
you want? I cannot read.'

'Never mind, look for it,' Oblomov said.

'You were reading some letter last night,' Zahar said,
'but I haven't seen it since.'

'Where is it, then?' Ilya Ilyitch retorted with vexation.
'I haven't swallowed it. I remember very well that you
took it from me and put it somewhere over there. Why,
there it is!'

He shook the blanket and the letter fell on the floor
from its folds.

'You are always blaming me!' . . . 'There, there, you
can go!' Zahar and Oblomov shouted at each other at the
same time. Zahar left the room and Oblomov began reading the letter, written as though in *kvass* on grey paper
and sealed with drab-coloured sealing-wax.

' "Dear Sir, your honour, our father and benefactor,
Ilya Ilyitch . . . " ' Oblomov began.

He omitted several greetings and good wishes and read
from the middle.

' "I inform you, our gracious master, that everything is well on your estate. There has been no rain for five weeks; the Lord God must be angry with us. The old people don't remember there ever having been such a drought; the spring crops are burned up as with fire. Winter crops have been ruined, some by caterpillars and some by early frosts; we ploughed them over to sow spring crops instead, but we don't know if anything will come up. We pray the merciful Lord may spare your honour, for ourselves we do not care if we have to rot. On St. John's Eve three more peasants ran away: Laptev, Balochov, and the blacksmith's son, Vaska, by himself. I sent the women after their husbands, but the women never returned, and are living at Tcholki, I hear. A mate of mine from Verhlyovo went to Tcholki, the steward sent him there; it appears a foreign plough had been brought to Tcholki and the steward sent my mate to have a look at it. I told him about the runaway peasants; he said: 'I went to the police captain and the police captain said, "Send in a petition and then I will do it and dispatch the peasants back to their proper homes," and did not say anything else, and I fell at his feet and begged him tearfully, and he bawled at the top of his voice, "Be off with you, I've told you I would do it if you send in a petition!"' But I never did send in a petition, and there is no one I can hire here; they have all gone to the Volga to work at the barges – the people are so foolish nowadays, dear father and benefactor, Ilya Ilyitch! There will be none of our linen at the fair this year: I have locked up the drying- and bleaching-house and put Sytchug to watch it night and day. He is a sober man, and lest he should filch any of my master's goods I watch over him night and day. Other peasants drink a lot and ask permission to go away and pay a tax instead of working at home; they haven't paid up their arrears. This year we will send you some two thousand less than last year, our father and benefactor, unless the drought ruins us altogether, but we will send what we say as I have put it to your honour." '

Then followed expressions of devotion and the signature: 'Your bailiff and most humble serf, Prokofy Vytyagushkin, has put his hand to it with his own hand.' Being illiterate he put a cross under the letter. 'Written from the words of the said bailiff by his brother-in-law, Dyomka Krivoy.'

Oblomov glanced at the end of the letter. 'There is no month or year,' he said; 'the letter must have been lying about at the bailiff's since last year: he talks of St. John's Eve and drought! He thought of sending it rather late in the day!' He sank into thought.

'How do you like his suggesting to send me some two thousand less, eh?' he went on. 'How much will that leave? What did I receive last year?' he asked, looking at Alexeyev. 'I didn't tell you then, did I?'

Alexeyev turned his eyes to the ceiling and pondered.

'I must ask Stolz when he comes,' Oblomov continued. 'I believe it was seven or eight thousand . . . it's bad not to put things down! So now he wants to reduce me to six thousand! Why, I shall starve! How can I live on it?'

'Why let it disturb you, Ilya Ilyitch?' Alexeyev said. 'One must never despair; it's a long lane that has no turning.'

'But do you hear what he says? Instead of sending me money or giving me some pleasant surprise, he does nothing but distress me, as though on purpose! Every year, you know! I am not myself now! Some two thousand less!'

'Yes, it's a great loss,' Alexeyev said; 'two thousand is no joke! They say Alexey Loginitch has also received this year only twelve thousand instead of seventeen.'

'Twelve and not six, anyway,' Oblomov interrupted him. 'The bailiff has quite upset me! Even if it really is true about the crops failing and the drought, why alarm one before he need?'

'Yes – that's true –' Alexeyev began, 'he shouldn't, but how can one expect refined feelings from a peasant? Those people don't understand.'

'Well, what would you do in my place?' Oblomov asked, looking inquiringly at Alexeyev in the vague hope that he might think of something reassuring.

'I must consider it, Ilya Ilyitch, I can't say off-hand,' Alexeyev said.

'I wonder if I ought to write to the Governor?' Ilya Ilyitch said meditatively.

'Who is your Governor?'

Ilya Ilyitch made no answer and sank into thought. Alexeyev did not speak any more and also pondered.

Crumpling the letter in his hands, Oblomov leaned his head on them, resting his elbows on his knees, and sat so for a time tormented by disturbing thoughts.

'I wish Stolz would make haste and come!' he said. 'He writes he is coming, but goodness knows where he is. He would settle it all.'

He looked doleful again. There was a long silence. Oblomov was the first to rouse himself at last.

'This is what I must do,' he said decidedly, and almost got out of bed, 'and do it at once too! It's no use wasting time. . . . To begin with. . . .'

At that moment there was a desperate ring at the front-door bell. Oblomov and Alexeyev started, and Zahar instantly jumped off his stove-shelf.

III

'AT home?' someone asked in the hall rudely and loudly.

'Where could he go at this hour?' Zahar answered, still more rudely.

The man who came in was about forty, tall, bulky, broad-shouldered, with a big head, large features, a short, thick neck, big protruding eyes, and thick lips. The merest glance at him gave one the impression of coarseness and untidiness. He obviously did not aim at elegance. It was not often that one saw him properly shaved, but he evidently did not care. He was not ashamed of his clothes and wore them with a kind of cynical dignity. He was Mihey Andreyevitch Tarantyev, and came from the same district as Oblomov.

Tarantyev looked at the world morosely and almost contemptuously, with obvious ill will for all around him; he was ready to abuse everyone and everything, as though he had suffered some injustice, had not received due recognition, or were persecuted by destiny and submitted to it, defiantly and unwillingly, like a man of strong character. His gestures were bold and sweeping; he spoke loudly, quickly, and almost always angrily; if one listened to him from a distance, it sounded like three empty carts going over a bridge. He had no regard for anyone, was never at a loss for a word, and was generally rude to everyone, including his friends, as though implying that he bestowed a great honour on a person by talking to him or sharing his dinner or supper.

Tarantyev was quick and cunning; no one could deal better than he with practical questions of a general character or complicated legal cases: he immediately decided how one ought to act in the circumstances, adduced subtle proofs of his theory, and in conclusion almost invariably snubbed the person who had asked his advice.

And yet, having entered an office twenty-five years before as a clerk, he remained at the same post till his hair began to turn grey. But it never occurred either to him or to anyone else that he might advance in the service. The fact was that Tarantyev was only good at talking; so long as it was a matter of words he settled everything simply and easily, especially where other people were concerned. But the moment he had to stir a finger, to make some move – in short, to apply his own theory in practice and to show quickness and energy – he became an utterly different man: he failed to rise to the occasion; he suddenly felt depressed or unwell or shy, or he found he had to attend to some other business – which he did not do either, or if he did, it was with disastrous results. He behaved just like a child: he overlooked things; proved to be ignorant of the merest trifles; was never in time for an appointment; and, finally, either threw up the business half-way or started at the wrong end and made such a mess of it that no one could put it right – and he abused other people afterwards.

His father, a provincial lawyer of the old-fashioned type, had meant his son to inherit his art and experience in seeing after other people's affairs, and to repeat his successful career in a Government office; but fate decided otherwise. The father, who had had no education, wanted his son to keep up with the times and to learn something besides the complicated art of conducting legal business. He sent him for three years to a priest to learn Latin.

The boy was clever and in three years mastered the Latin grammar and syntax and had just begun on Cornelius Nepos when his father decided that it was enough: the knowledge his son had acquired gave him, he thought, enormous advantages over the older generation, and further studies might perhaps interfere with his service in a Government office. Not knowing what to do with his Latin, Mihey, at sixteen, began to forget it in his father's house, but in the meantime, while waiting for the honour of attending the local or the district court, he attended all his father's drinking-parties; and in this school of candid talk the young man's mind developed thoroughly. He listened, with the impressionability of youth, to the stories told by his father and his friends of various lawsuits and of curious cases that had passed through the hands of all these old-fashioned lawyers. All this, however, had led to nothing. In spite of his father's efforts, Mihey did not grow up to be an attorney or a business man, though no doubt the old man would have had it his own way had not fate been against him. Mihey certainly did master his father's theories and had only to put them into practice when his father died without securing for him a post at the law courts. Mihey was taken to Petersburg by some benefactor, who found him a clerk's job in some Government department and then forgot all about him. And so Tarantyev remained a theoretical person all his life. His Latin and his subtle knowledge of how to settle all cases, fairly or unfairly, to his own liking, was of no use to him in Petersburg. And yet he was conscious of a force that lay dormant in him, prevented by hostile circumstances from ever finding an outlet. Perhaps it was this consciousness of useless powers that made Tarantyev rude, spiteful, abusive, and perpetually angry. He looked at his present occupation – the copying out of papers, putting them together, etc. – with bitterness and contempt. One last hope glimmered before him in the distant future – to get a berth in the liquor monopoly; this seemed to him the only profitable alternative to the career his father had intended for him. Meanwhile, his father's theory of life and work – the theory of crooked dealing and bribery – not having found its full and worthy application in the provinces, was applied by him to all the details of his miserable existence in Petersburg and coloured his relations with his friends, for lack of official outlet. He was a bribe-taker by temperament, by conviction, and having no cases or clients he managed to take bribes from his colleagues and friends; in all sorts of ways he forced whomever he could, either by cunning or by bullying, to stand him treat, demanded undeserved deference, made charges. He was never troubled about his shabby clothes, but he felt something like alarm if he could not look forward in the course of the day to an enormous dinner with a decent amount of wine and spirits. Among his friends he acted the part of a big watch-dog which barks at everyone, allows no one to stir, and is sure to catch a piece of meat in the air in whatever direction it may be thrown.

Such were Oblomov's two most assiduous visitors. Why did these two Russian proletarians go to him? They knew very well why: to eat, to drink, to smoke good cigars. They came to a warm and comfortable room and met always with the same reception – not distinctly cold, if not exactly warm. But why Oblomov allowed them to come he probably could hardly tell. Very likely it was for the same reason that even to this day, in our distant Oblomovkas, every well-to-do house is crowded with men and women of this description, penniless, without a trade, with no hands for producing, but with mouths for consuming, and almost always of a certain rank and social standing. There still exist sybarites who need such accessories to their life: they are dull without superfluous people. Who would hand them the snuff-box they cannot find or pick up a fallen handkerchief? To whom could they complain of a headache, expecting sympathy as their due, or tell a bad dream and demand an interpretation of it? Who would read aloud to them at bedtime and so put them to sleep? And sometimes the proletarian would be sent to the nearest town to do some shopping or would help in the house – their hosts could not be bothered with such tasks!

Tarantyev made a lot of noise and roused Oblomov from his dullness and immobility. He shouted, argued, and was as good as a show, thus saving his lazy host the necessity of speaking or acting. Tarantyev brought life, movement, and sometimes news to the room where sleep and sloth reigned supreme. Without stirring a finger, Oblomov could listen and look at something lively that was talking and moving in front of him. Besides, he was simple enough to believe that Tarantyev could really give him sensible advice.

Oblomov put up with Alexeyev's visits for another reason, no less important. If he wanted to live in his own way, i.e. to lie in silence, to doze, or to pace up and down the room, Alexeyev was as good as absent: he, too, was silent, dozed, or looked at a book or lazily examined pictures and knick-knacks, yawning till tears came into his eyes. He could go on like this for three days on end; and if Oblomov was bored of being by himself and wanted to talk, to read, to argue, to show emotion, he had always an obedient and ready listener who shared with equal willingness his silence, his conversation, his emotion, and his way of thinking, whatever it might be. Other visitors came seldom and for a little while, as the first three callers had done; Oblomov was getting more and more out of touch with them. He was sometimes interested in a piece of news, in a conversation lasting some five minutes; but he soon had enough and grew silent. They, however, wanted something in return, they expected him to take part in what interested them. They were at home in the human crowd; every one of them understood life in his own way differently from Oblomov, and yet they would not leave him alone; he disliked it, and it estranged him from them. There was one man who was after his own heart; he, too, gave Oblomov no peace; he, too, loved news, and society, and learning, and life as a whole, but somehow in his case it was deeper, warmer, more sincere; and although Oblomov was kind to everyone, he loved and trusted only him, perhaps because they had grown up, studied, and lived together. This man was Andrey Karlovitch Stolz. He was away, but Oblomov was expecting him back any hour.

IV

'How do you do, neighbour?' Tarantyev said abruptly, stretching a shaggy hand to Oblomov. 'And why are you lying like a log at this hour?'

'Don't come near, you come straight from the cold!' Oblomov said, covering himself up with the blanket.

'What an idea – from the cold!' Tarantyev bawled. 'There, now, take my hand, since I give it you! It will soon be twelve o'clock, and he is still lounging about!'

He wanted to lift Oblomov out of bed, but Oblomov did not give him a chance, quickly putting his feet on the floor and getting into both his slippers at once.

'I was just going to get up,' he said, yawning.

'I know how you get up; you would have lain here till dinner. Hey, Zahar, where are you, you old fool? Make haste and help your master to dress!'

'Have a Zahar of your own first and then swear at him!' said Zahar, walking in and looking spitefully at Tarantyev. 'The mess you have made on the floor, a regular navvy!' he added.

'He is answering back, the ugly creature!' Tarantyev said, lifting his foot to kick Zahar as he walked past him; but Zahar stopped and turned to him bristling.

'Just you try to touch me! What next? I'll go . . .' he said, walking back towards the door.

'There, there, Mihey Andreyitch! What a quarrelsome man you are! Why can't you leave him alone? Give me the things, Zahar.'

Zahar returned and, glancing sideways at Tarantyev, scuffled past him. Leaning on Zahar, Oblomov reluctantly rose from the bed like one very tired and as reluctantly walked to a big chair; he sank into it and sat still. Zahar took up the pomatum, a comb, and brushes from the table, oiled Oblomov's hair, made a parting in it, and then brushed it.

'Will you wash now?' he asked.

'I'll wait a bit,' Oblomov answered, 'you can go now.'

'Oh, you are here too?' Tarantyev said, suddenly turning to Alexeyev while Zahar was brushing Oblomov's hair. 'I hadn't noticed you. What are you doing here? What a pig that relative of yours is! I've been meaning to tell you. . . .'

'What relative? I haven't any.' Alexeyev was taken aback and answered timidly, looking wide-eyed at Tarantyev.

'Why, the one who is in the service here; whatever is he called? . . . Oh yes, Afanasyev. Of course he is a relation of yours.'

'But my name is Alexeyev, not Afanasyev, and I have no relations.'

'Of course he is a relation! He is as poor a specimen as you are, and his name is Vassily Nikolaitch too.'

'I swear he is a stranger to me; my name is Ivan Alexeyitch.'

'Well, anyway he is like you to look at. But he is a pig; you must tell him so when you see him.'

'I don't know him, I've never seen him,' Alexeyev said, opening his snuff-box.

'Give me some snuff,' Tarantyev said; 'but I believe yours is plain tobacco, not French? Yes, so it is,' he said, taking a pinch. 'Why isn't it French?' he added sternly.

'I have never seen such a pig as that relation of yours,' Tarantyev went on. 'I borrowed fifty roubles from him two years ago. Fifty roubles isn't much, is it? You might think he would forget; but not a bit of it, he remembered. After a month he began asking me wherever he met me, "What about that loan?" I got sick of him! And as though that wasn't enough, yesterday he came to our Department and said, "I expect you have just had your salary and can repay me now." I did go for him! I shamed him so in front of the others that he couldn't find the door soon enough.

"I am a poor man, I need the money." As though I didn't need it! I am not a millionaire to give him fifty roubles for the asking! Give me a cigar, neighbour.'

'The cigars are in a box over there,' Oblomov answered, pointing to a chiffonier. He was sitting dreamily in the easy-chair in his usual gracefully lazy attitude, not noticing what was happening round him or listening to what was being said. He was scrutinizing and stroking his small white hands with tender interest.

'They are the same as before, eh?' Tarantyev asked sternly, taking a cigar and looking at Oblomov.

'Yes, they are,' Oblomov answered absentmindedly.

'But I told you to buy some others, foreign ones! This is how well you remember what is said to you! Mind you buy some by next Saturday or I won't come to see you for weeks. Just see what wretched stuff!' He lighted a cigar, and sending out one cloud of smoke into the room swallowed another. 'One can't smoke it.'

'You have come early to-day, Mihey Andreyitch,' Oblomov said, yawning.

'Are you tired of me, or what?'

'No, I merely mentioned it; you generally come just in time for dinner and now it is only a little after twelve.'

'I have come early on purpose to find out what there is for dinner. You always give one wretched food, so I came to ask what you have ordered for to-day.'

'Ask in the kitchen,' Oblomov said.

Tarantyev went out.

'Upon my word!' he said, returning, 'Beef and veal! Ah, Oblomov, my dear, you don't know how to live, though you are a landowner! You live like a shopkeeper, not like a gentleman; you don't know how to treat a friend to a good dinner! Well, have you bought any Madeira?'

'I don't know, ask Zahar,' Oblomov answered, hardly listening. 'I expect there is some wine left.'

'The same as before, from the German? No, indeed! You must buy some in the English shop.'

'Oh, what we have will do,' Oblomov said. 'It's too much trouble to send.'

'Give me the money, I shall be going past the shop and will bring a bottle. I have still another call to make.'

Oblomov rummaged in a drawer and drew out a red ten-rouble note.

'Madeira costs seven roubles and this is ten,' he said.

'Give it to me, they'll give me change, don't you fear!' He snatched the note out of Oblomov's hand and quickly thrust it in his pocket.

'Well, I'll be going,' Tarantyev said, putting on his hat. 'I will be back by five o'clock; I have a call to make: I've been promised a place in a liquor depot and told to go and inquire. . . . By the way, Ilya Ilyitch, won't you hire a carriage to go to Ekaterinhof to-day? You might take me with you.'

Oblomov shook his head.

'Are you too lazy or do you grudge the money? Oh, you sluggard!' he said. 'Well, good-bye for the present.'

'Wait, Mihey Andreyitch,' Oblomov interrupted him. 'I want to ask your advice.'

'What is it? Be quick, I am in a hurry.'

'Why, two misfortunes have happened to me. I am being driven out of my flat.'

'You evidently don't pay your rent; serves you right,' Tarantyev said, making for the door.

'Oh, nonsense! I always pay in advance. No, they want to rebuild this flat. . . . But wait, where are you off to? Tell me what I am to do: they hurry me and say I must move within a week. . . .'

'Why should I bother to advise you? . . . You need not imagine. . . .'

'I don't imagine anything,' Oblomov said. 'Don't shout and scream, better think of what I am to do. You are a practical man. . . .'

Tarantyev no longer listened, but was pondering something.

'Well, so be it, you may thank me,' he said, taking off his hat and sitting down, 'and order champagne for dinner: your business is settled.'

'How is that?' Oblomov asked.

'Will there be champagne?'

'Perhaps, if your advice is worth it.'

'Yes, but you aren't worth the advice. Why should I advise you for nothing? There, you can ask him,' he added, pointing to Alexeyev, 'or his relative.'

'Come, come, tell me!' Oblomov asked him.

'Listen: you must move to-morrow. . . .'

'Oh, so that's your idea! I knew that much myself. . . .'

'Wait, don't interrupt!' Tarantyev shouted. 'Move to-morrow to a flat I know of on the Vyborg side – a friend of mine has one to let.'

'What next? The Vyborg side! They say wolves come there in winter.'

'They do sometimes run over from the islands, but what has that to do with you?'

'It's dull there, dreary; no one lives there.'

'Rubbish! My friend lives there; she has a house of her own with big kitchen-gardens. She is a widow with two children; her unmarried brother lives with her; he is a cute one, not like that man in the corner here,' he said, pointing to Alexeyev; 'he's sharper than you or I.'

'What has it all to do with me?' Oblomov said impatiently. 'I am not going there.'

'We shall see if you are not! No, if you ask for advice you must abide by it.'

'I will not go,' Oblomov said decisively.

'Damnation take you, then,' Tarantyev answered, and, ramming his hat on to his head, walked to the door.

'You queer fellow,' he said, coming back. 'What's the attraction for you here?'

'What's the attraction? Why, it's near to everything – to the shops and the theatre and my friends . . . it's central.'

'What?' Tarantyev interrupted him. 'And tell me, how long is it since you went out? How long is it since you've been to the theatre? What friends do you visit? Why the devil do you want to be "central," let me ask you?'

'Why? Oh, for lots of reasons.'

'You see, you don't know yourself! And then, just think: you will live in my lady friend's house, peacefully and quietly; no one will disturb you; no noise, no uproar, everything clean and tidy. Why, look, you live here just as at an inn – you, a gentleman and a landowner! And there it is clean and quiet; if you are bored there is someone to talk to. No one will trouble you with visits except me. There are two children; you can play with them as much as you like. What more do you want? And think of what you would save! What do you pay here?'

'Fifteen hundred.'

'And there you would pay a thousand for almost a whole house. And such jolly, light rooms! She has long been wanting a quiet, careful tenant – so I choose you. . . .'

Oblomov shook his head absentmindedly to say no.

'Nonsense, you will move!' Tarantyev said. 'Just think, it will cost you half of what you are spending now; on rooms alone you will gain five hundred roubles. Your food will be twice as good and clean; neither Zahar nor your cook will be able to steal. . . .'

A growl was heard behind the partition.

'There will be more order too,' Tarantyev continued. 'Now it's revolting to sit down to a meal in your flat: you look for pepper – there isn't any; vinegar – they have forgotten to buy it; the knives haven't been cleaned; you say you keep losing your linen, everything is covered with dust – it's disgusting! And there a woman will look after things: you and your stupid Zahar. . . .'

The growling behind the partition grew louder.

'That old dog,' Tarantyev went on, 'will not have to bother about anything – all will be provided. What is there to think about? Move, and make an end of it. . . .'

'But how could I, for no rhyme or reason, suddenly move to the Vyborg side? . . .'

'Look at him now!' Tarantyev said, wiping the perspiration off his face. 'It's summer: it will be as good as going to the country. Why are you rotting here in Gorohovy

Street? There you would have Bezborodkin Gardens, Ochta next door, the Neva two steps from you – no dust, no stuffiness! There's no need to think: I'll dash across to her before dinner – you'll give me the money for the cab – and to-morrow you must move. . . .'

'What a man!' Oblomov said. 'All of a sudden he thinks of a wild idea like moving to the Vyborg side. . . . It's easy enough suggesting that sort of thing. No, if you were really clever you would plan how I could stay on here. I have lived here for eight years, I don't want to change. . . .'

'It's settled: you are going to move. I shall go to my friend at once and call about my job some other time.'

He walked to the door.

'Stop, stop, where are you off to?' Oblomov detained him. 'There's something else, still more important. Read the letter I have had from my bailiff and decide what I should do.'

'What a creature you are!' Tarantyev retorted. 'You can't do anything by yourself. Always appealing to me! What's the good of a man like you? You might as well be a bundle of straw.'

'Where is the letter? Zahar, Zahar! He's put it away again!' Oblomov said.

'Here is the bailiff's letter,' said Alexeyev, picking up the crumpled letter.

'Yes, here it is,' Oblomov repeated, and began reading it aloud.

'What do you say? What am I to do?' he asked when he had finished. 'Drought, arrears. . . .'

'A lost man, utterly lost!' Tarantyev said.

'But why lost?'

'Of course you are lost.'

'Well, if I am, tell me what to do.'

'And what shall I have for it?'

'But you've been promised champagne; what more do you want?'

'Champagne was for finding you a flat. Why, I've

bestowed a benefit on you and you don't feel it, you argue! You are ungrateful. You just try and find a flat by yourself! But the flat is nothing; the chief thing is you will have perfect peace, as good as living at your own sister's. Two children, an unmarried brother; I shall be calling every day. . . .'

'Very well, very well,' Oblomov interrupted him. 'Tell me, now, what am I to do about the bailiff?'

'No, order some beer for dinner, then I'll tell you.'

'Now you want beer; as though you hadn't enough. . . .'

'Good-bye, then,' Tarantyev said, putting on his hat again.

'Oh, my goodness, the bailiff writes my income will be two thousand less, and he asks for beer! Very well, buy some.'

'Give me some more money,' Tarantyev said.

'But you will have the change out of the ten-rouble note!'

'And what about the cab to the Vyborg side?'

Oblomov took out another rouble and thrust it to him testily.

'Your bailiff is a rascal – that's what I will tell you,' Tarantyev put the rouble in his pocket, 'and you listen to him with your mouth open and believe him. He has pitched you a fine tale! Drought, failure of crops, arrears, runaway peasants – it's all lies. I have heard that in our parts, at Shumilovo, the harvest was so good last year that all the debts were paid off, and you, it appears, had drought and bad crops. Shumilovo is only thirty miles from you: why is it the crops there weren't burnt up? And then he talks of arrears. But what has he been thinking of? Why did he allow them to accumulate? Why should there be arrears? As though there were no demand for labour or no market in our parts! Oh, the wretch! I'd teach him! And I expect the peasants ran away because he let them go for a bribe and he never complained to the police captain at all.'

'Impossible,' Oblomov said. 'He actually quotes the
police captain's answer in his letter . . . it's all so convincing. . . .'

'Oh, you muff! You don't know a thing. Why, all
rascals write convincingly, believe me. Here, for instance,'
he said, pointing to Alexeyev, 'sits an honest man, a regular sheep, but can he write a convincing letter? Never!
While his relation, who is a pig and a rascal, can. And you
can't write convincingly, either. So your bailiff is a rascal
if only because he has written cleverly and convincingly.
You see how well he put it: "dispatch the peasants to
their proper homes!" '

'Well, what am I to do with him?'

'Dismiss him at once.'

'But whom shall I put in his place? What do I know
about the peasants? Another one might be worse. I
haven't been there for twelve years.'

'Go to your estate yourself – that's inevitable; spend
the summer there and in the autumn come to the new
flat. I will see that it's all ready for you.'

'Moving to a new flat, going to the country! What
desperate measures you suggest!' Oblomov remarked with
vexation. 'Instead of rushing to extremes you should try
and think of some compromise.'

'You know, Ilya Ilyitch, my dear, you will soon be past
praying for. Why, if I were you I would have long ago
mortgaged that estate and bought another or a house here
in a nice part of the town. And then I would have mortgaged the house also and bought another. . . . If I were
given your estate I'd make a figure in the world.'

'Stop boasting and invent some plan so that I need not
leave this flat or go to the country and yet that things
should come right. . . .' Oblomov remarked.

'But will you ever bestir yourself?' Tarantyev asked.
'Why, look at yourself! What's the good of you? Of
what use are you to your country? He can't go to his
estate!'

'It's too soon for me to go yet, I must finish my plan first. . . . I'll tell you what, Mihey Andreyitch,' Oblomov said suddenly, 'you go instead. You know what the business is, and you know those parts, and I wouldn't spare the expense.'

'Do you imagine I am your steward?' Tarantyev said haughtily. 'And besides, I've got out of the way of dealing with peasants. . . .'

'What am I to do!' Oblomov said dreamily. 'I simply don't know. . . .'

'Well, write to the police captain: ask him if the bailiff has spoken to him about the runaway peasants,' Tarantyev advised, 'and beg him to visit your estate; then write to the Governor and ask him to order the police captain to report on the bailiff's conduct. Say, "Your Excellency, take fatherly pity upon me and consider with an eye of mercy the terrible and inevitable misfortune that threatens me in consequence of my bailiff's riotous behaviour and the ruin which is bound to overtake me, together with my wife and twelve small children, who will be left starving and unprovided. . . ." '

Oblomov laughed.

'Where am I to get so many children from if they ask me to show them?' he asked.

'Nonsense! Say "twelve children"; it will not attract attention, no one will make inquiries, and it sounds "convincing." The Governor will pass the letter to his secretary and you will write to the secretary at the same time – with an enclosure, of course – and he will see to things. And ask your neighbours' help too; who is there? . . .'

'Dobrynin lives near,' Oblomov said. 'I have seen a good deal of him here; he is in the country now.'

'Write to him too, ask him nicely; say: "You will be doing me the greatest service and will oblige me as a Christian, a friend, and a neighbour"; and add some Petersburg present to the letter . . . say, some cigars. This is what you ought to do, but you have no sense. You are a lost soul! I would make that bailiff dance; he would catch it from me! When does the post go?'

'The day after to-morrow.'

'Well, sit down and write at once.'

'But if it is the day after to-morrow, why should I write now?' Oblomov observed. 'To-morrow will do. And look here, Mihey Andreyitch,' he added, 'you may as well bestow another "benefit" on me, and I will add fish or a bird for dinner.'

'What is it now?'

'Sit down and write. It won't take you a minute to scribble three letters! You tell the story so "convincingly," ' he added, trying to conceal a smile, 'and Ivan Alexeyitch would copy it out.'

'What next!' Tarantyev answered. 'The idea of my writing! I haven't written at the office for the last two days: as soon as I sit down to it my left eye begins to run, I must have a cold in it; and my head swims if I bend down. . . . Oh, you lazy fellow, you are simply going to the dogs, Ilya Ilyitch!'

'Oh, I wish Andrey would make haste and come,' Oblomov said, 'he would settle it all.'

'A fine sort of helper!' Tarantyev interrupted. 'A damned German and a thorough rogue!'

Tarantyev had an instinctive aversion for foreigners; for him the names of Frenchmen, Englishmen, or Germans were synonymous with rogue, rascal, fraud, or brigand. He made no distinction between nations – all were alike in his eyes.

'Look here, Mihey Andreyitch,' Oblomov said sternly, 'I must ask you to be more careful in what you say, especially when you are talking of my intimate friend.'

'Intimate!' Tarantyev retorted with hatred. 'He isn't related to you in any way! He is just a German.'

'He is closer than any relation: we have grown up and studied together and I will not allow any impertinence. . . .'

Tarantyev turned purple with rage.

'Ah, if you prefer the German to me I shall not set foot in your house again!' he said.

He put on his hat and walked to the door. Oblomov softened immediately.

'You should respect him as my friend and speak of him more carefully – that's all I ask of you; it isn't much of a service, I should have thought,' he said.

'Respect a German?' Tarantyev said with the utmost contempt. 'What for?'

'As I have told you, if only because we grew up and were at school together.'

'That's nothing! Any two people may be at school together.'

'If he were here, for instance, he would have settled all my difficulties without asking either for beer or champagne,' Oblomov said.

'Ah, you bring that up against me! Go to the devil, then, with your beer and champagne! Here, take back your money. . . . Where have I put it? I can't think what on earth I have done with the damned note!'

He pulled out of his pocket a greasy paper covered with writing.

'That's not it!' he said. 'Where could I have put it?'

He rummaged in his pockets.

'Don't bother to look for it,' Oblomov said. 'I don't reproach you, but only ask you to speak more decently of the man who has done so much for me. . . .'

'Done so much!' Tarantyev repeated maliciously. 'Wait a bit, he will do even more – you do as he tells you!'

'Why do you talk like that?'

'So that you may know, when your German fleeces you thoroughly, what it is to exchange a Russian and your own countryman for a wretched tramp. . . .'

'Listen, Mihey Andreyitch . . .' Oblomov began.

'There's nothing to listen to, I've heard a good deal and seen trouble enough through you! God knows what insults I have had to bear. . . . I expect in Saxony his father hadn't any bread to eat and he came here to lord it over us.'

'Why do you abuse the dead? How is his father to blame?'

'Both are to blame, father and son,' Tarantyev said gloomily, with a wave of his hand. 'It's not for nothing my father warned me against those Germans – and he knew all sorts of people in his time!'

'And what do you object to in Stolz's father, if you please?' Ilya Ilyitch asked.

'I object to his having come to our province with nothing but what he had on and then leaving his son a legacy – what is the meaning of that?'

'He only left his son some forty thousand roubles. Some of it was his wife's dowry and he made the rest by giving lessons and managing an estate: he received a good salary. . . . The father had not done anything wrong, as you can see. What's wrong with the son, now?'

'He is a fine one! He suddenly made three hundred thousand out of his father's forty and has the rank of a court councillor, and is a man of learning . . . and now he is on his travels! A Jack-of-all-trades! Would, now, a real good Russian do all that? A Russian would choose some one job and do it without haste, quietly, biding his time, and none too well at that; but this man, just look at him! Had he gone in for the liquor trade one could at least understand how he has grown rich, but there's nothing to account for it, it's a mere bubble! It's suspicious! I would prosecute a fellow like that. And now he is gadding about, the devil knows where!' Tarantyev continued. 'Why does he go knocking about in foreign parts?'

'He wants to study, to see everything, to know.'

'To study! Hasn't he studied enough? What is there to learn? It's all nonsense, don't you believe him: he deceives you to your face, like your bailiff. Just listen to it! As though a court councillor would want to study! You have been to school, but you are not studying now, are you? And he isn't' (pointing to Alexeyev), 'nor is his relative, nor any decent people! Is he sitting at a German school there, doing lessons? Fiddlesticks! I have heard he has gone to look at some machine and to order one like it: I expect it's a press for printing Russian money! I would put him in prison. . . . Oh, these stocks and shares . . . it makes me sick!'

Oblomov burst out laughing.

'What are you laughing at? Don't you believe what I say?' Tarantyev asked.

'There, we won't talk of it,' Ilya Ilyitch interrupted him. 'You go on your business now as you had meant to, and I'll write these letters with Ivan Alexeyitch's help; I will try, too, to jot down my plan as quickly as I can; I may as well make one job of it. . . .'

Tarantyev went out, but came back again immediately.

'I had quite forgotten! I came to you on business,' he began, in quite an amiable voice. 'I am invited to a wedding to-morrow: Rokotov is being married. Lend me your dress-coat, please, mine is a bit shabby. . . .'

'But how can I?' said Oblomov, frowning at this new request. 'It won't fit you. . . .'

'Oh yes it will!' Tarantyev interrupted him. 'Do you remember I tried on your frock-coat the other day: it might have been made for me! Zahar, Zahar! Come here, you old brute!'

Zahar growled like a bear, but didn't come.

'Call him, Ilya Ilyitch. What a creature he is!' Tarantyev complained.

'Zahar!' Oblomov called.

'Oh, damnation take you . . .' was heard behind the partition, together with the sound of feet jumping off the stove-shelf.

'Well, what do you want?' he asked, turning to Tarantyev.

'Bring my black dress-coat,' Ilya Ilyitch ordered. 'Mihey Andreyitch will try it on to see if it fits him – he has to go to a wedding to-morrow.'

'I won't bring the coat,' Zahar said decisively.

'How dare you, when your master orders you to?' Tarantyev shouted. 'Why don't you send him to a house of correction, Ilya Ilyitch?'

'Yes, that would be a nice thing to do – to send an old man to a house of correction! Don't be obstinate, Zahar, bring the coat!'

'I won't,' Zahar answered coldly. 'Let him first return our waistcoat and shirt – he has had them for five months. He borrowed them to go to somebody's name-day and that was the last we have seen of them. I won't give the dress-coat.'

'Well, good-bye for the present, curse you both,' Tarantyev said angrily, shaking his fist at Zahar as he went out. 'Mind, then, Ilya Ilyitch, I'll engage the flat for you – do you hear?' he added.

'Very well, very well,' Oblomov said impatiently, just to be rid of him.

'And you write your letters,' Tarantyev continued, 'and don't forget to tell the Governor that you have twelve young children, "one smaller than the other." And see that at five o'clock the soup is on the table. Why haven't you ordered a pie?'

But Oblomov said nothing; he had not been listening and had closed his eyes, thinking of something else.

When Tarantyev was gone, unbroken silence reigned for a good ten minutes. Oblomov was put out by the bailiff's letter and the prospect of moving to other lodgings and rather tired by Tarantyev's loud talk. At last he sighed.

'Won't you write?' Alexeyev said quietly. 'I would sharpen a pen for you.'

'Do, and then I think you had better go,' Oblomov said. 'I'll do the work alone and you can copy it out after dinner.'

'Very well,' Alexeyev answered. 'Or, indeed, I might disturb you. . . . I will go now and tell them not to expect you at Ekaterinhof. Good-bye, Ilya Ilyitch.'

But Ilya Ilyitch was not listening; he had tucked his

feet under him and, leaning his head on his hand, almost lay in the chair, plunged in thought or perhaps half asleep.

V

OBLOMOV, a gentleman by birth and a collegiate secretary by rank, had lived for the last twelve years in Petersburg.

At first, while his parents were still living, he had a lodging of two rooms only and was content with the services of Zahar, whom he had brought with him from the country. But when his father and mother died he became the sole owner of three hundred and fifty serfs, inherited by him in one of the distant provinces near the borders of Asia. Instead of five he now received from seven to ten thousand paper roubles a year, and his style of living expanded accordingly. He took a bigger flat, hired a chef, and kept a pair of horses. He was young then, and though one could not say he was lively, he was at any rate more alive than now; he was still full of plans, still hoped for something, expected a great deal both from fate and from himself; he was eager to achieve something, to play his part – in the first instance, of course, in the service for the sake of which he had come to Petersburg. He thought, too, of playing a part in society; and in the distant future, at the turning-point between youth and maturity, family happiness flitted brightly before his imagination. But days and years passed by: the soft down on his chin turned into stiff bristles, his shining eyes became dimmed, his waist broadened, his hair had begun to come out cruelly, he was turned thirty, and he had not advanced a step in any direction and was still standing at the threshold of his career as ten years before.

Life was divided, in his opinion, into two halves: one consisted of work and boredom – these words were for him synonymous – the other of rest and peaceful good-humour. This was the reason why his chief field of activity – Government service – proved to be an unpleasant surprise to him at the very outset.

Brought up in the depths of the country amidst the gentle and kindly manners and customs of his native province, he spent the first twenty years of his life in the embraces of his relatives, friends, and acquaintances, and was so permeated with the family principle that his future service appeared to him as a sort of family pursuit, such, for instance, as lazily putting down income and expenditure in a notebook, as his father had done. He imagined that the officials in the same Department were one friendly, closely knit family, unwearyingly striving for one another's peace and pleasure; that going daily to the office was by no means compulsory, and that bad weather, heat, or mere disinclination were sufficient and legitimate reasons for missing a day. How grieved he was when he saw nothing short of an earthquake could prevent an official in good health from going to his work – and unfortunately earthquakes never happened in Petersburg! A flood might, of course, also be regarded as an obstacle, but even floods happened rarely. Oblomov felt still more troubled when envelopes inscribed 'important' and 'very important' flitted before his eyes, and he was asked to make various inquiries and quotations, to look through papers, to write folios two inches thick, which were called, as though in mockery, 'notes.' To make matters worse, everything had to be done in a hurry – everyone seemed to rush and never to rest; they had no sooner finished one case than they furiously seized upon another, as though it were the one that mattered, and when they had done with that they forgot it and pounced upon a third – and there was no end to it! Twice he had been roused at night and made to write 'notes,' several times he had been fetched by a courier from a visit to friends – always because of those notes. All this frightened him and bored him terribly. 'But when am I to live?' he repeated in distress.

He had heard at home, in the country, that a superior officer was a father to his subordinates and had formed a most cheering and homely idea of such a person. He imagined him as a kind of fond parent whose only concern was constantly to reward his subordinates whether they deserved it or no, and to provide both for their needs and for their pleasures. Ilya Ilyitch had thought that a superior was so concerned with his subordinate's welfare that he would carefully ask him how he had slept, why his eyes looked dim, and whether his head ached. But he was bitterly disappointed on his very first day at the office. When the chief arrived there was a great deal of fuss, scurry, and confusion: the officials ran into one another, some began to pull their uniforms straight, for fear they were not tidy enough to appear before him. As Oblomov observed afterwards, all this commotion was due to the fact that some chiefs read in the stupidly frightened faces of their subordinates rushing out to meet them not only respect for themselves but zeal for the service, and some-times even ability for it. Ilya Ilyitch had no need to be afraid of his chief, a kind and pleasant man, who had never done any harm to anyone; his subordinates were highly satisfied and wished for nothing better. No one had ever heard an unpleasant word from him; he never shouted or made an uproar, never requested but always asked. He asked, whether it was a case of work, or of paying him a call, or of being put under arrest. He had never been rude to his subordinates either individually or collectively; but somehow they were timid in his presence; they answered his kind questions in an unnatural voice, such as they never used in speaking to other people. And Ilya Ilyitch, too, was suddenly afraid, without knowing why, when the chief came into the room, and he, too, began to lose his ordinary voice and to speak in an abject falsetto as soon as the chief addressed him.

Ilya Ilyitch was worn out with fear and misery serving under a kind and easy-going chief; Heaven only knows what would have become of him had he had a stern and exacting one! Oblomov managed to stay in the service for two years; he might have endured it for a third and obtained a rank had not a special incident caused him to resign. He once sent an important paper to Archangel instead of to Astrakhan. This was found out; a search was made for the culprit. All the others were waiting with interest for the chief to call Oblomov and ask him coldly and deliberately 'whether he had sent the paper to Archangel,' and everyone wondered in what sort of voice Ilya Ilyitch would reply. Some thought he would not reply at all – would not be able to. The general atmosphere infected Ilya Ilyitch; he was frightened, too, although he knew that the chief would do nothing worse than reprimand him. His own conscience, however, was much sterner than any reprimand; he did not wait for the punishment he deserved, but went home and sent in a medical certificate.

The certificate was as follows: 'I, the undersigned, certify and append my seal thereto that the collegiate secretary, Ilya Oblomov, suffers from an enlarged heart and a dilation of its left ventricle (*Hypertrophia cordis cum dilatione ejus ventriculi sinistri*), and also from a chronic pain in the liver (*hepatitis*), which may endanger the patient's health and life, the attacks being due, it is to be surmised, to his going daily to the office. Therefore, to prevent the repetition and increase of these painful attacks, I find it necessary to forbid Mr. Oblomov to go to the office and insist that he should altogether abstain from intellectual pursuits and any sort of activity.'

But this helped for a time only: sooner or later he had to recover and then there was the prospect of daily going to the office again. Oblomov could not endure it and sent in his resignation. So ended, never to be resumed again, his work for the State.

His social career was at first more successful. During his early years in Petersburg his placid features were more frequently animated; his eyes often glowed with the fire of life and shone with light, hope, energy. He was stirred to excitement like other people, hoped and rejoiced at trifles, and suffered from trifles too. But that was long ago, at that tender age when one regards every man as a sincere friend, falls in love with almost every woman, and is ready to offer her one's hand and heart – which some, indeed, succeed in doing, often to their profound regret for the rest of their lives. In those blissful days Ilya Ilyitch, too, had received not a few tender, soft, and even passionate glances from the crowd of beauties, a number of promising smiles, two or three stolen kisses, and many friendly handclasps that hurt to tears.

He was never held captive by the beauties, however, never was their slave or even a very assiduous admirer, if only because intimacy with a woman involves a lot of exertion. For the most part, Oblomov confined himself to admiring them from a respectful distance. Very seldom did fate throw him so much together with a woman that he could catch fire for a few days and believe that he was in love. His sentimental feelings never developed into love affairs; they stopped short at the very beginning, and were as innocent, pure, and simple as the loves of a schoolgirl.

He particularly avoided the pale, melancholy maidens, generally with black eyes reflecting 'bitter days and sinful nights'; hollow-eyed maidens with mysterious joys and sorrows, who always want to confide in their friend, to tell him something, and, when it comes to telling, shudder, burst into tears, throw their arms round his neck, gaze into his eyes, then at the sky, say that the curse of destiny is upon them, and sometimes fall down in a faint. Oblomov feared them and kept away. His soul was still pure and virginal; it may have been waiting for the right moment, for real love, for ecstatic passion, and then with years it seemed to have despaired of waiting.

Ilya Ilyitch parted still more coldly with the crowd of his friends. After the first letter from his bailiff about arrears and failure of crops, he replaced his chief friend, the chef, by a female cook, then sold his horses, and at last dismissed his other 'friends.'

Hardly any outside attractions existed for him, and every day he grew more firmly rooted in his flat.

At first he found it irksome to remain dressed all day, then he felt lazy about dining out except with intimate bachelor friends, at whose houses he could take off his tie, unbutton his waistcoat, and even lie down and have an hour's sleep. Evening-parties soon wearied him also: one had to put on a dress-coat, to shave every day. Having read somewhere that only the morning dew was good for one and the evening dew was bad, he began to fear the damp. In spite of all these fancies his friend Stolz succeeded in making him go and see people; but Stolz often left Petersburg for Moscow, Nizhni, the Crimea, and foreign parts, and without him Oblomov again wholly abandoned himself to solitude and seclusion that could only be disturbed by something unusual, out of the ordinary routine of life; but nothing of the sort happened or was likely to happen.

Besides, as Oblomov grew older he reverted to a kind of childish timidity, expecting harm and danger from everything that was beyond the range of his everyday life – the result of losing touch with external events.

He was not afraid of the crack in his bedroom ceiling – he was used to it; it did not occur to him that stuffy atmosphere and perpetual sitting indoors might be more perilous for his health than night dampness, or that continual overfeeding was a kind of slow suicide: he was used to it and was not afraid. He was not used to movement, to life, to seeing many people, to bustling about. He felt stifled in a dense crowd; he stepped into a boat feeling uncertain of reaching the other bank; he drove in a carriage expecting the horses to bolt and smash it. Sometimes he had an attack of purely nervous fear: he was afraid of the stillness around him or he did not know himself of what – a cold shiver ran down his body. He nervously peeped at a dark corner, expecting his imagination to trick him into seeing some supernatural apparition.

This was the end to which his social life had come. With a lazy wave of his hand he dismissed all the youthful hopes that had betrayed him or been betrayed by him, all the tender, melancholy, and bright memories that make some people's hearts beat faster even in their old age.

VI

WHAT did he do at home then? Read? Write? Study? Yes, if he happened to pick up a book or a paper, he read it. If he heard of some remarkable work, he still felt an impulse to acquaint himself with it; he tried to obtain the book, asked for it, and, if it arrived soon, he began it and formed some idea of the subject; a little more and he would have mastered it, but instead he lay, looking apathetically at the ceiling, with the book beside him, unfinished, not understood. He grew cold faster than he developed an enthusiasm: he never returned to a book he had once abandoned. And yet he had been brought up like everyone else – that is, was in a boarding-school till the age of fifteen; then, after a long struggle, the old Oblomovs had decided to send Ilyusha to Moscow, where he had to follow the course of studies to the end. His timid, apathetic nature prevented him from giving full scope to his laziness and caprices among strangers at school, where no exceptions were made for spoiled children. He had to sit straight in class and listen to what the teachers were saying, since there was no alternative, and he learned his lessons in the sweat of his brow, with sighs and much labour.

He never looked beyond the line which the teacher marked with his nail in setting the lesson, never asked any questions or required explanations. He was content with what was written in his notebook, and showed no troublesome curiosity even when he failed to understand all that he heard and learned. If he succeeded in wading through a book on statistics, history, or political economy, he was perfectly satisfied. But when Stolz brought him books that had to be read, in addition to what he had learned, Oblomov used to gaze at him in silence. 'You too are against me, Brutus!' he said with a sigh, opening the books. Such immoderate reading seemed to him hard and unnatural. 'What is the good of those notebooks that have taken so much paper, time, and ink? What is the good of text-books? What is the good of the six or seven years of seclusion, the strictness, the reprimands, the agony of sitting over lessons, of being forbidden to run, to play and amuse oneself, if there is no end to it?' 'When am I to live?' he asked himself again. 'When am I at last to make use of all this store of knowledge, most of which will never be required in life? Political economy, for instance, algebra, geometry – what use will it all be to me at Oblo-movka?' History merely reduced him to misery: one learned and read that years of calamity had come, that man was unhappy; now he mustered his forces, worked, took infinite trouble, endured incredible hardships labouring for the sake of better days. Here they came at last – one would think history might take a rest: no, clouds appeared again, the whole structure fell down, man had again to work and toil. . . . The bright days do not remain, they fly and life flows on, all things pass, swept away again and again.

Serious reading tired him. Philosophers had not succeeded in rousing in him a longing for speculative truth; but the poets touched him to the quick – youth came for him as it comes for everyone. The happy age that fails no one and smiles upon all had dawned for him too – the age when one's powers are at their best and one is full of hope and longs to do good, to work, to leave one's mark in the world, when the heart beats faster and the pulses quicken – the age of enthusiastic speeches, of emotion and happy tears. His heart and mind grew clearer; he shook off his drowsiness, his soul demanded activity. Stolz helped him to prolong that moment as long as it was possible for a nature like Oblomov's. He took advantage of Oblomov's love of poetry and for some eighteen months kept him under the spell of thought and learning. He made use of the enthusiastic flight of his friend's young dreams in order to introduce aims other than pure delight into his reading of poetry, pointed out sterner goals for Oblomov's life and his own, and made him think of their future. Both were deeply moved, shed tears, gave each other solemn promises of pursuing the path of light and reason. Stolz's youthful ardour infected Oblomov and he was consumed with a longing to work, to devote himself to a distant and enchanting aim.

But the flower of life blossomed and bore no fruit. Oblomov sobered down; occasionally, at Stolz's advice, he read this or that book, though without hurry or eagerness, lazily following the lines with his eyes. However interesting the passage he was reading might be, if it was time to go to bed or to have dinner he put the book face downwards and went to have dinner or blew out the candle and went to sleep. If he was given the first volume of a work he did not, after finishing it, ask for the second, but if the second were brought to him he slowly read it. As years passed he found even a first volume too much for him and spent most of his leisure with his elbow on the table, leaning his head on his arm; sometimes he leaned against the book which Stolz insisted he should read.

Such was the end of Oblomov's career as a scholar. The day when he heard his last lecture was the limit beyond which he never went. The director's signature on his certificate, as the schoolmaster's nail-mark in the old days, drew the line beyond which our hero did not think it necessary to go in his search for knowledge. His head was a complicated archive of past deeds, persons, figures, epochs, religions, of disconnected economical, mathematical and other truths, problems, contentions, etc. It was like a library consisting throughout of stray volumes only.

The years of study had a strange effect on Ilya Ilyitch; there was for him a chasm between life and learning and he did not attempt to bridge it. Life was one thing and learning another. He had studied all the existing and the no longer existing systems of law, had studied practical jurisprudence, and yet when he had burglars in the house and had to write to the police he took a sheet of paper and a pen and sat thinking over it, and at last sent for a clerk. His estate accounts were kept by his bailiff. 'How could the learning he had acquired be applied to it?' he asked himself in perplexity.

He returned to his seclusion without a store of knowledge which might have given a definite direction to his roving or idle and dreamy thoughts. What did he do, then? Well, he still went on drawing the pattern of his own life. He found in it, not without reason, so much wisdom and poetry that it provided an inexhaustible source of occupation apart from any books and learning. Having given up the service and society, he began to seek another meaning for his existence; he pondered what he could have been destined for, and at last discovered that he could find enough scope for activity in living his own life. He understood that his allotted portion was family happiness and the care of his estate. Hitherto he had never thoroughly gone into his affairs; Stolz sometimes looked after them for him. He did not know exactly what his income or his expenditure was, he never drew up any budget – he did nothing.

Oblomov's father passed on the estate to his son as he had received it from his own father. He had spent all his life in the country without trying to be clever or to puzzle his brains over various experiments as people do nowadays, seeking to discover new means of raising the productivity of the land or of increasing the old sources of income, and so on. The fields were sown with exactly the same kind of crops and in exactly the same way as they had been in his grandfather's time, and the methods of disposing of agricultural produce were unchanged. The old man was very pleased if, owing to a good harvest or a rise in prices, his income was more than it had been the previous year: he called it a Divine blessing. He merely disliked going out of his way to make money. 'God willing, we shall have enough to eat,' he used to say.

Ilya Ilyitch was not like his father or grandfather. He had studied, he had lived in the world: all this suggested to him ideas that had never occurred to them. He understood that, so far from acquisition being a sin, it was the duty of every citizen to keep up the general welfare by honest labour. Hence, the biggest part of the pattern of life which he drew in his seclusion was devoted to a new and fresh plan of administering the estate and managing the peasants in accordance with the needs of the day. The essentials of the plan had long been ready in his mind; only the details, the estimates and figures, remained. For several years he worked unwearyingly over his plan, thinking about it as he was lying down, walking, at home and in other people's houses; he kept completing or changing various points, recalling what he had thought of the day before and forgotten during the night; sometimes a new and unexpected idea flashed upon him like lightning and set his mind seething with activity. He was not a petty interpreter of another man's ready-made thoughts; he himself created and realized his own ideas. As soon as he got up in the morning and had had breakfast he lay down on the sofa, leaned his head on his hand, and thought without sparing himself until his head wearied of the hard work and his conscience said to him, 'You have done enough to-day for the common good.'

After finishing with business, Oblomov liked to withdraw into himself and live in the world of his imagination. He knew the delight of lofty thoughts; he was not a stranger to human sorrows. He sometimes bitterly wept in the depths of his heart over the sufferings of mankind; felt a vague, secret anguish, a yearning for something far off, for that world, perhaps, into which Stolz used to draw him. . . . Sweet tears flowed from his eyes. . . . Sometimes he was filled with contempt for human vice, falsity, slander, for all the evil rampant in the world, and was consumed with a desire to point out to man his sores; thoughts were kindled in him, sweeping through his mind like waves of the sea, developing into intentions and strivings, setting his blood on fire; moved by a spiritual force he rapidly changed his position two or three times in one minute, sat up in bed, with shining eyes stretched out his arms and looked round him like one inspired. . . . The striving was on the point of passing into action . . . and then, oh God! what wonders, what beneficent results would have followed from so lofty an effort! . . . But the morning fled by, the day was drawing to its close, and with it Oblomov's exhausted energies sought rest: the storms and emotions died down, his thoughts grew sober, his blood flowed slower through his veins. Slowly and thoughtfully he turned over on his back and, fixing sad eyes on the window, mournfully watched the sun setting magnificently behind a house of four storeys. How many times he had watched the sun set in this way.

In the morning once more there was life, excitement, dreams! He liked to imagine himself sometimes as some invincible conqueror to whom not only Napoleon but even Eruslan Lazarevitch could not hold a candle; he invented a war and a cause for it, for instance, the invasion of Europe by the peoples of Africa; or he held a new crusade and was fighting, settling the fate of nations, devastating towns, showing mercy or wreaking vengeance, performing wonderful deeds of goodness and magnanimity. Sometimes he chose for himself the part of a thinker or a great artist: everyone worshipped him, he gathered laurels; the crowd ran after him crying, 'Look, look, there goes Oblomov, our great Ilya Ilyitch!' At bitter moments he was tormented by his troubles, tossed from side to side, lay face downwards, and sometimes felt completely overwhelmed; then he rose from the bed, knelt down, and prayed earnestly, ardently, imploring the heavens to avert the storm that threatened him. After entrusting the care of his person to Providence, he grew calm and indifferent to everything in the world – and the storm might do what it liked.

This was how he used his spiritual powers, often spending a whole day in deep emotion, and recovering with a deep sigh from a charming dream or haunting anxiety only when the day passed into evening and the sun sank magnificently behind the four-storeyed house. He watched it as before with dreamy eyes and a melancholy smile, and peacefully rested from his spiritual exertions.

No one saw or knew Oblomov's inner life; people thought there was nothing special about him and that he merely lay about and ate good meals; nothing more was expected of him, and he was hardly credited with the power of coherent thought. This was what all his acquaintances said of him. Only Stolz, who knew him well, could have testified to his abilities and to the volcanic work of his ardent mind and tender heart; but Stolz was hardly ever in Petersburg. Zahar, who had spent all his life beside his master, knew his intimate ways even better than Stolz; but he was convinced that both he and his master were usefully employed and lived normally, as they should, and that nothing was amiss.

VII

ZAHAR was over fifty. He was not a direct descendant of those Russian *kalebs*, knights of the servants' hall, without fear or reproach, who were full of self-effacing devotion to their masters and had all the virtues and no vices. He was a knight with fear and reproach. He belonged to two different epochs, each of which had left its mark upon him. From one of them he inherited a boundless devotion to the Oblomov family, and from another, the later one, sophistication and corrupted morals. Though he was passionately devoted to his master, a day seldom passed without his telling him a lie. In the old days servants used to restrain their masters from extravagance and intemperance, but Zahar liked to have a drink with his friends at his master's expense; old-fashioned servants were chaste as eunuchs, but Zahar paid frequent visits to a lady friend of doubtful character. A servant of the old type guarded his master's money better than any safe, but Zahar always tried to cheat his master of ten copecks over some purchase and invariably appropriated any coppers lying on the table. Also, if Ilya Ilyitch forgot to ask Zahar for change, he never received it. Zahar did not steal bigger sums, perhaps because he measured his needs by coppers and ten-copeck pieces, or because he feared detection; it was certainly not from being over-scrupulous. A *kaleb* of the old times, like a well-trained dog, would rather die of starvation than touch the food entrusted to him, but Zahar was always watching for a chance to eat and drink something he had been particularly asked not to touch; the former was anxious that his master should eat as much as possible and was distressed if he had no appetite, but Zahar was distressed when his master ate up all that had been put on his plate.

Moreover, Zahar was a gossip. In the kitchen and at the meetings by the gate he complained every day that his life was not worth living, that there never had been a worse master, that Oblomov was capricious and stingy and bad-tempered, and there was no pleasing him and that he would sooner be dead than go on in his service. Zahar said this not from malice or a desire to injure Oblomov, but simply because he had inherited from his father and grandfather the habit of abusing his master at every opportunity. Sometimes he told some cock-and-bull story about Oblomov from sheer boredom or lack of a subject for conversation or just to thrill his listeners. 'He has taken to visiting that widow,' he would hiss confidentially; 'yesterday he wrote a note to her.' Or he said that his master was the greatest drunkard and gambler that ever was; he spent his whole nights playing cards and drinking. Not a word of it was true: Ilya Ilyitch never went to the widow, for he spent his nights sleeping peacefully, and did not touch cards.

Zahar was dirty. He seldom shaved, and although he did wash his face and hands it did not seem to make any difference; and, indeed, no soap could fetch the dirt off. When he went to the bath-house his hands, for a couple of hours, turned red instead of black, and then were black once more.

He was very clumsy; when he opened the doors, one-half would shut while he was opening the other, and as he ran to open it the other half would shut. He could never pick up a handkerchief or anything else from the floor at once, but had to dive for it two or three times; and if he caught hold of it at the fourth attempt he was sure to drop it again. If he carried a tray with things on it across the room, those at the top began to slide at the very first step he took; when the first thing dropped, he made a belated effort to stop it and dropped another two; as he gazed, open-mouthed, at the things on the floor instead of at those still on the tray, he held the tray aslant and dropped a few more. Sometimes all he succeeded in bringing to the other end of the room was one wine-glass or plate, and at other times, cursing and swearing, he deliberately flung down the last things that remained. Walking across the room he invariably caught his side or his foot against a table or a chair; he seldom passed through the open half of the door without banging his shoulder against the other half and swearing at both, or at the carpenter who had made them, or at the landlord. Almost all the articles in Oblomov's study, especially the fragile ones requiring careful handling, were broken or damaged, thanks to Zahar. He applied his strength to all things equally, without making any distinction in his method of treating them. He used as much force to snuff a candle or to pour out a glass of water as was needed to push open a heavy gate. It was no joking matter when Zahar, suddenly inspired with zeal and anxious to please his master, decided to tidy, clean, and rearrange everything quickly, at once! There was no end of damage done. An enemy soldier rushing into the house could not have done more mischief – things fell down and broke, crockery was smashed, chairs overturned; in the end Zahar had to be driven out of the room or went out of his own accord, grumbling and swearing.

He had drawn up for himself a definite programme of activity and never went beyond it if he could help it. In the morning he set the *samovar*, cleaned boots and clothes that his master wore, but never those which he did not wear, though they might have been hanging in the wardrobe for ten years. Then he swept – by no means every day – the middle of the room without touching the corners, and dusted only the table that had nothing on it so as to save himself the trouble of moving anything. After this he considered he had a right to doze care-free on the stove, or chatter to Anissya in the kitchen or to the servants at the gate.

If anything more was required of him he complied reluctantly, after a long argument to prove that what was asked of him was useless or impossible. Nothing could induce him to add a new regular duty to those he had once set for himself.

In spite of the fact that Zahar liked drink and gossip, took Oblomov's coppers, broke and spoiled things and shirked his work, he was profoundly devoted to his master. He would have jumped into fire or water for him without a moment's hesitation or thought of its being in any way heroic or worthy of admiration or reward. He would have done it as a matter of course, regarding it as inevitable, or rather he did not consider it at all but acted without reflection. He had no theories on the subject. He would have rushed to his death as simply as a dog rushes at a wild beast in the forest, without reasoning why it, and not its master, must attack it. But if, on the other hand, Oblomov's health or life depended on Zahar's keeping awake all night by his bedside, he would certainly have dropped asleep.

Outwardly he did not show any servility to his master; he treated him rudely and familiarly, was angry with him in good earnest over every trifle, and even, as we have said already, abused him to other people at the gate – all this, however, merely disguised but by no means diminished his instinctive inbred devotion, not to Ilya Ilyitch as such, but to everything that bore the name of Oblomov and was familiar, dear, and precious to him. Perhaps, indeed, this feeling was opposed to Zahar's opinion of Oblomov personally; very likely, intimate acquaintance with his master's disposition had induced a different attitude. Probably Zahar would have protested if someone had explained to him the degree of his devotion to Ilya Ilyitch. Zahar loved Oblomovka as a cat loves its attic, a horse its stable, a dog the kennel in which it has been born and grown up. Within the range of this love he developed certain individual preferences. Thus, for instance, he liked the coachman at Oblomovka better than the cook, the dairymaid Varvara better than either of them, and Ilya Ilyitch least of all; but still, the cook at Oblomovka was in his eyes better than any other cook in the world, and Ilya Ilyitch better than all other masters. He could not endure Taraska the footman, and yet he would not have exchanged this Taraska for the best man in the world, simply because Taraska was from Oblomovka. He treated Oblomov rudely and familiarly, just as a Siberian *shaman* treats his idol: he dusts it, drops it on the ground, sometimes, perhaps, slaps it in vexation, but the consciousness of the idol's superiority to himself dwells in his mind always. The least occasion was sufficient to call forth this feeling from the depths of Zahar's soul and to make him look at his master with reverence, sometimes with tears of emotion.

Zahar was inclined to look down on all other gentlemen; he waited upon Oblomov's visitors, handing them tea, and so on, with a kind of condescension, as though making them feel the honour his master bestowed upon them by receiving them. He refused them rather rudely: 'My master is asleep,' he would say, haughtily looking the visitors up and down. Sometimes, instead of telling tales about Ilya Ilyitch and abusing him, he began praising him immoderately at the shops and the meetings by the gate, and then his enthusiasm knew no bounds. He enumerated his master's virtues, his intelligence, kindness, good-nature, generosity; and if Oblomov's supply of splendid qualities ran short he borrowed them from others and ascribed to him high rank, wealth, and extraordinary influence. If he had to threaten the porter, the landlord's agent, or the landlord himself, he always made use of Oblomov: 'You wait,' he said menacingly, 'I'll tell my master and you will catch it then!' He did not suspect there could be a higher authority.

Outwardly, however, Zahar's relations with Oblomov were rather hostile. Having always lived together they were tired of each other. A close daily intimacy between two people has its price: a great deal of experience, logic, and warmth of heart is needed on both sides if they are to enjoy each other's good qualities without nagging at each other's failings or being worried by them. Ilya Ilyitch

knew at least one inestimable virtue in Zahar – his devotion to himself; and he was used to it, believing, like
Zahar, that this was as it should be and could not have
been otherwise; and, having grown used to the virtue once
and for all, he no longer enjoyed it; and yet, in spite of his
indifference to everything, he could not patiently endure
Zahar's innumerable shortcomings. Just as Zahar, in spite
of his profound devotion to his master, differed from the
old-fashioned servants by his modern failings, so Oblomov, although appreciating this devotion, differed from
the masters of the old days in not feeling as friendly and
affectionate to Zahar as they had done to their servants.
He sometimes indulged in serious quarrels with Zahar,
and Zahar, on his side, often tired of his master. In his
youth he had done his term of service as a valet in the
Oblomov household and had then been promoted to look
after the young master; from that day he looked upon
himself as an article of luxury, an aristocratic appendage
of the house, intended to enhance the brilliance and
opulence of the old family and not to be of any real
service. And so, having dressed the young master in the
morning and undressed him in the evening, he spent the
rest of his time doing nothing. Lazy by nature, he was
made more so by his life as a flunkey. He gave himself
airs before the other servants and never took the trouble
to set the *samovar* or sweep the floors. He either dozed in
the hall or went to have a chat in the servants' hall or the
kitchen, or he stood for hours by the gate, his arms
crossed, looking thoughtfully about him with sleepy eyes.
And after such a life he was suddenly burdened with the
task of doing the work of a whole flat single-handed! He
was to wait on his master, to dust and sweep and run
errands! All this made him sulky and his temper turned
harsh and sour; this was why he growled each time that
his master's voice caused him to leave the stove. In spite,
however, of his sullenness and uncouthness, Zahar had a
fairly soft and kind heart. He liked to spend his time with
children. He was often seen in the yard by the gate

surrounded by a crowd of them. He settled their quarrels, teased them, invented games, or simply sat with a child on each knee while a third little rogue would hug him from behind or play with his whiskers.

And so Oblomov interfered with Zahar's life by requesting every minute his services and his presence, while Zahar's heart, social nature, love of idleness, and a continual, never-ceasing need to be munching drew him to his lady friend or the kitchen, the shop or the gate.

Zahar and Oblomov had known each other and lived together for years. He had dandled his master in his arms as a baby, and Oblomov remembered him as a quick, sly young man with an enormous appetite. The old tie between them could not be severed. Ilya Ilyitch could not get up or go to bed or brush his hair or put on his shoes or have dinner without Zahar's help; Zahar could imagine no other master than Ilya Ilyitch and no other existence than that in which he dressed him, fed him, imposed upon him, lied to him, growled at him, and yet inwardly reverenced him.

VIII

WHEN Zahar had shut the door after Tarantyev and Alexeyev he did not sit down on the stove expecting his master to call him any minute, for he had heard that Oblomov
was going to write. But everything in the study was as
still as the grave. Zahar peeped through the crack – and
what did he see? Ilya Ilyitch was lying on the bed, his
head propped up by his hand, an open book was before
him. Zahar opened the door.

'Why are you lying down again?' he asked.

'Don't disturb me; you see I am reading,' Oblomov
said abruptly.

'It is time to wash and write,' Zahar persisted.

'Yes, so it is,' Ilya Ilyitch said, coming to himself.
'Directly. You go now. I'll think.'

'I wonder when he got back into bed?' Zahar grumbled,
jumping on to the stove. 'He is a quick one!'

Oblomov read the page that had turned yellow during
the month he had not touched the book. He put the book
down, yawned, and began thinking of the 'two misfortunes' that haunted him.

'What a bore!' he whispered, stretching his legs and
then tucking his feet under him again.

He felt disposed to lie snug and dream; he looked at
the sky in search of the sun he loved so much, but it was
right in the zenith, bathing in dazzling light the white-
washed wall of the house behind which Oblomov watched
it set in the evening. 'No, I must work first,' he said to
himself sternly, 'and then. . . .'

The morning would long have been over in the country
and in Petersburg was drawing to a close. A mingled
sound of human and non-human voices reached Oblomov
from the yard: some strolling players were singing to the
accompaniment of dogs' barking; a sea monster was

brought for show; produce of all sorts was offered for sale by different hawkers.

Ilya Ilyitch lay on his back and put both hands under his head. He was busy with his plan of estate management. In his mind he rapidly ran through several important, essential points about the tax the peasants were to pay and the amount of land to be ploughed, thought of a new and sterner measure against the idlers and absentees, and went on to arrange his own manner of life in the country. He was interested in the building of his future country house: he dwelt with pleasure for some minutes on the plan of the rooms, decided on the size of the dining-room and the billiard-room, thought on which side his study windows should look; he thought of the furniture and the carpets too. After that he planned the lodge and considered the number of visitors he intended to entertain, allotted the space for the stables, barns, the servants' quarters, and so on. At last he turned to the garden: he decided to leave all the old oaks and limes, but cut down the apple- and pear-trees and plant acacias instead; he thought of having a park, but, reckoning up the expenses, decided it would cost too much, and, putting it off for the present, passed on to the flower-beds and the hot-houses. The tempting thought of the fruit to be gathered appeared before his mind so vividly that he suddenly transferred himself to the country as it would be several years hence, when the estate was run according to his plan and he lived there permanently.

He imagined himself sitting dreamily one summer evening at the tea-table on the verandah, under a thick canopy of trees, lazily smoking a long pipe and enjoying the view, the stillness, the cool air; the fields showed yellow in the distance, the sun was setting behind the familiar birch copse, spreading a rosy glow over the mirror-like pond; mist was rising from the fields; it was getting cool, dusk was falling; the peasants were returning home in crowds. The servants were sitting idly by the gates; cheerful voices came from there, sounds of laughter and the *balalaika*; girls were playing and running after one another; his own children sported round him, climbed on his knees, put their arms round his neck; and at the *samovar* sat the queen of it all, his deity – a woman, his wife! Meanwhile, bright friendly lights were lighted in the dining-room, furnished with elegant simplicity, and a big round table was being laid. Zahar, promoted to be butler, his whiskers perfectly white by now, was laying the cloth and placing silver and glass on the table with a pleasant clink, constantly dropping a fork or a glass. They sat down to a plentiful supper; the comrade of his childhood, his faithful friend Stolz, was there too, and other familiar faces; then they went to bed. . . .

Oblomov's face was flushed with happiness; the dream was so vivid, so living, so poetical. He suddenly felt a vague longing for love, for peaceful happiness, for his native plains and hills, for a home, wife, and children of his own.

He lay for some five minutes with his face in the pillow, then turned over on to his back again. His face shone with tender, gentle feeling: he was happy. Slowly, and with delight, he stretched out his legs, and though the movement crumpled his trousers he never noticed this slight disorder. His obliging imagination had carried him lightly and freely into the distant future. Now he was engrossed with his favourite idea of a small colony of friends settling on farms and villages within some ten or fifteen miles from his estate, and going on a perpetual round of visits to one another, to dinners, suppers, dances; he saw nothing but bright days ahead, bright, laughing people, without cares or wrinkles, with rosy round faces, double chins, and unfailing appetites; it would be everlasting summer, everlasting gaiety, excellent food, and sweet idleness. . . .

'Oh, heavenly!' he said, brimming over with happiness, and came to himself. Five distinct voices were shouting in the yard: 'Potatoes! Sand for sale! Charcoal! Charcoal! Contribute something, kind ladies and gentlemen, towards

building a temple of God!' The sound of axes and shouts
of workmen came from a house that was being built next
door, the roar of traffic came from the street. There was
talk and movement all round.

'Ah!' Ilya Ilyitch sighed aloud dejectedly. 'What a life!
How disgusting this town noise is! When will the paradise
that I long for come at last? When shall I go to my native
fields and woods?' he thought. He wished he were lying
on the grass under a tree, looking at the sun through the
branches and counting the birds that alighted on them.
Some rosy-cheeked maid-servant with a sunburnt neck
and soft round elbows brought him his lunch and his
dinner; the sly creature looked down and smiled. . . .
When would this time come? 'And the plan, and the
bailiff, and the flat!' he suddenly remembered.

'Yes, yes, Ilya Ilyitch!' he said to himself harshly.
'Directly – this very minute.' He sat up quickly, put his
feet down, and, thrusting them into both slippers at once,
sat still for a time, then he got up and stood thinking for
a minute or two.

'Zahar, Zahar!' he called loudly, looking at the table
and the inkstand.

'What is it now?' was heard at the same time as the
jump. 'I wonder my feet still carry me. . . .'

'Zahar!' Ilya Ilyitch repeated dreamily, his eyes still
fixed on the table. 'I'll tell you what, brother . . . ' he said,
pointing to the inkstand, but the sentence remained
unfinished, and he sank into thought again. Then his
arms spread out, his knees gave way, and he began
stretching and yawning. 'We had some cheese left . . . ' he
began again, slowly, still stretching himself. 'And . . .
bring some Madeira; dinner won't be for some time, so I
will have a little lunch. . . .'

'Where was it left, now?' Zahar said. 'There wasn't any
left. . . .'

'Of course there was,' Ilya Ilyitch interrupted him. 'I
remember perfectly well; it was a piece like this. . . .'

'No, no! There wasn't any piece left,' Zahar repeated obstinately.

'There was,' Ilya Ilyitch said.

'There wasn't,' Zahar answered.

'Well, buy some, then.'

'Give me the money, please.'

'There's some change there, take it.'

'This is only a rouble forty copecks, and the cheese is one rouble sixty.'

'There were some coppers there too.'

'I haven't seen any,' said Zahar, shifting from one foot to another. 'There was some silver, and here it is still, but there were no coppers.'

'Yes there were – the pedlar gave them to me himself.'

'I was in the room,' said Zahar. 'I saw him give you some silver, but not any coppers. . . .'

'I wonder if Tarantyev took it?' Oblomov thought doubtfully. 'But, no, he would have taken the silver as well.'

'Well, what else is there left?' he asked.

'Nothing at all. There may perhaps be some ham left over from yesterday, I must ask Anissya,' said Zahar. 'Shall I bring it?'

'Bring what there is. But how is it there isn't any cheese?'

'Well, there isn't,' Zahar said, and went out. Ilya Ilyitch slowly and thoughtfully paced about the room.

'Yes, there is a lot to do,' he said softly. 'Take the plan, for instance – there is still a great deal to be done to it! . . . But there certainly was some cheese left,' he added thoughtfully; 'that Zahar has eaten it and says there wasn't any! And where could the coppers have gone to?' he said, fumbling on the table.

A quarter of an hour later Zahar pushed the door open with a tray which he held in both hands, and, coming into the room, wanted to shut the door with his foot, but missed it and kicked the air; a wine-glass, the stopper of the decanter, and a roll fell on the floor.

'You can't take a step without upsetting things!' Ilya Ilyitch said. 'Pick them up, at any rate; don't stand there admiring your handiwork!'

Holding the tray, Zahar stooped to pick up the roll, but suddenly saw that both his hands were busy and he had no means of doing so.

'Well, pick it up!' Ilya Ilyitch said, mocking him. 'Why don't you? What's preventing you?'

'Oh, damnation take you!' Zahar thundered furiously, addressing the articles on the floor. 'And whoever has lunch just before dinner?'

Putting the tray down he picked up the things he had dropped; he blew on the roll and put it on the table.

Ilya Ilyitch began his lunch; Zahar stood at some distance from him, glancing at him sideways and evidently intending to say something; but Oblomov went on eating without taking the slightest notice. Zahar coughed once or twice, but it had no effect.

'The landlord's agent has just sent another message,' Zahar began timidly at last; 'the contractor has been to see him and asks if he could have a look at our flat. It's about doing it up, you know. . . .'

Ilya Ilyitch was still eating and never answered a word.

'Ilya Ilyitch!' Zahar said in a voice still more subdued.

Ilya Ilyitch pretended not to hear.

'They say we must move next week,' Zahar hissed.

Oblomov drank a glass of wine and said nothing.

'What are we to do, Ilya Ilyitch?' Zahar asked almost in a whisper.

'I have forbidden you to talk to me about it!' Ilya Ilyitch said sternly, and rising from his seat walked up to Zahar.

Zahar drew away from him.

'What a venomous man you are, Zahar!' Oblomov added feelingly.

Zahar was offended.

'Venomous, indeed! I haven't killed anyone.'

'Of course you are venomous!' Ilya Ilyitch repeated. 'You poison my life.'

'I am not venomous,' Zahar insisted.

'Why do you pester me about the flat?'

'But what can I do?'

'And what can I do?'

'You were going to write to the landlord, weren't you?'

'Well, yes, I will write. One can't do it all at once.'

'You might very well write now.'

'Now! I have more important things to think of. You imagine it's like chopping wood, all done at one blow! There, there isn't any ink!' Oblomov said, turning a dry pen in the inkpot. 'How can I write?'

'I'll put some *kvass* in it,' Zahar answered, and taking the inkpot walked quickly out of the room while Oblomov searched for paper.

'I believe there's no paper either,' he said, fumbling in the drawer and passing his hand over the table. 'No, there isn't! Oh, that Zahar, he is the bane of my life!'

'Of course you are a venomous creature,' he said to Zahar when he returned, 'you never look after anything! Fancy having no paper in the house!'

'That's too much of a good thing, Ilya Ilyitch! I am a Christian, you have no business to keep calling me venomous! I was born and grew up in the old master's time, and he called one a puppy and pulled one's ears, but one never heard such a word from him, he didn't invent anything like that! There's no telling the mischief a word may do! Here is some paper.'

He took up half a sheet of grey paper from the chiffonier and handed it to Oblomov.

'How can one write on this?' Oblomov asked, throwing the paper down. 'I covered my glass with it in the night so that nothing . . . venomous should fall into it.'

Zahar turned away and looked at the wall.

'Well, never mind; give it me, I will write a rough draft and Alexeyev will copy it to-night.'

Ilya Ilyitch sat down at the table and quickly wrote: 'Dear Sir. . . .'

'What disgusting ink!' he said. 'Another time you must look sharp, Zahar, and do your work properly!'

He thought a little and began writing:

'The flat which I occupy on the second floor of the house in which you propose to make some alterations entirely suits my manner of life and habits acquired through continued residence in this house. Having heard through my servant, Zahar Trofimov, that you had told me that the flat I occupy. . . .'

Oblomov stopped and read what he had written.

'It's clumsy,' he said; 'here I have put *which* twice and there two *thats*.'

He whispered to himself and altered the words; *which* now seemed to refer to floor – it was awkward again. He managed to correct it and began thinking how he could avoid *that* twice. He scratched out a word, then put it in again. He moved *that* three times, but it either made nonsense or found itself in the immediate neighbourhood of another *that*.

'There's no getting rid of this second *that*!' he said impatiently. 'Oh, the letter be damned! I am not going to worry my head over such trifles. I've lost the habit of writing business letters. But I see it's nearly three o'clock.'

'Here you are, Zahar!' He tore the letter into four and threw the pieces on the floor.

'Did you see?' he asked.

'I did,' Zahar answered, picking up the bits of paper.

'So don't pester me any more about the flat. And what have you got there now?'

'Why, the bills.'

'Goodness me, you will be the death of me! What does it come to? Tell me quick.'

'The butcher's bill is 86 roubles 54 copecks.'

Ilya Ilyitch clasped his hands in dismay.

'Have you gone off your head? Such a pile of money for the butcher?'

'It does pile up if you don't pay for three months. It's all written down here, no one has been robbing you.'

'Venomous you are, no mistake!' Oblomov said.

'Fancy buying a million's worth of meat! And what good does it do you? If at least you fattened on it!'

'I haven't eaten it,' Zahar snarled back.

'Oh, indeed!'

'So you grudge me food now, do you? There, look for yourself!' and he shoved the bills to Oblomov.

'Who else is there to pay?' Ilya Ilyitch asked, pushing the greasy papers away with annoyance.

'There's 121 roubles 18 copecks owing to the baker and the greengrocer.'

'It's sheer ruination! It's beyond anything!' Oblomov said, beside himself. 'Are you a cow to have munched so much green-stuff? . . .'

'No, I'm a venomous man!' Zahar remarked bitterly, turning almost completely away from his master. 'If you didn't let Mihey Andreyitch come, you'd spend less,' he added.

'Well, what does it come to altogether? – Count!' Ilya Ilyitch said, and himself began counting.

Zahar was calculating on his fingers.

'The devil only knows what it comes to: each time I cast it up it's different!' Oblomov said. 'What do you make it? Two hundred, isn't it?'

'Wait a bit, give me time!' Zahar said, shutting his eyes and muttering: 'Eight tens and ten tens is eighteen plus two tens. . . .'

'You'll never finish at that rate,' Ilya Ilyitch said; 'you had better go now and give me the bills to-morrow, and see about paper and ink too. . . . Such a pile of money! I told you to pay as we go on – no, they want it all at once. . . . What a people!'

'Two hundred and five roubles seventy-two copecks,' Zahar said, having finished his calculation. 'Give me the money, please. . . .'

'Oh, certainly, at once! Wait a bit, I will check it to-morrow. . . .'

'But, Ilya Ilyitch, they are asking for it. . . .'

'There, there, leave me alone! I said to-morrow, and

to-morrow you shall have it. Go to your room now, and I must work; I have more important things to think of. . . .'

Ilya Ilyitch settled in his chair and tucked his feet under him, but before he had had time to sink into thought there was a ring at the bell. A short, rather portly man with a fair skin, rosy cheeks, and a bald head fringed at the back with thick black hair, came in. His bald head was as round, clean, and shiny as though it had been carved out of ivory. There was an expression of reserve in his eyes, of discretion in his smile, and of modestly official decorum in the studious attention with which he looked at everything. He was dressed in a comfortable frock-coat that opened widely and easily like a gate at a single touch. His linen was dazzlingly white, as though to match his bald head. On the forefinger of his right hand he wore a heavy ring with some dark stone in it.

'Doctor! What chance brings you?' Oblomov exclaimed, stretching one hand to the visitor and with another pushing a chair towards him.

'I've grown tired of your being well and not calling me in, so I have come uninvited,' the doctor answered jokingly. 'No,' he added seriously afterwards, 'I was with your neighbour upstairs and have called on you on my way.'

'Thank you. And how is he?'

'Oh, he may last three or four weeks or perhaps till the autumn and then . . . it's dropsy on the chest: we all know how that ends. And how are you?'

Oblomov shook his head sadly.

'Not at all well, doctor. I've been thinking of asking your advice. I don't know what to do. My digestion is very bad; there's a feeling of fullness in the stomach; I have fearful heartburn and breathlessness . . . ' Oblomov said, looking sorry for himself.

'Give me your hand,' said the doctor, and closed his eyes for a moment feeling Oblomov's pulse. 'Have you a cough?' he asked.

'At nights, especially after supper.'

'Hm! Palpitations? Headache?' The doctor asked

several more questions of the same kind, then bent his bald head and thought deeply. After two minutes he looked up and said decisively:

'If you spend another two or three years in this climate, lying about and eating rich, heavy food, you will die of a stroke.'

Oblomov was startled.

'What am I to do, then? Tell me, for Heaven's sake!' he asked.

'You must do as other people do – go abroad.'

'Abroad!' Oblomov repeated in surprise.

'Yes, why not?'

'Upon my word, doctor, abroad! How can I?'

'Why can't you?'

Oblomov looked in silence at himself, at his room, and repeated mechanically:

'Abroad!'

'What is there to prevent you?'

'Why, everything. . . .'

'What do you mean by everything? Have you no money?'

'That's it; I have no money at all,' Oblomov said in a lively voice, glad of this perfectly natural obstacle in which he could take refuge. 'See what my bailiff writes me. . . . Where is that letter? What have I done with it? Zahar!'

'Never mind, never mind,' said the doctor, 'that's none of my business; my duty is to tell you that you must change your manner of life, rooms, air, occupation – everything.'

'Very well, I will think about it,' Oblomov said. 'Where ought I to go and what must I do?'

'Go to Kissingen,' the doctor began, 'and spend June and July there; drink the water; then go to Switzerland or the Tyrol for a grape cure. Spend September and October there. . . .'

'The devil, to Tyrol!' Ilya Ilyitch whispered inaudibly.

'Then to some dry place – say, to Egypt. . . .'

'What next?' Oblomov muttered.

'Avoid worry and vexation. . . .'

'It's all very well for you to talk,' Oblomov remarked, 'you don't receive such letters from your bailiff. . . .'

'You must avoid thinking too.'

'Avoid thinking?'

'Yes, avoid intellectual strain.'

'And what about my plan of estate management? I am not a log, you know!'

'Well, that's your own look out. My duty is merely to warn you. You must avoid passions too; they hinder the cure. You must try and amuse yourself by riding, dancing, moderate exercise in the fresh air, pleasant conversation, especially with ladies, so that your heart should be stirred but slightly and by pleasant sensations only.'

Oblomov listened to him, hanging his head.

'And then?' he asked.

'Then you mustn't think about reading or writing – Heaven forbid! Hire a villa facing south, with plenty of flowers, have music and women about you. . . .'

'And what sort of food am I to have?'

'You must avoid meat and animal food in general, and also floury foods, brawns, and aspics. You may have light soups and vegetables, only remember there's cholera about, so you must be careful. . . . You may walk eight hours a day. Buy a gun. . . .'

'Good Lord!' Oblomov groaned.

'Finally,' the doctor concluded, 'go to Paris for the winter and amuse yourself there in the whirl of life; don't think. From a theatre go to a dance or a fancy-dress ball, go out of town, pay calls, have friends, noise, and laughter around you.'

'Anything else?' Oblomov asked with hardly concealed vexation.

The doctor pondered.

'Perhaps you ought to try sea air: you can get a steamer in England and take a trip to America. . . .'

He rose and began taking leave.

'If you carry it all out exactly . . .' he said.

'Oh, certainly, without fail,' Oblomov answered sarcastically as he saw him off.

The doctor went away, leaving Oblomov in a most pitiful condition. He closed his eyes, covered his face with his hands, huddled himself together in the chair, and sat so, feeling and seeing nothing.

A timid call was heard behind him.

'Ilya Ilyitch!'

'Yes?' he answered.

'What am I to tell the agent?'

'What about?'

'Why, about moving.'

'You are at it again?' Oblomov asked in surprise.

'But what am I to do, Ilya Ilyitch, sir? Judge for yourself. Life is none too easy for me, anyway. I am being worried to death.'

'No, it's me you will worry to death by your talk of moving,' Oblomov said. 'Just listen to what the doctor says!'

Zahar could not think of anything to say and merely heaved a sigh that shook the ends of the kerchief round his neck.

'You mean to be the death of me?' Oblomov asked again. 'You are tired of me, eh? Speak!'

'Mercy on us, live as long as you like! No one wishes you ill,' Zahar grumbled, utterly confused by the tragic turn the conversation was taking.

'You do!' Ilya Ilyitch said. 'I have forbidden you to mention our moving, but you remind me of it at least five times a day; it upsets me – understand that! My health is bad enough as it is.'

'I thought, sir, that . . . I thought, why shouldn't we move?' uttered Zahar in a voice shaking with emotion.

'Why shouldn't we move? You think nothing of it!' said Oblomov, turning together with his chair towards Zahar. 'But have you considered what moving means, eh? I don't believe you have!'

'No, I expect I haven't,' Zahar answered humbly, ready to agree with his master in everything so as to avoid a dramatic scene, which he loathed.

'If you haven't, then listen and see for yourself whether we can move. What does moving mean? It means your master has to go out for the whole day and walk about dressed from early morning. . . .'

'Well, what if you did go out?' Zahar remarked. 'Why shouldn't you be out all day? It's unhealthy to sit at home. See how bad you look! You used to be as fresh as a cucumber, and now that you always sit at home you look like nothing on earth. You might walk about the streets and look at the people or something. . . .'

'Stop your nonsense and listen!' Oblomov said. 'Walk about the streets, indeed!'

'Yes, really,' Zahar went on with added warmth. 'They say some unheard-of monster is on show; you might have a look at that. Or you might go to a theatre or a masquerade and we would do the moving without you!'

'Don't talk rubbish! So that's the way you look after your master's comfort! You would have me tramping about all day – it's nothing to you that I should have dinner Heaven knows where and how, and couldn't lie down after the meal? . . . They would move without me! If I don't look after it, everything will be smashed to smithereens. I know what moving means!' Oblomov went on, growing more and more impressive. 'It means noise, breakages; everything is heaped together on the floor. The portmanteau, the back of the sofa, pictures, pipes, books, all sorts of bottles one doesn't see at other times are sure to turn up from somewhere! One has to see to it all, so that things aren't broken or lost. . . . One half is here, another on the cart or at the new flat; one wants to smoke, takes up the pipe, but the tobacco is gone . . . wants to sit down, but there is nothing to sit on – all is covered with dust, and one can't touch anything without getting grimy; there's nothing to wash with and one has to go about with hands like yours. . . .'

'My hands are clean,' Zahar remarked, showing what looked like a pair of shoe soles rather than hands.

'Don't show them, at least!' said Ilya Ilyitch, turning away. 'And if one is thirsty,' he went on, 'the decanter is there, but there's no glass. . . .'

'One can drink out of the decanter just as well,' Zahar observed reassuringly.

'That's you all over: one can just as well not sweep and not dust and not shake the carpets. And at the new flat,' Ilya Ilyitch went on, carried away by the lively picture he had drawn, 'it will be at least three days before things are put straight; everything is in the wrong place, pictures on the floor by the walls, goloshes on the bed, boots in the same bundle with tea and the pomatum. An arm-chair leg is broken, the glass over some picture smashed, the sofa stained. Whatever one asks for is not to be had, no one knows where it is; it may be lost or left at the old flat and you have to run back for it. . . .'

'One may have to run a dozen times there and back,' Zahar interrupted.

'You see!' Oblomov continued. 'And getting up in the morning in a new flat, what a bore! There is no water, no charcoal, and in winter one would be simply frozen – the rooms are cold through and through and there is no fire-wood; you have to run and borrow some. . . .'

'And it depends on what neighbours God sends us,' Zahar remarked again. 'Some wouldn't lend one a cup of water, let alone a bundle of firewood. . . .'

'There it is!' Ilya Ilyitch said. 'You think the moving would be over by the evening, but, no, it will mean at least another fortnight's bother. You fancy everything is in its place . . . but there is still something left to do: cur-tains to hang, pictures to put up – it's enough to kill one, to make one's life a misery. . . . And the expense!'

'Last time, eight years ago, it cost us two hundred rou-bles; I remember as though it were to-day,' Zahar con-firmed.

'That's no joke, you know,' Ilya Ilyitch said. 'And how

queer it seems at first in a new flat! It takes a long time to grow used to it. I shan't be able to sleep for at least five nights in the new place; I shall be wretched when I get up and see something else instead of the carpenter's sign-board opposite; if that old woman with cropped hair doesn't peep out of the window before dinner, I feel I miss something. . . . Do you see now what you would let your master in for?' Ilya Ilyitch asked reproachfully.

'I see,' Zahar whispered humbly.

'Then why did you talk of moving? Why, no man could stand it!'

'I merely thought other people are no worse than us, and if they move we can . . .' Zahar said.

'What? What?' Ilya Ilyitch asked in surprise, rising from his chair. 'What did you say?'

Zahar was confused, not knowing what he could have said to cause his master's dramatic gesture and question. He was silent.

'Other people are no worse!' Ilya Ilyitch repeated with horror. 'This is what you have come to! I shall know now that I am the same as "other people" to you!'

Oblomov bowed to Zahar ironically, looking deeply insulted.

'But, Ilya Ilyitch, I've never said you were the same as anyone else. . . .'

'Out of my sight!' Oblomov commanded, pointing to the door. 'I can't bear to look at you. Ah, "other people"! Very well!'

With a deep sigh Zahar withdrew to his own quarters.

'What a life!' he grumbled, sitting down on the stove.

'Oh, heavens!' Oblomov groaned too. 'Here I wanted to devote the morning to useful labour and I'm upset for a whole day! And who has done it? My own servant! A tried, devoted servant; but what has he said? How could he have said it?'

Oblomov could find no peace; he lay down, got up, walked about the room and lay down again. Zahar's reducing him to the level of *others* was a violation of his right to Zahar's exclusive preference. He pondered over the comparison, considering what the *others* were, to what extent a parallel between him and them could be justly drawn, and how great was the insult Zahar had flung at him. Finally, he wondered whether Zahar had insulted him consciously, really believing that Ilya Ilyitch was no better than 'others', or the words had slipped out without thinking. Oblomov's vanity was piqued; he decided to show Zahar the difference between himself and 'others' and bring home to him the baseness of his action.

'Zahar!' he called, distinctly and solemnly.

Hearing the call, Zahar did not growl or noisily jump off the stove as usual; he slowly slid down and, catching at everything with his arms and sides, quietly and reluctantly walked to the door like a dog that knows by its master's voice that its tricks have been discovered and it is being called to be dealt with accordingly. Zahar half opened the door, but did not venture to go in.

'Come in!' Ilya Ilyitch said.

The door could be opened easily, but Zahar made it appear as though he could not pass through it and stuck in the doorway instead of walking in.

Oblomov was sitting on the edge of the bed.

'Come here!' he said insistently.

With difficulty Zahar disentangled himself from the door, immediately closed it behind him, and firmly leaned against it with his back.

'Here!' said Ilya Ilyitch, pointing to a place beside him. Zahar took another half-step and stopped fourteen feet away from the spot indicated.

'Nearer!' Oblomov said.

Zahar pretended to take another step, but merely swayed his body, brought his foot down with a noise, and remained where he was. Seeing that he could not induce Zahar to come any nearer, Ilya Ilyitch merely looked at him for some minutes reproachfully and in silence. Embarrassed by this mute contemplation, Zahar pretended not to notice his master, and stood turning away from him more than usual without even glancing at him. He gazed fixedly to the left; he saw there a sight familiar to him – a fringe of cobwebs round the pictures and a spider, a living reproach to his negligence.

'Zahar!' Ilya Ilyitch said quietly and with dignity.

Zahar made no answer; he seemed to be thinking, 'Well, what do you want? Some other Zahar? I am here right enough,' and transferred his glance to the right, past his master; there, too, he was reminded of himself by a mirror covered with thick dust as with muslin; his own sullen and unattractive countenance looked at him wildly and menacingly from there as from a mist. He turned away with annoyance from this sad and much too familiar object and decided to glance for a minute at Ilya Ilyitch. Their eyes met. Zahar could not endure the reproach in his master's eyes and looked down on the floor. There again, in the dusty carpet covered with stains, he read a poor testimony to his zeal for his master's service.

'Zahar!' Ilya Ilyitch repeated with feeling.

'What is it, sir?' Zahar whispered half audibly, and slightly shuddered at the prospect of a pathetic speech.

'Give me some *kvass*!' said Ilya Ilyitch.

Zahar breathed freely; in his joy he ran like a boy to the sideboard and brought some *kvass*.

'Well, how do you feel?' Ilya Ilyitch asked gently, taking a drink and holding the glass in his hands. 'You aren't happy, are you?'

The savage expression of Zahar's face was instantly softened by a ray of repentance which gleamed on his features. Zahar felt the first symptoms of reverence for his master awakening in his breast and melting his heart, and suddenly he began to look straight into Oblomov's eyes.

'Do you repent of your transgression?' Ilya Ilyitch asked.

'Whatever is this?' Zahar wondered bitterly. 'Something heart-rending, I expect; one is bound to cry if he goes for one like this.'

'Well, Ilya Ilyitch,' Zahar began on the lowest note in

his register, 'I haven't said anything except that. . . .'

'No, wait!' Oblomov interrupted him. 'Do you understand what you have done? Here, put the glass on the table and answer!'

Zahar made no answer, utterly failing to understand what he had done; but this did not prevent his looking at his master with reverence; he slightly bowed his head, conscious of his guilt.

'How can you deny being a venomous man?' Oblomov asked.

Zahar still said nothing and only blinked two or three times.

'You have grieved your master!' Ilya Ilyitch said slowly, and gazed fixedly at Zahar, enjoying his discomfiture.

Utterly wretched, Zahar did not know what to do with himself.

'You have grieved him, haven't you?' Ilya Ilyitch asked.

'Yes,' Zahar whispered, utterly overwhelmed by this new heart-rending word. He glanced from right to left in search of deliverance, and again there flitted before him the cobwebs, the dust, his own reflection in the mirror, and his master's face. 'I could sink through the floor! I wish I were dead!' he thought, seeing that, do what he would, there was no escaping a dramatic scene. He felt that he was blinking more and more often and tears might rush any moment from his eyes. At last he brought himself to answer his master.

'How have I grieved you, Ilya Ilyitch?' he said almost weeping.

'How?' Oblomov repeated. 'Why, have you considered what *other people* are?'

He paused, still looking at Zahar.

'Shall I tell you?'

Zahar turned like a bear in its den and sighed aloud.

'*Other people* – those whom you mean – are God-forsaken wretches, rough, uncultured people who live in some attic in dirt and poverty. They can sleep quite comfortably on a mat somewhere in a yard. All that is nothing to them. They guzzle herrings and potatoes. Poverty drives them from pillar to post and they keep on the run all day. They might be ready enough to move to new lodgings, I dare say. Lyagaev, for instance, would put the ruler under his arm, tie up two shirts in a handkerchief, and go off. . . . "Where are you going?" "I am moving," he would say. This is what "other people" are! And you imagine I am like them?'

Zahar glanced at his master, shifted from one foot to the other, and said nothing.

'What are "other people"?' Oblomov continued. 'They are people who clean their own boots, dress themselves, and though they sometimes look like gentlemen, it's mere pretence, they have never had a servant; if they have no one to send on an errand they run themselves; they think nothing of stirring the wood in the stove or of dusting. . . .'

'Lots of Germans are like that,' Zahar remarked gloomily.

'Exactly! And I? Do you imagine I am like that?'

'You are quite different!' Zahar said piteously, still failing to grasp what his master was driving at. 'Heaven only knows what has come over you. . . .'

'I am quite different, eh? Wait, think what you are saying! Consider how those "other people" live. They work without rest, they fuss, run about,' Oblomov went on. 'If they don't work they don't eat. They bow, they beg, they cringe. . . . And I? Well, say, what do you think, am I like other people, eh?'

'Don't torment me with heart-rending words, sir!' Zahar implored. 'Oh, my goodness!'

'Comparing me to "other people"! Why, do I rush about or work? Don't I eat enough? Do I look thin and wretched? Do I go short of things? I should hope I have someone to wait on me and do things for me. Thank Heaven I've never in my life put on my stockings myself! As though I would trouble! Why should I? And to whom am I saying this? Haven't you waited on me since I was a child? You know all this; you have seen that I have been brought up tenderly, have never suffered from cold or hunger or poverty, have never earned my living or done any dirty work. So how could you bring yourself to compare me with other people? Do you imagine I have health like theirs and can do and endure what they can?'

Zahar had lost all power of understanding Oblomov's words, but his lips were swollen with emotion; the pathetic scene was raging like a thunder-storm over his head. He said nothing.

'Zahar!' Ilya Ilyitch repeated.

'Yes, sir?' Zahar hissed almost inaudibly.

'Bring me some more *kvass*.'

Zahar brought the *kvass*, and when Ilya Ilyitch had drunk it and handed him the glass he rapidly made for the door.

'No, no, wait!' Oblomov began. 'I am asking you, how could you so bitterly insult your master, whom you used to carry in your arms as a baby, whom you have served all your life, and who is your benefactor?'

Zahar could not stand it. The word 'benefactor' was too much for him. He blinked oftener and oftener. The less he understood Ilya Ilyitch's dramatic speeches the sadder he felt.

'I am sorry, Ilya Ilyitch,' he hissed penitently. 'It was just my foolishness. . . .'

Not understanding what he had done, Zahar did not know how to finish his sentence.

'And here I work and worry night and day,' Oblomov went on in the injured voice of a man who is not rightly appreciated; 'sometimes I lie awake at night with a burning head and sinking heart, turning over from side to side, thinking how I can arrange things for the best . . . for whom? Why, for the peasants, and that means for you too. I dare say when you see me pull the blanket over my head you think I lie there like a log and sleep; but no, I don't sleep, I keep thinking hard what I can do that my peasants should not suffer any privations, should not envy other people, and complain against me to the Lord God on the Day of Judgment, but should pray for me and remember the good I have done them. Ungrateful men!' Oblomov concluded bitterly.

Zahar was completely overcome by the last heart-rending words. He began to sob.

'Ilya Ilyitch, sir, don't go on like this!' he implored. 'The Lord be with you, what are you talking about? Oh, Mother, Queen of Heaven, all this trouble coming upon us suddenly!'

'And you,' Oblomov went on, not listening to him, 'you should be ashamed to say such things! That's the snake I've warmed in my bosom!'

'Snake!' Zahar cried, clasping his hands and setting up such a howl that it sounded exactly as though two dozen bumble-bees had flown into the room and started buzzing. 'When have I mentioned a snake?' he said amidst his sobs. 'I never even dream of the cursed thing!'

Both had ceased to understand each other and now no longer understood themselves.

'How could your tongue have uttered it?' Ilya Ilyitch continued. 'And in my plan I had already assigned you a house and a kitchen-garden, so much flour per month, and a salary! You were to be my steward and butler and agent! The peasants would bow low to you, everyone would call you Zahar Trofimitch; and here he is not content, and compares me to "other people"! That's my reward! A nice way of treating his master!'

Zahar went on sobbing and Ilya Ilyitch was moved also. As he admonished Zahar he became deeply convinced for the moment of the benefits he had conferred on his peasants and uttered his last reproaches in a shaking voice with tears in his eyes.

'Well, now go in peace!' he said to Zahar conciliatingly. 'Wait, give me some more *kvass*! My throat is quite parched; you might have thought of it yourself – you heard your master was hoarse. This is what you've brought me to! I hope you have understood your transgression and are not going to compare your master to "other people" again. To atone for your fault, you must make some arrangement with the landlord so that I need not move. This is how you watch over your master's peace of mind: you have thoroughly upset me and made it impossible for me to think of anything new and useful. And who will be the worse for it? Why, yourselves; I have devoted my whole life to my peasants, it's for your sake I have retired from the service and sit within four walls. . . . Well, I forgive you. There, it is striking three! Only two hours left before dinner; there's no time to do anything in two hours, and there is a lot to be done. Very well, I will leave the letter till the next post and jot down the plan to-morrow. And now I will lie down for a bit; I am quite worn out. Pull down the curtains and shut me in properly so that I am not disturbed; I may sleep for an hour; wake me at half-past four. . . .'

Zahar began bottling up his master in the study; first he covered him with a blanket and tucked it under him, then pulled down the blinds, carefully shut all the doors, and went to his own room.

'May you choke, you demon!' he grumbled, wiping away the traces of tears and climbing on the stove. 'A demon and no mistake! A house, a kitchen-garden, a salary!' repeated Zahar, who had understood only the last words. 'He can talk well enough – it's simply cutting one's heart with a knife! Here is my house and kitchen-garden and here I'll breathe my last,' he went on, hitting the stove furiously. 'A salary! If I didn't pick up a few coppers when I have a chance I shouldn't have anything to buy tobacco with or to treat my friend! Curse you! . . . I wish it were all up with me. . . .'

Ilya Ilyitch lay on his back but did not go to sleep at once. He thought and thought and worried.

'Two misfortunes at once!' he said, covering himself up with the blanket, head and all. 'How can one stand it?'

In truth, however, the two *misfortunes*, i.e. the bailiff's sinister letter and the removal to new lodgings, no longer worried Oblomov; they were becoming merely disturbing memories. 'The troubles the bailiff is threatening me with are still a long way off,' he thought, 'a great deal may happen before then; the rain may save the crops, the bailiff may collect the arrears, and the runaway peasants be returned "to their proper homes," as he writes. Where could they have gone to, those peasants?' he wondered, and fell to considering this fact rather from the artistic point of view. 'I expect they ran away at night, in the damp, taking no bread. Where would they sleep? Surely not in the forest? Fancy people wanting to leave their homes! The cottage may smell nasty, but at least it's warm. And why should I worry?' he thought. 'My plan will soon be ready, so why be alarmed sooner than I need? It's foolish.' The thought of removal troubled him more. It was a new and more recent *misfortune*; but Oblomov's accommodating mind had already transferred it into the past. He was vaguely conscious that he would have to move, especially now that Tarantyev was mixed up in the business, but he put off this anxious event for at least a week in his mind and so gained a whole week of peace. 'And *perhaps* Zahar will contrive something so that I need not move; let's *hope* they'll manage without turning me out – put off the alterations till next summer, or not do them at all; well, things will be arranged *somehow*! After all, I really can't . . . move!' And so he worried and calmed himself alternately, and at last, as always, found in the comforting and conciliatory words '*let's hope, perhaps, and somehow,*' a fountain of hope and consolation, as in the ancient covenant of law, and succeeded in warding off the two misfortunes with their help. A slight, pleasant numbness spread over his limbs and his senses were clouded with sleep, just as the surface of water is clouded by the slight early frosts; another minute and his mind would have slipped Heaven knows where, when suddenly Ilya Ilyitch came to himself and opened his eyes.

'Why, I haven't washed! How is that? And I haven't done anything,' he whispered. 'I wanted to put down my

plan on paper and I haven't done it; I haven't written to
the police captain or the Governor; I began and didn't
finish the letter to the landlord; I haven't checked the
accounts or given Zahar the money – the morning has
been wasted!' He pondered. 'What does it mean? And
other people would have done it all,' flashed through his
mind. 'Other people . . . what are they?'

He began comparing himself to 'others.' He thought
and thought, and ideas, very different from those he had
expounded to Zahar, came into his mind. He had to admit
that 'others' would have found time to write all the letters
and write them so that 'which' and 'that' never jostled each
other; 'others' would have moved to a new flat, carried out
the plan, gone to the country. . . .

'I, too, could do all this, one would have thought,' he
reflected. 'I can write well enough and have written in my
time less simple things than letters! What has become of it
all? And what is there so dreadful about moving? One has
only to make up one's mind! Other people never wear a
dressing-gown . . . ' he added, by way of characterizing
'others' . . . then he yawned; 'they hardly sleep at all . . .
they enjoy life, go everywhere, see all there is to see, take
an interest in everything. . . . And I? I . . . am different,'
he said, sadly this time, and sank into thought. He
actually put his head out from under the blanket.

This was one of the lucid, conscious moments in Oblomov's life. Horror possessed him when there arose before
him a clear and vivid idea of what human destiny was
meant to be as compared with his own existence, when
the problems of life wakened within him and whirled
through his mind like frightened birds roused suddenly by
a ray of sunlight in a slumbering ruin. It grieved and hurt
him to think that he was undeveloped, that his spiritual
forces had stopped growing, that some dead weight ham-
pered him; he bitterly envied those whose lives were rich
and full, while he felt as though a heavy stone had been
thrown on to the narrow and pitiful path of his existence.
It hurt his timid mind to grasp that many sides of his

nature had never been awakened, others barely so, and
none had developed fully. And yet he was painfully conscious that something fine and good lay buried in him and
was, perhaps, already dead or hidden like gold in the
depths of a mountain, although it was high time for the
gold to be current coin. But the treasure was deeply
buried under a heavy load of rubbish and dirt. It was as
though the treasures bestowed on him by the world and
life had been stolen from him and hidden in the depths of
his own soul. Something hindered him from flinging himself into the arena of life and using his will and intellect to
go full speed forward. It was as though some secret enemy
had laid a heavy hand upon him at the beginning of his
journey and thrown him far back from the right road. . . .
And it did not seem that he could ever find his way to the
straight path from the thick jungle. The forest around
him and in his mind grew thicker and darker; the path
was more and more overgrown; clear consciousness
wakened more and more seldom, and his slumbering
forces were roused but for a moment. His mind and will
had been paralysed, hopelessly, it seemed. The events in
his life had dwindled down to microscopic proportions,
but even so they were more than he could cope with; he
did not pass from one to another, but was tossed to and fro
by them as by waves; he had not the strength of will to
oppose one course or to follow another rationally. He felt
bitter at having to confess all this to himself. Fruitless
regrets for the past, burning reproaches of conscience went
through him like stings; he struggled hard to throw off the
burden of these reproaches, to find someone else to blame
and turn the sting against. But against whom?

'It's all . . . Zahar's fault!' he whispered. He recalled
the details of the scene with Zahar and his face burned
with shame. 'What if someone had overheard it?' he
thought, turning cold at the idea. 'Thank Heaven Zahar
won't be able to repeat it to anyone; and, indeed, no one
would believe him, thank Heaven!'

He sighed, cursed himself, turned from side to side,

sought for someone to blame and could find no one. His groans and sighs reached Zahar's ears.

'The way he carries on after that *kvass*! ' Zahar muttered angrily.

'Why am I like this?' Oblomov asked himself almost with tears, and hid his head under the blanket again. 'Why?' After seeking in vain for the hostile power that prevented him from living like 'other people' he sighed, closed his eyes, and in a few minutes drowsiness began once more to benumb his senses. 'I, too . . . wished,' he said, blinking with difficulty, 'for something fine . . . has nature dealt unfairly with me? . . . No, thank Heaven, I can't complain that it has. . . . ' Then came the sound of a sigh of resignation. He was passing from agitation to his normal state of calm and apathy. 'It must be my fate. . . . What can I do?' he was hardly able to whisper, overcome by sleep. 'Some two thousand less than last year,' he suddenly said aloud, dreaming. 'Directly, directly, wait . . .' and he half awoke. 'And yet . . . I wish I knew why . . . I am . . . like this!' he said in a whisper again. His eyelids closed altogether. 'Yes, why? . . . It must be . . . because . . . ' he tried to say the word and could not.

He never arrived at the cause after all; his tongue and lips stopped in the middle of a word and remained half open. Instead of a word another sigh was heard, and then the even snoring of a man peacefully asleep.

Sleep stopped the slow and lazy flow of his thoughts and instantly transferred him to other times, other people, to another place, where the reader and I will follow him in the next chapter.

IX

OBLOMOV'S DREAM

WHERE are we? To what blessed spot has Oblomov's dream brought us? What a lovely country!

It is true there are no high mountains there, no sea, no rocks and precipices, no virgin forests – nothing grand, gloomy, or wild. But what is the good of the grand and the wild? The sea, for instance, God bless it! It merely makes one sad: looking at it, a man wants to cry. Fear clutches the heart at the sight of the boundless expanse of water, and there is nothing to rest the eyes aching with the endless monotony of the view. The roar, the wild onrush of the waves do not caress man's feeble hearing; they repeat a melody of their own, gloomy and mysterious, the same since the world began; and the same old wail is heard in it, the same complaint as though of a monster doomed to torture, and piercing, sinister voices. No birds twitter around; only silent gulls, as though condemned to it, mournfully fly to and fro by the beach and circle over the water.

The roar of a beast is powerless beside these cries of nature, the human voice is as nothing, and man himself is so little and weak, so completely lost among the small details in the vast picture. No, no sea for me! Its very calm and stillness give one no comfort: in the hardly perceptible swell of the water man sees the same boundless force, slumbering for the moment, that can mock so bitterly his proud will and bury so deeply his daring schemes and all his labour and toil.

Mountains and abysses, too, have not been created for man's enjoyment. They are as terrible and menacing as the teeth and claws of a wild beast threatening us; they remind us too vividly of our frailty and fill us with fear and anguish, and the heaven above them seems far and unattainable, as though it had forsaken man.

The peaceful spot where our hero suddenly found himself was of a different nature. The sky there seems to come nearer to the earth, not in order to fling sharper arrows at it, but to hug it more warmly and lovingly; it hangs as low overhead as the trusty roof of the parental home, to preserve, as it were, the chosen place from all calamities. The sun there shines warmly and brightly for about six months in the year and then withdraws gradually, as though reluctantly, turning back, as it were, to have another look or two at the place it loves and to give it a warm, clear day amidst the autumn rain.

The hills seem to be mere models of those terrible mountains far away that frighten one's imagination. They rise in gentle slopes, pleasant to slide down on one's back in play, or to sit on, dreamily watching the sunset.

The river runs cheerfully, sporting and playing; now it spreads into a wide pond, now flows on in a rapid stream or grows quiet, as though lost in thought, and hardly moves along the pebbles, sending out to all sides lively brooks, the ripple of which makes one delightfully drowsy.

The whole place, for ten or fifteen miles around, is a series of picturesque, bright, and smiling landscapes. The sandy, sloping banks of the clear river, the small bushes that come down from the hill to the water, the curving ravine with a brook running through it, the birch copse – all seem to have been fitted together on purpose and drawn with a masterly hand.

A heart worn out by troubles or wholly unfamiliar with them longs to hide in this secluded spot and live there happily, unnoticed by all. Everything there promises a calm, long life till the hair turns from white to yellow, and death comes unnoticed like sleep.

Nothing there disturbs the regular yearly round. As appointed by the calendar, spring comes in March, muddy streams run from the hills, the ground thaws, and a warm vapour rises above it like smoke. The peasant takes off his sheepskin, comes out into the open dressed only in his shirt, and, screening his eyes, stands there enjoying the sunshine, shrugging his shoulders with the pleasure of it from time to time; then he pulls the overturned cart first by one shaft then by another and kicks his foot against the plough that lies idly under the shelter in readiness for the usual labours. No sudden storms come in the spring, covering the fields with snow and breaking down the trees. Like a cold and unapproachable beauty winter remains true to its character till the lawfully appointed time for warmth; it does not tease one with sudden thaws or bend one double with unheard-of frosts; everything goes on in the usual way prescribed by nature. In November snow and frost begin, and by Epiphany the frost is so strong that if a peasant leaves his cottage for a minute he returns with hoar-frost on his beard; and in February a sensitive nose already feels the soft breath of approaching spring.

But the summer is particularly delightful in those parts. It is there one finds fresh, dry air filled with scent – not of lemons and laurels – but of wormwood, bird-cherry, and pine; it is there one finds clear days, slightly burning but not scorching sunshine, and cloudless sky for almost three months on end. Once fine weather comes, it lasts for three or four weeks; the evenings are warm and the nights are close. The stars look down from heaven with a friendly, kindly twinkle. If there is rain, refreshing summer rain, it falls quickly and abundantly, splashing merrily with big drops like the warm tears of a man overcome with sudden joy; and as soon as it stops the sun once more, with a bright smile of love, looks at the hills and meadows and dries them; and again the countryside smiles with happiness in response to the sun. The peasant welcomes the rain joyfully, 'The rain will wet and the sun will dry me,' he says, exposing with relish his face, shoulders, and back to the warm downpour. Thunder-storms are not a terror but a blessing in those parts; they happen invariably at the same set periods, hardly ever omitting St. Ilya's Day, as though to keep up the peasant's traditional belief. The strength and number of thunder-claps seem to be the same from year to year, as though a definite amount of electricity were annually allotted to the place. Hurricanes or devastating storms are unheard of in those parts. No one has ever read anything of the kind about this place, specially blessed by Providence, and nothing, indeed, would ever have been written or heard about it had not a peasant widow, Marina Kulkova, twenty-eight years of age, given birth to four babies at once, which was, dreadful to say, printed in the newspapers.

The Lord has never visited those parts either with the Egyptian or any other plagues. No one of the inhabitants has ever seen or remembers any terrible signs in heaven, fiery balls, or sudden darkness; no poisonous reptiles breed there, no locusts come; there are no roaring lions, no growling tigers, not even wolves or bears, for there are no forests. Only munching cows, bleating sheep, and cackling hens walk about the fields and villages in plenty.

Heaven only knows whether a poet or a dreamer would be content with nature in this peaceful spot. As everyone knows, these gentlemen love to gaze at the moon and to listen to the trilling of nightingales. They like a coquettish moon that dresses in pale amber clouds, peeps mysteriously through the branches, or flings sheaves of silvery rays into her admirer's eyes; and in that country the moon was the moon and nothing more. It looked good-naturedly, open-eyed, at the fields and villages, and strongly resembled a polished brass basin. It would be useless for the poet to gaze at it with ecstatic eyes: it would look at him as simple-heartedly as does a village beauty in response to the ardent and eloquent glances of a town Don Juan.

Nor are there any nightingales in those parts, perhaps because shady arbours and roses do not abound there; but what a number of quails! In harvest-time boys catch them with their hands. Let it not be thought, however, that quails are regarded by them as a luxury for the table – no, the inhabitants' morals have not been depraved to that extent: quail is not a prescribed article of diet. It delights the ear with its singing – this is why almost every house has a quail in a string cage under the eaves.

Poets and dreamers would not be satisfied with the general appearance of this modest and unpretentious neighbourhood. They would not succeed in seeing there an evening in the Swiss or Scotch style, when the whole of nature – the forest, the river, the cottage walls, and the sandy hills are all suffused with a glow of fire; the purple sunset would not reveal a cavalcade of men who, after escorting a lady on an excursion to some gloomy ruin, hasten along a sandy, winding road to a strong castle, where they will be treated to a story about the Wars of the Roses told by her grandfather, to wild goat's flesh for supper, and a ballad sung by a young lady to the sound of a harp – scenes with which Walter Scott has amply stocked our imagination. No, there is nothing like that in our parts.

How still and sleepy everything is in the three or four villages in that part of the country! They lie close to one another and look as though a giant's hand had thrown them down accidentally, scattering them about, and they had remained so ever since. One cottage has dropped on the edge of the ravine and has been hanging there from time immemorial with one-half of it in the air, propped up by three posts. Three or four generations have lived in it peacefully and happily. One would think a hen would be afraid to go into it, and yet Onisim Suslov, a man of an imposing figure, too big to stand up in his own dwelling, lived there with his wife. Not everyone would know how to enter Onisim's cottage, unless, indeed, the visitor persuaded it *to turn its back to the forest and its front to him*. The porch hangs over the ravine, and in order to step in one has to hold on to the grass with one hand and to the cottage roof with the other, and then plant one's foot on the steps. Another cottage clings to the hill like a swallow's nest; three have been accidentally placed side by side, and two others stand at the very bottom of the ravine.

Everything in the village is still and sleepy: the doors of the deserted cottages are wide open; not a soul is about; only the flies swarm in clouds and buzz in the stuffy air. If you walk in and call in a loud voice, dead silence will answer you. Occasionally some old woman, who is spending her remaining years on the stove, will reply with a painful groan or stifled cough, or a child of three, with long hair, bare feet, and only a smock on, will appear from behind the partition, gaze at the stranger in silence, and timidly hide again. In the fields there is the same profound peace and stillness; only here and there, stirring like an ant on the black earth, a peasant, bathed in sweat, presses his plough forward in the burning heat.

The same unruffled peace and quiet prevailed in the people's lives. No robberies or murders or terrible accidents of any sort ever happened there; no violent passions or daring enterprises agitated the inhabitants; and, indeed, what passions or enterprises could agitate them? Every one of them knew his own limitations. They lived far from other people – the nearest villages and the district town were some twenty or twenty-five miles away. At certain seasons the peasants carted corn to the landing-station nearest the Volga, which was their Colchis or Pillars of Hercules, and once a year some of them went to the fair; this was all the intercourse they had with the outside world. Their interests were centred in themselves and did not impinge upon or conflict with anyone else's. They knew that the chief town of the province was sixty miles distant, but very few of them ever went there; they knew that Saratov and Nizhni lay farther away in the same direction; they had heard of Petersburg and Moscow and of the Germans or the French who lived beyond Petersburg, but what lay farther was as full of mystery for them as for the ancients – unknown countries inhabited by monsters, by people with two heads, by giants; beyond this there was darkness, and the end of all was the fish

which held the world on its back. And since hardly
anyone ever travelled through their part of the country,
they could not learn from anywhere recent news of what
was going on in the world: the men who sold wooden
ware lived only fifteen miles away and knew no more than
they did. There was nothing with which they could compare their way of living so as to say whether they lived
well or no, whether they were rich or poor, and could
wish for something that others had. These lucky people
lived in the conviction that things could not, and ought
not to, be any different, that everyone lived as they did,
and that it would be a sin to live otherwise. They simply
would not believe it if someone told them that there were
other ways of ploughing, sowing, harvesting, selling. What
passions and excitements could they have? Like everyone
else they had their troubles and weakness – the payment
of taxes, laziness, love of sleep; but all this amounted to
very little and did not stir their blood. For the last five
years there had been no deaths at all among the several
hundred villages, not even natural deaths, to say nothing
of violent ones. And when someone had gone to his
eternal sleep, from old age or some chronic illness, the
people had gone on marvelling at such an extraordinary
event for weeks; and yet they did not think it at all
marvellous that, for instance, Taras the blacksmith had
nearly steamed himself to death in the bath-house and had
to be revived with buckets of cold water.

The only crime that was extremely prevalent was the
theft of peas, carrots, and turnips from the kitchen-
gardens; and one day two suckling pigs and a hen disappeared suddenly – an event which revolted the whole
neighbourhood and was unanimously attributed to the fact
that the day before traders in wooden ware had passed
through the village on their way to the fair. But, speaking
generally, accidents of any kind were extremely rare.
Once, however, a man had been found lying in the ditch
by the bridge outside – evidently one of the party of
workmen who had passed by on their way to town. The

boys were the first to see him and ran to the village horri-fied, saying that some terrible dragon or monster lay in the ditch, adding that he had chased them and very nearly eaten Kuzka. The pluckier of the peasants started off in a crowd towards the ditch, armed with forks and axes.

'Where are you going?' the old men tried to stop them. 'Are you so strong as all that? What do you want there? Leave it alone, no one is driving you.'

But the men went, and some three hundred feet from the spot began calling to the monster: there was no answer; they stopped, then went farther. A peasant lay in the ditch, leaning his head against the rising ground; a bag and a stick with two pairs of bark-shoes tied on to it lay beside him. The peasants did not venture to go near him or to touch him.

'Hey, there, brother!' they shouted in turn, scratching their heads or their backs. 'What's your name? Who are you? Hey, you! What do you want here?'

The man in the ditch tried to lift his head, but could not; he was evidently either ill or very tired.

One of the peasants very nearly ventured to touch him with the fork.

'Don't touch him! Don't touch him!' many of the others shouted. 'There's no knowing what he is; you see, he doesn't say anything; maybe there's something wrong about him. . . . Don't touch him, lads! Let us go,' some said. 'Let us, really! It's not as though he were a kinsman! He is nothing to us, it's merely courting trouble!'

And they all went back to the village, telling the old men that a stranger was lying there, that he did not speak, and God only knew what was the matter with him. . . .

'You let him alone if he is a stranger!' the old men said, as they sat outside their cottages with their elbows on their knees. 'Let him be! And there was no need for you to go!'

Such was the spot where Oblomov suddenly found himself in his dream. One of the three or four villages scattered there was called Sosnovka, and another, half a mile from it, Vavilovka. These were the hereditary property of the Oblomovs and were, therefore, known under the general name of Oblomovka. The master's house and residence was in Sosnovka. The village of Verhlyovo, that had once belonged to the Oblomovs, but had long since passed into other hands, and several scattered cottages that went with it, lay three miles from Sosnovka. Verhlyovo belonged to a rich landowner who rarely came to his estate – a German steward looked after it. Such was the geography of the place. . . .

Ilya Ilyitch woke up in his cot in the morning. He was only seven. He felt gay and light-hearted. How pretty, rosy, and plump he was! His cheeks were so round that many a little rogue could not puff his out to that shape if he tried. His nurse was waiting for him to wake. She began putting on his stockings; he did not let her, played about, kicking his legs; the nurse caught him and they both laughed. At last she succeeded in making him get up; she washed his face, combed his hair, and took him to his mother. Seeing his mother, who had been dead for years, Oblomov, even in his sleep, felt a tremor of joy and ardent love for her; two warm tears oozed slowly from under his eyelashes and rested on his cheeks. His mother covered him with passionate kisses, then looked at him with anxious, eager eyes to see if his eyes were clear, if anything ailed him; asked the nurse if he had slept well, if he had waked in the night, if he tossed about or had been feverish; then she took him by the hand and led him to the ikon. Kneeling before it and putting one arm round him she made him repeat after her the words of a prayer. The boy said them absentmindedly, looking out of the window through which the morning freshness and the scent of lilac poured into the room.

'Mamma, shall we go for a walk to-day?' he suddenly asked in the middle of praying.

'Yes, yes, darling,' she answered hurriedly, without taking her eyes off the ikon and hastening to finish the holy words.

The boy repeated them listlessly, but the mother put her whole soul into them. Then they went to see his father and then to have breakfast.

At the breakfast-table Oblomov saw their aunt, an old lady of eighty, who lived with them; she was constantly grumbling at her 'girl,' who stood behind her chair, nodding with old age as she waited upon her. Three elderly spinsters, his father's distant relatives; Tchekmenev, his mother's slightly mad brother-in-law, the owner of seven serfs, who was staying with them; and several old ladies and old gentlemen were there too. All these members and followers of the Oblomov family picked up Ilya Ilyitch in their arms and showered caresses and praise upon him; he had hardly time to wipe away the traces of the unwelcome kisses. Then he was fed with rolls, biscuits, cream. Then his mother kissed him once more and sent him for a walk in the garden, in the yard, and in the meadow, with strict injunctions to the nurse not to leave the child alone, not to let him go near the horses, the dogs, or the goat, or wander far from the house, and, above all, not to allow him to go to the ravine, which was the most terrible place in the neighbourhood and had a bad reputation. Once a dog was found there which was said to be rabid simply because it rushed away and disappeared behind the hill when men armed with forks and axes went for it; carcases were thrown into the ravine; wolves and robbers and other beings non-existent in those parts or anywhere in the world were supposed to live in the ravine.

The child did not wait for his mother to finish her warnings but ran out into the yard. With joyful surprise, as though for the first time in his life, he examined his parents' house and ran round it; it had various additions built on to it; the wooden roof was sunk in the middle and overgrown with tender green moss, the steps were shaky, the gate leaned on one side, the big garden was neglected. He dreadfully wanted to climb on to the projecting balcony that went right round the house and to have a look at the river from there; but the ancient balcony was rickety and only the servants were allowed to go there; the masters no longer ventured on it. Not heeding his mother's prohibition, he ran towards the alluring steps, but the nurse appeared in the porch and succeeded in catching him. He rushed towards the steep stairs that led to the hayloft, and she had no sooner reached the hayloft than she had to frustrate his designs of climbing into the dovecote, penetrating into the cattle-yard, and – Heaven forbid! – to the ravine.

'My goodness, what a child! A regular fidget! Are you ever going to sit still, sir? It's a shame!' the nurse said.

The whole day and every day and night of the nurse's life was full of fuss and fluster; she was wretched and happy in turns, now tortured by the fear that the child might fall and hurt himself, now deeply moved by his unfeigned childish affection, or vaguely disturbed about his distant future. This was all that her heart was beating for; the agitation warmed the old woman's blood and sustained her sleepy existence, which might otherwise have ebbed away many years before.

But the child was not always sprightly; sometimes he suddenly grew quiet and looked about him attentively as he sat by his nurse. His young mind was watching all that was happening before him; the impressions sank deeply into his soul, to grow and ripen with years.

It was a glorious morning – the air was cool, the sun was still low. Long shadows fell from the house, the trees, the dovecote, and the balcony. Cool recesses, inviting sleep and dreaminess, appeared in the yard and the garden. Only the rye-fields in the distance glowed like fire, and the river sparkled in the sun so brilliantly that it hurt one's eyes to look at it.

'Why is it dark there, nurse, and light here, and presently it will be light there as well?' the child asked.

'Because the sun is going to meet the moon, my dear, but cannot see it and frowns; and when it does catch sight of it in the distance presently it will grow brighter.'

The child pondered and went on looking about him; he saw Antip going to fetch water and another Antip ten times as big moving beside him along the ground; the water-barrel looked as big as the house and the shadow of the horse covered the whole of the meadow; the shadow took only two steps and shifted behind the hill before Antip had had time to leave the yard. The child also took two steps; another step and he would be by the hill. He would like to go there to see what had become of the horse. He ran to the gate, but heard his mother's voice from the window:

'Nurse, don't you see that the child has run out in the sun! Take him in the shade; if his head gets hot he will have a headache and won't eat his dinner. He will run to the ravine if you don't look out.'

'Oh, you naughty boy!' the nurse grumbled softly, taking him back to the porch.

The child looked about him, watching with keen impressionable eyes what the grown-ups were doing and how they were spending the morning. Not a single detail escaped the child's searching attention: the picture of his home life was being indelibly stamped on his memory; his pliable mind was nurtured on the examples before him, unconsciously planning his own life after the pattern of the life around him.

No one could say that the morning was wasted in the Oblomovs' house. The clatter of knives mincing the meat and the vegetables could be heard as far as the village. The hum of the spindle and a woman's gentle, high-pitched voice came from the servants' hall: one could hardly tell whether she was crying or improvising a melancholy song without words. As soon as Antip came back to the yard with the barrel of water, the women and the coachmen came towards it from all directions with buckets, troughs, and jugs. An old woman carried from the store-room to the kitchen a basin of flour and a heap of eggs; the cook suddenly threw out some water from the window, splashing the dog, Arapka, that sat all the morning with its eyes fixed on the window, licking its lips and wagging its tail ingratiatingly.

Oblomov's father was not idle either. He sat the whole morning by the window unremittingly watching all that was going on in the yard.

'Hey, Ignashka! What are you carrying, you stupid?' he would ask a man walking along the yard.

'I am taking the knives to the servants' hall to be sharpened,' he would answer, without so much as a glance at his master.

'Very well, go on, and mind you sharpen them properly.'

Then he would stop a woman:

'Hey, my good woman, where have you been?'

'To the cellar, sir,' she answered, and she stopped to gaze at the window, sheltering her eyes from the sun. 'I went to fetch some milk for dinner.'

'Very well, go on,' the master answered; 'and mind you don't spill the milk.' 'And where are you running again, Zaharka, you scamp?' he would shout again, 'I'll teach you to run about! It's the third time you are doing it, I see. Go back to the hall!'

And Zaharka went back to doze in the hall. If the cows came back from the fields the master would be the first to see that they were given drink; if he saw from the window that a dog was pursuing a hen he immediately took stern measures against such irregularities.

His wife, too, was very busy. She spent some three hours explaining to Averka, the tailor, how to make a coat for Ilyusha out of her husband's jacket, drawing the lines in chalk, and watching that Averka should not steal any cloth. Then she went to the maids' room and set each girl her daily task of lace-making; then she called Nastasya Ivanovna or Stepanida Agapovna, or some other member of her retinue, for a walk in the garden with practical purposes: to see how ripe the apples were, to look if the one that was ripe the day before had fallen off the tree, if there was any grafting or pruning to be done, and so on.

But her chief concern was the kitchen and the dinner. The whole household was taken into consultation about the dinner, and even the ancient aunt was invited to the council. Everyone suggested a dish: giblet or vermicelli soup, brawn, tripe, red or white sauce. Every advice was considered, fully discussed, and then finally accepted or rejected by the mistress of the house. Nastasya Petrovna or Stepanida Ivanovna was constantly being sent to the kitchen to remind the cook of this or of that, to add one dish and cancel another, to take sugar, honey, or wine for the cooking, and see whether the cook had used all that had been given him.

Food was the first and foremost interest in life at Oblomovka. What calves were fattened there for the feast-days! What birds were bred! What subtlety, knowledge, and care were needed to rear them! Turkeys and chickens intended for name-days and other solemn occasions were fed on nuts; geese were deprived of exercise and forced to hang motionless in a bag for a few days before the feast so that they should get coated with fat. What stores of jams, pickles, biscuits there were! What meads, what *kvasses* were brewed, what pies were baked at Oblomovka!

And so up to midday all was fuss and bustle, everyone was living the busy, conspicuously active life of an ant-hill. The industrious ants did not rest on Sundays or holy-days either; then the clatter of knives in the kitchen was louder than ever; the woman travelled several times from the store-room to the kitchen with a double quantity of eggs and flour: there were more shrieks and bloodshed than usual in the poultry-yard. A tremendous pie was baked, which was served to the family for two days in succession; on the third and fourth day the remnants descended to the maids' room; it lasted on till Friday, and at last one stale end without stuffing was handed down by way of special favour to Antip, who, crossing himself, fearlessly demolished the ossified relics, enjoying the con-sciousness that it was his master's pie more than the pie itself, just as an archæologist will enjoy drinking wretched wine out of the fragment of some vessel a thousand years old.

And the boy kept looking on and watching it all with his childish mind which missed nothing. He saw the busy and well-spent morning being followed by midday, when dinner was served. The day was burning hot, not a cloud in the sky. The sun stood right overhead, scorching the grass. There was not the faintest stir in the motionless air, not a rustle in the trees, nor a ripple on the water; unbroken stillness reigned over the fields and the village, as though everything were dead. The human voice echoed far in the empty air. A cockchafer could be heard flying and buzzing a hundred feet away, and there was a sound of snoring in the thick grass as though someone were fast asleep there.

Dead stillness reigned in the house. It was the hour of after-dinner sleep for everyone. The child saw that his father and mother and old aunt and their followers had all gone to their rooms; those who had no room of their own went to the hayloft, to the garden, or sought coolness in the passage, while some, protecting their faces from the flies with a handkerchief, dropped asleep wherever the heat and the heavy dinner had overcome them. The gardener stretched himself out under a bush in the garden beside his mattock, and the coachman was asleep in the stables. Ilya Ilyitch peeped into the servants' hall: everyone was lying down on the benches, on the floor, and in the entry; the children, left to their own devices, were crawling about the yard and rummaging in the sand. The dogs retreated into the depths of their kennels, since there was no one to bark at. One could walk right through the house and not meet anyone; one could steal everything there was about and cart it away unhindered – but there were no thieves in those parts. It was an overwhelming, irresistible sleep, a true semblance of death. There was no life anywhere: only sounds of snoring of various pitch and quality came from every corner. Occasionally some sleeper would raise his head, look in senseless surprise about him and turn over or spit without opening his eyes, and, munching with his lips or muttering something under his breath, drop asleep once more. Another one would suddenly, without any preliminaries, jump off his couch as though afraid of losing precious moments, seize the jug of *kvass*, blow away the flies that floated in it, causing them to move violently in the hope of improving their position, take a drink, and again fall on the bed as though shot dead.

The child watched and watched. He went out with his nurse again after dinner; but in spite of her mistress's strict injunctions and her own good resolutions the nurse could not resist the fascination of sleep. She, too, succumbed to the epidemic that raged at Oblomovka. At first she was quite brisk, did not let the child go far from her, scolded him for running about; then, feeling the symptoms of the infection, she begged him not to go out of the gate, not to tease the goat, not to climb the dovecote or the balcony. She settled down somewhere in the shade: on the steps, at the cellar door, or simply on the grass, evidently intending to knit her stocking and keep an eye on the child; but soon her reproofs grew slack and she began nodding. 'Dear me, that fidget is sure to climb the balcony,' she thought, half asleep, 'or what if he goes . . . to the ravine? . . .' Then the old woman's head bent forward, the knitting dropped out of her hands, and, slightly opening her mouth, she gave a gentle snore. The child had been waiting impatiently for that moment, for with it his independent life began. He seemed to be alone in the whole world; he tiptoed away from the nurse and went to see where people were sleeping; he stopped and looked attentively if someone woke up for a moment, spat, and mumbled in his sleep; then, with a sinking heart, he ran up to the balcony and raced round the creaking boards, climbed the dovecote, went into the depths of the garden, listened to a cockchafer buzzing and watched its flight in the distance, listened to something chirping in the grass and tried to catch the disturbers of peace; caught a dragon-fly and tore off its wings to see what would become of it, or stuck a straw through it and watched it fly with this appendage; with bated breath he watched delightedly a spider sucking a fly and the poor victim struggling and buzzing in its clutches. In the end the child killed both the victim and the torturer. Then he went to the ditch, dug up some special roots which he peeled and ate with relish, preferring them to the jam and apples which his mamma gave him. He ran out of the gate; he would have liked to go to the birch copse, which seemed only within five minutes' walk, not by the road but straight across the ditch, the hurdle fences, and the pits; but he was afraid — he had been told that wood demons and robbers and terrible beasts lived there. He wanted to go to the ravine, too, it was only three hundred feet from the garden; he ran to the very edge of it, closed his eyes, and was just going to peep as into the crater of a volcano . . . but suddenly all the stories and legends about the ravine rose before his imagination; terror-stricken he rushed back to his nurse, more dead than alive, and woke her, trembling with fear. Roused from her sleep, she straightened her kerchief and pushed the wisps of her grey hair under it; pretending that she had not been asleep at all, and glancing suspiciously at Ilyusha and at the house windows, she began, with trembling fingers, prodding with the needles at the knitting that lay on her lap.

Meanwhile, the heat had begun to abate a little; nature was reviving; the sun had moved nearer to the forest.

The house, too, was gradually waking; a door creaked somewhere; someone could be heard walking in the yard; somebody sneezed in the hayloft. Soon a servant brought in a huge *samovar* from the kitchen, bending under the weight. The family began assembling for tea; one had his eyes watering and creases on his cheek where he had lain on it, another had a red spot on his cheek and temple with lying down, a third was still husky from sleep. They all snorted, groaned, yawned, scratched their heads, and stretched, barely awake as yet. The dinner and the sleep

had made them desperately thirsty; their throats were
parched; each drank about twelve cups of tea, but this
did not help; there was groaning and sighing; they tried
whortleberry water, pear water, *kvass*; some had recourse
to medicinal drinks to relieve the dryness in their throats.
All sought deliverance from thirst as though it were some
terrible plague; all tossed about in anguish like a caravan
of travellers in the Arabian desert with no spring of water
in sight.

The child was there beside his mother; he was watching the strange faces around him, listening to the sleepy,
lazy conversation. It amused him to look at them, and
every stupid remark seemed to him interesting. After tea
everyone occupied himself in some way: one went down
to the river and slowly walked along the bank, shoving the
pebbles into the water with his foot; another sat by the
window on the look out for all that happened – if a cat
crossed the yard, or a crow flew by, the observer followed
them with his eyes and nose, turning his head from left to
right. Dogs like sometimes to sit in this way for the whole
day on the window-sill, basking in the sun, and carefully
examining every passer-by. Ilyusha's mother would put
his head on her lap and slowly comb his hair, admiring its
softness and making Nastasya Ivanovna and Stepanida
Tihonovna admire it too; she talked to them of his future,
picturing him as the hero of some brilliant romance of her
own imagining, and they predicted mountains of gold for
him.

Dusk began to fall. Once more a fire was kindled in the
kitchen and there was a clatter of knives: supper was
being cooked. The servants were assembled at the gate;
sounds of the *balalaika* and laughter were heard there.
They were playing catch-who-can. The sun was setting
behind the copse, throwing off a few warm rays, which
went through the wood like streaks of fire, clothing the
tops of the pines with brilliant gold. Then the rays faded
one after the other; the last one lingered, piercing the
thick branches like an arrow, but it, too, disappeared at

last. Objects lost their shapes; everything was merged first into a grey and then into a black mass. The birds gradually stopped singing and at last were silent altogether, except one, which as though from sheer contrariness chirped monotonously at intervals amidst the general stillness; but the intervals grew longer and longer and finally it gave one last, low whistle, slightly rustled the branches around it . . . and dropped asleep. All was still. Only the grasshoppers chirped louder than ever. White mist rose from the ground and spread over the meadows and the river. The river, too, was quieter; something splashed in it for the last time, and it stirred no more. There was a smell of damp. It grew darker and darker. Clumps of trees loomed like some strange monsters; it was eerie in the wood; something creaked there suddenly, as though one of the monsters were changing its place and dried branches cracked under its feet. The first star, like a living eye, gleamed brightly in the sky, and lights appeared in the windows of the house.

It was the moment of solemn stillness in nature, when the creative mind works more actively, poetic thoughts glow more fervently, the heart burns with passion more ardently or suffers more bitter anguish, when the seed of a criminal design ripens unhindered in a cruel soul, when . . . everything in Oblomovka is peacefully and soundly asleep.

'Let us go for a walk, mamma,' Ilyusha said.

'What are you thinking of? Going for a walk at this hour!' the mother answered. 'It's damp, you would get your feet wet, and it's dangerous too; the wood demon is about in the forest; he carries off little children.'

'Where to? What is he like? Where does he live?' the child asked.

The mother gave rein to her unbridled fancy. The child listened to her, opening and shutting his eyes until sleep overcame him at last. The nurse came and, taking him from his mother's lap, carried him off to bed, asleep, his head hanging over her shoulder.

'The day is over, and thank God!' the Oblomovka inhabitants said, getting into bed, sighing, and crossing themselves. 'We have lived through it safely; God grant it may be the same to-morrow! Thanks be to Thee, O Lord!'

Then Oblomov dreamt of another occasion: one endless winter evening he was huddling timidly by his nurse, while she was whispering to him a tale about a far-off, unknown country, where there is no night nor cold, where miracles keep happening, rivers flow with milk and honey, no one does any work all the year round, and fine lads, like Ilya Ilyitch, and maidens more beautiful than words can tell do nothing but enjoy themselves all day. A kind fairy lives there who sometimes takes the shape of a pike, chooses for her favourite some quiet, harmless man – in other words, some sluggard – ill-treated by everyone, and bestows all sorts of presents upon him, while he does nothing but eat to his heart's content, wear clothes that are provided for him, and ends by marrying some marvellous beauty, Militrissa Kirbityevna. The child, all eyes and ears, followed the story with passionate absorption. The nurse – or the tradition – so artfully avoided all reference to reality that one's intellect and imagination, nurtured on make-belief, remained enslaved by it till old age. The nurse told, simple-heartedly, the tale of Emelya the Fool, that bitter and insidious satire against our ancestors and perhaps against ourselves as well. Although when Ilya Ilyitch grew up he learned that there were no rivers flowing with milk and honey and no good fairies and smiled at the nurse's tales, his smile was insincere, and he sighed in secret. The fairy-tale had mingled with reality in his mind and he sometimes unconsciously grieved that the fairy-tale was not life and life not a fairy-tale. He could not help dreaming about Militrissa Kirbityevna; he was always attracted by the land where people did nothing but enjoy themselves and had no cares or sorrows; he preserved for the rest of his life a taste for lying on the stove, wearing clothes that had been provided for him, and eating at the good fairy's expense. Oblomov's father and grandfather had heard as children the same tales, which had passed through centuries and generations in the stereotyped form repeated by nurses.

Meanwhile, the nurse was drawing another picture for the child's imagination.

She was telling him about the exploits of our Achilles and Ulysses, of Ilya Muromets's prowess, of Dobrynia Nikititch and Alyosha Popovitch, of the giant Polkan, of the pilgrim Koletchishtche, of how they wandered about Russia, destroyed numberless hosts of infidels, vied with each other in drinking huge goblets of wine at one gulp without winking; then she told him of wicked brigands, sleeping princesses, of towns and men turned to stone; finally, she passed to our demonology, corpses, monsters, and changelings.

With Homer's simplicity and good humour, and a power like his of making every detail concrete and living, she filled the child's memory and imagination with the Iliad of Russian life, created by our Homers in the far-off days when man did not feel at home as yet with the dangers and secrets of nature; when he trembled at the thought of wood demons and changelings; sought Alyosha Popovitch's aid against the evils around him; and when air, water, forest, and plain were full of marvels. Man's life in those days was uncertain and fearful; it was danger-ous for him to leave his own threshold – a wild beast might pounce upon him any moment, a brigand might murder him, a wicked Tatar rob him of everything, or he might simply disappear leaving no trace.

Tokens from heaven appeared suddenly – pillars or balls of fire; a light glimmered above a new grave; a crea-ture with gleaming eyes walked about in the forest as though swinging a lantern, laughing terribly in the dark. Many strange things happened to people in those days: a man might live for years quite happily, and all of a sudden he would begin saying the queerest things or cry in a wild voice or walk about in his sleep, or, for no reason at all, writhe in convulsions and fall on the ground. And just before a hen had crowed like a cock and a raven cried over the roof. In his weakness man felt bewildered as he looked about him in terror, and he tried to find, in his imagination, the key to the mysteries of nature and of his own being.

And perhaps it was the everlasting quiet of the sleepy, sluggish life, the absence of movement, and of any real terrors, adventures, and dangers that made man create a fantastic world amidst the real, where his idle imagination could have free play and ordinary connections of events could be explained by causes that had nothing to do with the events themselves. Our poor ancestors fumbled their way through life; they neither practised self-control nor let their will soar on the wings of inspiration, and at the same time they marvelled naïvely at the discomforts and evils of life and tried to find the explanation of them in the dumb and confusing hieroglyphics of nature. A death was caused, in their opinion, by the fact that on a previous occasion a corpse had been carried from the house head foremost instead of feet foremost; a fire was due to a dog howling for three nights by the window: they took care that a corpse should always be carried out of the house feet foremost, but they went on eating as much as ever and slept on the bare earth as before; they beat or drove away the howling dog, but still shook the sparks from the burning splinters down the cracks of the rotten floor. And to this day the Russian people, in spite of the stern and prosaic reality around them, like to believe in the seductive legends of long ago – and it may be years and years before they renounce this faith.

Listening to the nurse's stories of our *Golden Fleece*, the Fire Bird, of the dangers and secret chambers of the enchanted castle, the child felt elated imagining himself to be the hero though shivers ran down his back, or grieved over the misfortunes of the brave. Story followed story. The nurse was carried away by her own tales and told them picturesquely, with fervour, sometimes with inspiration, for she half believed them herself. Her eyes sparkled, her head shook with emotion, her voice rose to unusual notes. The child, overcome by a mysterious terror, clung to her with tears in his eyes. She spoke of dead men rising from their graves at midnight, of the monster's victims pining away in captivity, of the bear with the wooden leg going in search of the leg that had been cut off – and the child's hair rose with horror; his imagination seemed paralysed and then worked feverishly; there was a sweet and painful feeling in his breast; his nerves were taut like cords. The nurse repeated menacingly the bear's words: 'Creak, creak, my limewood leg; I've walked through villages, I've walked through hamlets, all the women are asleep; one woman does not sleep, she is sitting on my skin, she is cooking my own flesh, she is spinning my own fur,' and so on; and when the bear entered the hut at last and was about to seize the ravisher of his leg, the child could bear it no longer: he rushed to his nurse's arms shrieking and trembling, crying with fright and laughing with joy because he was not in the beast's claws but on the stove beside his nurse. The boy's imagination was peopled with strange phantoms; fear and sadness were rooted in his soul for years, perhaps for ever. He looked about him mournfully, seeing harm and trouble everywhere in life, and he dreamed perpetually of the magic land where there were no evils, worries, or sorrows, where Militrissa Kirbityevna lived, and splendid food and clothes could be had for nothing.

Fairy-tales were not merely for the children at Oblomovka, they retained their influence over people all their lives. Everyone in the house and the village, from the master and mistress down to the burly blacksmith, Taras, was vaguely uneasy on a dark night; every tree looked to them a giant, every bush a robber's den. The rattling of the shutter and the howling of the wind in the chimney caused men, women, and children to turn pale. At Epiphany no one went out of the gate by himself after ten o'clock in the evening; on Easter night no one ventured into the stables, afraid of finding the goblin there. The people at Oblomovka believed in everything – in ghosts and changelings. If they were told that a stack of hay walked about the field they believed it unhesitatingly; if someone spread a rumour that a certain ram was not really a ram but something else, or that Marfa was a witch, they feared both the ram and Marfa; it never occurred to them to ask why the ram had changed its nature or why Marfa should be a witch, and, indeed, they would have turned against anyone who doubted it – so great was the faith in the miraculous at Oblomovka!

Ilya Ilyitch found later on that the world was arranged simply, that the dead did not rise from their graves, that as soon as any giants were about they were put in a booth for show and brigands were clapped in prison; but even if the belief in phantoms disappeared, fear and vague anxiety remained in its place. Ilya Ilyitch learned that no troubles were caused by monsters, and he hardly knew what troubles there were in the world at all, but every moment he expected something dreadful to happen and felt uneasy. Even now, if he were left in a dark room or saw a corpse, he felt the tremor of sinister apprehension, dating from childhood; he laughed at his fears in the morning, but in the evening they made him turn pale once more.

Then Ilya Ilyitch saw himself as a boy of thirteen or fourteen. He was studying at Verhlyovo, some three miles from Oblomovka, with the German steward of the estate, Stolz, who had started a boarding-school for the children of the local gentry. He had a son, Andrey, almost the same age as Oblomov, and there was another boarder, a boy who hardly worked at all, being scrofulous and almost always ill; he spent his whole childhood with either his eyes or his ears in bandages, and was always weeping in secret at having left his grandmother and having to live with strangers and wicked people, at having no one to pet him, no one to make him his favourite cakes. So far there were no other boarders at the school.

There was nothing for it. Oblomov's father and mother decided to set their spoiled darling to work in spite of his tears, caprices, and lamentations. At last he was taken to Stolz's. The German was a strict and business-like man, like most Germans. Ilyusha might have learned some good from him had Oblomovka been three hundred miles from Verhlyovo; but how could he learn anything? The charm of the Oblomovka atmosphere, habits, and way of life extended to Verhlyovo, which had also once belonged to the Oblomovs; everything there, except Stolz's house, was permeated by the same primeval laziness, simplicity, peace, and inertia. The child's heart and mind had been filled with the impressions of that life before he set eyes on a book; and who can tell how early a child's intellect begins to develop? How can one trace the birth of the first ideas and impressions in a child's mind? Perhaps before a baby can speak and walk, at the time when it merely gazes about it with the dumb, rapt look that seems blank to the grown-ups, it already perceives and guesses the significance and the connections of the events around it, though it cannot tell this either to itself or to others. Perhaps Ilyusha had understood long ago what was being said and done in his presence; had observed that his father, dressed in velveteen trousers and a quilted coat of brown cloth, did nothing but walk up and down the room all day with his hands behind his back, take snuff, and blow his nose, while his mother went on from coffee to tea, from tea to dinner; that his father never troubled to check the number of the hay- or corn-stacks and call the delinquents to task, although he turned the house upside down and shouted about disorder if his handkerchief was not handed him soon enough. Ilyusha's childish mind may have decided long ago that the way the grown-ups around him lived was the right way; and how could he have decided otherwise?

And how did the grown-ups live at Oblomovka? Did they ever ask themselves why life had been given them? God only knows. And how did they answer it? Probably they did not answer it at all: it seemed very simple and obvious. They had never heard of life being hard, of men being overwhelmed with anxious worries, rushing about from place to place, or devoting themselves to continuous, never-ending labour. They did not particularly believe in mental troubles either; they did not think that life could consist in striving for some distant aim; they were mortally afraid of strong feelings; and while in some places people's bodies are rapidly consumed by the volcanic action of inner, spiritual fire, the souls of the Oblomovka inhabitants rested, peaceful and undisturbed, in their comfortable bodies. Life did not brand them, as it does other people, with premature wrinkles, diseases, or devastating moral blows. The good people conceived of life as a state of perfect repose and idleness, disturbed at times by unpleasant accidents, such as illness, loss of money, quarrels, and work. They endured work as a punishment laid upon our forefathers, but they could not love it and avoided it whenever they could, believing it was possible and right to do so. They never troubled about any obscure moral or intellectual problems; this was why they enjoyed perfect health and good temper and lived long. At forty men looked like boys; old men did not struggle with a hard, painful death, but having lived till they could go on no longer, died as though by stealth, gradually dropping off and quietly breathing their last. This is why it is said that in the old days people were stronger. Yes, indeed, they were; in the old days they were not in a hurry to explain to a child the meaning of life and make him feel that living was a puzzling and difficult business; they did not worry him with books that rouse hosts of questions, wearing out one's heart and mind and shortening life. The way to live had been settled once and for all and taught to them by their parents, who had accepted the teaching ready-made from the grandparents and those from the great-grandparents, with the injunction of keeping it whole and undefiled like Vesta's fire. The same things were done in the same way in Ilya Ilyitch's father's time as they had been done for generations, and as, perhaps, they are still being done at Oblomovka.

What, then, was there to worry or grow excited about? What was there to learn, what aims to pursue? There was no need for anything; life flowed on like a quiet river, and all that remained for them was to sit on the bank watching the inevitable events that presented themselves, uncalled for, to everyone in his turn.

The three chief events that happened in the Oblomov family and in the families of their relations and friends – birth, marriage, death – unrolled themselves like living pictures, one by one, before the imagination of Ilya Ilyitch in his sleep. Then followed the motley series of their gay and mournful subdivisions: christenings, name-days, family celebrations, fasts, feast-days, dinner-parties, assemblies of relatives, greetings, congratulations, ceremonial tears and smiles. Everything was done meticulously, solemnly, imposingly. He saw the familiar faces and their expression on these different occasions, the look of preoccupation on them, and all the trouble people took. However ticklish the marriage settlement might be, however grand the wedding or the name-day, they managed it all in full accordance with tradition, without the least irregularity. No one at Oblomovka ever made the slightest mistake as to where the guests were to sit, what dishes were to be served, who were to drive together on a ceremonial occasions, what observances were to be kept. They knew all about rearing children. It was enough to look at the rosy, chubby babies that the mothers carried or led by the hand; it was their chief concern that the children should be plump, fair-skinned, and healthy. They would rather renounce the spring than omit baking larks made of pastry at the beginning of March. How should they forget or fail to do it? All their life and learning, all their joys and sorrows, were in these things: they banished all other griefs and worries, they knew of no other joys, because their life was full of these vital and inevitable events that provided endless food for their hearts and minds. Breathless with excitement, they waited for some ceremony, some feast, some rite, and then, having christened, married, or buried a man, forgot him altogether and sank into their usual apathy, from which some other similar occasion – a name-day, a wedding, etc. – roused them once more. As soon as a baby was born, the parents' first concern was to carry out as exactly as possible, without any omissions, all the traditional rites that decorum required, and have a feast after the christening; then they began carefully tending the baby. The mother set herself and the nurse the task of rearing a healthy child, of guarding him from colds, from the evil-eye, and other hostile influences. They took great care that the child should always be cheerful and eat a lot. As soon as the boy was on his feet and no longer needed a nurse, the mother's heart nurtured a secret desire to find him a mate – also as rosy and healthy as possible. Again there came a time for feasts and ceremonies and at last the wedding; the excitement of their whole life centred in this. Then came the repetitions: more children were born, more sacred rites to be observed, more feasts, until the decoration was changed for a funeral; but this too was not for long: one set of people made way for another, children grew up, married, and had children in their turn – and so life went on like a continual monoton-ous web, breaking off unnoticeably at the very edge of the grave.

Sometimes, it is true, other cares were thrust upon them, but the Oblomovka population met them for the most part with stoic immobility, and the troubles, after circling round their heads for a time, flew past like birds which, coming to a smooth wall and finding no resting-place there, flutter their wings in vain and fly farther on. Thus, for instance, one day a part of the balcony on one side of the house tumbled down suddenly, burying under the ruins a hen with its chickens; Aksinya, Antip's wife, who had settled down under the balcony with her spin-ning, would not have escaped but that, luckily, she had gone to fetch some more flax. There was great excitement in the house: everyone, small and great, ran to the spot and was terrified at the thought that instead of the hen and chickens the mistress herself, with Ilya Ilyitch, might have been walking under the balcony. All exclaimed and reproached one another that they had not thought of it before – that one had failed to remind another, another had failed to give orders, and the third to carry them out. All marvelled at the balcony falling down, although only the day before they marvelled at its having stood so long! A great deal was said of how things could be put right; regrets were expressed about the fowl and the chickens, and then all went back to where they had come from, strict orders being given that Ilya Ilyitch was not to be taken near the balcony. Some three weeks later Andryushka, Petrushka, and Vaska were told to take the fallen planks and banisters and put them near the barn out of the way. They lay there until the spring. Every time that the master saw them out of the window he thought of having the balcony repaired: he called the carpenter and consulted him whether it would be better to build a new balcony or break down all that remained of the old; then he let him go home, saying, 'You go now and I'll think about it.' This continued until Vaska or Motka informed his master that when he had climbed to what remained of the balcony that morning he saw the corners had broken away from the walls and the whole thing might tumble down any moment. Then the carpenter was invited for a final consultation, as a result of which it was decided to prop up the part that was still standing with the debris of the old, and this was actually done towards the end of the month.

'Why, the balcony is as good as new!' Oblomov's father said to his wife. 'See how finely Fedor has fixed the beams, just like the pillars in the Marshal's house! It is quite right now: it will last many years again.'

Someone reminded him that it would be a good opportunity to mend the gate and the front porch, for the holes between the steps were so big that cats and even pigs squeezed themselves through them into the cellar.

'Yes, yes, certainly,' Ilya Ivanovitch answered with concern, and went at once to have a look at the steps.

'Yes, indeed, just see how rickety it is!' he said, rocking the whole flight of steps with his feet like a cradle.

'Why, it rocked when it was first made,' someone observed.

'Well, what of it?' the master retorted. 'It hasn't fallen down, though it has stood for sixteen years without anything being done to it. Luka made it splendidly! . . . He was a carpenter, now! . . . He is dead, the Kingdom of Heaven be his! Carpenters are not what they were – they couldn't make it like that now.'

He looked away, and the steps, they say, still rock, but have not fallen down yet.

That Luka must have been a fine carpenter indeed.

One must do the Oblomovs justice, however: sometimes they put themselves out a great deal and actually lost their tempers when things went wrong. How could this or that have been neglected to such an extent? Something must be done at once, they said. They would talk of nothing but mending the little bridge across the ditch or of fencing in a part of the garden to prevent the cattle spoiling the trees, because a part of the hurdle had fallen down. Walking one day in the garden, Ilya Ilyitch's father actually went so far as to lift the hurdle fence with his own hands off the ground, groaning and sighing, and ordered the gardener to prop it up at once with two poles; owing to the master's promptness the fence remained standing like that through the summer and it was only in winter that the snow brought it down again. At last even the bridge had three new planks laid across it as soon as Antip had fallen from it into the ditch with the horse and the water-barrel. He had not had time to recover from his injuries before the bridge was as good as new. Nor did the cows and goats benefit much by the fresh fall of the hurdle fence round the garden: they had only had time to eat the currant bushes and to start stripping the tenth lime-tree, but had not reached the apple-trees, when an order was issued to fix the fence properly and dig a ditch round it. The two cows and a goat that were taken in the act caught it badly – they received a thorough beating!

Ilya Ilyitch dreamt, too, of the big dark drawing-room in his parents' house, with old-fashioned ash-wood arm-chairs that always had covers on, a huge hard and clumsy sofa, upholstered in a faded and stained light-blue stuff, and one big leather arm-chair.

A long winter evening was coming on. His mother sat on the sofa with her feet tucked under her, lazily knitting a child's stocking, yawning, and occasionally scratching her head with a knitting-needle. Nastasya Ivanovna and Pelagea Ignatyevna sat next to her, bending over their work and sewing diligently something for Ilyusha for the holiday or for his father or for themselves. His father walked up and down the room with his hands behind his back, perfectly pleased with himself; now and again he sat down in the arm-chair and then began pacing to and fro once more, listening attentively to the sound of his own footsteps. Now and again he took snuff, blew his nose, and snuffed again. One tallow candle dimly burned in the room, and even this was only allowed on autumn and winter evenings. During the summer months everyone made a point of getting up and going to bed by daylight. It was done partly from habit and partly for economy. The Oblomovs were extremely sparing with any articles that were not produced at home but had to be bought. They willingly killed an excellent turkey or a dozen chickens to treat a guest, but never put an extra raisin in the pudding; and they turned pale if the guest ventured to pour out his wine for himself. Though, indeed, such depravity was practically unheard of: only some desperate character, ruined in the opinion of society, could be guilty of it, and such a visitor would not be admitted within the gates. No, people's habits were very different: a visitor would not touch anything till it had been offered to him three times. He knew very well that if some dish or a glass of wine were offered him only once, he was, as often as not, expected to refuse it. It was not for every visitor, either, that two candles would be lighted: candles were bought in town for money and like all bought articles were kept by the mistress under lock and key. Candle-ends were carefully counted and put away. Altogether they did not like spending money at Oblomovka, and however necessary a purchase might be, the money for it was always given with the greatest regret, and then only if the sum was not considerable. Any big expense meant moaning, groaning, and swearing. The Oblomovs were ready to put up with any sort of inconvenience, and ceased, indeed, to regard it as such rather than spend money. This was the reason why the drawing-room sofa had been covered with stains for years and the master's leather arm-chair was leather only by name; in truth, it was all tow or string – a piece of leather remained only on the back and the rest had peeled off five years before. This, perhaps, was also the reason why the gate is aslant to this day and the steps are still rickety. To pay for something, however urgently necessary it might be, two or three or five hundred roubles at once seemed to them a kind of suicide. Hearing that a young neighbour had bought in Moscow a dozen shirts for three hundred rou-bles, boots for twenty-five roubles, and a dress-waistcoat for his wedding for forty roubles, Ilya Ilyitch's father crossed himself and muttered in horror that 'such a scamp ought to be put in prison.' They were altogether deaf to economic theories about the need for rapid turnover of capital, increased production, and exchange of goods. In the simplicity of their hearts they understood and put into practice only one way of using capital – keeping it in a chest.

Other inhabitants of the house and the usual visitors sat in different positions in the arm-chairs in the drawing-room. Deep silence reigned among them as a rule: they saw each other every day; the intellectual treasures in their possession had been explored and exhausted long ago, and news from outside was rare. All was still; only the tread of Ilya Ivanovitch's heavy home-made boots, the muffled ticking of a grandfather clock, and the sound of a thread being snapped by one of the ladies' teeth or hands disturbed the profound stillness. Half an hour passed in this way; occasionally someone yawned aloud and made the sign of the cross over his mouth, saying, 'Lord, have mercy!' His neighbour yawned after him, then the next person slowly opened his mouth, as though obeying a command, and so the infectious play of air in the lungs spread to them all, reducing some to tears. Sometimes Ilya Ivanovitch went up to the window, looked out, and said with mild surprise, 'It is only five o'clock, and how dark it is outside!'

'Yes,' someone answered, 'it is always dark at this time: the evenings are drawing in.'

In the spring they were surprised and delighted that the days were drawing out; but if you asked them what use long days were to them they could not answer.

There was a silence again. Then someone would snuff the candle and suddenly extinguish it; all would be roused and someone would be sure to say, 'An unexpected guest!' Sometimes this led to a conversation:

'Who would that be?' the mistress of the house said. 'Nastasya Faddeyevna, perhaps? I wish it were! But, no; she won't come before Christmas. How I should love to see her! How we should hug each other and have a good cry! And we would go to matins and Mass together. . . . But I can't keep up with her! Though I am the younger I can't stand so long as she can.'

'Let me see, when did she leave here?' Ilya Ivanovitch asked. 'Just after St. Ilya's Day, I believe.'

'What are you saying, Ilya Ivanitch? You always muddle everything. She went before Whitsuntide,' his wife corrected him.

'I believe she was here in St. Peter's fast,' Ilya Ivanovitch retorted.

'That's just like you!' his wife said reproachfully. 'You *will* argue and make yourself ridiculous!'

'Of course she was here in St. Peter's fast! I remember
we kept having mushroom pies because she liked them.'

'Why, that was Marya Onisimovna; she likes mushroom pies – I wonder you don't remember! And Marya
Onisimovna did not stop till St. Ilya's Day either, but
only till St. Prohor and Nikanor's Day.'

They reckoned the time by holy-days, seasons, various
family and domestic occurrences, and never referred to
dates or months. This may have been partly due to the
fact that everyone, except Oblomov himself, generally
muddled months and dates.

Ilya Ivanovitch, defeated, made no reply, and the
whole company sank into drowsiness once more. Ilyusha,
huddled behind his mother, was also drowsy and sometimes fast asleep.

'Yes,' one of the guests remarked after a time, with a
deep sigh, 'think what a strong man Marya Onisimovna's
husband was, God bless him, and yet he died! He did not
live to be sixty and one would have thought he would live
to be a hundred!'

'We shall all die in our proper time – it's God's will,'
Pelagea Ivanovna answered with a sigh. 'Some die, and
the Hlopovs can't christen their babies fast enough. I hear
Anna Andreyevna has had another – her sixth.'

'And there's not only Anna Andreyevna to think of!'
the lady of the house said. 'When her brother is married
and has children they will have much more trouble! The
other boys are growing up, too, and will soon be old
enough to marry; then the daughters will want husbands,
and where is one to find them? Everyone wants a dowry
nowadays, and wants it in cash too. . . .'

'What are you saying?' Ilya Ivanovitch asked, going up
to them.

'Why, we are saying that . . .' and the whole thing was
repeated to him.

'Such is life!' Ilya Ivanovitch pronounced sententiously.
'One person dies, another is born, a third one is getting
married, and we keep growing older: two days are not

alike, let alone two years! Why should it be so? How much better it would be if to-day were exactly like yesterday and yesterday like to-morrow! . . . It's sad to think. . . .'

'The old are ageing and the young are growing up!' someone in the corner of the room said in a sleepy voice.

'One must pray more and not think of anything!' the lady of the house observed sternly.

'That's so, that's so!' Ilva Ivanovitch muttered apprehensively, and, not attempting to philosophize any more, paced up and down the room again.

There was another long pause; only the swish of the cotton was heard as the needles moved to and fro. Sometimes the mistress of the house broke the silence:

'Yes, it's dark outside,' she said. 'God willing, at Christmas-time, when our people come to stay, it will be merrier and we won't notice the evenings pass. If Malanya Petrovna comes there will be no end of fun! She is up to all sorts of tricks: telling fortunes by melted tin and wax and running out of the gate; my maids simply go off their heads when she is here! She invents all kinds of games . . . she is a one!'

'Yes, she is a society lady,' one of the company remarked. 'Two years ago she insisted on tobogganing, you remember, when Luka Savitch bruised his head. . . .'

Everyone was roused suddenly and roared with laughter, looking at Luka Savitch.

'However did you do it, Luka Savitch? Come, tell us!' said Ilya Ivanovitch, rocking with laughter.

All went on laughing; Ilyusha woke up and laughed also.

'Oh, there's nothing to tell,' Luka Savitch said in confusion. 'Alexey Naumitch has invented it all; it was nothing whatever. . . .'

'What!' the others cried in a chorus. 'Nothing whatever? Why, we are all here and saw it with our own eyes! And look at your forehead, why, there's a scar on it still!'

And they laughed.

'What are you laughing at?' Luka Savitch tried to say in the intervals. 'I wouldn't . . . have fallen . . . but that rascal Vaska . . . gave me an old toboggan . . . and it came to pieces under me . . . and so I. . . .'

His voice was drowned in the general laughter. He tried in vain to finish the story of his fall: the laughter had infected everyone, penetrated to the hall and the maids' room, spread throughout the house; all had recalled the amusing incident, and for many minutes laughed in unison like the Olympian gods. When the laughter seemed to abate somebody would start it again and it would break out afresh. At last they managed some-how to compose themselves.

'Will you go tobogganing this Christmas, Luka Savitch?' Ilya Ivanovitch asked after a pause.

Again there was a general outburst of laughter lasting for about ten minutes.

'Hadn't we better tell Antipka to make a hill before the holidays?' Oblomov said again. 'We'll tell him Luka Savitch is very keen on it, and can't bear to wait. . . .'

General laughter interrupted him.

'But is that sledge still to be had?' one of the company asked, hardly able to articulate through laughter.

There was more laughter.

They all laughed for some minutes, then gradually began to subside; one person was wiping his eyes, another blowing his nose, a third coughing violently and clearing his throat, saying with difficulty:

'Oh, dear, this cough will be the death of me. . . . He did make us laugh then, upon my word! The way he rolled over, with the skirts of his coat sticking out. . . .'

This was followed by a final burst of laughter, the longest of all, and at last all was still. One of the company sighed, another yawned aloud, muttering something, and then there was general silence.

As before the only sounds were the ticking of the clock, the tread of Oblomov's boots, and now and again the slight snapping of the thread. Suddenly Ilya Ivanovitch stopped in the middle of the room, anxiously touching the tip of his nose.

'I say, what trouble is this?' he said. 'There's sure to be a death: the tip of my nose keeps itching. . . .'

'Goodness me!' said his wife, clasping her hands. 'How can it be a death if it's the tip of the nose itching? It's death when the bridge of the nose is itching. What a man you are for never remembering anything, Ilya Ivanitch! You may say a thing like that before strangers one day and disgrace yourself.'

'And what does it mean when the tip of the nose is itching?' Ilya Ivanovitch asked shamefacedly.

'Looking into a wine-glass. A death, indeed! What next?'

'I keep mixing it up,' Ilya Ivanovitch said; 'how can one remember – the nose itching at the side, at the tip, or the eyebrows itching. . . .'

'If it is at the side,' Pelagea Ivanovna chimed in, 'it means news; if the eyebrows itch, it means tears; if the forehead, bowing; if on the right side, bowing to a man, if on the left, to a woman; ears itching means rain; lips, kissing; moustache, eating sweets; elbows, sleeping in a new place; soles of the feet, a journey. . . .'

'Well done, Pelagea Ivanovna!' Ilya Ivanovitch said. 'And isn't there something about the back of one's head itching when butter is going to be cheap?'

The ladies laughed and whispered together; some of the men were smiling; a new outburst of laughter was preparing, but at that moment there came a sound of something like a dog growling and a cat hissing when they are about to attack each other. It was the clock striking.

'Why, it's nine o'clock!' Ilya Ivanovitch said with joyful surprise. 'Just think of it, I never noticed how the time passed. Hey, Vaska! Vanka! Motka!'

Three faces heavy with sleep appeared in the doorway. 'Why don't you set the table?' Oblomov asked with surprise and vexation. 'You never think of your masters!

What's the good of your standing there? Make haste and bring the vodka!'

'That's why the tip of your nose itched,' Pelagea Ivanovna remarked briskly; 'you will drink vodka and look into the glass!'

After supper they kissed and blessed one another and all went to bed, where sleep soon descended upon their untroubled heads.

Ilya Ilyitch was dreaming not of one such evening, but weeks, months, and years of evenings spent in this way. Nothing disturbed the monotony of the life at Oblomovka, and its inhabitants did not resent it, for they could not imagine any other existence; and if they could, they would have turned away from it in horror. They did not desire any other life and they would have disliked it. They would have been sorry if circumstances had brought any changes into their manner of living. They would have been wretched if one day was not like another, if the morrows were not like the yesterdays. What did they want with variety, change, and adventure that other people seek? Let those others make the best of it; the folk at Oblomovka did not care for that sort of thing. Others could live as they liked. Adventures, even if they brought luck, were disturbing; they involved trouble, care, running about, having no rest, buying and selling, or writing, in short, being on the go – and that was no joke! They went on for years yawning and drowsing, laughing good-humouredly at the country jokes or sitting around and telling their dreams to one another. If the dream had been terrible they all were seriously perturbed and afraid; if it was prophetic, they unfeignedly grieved or rejoiced according to the nature of the prophecy. If the dream required that some observance should be complied with, active measures were at once taken to do so. Or they played cards – simple nursery games on weekdays and Boston with visitors on holy-days, played patience, told fortunes for a king of hearts or a queen of clubs and foretold marriage. Sometimes a Natalya Faddeyevna would come to stay for a week or a fortnight. The ladies began by talking over all the neighbours, their occupations and way of living; they penetrated not only into their family life and behind the scenes generally, but into their secret thoughts and intentions, into their very souls; disapproved, condemned the unworthy, especially the faithless husbands; then they discussed the various social occasions – name-days, christenings, and so on, recalling who had been invited and what fare had been offered. Tired of this, they showed each other their new clothes, dresses, coats, even stockings and petticoats. The hostess boasted of her home-made linen, yarn, or lace. But this subject, too, would be exhausted. Then they fell back upon coffee, tea, jam. Then they sank into silence. They sat for hours looking at each other, sighing heavily at times. Occasionally one of them began to cry. 'What is it, my dear?' the other asked anxiously. 'Oh, I feel sad, darling,' the visitor replied; 'we have angered the Lord God, wretched sinners that we are. No good will come of it.' 'Oh, don't frighten, don't alarm me, dear!' the hostess interrupted. 'Yes, yes,' the other went on, 'the last days will come, nation will rise against nation, kingdom against kingdom . . . the end of the world is coming!' Natalya Faddeyevna uttered at last, and both ladies wept bitterly. Natalya Faddeyevna had no grounds for her conclusion, for no nations had risen up and there had not even been a comet that year; but old ladies have dark forebodings at times.

Occasionally their usual trend of life at Oblomovka was disturbed by some accident, such, for instance, as the whole household being overpowered by the fumes from the stoves. Other accidents were practically unheard of in the house or the village; sometimes, perhaps, a man would stumble against a post in the dark or fall from the hayloft or be hit by a plank dropping off the roof. But this seldom happened, and there were homely, well-tried remedies against the effect of such accidents: the bruise was rubbed with water-weed or angelica, the patient was given holy water to drink or had a spell whispered over him – and he was perfectly well again. But headaches from the stove fumes happened fairly often, then all took to their beds; there was moaning and groaning; some tied sliced cucumber round their heads, some put cranberries in their ears and sniffed horse-radish, some went out into the frost with nothing but a shirt on, others simply lay senseless on the floor. This happened regularly once or twice a month, because they did not like to waste warmth and shut the flues while bluish flames, like those in *Robert le Diable*, still flickered in the stove. One could not touch a single stove without blistering one's hand.

Only once the monotony of their life was disturbed by a truly unexpected event. When, having rested after an exacting dinner, they had all gathered for tea, an Oblomovka peasant, who had returned from town, came into the room suddenly, and with much difficulty pulled out from the breast of his coat a crumpled letter addressed to Ilya Ivanovitch Oblomov. Everyone was dumbfounded; the lady of the house turned slightly pale; everyone craned towards the letter, their eyes fixed upon it.

'How extraordinary! From whom could it be?' Madame Oblomov said at last, coming to herself.

Her husband took the letter and turned it about in perplexity, not knowing what to do with it.

'But where did you get it from?' he asked the peasant. 'Who gave it you?'

'Well, it was like this,' the peasant answered; 'a man from the post office came twice to the inn where I had put up asking if there were any peasants from Oblomovka there, because there was a letter for the master.'

'Well? . . .'

'Well, at first I hid myself and so the soldier went back with the letter. But the sexton from Verhlyovo had seen me and he gave me away. They came again, and the second time they came they swore at me and gave me the letter, and charged me five copecks for it too. I asked what I was to do with it, and they said I was to give it to your honour.'

'You shouldn't have taken it,' Madame Oblomov remarked angrily.

'Well, I didn't want to take it. I said we had no use for it and wouldn't have it; we hadn't been told to bring letters and I didn't dare take it; be off with your letter, I said. But the soldier swore dreadfully and said he would complain to his chief, so I took it.'

'Idiot!' the lady said.

'From whom could it be?' Oblomov said thoughtfully, examining the address. 'The writing seems familiar!'

The letter was passed round. Everyone conjectured what it could be about and from whom it could have come. All were completely puzzled. Ilya Ivanovitch asked for his spectacles; a good hour and a half were spent searching for them. At last he put them on and was about to open the letter.

'I shouldn't open it, Ilya Ivanitch,' his wife stopped him anxiously; 'who knows what sort of letter it is? It may be something dreadful and bring us trouble. You know what people are nowadays! You will have time to read it to-morrow or the day after – it won't run away from you.'

The letter was locked up with the spectacles and they all sat down to tea. It might have lain in the drawer for years had not their minds been too deeply affected by so unusual an event. At tea and all the next day they could talk of nothing but the letter. At last they could endure it no longer, and on the fourth day, gathering together, they opened the letter in trepidation. Oblomov glanced at the signature.

'Radishtchev,' he read; 'why, that's from Filip Matveyitch.'

'Oh, so it's from him!' was heard on all sides. 'So he is still alive then! Just think of it, he isn't dead yet! Well, thank God! What does he say?'

Oblomov read the letter aloud. It appeared that Filip Matveyitch was asking for a recipe of beer that was brewed particularly well at Oblomovka.

'Send it him! Send it him!' everyone said. 'You must write to him.'

A fortnight passed.

'I must write to him, I certainly must!' Ilya Ivanovitch kept repeating. 'But where is the recipe?'

'Where can it be, now?' his wife answered. 'I must try and find it; but there is no hurry. Now Christmas will soon be here, the fast will be over, and then, God willing, you can write to him; there will be plenty of time.'

'Yes, indeed, I had better write during the holidays,' Ilya Ivanovitch said.

At Christmas the subject came up again. Ilya Ivanovitch quite made up his mind to write. He withdrew to his study, sat down at the table, and put on his spectacles. Profound stillness reigned in the house; the servants were told not to stamp or shout. 'The master is writing,' everyone said, speaking in a timid and respectful voice as though there were a death in the house. He had just written: 'Dear Sir' in a trembling and uneven hand, slowly and cautiously, as though engaged on some dangerous task, when his wife came into the room.

'I've looked for that recipe all over the place and I can't find it,' she said. 'I must have another look in the bedroom cupboard. But how are you going to send the letter?'

'By post,' Ilya Ivanovitch answered.

'What will the postage be?'

Oblomov produced an old calendar.

'Forty copecks,' he said.

'What a waste!' she remarked. 'We had better wait till someone from the town is going that way. Tell the peasants to find out.'

'Yes, it would certainly be better to send it by hand,' Ilya Ivanovitch answered, and drying his pen he stuck it into the inkstand and took off his spectacles.

'It certainly will be better,' he concluded. 'There is no hurry; there's plenty of time to send it.'

History does not say whether Filip Matveyitch ever received the recipe.

Sometimes Ilya Ivanovitch picked up a book – he did not mind what book it was. He never suspected that reading could be an essential need, but regarded it as a luxury that could be easily dispensed with – of no more importance than whether one hung up a picture or went for a walk; and so it did not matter to him what the book was: he thought it was merely something to distract one, to be picked up when one was bored and had nothing better to do. 'I haven't read a book for ages,' he would say, though sometimes he changed the phrase to 'I think I'll read a book.' Or he would simply happen to see the small pile of books left him by his brother and pick up one at random. Whether it chanced to be Golikov, or the latest *Dream Book*, or Heraskov's *Rossiada*, or Sumarokov's tragedies, or a newspaper of two years ago, he read it with equal pleasure, remarking from time to time: 'Just fancy now, what he is up to, the rascal! Ah, plague take the fellow!' These exclamations referred to authors – a calling for which he had no respect whatever; he had, indeed, a certain contempt for writers, usual in old-fashioned people. Like many men of his day he thought that an author was sure to be a gay dog, a rake, a drunkard, and a mountebank, something like a clown.

Sometimes he read the two-year-old papers aloud for everyone's benefit, or simply announced the news from them. 'They write from Hague,' he said, 'that His Majesty the King has safely returned to his palace after a short journey,' and looked through his spectacles at his listeners. Or, 'The ambassador of such and such a country has presented his letters of credit in Vienna.' 'And here they write,' he read, 'that the works of Madame Genlis have been translated into Russian.'

'I expect they do all these translations just to extract money from us gentry,' one of the listeners, a small landowner, remarked.

And poor Ilyusha still went to Stolz's for his lessons. He woke up on Monday mornings feeling thoroughly depressed. He heard Vanka's strident voice shouting from the porch:

'Antipka, harness the piebald to take the young master to the German.'

His heart sank. He sadly went in to his mother. She knew what was the matter and began gilding the pill, although she secretly sighed herself at the thought of parting from him for a whole week. She could not give him things good enough to eat that morning: special rolls and twists were baked for him; he was given pickles, biscuits, jam, fruit, cheeses, and all sorts of home-made sweets and victuals to take with him, the idea being that the German did not give him enough to eat.

'It's frugal fare there,' the people at Oblomovka said; 'you would be given soup, roast meat and potatoes for dinner and butter with your tea, but you may whistle for your supper!'

Ilya Ilyitch, however, was dreaming chiefly of Mondays on which he did not hear Vanka's voice saying that the piebald was to be harnessed but his mother met him at breakfast with a smile and pleasant news:

'You are not going to-day: Thursday is a great holy-day, and it isn't worth while to go there and back just for three days.'

Or sometimes he would be told it was a commemoration week: 'No time for lessons; we shall be baking pancakes.'

Or his mother would look at him attentively on a Monday morning and say, shaking her head:

'Your eyes look heavy this morning – are you quite well?'

The sly boy was perfectly well, but he said nothing. 'You had better stay at home this week,' his mother said, 'and then we shall see.'

And everyone in the house was convinced that lessons and commemoration week were incompatible, and that Thursday, being a holy-day, was an insurmountable obstacle to lessons during the rest of the week. Only occasionally a servant, who had been scolded because of the boy, would grumble:

'Oh, you spoiled baby! I wish you'd clear out and go to your German!'

At other times Antipka, on the familiar piebald, would turn up at the German's at the beginning or in the middle of the week to fetch Ilya Ilyitch.

'Marya Savishna or Natalya Faddeyevna or the Kuzov-kins with all their children have come on a visit, so please come home!'

And Ilyusha stayed at home for three weeks; then Holy Week was not far off, then Easter came, and then some-one in the house would declare that no one worked in the week after Easter; and then it would be only a fortnight to the summer holidays, when the German himself had a rest, so the lessons were put off till the autumn. Ilya Ilyitch picked up wonderfully in the six months; he grew taller, stouter, and how well he slept! His family could not admire him enough, observing that on the Saturdays when the child returned from the German he looked pale and thin.

'One must be careful,' his father and mother said; 'les-sons can be had any time, but health cannot be bought for money; health is the most precious thing in life. You see, he returns from school as from a hospital: all his fat is gone, he is so thin . . . and so naughty too; wants to be running about all the time.'

'Yes,' his father would remark, 'learning is no man's friend; it will wear anyone to a shadow.' And the tender parents went on finding pretexts for keeping their son at home; there were plenty of pretexts to be found besides holy-days. In winter they thought it was too cold; in the summer he could not go because of the heat, and some-times it rained; in the autumn the weather was bad. Sometimes they had doubts about Antipka: he was not drunk, apparently, but there was a wild sort of look in his eyes; there might be trouble, he might get the carriage stuck in the mud or fall into a ditch.

The Oblomovs tried, however, to make those pretexts as legitimate as possible in their own eyes and in the eyes of Stolz, who did not stint *Donnerwetters*, both to their faces and behind their backs, for their pampering the child. The times of the Prostakovs[1] and the Skotinins[1] had disappeared years before. The proverb 'Learning is light and ignorance is darkness' was already making its way into the villages together with the books sold by book-pedlars. Ilya Ilyitch's parents understood the advantages of education, but only its material advantages. They saw that people could not make their way in life – that is, acquire rank, orders of merit, and money – except through education; that old-fashioned attorneys, case-hardened officials, who had grown old in their pettifogging ways, had a bad time of it. Sinister rumours were about that not merely a knowledge of reading and writing but of other hitherto unheard-of subjects was required. An abyss opened between a titular councillor and a collegiate assessor that could only be bridged by something called a diploma. Officials of the old type, reared on office routine and bribery, were becoming extinct. Many of those that still survived were dismissed as unreliable, others were committed for trial; the luckiest were those who, seeing that the new order of things was too much for them, retired of their own accord to their well-feathered nests.

The Oblomovs grasped all this and understood the advantages of education, but merely in this obvious sense. They had only the vaguest and remotest idea of education being necessary for its own sake, and were anxious to secure for their Ilyusha simply the brilliant external advantages. They dreamed of a gold-embroidered uniform for him, pictured him as a Councillor, his mother saw him as a Governor; but they wanted to secure all this on the cheap, by cunning, by secretly dodging the obstacles scattered on the path of learning and ambition instead of overcoming them. They meant the boy to work just a

1 Characters in von Vizin's play *Nedorosl*, published at the end of the eighteenth century. – TRANSLATOR'S NOTE.

little, not to exhaust his body and mind nor to lose the blessed plumpness acquired in childhood, but merely to comply with the necessary standards and somehow gain a diploma which said that Ilyusha *had mastered all the arts and sciences.*

The Oblomov system of education met with sharp opposition on the part of Stolz. It was a stubborn fight. Stolz struck at his opponents directly, persistently, and openly, while they warded off the blows by stratagems, some of which have been described already. Victory went to neither side; German pertinacity might have overcome the Oblomovs' obstinacy and obtuseness had not the German found an opponent in his own camp. The fact was that Stolz's son spoiled Oblomov, prompted him at lessons, and wrote exercises for him.

Ilya Ilyitch clearly saw his life at home and at Stolz's. As soon as he woke up in the morning he saw Zaharka, later his famous valet, Zahar Trofimitch, standing by his bed.

Zahar pulled on his stockings for him like the nurse used to do, put on his shoes, while Ilyusha, a boy of fourteen by now, did nothing but stretch out to him first one leg then the other as he lay in bed; and if something seemed to him amiss he gave Zaharka one on the nose with his foot. If Zaharka resented it and complained he received a blow from the grown-ups as well. Then Zaharka combed his hair, pulled on his coat, carefully thrusting Ilya Ilyitch's arms into the sleeves so as not to disturb him unduly, and reminded him of the things that had to be done in the morning – washing, and so on.

If Ilya Ilyitch needed anything he had merely to wink and three or four servants rushed to do his bidding; if he dropped a thing or found that it was out of his reach or if there was an errand to be done, he, being a lively boy, sometimes wanted to help himself and ran to fetch what was wanted, but his father and mother and three aunts shouted all at once:

'Where are you off to? What is it? And what are Vaska

and Vanka and Zaharka for? Hey, Vaska! Vanka! Zaharka! What are you thinking of, you ninnies? I'll give it you! . . .'

And so Ilya Ilyitch never succeeded in doing anything for himself. Later on he found it was much less trouble and learned to shout like his elders: 'Hey, Vaska! Vanka! give me this, bring me that! I don't want this; I want that! Run and fetch it!'

At times his parents' tender solicitude wearied him. If he ran down the steps or in the yard ten voices shouted desperately after him: 'Oh, hold his hand! Stop him! He will fall and hurt himself . . . stop, stop!' If in winter-time he rushed out into the entry or tried to open a window-pane there were again shouts of 'Aïe, where are you off to? You can't! Don't run, don't go there, don't open the window, you will hurt yourself, you will catch cold. . . .' And Ilyusha sadly remained indoors, protected like an exotic flower in a hot-house, and like the latter he developed slowly and tardily. Finding no outlet, his energies turned inwards and gradually drooped.

And sometimes he woke up so gay, active, and fresh; he felt as though something were playing within him, bubbling over; some little imp seemed to have gained possession of him, inviting him to climb on the roof or mount the piebald and gallop to the meadows where they were haymaking, or sit astride on the fence or tease the village dogs; or he suddenly wanted to run down the village street and then into the fields, over the rough ground to the birch copse, rush in three big jumps to the bottom of the ravine, or try his hand at a game of snowballs with the village boys. The little imp kept egging him on; he resisted as long as he could, and at last skipped down the steps into the yard in winter, without his cap on, seized a ball of snow in each hand, and flew towards a group of boys. His face smarted with the keen wind, the frost was pricking his ears, the cold air was in his mouth and throat, and his heart was filled with joy; he ran along, faster than he thought he could run, laughing and screaming. Here

were the boys: he threw a snowball and missed, not being
used to it; he was just going to pick up some more snow
when a regular avalanche descended on his face – he fell;
his face was smarting with the new sensation, and yet it
was such fun, he was laughing and there were tears in his
eyes. . . . Meanwhile, there was a hullabaloo in the house!
Ilyusha was missing! There were shouts and noise. Zaharka
rushed into the yard, followed by Vaska, Mitka, Vanka,
and ran headlong, not knowing what to do. Two dogs flew
after them, catching them by the heels, for, as everyone
knows, a dog cannot bear to see a man running. The men
shouting and yelling, the dogs barking, raced through the
village. At last they found the boys and set to administering justice: pulled their hair and ears, distributed blows,
threatened the boys' fathers. Then they took possession of
the young master, wrapped him up in the sheepskin coat
they had brought, then in two blankets, and carried him
home in triumph. His family had given him up for lost
and despaired of ever seeing him again; his parents' joy at
seeing him alive and unhurt was indescribable. They
thanked the Lord God, then gave him mint and elder-
berry-tea to drink, then raspberry-tea in the evening, and
kept him three days in bed, though only one thing would
have done him good – playing snowballs again. . . .

X

As soon as Ilya Ilyitch's snoring reached Zahar's ears he jumped quietly and noiselessly off the stove-shelf, tip-toed to the entry, locked his master in, and went to the gate.

'Ah, Zahar Trofimitch, welcome! Haven't seen you for ages!' coachmen, valets, women, and children by the gate said in different voices.

'What has become of your gentleman? Has he gone out?' the porter asked.

'Sleeping like a log,' Zahar responded gloomily.

'How so?' a coachman asked. 'It seems a bit early, at this time of the day. . . . I suppose he is unwell?'

'Unwell, indeed! He is half-seas over!' said Zahar in a voice of conviction. 'Would you believe it? He has drunk by himself a bottle and a half of Madeira and two bottles of *kvass*, so now he is sleeping it off.'

'Just fancy!' the coachman said enviously.

'What made him so festive to-day?' one of the women asked.

'No, Tatyana Ivanovna,' Zahar said, casting his side-long glance at her, 'it's not merely to-day; he is simply no good at all – it's too sickening for words!'

'He must be like my mistress!' she remarked with a sigh.

'Do you know if she is going anywhere to-day, Tatyana Ivanovna?' the coachman asked. 'I want to go to a place not far from here.'

'Not she!' Tatyana said. 'She is sitting with her sweet-heart, and they can't take their eyes off each other.'

'He comes to you pretty often,' the porter said. 'He is a nuisance at nights, damnation take him! Everyone is in, all the visitors gone, but he is always the last to leave, and swears, if you please, about the front door being locked. . . . I am not going to mount guard at the door for his benefit!'

'What a fool he is, brothers,' Tatyana said; 'you can hardly find another such! He gives her no end of things! She puts on all her finery and struts about like a peacock, but if you only saw what her petticoats and stockings are like you'd be ashamed! She doesn't wash her neck for a fortnight on end, but she paints her face . . . sinner that I am, I can't help thinking to myself sometimes, "Oh, you God-forsaken creature, you'd much better tie a kerchief over your head and go to a convent as a pilgrim. . . ." '

All laughed except Zahar.

'Tatyana Ivanovna is a sharp one, she does hit one off!' approving voices said.

'But it's quite true,' Tatyana continued. 'I wonder gentlemen can go about with a woman like that!'

'Where are you going?' someone asked. 'What's this bundle you have?'

'I am taking a dress to the dressmaker's; my fine lady has sent me – it's too full, if you please! But when Dunyasha and I have to lace the elephant's corsets we can't do a thing for three days afterwards – our arms ache so! Well, it's time I was going. Good-bye for the present.'

'Good-bye, good-bye!' said some.

'Good-bye, Tatyana Ivanovna,' the coachman said; 'come out in the evening. . . .'

'I don't know if I can; perhaps I will, but if not. . . . Good-bye!'

'Good-bye,' everyone said.

'Good-bye . . . good luck to you!' she replied, going away.

'Good-bye, Tatyana Ivanovna!' the coachman called after her once more.

'Good-bye!' her voice sang out in the distance. When she had gone Zahar looked as though he were waiting for his turn to speak. He sat down on the iron post by the gate, swinging his legs and watching the passers-by and the traffic morosely and absentmindedly.

'Well, how is your master to-day, Zahar Trofimitch?' the porter asked.

'Playing antics as usual,' Zahar said. 'And it's all your doing: I've had no end of trouble on your account, about the flat, you know. He is simply frantic, he doesn't want to leave. . . .'

'But how am I to blame?' the porter asked. 'For aught I care he might live here for the rest of his life. I am not the landlord, am I? I do as I am told. . . . If the house were mine – but then it isn't. . . .'

'Does he swear, or what?' some coachman asked.

'He swears something dreadful, I wonder God gives me strength to endure it!'

'Oh, that's nothing! If a master swears he is a good sort,' said a footman, slowly opening a creaking round snuff-box. All except Zahar stretched their hands for a pinch. There was general sniffing, sneezing, and spitting. 'If he swears, it's all the better,' the man went on; 'the more he swears the better – at any rate he won't beat you if he swears. But I had a master once who grabbed you by the hair before you knew what was amiss.'

Zahar was contemptuously waiting for him to finish and then went on, turning to the coachman:

'He thinks nothing of reviling a man for no reason at all!' he said.

'Hard to please, is he?' the porter asked.

'Oh, I should think he is, fearfully hard!' Zahar hissed significantly, closing his eyes. 'This is wrong and this isn't right, and I don't know how to walk and how to serve a meal, and I break everything and I don't clean the place, and I steal and I eat up his food. . . . Curse the man! He made an awful row to-day, it was shocking to hear him, and all because there had been a piece of cheese left from last week – one would be ashamed to throw it to a dog – but no, a servant must not touch it! He asked for it, and when I said there wasn't any he did carry on! "You ought to be hanged," he said; "you ought to be boiled in pitch and pinched with red-hot pincers; you ought to have an aspen post driven into you!" he said. And he was edging up to me trying to hit me all the time. . . . What do you think, mates? The other day I scalded his foot – I don't know, I am sure, how I did it – and the way he yelled! If I hadn't jumped back he would have struck me on the chest with his fist . . . he really would! That's what he was aiming at. . . .'

The coachman shook his head and the porter said, 'He must be a lively gentleman: he doesn't give you much rope!'

'Oh, if he swears he must be a good sort,' the footman remarked phlegmatically. 'One that doesn't swear is worse: he looks and looks at you and suddenly grabs you by the hair before you've guessed what it is for!'

'But that's done him no good,' Zahar went on, taking again not the slightest notice of the interruption; 'his foot has not healed yet, though he keeps putting ointment on it – let him!'

'A difficult gentleman!' the porter said.

'Simply dreadful!' Zahar went on. 'He will kill a man one day, upon my word he will! And for every little trifle he calls me "a bald-headed ——" I don't want to repeat the rest. And to-day he's invented something new: I am "venomous"! he said. To think of his tongue turning to say a thing like that!'

'Oh, that's nothing!' the footman went on. 'If he swears it's right enough, God bless him. . . . But when a man says nothing, and you go past him and he just looks and looks and then grabs you by the hair, like that master I once had . . . and if he swears, that's nothing. . . .'

'And it served you right,' observed Zahar, annoyed by his intruding into the conversation. 'I would have given it you worse!'

'And what does he call you, Zahar Trofimitch – a bald-headed devil, or what?' asked a page-boy of fifteen.

Zahar slowly turned his head and fixed his dim eyes upon him.

'Look out, my lad,' he said sharply; 'you are much too

clever for your age! You may be employed at a general's, but I'll pull your hair sure enough! Go back to your place!'

The page walked a step or two away and stood looking at Zahar with a smile.

'What are you grinning at?' Zahar hissed furiously. 'Wait till I catch you and twist your ears: I'll teach you to grin!'

At that moment a huge footman in patent-leather boots, with his braided livery coat unbuttoned, rushed out of the front door. He ran up to the page-boy, gave him a slap on the face, and called him a fool.

'What's the matter, Matvey Moseitch, what have I done?' asked the page-boy, dazed and ashamed, holding his cheek and blinking convulsively.

'Ah, so you answer back?' the footman said. 'I am looking all over the house for you, and you are here!'

He took him by the hair, bent down his head, and hit him three times with his fist on the neck, slowly and methodically.

'The master has rung three times,' he added by way of a moral; 'and they find fault with me because of you, you puppy! Be off!'

And he pointed to the staircase with a commanding gesture. The boy stood blinking for a minute in a kind of bewilderment, glanced at the footman, and seeing that nothing was to be expected from him except fresh blows, tossed his hair and ran up the staircase.

What a triumph for Zahar!

'Go for him, give it to him, Matvey Moseitch! Give him another,' he said with malicious joy; 'that's not enough! Well done, Matvey Moseitch! Thanks! He is much too clever. . . . Here's a "bald-headed devil" for you! That will teach you to jeer!'

The servants laughed, sympathizing with the footman who had beaten the page-boy and with Zahar's malicious joy. No one pitied the page-boy.

'That's exactly how my old master used to go on,' the

footman who had been interrupting Zahar began again;
'just when you felt like having a bit of fun he seemed to
guess what was in your mind and grabbed you suddenly,
like Matvey Moseitch grabbed Andryushka. And if a master merely swears at you, it's nothing at all. What does it
matter if he calls you a bald-headed devil?'

'His master, too, might grab at you,' said the coachman, pointing at Zahar. 'See what a mat of hair you have!
But how is he to grab at Zahar Trofimitch? His head is
like a pumpkin. . . . Unless, indeed, he caught him by
these two beards on his jaws – there's plenty to seize hold
of there!'

They all laughed, but Zahar was thunderstruck by this
sally of the coachman, to whom he had been talking as a
friend.

'And if I go and tell my master,' he hissed furiously at
the coachman, 'he will find how to seize hold of you: he'll
smooth out your beard for you; it's all in icicles!'

'Your master must be a sharp one if he goes for other
people's coachmen! First have coachmen of your own and
then smooth their beards if you like, but now you are a bit
too quick!'

'We wouldn't engage a rascal like you,' Zahar hissed.
'You aren't good enough for my master to drive you
instead of a horse!'

'A fine sort of master!' the coachman observed sarcastically. 'Where did you unearth him?'

He laughed, and so did the porter and the barber, and
the footman who defended the practice of swearing.

'You may laugh, but I'll tell my master!' Zahar hissed.
'And you,' he added, turning to the porter, 'you ought to
muzzle these rascals instead of laughing. What is your job
here? To keep order. And what do you do? I'll go and tell
my master, you will catch it then!'

'Come, come, Zahar Trofimitch,' the porter said,
trying to pacify him, 'what has he done to you?'

'How does he dare to speak of my master in that way?'
Zahar answered with heat, pointing to the coachman.

'Does he know what my master is?' he asked with reverence. 'Why, you wouldn't see a master like that in your dreams,' he went on, turning to the coachman – 'handsome, clever, kind! And yours is just like an underfed nag! It's a disgrace to see you driving out with your grey mare, like beggars! You have nothing but radish and *kvass* to eat. Look at your coat, it's nothing but holes!'

It should be observed that the coachman's coat had not a hole in it.

'I couldn't find one like yours if I tried!' the coachman interrupted, quickly pulling out the piece of shirt that was showing under Zahar's arm.

'Come, come, that will do!' the porter repeated, trying to part them.

'Ah, you tear my clothes!' Zahar shouted, pulling out still more of his shirt through the tear. 'Wait, I'll show it to my master! Here, look, brothers, what he has done: he has torn my coat!'

'I, indeed!' the coachman said, somewhat alarmed. 'Your master must have given you a hiding!'

'As though he would!' Zahar cried. 'So kind a man! He is a perfect treasure of a master, God bless him! Living with him is as good as being in heaven; I have all I need, and he has never so much as called me a fool. I live in comfort and peace, have the same food as he has, go out when I like – so there! And in the country I have a house of my own with a kitchen garden, a special allowance of cash, the peasants bow to me! I am steward and *majodom*! And you with your master. . . .'

Rage choked his voice so that he could not finally demolish his adversary. He stopped for a moment to gather strength and invent some venomous word, but could not do so from excess of bitterness.

'You wait and see what happens to you for tearing my clothes: they'll teach you to tear them!' he brought out at last.

A slight to his master was a slight to Zahar himself. His ambition and vanity were roused, his devotion was awakened and expressed itself in all its force. He was ready to pour venom not only on his opponent but on his opponent's master and the master's friends and relatives, though he did not know whether he had any. He repeated with marvellous precision all the gossip and slander that he had picked up from his previous talks with the coachman about their masters.

'You and your master are wretched paupers, Jews, worse than the Germans!' he said. 'I know what your master's grandfather was – a hawker in a street-market! And when your visitors left last night I wondered if they were pickpockets that had found their way into the house – miserable sight! And his mother used to sell stolen and worn-out clothes from a stall.'

'Come, that will do!' the porter intervened.

'Yes,' Zahar said, 'and mine, thank God, is a born gentleman and has generals, counts, and princes for friends. And it's not every count he will admit into his presence either; some come and have to wait in the hall. . . . Authors keep coming too. . . .'

'What are these authors now, brother?' asked the porter, hoping to stop the quarrel. 'Are they special officials, or what?'

'No, they are gentlemen who lounge about on sofas, drink sherry, and smoke pipes. Sometimes they make a fearful mess on the floor with their feet . . .' said Zahar, and stopped, seeing that almost everyone was smiling derisively.

'And you are all blackguards, every one of you!' he rapped out with a sidelong glance at the company. 'He'll teach you to tear other people's clothes! I'll go and tell my master!' he added, and walked home with rapid strides.

'Come, come, that will do! Stop, stop!' the porter shouted. 'Zahar Trofimitch, let's go to the pot-house, please, let us. . . .'

Zahar stopped half-way, turned back quickly, and, without looking at the servants, rushed into the street. Without a glance at anyone he walked to the door of the pot-house, which was just opposite the gate; there he turned round, threw a gloomy glance at the company, and, still more gloomily motioning them to follow him, disappeared in the doorway.

The crowd had dispersed: some went to the pot-house, others home, only the footman remained.

'Well, what will it matter if he does tell his master?' he said meditatively and phlegmatically to himself, slowly opening his snuff-box. 'One can see from everything his master is a kind man: he would merely swear! And what if he did? It's not like some people who keep looking and looking at you and suddenly grab you by the hair. . . .'

XI

SOON after four Zahar carefully and noiselessly opened the front door and tiptoed to his room; then he went to his master's study door and after listening at the keyhole bent down and peeped into it.

Regular sounds of snoring came from the study.

'He is asleep,' he whispered. 'I must wake him, it's just on half-past four.'

He coughed and went into the study.

'Ilya Ilyitch! Ilya Ilyitch, I say!' he began quietly, standing by Oblomov's pillow.

The snoring continued.

'He does sleep!' Zahar said. 'He might be a navvy!'

'Ilya Ilyitch!'

Zahar lightly touched Oblomov on the sleeve.

'Get up! It's half-past four.'

Ilya Ilyitch made an inarticulate sound, but did not wake.

'Get up, Ilya Ilyitch! It's a disgrace!' Zahar said, raising his voice.

There was no answer.

'Ilya Ilyitch!' Zahar repeated, touching his master on the sleeve. Oblomov slightly turned his head and looked at Zahar with one eye that might have been the eye of a paralytic.

'Who is it?' he asked hoarsely.

'It's me. Get up!'

'Get away!' Ilya Ilyitch muttered and sank into heavy sleep again. Instead of snoring he now whistled with his nose. Zahar pulled at his dressing-gown.

'What do you want?' Oblomov asked fiercely, suddenly opening both his eyes.

'You told me to wake you.'

'Yes, I know. You have done your duty and now begone! The rest is my own business. . . .'

'I won't go,' Zahar said, pulling him by the sleeve again.

'There, don't disturb me,' Ilya Ilyitch said gently, and burying his face in the pillow began snoring again.

'You mustn't, Ilya Ilyitch,' Zahar said. 'I would be glad enough to leave you in peace but I can't!'

And he pulled at his master's clothes.

'Please do me the favour not to disturb me,' Oblomov said persuasively, opening his eyes.

'Yes, and if I did you the favour you would be angry with me afterwards for not waking you. . . .'

'Oh my goodness, what a man!' Oblomov exclaimed. 'Let me have just one minute's sleep; a minute is nothing! I know. . . .'

Ilya Ilyitch stopped suddenly, struck down by sleep.

'You know how to sleep,' said Zahar, certain that his master did not hear him; 'there he lies like a log! What was the good of a man like that being born?

'Get up, you! I tell you . . .' Zahar roared.

'What? What?' Oblomov said menacingly, raising his head.

'I said, why don't you get up, sir?' Zahar answered blandly.

'Yes, but how did you say it, eh? How did you dare to?'

'Dare what?'

'Speak so rudely.'

'You must have dreamt it . . . upon my soul, you dreamt it.'

'You think I am asleep? I am not, I hear everything. . . .'

He was asleep again.

'Oh dear, what am I to do?' Zahar said in despair. 'Why do you lie there like a block? It sickens me to look at you. See him, good people! . . . Tfoo!

'Get up, get up!' he began suddenly in a frightened voice. 'Ilya Ilyitch, see what's happening!'

Oblomov quickly raised his head, looked about him, and lay down again with a deep sigh.

'Leave me in peace!' he said impressively. 'I told you to wake me and now I cancel my order – do you hear? I will wake up myself when I feel like it.'

Sometimes Zahar left him at that, saying, 'Well, sleep on, damn you!' but sometimes he carried his point, and so he did this time.

'Get up, get up!' he yelled with all his might, seizing Oblomov with both hands by the skirt of his dressing-gown and by the sleeve. Oblomov jumped up suddenly and rushed at Zahar.

'Wait a bit, I'll teach you to disturb your master when he wants to rest!' he said.

Zahar darted away from him, but at the third step Oblomov shook off the glamour of sleep and began yawning and stretching himself.

'Give me . . . some *kvass*!' he said between his yawns.

At that moment someone behind Zahar broke into a peal of laughter. Both looked round.

'Stolz! Stolz!' Oblomov cried delightedly, rushing towards his friend.

'Andrey Ivanitch!' Zahar said with a grin. Stolz was still roaring with laughter; he had watched the scene that had just taken place.

PART II

PART II

I

Stolz was only half German, on his father's side: his mother was Russian; he belonged to the Orthodox Church. Russian was his native tongue – he learned it from his mother and from books, in the University lecture-rooms, in his games with the peasant children, in conversations with their fathers, and on the markets in the streets of Moscow. He learned the German language from his father and from books. Stolz had been brought up in the village of Verhlyovo, where his father was steward. From eight years upward he had been sitting over a map with his father, spelling out verses from the Bible and from Herder and Wieland, casting up the totals of the badly written accounts presented by peasants, artisans, and factory hands, and reading with his mother Bible histories, learning Krylov's fables, and struggling through *Télémaque*. When the lessons were over he went bird-nesting with the peasant boys, and not infrequently, at prayers or in the middle of a lesson, the sound of young jackdaws squeaking came from his pocket. Sometimes in the afternoon, when his father was sitting under a tree in the garden smoking his pipe and his mother was knitting or embroidering, there would be noise and shouts outside and a whole crowd of people broke into the house.

'What is it?' the mother asked in alarm.

'I expect they have brought Andrey again,' the father answered coolly.

The doors burst open and a crowd of peasants, women and children, rushed into the garden. They really had brought Andrey, but in what a state! Without his boots, his clothes torn, his nose bleeding – or some other boy's nose. The mother was always anxious when Andryusha disappeared for half a day, and had not her husband definitely forbidden her to interfere with the boy she would have kept him at her side. She washed him, changed his clothes, and for half a day Andryusha walked about looking such a clean, well-behaved little boy; but in the evening and sometimes in the morning someone again brought him home dirty, dishevelled, unrecognizable; or he returned with the peasants on the top of a hay-cart or in the fisherman's boat, lying asleep on the net. His mother shed tears, but his father did not trouble; he actually laughed.

'He will be a good *Bursch*,' he said sometimes.

'Why, Ivan Bogdanitch,' the mother complained, 'not a day passes but he comes home with a bruise, and last week he made his nose bleed.'

'What sort of a child would he be if he never made his nose bleed – or somebody else's?' his father said, laughing.

His mother would cry a little, then sit down to the piano, and forget her troubles over Herz while her tears dropped on the keys. Then Andryusha was brought or came back by himself and began telling his adventures in such a jolly, lively way that she could not help laughing, and he was so quick too! He was soon able to read *Télémaque* as well as she and to play duets with her. Once he disappeared for a whole week: his mother cried her eyes out, but his father did not trouble and walked in the garden smoking his pipe.

'If Oblomov's son had been lost,' he said in answer to his wife's entreaty to go and look for Andrey, 'I would have roused the whole village and the police, but Andrey will return. Oh, he is a good *Bursch*!'

Next morning Andrey was found sleeping peacefully in his bed, and under the bed lay a gun and a pound of powder and shot.

'Where on earth have you been? Where did you get the gun from?' his mother bombarded him with questions. 'Why don't you speak?'

'I don't know,' was all he said.

His father asked whether he had prepared the German translation from Cornelius Nepos.

'No,' he answered.

His father took him by the collar, led him out of the gate, put his cap on for him, and gave him such a kick from behind that the boy fell down.

'Go back to where you have come from,' he added, 'and come back with a translation of two chapters instead of one; and mind you prepare for your mother the part in the French comedy she gave you to learn – don't show yourself until you have done it!'

Andrey returned in a week; he brought the translation and had learned the part.

When he grew older his father took him in the trap with him, gave him the reins, and told him to drive to the factory, to the fields, to the town, to Government offices, to the shops, then to see some special clay which he took in his fingers, sniffed, licked, and gave his son to sniff, explaining what kind of clay it was and what it was fit for. Or they went to see the workmen making potash or tar or melting lard. At fourteen or fifteen the boy often went by himself in the trap or on horseback with a bag at the saddle to do some errand for his father in the town, and he never forgot or muddled or omitted anything. '*Recht gut, mein lieber Junge,*' the father said, patting him on the shoulder after hearing his account, and gave him two or three roubles according to the importance of the errand. It took his mother a long time to wash Andryusha clean from the soot, mud, clay, and oil.

She was not altogether pleased with this workmanlike, practical education. She was afraid her son would become a German *Bürgher* like his father's people. She considered the whole German nation as essentially bourgeois, and disliked the crudity, independence, and self-assertion with which the German masses insist on the civic rights won in the course of centuries, like a cow that can never keep her horns out of sight. In her opinion there was not and there could not be a single gentleman in the whole German nation. She could detect in the German character no softness, no delicacy, no faculty for making allowances,

nothing of what makes social life so agreeable and enables
one to avoid a rule, to set aside a general custom, to overlook a convention. No, those rude creatures rode rough-
shod over everything, determined to do what they were
bent on, what they considered the proper thing, and were
ready to smash a wall with their own heads for the sake of
acting according to rule. She had been a governess in a
rich family and had an opportunity of going abroad and
travelling all over Germany; the Germans seemed to her
just one crowd of men smoking short pipes and spitting
through their teeth – shopmen, artisans, merchants, officers
straight as sticks with soldierly faces, commonplace-looking
clerks; they were in her view capable only of dirty work,
of slaving for a livelihood, of living dull, regular lives
ruled by routine and of pedantically discharging their
duties – all these *Bürghers* with angular manners, huge
clumsy hands, rude speech and plebeian freshness of complexion. 'Whatever a German puts on,' she thought, 'the
finest and whitest shirt, patent boots, yellow gloves, he
will still look as though he were made of shoe-leather; the
white cuffs show rough and reddened hands, and in spite
of the elegant suit one can see he is a baker or a restaur-
ant-keeper. His rough hands seem to be asking for an awl
or at best for a fiddle in the orchestra.' She dreamed that
her son should be the ideal of a gentleman, for although
his father was a plebeian his mother was a Russian lady,
and he was a fair-skinned, beautifully made boy, with
small hands and feet, a smooth face, and clear alert eyes –
a boy such as she had seen in rich Russian families and
abroad, though not, of course, among the Germans. And
to think of his working on a mill, of his returning from
factories or fields like his father, covered with oil and
manure, with rough, red hands and a wolfish appetite!
She made haste to trim Andryusha's nails, to curl his hair,
to make him elegant collars and cuffs, ordered his coats in
the town; she accustomed him to listen to the dreamy
music of Herz, sang to him about flowers, about the
poetical side of life, whispered to him of the brilliant call-

ing of a soldier or a writer and dreamed with him of the noble part that some men are destined to play. . . . And all these prospects were to be ruined by his clicking beads on the counting-frame, sorting out the peasants' dirty receipts, and dealing with factory hands! She grew to hate the trap in which Andryusha drove to the town, the oilskin cape his father had given him, and the green chamois-leather gloves – symbols of a life of labour. To make matters worse, Andryusha was very good at his studies and his father made him coach the other boys. This would not have mattered, but he paid him a salary, just as to an artisan, in regular German style: ten roubles a month, for which he made him sign in a book.

Do not worry, good mother, your son has grown up on Russian soil, not in a workaday crowd of bovine *Bürghers* with hands used to turning mill-stones. Oblomovka was close by: there it was perpetual holiday! There the master did not get up at dawn and walk about the factory – close to oily wheels and springs. Verhlyovo itself had a big house, shut up most of the year, and when the lively boy found his way there, as he often did, he saw spacious halls and galleries hung with dark portraits of people who did not have coarse big hands or ruddy plebeian complexions; he saw dark-blue eyes, powdered hair, full bosoms, delicate fair-skinned faces, fine blue-veined hands showing from lace cuffs and resting proudly on the hilt of the sword; he saw a series of generations that had lived refined, luxurious, and useless lives, and worn brocade, velvet, and lace. Those figures told him a tale of glorious days, of battles and heroes of long ago; he read the story of a past very different from the one his father had told him a hundred times, spitting and smoking his pipe, of the life in Saxony, spent between the market and the kitchen garden with its potatoes and kohlrabi.

Once in three years the mansion suddenly filled with people and brimmed over with life; there were fêtes and balls, the long galleries were resplendent with lights. The prince and the princess arrived with their family. The prince was grey and bald, with dull protruding eyes and a colourless, parchment-like face; he had three stars on his coat, wore velvet boots, and carried a gold snuff-box and a cane with an emerald top. The princess was a majestic-looking woman, handsome, tall, and stout; it seemed incredible that anyone, including the prince, had ever come near her, embraced her or kissed her, although she had five children. She seemed to be above the world into which she descended once in three years; she did not speak to anyone or go anywhere, and spent her time in the green corner-room with three old ladies; she walked to church down a covered way across the garden and sat there on a chair behind a screen.

But in addition to the prince and the princess the house contained a gay and lively company, and Andryusha's childish green eyes could see into three or four social sets at once, and his quick mind eagerly and unconsciously watched the various types as one watches the characters at a fancy-dress ball. There were the young princes, Pierre and Michel; the first immediately showed Andryusha how they sound the réveillé in the cavalry and the infantry, explained the difference between the sabres and spurs of the dragoons and the hussars, told him what coloured horses were used by the different regiments and what career one ought to choose on leaving school if one were not to be disgraced. The second, Michel, on being introduced to Andryusha, placed him in position and began doing wonderful things with his fists, hitting Andryusha in the nose or the belly; he said afterwards that it was English boxing. Three days later Andryusha smashed Michel's nose both in the English and the Russian fashion with the sole aid of his muscular arms and country vigour, having had no lessons in boxing; this gained him the young princes' respect. Then there were the two young princesses, tall and graceful girls of eleven and twelve, always smartly dressed; they did not speak or bow to anyone, and were afraid of the peasants. There was their governess, Mlle. Ernestine, who used to take coffee with Andryusha's mother, and taught her to curl his hair. Sometimes she put his head on her lap, twisted his hair in paper curlers till it hurt, then took his cheeks in her white hands and kissed him affectionately. There was the German teacher who made snuff-boxes and buttons on a turner's wheel, then the teacher of music who was drunk from one Sunday to another, then a whole bunch of maids and a pack of dogs, big and little. All this crowd filled the house and village with noise, uproar, clatter, shouts, and music.

Oblomovka, on the one hand, and the ease and luxury of the prince's house on the other, counteracted the German element and Andrey did not grow up to be a good *Bursch* or even a Philistine.

Andrey's father was an agriculturist, a technician, and a teacher. He had received practical training in agriculture on his father's farm, had studied technology in Saxon factories; the neighbouring university, where there were about forty professors, had given him a taste for teaching what the forty wise men had succeeded in driving into his head. He did not go any farther, but obstinately turned back, deciding that he must do something practical. He returned to his father, who gave him a hundred thalers and a new knapsack and sent him out into the world. From that time onwards Ivan Bogdanovitch had never seen his father or his native land. He had wandered about for six years in Switzerland and Austria and had lived for twenty years in Russia, blessing his lucky stars.

As he had been to a university, he decided that his son must do the same, although it could not be a German university but a Russian one, which was bound to revolutionize the young man's life and take him far from the path which his father had mentally marked out for him. The father had done it very simply: he drew a straight line from his grandfather to his future grandson and troubled no further, never suspecting that Herz's melodies, the mother's tales and dreams, the gallery and the boudoir in the prince's castle would turn the narrow

German rut into a wider road than either his grandfather, his father, or himself had ever dreamed of. He was not a pedant, however, in this respect and would not have insisted on his own scheme; it was only that he could not conceive of any other path in life for his son.

He did not trouble much about Andrey's future. When his son returned from the university and had spent some three months at home, his father said that there was nothing more for him to do at Verhlyovo, that even Oblomov had been sent to Petersburg, and so it was time for him to go too. The old man did not ask himself why Andrey had to go to Petersburg, why he could not stay at Verhlyovo and help him with the management of the estate; he merely remembered that when he had finished his course of studies his father had sent him away. And so he did the same – such was the custom in Germany. His wife was dead and there was no one to oppose him.

On the day of Andrey's departure Ivan Bogdanovitch gave his son a hundred paper roubles.

'You will ride to the town,' he said, 'there Kalinnikov will pay you three hundred and fifty roubles he owes me, and you can leave the horse with him. If he hasn't the money, sell the horse; there is soon going to be a fair in the town and anyone will give you four hundred roubles for it. It will cost you forty roubles to go to Moscow and another seventy-five to go from there to Petersburg; you will have enough money left. Afterwards you may do what you like. You have done business with me and so you know that I have a small capital; but you must not reckon upon it till after my death, and I am likely to live another twenty years unless a stone falls on my head. The lamp burns brightly and there is plenty of oil in it. You have had a good education – all the roads are open before you; you can go into Government service or go in for business, or be a writer if you like – I don't know which you will choose, which attracts you most. . . .'

'I'll see whether I can't do everything at once,' Andrey said. The father laughed with all his might and patted his son on the shoulder so vigorously that a horse would not have stood it – Andrey did not budge.

'Well, and if you are not clever enough, if you cannot hit upon the right thing straight away and want guidance and advice, call on Reinhold, he will teach you. Oh,' he added, raising his hands and shaking his head, 'he is – he is a ——' he could not find a suitable word of praise. 'We came together from Saxony. He has a house of four storeys. I'll give you his address. . . .'

'Don't trouble,' Andrey interrupted him, 'I'll go to him when I, too, have a house of four storeys, and for the present I will do without him. . . .'

There was more patting on the shoulder.

Andrey jumped on to his horse. Two bags were tied to the saddle: one contained an oilskin cape, thick hob-nailed boots, and several shirts made of Verhlyovo linen – things he had bought at his father's insistence; the other had in it an elegant dress-coat of fine cloth, a thick overcoat, a dozen fine shirts and shoes that had been ordered in Moscow, in remembrance of what his mother had told him.

'Well?' the father said.

'Well?' said the son.

'Is that all?' the father asked.

'That's all,' the son answered.

They looked at each other in silence as though trying to pierce each other with their eyes.

Meanwhile, a group of inquisitive neighbours had assembled and was gazing open-mouthed at the steward taking leave of his son. The father and son pressed each other by the hand. Andrey set off at a quick pace.

'Just think of it, the puppy hasn't shed a tear!' the neighbours said. 'Those two crows on the fence are cawing their loudest – he'd better look out!' 'What does he care about crows? He walks about in the wood by himself on St. John's Eve – all that is nothing to them. A Russian would have paid for it!' 'And the old infidel is a nice one too,' a mother observed; 'he chucked him out like a kitten: never embraced him or wailed over him.'

'Stop, stop, Andrey!' the old man shouted.

Andrey stopped his horse.

'Ah, so his heart has pricked him after all!' the crowd said approvingly.

'Yes?' Andrey asked.

'The saddle-strap is loose, you must tighten it.'

'I'll put it right when I get to Shamshevka. It's no use wasting time, I want to be there before dark.'

'Right!' said the father with a wave of his hand.

'Right!' the son repeated, nodding, and bending down slightly, he was about to spur his horse.

'Oh, you dogs! Dogs and no mistake! Why, they might be strangers!' the neighbours said. Suddenly a loud wail was heard in the crowd: some woman could stand it no longer.

'Darling, sweet boy,' she said, wiping her eyes with a corner of her kerchief, 'poor little orphan! Your dear mother is dead and gone, there is no one to bless you. . . . Let me, at least, give you a blessing, my beauty!'

Andrey rode up to her, jumped off his horse, threw his arms round the old woman's neck, then wanted to ride on – and suddenly burst into tears while she was kissing him and making the sign of the cross over him. The woman's affectionate words seemed to him to have been said by his mother, and her tender image rose for an instant before his mind. He gave the woman another good hug, hastily wiped his tears and jumped on to his horse. He struck it with the whip and disappeared in a cloud of dust; three dogs rushed after him barking desperately.

II

Stolz was the same age as Oblomov; he, too, was over thirty. He had been in Government service, retired, went in for business, and really had succeeded in acquiring a house and capital. He belonged to some trading company that shipped goods abroad. He was continually on the move: if the company needed to send an agent to Belgium or England, they sent him; if some new scheme was to be devised or put into practice, he was chosen to do it; and yet he kept up his social life and his reading; Heaven only knows how he found time for it.

He was all bone, muscle, and nerve, like an English race-horse. He was lean: he could hardly be said to have cheeks, for though there was bone and muscle there was no sign of fat or roundness; his skin was smooth and dark with no touch of red in it; his eyes were rather green but expressive. He made no superfluous movements. If he was sitting, he sat still; if he was active, he used only such gestures as were necessary. Just as nothing was excessive in his physique, so in his mental activities he aimed at a balance between the practical side of life and the finer claims of the spirit. The two sides ran parallel with each other, twisting and twining on the way, but never becoming entangled in heavy, hopeless knots. He went his way firmly and cheerfully; he lived on a fixed plan and tried to account for every day as for every rouble, keeping unremitting watch over his time, his labour, and the amount of mental and emotional energy he expended. It seemed as though he controlled his joys and sorrows like the movements of his hands and feet and treated them as he did the weather. He put an umbrella up while the rain fell – that is, he suffered while the sorrow lasted, and even then with vexation rather than a timid submissiveness; he bore it patiently only because he blamed himself for his

troubles and did not lay them at other people's doors. He
enjoyed pleasure as one enjoys a flower plucked by the
roadside – until it begins to fade, and never drained the
cup to those last dregs of bitterness which lie at the bottom of every delight. He aimed at a simple – that is, at a
true and direct view of life, and as he gradually achieved
it he grasped how difficult the task was and felt proud and
happy each time that he noticed some deviation in his
course and set it right. 'It's hard and complicated to live
simply!' he often said to himself, and hastened to see what
was wrong, where the thread of life was beginning to coil
into a tangled, irregular knot. Above all things he feared
imagination, that double-faced companion, friend on one
side and foe on the other – friend in so far as one distrusts
it, and enemy if one goes trustfully to sleep to the sound
of its sweet murmur. He was afraid of day-dreaming, and
if he did enter the land of dreams it was as one enters a
grotto inscribed *'ma solitude, mon hermitage, mon repos,'*
knowing the hour and the minute when one would leave
it. There was no room in his soul for dreams, enigmas,
and mysteries. All that could not be practically verified
was for him an optical illusion, a particular reflection of
rays and colours on the retina, or at most a fact which had
not yet been established. He had none of the dilettante's
love for adventuring into the realm of the miraculous or
making wild guesses about the discoveries of a thousand
years hence. He obstinately stopped at the threshold of a
mystery showing neither childish belief nor fatuous doubt,
but waiting for the formulation of a law that would provide the key to it.

He kept as careful and subtle a watch over his heart as
over his imagination. Stumbling frequently, he had to
confess that feelings were still a *terra incognita* to him. He
warmly thanked fate if he managed to distinguish in time
the painted sham from the pale truth in this unfamiliar
domain; he did not repine when a deception artfully hidden in flowers caused him merely to stumble and not to
fall, and was only too happy if his brow was not covered

with cold sweat, if his heart merely throbbed instead of bleeding, and a long shadow was not cast over his life for years to come. He considered himself lucky because he could at least remain at a certain level: he was never carried away by feeling beyond the fine line that divides real emotion from false sentimentality, the true from the ridiculous, and his reactions against emotion never took him to the sandy desert of hard-heartedness, sophistication, distrust, pettiness, and callousness.

He was never swept off his feet and always felt strong enough to wrench himself free if need be. He was not blinded by beauty and therefore never forgot or lowered his manly dignity; never was a slave or 'lay at beauties' feet' – though he also never experienced fiery joys. He had no idols, but he had preserved the powers of his soul and body and a chaste pride; there was a freshness and strength about him which unconsciously made even the least modest of women draw back. He knew the value of these rare and precious qualities and used them so sparingly that he was thought to be selfish and insensible. People blamed him for his self-control, for his power of retaining his spiritual freedom, while they excused and sometimes envied and admired other people for flying headlong into trouble and ruining their own and others' lives. 'Passion justifies everything,' his friends said, 'and you in your egoism are only thinking of yourself; we shall see for whom you are saving yourself up.' 'It must be for somebody,' he said dreamily, as though looking into the distance, and continued to disbelieve in the poetic beauty of passions. He did not admire their tempestuous expression and devastating consequences; his ideal lay as before in a lofty conception of life and its functions. The more his friends argued with him, the more obstinate he grew in his convictions, erring at times, especially in discussion, on the side of puritanical fanaticism. He said that 'man's normal destiny was to live through the four seasons of life without sudden jumps and to bring the cup of life down to the last day not having wasted a single drop, and that a slowly and evenly burning fire was better than a violent conflagration, however poetical the latter might be.' He added, in conclusion, that 'he would be happy to prove his conviction in practice, but that he could not hope for it since it was much too difficult – human nature was too depraved, and there was as yet no proper education.' But he steadily followed the path he had chosen. No one saw him plunged in painful and morbid brooding; he did not seem to be tortured by the reproaches of a weary heart; his soul did not ache; he never lost his head in new, difficult, or complex circumstances, but tackled them as old acquaintances, as though he were living his old life over again. He at once applied the right method in every emergency, as a housekeeper chooses from the bunch hanging at her waist the right key for every door. Persistence in pursuing an aim was a quality he prized above all: it was a mark of character in his eyes and he never denied respect to people who had it, however poor their aims might be. 'They are real people,' he said. It need not be added that he pursued his own aims with bold disregard for obstacles and turned aside only when a wall rose before him or an abyss opened at his feet. He was incapable of the kind of daring which enables a man to jump across an abyss with his eyes shut or to fling himself recklessly at a wall. He measured the wall or the abyss, and if there were no certain way of overcoming the obstacle he turned back, regardless of what might be said of him.

Such a character, perhaps, could not be formed without the mixed elements of which Stolz was made up. Our men of action have always been of five or six stereotyped patterns; lazily looking round them with half-closed eyes, they put their hand to the machine of the State, sleepily pushing it along the beaten track, treading in their predecessors' footprints. But, behold, their eyes are awakening from sleep, bold, lively footsteps can be heard, and there is a sound of animated voices. . . . Many Stolzes with Russian names are bound to come soon!

How could a man like Stolz be intimate with Oblomov, whose whole existence, every characteristic, every movement, was a flagrant protest against Stolz's way of living? It seems to be an established truth that extreme opposition is not a bar to affection even if it does not actually give rise to it, as people once believed. Besides, they had been children and gone to school together – two very strong ties; there was much affectionate, solid Russian kindness lavished upon the German boy in Oblomov's family; then there was the fact that Stolz had always played the part of the stronger, both morally and physically, and, most of all, that there was in Oblomov's nature something essentially good, pure, and lofty, which was in profound sympathy with everything noble, with everything that responded to the call of his simple, guileless, and trustful heart. Anyone who once looked, by accident or of design, into his pure, childlike soul could not, however gloomy or bitter he might be, fail to love it, or at any rate, if circumstances made intimacy impossible, to preserve a lasting and good memory of Oblomov.

Often, tearing himself away from work or from the fashionable crowd, Andrey went from a party or a ball to sit on Oblomov's wide sofa and find in his lazy conversation relief and rest for his agitated or weary mind; and he always had the comforting feeling a man has on coming away from magnificent halls and entering his own humble home, or returning from the beautiful South to the birch copse where he used to walk as a child.

III

'How do you do, Ilya? How glad I am to see you! Well, how are things going with you? Are you well?' Stolz asked.

'Oh, no, not at all well, brother Andrey!' Oblomov said with a sigh. 'My health is very poor.'

'Why, what's the matter?' Stolz inquired anxiously.

'Styes will be the death of me: last week I had one on my right eye and now I am getting one on the left.'

Stolz laughed.

'Is that all?' he asked. 'That's with sleeping too much.'

'All, indeed! I have terrible heartburn. You should have heard what the doctor said this morning. "You must go abroad," he said, "or things will go badly with you: you may have a stroke."'

'Well, are you going?'

'No, I am not.'

'Why not?'

'How could I! You should have just heard all he said – I was to live on a mountain somewhere, go to Egypt or to America.'

'Well, what of it?' Stolz remarked coolly. 'You can be in Egypt in a fortnight and in America in three weeks.'

'What, you too! You were the only reasonable man I knew and now you are off your head. Whoever goes to America or Egypt? The English do; but then that's the way the Lord God made them, and besides, they have no room to live at home. But which of us would dream of going? Some desperate fellow, perhaps, whose life is worth nothing to him.'

'Yes, indeed, there would be terrible hardships to face: to step into a carriage or go on board ship, breathe pure air, look at foreign countries, towns, customs, at all the marvels. . . . Ah, you are hopeless! Well, tell me how

things are going with you, what's happening at Oblomovka?'

'Ach!' Oblomov said with a gesture of despair.

'What has happened?'

'Why, life doesn't leave me in peace.'

'Good thing it doesn't!'

'A good thing? Yes, if it patted me on the head, but
it pesters me just as naughty boys pester a quiet one at
school, pinching him on the sly or dashing straight at him
and chucking sand into his face!'

'You are much too quiet. What has happened?'

'Two misfortunes.'

'What are they?'

'I am ruined!'

'How so?'

'I will read to you what my bailiff writes. . . . Where is
the letter? Zahar, Zahar!'

Zahar found the letter. Stolz read it and laughed,
probably at the bailiff's style.

'What a rogue that bailiff is!' he said. 'He has lost his
hold on the peasants and then he complains! It would be
better to give them passports and let them go where they
like.'

'Why, at that rate they might all want to go!' Oblomov
exclaimed.

'Let them!' Stolz said with unconcern. 'Those who are
happy and find it to their advantage to stay will not go,
and those who can't make both ends meet are of no
benefit to you either, so why keep them?'

'What an idea!' Ilya Ilyitch said. 'The peasants at
Oblomovka are quiet, stay-at-home people, why should
they wander about?'

'You don't know,' Stolz said, 'a landing-stage is going
to be made at Verhlyovo and it is proposed to make a
highroad so that it will run near Oblomovka too, and an
annual fair is going to be held in the town.'

'Oh dear,' Oblomov said, 'that's the last straw!
Oblomovka was such a quiet spot, away from everything,

and now there will be the highroad, the fair! The peasants will take to going to town, tradesmen will be coming to us – we shall be done for! It's simply dreadful!'

Stolz laughed.

'Of course it's dreadful!' Oblomov repeated. 'The peasants were right enough, one heard nothing, either good or bad, about them, they did their work and were contented, and now they will be demoralized! They will take to tea and coffee and velvet trousers and leather boots and accordions . . . no good will come of it!'

'Yes, if that's all, it is certainly not much good,' Stolz remarked; 'but you ought to open a school in your village.'

'Isn't it too soon?' Oblomov said. 'Education is bad for peasants; if you teach them they may not want to plough any more. . . .'

'Why, but they will read of how ploughing should be done, you queer man! But I say, you really ought to go to your estate this year.'

'Yes, that's true; only my plan isn't quite ready . . .' Oblomov remarked timidly.

'There is no need for it,' Stolz said. 'When you arrive you will see on the spot what there is to be done. You have been at this plan for years: isn't it ready yet? What do you do with yourself?'

'Oh, my dear, as though I had nothing but the estate to think of! There's the other misfortune.'

'What is it?'

'I am being driven out of my flat.'

'How so?'

'They say I must leave, and that's all about it.'

'Well, what of it?'

'How can you say that? Why, I've worn myself out tossing in bed with all this worry. I am all alone, and there's this and that to be seen to, accounts to be checked, bills to be paid, and then there's the moving! Money simply flies and I don't know where it goes to! I may find myself penniless any day. . . .'

'You are a spoiled creature! Moving to new lodgings seems a hardship to you!' Stolz remarked in surprise. 'By the way, talking of money, how much have you here? Lend me five hundred roubles, I must send it off to-day; I will draw the money from our office to-morrow. . . .'

'Let me see now. . . . The other day I received a thousand from the country, and now there is left . . . wait a minute. . . .'

Oblomov began rummaging in his drawers.

'Here is ten . . . twenty, two hundred . . . another twenty. There were some coppers too. . . . Zahar, Zahar!'

Zahar jumped off the stove-shelf in his usual way and came into the room.

'Where are the two ten-copeck pieces that were on the table? I put them here yesterday. . . .'

'The way you keep on about those coppers, Ilya Il-yitch! I have already told you there weren't any on the table.'

'Of course there were! The change from the oranges. . . .'

'You must have given it to somebody and forgotten,' Zahar said, turning to the door.

Stolz laughed.

'Ah, you Oblomovs,' he taunted him; 'you don't know how much money you have in your pockets!'

'You gave some money to Mihey Andreyitch, you know,' Zahar reminded him.

'Oh yes, Tarantyev took ten roubles,' Oblomov said, turning quickly to Stolz, 'I had forgotten.'

'Why do you receive that brute?' Stolz remarked.

'Receive him, indeed!' Zahar intervened. 'He comes as though this were his own house or an inn. He has taken the master's shirt and waistcoat, and it is the last we shall see of them! This morning, if you please, he came to borrow a dress-coat – let him wear it! I wish you'd check him, Andrey Ivanitch, sir!'

'It's not your business, Zahar. Go to your room!' Oblomov remarked sternly.

'Give me a sheet of note-paper,' Stolz said, 'I must write a few lines.'

'Zahar, Andrey Ivanitch wants paper, give him some,' Oblomov said.

'But there isn't any! You looked for it this morning,' Zahar answered from the hall without troubling to come in.

'Any scrap will do,' Stolz persisted. Oblomov searched on the table; no, there was not a scrap.

'Well, give me a visiting-card at least.'

'I haven't had any for months,' Oblomov replied.

'What is the matter with you?' Stolz asked ironically. 'And yet you talk of moving, and are writing a plan! Tell me, please, do you go out anywhere? What people do you mix with? Whom do you see?'

'Oh, I don't go anywhere much, I mostly sit at home: the plan worries me, you know, and then there's the moving. . . . Luckily, Tarantyev promised to try and find something for me. . . .'

'Do people come to see you?'

'Yes . . . there's Tarantyev and Alexeyev. This morning the doctor called. . . . Penkin, too, Sudbinsky, Volkov.'

'I don't see any books in your room,' Stolz said.

'Here's a book!' Oblomov remarked, pointing to a book that lay on the table.

'What's this?' Stolz asked, glancing at it. '*A Journey to Africa*. And the page you have stopped at has gone mildewy. There isn't a newspaper to be seen either. . . . Do you read the papers?'

'No, the print is too small, it's bad for the eyes . . . and there is no need to: if there is any news everyone talks of nothing else all day long.'

'Good heavens, Ilya!' said Stolz, looking at Oblomov in surprise. 'But what do you do? – You simply lie here like a piece of dough.'

'That's true, Andrey,' Oblomov admitted sadly.

'A confession is not a justification, you know.'

'No, it's merely an answer to your words. I don't justify myself,' Oblomov remarked with a sigh.

'But you must rouse yourself.'

'I have tried, but never succeeded, and now. . . . Why should I? There is no inducement, my heart is at rest, my mind is sound asleep!' he concluded with hardly perceptible bitterness. 'Don't let us speak of it. . . . Better tell me where have you come from?'

'From Kiev. In another fortnight I shall be going abroad. Come with me. . . .'

'Very well, perhaps I will . . .' Oblomov decided.

'Then sit down and write the application for your passport, you can give it in to-morrow.'

'To-morrow!' Oblomov was alarmed. 'The hurry these people are in, as though they were being driven! We'll think and talk about it and then we shall see. Perhaps I might go to the country first . . . and abroad afterwards.'

'Why afterwards? You say the doctor told you to go. Get rid of your fat, of the bodily heaviness, and then your mind will no longer be sleepy. You need both physical and mental gymnastics.'

'No, Andrey, it would tire me too much. I am in very poor health, you know. No, you had better leave me and go alone. . . .'

Stolz looked at Oblomov as he lay there, Oblomov looked at him. Stolz shook his head and Oblomov sighed.

'You seem to be too lazy to live!' Stolz remarked.

'I believe I am, Andrey, it's true.'

Andrey was turning over in his mind how he could touch him to the quick and what was still 'quick' in him; meanwhile, he scrutinized Oblomov in silence and suddenly laughed.

'Why, you have one thick and one thin stocking on,' he remarked, pointing to Oblomov's feet, 'and your shirt is inside out!'

Oblomov looked at his feet, then at his shirt.

'Yes, indeed,' he confessed in confusion, 'this Zahar has been sent me for my sins! You wouldn't believe what a time I have with him! He argues, he is rude, he doesn't do his work!'

'Ach, Ilya, Ilya!' Stolz said. 'No, I am not going to leave you in this state. In a week's time you won't know yourself. I'll tell you in the evening all I intend doing with you and myself, and now dress! Wait, I will rouse you. Zahar,' he cried, 'give Ilya Ilyitch his clothes!'

'What are you thinking of? Why, Tarantyev and Alexeyev are just coming to dine with me, and then we had thought we . . . .'

'Zahar,' Stolz said, without heeding him, 'give him his clothes.'

'Yes, Andrey Ivanitch, sir, I'll just polish the boots,' Zahar said readily.

'What! You don't begin polishing boots till five o'clock?'

'I did polish them last week, but master hasn't been out so they have grown dull again. . . .'

'Well, bring them as they are. Take my portmanteau to the drawing-room; I will stay here. I am just going to dress, and you be ready too, Ilya. We'll dine somewhere on the way, then call at two or three places and. . . .'

'But look here . . . it's too sudden . . . wait . . . let me think. . . . I haven't shaved, you know.'

'It's no use thinking and scratching your head. . . . You'll shave on the way; I'll drive you to a barber's.'

'Where are you taking me?' Oblomov cried sorrowfully – 'to strangers? What an idea! I would rather go to Ivan Gerasimitch, I haven't been there for three days or more.'

'Who is Ivan Gerasimitch?'

'He was at the office with me. . . .'

'Ah, that grey-headed clerk! What do you see in him? What pleasure is there in wasting your time with that blockhead?'

'How sharply you speak of people at times, Andrey, bless you! He is a good man, though he doesn't wear shirts of Dutch linen. . . .'

'What do you do there? What do you talk to him about?' Stolz asked.

'You know, one somehow feels so cosy, so at home in his house. The rooms are small, the sofas are so deep that one sinks into them and can't be seen. The windows are covered with ivy and cactus leaves, there are more than a dozen canaries and three dogs, such affectionate ones! There is always food on the table. The prints on the walls are scenes of family life. You come and don't want to go away. You sit without thinking or worrying about anything, and you know there is a man beside you . . . not a brilliant one, of course, it's no use exchanging ideas with him, but kind, simple, unpretentious, one who won't revile you behind your back!'

'But what do you do there?'

'What do I do? Why, I come and settle down on a sofa with my feet up, and he does the same on the sofa opposite; he smokes. . . .'

'And you?'

'I . . . I also smoke, I listen to the canaries trilling. Then Marfa brings the *samovar*.'

'Tarantyev, Ivan Gerasimitch!' Stolz said, shrugging his shoulders. 'Well, make haste and dress,' he hurried him. 'Tell Tarantyev when he comes,' he added, turning to Zahar, 'that we are dining out, that Ilya Ilyitch will be dining out all the summer, and in the autumn he will have a lot of work and will not be able to see him.'

'I'll tell him everything, I won't forget,' Zahar said; 'and what shall I do about the dinner?'

'You may eat it up with some friend and welcome.'

'Yes, sir.'

Ten minutes later Stolz came out of the next room, having changed his clothes, shaved, and brushed his hair, and found Oblomov sitting in a melancholy attitude on the bed slowly buttoning his shirt-front and struggling with the buttonholes. Waiting for him to finish, Zahar knelt before him on one knee holding an unpolished boot as though it were a dish.

'You haven't put your boots on yet!' Stolz said in surprise. 'Make haste, Ilya, make haste!'

'But where are we to go? What for?' Oblomov said with anguish. 'What's the attraction? I've lost the habit, I don't want to go. . . .'

'Hurry up, hurry up!' Stolz said.

IV

ALTHOUGH it was late, they managed to make a business call; then Stolz took some gold-mine owner along to dinner with them, then they went to the man's summer villa to tea and found a large company there, and Oblomov after his complete seclusion found himself in a crowd. They returned home late at night.

The next day and the day after it was the same thing, and so a whole week flew by. Oblomov protested, complained, argued, but gave in and followed his friend everywhere. One evening, when they came home late, he was particularly emphatic in his protests.

'I am wearing boots from morning till night,' he grumbled, 'my feet are aching dreadfully. I don't like this Petersburg life,' he continued, lying down on the sofa.

'What kind of life do you like?'

'Different from this.'

'What, precisely, do you dislike about this one?'

'Everything: the everlasting running to and fro, the constant play of petty passions – of greed especially – the gossip, the backbiting, the mutual affronts, the way they look one up and down and trip up one another. Listening to their talk is enough to turn one silly. At first sight they look so intelligent, such dignity in their faces, but all you hear from them is: "So and so has received this; so and so has obtained a contract." "Mercy on us, what for?" someone will shout. "This one lost at cards at the club yesterday; that one is making three hundred thousand!" The boredom of it! Where is the real man in all that? Where is his sterling worth? What has become of it? How has it been changed into base coin?'

'But, after all, society must have something to occupy it,' Stolz said; 'everyone has his own interests. It's life. . . .'

'Society! You must be sending me into society on purpose to make me dislike going there still more than I did,
Andrey. Life! Nice sort of life! What does one find in it?
– Intellectual interests, genuine feeling? There is no
centre round which it all revolves, there is nothing deep,
nothing vital. All these society people are dead men, men
fast asleep, they are worse than I am! What is their aim in
life? They do not lie in bed like me, they dash backwards
and forwards every day like flies, but what is the good?
You come into a room and can't admire enough the sym-
metrical way the guests are seated; how quiet and
thoughtful they are at the card-tables! There's no gain-
saying it, it is a fine aim to live for, a splendid example
for a mind that wants something to stir it! Don't you see
that they are dead, that all their life long they are asleep
as they sit there? Why am I more to blame because I lie in
bed and don't poison my head with aces and knaves?'

'All this is stale, it has been said a thousand times,'
Stolz remarked. 'Have you anything fresher!'

'And our best young people, what do they do? Don't
they sleep walking or dancing or driving along the Nevsky? Empty reshuffling of days! And see with what
groundless pride and dignity and haughty aloofness they
look upon those who are not dressed as they are, who are
not of the same rank and class. And the unfortunate creatures imagine they are above the common herd: "We have
posts that no one else has; we sit in the front row of the
stalls, we go to Prince N.'s balls where other people aren't
invited. . . ." And when they meet together they get drunk
and fight just like savages! Are they real, wide-awake
people? And it isn't only the young ones: look at the
grown-ups. They meet together, invite one another to
meals, but there is no hospitality, no kindness, no mutual
liking! They come to a dinner or to an evening-party as to
their office, coldly, without gaiety, simply to boast of their
cook or their drawing-room, and to make mischief and
jeer at one another afterwards. The other day at dinner I
didn't know where to look and was ready to hide under

the table when they began pulling to pieces those who weren't present: "So and so is stupid; so and so is low; that one is a thief, the other is ridiculous" – a regular massacre! And they were looking at one another as though to say, "The moment you go out of the door, the same will be done to you!" . . . Why do they meet if they are like that? No genuine laughter, not a glimmer of sympathy! They strive for a name, for high rank: "So and so has called on me, I've been to see so and so," they boast. What kind of life is that? I don't want it. What shall I learn there, what can I derive from it?'

'Do you know, Ilya,' Stolz remarked, 'you argue just like the ancients did; that's how they used to write in old books. But, after all, it's a good thing: anyway, you reason and don't sleep. Well, what more? Go on.'

'What more is there to say? Just look: not a single person here looks fresh and healthy.'

'It's the climate,' Stolz interrupted. 'Your face, too, looks puffy, though you lie in bed and don't run about.'

'Not one of them has calm, clear eyes,' Oblomov went on. 'All infect one another with misery and bitter worry, all are painfully striving for something. And if, at least, it were for truth, for their own and other people's good! – But no, a comrade's success makes them turn pale. One man's sole concern is to call every day at the law courts: his case has been going on for five years, his opponent is winning, and for five years he has had but one thought, one desire in his mind – to bring the other man down and to build his own welfare on the enemy's ruin. To sit and sigh in a waiting-room for five years – here's an aim and ideal of life for you! Another one is wretched because he has to go to the office every day and sit there till five o'clock, and a third one is sighing deeply because this happiness has been denied him. . . .'

'You are a philosopher, Ilya,' Stolz said: 'everyone is worrying, you alone don't need anything.'

'That yellow-faced gentleman in spectacles,' Oblomov continued, 'kept asking me whether I had read the speech of some deputy or other and stared at me open-eyed when I told him I didn't read the newspapers. He carried on about Louis Philippe as though he were his own father. Afterwards he pestered me why, did I think, had the French Ambassador left Rome? Good heavens, to condemn oneself to swallowing a daily supply of world news and shouting about them all the week till the supply runs out! To-day Mehmet Ali has sent a ship to Constantinople and he puzzles his head why. To-morrow Don Carlos has a reverse, and he is fearfully worried. Here they are digging a canal, there a detachment of troops has been sent to the East – dear me, you might think there was a fire! He is dreadfully upset, he fusses and shouts as though the troops were after him! They argue and reckon things out this way and that, but they are bored, they don't really care; one can see they are fast asleep in spite of all their shouting. It has nothing to do with them; it's like borrowed clothes. They have no work of their own and so they scatter their energies in all directions. Their all-embracing interests are a cloak for emptiness, for being out of sympathy with everything! To choose a modest path of labour and follow it drawing a deep furrow is dull and unnoticeable; knowing everything would be of no use for it and there would be no one to dazzle!'

'Well, Ilya, you and I haven't scattered our energies. Where is our modest path of labour?' Stolz asked.

Oblomov was silent.

'I have just to finish my . . . plan,' he said. 'But bless them, I am not interfering with them,' he added with vexation, 'I am not after anything; I merely do not think that their life is normal. No, it is not life but a violation of the norm, of the ideal which nature has put before man. . . .'

'What is this ideal, this norm of life?'

Oblomov made no answer.

'Well, tell me how would you arrange your life?' Stolz insisted.

'I have thought it all out.'

'How? Do tell me.'

'How?' Oblomov repeated, turning over on his back and looking at the ceiling. 'Why, I would go to the country.'

'What is there to prevent you?'

'My plan isn't ready. And then I would go with a wife, and not alone. . . .'

'Oh, so that's it! Well, God speed to you. What are you waiting for? In another three or four years' time nobody will marry you.'

'Well, it's fate, there is nothing for it,' Oblomov said with a sigh. 'I am too poor to marry.'

'Why, but there is Oblomovka! Three hundred serfs!'

'What of it? That's not enough to live on with a wife.'

'Not enough for two people to live on?'

'But when we have children?'

'If you bring them up properly, the children will fend for themselves; you must start them in the right direction.'

'No, what's the good of making well-born children into artisans?' Oblomov interrupted him dryly. 'But apart from children, we shouldn't be just by ourselves. One says "alone with my wife," but in truth you are no sooner married than all sorts of females invade your house. Look at any family you know: one can't make out whether they are relatives or housekeepers, but they either live in the house or come every day to dinner and to coffee. . . . How could one keep such a boarding-house with three hundred serfs?'

'Very well; suppose someone made you a present of three hundred thousand roubles, what would you do?' asked Stolz, extremely interested.

'I would put it at once into a bank and live on the interest,' Oblomov said.

'They don't give a high interest there; why not invest it in some company – ours, say?'

'No, Andrey, you won't catch me.'

'What, wouldn't you trust even me?'

'Certainly not; it isn't that I wouldn't trust you,

but anything might happen: your company might go bankrupt and I would be left penniless. It's safer in the bank.'

'Very well; what would you do then?'

'Well, I would move into a new comfortable house. . . . There would be good neighbours living near – you, for instance. . . . But no, you wouldn't be able to settle down anywhere. . . .'

'But would you settle there for ever? Would you never go anywhere?'

'Never.'

'Why are they taking the trouble to build railways everywhere and run steamers if the ideal of life is to sit still? Let us send in a proposal for them to stop, Ilya: we are not going anywhere.'

'There are plenty of people apart from us; aren't there enough agents, bailiffs, tradesmen, officials, idle travellers, who have no home? Let them travel to their hearts' content!'

'And who are you?'

Oblomov said nothing.

'In which social class do you include yourself?'

'Ask Zahar,' Oblomov said.

Stolz carried out Oblomov's wish literally.

'Zahar!' he shouted.

Zahar came in looking very sleepy.

'Who is it lying there?' Stolz asked.

Zahar woke up suddenly and threw a suspicious, side-long glance first at Stolz and then at Oblomov.

'How do you mean? Don't you see?'

'No, I don't,' Stolz said.

'That's a funny thing! It's the *barin*, Ilya Ilyitch.' He grinned.

'Very well, you may go.'

'*Barin!*' Stolz repeated, and roared with laughter.

'Well, a gentleman,' Oblomov corrected him with vexation.

'No, no, you are a *barin!*' Stolz went on, laughing.

'What's the difference?' Oblomov said. 'Gentleman is the same as *barin*.'

'A gentleman is the kind of *barin* who puts on his stockings and takes off his boots himself,' Stolz defined.

'Yes, the English do it themselves because they haven't very many servants, but the Russian. . . .'

'Go on painting your ideal of life to me. . . . Very well, there are good friends in the neighbourhood; what next? How would you spend your days?'

'Well, I get up in the morning . . .' Oblomov began, putting his hands behind his neck; his face assumed a peaceful expression as though he were already in the country. 'The weather is lovely, the sky is a deep, deep blue, not a cloud in it,' he said; 'the balcony on one side of the house in my plan faces east towards the garden and the fields, and on the other towards the village. Waiting for my wife to wake, I put on my dressing-gown and stroll about the garden to breathe the morning freshness; I find the gardener there, we water the flowers and prune the trees and the bushes. I make a nosegay for my wife. Then I go to the bathroom or the river to have a bathe, and when I come back the balcony door is open; my wife is waiting for me in a morning-dress and a flimsy cap that lightly rests on her head and looks as though it might be blown off any moment. . . . "Tea is ready," she says. What a kiss! What tea! What a comfortable arm-chair! I sit down by the table; there are home-made rusks on it, cream, fresh butter. . . .'

'Then?'

'Then I put on a loose coat or a jacket of some sort and we go, my arm round my wife's waist, down an endless dark avenue of trees; we walk along in silence slowly and dreamily; or we think aloud, we dream, we count the moments of happiness as the beating of one's pulse; we listen to our hearts throbbing; we look to nature for sympathy . . . and imperceptibly we come to the river and the fields. . . . The river barely stirs, the ears of corn wave in the slight breeze, it's hot . . . we step into the boat; my wife guides it, scarcely lifting the oars. . . .'

'Why, Ilya, you are a poet!' Stolz interrupted him.

'Yes, a poet in life because life is poetry, if people don't distort it! Then we might go into the hot-house,' Oblomov continued, carried away by the ideal of happiness he was depicting.

He was talking of scenes which he had drawn in his imagination many a time, and spoke with animation, never stopping for a pause.

'To have a look at the peaches, the grapes,' he went on, 'to say what was to be sent in for the table; then we would return, have a light lunch, and wait for visitors. . . . Meanwhile, there would be a note for my wife from some Marya Petrovna or other sending her a book or music, or somebody would send us a pineapple as a present, or in my hot-house a monstrous water-melon would ripen and I would send it to a friend for to-morrow's dinner – and go there myself. . . . And, meanwhile, there is tremendous activity in the kitchen; the chef, in a snow-white cap and overall, is fearfully busy, putting one saucepan on the stove, taking off another, stirring something in the third, throwing away the water, making pastry . . . the vegetables are being chopped . . . the ice cream is being made. . . . It is nice to peep into the kitchen before dinner, to lift a saucepan-lid and have a sniff, to see them rolling up the pies or whipping cream, and then to lie down on the sofa. My wife is reading some new book; now and again we stop to argue about it. . . . But visitors come, you and your wife, for instance.'

'Oh, you will have me married too?'

'Certainly! Two or three friends more, always the same people; we begin the conversation we had not finished the day before; we joke and sometimes there is an eloquent silence, and we are thoughtful – not because so and so has lost his job, or because the case in the Senate troubles us, but thoughtful with the fullness of satisfied desires, with happiness. . . . You will not hear anyone thundering against an absent friend or catch a glance that promises the same to you the moment you walk out of the door.

You are not going to eat at the same table with those whom you don't like and respect. You will read sympathy in your companions' eyes, you will hear sincere, kindly laughter in their jokes. . . . It is all genuine! They look and feel what they say! After dinner there is Mocha coffee and Havannah cigars on the verandah. . . .'

'You are telling me of how our fathers and grandfathers used to live.'

'No, I am not,' Oblomov answered almost touchily, 'it's quite different. My wife would not spend her time making jam and pickling mushrooms. She wouldn't be measuring yarn and sorting out home-spun linen; she would not box her maids' ears. Don't you hear what I said – music, piano, elegant furniture?'

'And you?'

'I should not be reading last year's papers and driving in a clumsy old chaise, and instead of eating vermicelli soup and roast goose I should have my chef trained at the English Club or at a foreign legation.'

'Well, and then?'

'Then when the heat subsides we would send a cart with the *samovar* and dessert to the birch copse or the meadow, spread carpets on the newly mown grass and enjoy ourselves there till it was time for cold soup and beefsteak. The peasants are returning from the fields with scythes on their shoulders; a load of hay crawls past so big that you can't see the cart or the driver, a peasant cap with flowers round it and a child's head peep out of the hay on the top; there comes a crowd of women, bare-footed, carrying sickles and singing. . . . They suddenly catch sight of us, grow quiet, and bow. One of them, with bare elbows and a sunburnt neck, her sly eyes timidly cast down, pretends to push away her master's arm, but is really pleased at his caress. . . . Hush, my wife mustn't see it, Heaven forbid!'

Both Oblomov and Stolz roared with laughter.

'It's damp in the meadow,' Oblomov concluded; 'it's dark: a sea of mist hangs low over the rye; the horses shiver and stamp on the ground; it's time to go home. There are lights in the house windows: five big knives are clattering in the kitchen; a frying-pan full of mushrooms, minced-meat balls, strawberries. . . . Then there is music. . . . *Casta diva . . . Casta diva!*' Oblomov sang the beginning of the aria. 'I cannot bear to recall *Casta diva*,' he said. 'The way that woman cries her heart out! What sorrow there is in those sounds! . . . No one around her knows anything. . . . She is alone. . . . Her secret is a burden to her; she tells it to the moon. . . .'

'You are fond of that aria! I am so glad: Olga Ilyinsky sings it beautifully. I will introduce you – she has a wonderful voice; and how she sings! And she herself is such a charming child. Though perhaps I am partial, I have a weakness for her. . . . Don't lose the thread, though,' Stolz added, 'go on telling me!'

'Well,' Oblomov went on, 'what else is there? . . . That's all. The visitors go to their rooms at the lodge or the pavilion and the next day some of them go fishing or shooting, and some simply sit still. . . .'

'Simply? With nothing in their hands?' Stolz asked.

'What would you like them to have? Well, a handkerchief, perhaps. Now, don't you want to live like that, eh?' Oblomov asked. 'Isn't that the real thing?'

'All your life?' Stolz asked.

'Till old age, till death. That is life!'

'No, it isn't.'

'It isn't? What's wrong with it? Just think, you wouldn't see a single pale, unhappy face, there wouldn't be any worries, any questions about the Senate, the stock exchange, shares, reports, the minister's reception, ranks, bonuses. Instead, there would be real heart-to-heart conversations. You would never have to change your lodgings – that alone is worth something! And you say it isn't life?'

'It isn't,' Stolz repeated obstinately.

'It's –' Stolz broke off, trying to think of a word to describe this kind of existence – 'it's a sort of . . . Oblomovism,' he said at last.

'Ob-lo-movism!' Ilya Ilyitch pronounced slowly, marvelling at the strange word and dividing it into syllables, 'Ob-lo-movism!'

He looked at Stolz with a strange fixity.

'What, then, is the ideal life, you think? What is not Oblomovism?' he asked timidly and without enthusiasm. 'Doesn't everyone strive for the very same things that I dream of? Why,' he added more confidently, 'isn't it the purpose of all your running about, your passions, wars, trade, politics – to secure rest, to attain this ideal of a lost paradise?'

'Your very Utopia is that of an Oblomov,' Stolz retorted.

'Everyone seeks peace and rest,' Oblomov defended himself.

'No, not everyone, and ten years ago you, too, sought something very different.'

'What was it?' Oblomov asked in perplexity, turning his thoughts on the past.

'Think, try to remember. Where are your books, your translations?'

'Zahar put them away,' Oblomov answered. 'I expect they are in a corner somewhere.'

'In a corner!' Stolz said reproachfully. 'In the same corner as your plans "to work so long as you have any strength left, because Russia needs hands and brains to make use of her inexhaustible wealth" (these were your words); to work in order to rest more happily, and to rest meant to live in another artistic, beautiful aspect of life, the life of poets and artists. Has Zahar put all these plans of yours in a corner too? Do you remember how after you had finished with books you wanted to visit foreign countries so as to know and to love your own the better? "The whole of life is work and thought," you used to repeat then; "obscure, unrecognized but unremitting work"; "to die knowing that you have done your share" – in what corner have you put that?'

'Yes . . . yes . . .' Oblomov repeated, following anxiously

every word of Stolz's. 'I remember that I really did . . . I believe. . . . Yes, of course!' he said, suddenly recalling the past. 'Why, Andrey, we had intended to travel all over Europe, to walk right through Switzerland, to scorch our feet on Vesuvius, to go down to see Herculaneum. We were nearly mad then! What silly things we said!'

'Silly!' Stolz repeated reproachfully. 'Didn't you say, with tears in your eyes, as you looked at the prints of Raphael's Madonnas, · of Correggio's *Night*, of Apollo Belvedere: "Oh dear, shall I never be able to see the originals, to stand awestruck before the work of Michel-Angelo and Titian, to tread upon the soil of Rome? Shall I never in my life see those myrtles, cypresses, and citrons in their native land instead of in hot-houses? Shall I never breathe the air of Italy and drink in the blue of its skies?" You used to let off many magnificent fireworks of eloquence in those days! Silly things!'

'Yes, yes, I remember!' said Oblomov, thinking of the past. 'You took me by the hand one day and said, "Let us promise not to die before we have seen it all." '

'I remember,' Stolz went on, 'how you brought me once on my name-day a translation from a book of Say's dedicated to me; I have it still. And how you used to lock yourself in with the teacher of mathematics because you were determined to understand why one needed to know about squares and circles, but you threw it up half-way! You began to learn English . . . and you gave that up too. And when I planned a journey abroad and asked you to have a look at the German universities with me, you jumped up, hugged me, and solemnly held out your hand: "I am yours, Andrey, I will go with you anywhere," you said; you were always a bit of an actor, you know. Well, Ilya, I have been abroad twice; after all the wisdom learned at our university here I humbly sat with the students at Bonn, Jena, Erlangen, I learned to know Europe as my own estate. But, after all, foreign travel is a luxury and not everyone is able and obliged to go abroad; but Russia? I have been all over Russia. I work. . . .'

'You will stop working some day,' Oblomov remarked.

'Never. Why should I?'

'When you have doubled your capital,' Oblomov said.

'I won't stop when I have squared it.'

'Then why do you work so hard,' Oblomov began after a pause, 'if it isn't for the sake of providing for your future and then retiring to the country?'

'Oblomovism in the country!' Stolz said.

'Or to attain a high rank and social position and then enjoy in honourable inactivity a well-earned rest? . . .'

'Oblomovism in Petersburg!' Stolz answered.

'When, then, are you going to live?' Oblomov asked, annoyed at his remarks. 'Why slave all your life?'

'For the sake of the work itself and nothing else. Work gives form, and completeness, and a purpose to life, at any rate for me. Here, now, you have banished work from your life, and what is the result? I shall try to raise you up, perhaps for the last time. If after this you will still go on sitting here with the Tarantyevs and Alexeyevs you will be done for, you will be a burden to yourself. Now or never!' he concluded.

Oblomov listened, looking at him with anxious eyes. It was as though his friend were holding a mirror before him and he was frightened when he recognized himself.

'Don't scold me, Andrey, better help me!' he began with a sigh. 'I suffer from it myself; had you seen me earlier in the day and heard the way I was bewailing my fate and digging my own grave you would not have had the heart to reproach me. I know and understand it all, but I have no strength, no will. Give me some of your will and intelligence and lead me where you like. I may perhaps follow you, but alone I shall not stir from the spot. You are quite right, it is now or never. In another year it will be too late!'

'Is this you, Ilya?' Stolz said. 'I remember you a slender, lively boy, walking every day from Pretchistenka to Kudrino; in the garden there . . . you haven't forgotten the two sisters? You haven't forgotten Rousseau, Schiller,

Goethe, Byron, and how you used to bring their works to
the girls, and take away from them Genlis and Cottin . . .
how you used to show off before them and wanted to
improve their taste?'

Oblomov jumped off the bed.

'What, you remember that too, Andrey? Yes, of course!
I dreamed with them, whispered hopes of the future,
unfolded plans, ideas . . . and feelings too, though I hid it
from you so that you shouldn't make fun of me. It all died
there and was never repeated again! Where has it all gone
to? Why has it all burnt out? I can't understand it! I had
no storms, no shocks of any kind; I did not lose anything;
I have nothing on my conscience – it is clear as glass; no
blow of any kind has shattered my ambitions, and God
only knows why my life is such a waste!'

He sighed.

'Do you know, Andrey, there has never been a flame
burning in my life, either to save or to destroy me! My
life, unlike other people's, was never like a morning which
gradually acquires colour and turns into a blazing day,
when everything is seething with movement in the vivid
noonday light and then gradually subsides and grows dim-
mer, fading naturally into the evening twilight. No, my
life began by fading out. It is strange, but it was so! From
the moment I became aware of myself I felt that I was
already withering. My decline began when I sat copying
papers in the office, continued when I read in books
truths which I did not know how to apply in life, when I
sat with friends listening to rumours, gossip, gibes, malicious, cold, empty chatter, watching friendship that was
kept up by meeting one another without aim or affection;
I was losing ground and wasting my powers when I was
with Minna, on whom I spent more than half my income
imagining that I loved her, when I idly and despondently
walked up and down the Nevsky among people in marmot
coats with beaver collars, went to receptions and parties
where I was received well as a fairly eligible young man. I
was losing ground and wasting my life and mind on trifles

when I moved from the town to a summer villa, from the summer villa back to Gorohovy Street. When spring meant for me that lobsters and oysters were in season, autumn and winter meant *jours fixes*, summer – the usual outings, and life in general – lazy and comfortable, slumber just as it does for others. . . . My ambition – what was it spent on? On ordering clothes at a fashionable tailor's! Being received in well-known families! Shaking hands with Prince P.! And ambition is the salt of life! Where has it all gone? Either I have failed to understand the life around me or it was utterly worthless and I did not know of a better one, no one showed it me. You appeared and swiftly disappeared again like a bright comet. I forgot it all and was sinking lower and lower.'

Stolz no longer answered Oblomov with light mockery. He listened in gloomy silence.

'You said just now that my face looked puffy and flabby,' Oblomov went on. 'Yes, I am like an old worn-out coat, and it isn't because of the climate or of work, but because for twelve years a fire has been shut up within me which could not find an outlet, it merely ravaged its prison and died down. Twelve years have passed, my dear Andrey; I did not want to wake up any more.'

'Why didn't you tear yourself away? Why didn't you escape instead of perishing in silence?' Stolz asked impatiently.

'Where to?'

'Where to? Why, if only to the Volga with your peasants: there is more to do there; anyway, you could find an interest in life, a purpose, some work! I would have gone to Siberia, to Sitkha. . . .'

'You always prescribe such violent remedies, you know,' Oblomov remarked despondently. 'And I am not the only one: look, there's Mihailov, Petrov, Semyonov, Stepanov . . . too many to count; our name is legion!'

Stolz was still under the influence of Oblomov's confession and said nothing. Then he sighed.

'Yes, much water has flowed past,' he said. 'I am not

going to leave you like this; I will take you away, first abroad and then to the country; you will grow thinner, recover your spirits, and then we will find you work. . . .'

'Yes, let us go away from here!' Oblomov cried out.

'To-morrow we will apply for foreign passports and then make ready. . . . I won't leave you alone, Ilya – do you hear?'

'You want to do everything to-morrow!' Oblomov retorted, as though falling from the clouds.

'And you would like "not to put off till to-morrow what can be done to-day"? What energy! It is too late to-day,' Stolz added, 'but in a fortnight's time we shall be far from here. . . .'

'What are you talking of, brother? In a fortnight, so suddenly!' Oblomov said. 'Let me think it over properly and get ready. . . . We must buy a carriage of some sort. . . . In three months perhaps.'

'Buying a carriage! What next? We shall go in a post-chaise as far as the frontier, or perhaps by boat as far as Lubeck, whichever is more convenient; and abroad there are railways in many places.'

'And the flat, and Zahar, and Oblomovka? I must see to it all,' Oblomov protested.

'Oblomovism, Oblomovism!' Stolz laughed, and taking his candle said good night and went to his room. 'It's now or never, remember!' he added, turning to Oblomov and shutting the door behind him.

V

'NOW or never' were the menacing words that appeared before Oblomov's mind as soon as he woke in the morning. He got up, walked three times up and down the room, peeped into the drawing-room – Stolz sat writing. 'Zahar!' he called, but there was no sound of Zahar jumping off the stove, and he did not come – Stolz had sent him to the post. Oblomov sat down at his dusty table, dipped the pen in the inkstand, but there was no ink; he looked for paper – there was none either. He sank into thought and mechanically began writing on the dusty surface, then looked at what he had written – it was *Oblomovism*. He hastily wiped it off with his sleeve. He had dreamt of that word in the night, written on the walls in letters of fire as at Belshazzar's feast. Zahar came in and looked at his master vacantly, astonished that he was not in bed. *Oblomovism* was written in that dull look of surprise. 'A single word,' Ilya Ilyitch thought, 'but how . . . venomous it is!'

Zahar took up the brush, comb, and towel, and went up as usual to do his master's hair.

'Go to the devil!' Oblomov said angrily, and knocked the brush out of Zahar's hands. Zahar dropped the comb.

'Aren't you going to lie down again?' Zahar asked. 'Then I will make the bed.'

'Bring me some paper and ink,' Oblomov answered. He was thinking about the words 'now or never!' As he pondered on this desperate appeal of reason and energy, he was considering and weighing how much will-power he still had left and what use he could make of that poor remnant. After some minutes of painful thought he pulled a book out of the corner and wanted in one short hour to read, write, and think over what he had not read, written, and thought over in ten years. What was he to do now?

Go forward or remain where he was? This Oblomov question was for him deeper than Hamlet's. To go forward
meant to throw the loose dressing-gown not only off his
shoulders but off his mind and soul; to sweep the dust
and cobwebs from his eyes as well as from the walls, and
to regain his sight! What was the first step towards it?
How was he to begin? 'I don't know, I can't . . . no, I am
prevaricating, I do know. . . . And besides, Stolz is here,
he will tell me at once. And what will he say? He will say
that during the week I must write detailed instructions to
my agent and send him to the country; mortgage Oblomovka; buy some more land; send down a plan of buildings to be put up; give up the flat; take a passport and go
abroad for six months; get rid of my fat; throw off my
heaviness; refresh my soul with the air of which I once
dreamed with my friend; live without a dressing-gown,
without Zahar and Tarantyev; put on my stockings and
take off my boots myself, unaided; sleep at night only; go
where everybody goes – by rail, on steamers, and then . . .
then . . . settle down at Oblomovka; learn what sowing and
harvesting means, why peasants are rich and poor; go to
the fields; take part in the elections; drive to the works, to
the mill, to the harbour. At the same time read newspapers and books; worry why the English have sent a ship
to the East. . . . That's what he will say! This means to go
forward. . . . And to do this all my life! Good-bye, my
poetic ideal! It's like being in a smithy, it isn't life; it's
continual noise, flame, heat, clatter. . . . When am I to
live? Hadn't I better stay? To stay means putting on my
shirt inside out; listening to Zahar jumping off the
stove; dining with Tarantyev; thinking less and less; never
finishing *The Journey to Africa*; and growing peacefully
old at the house of Tarantyev's friend. . . . "Now or
never!" "To be or not to be!" ' Oblomov got up from the
chair, but failed to find his slippers at once with his feet
and sat down again.

In another fortnight Stolz went to England, making
Oblomov promise to come straight to Paris. Ilya Ilyitch's

passport was ready, he had ordered a coat for travelling
and bought a cap. Things had advanced as far as that!
Zahar had been arguing earnestly that it was enough to
order one pair of boots and have the other re-soled. Oblomov had bought a blanket, a jersey, a travelling-bag, and
had been on the point of buying a bag for provisions, but
ten people told him that abroad people do not carry food
with them. Zahar had been dashing about shops and
work-rooms bathed in perspiration, and although he pock-
eted a good many coppers out of the change in the shops,
he cursed both Stolz and all those who had invented
travel. 'Whatever is he going to do there by himself?' he
said to his friends at the shop. 'People say all the servants
in those parts are girls. How can a girl pull off a gentleman's boots? How will she put the stockings on the
master's bare feet?' He shook his head and grinned so that
his whiskers moved sideways. Oblomov was not too lazy
to write down what was to go with him and what was to
be left at home. Tarantyev was commissioned to take the
furniture and other things to his friend's house at the
Vyborg side and lock them up in three rooms pending
Oblomov's return from abroad.

Oblomov's friends had already said, some incredulously,
others laughing, and some with a kind of alarm: 'He is
going; would you believe it, Oblomov is actually on the
move!'

But a month and then three months passed and Oblomov did not go.

On the eve of the departure his lip had swollen. 'A fly
has bitten me, I can't go on board ship with a lip like
this!' he said, and decided to wait for the next ship. Now
it was August; Stolz had been in Paris for some time and
was writing desperate letters to Oblomov, who did not
reply.

Why? Probably because the ink had gone dry in the
inkstand and there was no paper? Or perhaps because
that and *which* jostle against each other too often in

Oblomov's style? Or because Ilya Ilyitch had stopped at the last of the two menacing words, '*now* or *never*,' had put his arms behind his head, and Zahar tried in vain to wake him?

No, his inkstand was full of ink; letters, paper, and even stamped paper covered with his own handwriting lay on the table.

Having written several pages he never put *which* twice in the same sentence; he wrote easily and at times expressively and eloquently, as in the days when he had dreamed with Stolz about a life of labour and of travelling, when he used to fill notebooks with prose and verse and shed tears over poetry.

He got up at seven, read, carried books about. He looked neither bored nor tired nor sleepy. There was colour in his face, a light in his eyes – something like courage, or at any rate like self-confidence. He did not wear his dressing-gown: Tarantyev had taken it to his friend's flat, together with the other things. Oblomov sat reading or writing, dressed in a light overcoat with a kerchief round his neck; his shirt-collar showed above his tie and was white as snow. When he went out he wore an excellently made frock-coat and an elegant hat. . . . He was cheerful, he sang to himself. . . . Why was this? . . . Here he was sitting by his window (he was staying at a summer villa, some miles out of town) with a nosegay lying by him. He was hurriedly writing something, glancing every moment over the bushes at the path and again writing hastily. Suddenly the sand of the path crunched under light footsteps; Oblomov threw down the pen, seized the bouquet, and ran to the window. 'Is it you, Olga Sergeyevna? I shan't be a minute,' he said, seized his cap and cane, ran out of the gate, offered his arm to some beautiful woman, and disappeared with her in the forest, in the shadow of the enormous pine-trees. . . . Zahar appeared from behind a corner, looked after him, shut the door of the room and went to the kitchen.

'He is gone!' he said to Anissya.

'Will he be in to dinner?'

'Heaven only knows,' Zahar answered sleepily. Zahar was the same as ever: huge whiskers, unshaven chin, a grey waistcoat and a tear in his coat, but he was married to Anissya, either owing to a breach with his 'lady friend' or simply from conviction that a man ought to have a wife; he was married, but, contrary to the proverbs, he had not changed.

Stolz had introduced Oblomov to Olga and her aunt. When he brought Oblomov to Olga's aunt's house for the first time there were visitors there. Oblomov felt depressed and shy as usual. 'I wish I could take off my gloves,' he thought, 'the room is quite warm. I've got so out of it all!'

Stolz sat down by Olga, who was leaning back in an arm-chair near the lamp, at some distance from the tea-table, by herself, taking little part in what was happening around her. She was very glad to see Stolz; her eyes did not sparkle and her cheeks were not flushed at the sight of him, but an even, calm light spread over her face and she smiled. She called him her friend, she liked him because he always amused her and did not let her be bored, but she was a little afraid of him, too, for she felt too much of a child in his presence. When some question or perplexity arose in her mind she did not venture at once to trust it to him: he was too far ahead of her, too much above her, so that her vanity sometimes suffered from the sense of her own childishness, of the difference in their years and intelligence. Stolz admired her disinterestedly, as a lovely creature with a fragrant freshness of mind and heart. She was, in his eyes, simply a charming and a very promising child. And yet he talked to her oftener and more readily than to other women because, without knowing it, she lived simply and naturally, and, owing to her happy nature, her healthy, unsophisticated upbringing, did not shrink from expressing her thoughts, feelings, and desires, and there was nothing artificial about the tiniest movement of her lips, her eyes, her hands. Perhaps she followed her path in life so confidently because she heard at times beside her the still more confident tread of her 'friend,' whom she trusted and with whom she tried to keep in step. However that might be, there were few girls whose words, opinions, and actions were as simple and spontaneous as Olga's. One never read in her eyes, 'Now I will purse up my lips a little and be thoughtful – it rather suits me. I will glance over there, be frightened, and give a slight scream; they will run up to me. I will sit down by the piano and show the tip of my foot. . . .' There was nothing showy about her, no affectation, no coquetry, no falsity, no calculation. In consequence, hardly anyone but Stolz appreciated her; she had sat through more than one mazurka alone, looking frankly bored; the most amiable of the young men were silent in her presence, not knowing what to say to her and how to say it. . . . Some thought her simple, shallow, and rather stupid because she did not shower upon them either profound aphorisms about life and love or rapid, bold, and unexpected repartees, or musical and literary criticisms borrowed from books or overheard; she spoke little, and only her own, unimportant thoughts – and so, clever and lively partners avoided her; the quiet ones, on the contrary, thought her much too clever and were a little afraid of her. Stolz alone made her laugh and could never stop talking to her. She was fond of music, but sang for the most part either to herself or to Stolz or to some school friend; and, according to Stolz, she sang better than any professional singer. No sooner had Stolz settled beside her than her laughter resounded in the room, so musical, so sincere and infectious, that whoever heard it was sure to laugh too, without knowing why. Stolz did not, however, amuse her all the time: in another half-hour she was listening to him with interest and looking from time to time at Oblomov with still greater interest – and Oblomov felt ready to sink through the ground because of those glances.

'What are they saying about me?' he thought, looking

at them sideways anxiously. He was on the point of going away when Olga's aunt called him to the table and made him sit down beside her, under the cross-fire of the other visitors' glances. He looked round at Stolz timorously, but Stolz had gone; he looked at Olga and met the same interested gaze fixed upon him. 'She is still looking at me!' he thought, looking in confusion at his clothes. He wiped his face with his handkerchief, thinking that perhaps he had a smut on his nose; touched his tie to see if it had come undone – it sometimes happened to him; no, everything seemed to be in order, but she was still looking! A footman brought him a cup of tea and a tray with cakes and biscuits. He wanted to control his confusion, to be free and easy and, in the effort to do so, picked up such a heap of biscuits and rusks that a little girl who sat next to him laughed. Others glanced at the heap with interest. 'My goodness, she is looking at it too!' Oblomov thought. 'What shall I do with this heap?' He could see without looking that Olga got up from her seat and walked to another corner of the room. He felt relieved. The little girl watched to see what he would do with the biscuits.

'I must hurry up and eat them,' he thought, and began demolishing them; fortunately they simply melted in the mouth. Only two remained; he breathed freely and ventured to look where Olga had gone. She was standing by a bust, leaning against the pedestal and watching him. It seemed as though she had left her corner on purpose to watch him the more freely: she had noticed his mischance with the biscuits. At supper she sat at the other end of the table and was talking and eating without apparently taking any notice of him; but no sooner did Oblomov timidly turn in her direction in the hope that she was not looking at him, than he met her eyes, full of curiosity and yet so kind. . . .

After supper Oblomov hastily took leave of Olga's aunt; she invited him to dinner the next day, asking him to give the invitation to Stolz too. Ilya Ilyitch bowed and walked across the room without raising his eyes; just behind the

piano was the screen and the door. He looked up – Olga
sat at the piano, looking at him with great interest. He
fancied she smiled.

'Andrey must have told her I had odd stockings on
yesterday or that my shirt was inside out!' he concluded,
and went home out of spirits, both because of this suspicion and still more of the invitation to dine, which he had
answered with a bow – that is, he had accepted it.

From that moment Olga's persistent gaze never left
Oblomov's mind. It was no use his stretching full length
on his back and lying in the laziest and most comfortable
position – he simply could not go to sleep. His dressing-
gown seemed disgusting to him; Zahar was stupid and
intolerable, dust and cobwebs – unendurable. He ordered
him to take down several wretched pictures, which some
patron friend of poor artists had forced upon him; he
himself put right the blind, which had been out of order
for months, called Anissya and told her to clean the
windows, brushed away the cobwebs, and then lay on his
side and spent an hour thinking of Olga.

At first he carefully considered her appearance and
drew her portrait in his memory. Olga was not a beauty in
the strict sense of the word – that is, her skin was not
dazzling white, her lips and eyes were not vividly coloured, and her eyes did not sparkle with an inward fire;
her lips were not corals or her teeth pearls, nor were her
hands as tiny as those of a child of five with fingers
shaped like grapes, but if she had been turned into a
statue it would have been a model of grace and harmony.
She was rather tall, and her height, the size of her head,
the oval of her face, her shoulders, her waist, were all
perfectly proportioned. Even an absentminded man could
not help stopping for a moment before a creature so nobly
designed and exquisitely made. Her beautifully shaped
nose was slightly aquiline; her fine lips were for the most
part tightly closed – a sign of concentrated thought. Her
keen, wide-awake blue-grey eyes, that never missed
anything, shone, too, with the light of thought. The brows

gave them a peculiar beauty: they were not arched, they had not been thinned out into delicate lines above the eyes; no, they were two brown, fluffy streaks that were almost straight and seldom lay symmetrically – one was the tiniest bit above the other and there was a slight wrinkle above it that seemed to mean something, as though some idea rested there. Olga's head was poised nobly and gracefully on her slender, proud neck, and she walked bending it slightly forward, her whole body moving evenly, her tread so light that it seemed imperceptible. . . .

'Why did she look at me so fixedly yesterday?' Oblomov wondered. 'Andrey swears he did not say anything about the odd stockings or the shirt, but was speaking of his friendship for me, of how we had grown up and been at school together – all the good things, and he said how unhappy I was, how everything fine in me was perishing from lack of sympathy and activity, how feebly the flame of life flickered in me and how. . . . What was there to smile at, anyway?' Oblomov thought. 'If she has a heart it ought to have throbbed or bled with pity, but she . . . well, bless her, I won't think of her! I will go and dine there to-day – and then will not set foot in her house.'

Day followed day, and he not only set foot there, but he transplanted himself altogether. One fine morning Tarantyev moved all his belongings to his friends' house on the Vyborg side and Oblomov spent three days as he had not done for years – without a bed or a sofa, dining with Olga's aunt. It appeared there was a villa to let opposite to theirs. Oblomov hired it without looking at it and settled there. He was with Olga from morning till night; he read to her, sent her flowers, went with her on the lake, on the hills . . . he, Oblomov! Strange things happen in the world! How could it have come to pass? It was like this.

When Stolz and he dined at Olga's, Oblomov suffered the same agonies at dinner as he had done the evening before; he ate and talked, feeling her gaze upon him like sunshine, burning him, exciting him, stirring his nerves, his blood. Only when smoking a cigar on the balcony he managed to hide for a moment from this silent, persistent gaze.

'What does it mean?' he said, turning first to one side then to another. 'It's perfect agony! Why should she laugh at me? She does not look at anyone else in that way – she doesn't dare to. I am quieter than the others and so she . . . I will talk to her!' he decided. 'I will say in words what she is dragging out of my soul with her eyes!'

Suddenly she appeared before him at the balcony door; he gave her a chair and she sat down beside him.

'Is it true that you find life very dull?' she asked him.

'Yes, but not so very. . . . I have something to occupy me.'

'Andrey Ivanitch said you were writing some plan?'

'Yes, I want to go and live in the country, so I am gradually preparing for it.'

'And are you going abroad?'

'Yes, certainly, as soon as Andrey Ivanitch is ready.'

'Are you pleased you are going?' she asked.

'Very much so. . . .'

He looked at her: a smile was all over her face, shining in her eyes, spreading over her cheeks, only her lips were closed. He had not the heart to lie with composure.

'I am a little . . . lazy,' he said, 'but. . . .' He was rather annoyed that she should have so easily, almost silently, extracted from him a confession of laziness. 'What is she to me? Am I afraid of her, or what?' he thought.

'Lazy?' she retorted, with a hardly perceptible slyness. 'Is it possible? How can a man be lazy – I don't understand it.'

'What is there to understand?' he reflected. 'It's simple enough, I should have thought – I sit at home most of the time, that's why Andrey thinks that I. . . .'

'But no doubt you read and write a great deal,' she said. 'Have you read . . . ?'

She was looking at him very intently.

'No, I haven't,' he suddenly blurted out, terrified of her cross-examining him.

'What?' she asked, laughing. He laughed too.

'I thought you were going to ask me about some novel. I don't read them.'

'You've guessed wrong: I was going to ask you about a book of travel.'

He looked at her keenly; her whole face was laughing, but not her lips.

'Oh, she is . . . one must be careful with her,' Oblomov thought.

'What do you read?' she asked curiously.

'It is true I prefer books on travel. . . .'

'To Africa?' she asked softly and roguishly.

He flushed, guessing with good reason that she knew not only what he read, but how he read it.

'Are you a musician?' she asked, to put him at his ease.

At that moment Stolz came up to them.

'Ilya, I have told Olga Sergeyevna that you passionately love music and asked her to sing something . . . *Casta diva*.'

'Why do you slander me?' Oblomov grumbled. 'I certainly don't love music passionately. . . .'

'What a man!' Stolz interrupted. 'He seems offended! I present him as a decent man and he hastens to disillusion you!'

'I merely object to being described as a lover of music: it is a doubtful and a difficult part to play.'

'What music do you like best?' Olga asked.

'It is hard to say – every kind! I may listen with pleasure to a hoarse barrel-organ playing some tune that has remained in my memory, and at other times I can't sit through an opera; Meyerbeer may stir me, or even the bargemen's song: it all depends on the mood! Sometimes one feels like stopping one's ears to Mozart. . . .'

'That means you are really fond of music.'

'Sing something, Olga Sergeyevna,' Stolz asked.

'And what if Mr. Oblomov wants to stop his ears?' she said, turning to him.

'I ought to pay some compliment at this point, but I am no good at it,' Oblomov replied; 'and even if I were, I wouldn't venture to. . . .'

'Why not?'

'But what if you sing badly?' he remarked naïvely. 'I should feel awkward afterwards.'

'As with the biscuits yesterday . . .' she said unexpectedly to herself, and flushed crimson; she would have given anything not to have said it. 'Forgive me – I am sorry!' she said.

Oblomov was taken by surprise – utterly confused.

'It is wicked treachery!' he said in an undertone.

'No, only, perhaps, a slight revenge – and even that quite unpremeditated, I assure you – because you hadn't even a compliment for me.'

'Perhaps I shall have when I hear you.'

'Do you want me to sing?' she asked.

'He wants you to,' Oblomov answered, pointing to Stolz.

'And you?'

He shook his head negatively.

'I cannot want what I do not know.'

'You are rude, Ilya!' Stolz remarked. 'This is what comes of lying at home – having stockings that. . . .'

'Why, Andrey,' Oblomov interrupted him quickly, not letting him finish, 'it's no trouble to me to say, "Oh, I shall be delighted, no doubt you sing admirably," ' he continued, turning to Olga; ' "it will give me the greatest pleasure . . ." and so on. But is it necessary?'

'But you might wish me to sing . . . out of mere curiosity.'

'I daren't, you are not an actress.'

'Well, I will sing for you,' she said to Stolz.

'Ilya, have your compliment ready.'

Meanwhile, evening had come on. The lamp was lit, and it looked like the moon through the vine-covered trellis. The dusk had hidden the outlines of Olga's face and figure and had thrown, as it were, a veil over her; her face was in the shadow; there was only the sound of her mellow but powerful voice with the nervous tremor of feeling in it. She sang many songs and arias at Stolz's request; some expressed sorrow, with a vague presentiment of happiness, others joy, though there was a hidden spring of sadness in the sounds. The words, the music, the pure, strong, girlish voice set the heart throbbing and the nerves quivering, made the eyes shine and fill with tears. One wanted to die listening to the sounds and at the same time was eager for more life. . . . Oblomov was thrilled, overcome; he struggled to hold back his tears and still more to stifle a shout of joy that was ready to escape him. He had not felt for years the courage and strength that seemed now to have risen from the depths of his soul, prompting him to heroic deeds. He would have gone abroad that very minute if all that was left him was to step into the carriage and depart.

In conclusion she sang *Casta diva*; the delight, the thoughts that flashed through his mind like lightning, the shiver of ecstasy that ran through his body, were too much for Oblomov; he was overwhelmed.

'Are you pleased with me to-day?' Olga asked Stolz suddenly, as she finished singing.

'Ask Oblomov what he thinks,' Stolz said.

'Oh!' Oblomov cried out. He suddenly seized Olga's hand, but at once let it go in confusion.

'Excuse me . . .' he muttered.

'Do you hear?' Stolz said. 'Tell me honestly, Ilya, how long is it since you have felt like this?'

'This morning, perhaps, if a raucous barrel-organ passed by your windows . . .' Olga interposed, so gently and kindly that she took the sting out of the sarcasm.

He looked at her reproachfully.

'He still has double windows, so he does not hear what goes on outside,' Stolz said.

Oblomov looked at Stolz reproachfully.

Stolz took Olga's hand.

'I don't know what the reason is, Olga Sergeyevna, but you sang to-night as you have never sung before – at any rate, I haven't heard such singing for years. This is my compliment,' he said, kissing every finger of her hand.

Stolz was going. Oblomov wanted to go too, but Stolz and Olga tried to detain him.

'I have some work to do,' Stolz remarked, 'but you would merely go to lie down . . . and it is still early. . . .'

'Andrey! Andrey!' Oblomov said imploringly. 'No, I cannot stay, I must go,' he added, and went.

He could not sleep all night. Sad and thoughtful he walked up and down the room; he went out at dawn and walked along the Neva and down the streets, hardly knowing what he was thinking and feeling. . . .

Three days later he was at Olga's again, and in the evening, when the other visitors had sat down to play cards, he found himself by the piano, alone with her. Her aunt had a headache; she was sitting in the study sniffing smelling-salts.

'Would you like me to show you the collection of drawings Andrey Ivanitch has brought me from Odessa?' Olga asked. 'He hasn't shown it to you, has he?'

'You seem to feel it your duty as hostess to entertain me?' Oblomov asked. 'You need not!'

'Why not? I don't want you to be bored, I want you to feel at home here, to be comfortable, free, at your ease, so that you shouldn't go away . . . to lie down.'

'She is a cruel, mocking creature,' thought Oblomov, admiring, in spite of himself, her every movement.

'You want me to feel free and at my ease and not be bored?' he asked.

'Yes,' she answered, looking at him as she had done the time before, but with still greater curiosity and kindness.

'In that case, first of all you must not look at me as you are looking now and as you did the other day. . . .'

She looked at him with redoubled curiosity.

'There, that is just the look that makes me very uncomfortable. . . . Where is my hat?'

'But why uncomfortable?' she asked softly, and no longer looked curious, but merely kind and friendly.

'I don't know; I seem to feel as though with that look you extracted from me all that I don't want other people to know – and you especially.'

'Why? You are Andrey Ivanitch's friend and he is mine, so that ——'

'So that there is no reason why you should know about me all that Andrey Ivanitch knows,' he finished.

'There is no reason, but there is a chance. . . .'

'Owing to my friend's indiscretion – a bad service on his part!'

'Why, have you any secrets?' she asked. 'Crimes, perhaps?' she added, laughing and drawing away from him.

'Perhaps!' he answered, with a sigh.

'Yes, it is a great crime,' she said softly and timidly, 'to wear odd stockings. . . .'

Oblomov seized his hat.

'I can't stand it!' he said. 'And you want me to be at my ease! I won't love Andrey any more. . . . He has told you that too?'

'He did make me laugh so about it to-day,' Olga said. 'He always makes me laugh. Forgive me, I won't, I won't, and I will try to look at you differently. . . .'

She made a roguishly serious face. 'All this is in the first place,' she went on. 'Well, now, I don't look at you as I did yesterday, so you must be feeling comfortable and at your ease. Now what must I do in the second place so that you shouldn't be bored?'

He was looking straight into her grey-blue, friendly eyes.

'Now you, too, are looking at me strangely . . .' she said.

He really was looking at her not, as it were, with his eyes, but with his thought, with his whole will, like a hypnotizer, yet he did so involuntarily, could not resist looking. 'My goodness, how pretty she is! To think of anyone being so pretty!' he thought, looking at her almost in alarm. 'This white skin, these eyes, dark as deep pools, and yet there is a light in them – of the soul, beyond doubt! One can read her smile like a book; it shows such beautiful teeth . . . and her whole head . . . how tenderly it rests on her shoulders, swaying like a flower, breathing with fragrance! . . . Yes, I am drawing something from her,' he thought, 'something passes from her into me. There, my heart is beginning to throb and surge. . . . I have a new sensation there. . . . Oh dear, what a joy it is to look at her, it takes my breath away! . . .'

These thoughts were whirling through his mind and he went on gazing at her as one gazes into endless distance, into a bottomless abyss, with delight and self-oblivion.

'Come, Mr. Oblomov, see how you are looking at me now!' she said shyly, turning away, but she was too interested to keep her eyes off his face.

He heard nothing. He gazed at her without hearing her words, silently taking stock of what was passing within him; he touched his head – it, too, was in a turmoil. He could not catch his thoughts – they had flown away like a flock of birds and there seemed to be a pain in his left side, by the heart.

'Don't look at me so strangely,' she said. 'I, too, feel awkward. . . . I expect you also want to extract something from me?'

'What can it be?' he asked mechanically.

'I, too, have *plans*, begun and unfinished,' she said. He was brought to himself by this hint about his unfinished plan.

'It is strange,' he said, 'You are malicious, but your eyes are kind. It's not for nothing people say that women are not to be trusted: they lie both intentionally with their tongue and unintentionally with their eyes, their smile, the colour of their cheeks, even with fainting fits. . . .'

She did not allow the impression to grow stronger, gently took his hat from him and sat down.

'I won't, I won't,' she said quickly. 'Forgive me, my tongue is my enemy! But I swear I wasn't mocking you!' she almost sang, and her voice trembled with feeling.

Oblomov was reassured.

'That Andrey!' he said reproachfully.

'Well, in the second place, tell me what must I do so that you shouldn't be bored?'

'Sing!' he said.

'There, that is the compliment I have been waiting for!' she cried, flushing with joy. 'Do you know,' she continued with animation, 'if you hadn't said "Oh!" in the way you did after my singing that evening, I think I could not have slept. I should have cried, perhaps.'

'Why?' Oblomov asked in surprise.

She pondered.

'I don't know, myself,' she said, after a pause.

'You are proud, that's what it is.'

'Yes, of course,' she said thoughtfully, touching the keys with one hand, 'but then everyone has pride and very much so. Andrey Ivanitch says that pride and ambition are the only motives that stir people's will. I expect you haven't any and that's why you. . . .'

She broke off.

'What?' he asked.

'No, nothing.' She changed the subject. 'I love Andrey Ivanitch, not only because he amuses me – sometimes his words make me cry – and not because he loves me, but I believe because . . . he loves me more than he does others . . . you see how pride comes in!'

'You love Andrey?' Oblomov asked, looking fixedly and searchingly into her eyes.

'Yes, of course, if he loves me more than others it's only natural I should,' she answered seriously.

Oblomov gazed at her in silence, she answered him with a simple, silent look.

'He loves Anna Vassilyevna too, and Zinaida Mihailovna, but not so much as me,' she went on. 'He won't sit with them for two hours on end, making them laugh or

telling them his thoughts; he talks about business, about
the theatre, the news, but to me he talks as to a sister . . .
no, as to a daughter,' she added hastily. 'Sometimes he
scolds me if I don't understand or agree with him or do as
he tells me; but he does not scold them, and I think I love
him all the more because of it. Pride!' she added thoughtfully. 'But I don't know how it could come into my singing. I have often been complimented on it, and you
wouldn't even listen to me, you were made to almost by
force. And if you had gone away without saying a word to
me, if I hadn't noticed anything in your face . . . I believe
I should have been ill! . . . Yes, it certainly was pride!' she
concluded decisively.

'And what did you notice in my face?' he asked.

'Tears, although you concealed them; it's a bad habit
with men to be ashamed of their heart. That is false
pride. They had better be sometimes ashamed of their
intellect – it goes astray more often. Even Andrey Ivanitch
is ashamed of his heart. I told him and he agreed. And
you?'

'One would agree with anything as one looked at you!'
he said.

'Another compliment, and such a. . . .'

She was at a loss for a word.

'Vulgar one!' Oblomov finished, not taking his eyes off
her.

She smiled assent.

'That was just what I feared when I would not ask you
to sing. . . . What can one say, after hearing a singer for
the first time? And yet one has to say something. It is
difficult to be intelligent and sincere at the same time,
especially about one's feelings, when one is so impressed
as I was then. . . .'

'I really did sing then as I had not done for years, perhaps as I had never done. . . . Don't ask me, I shall not be
able to sing so again. . . . Wait, though, I will sing just one
thing. . . .' she said. Her face seemed to light up, her eyes
shone; she struck two or three chords and began.

Oh, how much there was in her singing! Hope, vague fear of storms, the storms breaking out, the rush of happiness – all this could be heard, not in the song, but in her voice. She sang on and on, turning to him at times to ask like a child: 'Had enough? No, just this then!' and went on singing. Her cheeks and ears were burning with excitement, sometimes her girlish face reflected the lightning play of emotion, a ray of passion as mature as though in her heart she were living through what a distant future held for her; and then this momentary ray suddenly faded again and her voice once more was fresh and silvery. There was the same play of life in Oblomov; he felt as though he had been living through all this and feeling it, not for the last hour or two, but for years. . . . Both, though outwardly motionless, were rent by an inward fire, shaken by the same tremor; the tears in their eyes were called forth by a similar mood. It was all a token of the passions which were bound one day to spring up in her young soul, disturbed as yet only by the faint and fleeting stirrings of the life force slumbering in her. She finished on a long-drawn-out note and her voice died away. She stopped, tired suddenly, put her hands on her knees, and, deeply moved and excited, herself looked at Oblomov to see what he was feeling. His face was radiant with happiness that had dawned in the very depths of his soul; his eyes, brimming with tears, were fixed upon her.

This time it was she who took his hand unconsciously. 'What is it?' she asked him. 'Why do you look like that?'

But she knew why, and in her mind she triumphed modestly, enjoying this testimony to her power.

'Look at yourself in the glass,' she went on with a smile, pointing to his reflection in the mirror. 'Your eyes are shining. Why, there are tears in them! How deeply you feel music!'

'No, it isn't music I feel . . . it's . . . love!' Oblomov said softly.

She instantly let go his hand and changed colour. Their eyes met: his almost frenzied gaze was fixed upon her; it was not Oblomov but passion itself looked at her. Olga understood that his words had escaped him involuntarily and that they were true.

He came to himself, picked up his hat, and ran out of the room without turning round. She did not follow him with questioning eyes; she stood for several minutes by the piano, motionless as a statue, her eyes fixed on the ground, her bosom heaving.

VI

WHENEVER Oblomov lay idly absorbed in drowsy stupor or in flights of fancy, in the foreground of his dreams always stood a woman – his wife, never his mistress. In his dreams he saw the image of a tall, graceful woman, with gentle yet proud eyes and a dreamy expression, her head gracefully poised on her shoulders, her arms serenely folded on her breast as she sat in an easy attitude among the creepers on the balcony or stepped lightly on the carpets or on the sandy avenues, her waist swaying as she walked; she was his ideal, the embodiment of a whole life filled with ease and serene repose, she was peace itself. He dreamed of her first at the altar wearing a long veil and wreathed in flowers, at the head of the marriage-bed with her eyes shyly cast down, then as a mother among a group of children. He dreamed of her smile, not a smile of passion, but of sympathetic understanding for him, her husband, and of indulgence for others; he dreamed of her eyes, not moist with passion, but kind only to him and shy, even severe, to others. He never wanted to see tremors in her, to hear of ardent dreams, of sudden tears, of longings, languors, and then frenzied outbursts of joy. He did not want moonlight and melancholy. She was not to turn pale suddenly, to faint, to feel overwhelming emotions. . . . 'Women of that sort have lovers,' he used to say, 'and they are a lot of trouble too: doctors, watering-places, and no end of caprices. One couldn't sleep in peace!' But a man could sleep care-free beside a wife who was modest, proud, and serene. He could go to sleep confident that on waking he would meet the same gentle and kind gaze. In twenty or thirty years' time, in response to his affectionate look, there would be the same soft and gentle ray of sympathy in her eyes. And so it would be to their dying day! 'Is it not the secret aim of every man and woman to find in their friend unchanging repose, an even and abiding flow of feeling? That is the norm of love, and if there is any deviation from it, any coldness or change – we suffer; so, then, my ideal is the common ideal of all,' he thought. 'Is it not the crowning conception, the supreme solution of the relations of the sexes? To give passion a legitimate outlet, to let it flow in a certain direction like a river for the benefit of the whole country, is the problem of all humanity; the solution of it is the pinnacle of progress towards which all these advanced people are striving, although they perpetually go astray. Once it is solved there can be no unfaithfulness, no cooling down, but only everlasting moral health, the even beating of a calm and happy heart and therefore a life that is for ever rich and full. There are cases of such blessedness, but they are rare; they are pointed out as a marvel. People say one must be born for it. But who knows, perhaps one ought to be educated for it and seek it consciously. . . . Passion! It is all very well in poems and on the stage, where actors with knives walk about in cloaks and afterwards the murderers and the murdered go and have supper together. . . . It would be a good thing if passions ended like that, too, but they leave nothing but smoke and stench behind and no happiness, and the memories are nothing but shame and despair. And if such a misfortune did happen and one were possessed by passion it would be like finding oneself on a rough, hilly, bumpy road where horses slip and the rider is exhausted, but the native village is already in sight: one must keep it in view and make desperate haste to leave the dangerous spot. . . . Yes, passion must be limited, stifled, and destroyed by marriage.'

Oblomov would have run away in horror from a woman who suddenly shot an ardent glance at him, or fell groaning on his shoulder with her eyes closed and then, coming to herself, tightly wound her arms round his neck. . . . That would be like a firework, like the explosion of a barrel of gunpowder – and deafness, blindness, and singed hair would be the result.

But let us see what kind of woman Olga was.

She and Oblomov did not see each other alone for some days after his avowal. He hid like a schoolboy the moment he caught sight of Olga. She had changed to him, though she did not avoid him and was not cold with him; she had merely grown quieter. She seemed to be sorry that something had happened which prevented her from tormenting Oblomov by her inquisitive gaze and mocking good-humouredly at his indolence, his staying in bed, his clumsiness. . . . She enjoyed making fun of him, but it was the mockery of a mother who cannot help smiling when she sees her son's comical dress. Stolz had gone away and she missed having no one to whom she could sing; her piano was shut up – in short, they both felt constrained and awkward. And how well they had got on at first! How simply they had come to know each other! How easily they had made friends! Oblomov was simpler and kinder than Stolz; it was true he did not amuse her as well, though he amused her by being what he was and forgave her mockery so easily. Besides, when Stolz went he left Oblomov in her charge, asking her to keep an eye on him and prevent him from sitting at home. She had devised, in her pretty, clever head, a detailed plan of how she would break Oblomov of the habit of sleeping after dinner, and would not allow him to lie down in the day-time: she would make him promise. She dreamed of how she would tell him to read the books Stolz had left, to read the papers every day and tell the news to her, to write letters to the country, to finish his plan of estate management, to get ready to go abroad – in short, she would not let him drowse; she would hold up a purpose before him, make him love once more the things to which he had grown indifferent, and Stolz would not recognize him when he came back. She, the shy, silent Olga, who had not yet begun to live and whom, so far, no one obeyed, would work the miracle! She would be the cause of the transformation! It had begun already: Oblomov had changed as soon as he heard her sing. . . . He would live and work, bless life and her. To restore a man to life! What praise was lavished on a doctor who saved a hopeless invalid! And what about saving a mind and soul that were perishing morally? . . . A tremor of joy and pride ran through her; she thought it was a task appointed her from heaven. In her mind she made him her secretary, her librarian. And now suddenly it was all to come to an end! She did not know what she ought to do and so was silent when she met Oblomov.

Oblomov was tortured by the thought that he had shocked and offended her, and, expecting lightning-like glances and cold severity, trembled and turned aside whenever he saw her at a distance. Meanwhile, he had already moved to the summer villa, and for three days on end went by himself across the marsh to the forest or walked to the village and sat idly by some cottage gate, watching the children run about and the ducks dive and swim in the pond. Close to the villa there was a lane and a huge park: he was afraid to go there for fear of meeting Olga by herself. 'Whatever induced me to blurt it out!' he thought, without even asking himself whether his words were true or merely due to the momentary effect of the music on his nerves. The feeling of awkwardness, shame, or 'disgrace,' as he called it, prevented him from analysing his outburst or from asking what Olga was to him. He no longer questioned himself what it was that had entered his heart – a kind of lump that had not been there before. All his feelings were merged into one overwhelming load of shame. But when for a moment Olga appeared before his imagination, there rose at the same time that other image, that ideal of incarnate peace, life, happiness: it was exactly like Olga! The two images drew nearer and nearer together and merged into one. 'Oh, what have I done!' he said. 'I have ruined it all! Thank God that Stolz has gone: she has not had time to tell him, or I should have been ready to sink through the ground! Love, tears – it's not in my line at all! Olga's aunt hasn't sent me a message or invited me: Olga must have told her. . . . Oh, my God!'

This was what he thought as he walked into the depths of the park, down a side avenue.

The only difficulty Olga felt was how she should meet him: ought she to say something, or to behave as though nothing had happened? But what was she to say? Should she make a stern face, look at him proudly, or not look at all, but remark dryly and haughtily that 'she never expected it of him; whom did he take her for that he was so impertinent?' That was how Sonitchka, during a mazurka, answered a sub-lieutenant, although she had taken a great deal of trouble to turn his head. 'But is it an impertinence?' she asked herself. 'If he really feels it, why shouldn't he say it? . . . But how could that be? So suddenly, he hardly knows me. . . . No one else would have said such a thing seeing a woman for the third time in his life; and no one would have fallen in love so soon. Only an Oblomov could. . . .' But then she recalled she had read and heard that love sometimes comes suddenly. 'He was carried away, it was a sudden rush of feeling; now he doesn't come near me: he is ashamed, so it wasn't an impertinence. And whose fault is it?' she wondered. Andrey Ivanitch's, of course, because he made her sing. But Oblomov did not want to listen at first – she was vexed and she . . . tried . . . (she blushed violently) – yes, she did her utmost to rouse him. Stolz had said that he was apathetic, that nothing interested him, that all was dead within him. . . . So she wanted to see whether it really was so, and she sang . . . sang as she had never done before. . . .

'Oh, dear, it was my fault: I must ask him to forgive me. . . . What for, though?' she asked herself. 'What am I to tell him? "Mr. Oblomov, I am to blame, I tried to attract you." . . . What a disgrace! It isn't true,' she cried, flushing and stamping her foot. 'Who would dare to think such a thing? . . . How could I know what would happen? And if it hadn't happened, if the words hadn't escaped him, what then? I don't know,' she thought. Ever since that evening she had had a queer feeling in her heart . . .

she must have been very much offended . . . she felt positively feverish and her cheeks were flushed. . . . 'Nervous
irritation . . . a slight fever,' the doctor had said. 'It's all
Oblomov's doing! Oh, I must teach him a lesson so that it
doesn't happen again! I'll ask *ma tante* to refuse him the
house: he mustn't forget himself . . . how did he dare!' she
thought, as she walked in the park, her eyes flashing.

Suddenly she heard someone coming.

'There's someone coming,' Oblomov thought.

And they met face to face.

'Olga Sergeyevna!' he said, shaking like an aspen-leaf.

'Ilya Ilyitch!' she answered timidly, and they both
stopped.

'Good morning,' he said.

'Good morning,' she answered.

'Where are you going?' he asked.

'Nowhere in particular,' she answered, not raising her
eyes.

'I don't disturb you?'

'Oh, not at all,' she answered, glancing at him quickly
and curiously.

'May I come with you?' he asked suddenly, with a
searching glance at her.

They walked along the path in silence. Neither the
teacher's ruler nor the director's eyebrows had ever made
Oblomov's heart thump as it was doing now. He wanted
to say something and tried hard to speak, but his tongue
would not move; only his heart was beating frantically, as
though in dread of a misfortune.

'Have you had a letter from Andrey Ivanitch?' she
asked.

'Yes, I have.'

'What does he say?'

'He urges me to come to Paris.'

'And what are you going to do?'

'I shall go.'

'When?'

'Later on . . . no, to-morrow . . . as soon as I am ready.'

'Why so soon?' she asked.

He did not answer.

'Don't you like your villa or . . . tell me, why do you want to go?' Insolent creature, wanting to go away into the bargain! she thought.

'Something is making me wretched, awkward . . . tormenting me,' he said in a whisper, without looking at her.

She was silent. Then she picked a spray of lilac and buried her face in it, sniffing it.

'Doesn't it smell delicious,' she said, covering his nose with it too.

'And here are some lilies of the valley! Wait, I'll pick you some,' he said, bending down to the grass, 'they smell better, of fields, of woods; there is more nature about them. And lilac always grows close to houses, the branches thrust themselves in at the windows and the smell is too sweet. Look, the lilies of the valley are still wet with the dew.'

He gave her several of them.

'And do you like mignonette?' she asked.

'No, the smell is too strong; I don't care either for roses or for mignonette. And altogether I don't care for flowers; in the fields they are well enough, but indoors they mean a lot of trouble . . . such a litter. . . .'

'And you like to have your rooms clean?' she asked, looking at him roguishly. 'You can't bear to have any litter about?'

'No; but I have such a servant . . .' he muttered. 'Oh, wicked one!' he added to himself.

'Will you go straight to Paris?' she asked.

'Yes; Stolz has been expecting me for some time.'

'Take a letter for me; I am going to write to him.'

'Give it to me to-day; I am moving to town to-morrow.'

'To-morrow?' she asked. 'Why so soon? It's as though you were being driven away.'

'I am. . . .'

'How?'

'By shame . . .' he whispered.

'Shame!' she repeated mechanically, and thought: 'Now I will tell him. Mr. Oblomov, I never expected. . . .'

'Yes, Olga Sergeyevna,' he brought himself at last to say, 'I imagine you are surprised . . . angry. . . .'

'Now is the time . . . this is the moment.' Her heart throbbed. 'Oh dear, I cannot!'

He tried to peep into her face and discover what she felt, but she was sniffing the lilac and the lilies of the valley, not knowing herself what she was feeling . . . what she ought to say and do. 'Sonitchka would have thought of something at once, but I am so silly! I can never do the right thing . . .' she thought desperately.

'I had quite forgotten . . .' she said.

'Believe me, I couldn't help it . . . it escaped me,' he began, gradually growing bolder. 'If a thunderbolt had fallen, if a stone had crashed down beside me, I should have still said it. No power could have held me back. . . . For God's sake, don't think that I wanted. . . . A minute later I would have given anything to take back the rash word. . . .'

She walked with her head bowed, sniffing the flowers.

'Forget it,' he continued, 'forget it, especially since it was not true. . . .'

'Not true?' she repeated, suddenly raising her head and dropping the flowers.

Her eyes opened wide and there was a gleam of surprise in them.

'How not true?' she repeated once more.

'Yes, for Heaven's sake, forget it, and don't be angry. I assure you I was simply carried away for a moment . . . because of the music. . . .'

'Only because of the music!'

She changed colour; her cheeks were no longer flushed and the light had gone out of her eyes.

'There, it's all gone! He has taken back his rash words and there is no need to be angry! . . . All is well, now. . . . There is nothing to worry about. . . . We can talk and joke as before . . .' she thought, and as she walked she tugged at a branch, broke it off, bit a leaf, and immediately threw down on the path both the branch and the leaf.

'You are not angry? You have forgotten?' Oblomov said, bending over her.

'But what is it? What do you want of me?' she answered nervously, almost with vexation, turning away from him. 'I have forgotten all about it. . . . I have no memory!'

He said nothing and did not know what to do. He saw her sudden vexation, but did not see the cause of it.

'Oh dear,' she thought, 'everything is put right, that scene has been wiped out, thank Heaven! What then. . . . Oh dear, what does it mean? Ah, you lucky Sonitchka!'

'I am going home,' she said suddenly, quickening her steps and turning into another avenue.

There was a lump in her throat. She was afraid she would cry.

'That's not the way, this is nearer,' Oblomov observed. 'Fool,' he said to himself dejectedly, 'much good it was having an explanation! Now I have offended her all the more. I ought not to have reminded her: it would have gone off of itself and been forgotten. There is nothing for it, I must beg her forgiveness.'

'I suppose I am so vexed,' she thought, 'because I have not had time to say to him, "Mr. Oblomov, I never thought that you would presume. . . ." He has forestalled me. . . . "Not true!" So he was lying into the bargain, if you please! How dared he?'

'Is it true you have forgotten?' he asked in a lower voice.

'Yes, everything,' she said hurriedly, anxious to get home.

'Give me your hand to show you are not angry.'

Without looking at him she gave him the tips of her fingers and drew her hand away the moment he touched them.

'No, you are angry!' he said with a sigh. 'How can I assure you that it was an aberration, that I would never have presumed? . . . No, that's the end of it, I will not listen to your singing any more. . . .'

'You need not assure me: I don't want your protestations . . .' she said quickly. 'I won't sing, in any case.'

'Very well, I will say nothing, only for Heaven's sake don't go away like this, or there will be such a load on my heart. . . .'

She walked slowly, listening intently to his words.

'If it's true that you would have wept if I hadn't cried out after your singing, this time, I . . . if you go away like this, without smiling, without holding out your hand to me in a friendly way . . . have pity on me, Olga Sergeyevna! I shall be ill. My knees tremble, I can hardly stand. . . .'

'Why?' she asked suddenly, glancing at him.

'I don't know myself,' he said. 'The shame is gone now: I am not ashamed of my words. . . . I think they were —'

Again he felt a shiver in his heart, again a kind of lump was there, again her kind and curious gaze began to burn him. She had turned to him so gracefully, was watching for his answer so anxiously.

'They were — what?' she asked impatiently.

'No, I am afraid to say it: you will be angry again.'

'Tell me!' she said imperatively.

He was silent.

'Well?'

'I again want to shed tears as I look at you. . . . You see, I have no pride, I am not ashamed of my feelings. . . .'

'But why shed tears?' she asked gently, and the colour came back to her cheeks.

'I keep hearing your voice . . . I again feel. . . .'

'What?' she asked, and there was no longer a lump in her throat; she was tense with expectation.

They came up to her house.

'I feel . . .' Oblomov was in a hurry to finish, but kept stopping.

She was going up the steps slowly and as it were with difficulty.

'The same music . . . the same . . . emotion . . . the same . . . feel — Forgive me, forgive me – really, I cannot help it. . . .'

'Mr. Oblomov . . .' she began sternly, but suddenly her face lit up with a smile, 'I am not angry, I forgive you,' she added gently, 'only in the future. . . .'

Without turning round she stretched out a hand to him; he seized it and kissed her palm; she softly pressed it to his lips and instantly disappeared behind the glass door while he remained rooted to the spot.

VII

HE gazed after her open-eyed, open-mouthed, then looked vaguely at the bushes. . . . Some strangers walked by, a bird flew past. A peasant woman going by asked him if he wanted some strawberries, but his stupor continued. He walked slowly down the same avenue, and in the middle of it came across the lilies of the valley and the lilac branch she had plucked and thrown down in vexation. 'Why had she done it? . . .' he wondered, recalling it all. 'Idiot that I am!' he said aloud suddenly, seizing the flowers and the branch, and he almost ran down the avenue. 'I begged her forgiveness, and she. . . . Oh, can it be true? . . . What an idea!' Happy and radiant, 'a crescent moon over the brows,' as his nurse used to say, he came home, sat down in the corner of the sofa and quickly wrote in big letters on the dusty surface of the table: 'Olga.' 'Oh, what dust!' he remarked, recovering from his delight. 'Zahar, Zahar!' He shouted for some time, because Zahar was sitting with some coachmen by the gate that faced the road.

'Come along,' Anissya said in a menacing whisper, pulling him by the sleeve, 'master has been calling you for I don't know how long!'

'Look, Zahar, what's this?' Ilya Ilyitch said gently and kindly: he could not be angry just then. 'You want to have dust and cobwebs here too? No, you must excuse me, I won't have it! Olga Sergeyevna gives me no peace as it is: "You like dirt," she says.'

'It's all very well for her to talk, they have five servants,' Zahar said, turning to the door.

'Where are you off to? Take a brush and dust the room: one can't sit down here or lean on the table. . . . It's disgusting, you know, it's . . . Oblomovism!'

Zahar turned sulkily and looked at his master sideways. 'There now,' he thought, 'he's invented one more high-flown word! And yet it sounds familiar!'

'Well, why don't you do as I tell you?' Oblomov asked.

'What's the good? I've swept the floor to-day,' Zahar answered obstinately.

'Where does the dust come from, if you have swept the room? There, do you see? I won't have it! You must clean the place at once.'

'I did clean it,' Zahar repeated. 'I can't sweep ten times a day! And the dust comes from the road . . . the fields are near, it's a summer villa; there is a lot of dust in the road.'

'I'll tell you what, Zahar Trofimitch,' Anissya began, suddenly peeping out of the other room, 'it's a mistake to sweep first and brush the furniture afterwards: the floor gets dusty again. . . . You ought first to. . . .'

'You've come to teach me, have you?' Zahar hissed furiously. 'Go back to your place!'

'I never heard of such a thing – sweeping the floor first and then brushing the tables! No wonder the master is angry. . . .'

'Now then!' he shouted, aiming with his elbow at her breast.

She smiled and disappeared. Oblomov motioned Zahar to go out too. He put his head on the embroidered cushion, put his hand to his heart and listened to its throbbing.

'It must be bad for me,' he said to himself. 'What's to be done? If I ask the doctor's advice he may send me to Abyssinia!'

Before Zahar and Anissya were married they did their own work without interfering with each other: Anissya did the cooking and marketing and took part in cleaning the rooms only once a year, when the floors were scrubbed. But after her marriage she had easier access to her master's rooms. She helped Zahar and the place was cleaner; she took some of her husband's duties upon herself, partly of her own will and partly because Zahar despotically laid them upon her. 'Here, beat this carpet,' he hissed imperatively, or, 'You'd better sort out those things in the corner and take what isn't wanted to the kitchen.' This happy state of things lasted for about a month: the rooms were clean, his master did not grumble or say any 'heart-rending' words, and Zahar had nothing to do. But the happiness came to an end – and this was why. As soon as Anissya and he began looking after Oblomov's rooms together, everything Zahar did proved to be stupid. Every step he took was all wrong. He had lived in the world for fifty-five years in the conviction that nothing he did could be done better or differently. And suddenly, now, Anissya proved to him within a fortnight that he was good for nothing, and she did it with mortifying condescension and gentleness, as though he were a child or a perfect fool, actually smiling as she looked at him. 'It's a mistake, Zahar Trofimitch, to open the windows after shutting the flues,' she said kindly, 'the room gets cold at once.' 'When should I open them, you think?' he asked, with the rudeness of a husband. 'When you light the stove: the stale air will be drawn away and the room will be warm,' she answered softly. 'You stupid!' he said. 'I have done it my way for twenty years and am not likely to change for you. . . .' He kept on the same shelf in the cupboard: tea, sugar, lemon, silver, blacking, brushes, and soap. He came home one day and found that the soap was lying on the washing-stand, the blacking and brushes on the kitchen window, the tea and the sugar in a separate drawer. 'What do you mean upsetting my things, eh?' he asked menacingly. 'I have put it all together on purpose to have everything handy and you have shoved it all into different corners!' 'It's so that tea shouldn't smell of soap,' she remarked gently. Another time she pointed out to him two or three moth holes in Oblomov's clothes and said that he must be sure to shake and brush the clothes once a week. 'Let me brush the coat,' she said kindly, in conclusion. He snatched from her both the brush and the coat and hung the coat back in the wardrobe. When one day he began complaining as usual that his master blamed him for the beetles although 'he hadn't invented them,' Anissya, without a word, cleared from the shelves the pieces and crumbs of black bread that had been lying there from times immemorial, swept out and washed all the cupboards and crockery – and the beetles almost completely disappeared. Zahar still failed to grasp what it all meant and put it down to her zeal for work. But one day, when he dropped two glasses off a tray he was carrying and, swearing as usual, was about to throw the whole tray on the floor, Anissya took it from him, replaced the glasses, put the bread and the sugar-basin on the tray and, arranging it so that not a cup moved, showed him how to pick up the tray with one hand and hold it firmly with the other; she walked up and down the room, turning the tray to left and to right, and not a single spoon stirred – and Zahar suddenly saw clearly that Anissya was cleverer than he! He snatched the tray from her, dropped the glasses, and could never forgive her for it. 'You see, that's the way to do it,' she added gently. He looked at her with stupid haughtiness, and she actually smiled.

'So you are trying to be clever, you wretched peasant woman! Why, don't you know what our house at Oblomovka was like? I had fifteen footmen and pages under me, to say nothing of other servants! And you women were so many one didn't know you by name. . . . And now you presume . . . you! . . .'

'I mean it for the best,' she began.

'Now then,' he hissed, raising his elbow menacingly, 'clear out of the master's rooms! The kitchen is the place for you women.'

She smiled and walked away while he gloomily looked after her out of the corner of his eye. His pride suffered and he was sulky with Anissya. When, however, Ilya Ilyitch asked for something that could not be found, or had been broken, or generally when things went wrong and a storm, accompanied by 'heart-rending words,' gathered over Zahar's head, Zahar winked at Anissya, nodded towards Oblomov's study, and, pointing to it with his thumb, commanded in a whisper, 'You go to the master; what does he want?' Anissya went, and the storm resolved itself into a simple explanation. As soon as Oblomov began to talk pathetically, Zahar suggested calling in Anissya. Oblomov's rooms would have reverted to their original condition had it not been for Anissya: she considered herself now as belonging to the Oblomov household, and felt as indissolubly connected with Ilya Ilyitch's person, life, and house as her husband. Her feminine eye kept careful watch over the desolate rooms. As soon as Zahar was out of the way Anissya dusted the tables and sofas, opened the window, set the blinds right, put away the boots left in the middle of the room and the trousers thrown on an arm-chair, looked through all the clothes, put in order the papers, pencils, penknife, and pens on the table, remade the crumpled bed – and did all in the twinkling of an eye; then she glanced round the room, moved a chair, shut a half-open drawer, took a napkin off the table, and slipped into the kitchen the moment she heard Zahar's creaking boots. She was a quick, lively woman of about forty-seven, with a smile that betrayed an anxiety to please, eyes that darted rapidly from side to side, a firm neck and breast, and red, tenacious, never weary hands. She had hardly any face to speak of: the nose was the only noticeable feature of it; it was small, but it seemed to stand out as though it had not been properly fixed; the end of it was turned up and made the rest of her face not noticeable; it was so thin and faded that one gained a clear idea of the nose before observing her other features.

There are many husbands like Zahar in the world. A diplomatist will sometimes carelessly listen to his wife's advice, shrug his shoulders, and secretly write what she told him. A Government official will whistle and make a contemptuous grimace at his wife's chatter about some important affair – and the next day he will solemnly repeat this chatter to the Minister. These gentlemen treat their wives morosely or lightly, despising them, like Zahar, as mere women, or regarding them as a pleasant relaxation from the serious life of business.

The bright midday sun had long been scorching the paths in the park. Most people were sitting in the shade of the canvas awnings and only groups of nurses and children boldly walked or sat on the grass in the sunshine. Oblomov still lay on the sofa, believing and disbelieving the meaning of his conversation with Olga that morning. 'She loves me, she cares for me. Is it possible? She dreams of me; it was for me she sang so passionately, and music has made us feel the same!' Pride was sweetly stirring within him, life was suddenly aglow with light and colour, and a magic vista opened before him. He saw himself with her, abroad, on the lakes in Switzerland, in Italy, walking among the ruins in Rome, riding in a gondola, then lost in a crowd in Paris and London, then . . . then in his earthly paradise, Oblomovka. She is adorable with her charming prattle, her exquisite, fair-skinned face, her fine slender neck . . . the peasants have never seen anyone like her; they fall at the angel's feet. Softly treading on the grass, she walks with him in the shadow of the birch copse; she sings to him. . . . He is conscious of the gentle flow of life, of the delicious splashing of its stream . . . he is thought-ful because of the fullness of his happiness, of the complete realization of his desires. . . .

Suddenly his face clouded.

'No, that cannot be!' he said aloud, getting up from the sofa and pacing up and down the room. 'To love an absurd creature like me, with sleepy eyes and flabby cheeks. . . . She must be laughing at me. . . .'

He stopped before the mirror and examined himself, disapproving, but presently his eyes cleared; he actually smiled.

'I seem to look better, fresher than I did in town,' he said, 'and my eyes are not dull. . . . I was beginning to have a stye, but it has gone off. . . . I expect it's because of the air here; I walk a lot, don't drink any wine, don't lie down in the daytime. . . . There is no need for me to go to Egypt. . . .'

A servant from Olga's aunt brought him an invitation to dinner.

'I am coming,' said Oblomov.

The servant turned to go.

'Wait, here is something for you!'

He gave him some money.

He felt gay and light-hearted. The day was so sunny. The people were kind, everyone was enjoying himself and looking happy. Zahar alone was gloomy and kept looking at his master sideways, but Anissya smiled good-humouredly. 'I'll keep a dog,' Oblomov decided, 'or, better, a cat . . . cats purr and are affectionate.'

He ran off to Olga's.

'But then . . . Olga loves me!' he thought on the way. 'She, so young, so fresh! The most poetic aspect of life is now open to her imagination: she must be dreaming of tall, graceful youths with black curly hair and a proud smile, with that melting and trembling light in the eye which so easily touches the heart, a fresh and gentle voice that sounds like a harp-string and an expression of thoughtful, hidden power and courage in their faces. Though, indeed, a woman may love other things than youth, courage, good dancing, and clever riding. . . . Olga is not an ordinary girl who can't resist the sight of a moustache or the clank of a sword; but then, one must have other things . . . intelligence, for instance, so that a woman could humble herself before it and bow down to it as the rest of the world does. . . . Or one must be a famous artist. . . . But what am I? Oblomov – and nothing more. Stolz, now, is different; Stolz has intelligence, character, he knows how to rule himself and others, how to order life. Wherever he comes, he seems to gain possession of all the people he meets and to play on them as on an instrument. . . . And I? . . . I can't manage Zahar even . . . nor myself. . . . I am an Oblomov! Stolz! Good heavens! . . . she loves him,' he thought in terror, 'she told me so herself; she loves him as a friend, she says; but it is a lie, perhaps an unconscious one. . . . There is no such thing as friendship between man and woman. . . .' He walked slower and slower, possessed by doubt. 'What if she is merely playing with me? . . . If only. . . .' He stopped and stood stark still for a moment. 'What if it is perfidy, a plot. . . . And whatever made me imagine that she loves me? She never said so: it was just the diabolical prompting of vanity! Andrey, can it be? . . . No, it cannot: she is so. . . . This is what she is!' he said joyfully, seeing Olga walking to meet him.

Smiling gaily, Olga gave him her hand. 'No, she is not like that, she is not deceitful,' he decided; 'deceitful women don't look so kind, don't laugh so candidly . . . they squeak so affectedly. But . . . she hasn't said that she loves me,' he suddenly thought again in alarm: it was his own interpretation. . . . 'But, then, why should she have been vexed? . . . Oh, dear, what a quagmire I am in!'

'What have you there?' she asked.

'A branch.'

'What branch?'

'You can see for yourself: it's lilac.'

'Where did you pick it? There is no lilac on the path you have come by.'

'You plucked it and threw it away.'

'Why did you pick it up?'

'Oh, I was pleased at your . . . throwing it away in vexation.'

'Pleased at my being vexed – that's something new! Why?'

'I won't tell you.'

'Oh, please, do tell me!'

'Not for anything in the world!'

'I implore you!'

He shook his head.

'And if I sing?'

'Then . . . perhaps. . . .'

'So music alone has an effect on you?' she said, frowning. 'It's true, then?'

'Yes, music interpreted by you.'

'Very well, I will sing . . . *Casta diva; Casta di . . .*' she sounded the first notes of Norma's invocation and stopped. 'Well, tell me now!' she said.

He hesitated.

'No, no,' he said, more decisively than ever, 'not for anything . . . never! Suppose it isn't true, and I have merely fancied it? . . . Never, never!'

'What can it be? Something dreadful?' she said, pondering and turning a searching glance on him.

Her face gradually became more and more conscious; a ray of thought penetrated to every feature of it and suddenly it was all lit up – she had guessed. This is how the sun, coming out from behind a cloud, gradually lights one bush, then another, then the roof of a house, and suddenly floods the whole landscape with light. Olga knew Oblomov's thought.

'No, no, I could never bring myself to say it . . .' Oblomov repeated, 'it is no use your asking.'

'I am not asking,' she said indifferently.

'Why, but just now you. . . .'

'Let us go home,' she said seriously, without listening to him, '*ma tante* is waiting.'

She walked in front of him and, leaving him alone with her aunt, went straight to her room.

VIII

THAT day was one of gradual disappointment for Oblomov. He spent it with Olga's aunt, a very intelligent, tactful, well-dressed woman, who always wore an excellently made silk gown with an elegant lace collar and a becoming cap with ribbons that coquettishly matched her complexion – fresh, in spite of her being nearly fifty. A golden lorgnette hung on a chain round her neck. Her gestures and attitudes were full of dignity; she skilfully draped herself in a beautiful shawl, very appropriately leaned her elbow on an embroidered cushion, majestically reclined on the sofa. One never saw her at work: bending down, sewing, attending to small things, did not suit her face, her imposing figure. She gave orders to her servants briefly, in a dry and careless tone. She sometimes read but never wrote; she spoke well, though for the most part in French. She noticed at once that Oblomov was not quite at home with French and after his first visit spoke to him in Russian. She did not indulge in flights of fancy or try to be too clever in her conversation; she seemed to have drawn a line in her mind beyond which she never went. One could see from everything that feeling, sympathy, love, did not occupy a foremost place in her life, while in the case of other women love obviously enters into everything, at any rate in words, and all other aspects of life exist only in so far as love leaves room for them. The thing that mattered most to this woman was the art of living, being mistress of herself, keeping the balance between thought and intention, intention and realization. Like a watchful enemy whose expectant gaze is fixed upon you every moment, she could never be caught unawares. Society was her element, and therefore tact and caution inspired her every thought, word, and movement. She never opened her inmost heart or confided her secret feelings to anyone;

one did not see her whispering with some good old lady friend over a cup of coffee. Baron von Langwagen was the only person with whom she often remained *tête-à-tête*; in the evenings he sometimes stayed with her till midnight, though Olga was generally there as well. They were silent most of the time, but intelligently, significantly silent, as though they knew something that other people did not – but that was all. They apparently liked being together – that was the only conclusion one could draw; she treated him exactly as she did everyone else: she was gracious and kind, calm and even-tempered as usual. Malicious people hinted at an old friendship, at a visit abroad together, but not a trace of any special secret sympathy could be detected in her attitude to him, and yet it would surely have shown itself had it been there. He was trustee of Olga's small estate, which had by some sharp practice been unjustly mortgaged. The baron was engaged in a lawsuit about it – that is, he made some clerk write papers, read them through his lorgnette, signed, and sent the clerk with them to the law courts while he himself made use of his social connections to secure the success of his case. He said there was reason to hope the case would soon end favourably. This put an end to malicious gossip, and people grew accustomed to see the baron in the house of Olga's aunt as one of the family. He was nearly fifty, but he was very well preserved; he dyed his moustache and had a slight limp. He was exquisitely polite, never smoked in the presence of ladies or crossed his legs, and severely blamed young men who allowed themselves in the drawing-room to lean back in an arm-chair and to raise their knees and boots to the level of their nose. He kept his gloves on even indoors and only removed them when he sat down to dinner. He dressed in the latest fashion and wore several ribbons in his buttonhole. He always drove in a closed carriage and took great care of his horses: before stepping into the carriage he walked round it, examined the harness, the horses' hoofs, and sometimes rubbed their flanks or backs with a white handkerchief to

see whether they had been groomed well. He met his
acquaintances with a polite and affable smile and was cold
to persons who had not been introduced to him; but as
soon as the introduction was made coldness was replaced
by the smile and his new acquaintance could henceforth
confidently expect it in the future. He reasoned with
equal precision – about virtue, high prices, sciences, and
society, expressing his opinions in clear-cut, ready-made
sentences that might have been written down in some
textbook and circulated for general guidance.

Olga's relations with her aunt had so far been very
simple and calm: they were moderately affectionate to
each other and there never was a shadow of unpleasant-
ness between them. This was due partly to Marya
Mihailovna's disposition and partly to the absence of any
reason for them to quarrel. The aunt never thought of
requiring from Olga anything to which she was strongly
opposed, and Olga never dreamed of refusing to comply
with her aunt's wishes or advice. And these wishes had
reference only to the choosing of clothes or the style of
doing her hair, or deciding whether they should go to the
opera or the French theatre. Olga obeyed in so far as her
aunt expressed a desire or gave advice, but no further, and
Marya Mihailovna was moderate to the point of dryness
in her requests and never trespassed upon her rights as an
aunt. Their relations were so colourless that one could not
possibly tell whether the aunt made claims upon Olga's
obedience and any special tenderness on her part and
whether Olga responded. On the other hand, one could
tell at the first glance that they were aunt and niece and
not mother and daughter.

'I am going shopping; is there anything you want?' the
aunt asked.

'Yes, *ma tante*, I want to change the lilac dress,' Olga
said, and they went together; or, 'No, *ma tante*, I went the
other day.'

The aunt touched Olga's cheeks with two fingers and
kissed her on the forehead, and she kissed her aunt's

hand, and one went and the other stayed behind.

'Shall we take the same villa as last year for the summer?' the aunt said, neither questioningly nor decisively, but as though talking to herself and unable to make up her mind.

'Yes, it is very nice there,' Olga said.

And the villa was taken.

But if Olga said: 'Oh, *ma tante*, aren't you tired of that forest and sand? Hadn't we better look round somewhere else?'

'Let us,' the aunt replied.

'Let us go to the theatre, Olenka,' the aunt said. 'This play has been so much talked of.'

'With pleasure,' Olga answered, without any hurried obsequiousness or expression of obedience.

Sometimes they had a slight disagreement.

'Green ribbons would not suit you at all, *ma chère*,' the aunt said; 'take yellow.'

'Oh, *ma tante*, I've worn yellow six times already, people will be tired of it!'

'Well, take *pensée*.'

'And do you like these?'

The aunt looked carefully and shook her head. 'As you like, *ma chère*, but if I were you I would take yellow or *pensée*.'

'No, *ma tante*, I think I will take these,' Olga said gently, and bought what she wanted.

Olga asked her aunt for advice not as though she were an authority whose word was law, but as she would have asked any woman more experienced than herself.

'*Ma tante*, you have read this book – what is it like?' she asked.

'Oh, disgusting!' the aunt said, pushing the book away, but not hiding it or taking any measures to prevent Olga reading it.

And it would never have occurred to Olga to read it. If neither of them knew what the book was like, they asked Baron von Langwagen, or Stolz if he was available, and accepted his verdict as to whether it was worth reading.

'*Ma chère* Olga,' the aunt said sometimes, 'I was told something yesterday about that young man who often talks to you at the Zavadskys' – a rather silly story.' That was all. It was for Olga to decide whether she would talk to the young man any more.

Oblomov's appearance in the house gave rise to no questions and attracted no special attention on the part of the aunt or the baron or Stolz himself. He wanted to introduce his friend to people who were inclined to stand on ceremony, in whose house one was not offered to have a nap after dinner or even supposed to sit with one's legs crossed, where one had to be carefully dressed, to remember what one was talking about, where there was always lively conversation on up-to-date topics and one had to be alert and not go to sleep. Besides, Stolz thought that to bring a clever, attractive, humorous and lively girl into Oblomov's sleepy life would be like bringing into a dark room a lamp that would shed an even light into the corners, raise the temperature, and make the place brighter. This was all he had aimed at when he introduced his friend to Olga. He had not foreseen he was bringing an explosive – nor, of course, had Olga, nor Oblomov.

On his first visit Ilya Ilyitch had sat for a couple of hours with the aunt without crossing his legs once and talked very properly about everything; twice he cleverly put the footstool under her feet. The baron came, smiled politely, and affably shook his hand. Oblomov behaved still more decorously and all three were extremely pleased with one another. The aunt considered Olga's walks and private conversations with Oblomov as . . . or rather, she did not consider them at all. Going out for walks with a young dandy would have been a different matter; even then she would not have said anything, but with her usual tact would have arranged matters imperceptibly: she would have gone with them herself once or twice or sent somebody and the walks would have come to an end of themselves. But going for walks with Oblomov, sitting

with him in a corner of the drawing-room or on the balcony. . . . What did it matter? He was over thirty: he was
not likely to talk foolishly to her or to give her unsuitable
books. . . . No one suspected anything of the kind.
Besides, Marya Mihailovna had heard Stolz, on the eve of
his departure, ask Olga not to let Oblomov grow slack, not
to allow him to sleep in the daytime but to keep him on
the go, to worry him, to give him various commissions –
in short, to take charge of him. Stolz had asked
Marya Mihailovna, too, not to lose sight of Oblomov, to
invite him often, to take him for walks and excursions and
to rouse him in every possible way, if he did not go
abroad.

Olga did not show herself while Oblomov sat with her
aunt, and the time passed slowly. Oblomov was again hot
and cold in turns. Now he guessed the reason of this new
change in Olga and it pained him more than the first. His
first blunder made him feel frightened, but now his heart
was heavy and he felt awkward, chilled, and miserable, as
in cold rainy weather. He had let her see that he had
guessed she loved him, and perhaps he had guessed
wrongly too. This was indeed an insult, perhaps an
irreparable one. And even if he had guessed rightly, how
clumsy he had been! He was fatuous. He might have
frightened away the feeling that was timidly knocking at
her young, virginal heart, resting there lightly and timorously like a bird on a branch, ready to fly away at the least
sound. He waited with a sinking heart for Olga to come
down to dinner, wondering what she would say, how she
would speak and look at him.

She came down – and he could not marvel enough at
her; he hardly recognized her. Her face was different,
even her voice was not the same. The young, naïve,
almost childish smile never once appeared on her lips, she
did not once look with wide-open eyes questioningly or in
perplexity or with simple-hearted curiosity: it was as
though she had nothing more to ask, nothing to find out,
nothing to wonder at! Her eyes did not follow him as

before. She looked at him as though she had known him for years and had studied him thoroughly, as though he were nothing to her, no more than the baron – in short, he might be seeing her after a year's absence, seeing her a year older. She was not stern or vexed as she had been, she joked and laughed, replied fully to questions which she would have left unanswered before. It was obvious that she had decided to behave like other people – a thing she had never done before. The freedom, the lack of restraint that had made it possible for her to speak her mind was no longer there. Where had it all gone? After dinner he went up to ask her if she would go for a walk. Without answering him she turned to her aunt and asked:

'Shall *we* go for a walk?'

'We might go a little way,' the aunt said. 'Ask for my umbrella.'

They all set out together. They sauntered along lazily, looked at Petersburg in the distance, walked as far as the forest, and returned to the balcony.

'You don't seem inclined to sing to-day? I am afraid to ask you,' Oblomov said, wondering if the restraint would end and she would be gay again, hoping to catch a glimpse of her candid, naïve, and trustful self in a word, a smile, in her singing perhaps.

'It is too hot!' her aunt remarked.

'Never mind, I will try,' Olga said, and sang one song.

He listened and could not believe his ears. It was not she: where was the old passionate note? She sang so clearly, so correctly, and at the same time so . . . so like all young ladies when they are asked to sing in company – without feeling. She took her soul out of her singing and not a single nerve stirred in the listener. Was she playing with him, pretending, angry? It was impossible to tell: she looked at him kindly, she spoke readily, but she spoke and sang like everyone else. . . . What did it mean?

Without waiting for tea, Oblomov took his hat and said good-bye.

'Come oftener,' Marya Mihailovna said. 'On weekdays

we are always alone, if it doesn't bore you, and on Sundays we have visitors, so you won't be dull.'

The baron got up politely and bowed to him.

Olga nodded to him as to an old friend, and when he walked away she turned to the window and listened with indifference to Oblomov's retreating steps.

These two hours and the three or four days, or at most a week, that followed had a profound effect on her and moved her a long way forward. Only women are capable of this rapid development of their powers, this blossoming of all sides of their nature. Olga seemed to be absorbing by the hour all that life had to teach her. Hardly perceptible experiences that flit past a man before he has become aware of them are caught by a girl with inexpressible quickness: she follows their distant flight with her eyes and the curve they describe remains in her memory indelibly as a sign or a warning. Where a man needs a signpost with an inscription over it, a rustle of wind, a hardly audible tremor of the air is enough for a girl. Why does the absurdly naïve face of a girl, so care-free only the week before, suddenly bear the imprint of grave thought? And what thought? What about? It seems to contain the whole of a man's logic, of his speculative, experimental, and practical philosophy, a whole system of life! The cousin who left her not so long ago a little girl has finished his course of studies, donned his epaulettes, runs up to her gaily, intending, as before, to pat her on the shoulder, to spin her round, to jump with her over chairs and sofas . . . and suddenly, after one attentive look at her face, grows shy and draws back in confusion, conscious that he is still a boy while she is already a woman! Why? What has happened? A tragedy? Some great event? Some news that all the town knows? No, neither *maman* nor *ma tante*, nor *mon oncle*, nor the nurse, nor the maid, knows anything about it. And there has not been time for anything to happen: she has danced two mazurkas and a few quadrilles and then, somehow, she had a headache and did not sleep the night. . . . And then it all passed off, only

there was something new in her face: she looked at one
differently, she no longer laughed aloud, or ate a whole
pear at one go, or told how 'at school they used to. . . .'
She, too, had finished her studies.

The next day and the day after, Oblomov, like the
cousin, hardly recognized Olga, and looked at her timidly,
while she looked at him simply, just as at other people,
without curiosity or friendliness, as before. 'What is the
matter with her? What is she feeling and thinking now?'
he worried himself with questions. 'I cannot make it out
for the life of me!' And how, indeed, could he grasp that
the same thing had happened to her as happens to a man
of twenty-five with the help of twenty-five professors and
libraries, after wandering about the world and sometimes
at the cost of losing some of his moral, intellectual, and
physical freshness – that is, that she had entered the realm
of fully awakened consciousness. It had been accom-
plished so easily and had cost her so little.

'No, it's dull, it's depressing!' he concluded. 'I will
move to the Vyborg side, will work, read, go to Oblomovka
. . . alone,' he added with profound dejection, 'without
her! Good-bye, my paradise, my bright, peaceful ideal of
life!'

He did not go to Olga's on the fourth or the fifth day;
he did not read or write; he attempted a walk, but when
he came out on to the dusty road which went up hill he
said to himself: 'Fancy going there in this heat!' yawned,
and, coming home, lay down on the sofa and dropped into
a heavy sleep as he used to do in his dusty room in Gorohovy Street with the curtains drawn. His dreams were
confused. Waking up, he saw the table set for dinner,
kvass, soup, roast meat. Zahar stood looking sleepily out
of the window; in the next room Anissya was rattling the
plates. He ate his dinner and sat down by the window. It
was all so dull and stupid, and he was alone! Again he did
not want to go anywhere or to do anything.

'Look, sir, our neighbours have brought us a kitten:
shall we take it? You asked for one yesterday,' Anissya

said, trying to distract him, and put the kitten on his knee.

He began stroking the kitten; but he was bored with the kitten too!

'Zahar!' he said.

'Yes, sir?' Zahar responded listlessly.

'I may be moving to town.'

'Where to? We haven't a flat.'

'Why, to the Vyborg side.'

'What's the good of moving from one summer villa to another? What's the attraction there? Is it Mihey Andreyitch you miss?'

'Oh, it's uncomfortable here. . . .'

'Moving again? Good Lord! We've hardly recovered as it is, and I haven't yet found those two cups and the broom; if Mihey Andreyitch hasn't taken them with the other things, they must have been lost.'

Oblomov said nothing. Zahar went out and returned immediately, dragging a suit-case and a travelling-bag.

'And what are we to do with this? We might as well sell it,' he said, giving a kick to the suit-case.

'Have you gone off your head? I am going abroad in a few days,' Oblomov interrupted angrily.

'Abroad!' Zahar brought out with a sudden grin. 'You've had your talk about it, but as to going! . . .'

'What do you see strange in that? I am going and that's the end of it. . . . My passport is ready.'

'And who will take your boots off out there?' Zahar remarked ironically. 'Maid-servants, I suppose? Why, you will be lost there without me!'

He grinned again so that his whiskers and eyebrows moved.

'The nonsense you talk! Take these things out and go away!' Oblomov answered with vexation.

As soon as Oblomov woke up at nine o'clock next morning, Zahar brought him his breakfast and said that on the way to the baker's he had met the young lady.

'Which young lady?'

'Which? Why the Ilyinsky young lady, Olga Sergey-evna.'

'Well?' Oblomov asked impatiently.

'Well, she sent you her greetings and asked how you were and what you were doing.'

'And what did you say?'

'I said you were well – what could ail you?'

'Why do you add your stupid reflections?' Oblomov remarked. ' "What could ail me!" How do you know? Well, what else?'

'She asked where you had dinner yesterday.'

'Well?'

'I said you had dinner at home, and supper too. "Why, does he have supper?" the young lady asked, and I said "He only ate two chickens." '

'Idiot!' Oblomov said energetically.

'Why idiot? Isn't it true?' Zahar said. 'I can show the bones if you like. . . .'

'Idiot, and no mistake,' Oblomov repeated. 'Well, and what did she say?'

'She smiled and said, "Why so little?" '

'Oh, you idiot!' Oblomov exclaimed. 'You might as well have told her you put on my shirt inside out.'

'She didn't ask, so I didn't mention it,' Zahar replied.

'What else did she ask?'

'She asked what you had been doing these days.'

'And what did you tell her?'

'I said you did nothing and just lay about.'

'Oh!' Oblomov cried in exasperation, raising his fists to his temples. 'Go away!' he added menacingly. 'If ever again you dare tell such stories about me you will see what I shall do to you! Venomous creature that man is!'

'Do you want me to tell lies in my old age?' Zahar protested.

'Begone!' Ilya Ilyitch repeated.

Zahar did not mind abuse so long as his master said nothing 'heart-rending.'

'I said you think of moving to the Vyborg side,' Zahar concluded.

'Go!' Oblomov shouted imperatively.

Zahar went out with a sigh that could be heard all over the room. Oblomov began drinking tea; out of the enormous supply of rolls and bread rings he ate only one roll, afraid of some fresh indiscretion on Zahar's part. Then he lit a cigar and, sitting down to the table, opened a book; he read one page and was going to turn it over, but the pages had not been cut. Oblomov tore the pages with his finger, making festoons round the edges; and it was not his book, but Stolz's, who was so strict and absurdly methodical about everything, books especially! Every little thing, papers, pencils, were to lie in the precise way he had arranged them. Oblomov ought to have taken a paper-knife, but it was not there; he might, of course, have asked for a table-knife, but he preferred instead to put the book in its place and go to the sofa; he had just put his hand on the embroidered cushion and was going to lie down comfortably when Zahar came into the room.

'The young lady asked you to come to that — Oh, whatever is it called?' he announced.

'Why didn't you tell me before, two hours ago?' Oblomov asked hastily.

'You ordered me out of the room and did not let me finish . . .' Zahar answered.

'Zahar, you are my undoing!' Oblomov pronounced tragically.

'He is at it again,' Zahar thought, turning his left whisker to his master and gazing at the wall, 'like the other day . . . sure to say something to upset one!'

'Where did she ask me to come?' Oblomov asked.

'Why, whatever is it called? The garden, you know. . . .'

'The park?' Oblomov said.

'The park, that's it, "to go for a walk, if he would like to; I shall be there," she said.'

'Give me my clothes!'

Oblomov ran all over the park, peeping into every glade, every arbour – Olga was not there. He walked along

the avenue where they had had their explanation and
found her there, on a seat near the place where she had
plucked and thrown away a lilac branch.

'I was afraid you weren't coming,' she said kindly.

'I have been looking for you all over the park,' he
answered.

'I knew you would be looking for me and sat down in
this avenue on purpose: I thought you would be sure to
walk through it.'

He was on the point of asking, 'Why were you sure?'
but glanced at her and said nothing. She looked not as she
had done when they walked here, but as he had seen her
last, when he was so alarmed by her expression. Even her
kindness somehow seemed restrained, she had such a set,
such a concentrated expression; he saw he could no longer
play with her at guesses, hints, and naïve questions, that
that gay, childish moment had passed. Much of what had
remained unsaid and might have been approached with a
sly question had already been settled between them without words, without explanations, Heaven only knew how –
there was no returning to it.

'How is it we haven't seen you all this time?' she asked.

He said nothing. He would have liked to make her feel
that the secret charm of their relations had gone, that
he was oppressed by the air of concentration she had
assumed, hiding herself as with a cloud, and that he did
not know what to do, how to behave towards her. But he
felt that the least hint of this would make her look surprised and grow still colder towards him, and perhaps
finally extinguish the spark of sympathy that he had so
clumsily put out at the very beginning. It had to be
rekindled slowly and imperceptibly, but he did not know
in the least how this was to be done. He vaguely understood that she had grown up and was, perhaps, ahead of
him; there was no returning to childlike confidence, a
Rubicon lay before him and the lost happiness lay on the
opposite bank – he had to cross over to it. But how? What
if he crossed over alone? She understood better than he

did what was going on in his mind and so she had the advantage over him. His soul was open to her; she saw how feeling was born in it, how it was seeking an outlet; she knew that feminine slyness, cunning, and coquetry – Sonitchka's weapons – were not needed in his case, because there would be no struggle. She even knew that in spite of her youth she would have to take the initiative, since all that could be expected of him was deep impressionability, ardent but passive devotion, perpetual harmony with every beat of her heart, but no movement of will, no active thought. She instantly weighed her power over him and liked her part of the guiding star, the ray of light that beams over the still water of the lake and is reflected in it. She made use of her supremacy in their duel in various ways. In the comedy, or it may be the tragedy, of love the two actors appear almost invariably in the characters of tormentor and victim. Like every woman in the leading part – that is, the part of tormentor – Olga could not deny herself the pleasure of playing cat and mouse with her victim, though she did it unconsciously and not so much as other women; sometimes she would capriciously show a sudden, lightning-like glimpse of feeling and then draw back immediately and be composed and restrained once more. For the most part, however, she urged him forward, knowing that he would not take a single step by himself but remain where she had left him.

'Have you been busy?' she asked, embroidering a bit of canvas.

'If it hadn't been for Zahar I should have said yes,' Oblomov groaned inwardly.

'Yes, I have been reading,' he answered carelessly.

'What, a novel?' she asked, and raised her eyes from her work to see what he would look like when telling a lie.

'No, I hardly ever read novels,' he answered very calmly. 'I have been reading *The History of Inventions and Discoveries*.'

'Thank Heaven, I have read through a page of it to-day,' he thought.

'In Russian?' she asked.

'No, in English.'

'Do you read English?'

'Yes, I do, though with difficulty. And have you been to town?' he asked, chiefly to shift the conversation from books.

'No, I was at home all the time. I generally work here, in this avenue.'

'Here?'

'Yes, I like this avenue very much; I am grateful to you for having shown it me; hardly anyone comes here. . . .'

'I didn't show it you,' he interrupted, 'we met here accidentally, you remember?'

'Yes, so we did.'

Both were silent.

'Has your stye quite gone?' she asked, looking straight at his right eye.

He blushed.

'Yes, thank Heaven!' he said.

'When your eye begins to itch, bathe it with vodka, it prevents styes. My nurse told me that.'

'Why does she keep on about styes?' Oblomov thought.

'And don't take supper,' she added seriously.

'Zahar!' He furiously swore at Zahar under his breath.

'A good supper,' she went on, without raising her eyes, 'and two or three days spent lying down, especially on one's back, are sure to give one a stye.'

'Idiot!' Oblomov thundered inwardly against Zahar.

'What are you embroidering?' he asked, to change the subject.

'A bell-bag,' she said, unfolding the roll of canvas and showing him the pattern, 'for the baron. Pretty?'

'Yes, very pretty, the pattern is charming. It is a lilac branch, isn't it?'

'Yes . . . I think it is,' she answered carelessly. 'I took at random the first pattern that turned up. . . .' And, blushing slightly, she quickly rolled up the embroidery.

'Well, it isn't much fun if things go on like this and I can't get anything out of her,' he thought. 'Other people could – Stolz, for instance, but I cannot.'

He frowned and looked sleepily around him. She glanced at him and put her work into a basket.

'Let us walk as far as the wood,' she said, and, giving him the basket to carry, she straightened her dress, put up her parasol, and walked on.

'Why are you depressed?' she asked.

'I don't know, Olga Sergeyevna. But why should I be happy, and how?'

'Work, spend more time with other people.'

'One can work if one has a purpose. But what is my purpose? I haven't any.'

'The purpose is – to live.'

'When one doesn't know what to live for, one simply lives from day to day, glad that the day is over, that the night has come, and one can forget in sleep the dull question why one has lived this day and is going to live the next.'

She listened to him in silence, with a severe expression; she frowned sternly and a look of incredulity or contempt hovered about her lips.

'Why you have lived!' she repeated. 'Can anyone's life be useless?'

'It can. Mine, for instance.'

'You don't yet know what the purpose of your life is?' she asked, stopping short. 'I don't believe it: you are slandering yourself; if it were true you wouldn't be worthy of life. . . .'

'I have passed the point at which I ought to have found it and now there is nothing before me.'

He sighed, and she smiled.

'Nothing before you?' she repeated questioningly, with gay mockery, as though she disbelieved him and saw that he had a future.

'You may laugh, but it is so,' he continued. She slowly walked on, bending her head.

'Whom am I to live for, to what purpose?' he said, following her. 'What am I to seek, to strive for, to dream about? The blossom of life has fallen, only the thorns are left.'

They were walking slowly; she listened absentmindedly, plucked a branch of lilac by the way, and gave it to him without looking.

'What is it?' he asked, taken aback.

'You see, it's a branch.'

'What branch?' he asked, looking at her open-eyed.

'Lilac.'

'I know . . . but what does it mean?'

'The flower of life . . . and. . . .'

He stopped and she stopped too.

'And?' he repeated questioningly.

'My vexation,' she said, looking straight at him, and her smile showed that she knew what she was doing.

The impenetrable cloud around her had dispersed. The language of her eyes was clear. It was as though she had opened on purpose a certain page of a book and allowed him to read the secret passage.

'Then I may hope . . .' he cried, suddenly flushing with joy.

'All things! But. . . .'

She said nothing more. He seemed to have suddenly come to life. She in her turn did not recognize Oblomov. The sleepy, clouded face was transfigured; his eyes were wide open, colour came into his cheeks; thoughts stirred in his mind, desires and determination sparkled in his glance. She clearly saw from the dumb play of his features that Oblomov had instantly acquired a purpose in life.

'Life is opening to me once more!' he said, speaking as though in a trance. 'Here it is, in your eyes, your smile, in this lilac, in the *Casta diva* . . . it's all here.'

She shook her head.

'No, not all . . . only half.'

'The best.'

'Perhaps,' she said.

'Where is the other half? What more can there be?'

'You must look for it.'

'Why?'

'So as not to lose the first,' she answered, taking his arm and starting to walk home.

He kept glancing stealthily and with delight at her face, her curls, her figure, and convulsively grasped the lilac branch.

'Life and hope once more!' he repeated dreamily, unable to believe it.

'You are not moving to the Vyborg side?' she asked when he was going home.

He laughed and did not even call Zahar a fool.

IX

AFTER that there were no sudden changes in Olga. She was calm and even-tempered with her aunt and her friends, but lived and felt that she was living only when she was with Oblomov. She did not ask any more what she ought to do, how she ought to act, and did not appeal in her mind to Sonitchka's authority. As the different phases of life – that is, of feeling – opened before her, she keenly watched all that happened, listened intently to the voice of her own instinct, and, checking her experiences by the few observations she had gathered, moved forward warily, trying with her foot the ground she was going to tread. She had no one she could consult. Her aunt? But she glided over such subjects so lightly and cleverly that Olga never succeeded in formulating her opinions and imprinting them on her memory. Stolz was not there. Oblomov? But he was a kind of Galatea to whom she had to act Pygmalion. Her life was filled so quietly, so imperceptibly to the others that she lived in her new sphere without attracting attention or showing any sign of emotional crises and anxieties. She did the same things as before, but she did them all differently. She went to the French theatre and the play became somehow connected with her life; she read a book and invariably found lines reflecting her own mind, glowing with her own feeling, repeating the words she had said the day before; it was as though the author had overheard her heart beating. The trees in the forest were the same, but their rustle had a special meaning for her: a living harmony existed now between her and them. The birds were not simply twittering and chirruping, but saying something to one another; and everything around her was speaking, everything was responding to her mood; if a flower opened, she seemed to hear it breathe. Her dreams had a new life in them:

they were peopled with visions and images to which she sometimes spoke aloud . . . they told her something, but so vaguely that she could not understand; she tried to speak to them, to question them, but what she said was incomprehensible; Katya told her in the morning that she had been talking in her sleep. She recalled what Stolz had said: he often told her she had not begun to live, and she was sometimes offended at his regarding her as a child when she was twenty. But now she understood that he had been right. 'When all your powers are awakened, life around you, too, will be all astir; you will see things to which you are now blind, you will hear what you don't hear now; your nerves will sing melodies, you will hear the music of the spheres, will listen to the grass growing. Wait, don't be in a hurry, it will come of itself!' he threatened her. It had come. 'It must be my powers coming into play, my nature awakening . . .' she repeated his words, listening intently to the strange tremor within her and watching keenly and timidly every fresh expression of the awakening forces. She did not give way to day-dreaming, was not enthralled by the sudden rustle of the leaves, the night visions, and mysterious whispers, when someone seemed to bend over her and say something vague and incomprehensible in her ear; 'it's my nerves,' she would murmur with a start, smiling through tears, hardly able to master her fear – her nerves were as yet hardly strong enough to bear the strain of the newly awakened emotions; she got out of bed, drank a glass of water, opened the window, fanned her face with her handkerchief, and recovered from dreaming.

As soon as Oblomov woke up in the morning the image of Olga with a spray of lilac in her hand arose before him. He thought of her as he went to sleep, she was with him when he read or went for a walk. Day and night he carried on an endless conversation with her in his mind. He kept adding to the *History of Discoveries and Inventions* fresh discoveries about Olga's appearance or character, and invented occasions for meeting her accidentally, for sending her a book, arranging some little surprise for her.

After talking to her he would continue the conversation at home, so that sometimes when Zahar came in he said to him in the very soft and tender voice in which he had been mentally addressing Olga: 'You have again left my boots unpolished, you bald devil; take care or you will catch it. . . .'

But his peace of mind had left him from the moment she had first sung for him. He no longer lived his old life, when it was all the same to him whether he lay on his back or with his face to the wall, whether he was at Ivan Gera-simovitch's or had Alexeyev sitting in his room, when he expected nothing and no one either by day or by night. Now both day and night, every hour of the morning or the evening, had an individuality and was either shining with rainbow glory or colourless and gloomy, according to whether it was filled with Olga's presence or passed dully and listlessly without her. All this affected him deeply; his mind was a regular network of continual conjectures, guesses, agonies of uncertainty – all to do with the questions: Would he see her or not? What would she say and do? How would she look? What would she ask him to do? Would she be pleased or not? These questions had become vital to him. 'Oh, if one could feel only the warmth of love without its anxieties!' he dreamed. 'No, it's like fire, life gives one no peace, there is no escaping from it! What a lot of movement and occupation has suddenly been crowded into it! Love is a very difficult school of life!'

He read several books: Olga asked him to tell her the subject and listened with incredible patience. He wrote several letters to the country, changed his bailiff and, through Stolz, entered into communication with one of his neighbours. He would have actually gone to Oblomovka had he thought it possible to part from Olga. He gave up having supper, and it was a fortnight since he had lain down in the daytime. In two or three weeks they had visited all the places round Petersburg. Olga and her aunt, the baron and Oblomov appeared at suburban concerts and festivities. They talked of going to Imatra in Finland. So far as Oblomov was concerned, he would not have stirred anywhere farther than the park, but Olga kept making plans, and if he hesitated in accepting an invitation to go somewhere the excursion was sure to take place; and then there was no end to Olga's smiles. There was not a hill within three miles of their villa that he had not climbed several times.

Meanwhile, their sympathy grew and developed, expressing itself in accordance with its own inexorable laws. Olga blossomed out as her feeling grew stronger. Her eyes were brighter, her movements more graceful; her bosom had filled out so beautifully and heaved so evenly. 'You have grown prettier since we came here, Olga,' her aunt said, and the baron's smile expressed the same compliment. Olga blushed and put her head on her aunt's shoulder, and the aunt patted her affectionately on the cheek.

'Olga! Olga!' Oblomov called cautiously, almost in a whisper, standing at the foot of a hill where she had told him to meet her before going for a walk.

There was no answer; he looked at his watch. 'Olga Sergeyevna!' he added aloud. All was still.

Olga was sitting at the top of the hill and heard him call, but she said nothing and tried not to laugh. She wanted to make him climb up.

'Olga Sergeyevna!' he called, glancing towards the top when he had climbed half-way between the bushes. 'She did say half-past five,' he said to himself.

She could not help laughing.

'Olga, Olga! Ah, you are there!' he said, and went on climbing.

'Oof! The idea of hiding at the top of a hill!' He sat down beside her. 'For the sake of tormenting me, you torment yourself.'

'Where do you come from? Straight from home?' she asked.

'No, I have been to your house; they told me you had gone.'

'What have you been doing to-day?'

'To-day. . . .'

'Quarrelling with Zahar?' she finished for him.

He laughed at this as at something utterly impossible.

'No, I have been reading *La Revue*. But listen, Olga. . . .'

He said nothing, however, and sitting down beside her sank into the contemplation of her profile, of her head, of her hand moving up and down as she pulled the needle through the canvas. He could not take his eyes off her. He did not move, only his glance moved to right or to left, up or down, following her hand. All was astir within him: the blood raced rapidly through his veins, his pulse was beating twice as fast, his heart was seething, and it all had such an effect on him that he breathed slowly and painfully, as people do before the scaffold or at moments of highest spiritual enjoyment. He was silent and could not make the least movement; his eyes, moist with emotion, were fixed upon her.

She threw a deep glance at him from time to time, read the obvious meaning written on his face and thought: 'Oh, how he loves me! How tenderly he loves me!' And she looked with pride and admiration at the man who lay at her feet, brought there by her own power. The time of symbolic allusions, significant smiles, and lilac sprays was irrevocably past. Love had grown sterner, more exacting, was becoming a kind of duty; they now had rights over each other. They had both come into the open; misunderstandings and doubts were disappearing or giving way to clearer and more definite questions. She still slightly mocked him for the years he had wasted in idleness; she passed a severe sentence upon him and punished him for his apathy more deeply and effectively than Stolz had done; then as they grew more intimate, instead of mocking his listless and flabby existence, she began despotically to impose her will upon him; she boldly reminded him of the purpose and the duties of life and sternly demanded that he should act; she constantly kept his mind employed, either by drawing him into a subtle discussion of some practical question that she was familiar with or by asking him about something she did not understand and could not find out by herself. He struggled, thought hard, did all he could not to lose her good opinion but to help her to unravel a knot or boldly to cut it. All her feminine tactics were inspired by tenderest sympathy; all his efforts to keep up with her active mind breathed of passion. But more often he lay down at her feet exhausted, put his hand to his heart and listened to its beating, never taking off her his wondering, rapturous gaze. 'How he loves me!' she repeated at those moments, looking at him with admiration. If she noticed the least weariness or apathy still lurking in Oblomov's mind – and she could see deep into it – she overwhelmed him with reproaches, which were at times tinged with the bitterness of regret, the fear of having made a mistake. Sometimes, just as he was going to yawn, he met her look of surprise and instantly shut his mouth with a snap. She persecuted the least shadow of sleepiness in his face. She asked him not only what he had been doing, but also what he was going to do. What roused him even more effectively than her reproaches was the fact that his weariness made her weary too, and she grew cold and indifferent. Then he became feverishly active and lively; the shadow disappeared and the spring of their sympathy again ran clear and strong. But so far all these troubles did not extend beyond the magic circle of love; his activity was of a negative character: he did not sleep, he read, he sometimes thought of writing his plan of estate management, he walked and drove a great deal. But what he was to do further, what the work of his life was to be, was still a matter of intentions only.

'What other kind of life and work is Andrey expecting of me?' Oblomov thought, trying hard to keep his eyes open after dinner. 'Isn't this life? Isn't love as good as work? I should like him to try it! Walking a good seven miles every day! I slept last night at a wretched inn in

town, with all my clothes on, I only took off my boots, no
Zahar to help me – and all through her sending me on
errands!'

He suffered most when Olga asked him some question
that required special knowledge, expecting him to answer
it as fully as though he were a professor of the subject. In
doing so she often forgot her ulterior aims with regard to
Oblomov and was absorbed in the question for its own
sake. 'Why don't they teach us these things?' she said
with thoughtful vexation as she listened eagerly to snat-
ches of conversation on some subject generally regarded
unnecessary to women. On one occasion she accosted
Oblomov with questions about double stars: he incautiously referred to Herschel and was sent to town for a
book which he had to read and to expound to her till she
was satisfied. Another time, talking to the baron, he again
incautiously said something about schools of painting –
and again he was given work for a week: to read and to
tell her what he had read; then they went to the Hermitage and he had to give her concrete instances of what he
had read. If he said anything at random she saw through
it at once and gave him no peace. Then he spent a week
going to different shops in search of the engravings of the
best pictures. Poor Oblomov was either looking up what
he had once learned or rushing to the bookshops in search
of new books, and sometimes spent a whole night without
sleep, reading, rummaging for information, so that in the
morning he could deal with the question of the day before
with the casual air of having just remembered the answer.
She put her questions, not with feminine absentminded-
ness, not because of a sudden caprice, but insistently and
impatiently, and if Oblomov was silent she punished him
by a long, searching look. How he used to tremble under
that look!

'Why are you so silent?' she asked. 'One might think
you were bored.'

'Oh,' he said, as though coming to himself after a fainting fit, 'how I love you!'

'Indeed? And if I hadn't asked, it would have looked far from it.'

'But don't you feel what is happening in me?' he began. 'Do you know, I can hardly speak? Just here . . . give me your hand – something seems in the way, as though a heavy stone lay there – as in deep sorrow. Isn't it strange that the same thing happens to one both in joy and in sorrow? – it's hard to breathe, it almost hurts one and one wants to cry! If I wept, tears would make me feel easier, just as in sorrow. . . .'

She looked at him silently, as though checking his words by his expression, and smiled; she was satisfied with the result. Her face, too, breathed of happiness, but of peaceful happiness which nothing, it seemed, could disturb. One could see that her heart was not heavy, but as serene as nature itself on that quiet evening.

'What is the matter with me?' Oblomov asked in wonder, as though talking to himself.

'Shall I tell you?'

'Do.'

'You are . . . in love.'

'Yes, of course,' he confirmed, taking her hand away from her embroidery. He did not kiss it but only firmly pressed her fingers to his lips, apparently intending to hold them indefinitely.

She gently tried to release her hand, but he held it firmly.

'There, that's enough, let me go,' she said.

'And you?' he asked. 'You . . . are not in love. . . .'

'In love – no . . . I don't know, I am afraid of it. I love you!' she said, with a long, thoughtful look at him as though she wanted to make sure that she really did love him.

'Love!' Oblomov said. 'But one may love one's mother, father, nurse, even one's dog; all this is covered by the general, collective term "love" as by an old. . . .'

'Dressing-gown?' she said, laughing. 'By the way, where is your dressing-gown?'

'What dressing-gown? I have never had one.'

She looked at him with a reproachful smile.

'Here you are talking of my dressing-gown!' he said. 'I am waiting, I am longing to hear you speak of your feeling, to know what name you will give it, and you . . . Well, so be it! Yes, I am in love with you, and I say that without that there can be no real love: one does not fall in love with one's father or mother or nurse, one simply loves them. . . .'

'I don't know,' she repeated, almost to herself, still intent on grasping what was passing within her. 'I don't know if I am in love with you; if not, perhaps the moment has not yet come for it; I only know that I haven't loved in this way either my father, or my mother, or my nurse. . . .'

'But what is the difference? Do you feel anything special?' he insisted.

'Do you want to know?' she asked roguishly.

'Yes, yes, yes! Don't you yourself want to put it into words?'

'But why do you want to know?'

'So as to live by it every minute; to-day, all night, to-morrow – till we meet again. . . . This is all I live by.'

'You see, you want to renew the supply of your tenderness every day: this is just the difference between loving and being in love. I. . . .'

'You?' he said impatiently.

'I love differently,' she said, leaning back on the seat and watching dreamily the moving clouds. 'I miss you; I am sorry to part from you, and it would hurt me if the parting were for long. I have seen and learned once for all that you love me – I believe it and am happy, though you may never tell it me again. I cannot love more and better than this.'

'It might be . . . Cordelia speaking,' Oblomov thought, looking at Olga passionately.

'If you . . . died,' she went on with a catch in her voice, 'I should wear mourning for you all my life and never

smile again. If you fell in love with another woman I
would not repine or curse you, but in my mind would
wish you happiness. . . . Love for me is the same as . . .
life, and life is. . . .'

She sought for a word.

'What is life, do you think?'

'Life is a duty, an obligation, and so love, too, is a
duty; it is as though God has sent it me,' she concluded,
raising her eyes to heaven, 'and commanded me to love.'

'Cordelia!' Oblomov said aloud. 'And she is twenty-
one! So this is what love means to you!' he added
thoughtfully.

'Yes, and I think I shall have the strength to live and
love all my life. . . . One cannot be without the other.'

'Who has taught her this?' Oblomov thought, looking
at her almost with reverence. 'It is not through experience, torture, fire, and smoke, that she has reached this
simple and clear understanding of life and love.'

'And are there lively joys, are there passions?' he
began.

'I don't know,' she said. 'I have not felt them and I
don't understand what they are.'

'Oh, how I understand it now!'

'I, too, may feel it in time, may go through the same
emotions as you, and perhaps when I meet you I shall also
look at you and not believe that it is really you. . . . It
must be very funny,' she added gaily, 'you do make such
eyes sometimes! I think *ma tante* notices it.'

'Then what happiness do you find in love if you don't
feel the intense joy I feel?'

'What happiness? Why, this!' she said, pointing to him,
to herself, to the solitude around them. 'Is this not happiness? Have I ever lived like this before? In the old days I
should not have sat here for a quarter of an hour alone
among these trees without a book, without music. Talking
to men, except to Andrey Ivanitch, used to bore me, I had
nothing to say to them. . . . And now . . . even being silent
together is delightful!'

She looked round at the trees, the grass, then at him, and smiling gave him her hand.

'Don't you know that it will hurt me to part from you?' she added. 'Don't you know that I shall hurry to bed so as to drop asleep and not see the dull night? That I shall send a message to you in the morning?'

With every fresh sentence she uttered Oblomov's face filled with happiness and his eyes shone.

'Yes, yes,' he repeated, 'I, too, long for the morning, I, too, find the night dull, I, too, will send a message to you to-morrow simply for the sake of uttering your name and hearing the sound of it, of learning something about you from the servants and envying them for having seen you already. . . . We think, wait, live, and hope in the same way. Forgive me my doubts, Olga: I am certain now that you love me as you have not loved your father or your aunt or. . . .'

'My lap-dog,' she added. 'Trust me, then,' she concluded, 'as I trust you; do not be uncertain, do not disturb this happiness with empty doubts or it will fly away. I will not give back what I have once called my own – unless it is taken from me by force. I know this, although I am young, I. . . . Do you know,' she said with confidence, 'for the last month, since I have known you I have thought and felt a great deal; it's as though I had read a big book all by myself, little by little. . . . Don't doubt me then. . . .'

'I cannot help doubting,' he interrupted. 'Don't ask me that. Now, in your presence I am certain of everything: your voice rings true, your look is full of feeling. Your eyes seem to speak: I do not need words, I can read your expression. But when you are not here, such an agonizing whirl of questions and doubts begins that I must run to you again to have a look at you or I lose faith. Why should it be so?'

'But I have no doubts about you: how is that?'

'I should think not! You have a madman before you, a man possessed by passion! I expect you see yourself in my eyes as in a mirror. Besides, you are twenty; look at

yourself: how could a man fail to admire you . . . if only at
a distance? And to know you, to listen to you, to look at
you for hours, to love you – oh, that's enough to drive one
mad! And you are so calm, so even; and if two or three
days pass without your saying "I love you" . . . there's
trouble here,' he pointed to his heart.

'I love you, I love you, I love you – here is a three
days' supply for you!' she said, getting up.

'You are always joking, but it's no joke to me!' he said
with a sigh, following her down the hill.

Thus one and the same tune was played by them in
endless variations. Their meetings, their conversations,
were like one continuous song, one single bright light, the
rays of which, broken up in the surrounding atmosphere,
shimmered with rose, amber, and green. Every day and
every hour brought new sounds, new colours, but the tune
and the light were the same. Both he and she listened,
trying to catch these sounds, and hastened to sing to each
other what they heard without suspecting that the next
day new sounds would be heard, new colours would
appear, and forgetting, when the morrow came, that the
day before the music was different. She clothed her emotions in the colours with which her imagination glowed at
the moment, believing they were true to nature, and with
innocent and unconscious coquetry hastened to show herself to her friend in that lovely guise. He had even greater
faith in the magic sounds, in the enchanting light, and
hurried to appear before her in the full armour of passion,
to show her all the brilliance and power of the fire that
was consuming his soul. They did not lie either to themselves or to each other; they put into words what the heart
said, and its voice was inspired by imagination. Oblomov
did not really care whether Olga appeared as Cordelia and
remained true to that image or followed a new path and
was transformed into another vision, so long as she was
surrounded by the coloured radiance in which she lived
in his heart and so long as he was happy. Olga did not
inquire if her passionate friend would pick up her glove if

she threw it into the lion's mouth or would jump into an abyss for her sake, so long as she could see the signs of his passion and he remained true to her ideal of a man – and of a man coming to life through her; so long as the light of her eyes, her smile, kept his courage aflame and she remained the purpose of his life. And so the fleeting image of Cordelia, the fire of Oblomov's passion, were only the reflection of a single moment of the morning of love, its one ephemeral breath, one fanciful pattern. And the morrow would be aglow with a different light, as beautiful, perhaps, but not the same! . . .

X

OBLOMOV was like a man who has just seen the summer sun go down and is enjoying the rosy afterglow, thinking of nothing but the return of light and warmth on the morrow, and never taking his eyes off the western sky or turning back to see the approach of night. He lay on his back enjoying the impressions of his meeting with Olga. The 'I love you, I love you, I love you' still sounded in his ears, clearer than anything Olga had sung; the last rays of the deep look she gave him still rested upon him. He was reading the meaning of it and determining the degree of her love as he was dropping asleep, when suddenly. . . .

The following morning Oblomov got up pale and gloomy; his face bore the traces of a sleepless night; his forehead was wrinkled; his eyes were dull and apathetic. The proud, cheerful, and energetic expression, the quick, determined movements of a busy man, had all gone. He listlessly drank his tea, and without sitting down to his table or opening a book settled down on the sofa and dreamily lighted a cigar. In the old days he would have lain down, but he had lost the habit of it and did not even feel tempted to put his head on the pillow, though he did lean his elbow on it – a symptom of his former inclinations. He was depressed, sighed from time to time, shrugged his shoulders suddenly, shook his head in dejection. Something was violently at work in him, but it was not love. Olga's image was before his mind, but it seemed to be distant, misty, with no radiance around it, a stranger to him; he looked at it sorrowfully and sighed.

'To live as God commands and not as one would like is a wise rule, but. . . .' He sank into thought. 'No, one cannot live as one would like, that's clear,' some sullen rebellious voice in him began speaking; 'one is bound to fall into a chaos of contradictions that no human intellect,

however deep and bold, can unravel! One desired a thing
yesterday, has been passionately, desperately longing for it
to-day, and the day after to-morrow will be blushing for
having desired it and then cursing life because the desire
has been fulfilled – this is what comes of going along
boldly and independently, of following one's own will!
One must fumble one's way, shut one's eyes to many
things, and not dream of happiness, not dare to repine at
its slipping away – that is what life is! Whose notion was
it that life means delight, happiness? A mad idea! Life is
life – "duty," as Olga says, "obligation" – and duty may
be hard. Let us do our duty, then. . . .' He sighed. 'Not to
see Olga. . . . My God, you have opened my eyes and
pointed my duty to me,' he said, looking up at the sky,
'but where is the strength to do it? To part! I can still do
it now, though it will hurt me, and at any rate I shall not
curse myself afterwards for not having parted from her. . . .
And she is just going to send a message to me, she said
she would. . . . She doesn't expect. . . .'

What was the cause of it all? What wind had suddenly
blown on Oblomov? What clouds had it brought? And
why did he think of inflicting such suffering on himself?
Why, only the day before he had looked into Olga's heart
and seen there the world and his whole life bathed in
light, had read his horoscope and hers. What had happened, then? He must have taken supper or lain on his
back, and the poetic mood was replaced by horrors. It
often happens that one goes to sleep in the twinkling star-
light of a still, cloudless summer night thinking how lovely
the fields will look the next day in the bright morning
light, how delightful it will be to plunge into the depths
of the forest to escape from the heat! . . . And suddenly
one wakes to the patter of rain on the roof, to grey melancholy clouds, to the cold and damp. . . . In the evening
Oblomov had been listening as usual to the beating of his
heart and analysing his happiness when he suddenly came
upon a drop of bitterness that poisoned him. The poison
acted quickly and violently. He ran through the whole of

his life: for the hundredth time repentance and belated regret for the past gnawed at his heart. He imagined what he would have been now had he gone boldly forward, how much fuller and more varied his life would have been had he been active, and then he began to consider what he was now, and how could Olga love him, what could she love him for? Was it not a mistake? the thought flashed through his mind like lightning and the lightning struck him right in the heart and broke it. He groaned. 'A mistake, yes . . . that's what it is!' persisted in his mind.

'I love you, I love you, I love you,' he suddenly remembered, and his heart grew warmer for a moment but then was chilled again. What did Olga's 'I love' mean? An optical illusion on her part, a deceptive whisper of a heart that was still unoccupied? It was not love but merely a presentiment of love. Her voice would sound one day so powerfully, in such striking notes, that the world would hear it! The aunt and the baron would know, and the echo would spread far away! That feeling would not wind its way as gently as a little brook hiding in the grass with a hardly audible murmur. She loved now in the same way as she embroidered: she worked out the pattern slowly and lazily, still more lazily unfolded it to admire what she had done, then put it down and forgot all about it. Yes, this was only the preparation for love, an experiment, and he happened to be the first fairly passable subject that had turned up. . . . It was mere accident that had brought them together. She would not have noticed him: Stolz had pointed him out to her and infected her young impressionable heart with sympathy; she felt compassion for him, and took a pride in rousing his lazy mind; and then she would leave him. 'That's what it is!' he said in horror, getting out of bed and lighting a candle with a hand that trembled. 'It has never been anything more than that! She was ready for love, her heart was waiting eagerly and I came into her life accidentally, by mistake. . . . As soon as the right man comes along she will recognize her mistake with horror! How she will look at me then! How she will turn away . . . it's awful! I am stealing what does not belong to me: I am a thief! What am I doing! How blind I have been – good God!'

He looked at himself in the glass: he was pale and sallow, his eyes were dull. He thought of the lucky young men with a confident smile, a sprightly step, a ringing voice, with eyes that were moist and dreamy but could sparkle tremulously and had a look of depth and strength like Olga's eyes. And the day would come for one of these men to appear: she would flush suddenly, glance at Oblomov, and . . . burst out laughing!

He looked at himself in the glass once more. 'No one could love a man like me!' he said.

Then he lay down, burying his face in the pillow. 'Good-bye, Olga, be happy,' he concluded.

'Zahar!' he called in the morning. 'If a servant comes from the Ilyinskys' with an invitation for me, say I am not at home, I have gone to town.'

'Yes, sir.'

'Yes . . . no, I had better write to her,' he said to himself, 'or she will think it strange that I have suddenly disappeared. I must explain.'

He sat down to the table and began writing quickly, eagerly, with feverish haste, very differently from the way he wrote to his landlord on the first of May. Two *which's* and two *thats* never once had an unpleasant encounter.

'You will be surprised, Olga Sergeyevna [he wrote], to receive this letter instead of me, when we see each other so often. Read it to the end and you will see that I could not have acted differently. I ought to have begun by writing it, then we should have both been saved much remorse in the future; but it is not yet too late. We fell in love with each other so quickly and unexpectedly that it was like suddenly falling ill, and this was why I had not come to myself sooner. Besides, who could, looking at you and listening to you by the hour, voluntarily undertake the hard task of recovering from the enchantment? How

could one have sufficient caution and strength of will to
stop at every slope instead of gliding down it? Every day I
thought, "I will not go any farther, I will stop where I am;
it rests with me," but I was carried away, and now comes
the struggle in which you must help me. It was not till
last night I understood how rapidly I am sliding down:
yesterday I succeeded in looking deeper into the abyss
into which I am falling and I decided to stop. I am only
speaking of myself – not from selfishness, but because
when I shall be lying at the bottom of that abyss you will
still be soaring high above it like an angel of purity, and I
don't know whether you will want to cast a glance at it.
Listen, I will say simply and clearly, without any circum-
locution: you don't and you cannot love me. Trust my
experience and believe me completely. You see, my heart
began beating long ago, and though it was all wrong and
out of tune it taught me to distinguish its regular beating
from occasional throbbing. You cannot, but I can and
ought to, know truth from error, and it is my duty to
warn one who has not had time to discover it. And so I
warn you, you are in error, turn back!

'So long as love appeared to us as a light, smiling
vision, so long as it sounded in the *Casta diva*, breathed in
the smell of lilac, took the form of unexpressed sympathy,
of timid looks, I did not believe in it, thinking it was mere
play of imagination and whisper of vanity. But the light
stage has passed; love has become a disease with me, I
have felt the symptoms of passion; you have grown
thoughtful and serious; you have given me your leisure;
your nerves are unstrung; you feel restless, and now I am
frightened and feel that it is my duty to stop and tell you
what it means. I have told you that I love you and you
answered that you love me – don't you hear how discord-
ant it sounds? You don't hear? Then you will hear later,
when I am in the abyss. Look at me, think carefully of
what I am: is it possible for you to love me, do you love
me? "I love you, I love you, I love you!" you said yesterday. No, no, no! I answer firmly. You don't love me, but

you are not lying – I hasten to add this – you are not deceiving me; you are incapable of saying *yes* when you are feeling *no*. I merely want to convince you that what you feel now is not real love, but only an expectation of it; it is merely an unconscious need of love which for lack of proper fuel burns with a false flame that has no warmth in it and with women sometimes finds expression in caressing a child, in loving another woman, or sometimes simply in tears or attacks of hysteria. I ought to have sternly said to you at the beginning, "You have made a mistake, the man before you is not the one whom you have been expecting and dreaming of. Wait, he will appear and then you will come to yourself: you will be vexed and ashamed of your mistake and this shame and vexation will hurt me" – this is what I ought to have said to you had nature given me a keener mind and more energy, and, also, had I been more sincere. . . . I have said it, but you remember how: with fear lest you should believe me, lest it should really happen; I told you beforehand all that other people might say later so as to prepare you not to listen to them and not to believe them, and at the same time I hastened to meet you and thought, "The right man may not be coming yet, and meanwhile I am happy." Such is the logic of seduction and passion!

'Now I think differently. What will happen, I ask myself, when I grow attached to her, when her presence is no longer a luxury but a necessity, when love fastens on my heart for good (it's not for nothing I feel a lump there!)? How shall I tear myself away then? Shall I survive it? It will go badly with me. Even now I cannot think of it without horror. If you were older, more experienced, I would have blessed my happiness and given you my hand for ever. But now. . . .

'Why, then, do I write all this? Why haven't I come to tell you straight that my desire to see you grows every day and yet I ought not to see you? But think for yourself: how could I have the courage to say it to your face? Sometimes I do want to say something of the kind, but say something utterly different instead. Perhaps you would look sad (if it is true that you haven't been bored with me) or you might misunderstand my good intentions and be offended. I could not bear it, I would again say something different, my honourable intentions would crumble into dust and end in my arranging to meet you the next day. Away from you, it is different: your gentle eyes, your kind, pretty face is not before me, the paper is silent and long-suffering and I write calmly (this is not true): *We shall not meet again* (this is true). Another man might add, "*I write this bathed in tears*," but I don't pose before you, I don't parade my grief because I don't want to make the pain worse, to increase regret and sorrow. Such posing generally conceals the hope of making the feeling take deeper root, while I want to destroy the seeds of it both in you and in myself. And besides, tears are suitable either to languid dreamers or to seducers who try to capture a woman's incautious vanity by phrases. I say this, taking leave of you as one takes leave of a dear friend who sets out on a long journey. In another three or four weeks it would be too late, too difficult: love makes incredible progress, it's a gangrene of the soul. I am bad enough as it is, I don't reckon time by hours or minutes, by the sun rising or setting, but only reckon: I have seen her; I haven't; I shall see her, I shall not; she has been; no, she hasn't; she will come. . . . All this is very well in youth, when both the pleasant and the unpleasant emotions are borne easily, but mine is the age for peace – the dull, sleepy peace that is familiar to me; I cannot weather storms.

'Many people would wonder at my action: "Why is he running away?" some will say, and others will laugh at me: so be it, I am ready to face it. If I am ready not to see you, it means I am ready for anything.

'It is a slight comfort to me in my deep anguish to think that this short episode of our lives will leave for ever so pure and fragrant a memory behind it that it alone will be enough to prevent me from sinking once more into spiritual slumber, and without harming you will serve you as a guide in a real love in the future. Good-bye, my angel, make haste and fly away as a frightened bird flies from a branch on which it has settled by mistake, and do it as gaily, swiftly, and lightly.'

Oblomov was writing with inspiration: his pen was flying over the pages, his eyes were shining, his cheeks were flushed. The letter turned out to be long, as all love-letters are: lovers are dreadfully talkative.

'Strange! I no longer feel bored or distressed!' he thought, 'I am almost happy. . . . Why is it? It must be because I have thrown the load off my mind into the letter.'

He read the letter over, folded and sealed it.

'Zahar,' he said, 'when the servant comes give him this letter for the young lady.'

'Yes, sir,' Zahar said.

Oblomov really felt almost cheerful. He sat down on the sofa with his feet under him and asked if there was anything for lunch. He ate two eggs and lighted a cigar. His heart was full, his mind active; he was living. He was picturing to himself how Olga would receive his letter, how surprised she would be, what she would look like after reading it. What would happen then? . . . He enjoyed the possibilities of that day, the newness of the situation. . . . He listened with a sinking heart for a knock at the door, was wondering if the servant had been, if Olga was already reading his letter. . . . No, all was quiet in the hall.

'What can it mean?' he thought anxiously. 'No one has called; how could that be?'

A secret voice whispered to him at once, 'Why do you worry? This is just what you want, that no one should come and you should break off all relations.' But he stifled that voice.

After half an hour he succeeded in calling in Zahar, who had been sitting in the yard with the coachman.

'Has anyone been?' he asked. 'Was there a message?'

'Yes, there was,' Zahar answered.

'What did you say?'

'I said you were not at home, you had gone to the town.'

Oblomov stared at him open-eyed.

'But why did you say that?' he asked. 'What did I tell you to do when the man came?'

'But it wasn't a man, it was a maid,' Zahar answered with unruffled coolness.

'Did you give her my letter?'

'No, sir: you told me first to say you were not at home and then give the letter. When the man-servant comes, I will give it him.'

'Why, you – you are as good as a murderer! Where is the letter? Give it me!'

Zahar brought the letter, a good deal soiled by now.

'Mind you wash your hands!' Oblomov said angrily, pointing to the finger-marks.

'My hands are clean,' Zahar responded, looking aside.

'Anissya, Anissya!' Oblomov called.

Anissya thrust her head in at the door.

'Just see what Zahar has done!' he complained to her. 'Take this letter and give it to the Ilyinskys' footman or their maid for the young lady – do you hear?'

'Yes, sir. Let me have the letter, I will see to it.'

But as soon as she left the room Zahar snatched the letter from her.

'Go along,' he shouted, 'mind your own business, woman!'

The maid soon came again. Zahar was opening the door to her and Anissya had gone up too, but Zahar looked at her furiously.

'What are you doing here?' he asked hoarsely.

'I have just come to hear what you would say. . . .'

'Out with you!' he thundered, threatening her with his elbow. 'What next!'

She smiled and went out, but peeped through the crack

in the door to see if Zahar was carrying out his master's orders.

Hearing a noise, Ilya Ilyitch himself came to the door.

'What is it, Katya?' he asked.

'Olga Sergeyevna sent me to ask where you have gone, and you haven't gone anywhere! I'll run and tell her,' she said, turning to go.

'I am at home. Zahar is always telling stories,' Oblomov said. 'Here, give this letter to Olga Sergeyevna.'

'Yes, sir, I will.'

'Where is she now?'

'She has gone down the village street, and she says if you have finished the book will you please come to the park about two o'clock.' Katya went away.

'No, I won't go . . . why rouse the emotion when all ought to be over?' Oblomov thought, walking towards the village.

From a distance he saw Olga walking up the hill; Katya overtook her and gave her the letter; Olga stopped for a moment, looked at the letter, and thinking for a moment, nodded to Katya and turned down an avenue into the park.

Oblomov walked round the hill, entered the same avenue from the other end, and half-way down it sat down in the grass among the bushes, waiting for Olga.

'She will pass by me,' he thought. 'I will not show myself, but just see how she is and go away for ever.'

With a sinking heart he listened for her footsteps. No, all was still. Nature was busy around him: the bustle of unseen tiny life was stirring all about him, and yet nature seemed to be lying in majestic repose. But everything in the grass was moving, creeping, hurrying. Ants were racing in all directions, so busily jostling each other, running about, hastening; it was exactly like looking from a height at a market-place: the same groups scattered about, the same pushing and bustling. Here was a bumble-bee buzzing about a flower and crawling into its bell; here masses of flies were clustering round a drop of sap oozing from the cracked bark of a lime-tree; a bird somewhere in the thicket had long been repeating one and the same note, perhaps calling to its mate. Two butterflies, twirling round one another as in a waltz, whisked past the tree-trunk. A strong scent came from the grass, and the clamour that rose from it was unceasing.

'What a lot there is going on here,' Oblomov thought, watching the busy life of nature and listening to its gentle noise, 'and from the outside it all seems so still and peaceful!'

But there was no sound of footsteps. At last he thought he could hear her. 'Oh!' Oblomov sighed, parting the branches quietly. 'Yes, it's she. . . . What is it? She is crying! Oh, dear!'

Olga walked slowly along, wiping her tears with a handkerchief; but no sooner had she wiped them than fresh tears came. She tried to swallow them, to hide them from the very trees in her shame, but she could not. Oblomov had never seen Olga cry; he did not expect it, and her tears seemed to burn him, but in a way that made him warm, not hot.

He walked quickly after her.

'Olga, Olga!' he said tenderly, as he followed her.

She started, looked round, gazed at him in surprise, then turned away and walked on.

He walked beside her.

'You are crying!' he said.

Her tears fell faster than ever. She could no longer control them, and pressing her handkerchief to her eyes burst into sobs and sank down on the nearest seat.

'What have I done?' he whispered in horror, taking her hand and trying to draw it away from her face.

'Leave me!' she said. 'Go away! Why are you here? I know I must not cry – why should I? You are right; yes, anything might happen.'

'What can I do to stop your tears?' he asked, kneeling down before her. 'Tell me, command me, I am ready to do anything. . . .'

'You've made me cry, but it's not in your power to stop my tears. . . . You are not so strong as all that! Let me go!' she said, fanning her face with her handkerchief.

He looked at her and cursed himself inwardly.

'That ill-fated letter!' he said remorsefully.

She opened her basket, took out the letter and gave it him.

'Take it,' she said, 'carry it away so that I don't weep much longer looking at it.'

He put it in his pocket and sat in silence, hanging his head.

'At any rate you will do justice to my intentions, Olga,' he said softly, 'it proves how dear your happiness is to me.'

'Yes, very dear!' she said with a sigh. 'No, Ilya Ilyitch, I think you must have envied me my peaceful happiness and so hastened to disturb it.'

'To disturb it! Then you have not read my letter? I will repeat it to you. . . .'

'I haven't read to the end because I could not see for tears: I am still so silly! But I have guessed the rest; don't repeat it if you don't want to make me cry once more.'

Her tears began to flow again.

'But surely I am giving you up for the sake of your future happiness?' he began. 'I am sacrificing myself to it! Do you imagine I am doing it calmly, without weeping inwardly? Why do you suppose I am doing it?'

'Why?' she repeated, suddenly leaving off crying and turning to him. 'For the same reason that you have now hidden in the bushes to see if I would cry and how I would do it – that's why! Had you honestly wished what you have written, had you been really convinced that we ought to part, you would have gone abroad without seeing me!'

'What an idea! . . .' he said reproachfully and broke off. He was struck by her suggestion because he suddenly saw that she was right.

'Yes,' she confirmed, 'yesterday you wanted me to say I loved you, to-day you wanted my tears, and to-morrow you may want to see me die.'

'Olga, how can you wrong me so! Surely you know I would give half my life just now to hear you laugh instead of seeing your tears. . . .'

'Just now, perhaps, when you have already seen a woman cry about you. . . . No,' she added, 'you are heartless. You say you didn't want my tears, but if it were true you wouldn't have made me cry. . . .'

'But how could I have known?' he cried out, pressing both his hands to his chest.

'The heart has a wisdom of its own when it loves,' she answered, 'it knows what it wants and knows what is going to happen. Yesterday I ought not to have come here because some visitors arrived suddenly, but I knew you would have been wretched waiting for me and might have slept badly, and so I came because I did not want you to suffer. . . . And you . . . you are glad because I am crying. Very well, look, gloat over it!'

And she began to cry again.

'I have slept badly as it is, Olga; I was wretched all night. . . .'

'And so you regretted that I slept well, that I wasn't wretched – isn't that so? If I weren't crying now you would sleep badly.'

'What am I to do now – to beg your pardon?' he said with submissive tenderness.

'Only children do that, or one begs pardon for treading on a person's foot in a crowd, but in a case like this it's no good,' she said, fanning herself again.

'But, Olga, what if it is true, if I am right, and your love is a mistake? What if you fall in love with another and blush when you look at me . . . ?'

'Well, what of it?' she asked, looking at him with such deep, ironical, and penetrating eyes that he was confused.

'She is after something!' he thought. 'Take care, Ilya Ilyitch!'

'How "what of it?"' he repeated, looking at her anxiously, unable to guess her thoughts and to see how she would explain her question – since obviously there could be no justification for their love if it was a mistake.

She was looking at him deliberately and confidently, certain of what she meant.

'You are afraid,' she said maliciously, 'of falling "to the bottom of the abyss"; you are afraid of what you are going to suffer when I cease loving you! "It will go badly with me," you write. . . .'

He still failed to understand her.

'But don't you see I shall be happy if I fall in love with somebody else, so that all will be well with me! And you say you know I shall be happy and are ready to sacrifice everything, your very life, for my sake?'

He looked at her attentively, blinking from time to time.

'So that's the logic of it!' he whispered. 'I confess I didn't expect this. . . .'

She looked him up and down with poisonous irony.

'And the happiness that is driving you mad,' she went on, 'and these mornings and evenings, this park, my saying *I love you* – isn't all this worth something, worth some sacrifice, some pain?'

'I wish I could sink through the ground!' he thought in misery, as he grasped Olga's meaning.

'And what if you grow tired of this love,' she continued warmly, 'as you have grown tired of books, of your work, of society? What if, in time, without any rival love, you simply drop asleep beside me as on your sofa and my voice fails to waken you? What if the lump in your heart disperses and you prefer to me not another woman even, but your dressing-gown?'

'Olga, it's impossible!' he interrupted with annoyance, drawing away from her.

'Why impossible? You say that I am mistaken, that I will fall in love with somebody else, and I think sometimes that you will simply fall out of love with me. And what then? How shall I justify myself for what I am doing now? Not to mention other people and society, what shall I say to myself? This keeps me also awake at times, but I don't torture you with surmises about the future because I hope for the best. With me happiness outweighs fear. I do think it is worth something when I make your eyes shine, when you climb hills in search of me, when you forget your indolence and rush off in the heat to the town for a book or some flowers for me, when I see that you smile and are eager to live because of me. . . . If I am making a mistake, if it is true that I shall bewail it, at any rate I feel here' (she put her hand to her heart) 'that the future will not be my fault; it will mean that fate was against me, that it wasn't God's will. But I am not afraid of having to shed tears in the future; I shall not be weeping for nothing: it will be a price worth paying! . . . I was so happy . . . till now!' she added.

'Do let yourself be happy again!' Oblomov implored.

'And you see nothing but gloom ahead; happiness is nothing to you. . . . It's ingratitude,' she went on; 'it isn't love, it's. . . .'

'Selfishness!' Oblomov finished the sentence for her, not daring to look at Olga or to speak or to beg her forgiveness.

'Go on to where you were going,' she said gently.

He glanced at her. Her eyes were dry. She was looking down thoughtfully and drawing with her umbrella in the sand.

'Lie on your back again,' she added, 'you will not be making a mistake then or "falling into an abyss". . . .'

'I have poisoned myself and poisoned you instead of being happy simply and straightforwardly . . .' he muttered remorsefully.

'Drink *kvass*: that won't poison you,' she mocked him.

'Olga, it's ungenerous,' he said, 'when I have been torturing myself. . . .'

'Yes, in words you torture yourself, fling yourself into abysses, give half your life – and then doubt comes and a sleepless night; how tender you are with yourself then, how cautious, how solicitous and far-seeing!'

'That is the truth and how simple it is!' Oblomov thought, but he was ashamed to say it aloud. Why was it he had not discovered this truth for himself, but a woman who had hardly begun to live had to explain it to him? How quickly she had grown up: quite a short time ago she had seemed a child!

'We have nothing more to say to each other,' she concluded, getting up. 'Good-bye, Ilya Ilyitch, and be . . . calm; that's what happiness means for you.'

'Olga, no, for God's sake, no! Don't drive me away now, when everything has been made clear again . . .' he said, taking her hand.

'But what do you want of me? You wonder if my love for you isn't a mistake: I cannot calm your doubt; perhaps it is a mistake – I don't know.'

He let go her hand. The knife was raised over him again.

'How, you don't know? Don't you feel it?' he asked, looking doubtful once more. 'Don't you suspect? . . .'

'I don't suspect anything; I told you yesterday what I felt, but I don't know what is going to happen in a year's time. But can one happiness be followed by another and then by a third just like it?' she asked, looking at him open-eyed. 'Tell me, you have had more experience than I.'

But he no longer wanted to confirm her in the idea and said nothing, shaking an acacia-branch with one hand.

'No, love only comes once!' he said, like a schoolboy repeating a lesson.

'There, you see; I believe it too,' she added. 'But if it is not so, perhaps I shall fall out of love with you, perhaps my mistake will make me suffer, perhaps we shall part! . . . To love twice, three times . . . no, no . . . I don't want to believe it!'

He sighed. The *perhaps* was rankling in his soul and he walked after her listlessly, lost in thought. But his heart felt lighter at every step; the *mistake* he had invented in the night seemed to be so far ahead. . . . 'After all, it's not only love, but all life is like this . . .' he thought suddenly, 'and if one rejects every opportunity as a mistake, when will the real thing come? What is the matter with me? I seem to have gone blind. . . .'

'Olga,' he said, lightly touching her waist with two fingers (she stopped), 'you are cleverer than I am.'

She shook her head.

'No, I am simpler and have more courage. What are you afraid of? Do you mean to say you seriously think one may fall out of love?' she asked, with proud confidence.

'I am not afraid any longer,' he said gaily. 'With you I do not fear the future!'

'I have read that phrase somewhere recently . . . in Sue, I think,' she suddenly said, mockingly, turning to him, 'only there it's a woman who says it to a man. . . .'

Oblomov flushed crimson.

'Olga, let everything be as yesterday,' he implored her, 'I will not be afraid of *mistakes!*'

She said nothing.

'Yes?' he asked timidly. 'Well, if you won't say it, give me some sign . . . a spray of lilac. . . .'

'Lilac . . . is over, it's done for,' she answered. 'You see what is left of it – it's all withered.'

'It's over, it's withered!' he repeated, looking at the lilac. 'And it's all over with the letter too!' he said suddenly.

She shook her head. He walked after her thinking about the letter, the happiness of yesterday, the withered lilac.

'Lilac certainly is over!' he thought. 'Why did I write that letter? What kept me awake all night and made me write it this morning? Now that my mind is at rest once more . . .' (he yawned) 'I feel dreadfully sleepy. And if I hadn't written the letter there would have been nothing of this: she wouldn't have cried, everything would have been as yesterday; we should have sat quietly in this avenue, looking at each other and talking of happiness. It would have been the same to-day and to-morrow . . .' he gave a big yawn.

Then it suddenly struck him what would have happened had his letter achieved its purpose and she had agreed with him and been as afraid of mistakes and distant future storms as he was; if she had listened to his so-called experience and good sense and consented to part from him, to forget each other! God forbid! To say good-bye, to return to the town, to go to the new flat! An interminable night would have followed, a dull to-morrow, an unbearable after-to-morrow, and a series of days one more colourless than the other. . . . How could that be? It would have been death! And that is what would have happened! He would have fallen ill. He had not wanted to part from her, he could not have endured it, he would have come to her and implored her to see him. 'What did I write the letter for?' he asked himself.

'Olga Sergeyevna,' he said.

'Yes?'

'I must confess something else to you. . . .'

'What is it?'

'Why, there was no need whatever for that letter. . . .'

'Oh yes, it was necessary.'

She turned round and laughed when she saw what a face he made; his sleepiness vanished suddenly and he opened his eyes wide with surprise.

'Necessary?' he repeated, slowly staring at her back with amazement. But all he could see there were the two tassels of her mantle.

What, then, did her tears and reproaches mean? Was it a ruse? But Olga was not cunning – he saw that clearly. It is only women of inferior mind that have recourse to cunning. For lack of direct intelligence they move the springs of their everyday, petty life by means of cunning, and weave the network of their domestic policy without observing the direction which the main currents of life around them are taking. Cunning is like small coin with which one cannot buy much. Just as small coin can keep one going for an hour or two, so cunning may serve to conceal something, to deceive someone, to put a wrong construction on things, but does not enable one to see a far horizon, to connect the issues in the case of any big event. Cunning is short-sighted: it sees well only what is close at hand and is often caught in the trap it has set for others. Olga was simply intelligent: how well and clearly she had solved the problem to-day, as, indeed, she always did! She saw at once the true meaning of anything and went straight to the point. And cunning was like a mouse running round things and hiding. . . . And altogether it was not in Olga's character. What did her words mean, then? What new thing was this?

'Why was the letter necessary?' he asked.

'Why?' she repeated gaily, turning round to him, delighted with her power to nonplus him at any moment. 'Because,' she began slowly, 'you were awake all night and wrote it all for me; I, too, am selfish! This is the first reason. . . .'

'Then why did you reproach me just now if you agree with me?' Oblomov interrupted her.

'Because you invented trouble. I did not invent it, it simply came, and I am happy it's over, but you prepared it all beforehand and enjoyed the prospect. You are heartless and I reproached you for that. Then . . . there is a play of thought and feeling in your letter . . . last night and this morning you lived, not in your usual way, but as your friend and I like you to live – that's the second reason; and the third reason. . . .'

She walked up so close to him that the blood rushed to his heart and his head; he could hardly breathe with emotion. She looked him straight in the eyes.

'The third reason is that this letter reflects, as in a mirror, your tenderness, your solicitude, your care for me, your fear for my happiness, your pure conscience . . . all that Andrey Ivanitch pointed out to me in you and all that made me love you, that makes me forget your

indolence . . . your apathy. . . . You gave yourself away in
that letter: no, you are not selfish, Ilya Ilyitch, you wrote
it not because you wanted to part from me – you
didn't want that – but because you were afraid of deceiving me . . . it was your honesty speaking; had it been
otherwise your letter would have wounded me and I
wouldn't have wept – from pride! You see, I know what I
love you for and I am not afraid of making a mistake: I am
not mistaken in you. . . .'

It seemed to Oblomov there was a halo, a radiance
around her as she spoke. Her eyes were shining with the
triumph of love, with the consciousness of her own
power; her cheeks were flushed. And he – he was the
cause of it! An honest impulse of his heart had kindled
that fire in her soul, given rise to this play, this brilliance!

'Olga . . . you are the best of women, you are the finest
woman in the world!' he said in ecstasy, and beside himself he put out his arms and bent over her.

'For God's sake . . . one kiss as a token of unspeakable
happiness . . .' he whispered deliriously.

She stepped back instantly; the triumphant radiance,
the colour, left her face and her gentle eyes blazed with
indignation.

'Never! Never! Don't come near me!' she said in alarm,
almost in horror, and stretching out both arms and parasol
to ward him off, she stood breathless and motionless in a
forbidding attitude, her head half turned, her eyes bright
with anger.

He subsided suddenly; it was not the gentle Olga
before him, but an offended goddess of pride and wrath,
with compressed lips and lightnings in her eyes.

'Forgive me! . . .' he whispered in confusion, feeling
utterly crushed.

She turned slowly and walked on, glancing timidly over
her shoulder to see what he was doing. But there was
nothing alarming about him: he lagged behind like a dog
that has been scolded and walks with its tail between its
legs. She had quickened her pace, but when she saw his

face she suppressed a smile and walked more leisurely, though she still shuddered from time to time. The colour came and went in her cheeks. As she walked her face cleared, her breath grew more even, and her pace slackened. She saw how sacred her '*never*' was for Oblomov and her anger gradually gave way to regret. She walked slower and slower. . . . She wanted to make amends for her outburst; she was trying to find a pretext to speak.

'I've ruined everything! This, now, is a real mistake! "Never!" Oh dear, the lilacs are over,' he thought, looking at the faded flowers, '*yesterday* has faded away, and my letter too, and this moment, the best in my life, when a woman has told me for the first time, like a voice from heaven, what good there is in me, it, too, has faded away! . . .' He looked at Olga – she stood waiting for him, with her eyes cast down.

'Give me the letter,' she said softly.

'It has faded away!' he answered sadly, giving it to her. She drew close to him once more and bent down her head; her eyes were almost closed. She was nearly trembling. He gave her the letter; she did not raise her head or move away.

'You frightened me!' she added gently.

'Forgive me, Olga,' he muttered.

She said nothing.

'That terrible *never!*' he said sadly, with a sigh.

'It will fade away!' she whispered, hardly audibly, flushing crimson. She cast a shy, tender glance at him, took both his hands, and, pressing them warmly, put them to her heart.

'Do you hear it throbbing?' she said. 'You frightened me! Let me go!'

And without looking at him she turned round and ran along the path, slightly lifting the hem of her skirt.

'Where are you off to?' he said. 'I am tired, I cannot keep pace with you. . . .'

'Leave me. I am running to sing, sing, sing!' she

repeated with burning cheeks. 'My heart is so full, it almost hurts me!'

He remained standing, and gazed long after her as though she were an angel flying away.

'Can it be that this moment, too, will fade away?' he asked himself almost sadly, without noticing whether he was walking or standing.

'The lilacs are over,' he thought, 'and so is yesterday, and so is last night with its phantoms, its choking misery. . . . Yes, and this moment, too, will be over like the lilacs! But while last night was passing away, this morning was coming into flower. . . .'

'What does it mean?' he said aloud in his absent-mindedness. 'Then love too. . . . And I had thought that it would hang over lovers like a sultry noon when nothing moves or breathes; but there is no rest in love either, it, too, keeps changing, moving on and on . . . "like all life," Stolz said. And the Joshua who would tell it "Stand still!" has not yet been born. What will happen to-morrow?' he asked himself anxiously, as he lazily walked home lost in thought. Passing under Olga's windows he heard the strains of Schubert in which her heart was finding relief from its burden and seemed to be sobbing with happiness.

Oh dear! How delightful life was!

XI

At home Oblomov found another letter from Stolz beginning and ending with the words 'now or never,' and full of reproaches for his inertia; Stolz insisted on his coming to Switzerland, where he himself was going, and then to Italy. Failing this he suggested that Oblomov should go to the country, see to his affairs, rouse the peasants to work, ascertain his income, and begin building his new house. 'Remember our pact: now or never!' he concluded. 'Now, now, now!' Oblomov repeated. 'Andrey doesn't know what romance has come into my life. What more does he want of me? Can I ever be as busy as I am now? I should like him to try it! One reads about the French and the English always being at work, always busy; but they travel about Europe or even Asia or Africa just for their pleasure – for drawing in their albums or excavating antiquities or shooting lions or catching snakes. Or they sit at home in noble idleness, having lunches and dinners with their friends and ladies – that's all their work comes to! Why should I be sentenced to hard labour? It's only Andrey thinks one must work like a horse! Why should I? I have enough to eat and have clothes to my back. Olga did ask me, though, if I meant to go to Oblomovka. . . .'

He spent feverish hours writing and reckoning, and actually went to consult an architect. Soon the plan of the house and the garden lay on his little table. It was a roomy house with two balconies. 'Here is my room, here is Olga's, this is the bedroom, this the nursery . . .' he thought with a smile. 'But the peasants, the peasants . . .' the smile left his lips and he frowned anxiously. 'My neighbour goes into all sorts of details in his letter, talks of land under the plough, of the yield per acre. Such a bore! And he suggests, too, that we should share the expense of making a road to a big trading village and a bridge over the river, asks for three thousand roubles and wants me to mortgage Oblomovka. . . . But how do I know if it's really necessary? Will any good come of it? Isn't he cheating me? Granted that he is an honest man – Stolz knows him, but he may be mistaken and my money will be gone! Three thousand is a lot – where am I to get it? No, it's too great a risk! He also writes that some of the peasants ought to be settled on the waste land and wants an answer at once – he is always in such a hurry! He promises to send me all the documents necessary for the mortgage. I am to send him a deed of trust, to go to the courts to have it witnessed – what next! I don't even know where the courts are and which door to try!'

Oblomov had left the letter unanswered for a fortnight, and meanwhile even Olga asked him if he had been to the courts. Stolz sent another letter to him and one to Olga asking what he was doing. But Olga could keep only a superficial watch over his doings and that only in her own sphere. She knew whether he looked happy, went everywhere readily, came to the copse at the appointed hour, was sufficiently interested in the current news, in general conversation. She watched still more jealously that he should not lose sight of the main purpose of his life. She asked him about the courts merely so that she could answer Stolz's question.

The summer was at its height; it was the end of July; the weather was perfect. Oblomov hardly ever parted from Olga. On fine days they were in the park, in the hot noonday hours they found shelter under the fir-trees in the copse; he sat at her feet reading to her; she had started another piece of embroidery – this time for him. Summer was hot in their hearts too: clouds would sometimes flit across their sky and float away. If he had troubled dreams and doubt knocked at his heart, Olga stood by him like a guardian angel: she looked with her bright eyes into his face, discovered what he had on his mind, and all was well again and the stream of feeling flowed peacefully like a river reflecting the changing clouds. Olga's convictions about life and love and everything had grown still clearer and more definite. She had more confidence in herself and was not afraid of the future; her mind was developing in new directions; her character betrayed new qualities. Her mind now displayed depth and poetic variety and now worked clearly, accurately, consistently, and naturally. . . . She had a kind of tenacity which triumphed, not merely over destiny, but over Oblomov's indolence and apathy. If she fixed upon some plan the work made rapid progress. One heard of nothing else; or if she did not speak one could see that she had the thing in mind, that she would not forget or give it up or lose her bearings, but would take everything into consideration and attain her object. Oblomov could not understand what was the source of her strength, of her instinctive knowledge of what to do and how to do it whatever circumstances might arise. 'It's because one of her eyebrows is never straight, but is raised a little and there is a tiny, hardly perceptible fold above it . . .' he thought. 'It's there that her tenacity is hidden.' However calm and happy her expression might be, her eyebrows did not lie level, and the line was never smoothed out. But there was nothing bold or self-assertive about her manner. Tenacity and determination did not make her a whit less feminine. She had no ambition to be a lioness, to pull up sharply a tactless admirer, to surprise the company by the smartness of her wit, so that someone in the corner of the drawing-room should cry, 'Bravo!' Like many women she was actually timid in some ways; it is true she did not tremble at the sight of a mouse or faint if a chair fell down, but she was afraid to walk too far from home, she turned aside if she saw a suspicious-looking peasant, she closed her window at night lest burglars should climb in – like a true woman! Besides, she easily felt pity and compassion. It was not difficult to make her cry; the way to her heart was easily found. In love she was very tender; her relations with everyone were full of kindness, of affectionate solicitude – in short, she was a woman! Sometimes there was a sparkle of irony in her speech, but it was so gracious and reflected such a charming, gentle nature that one was only too glad to be its victim. She was not afraid of draughts and went lightly clad after sunset – it did not hurt her! She was brimming over with health, her appetite was excellent, she had her favourite dishes and knew how to cook them. All this, of course, can be said of many other women, but then they do not know what to do in an emergency; they only know what they have learned once for all or have heard from others, and cannot tell why they act in the way they do, but refer to the authority of a cousin or an aunt. . . . Many do not even know what it is they want, and if they decide upon something they do it so listlessly that one cannot make out whether they really care. This must be because their eyebrows lie in even arches that have been plucked with the fingers and there is no wrinkle on their forehead.

A secret understanding, invisible to the others, existed between Olga and Oblomov: every look, every insignificant word uttered in the presence of others, had a special meaning for them. They saw in everything a reference to love. In spite of her self-confidence, Olga sometimes flushed crimson if somebody told at table a love-story that resembled her own; and since all love-stories are very much alike she often had to blush. Oblomov, too, at the mention of love would seize in his confusion such a heap of biscuits at tea that someone was sure to laugh. They had grown cautious and sensitive. Sometimes Olga omitted to tell her aunt that she had seen Oblomov, and he would say at home that he was going to town and walk to the park instead.

But although Olga's mind and her general outlook were so clear she began to develop some morbid symptoms in spite of her health and vigour. A restlessness that she could not account for came over her at times. Holding Oblomov's arm as she walked in the noonday heat she sometimes leaned lazily against his shoulder and moved mechanically, in a kind of exhaustion, never saying a

word. Her liveliness deserted her; tired and listless, she
fixed her eyes on some one point and felt too lazy to shift
them. Something seemed to weigh her down, to press on
her breast, to disturb her. She took off her mantle, her
fichu, but it did not help – she felt as oppressed as ever.
She would have liked to lie down under a tree and stay
there for hours. Oblomov was at a loss; he fanned her
with a branch, but she made an impatient sign for him to
stop and still could find no peace. Then she sighed
suddenly, glanced around with conscious eyes, and looking at him pressed his hand; she was once more gay and
vigorous and regained her self-control.

One evening she had a bad attack of this restlessness;
she was, as it were, moonstruck with love, and Oblomov
saw a new aspect of her. It was hot and sultry; the dull
murmur of a warm wind came from the forest; the sky
was overcast. It was growing darker and darker. 'It is
going to rain,' said the baron, and went home. Marya
Mihailovna retired to her room. Olga played the piano
dreamily, but at last she stopped.

'I can't, my fingers are trembling; I feel choked,' she
said to Oblomov. 'Let us go into the garden.'

They walked for some time along the avenues, hand in
hand. Her hands were moist and soft. They entered the
park. The trees and bushes were merged into a gloomy
mass; one could not see two paces ahead, and only the
winding, sandy paths showed white. Olga looked intently
into the darkness and pressed herself against Oblomov.
They roamed about in silence. 'I am afraid!' she said,
starting suddenly as they were almost fumbling their way
down a narrow avenue between two black, impenetrable
walls of trees. 'What of?' he asked. 'Don't be afraid, Olga,
I am with you.' – 'I am afraid of you too,' she said in a
whisper, 'but it is a pleasant fear, somehow. There's a
flutter at my heart. Give me your hand, feel how it beats.'
She trembled and looked round. 'There, do you see?' she
whispered with a start, clutching at his shoulder with
both hands. 'Do you see something flitting in the dark-

ness?' She pressed herself close to him. 'There is no one here . . .' he said, but he, too, felt a cold shiver run down his back. 'Cover up my eyes with something . . . cover them close!' she whispered. 'I am better now. . . . It's my nerves,' she added uneasily. 'There, again! Look! Who is it? Let us sit down. . . .' He felt his way to a garden seat and led her to it. 'Let us go home, Olga,' he urged her, 'you are not well.' She put her head on his shoulder. 'No, the air here is fresher,' she said, 'I feel so stifled,' her breath was hot against his cheek. He touched her head – it was hot too. She breathed unevenly and often heaved a sigh. 'Hadn't we better go home?' Oblomov insisted anxiously. 'You ought to lie down.' – 'No, no, let me be, don't disturb me,' she said languidly, hardly audibly, 'my heart seems on fire.' – 'Do let us go home!' Oblomov hurried her. – 'No, wait, I shall be better in a minute. . . .' She pressed his hand and now and again looked close into his eyes. She did not speak for several minutes and suddenly began to cry, quietly at first, and then broke into sobs. He was utterly at a loss. 'For God's sake, Olga, let's hurry home,' he said in alarm. 'It's nothing,' she answered, sobbing, 'don't disturb me, let me have a cry. . . . The fire will find vent in tears and I shall be better; It's just my nerves. . . .' He listened in the darkness to her heavy breathing, felt her warm tears on his hand, the convulsive pressure of her palm. He did not dare to breathe, to stir a finger. Her head lay on his shoulder, he felt her hot breath on his cheek. . . . He, too, was trembling, but he did not dare to touch her cheek with his lips. She grew still after a time and breathed more evenly. . . . She did not speak. He wondered if she were asleep and was afraid to stir. 'Olga!' he called in a whisper. – 'What?' she answered in a whisper too, and sighed aloud. 'There, it's over . . . I am better,' she said languidly. 'I can breathe freely.' – 'Let us go,' he said. – 'Let us,' she answered reluctantly. 'Darling!' she whispered tenderly, pressing his hand, and leaning against his shoulder walked home with unsteady steps. He looked at her when they were in the drawing-room: she seemed exhausted and was smiling a strange, unconscious smile as though she were dreaming. He made her sit down on the sofa, knelt beside her, and, deeply touched, kissed her hand again and again. She looked at him with the same smile, abandoning both hands to him, and her eyes followed him as he walked to the door. In the doorway he turned round: she was still looking after him and there was the same languor in her face, the same ardent smile that she seemed unable to restrain. . . . He went away pondering. He had seen that smile somewhere; he was trying to recall the picture of a woman with a smile like that . . . only it was not Cordelia.

The next day he sent to inquire after her health. The answer was that she was quite well and would he please come to dinner, and in the evening they were going for a three-mile drive to see the fireworks.

He could not believe it and went to see for himself. Olga was fresh like a flower: her eyes were bright and lively, her cheeks rosy, her voice had a ringing note in it. But she was suddenly confused and almost cried out when Oblomov came up to her, and flushed all over when he asked her how she was feeling after last night. 'It was a slight attack of nerves,' she said hurriedly. '*Ma tante* says I ought to go to bed earlier. It's come over me only lately. . . .'

She broke off and turned away as though begging for mercy. But she did not know herself why she was so confused. Why should the memory of that evening and of her attack of nerves torment her so? She felt ashamed of something and vexed, too, though she did not know whether it was with herself or with Oblomov. At moments it seemed to her that Oblomov had grown nearer and dearer to her, that she loved him to tears, as though the night had united them by some mysterious bond. . . .

She could not go to sleep for hours, in the morning walked alone in agitation up and down the avenue that led from the house to the park, lost in conjectures, thinking hard, frowning, blushing suddenly, smiling at something –

and yet could arrive at no conclusion. 'Ah, that lucky Sonitchka would have settled it at once!' she thought in vexation.

And Oblomov? Why had he been mute and motionless the night before, though her breath was burning his cheek, her hot tears fell on his hand, and he had almost carried her home in his arms, and overheard the tell-tale whisper of her heart? Another man in his place would have. . . .

Although Oblomov's youth had been spent among companions who knew all about everything and believed in nothing, who had settled all vital problems long ago, and analysed everything with cold wisdom, he still believed in friendship, in love, in honour, and however many mistakes he made or might still make about people they did not undermine his conception of goodness and his faith in it. He secretly worshipped feminine purity, admitted its rights and power, and was ready to make sacrifices for its sake. But he had not enough character openly to recognize the principles of goodness and of respect for innocence. He enjoyed its fragrance in secret, but in words he sometimes joined the cynics who dread being suspected of chastity or of having respect for it, and added his frivolous remarks to their ribald conversation. He never clearly grasped what tremendous weight attaches to a good, true, and pure word thrown into the stream of talk and how deeply it alters the course of it; he did not know that when uttered boldly and aloud, with courage instead of a blush of false shame, it is not drowned by the hideous shouts of worldly satyrs, but sinks like a pearl to the depths of social life and always finds a shell to hold it. Many people turn crimson with shame when they try to utter a good saying, while they boldly and loudly speak frivolous words, not suspecting that these words are not, unfortunately, uttered in vain either, but leave behind a long trail of evil, sometimes irremediable. But however wrong Oblomov's words may have been he did not put them into practice: there was not a single stain on his conscience, and no one could reproach him with cold, soulless cynicism that knows neither emotion nor struggle. He could not bear to hear the everyday talk of how one man had bought new horses or new furniture and another – a new woman . . . and what the cost of the purchase was. He often grieved for a man who had lost his honour and dignity, or for a woman – an utter stranger to him – who had fallen into the mire, but he said nothing, afraid of public opinion. One had to guess his feeling: Olga did guess it.

Men laugh at such queer characters and women recognize them at once: pure and chaste ones love them from affinity; and depraved ones seek intimacy with them as a relief from their own depravity.

Summer was drawing to its close. The mornings and evenings were growing dark and damp. Not only lilac but lime blossom was over, strawberries and raspberries were over. Oblomov and Olga saw each other every day. He was once more keeping pace with life – that is, he caught up all the things he had let go for years; he knew why the French ambassador had left Rome, why the English were sending battleships to the East, he was interested in a new railway being made in France or Germany. But he gave no thought to the road from Oblomovka to the big village, he had not had the deed of trust witnessed at the courts, and had not answered Stolz's letter. He was well informed only about the things that formed the subject of daily conversation at Olga's house, or were read in the papers received there, and owing to Olga's insistence he followed current foreign literature fairly closely. Everything else was drowned in love. In spite of frequent changes in the rosy atmosphere, there were no clouds on his horizon. Olga, it is true, wondered sometimes about Oblomov and her love for him – when that love left her any time and energy to spare; if some of her questions failed to find a complete and ready answer in his mind, if his will did not respond to hers, and he replied only by a heavy, passionate glance to her vigour and liveliness, she sank into despondent brooding: something cold as a snake crept into her heart, wakened her from her dream, and the warm, fairy-like world of love turned into a grey autumn day. She asked herself why she was dissatisfied, why her happiness was incomplete. What was lacking? What more did she want? Surely it was what she had been destined for – to love Oblomov? That love was justified by his gentleness, by his pure faith in goodness, and above all by his tenderness – a tenderness she had never seen in a man's eyes. What did it matter, then, if he did not always look as though he understood the expression of her eyes, if his voice sometimes sounded differently from what she seemed to have heard once in her dreams or perhaps in reality. . . . It was her nerves, her imagination; what was the good of listening to it and inventing trouble? And besides, even if she did want to escape this love, how could she? The thing was done: she was in love already and it was impossible to discard love at will, like a dress. 'One does not love twice,' she thought. 'They say it's immoral. . . .'

This was how she was learning love, testing it, marking every fresh step with a smile or a tear and thinking deeply about it. This was why she had the concentrated expression that held both smiles and tears and alarmed Oblomov so much. But she never even hinted to him about her thoughts and struggles. Oblomov did not think about love; he abandoned himself to a kind of sweet drowsiness of which he had once dreamt aloud before Stolz. At times he began to believe in life being always cloudless, and once more dreamed of Oblomovka full of kind, friendly, untroubled faces, of sitting on the verandah, absorbed in the contemplation of complete and perfect happiness. He sometimes indulged in it even now, and on two occasions, which he concealed from Olga, dropped asleep in the forest while waiting for her. But suddenly there was a cloud. . . .

One day they were lazily and silently returning from a walk, and just as they were going to cross the high road a carriage, flying along in a cloud of dust, met them. Sonitchka and her husband, and another lady and gentleman, were in the carriage. . . .

'Olga! Olga! Olga Sergeyevna!' they cried.

The carriage stopped. The ladies and gentlemen stepped out, surrounding Olga, and there were greetings and kisses; they all spoke at once, taking no notice of Oblomov. Then they all looked at him suddenly, one gentleman through a lorgnette.

'Who is this?' Sonitchka asked quietly.

'Ilya Ilyitch Oblomov!' Olga introduced him. They all set off to walk home together. Oblomov felt uncomfortable; he lagged behind and had just raised his leg to climb over a fence and escape home through the rye when a look from Olga bid him stay. He would not have minded, but all these ladies and gentlemen looked at him so strangely. This, too, would not have mattered; in the old days people had always looked at him like this because of his sleepy, bored expression and his slovenly clothes. But they looked in the same strange way at Olga, too, and their suspicious glances suddenly made his heart turn cold; he felt such pangs that he could endure it no longer and went home thoughtful and morose. The following day Olga's charming chatter and affectionate playfulness could not cheer him. He had to plead headache in answer to her insistent questions, and patiently submitted to having seventy-five copecks' worth of eau-de-Cologne poured on his head. The day after that, when they came home late in the evening, Olga's aunt looked somehow too knowingly at them, especially at him, and then lowering her heavy, slightly swollen eyelids, thoughtfully sniffed her smelling-salts for a minute, while her eyes seemed to be still fixed upon him. Oblomov suffered in silence. He did not venture to confide his doubts to Olga, afraid of alarming her, and also, if the truth be told, afraid of disturbing their peaceful and cloudless world by so grave a question. It was no longer a question of whether she had fallen in love with him by mistake, but of whether the whole of their love – their meeting in the forest, alone, sometimes late at night, was not a mistake. 'I presumed to ask for a kiss,' he thought with horror, 'and that's a crime in the moral code, and not a small one either! There are many stages before it: pressing the hand, avowal, letter. . . . We have been through all that. But, after all,' he thought, raising his head, 'my intentions are honourable, I. . . .' And suddenly the cloud vanished and a bright vision of Oblomovka, basking in brilliant sunshine with its green hills and sparkling river, appeared before him; he was dreamily walking beside Olga down a long avenue, his arm round her waist; they were sitting in the arbour, on the verandah. . . . Everyone bowed down before her in adoration – in short, it was just what he had described to Stolz. 'Yes, yes; but I ought to have begun by that,' he thought anxiously again, 'those three, "I love you," the lilac branch, the avowal – all that ought to be the token of lifelong happiness, and never be repeated again in the case of a pure woman. What am I then? What am I?' the question hammered in his head. 'I am a seducer, a lady-killer! I might as well, like that nasty old rake with oily eyes and a red nose, stick in my buttonhole a rose stolen from a woman and whisper to my friends about my conquest, so that . . . so that. . . . Oh, my goodness, what have I come to! This indeed is an abyss! And Olga is not soaring high above it, but is at the bottom. . . . Why, what has she done to deserve it?'

He was overwhelmed and wept like a child at the thought that the rainbow colours of his life had suddenly faded, and that Olga was going to be sacrificed. His love was a crime, a stain on his conscience. The storm in his mind subsided for a moment when he reflected that there was a lawful issue to it all: to give Olga his hand with a wedding-ring. . . .

'Yes, yes,' he said, with a joyful flutter, 'and her answer will be a look of shy consent. She will not say a word, but flush crimson, smile with all her heart, and then her eyes will fill with tears. . . .' Tears and smiles, a hand silently stretched towards him, then lively, playful joy, the flurry of happiness in all her movements, a long, long conversation, whispered confidences and a secret pact to merge two lives into one! A love unseen to everyone but themselves will shine in every trivial thing, in every commonplace conversation. And no one will dare to insult them with a look. . . .

His face suddenly looked grave and stern.

'Yes,' he said to himself, 'that's where the world of secure, straightforward and honourable happiness is to be found! I ought to be ashamed to have been all this time plucking flowers, bathing in the fragrance of love like a boy, keeping trysts, walking about in the moonlight, listening to her heart-beats, catching her fluttering dreams. . . . My God!'

He flushed crimson.

'This very evening Olga shall know what stern duties are imposed by love; this shall be our last meeting alone. . . .'

He put his hand to his heart: it was beating vigorously but evenly, as an honourable man's heart ought to beat.

He was once more excited at the thought of how grieved Olga would be when he told her that they must not meet, he would find out what she thought, would enjoy her confusion, and at last timidly declare his intentions. . . . Then he dreamed of her shy consent, her smile and tears, of the hand she would silently give him, of their secret whispers together, of the kiss in front of the whole world.

XII

HE ran to find Olga. They told him at her house that she had gone out; he went to the village – she was not there. He saw her climbing a hill in the distance, looking like an angel ascending to heaven, so light was her tread, so graceful her movements. He followed her, but she seemed hardly to touch the grass with her feet, as though she were really flying. Half-way up the hill he began calling to her.

She waited for him, but as soon as he came within fifteen feet of her, she walked on again, leaving a big space between them, then stopped again and laughed. He stopped at last, certain that she would not escape him. She ran down a few steps towards him, gave him her hand, and, laughing, dragged him after her. They entered the copse; he took off his hat, she wiped his forehead with a handkerchief and began fanning him with her parasol.

Olga was particularly lively, gay, and chatty; she had sudden outbursts of affection and then all at once grew thoughtful.

'Guess what I was doing yesterday?' she asked him when they sat down in the shade.

'Reading?'

She shook her head.

'Writing?'

'No.'

'Singing?'

'No. Telling fortunes!' she said. 'The countess's housekeeper came yesterday; she can tell fortunes by cards, so I asked her to tell mine.'

'Well, what did she tell you?'

'Nothing special. A journey, a crowd of people, and a fair man beside me all the time. . . . I blushed all over when she said in Katya's presence that a king of diamonds was thinking about me. When she wanted to tell me whom I was thinking of I mixed up the cards and ran away. You are thinking of me, aren't you?' she asked suddenly.

'Ah, I wish I could think of you less!' he said.

'And I . . .' she said thoughtfully. 'I seem to have forgotten that life can be different. When you were sulky last week and did not come for two days – you remember, you were cross? – I suddenly changed and grew so bad-tempered! I quarrelled with Katya as you do with Zahar; I saw she was crying to herself and I did not feel in the least sorry for her. I didn't answer *ma tante* and did not hear what she said, I didn't do anything or go anywhere. And as soon as you came I grew quite different again. I gave Katya my lilac dress. . . .'

'It's love!' he pronounced dramatically.

'What, the lilac dress?'

'Everything! I recognize myself in all you say; for me, too, there is no daylight or life without you; I keep dreaming of flowering valleys at night. When I see you I feel good and want to do things, and without you I am bored and lazy, I want to lie down and think of nothing. . . . Love me, don't be ashamed of your love. . . .'

He suddenly stopped. 'What am I saying? It wasn't for this I came,' he thought, and frowning started to cough.

'And what if I die?' she asked.

'What an idea!' he said carelessly.

'Yes,' she went on, 'I will catch cold and fall ill with fever; you will come here and not find me; you will come to us and they will tell you I am ill, and the same thing next day; the shutters in my room will be closed; the doctor will shake his head; Katya will come out to you on tiptoe, in tears, and whisper, "She is ill, she is dying. . . ." '

'Oh!' Oblomov cried out suddenly.

She laughed.

'What will become of you then?' she asked, looking into his face.

'What? I shall go mad or shoot myself, and you may recover after all!'

'No, no, don't!' she said nervously. 'What are we talking about! Only you mustn't come to me as a ghost, I am afraid of corpses. . . .'

He laughed and so did she.

'Oh dear, what children we are!' she said, growing sober.

He cleared his throat again.

'I say . . . I meant to tell you. . . .'

'What?' she asked, turning to him quickly.

He was silent with apprehension.

'Go on!' she urged him, pulling him lightly by the sleeve.

'No, it's nothing,' he said in a panic.

'Yes, you have something on your mind.'

He said nothing.

'If it's something dreadful, better not tell me,' she said. 'Yes, do!' she added suddenly.

'But it's nothing, nothing at all.'

'Yes, yes, you have something on your mind, tell me!' she insisted, holding him tight by the lapels of his coat so closely that he had to keep turning his head from side to side so as not to kiss her.

He would not have turned it but that her terrible *never* was still thundering in his ears.

'Tell me!' she kept on.

'I can't, it's not necessary . . .' he pleaded.

'How is it you used to say that "confidence is the basis of happiness," that "not a single flutter of one's heart should be hidden from the friend's eye"? Whose words are those?'

'I only meant to say,' he began slowly, 'that I love you so much, so much, that if. . . .'

He hesitated.

'Yes?' she asked impatiently.

'That if you fell in love with someone who could make you happier than I could, I'd . . . swallow my grief in silence and give up my place to him.'

She suddenly let go of his coat.

'Why?' she asked in surprise. 'I don't understand it. I wouldn't give you up to anyone; I don't want you to be happy with another woman. It's too deep for me, I don't understand it.'

Her glance wandered thoughtfully over the trees.

'Then you don't love me?' she asked afterwards.

'On the contrary, I love you devotedly, I am ready to sacrifice myself for you.'

'But why? Nobody asks you.'

'I mean, in case you fell in love with somebody else. . . .'

'With somebody else! Are you mad? Why should I, if I love you? Are you going to fall in love with another woman?'

'You mustn't listen to me! Heaven only knows what I am saying, and you believe me! It wasn't this at all I meant to tell you. . . .'

'What then?'

'I meant to tell you that I have wronged you, have been wronging you all this time. . . .'

'What do you mean? How? Don't you love me? Was it a joke, perhaps? Tell me at once!'

'No, no, it isn't that!' he said in anguish. 'You see,' he began irresolutely, 'we meet . . . secretly. . . .'

'Secretly? Why secretly? I tell *ma tante* almost every time that I have seen you. . . .'

'Every time?' he asked anxiously.

'What's the harm?'

'It's my fault: I ought to have told you long ago that it isn't . . . done. . . .'

'You did tell me.'

'Did I? I believe I did . . . hint at it. Well, then I have done my duty.'

He cheered up, glad that Olga so lightly relieved him of the responsibility.

'What else?' she asked.

'Else? . . . that was all.'

'It isn't true,' Olga said positively, 'there is something else; you haven't told me all.'

'Well, I had thought,' he began, trying to speak carelessly, 'that. . . .'

He stopped; she waited.

'That we ought to meet less often . . .' he glanced at her timidly.

She did not speak.

'Why?' she asked after a pause.

'My conscience torments me. . . . We spend so much time alone: I grow excited, my heart throbs, you, too, are agitated. . . . I am afraid,' he concluded, speaking with difficulty.

'What of?'

'You are young and don't know all the dangers, Olga. A man may lose his self-control; at times an evil power gains possession of him, his heart is in darkness, his eyes throw lightning. His mind is clouded; respect for purity and innocence is carried away by the whirlwind; he does not know what he is doing, he is swayed by passion and is no longer master of himself – then an abyss opens at his feet. . . .'

He positively shuddered.

'Well, what of it? Let it!' she said, looking at him open-eyed.

He was silent; there was nothing more for him to say, or perhaps no need of more.

She gazed at him for a few minutes as though trying to read the wrinkles on his brow and recalling his every word and look; she ran in her mind through the whole history of their love, got as far as the dark evening in the garden, and suddenly blushed.

'You talk such nonsense!' she said quickly, looking away. 'I haven't seen your eyes flash like lightning . . . you look at me for the most part like . . . my nurse, Kuzmin-ishna,' she added, laughing.

'You are joking, Olga, but I am in earnest . . . and I haven't said everything yet.'

'What else?' she said. 'Something about an abyss?'

He sighed.

'Why, that we oughtn't to meet . . . alone.'

'Why?'

'It isn't right. . . .'

She was thoughtful.

'Yes, people say it isn't right,' she said doubtfully, 'but why?'

'What will people say when they know, when the rumour spreads? . . .'

'But who is to say anything? I have no mother; she alone could have asked me why I saw you, and it's only in answer to her I would have cried and said I wasn't doing any wrong, or you either. She would have believed me. Who else is there?' she asked.

'Your aunt,' Oblomov said.

'My aunt?' Olga sadly shook her head. 'She would never ask. If I left home altogether she would not go to look for me or ask me questions, and I would not return to tell her where I had been and what I had done. Who else can there be?'

'Others, everybody . . . the other day Sonitchka looked at you and me with a smile, and all the ladies and gentlemen with her smiled too.'

He told her how uneasy he had been ever since.

'While she looked only at me,' he added, 'I didn't mind; but when she looked in the same way at you, my hands and feet went numb. . . .'

'Well?' she asked coldly.

'Well, I have been in agonies day and night since then, racking my brains how to prevent its becoming public property; I was anxious not to alarm you. . . . I have long wanted to talk to you about it. . . .'

'You need not have troubled,' she answered, 'I have known it all along!'

'How do you mean?' he asked in surprise.

'Very simply. Sonitchka talked to me, cross-questioned me, was sarcastic, and even told me how I should behave with you. . . .'

'And you haven't told me a word of it, Olga!' he reproached her.

'But you haven't spoken to me of your troubles either!'

'What did you answer her?'

'Nothing! What could I say? I merely blushed.'

'My God! What have we come to: you blush! How incautious we are! What will come of it?'

She looked at him with a question in her eyes.

'I don't know,' she said shortly.

Oblomov had thought he would find comfort in sharing his trouble with Olga and draw strength from her clear words and look, but discovering she had no lively and decisive answer to give he suddenly lost courage. His face expressed hesitation, his glance wandered dejectedly. He was feeling slightly feverish. He had almost forgotten Olga; Sonitchka, her husband, and the visitors occupied his mind; he heard their laughter and gossip. Olga, usually so resourceful, was looking at him coldly and silently, and still more coldly said, 'I don't know.' And he did not trouble to grasp the secret meaning of this 'I don't know,' or perhaps could not do so.

And so he was silent: his thoughts and intentions never matured without another person's help; they were not like ripe apples that fall to the ground of themselves, but had to be gathered.

Olga looked at him for a few minutes, then put on her mantle, picked up her fichu she had hung on a branch, and, slowly tying it round her head, took her parasol.

'Where are you off to? It's quite early!' he said, coming to himself suddenly.

'No, it's late. You are right,' she said sadly and thoughtfully, 'we have gone too far and there is no way out; we must make haste and part so as to bury the past. Good-bye!' she added dryly and bitterly, and bending her head she walked down the path.

'Olga, for Heaven's sake! What are you thinking of? How can we part? Why, I . . . Olga!'

She walked faster, not heeding him; the dry sand crunched under her feet.

'Olga Sergeyevna!' he cried.

She did not hear and walked on.

'For God's sake, come back!' he cried with tears in his voice. 'One should give a hearing even to a criminal. . . . Good heavens, she must be heartless! That's what women are!'

He sat down and buried his face in his hands. He could hear her footsteps no longer.

'She has gone!' he said, almost in terror, and raised his head.

Olga was before him.

He joyfully seized her hand.

'You haven't gone, you will not go?' he said. 'Don't go; remember, if you go away – I am a dead man!'

'And if I don't go away I am a criminal, remember that, Ilya.'

'Oh, no. . . .'

'How no? If Sonitchka and her husband discover us together once more – I am ruined.'

He shuddered.

'Listen,' he began hurriedly, stumbling for words. 'I haven't said all . . .' and he stopped.

What at home had seemed so simple, natural, necessary, what he had been looking forward to as his happiness, suddenly appeared as a kind of abyss. He had not the heart to cross it. The step he had to take was bold and decisive.

'There is someone coming!' Olga said.

A sound of footsteps came from the path.

'Can it be Sonitchka?' Oblomov asked, his eyes fixed with terror.

Two men and a lady, strangers, went past. Oblomov felt easier.

'Olga,' he began hurriedly, taking her by the hand, 'let us go over there, where there is no one. Let us sit down.'

He made her sit on the bench and sat down on the grass beside her.

'You flared up and walked away and I hadn't finished what I had to say,' he began.

'And I will go away again and not return if you play with me. You enjoyed my tears once and now you would like, perhaps, to see me at your feet, reduce me to being your slave, so that you can be capricious, moralize, shed tears, be frightened, and frighten me and then ask me what we are to do. Remember, Ilya Ilyitch,' she added, getting up with sudden pride, 'I have grown up a lot since I met you, and I know what game you are playing with me . . . but you shan't see my tears any more!'

'I swear I am not playing with you!' he said convincingly.

'So much the worse for you,' she remarked dryly. 'I will say one thing to all your apprehensions, riddles, and warnings: till to-day I have loved you and did not know what I ought to do; now I know,' she concluded decisively, making ready to go, 'and I am not going to ask your advice.'

'And I know too,' he said, retaining her by the hand and making her sit down again, and then he stopped for a minute plucking up his courage.

'Would you believe it,' he began, 'my heart is full of one desire, my head of one thought, but my will and my tongue will not obey me: I want to speak and I can't utter the words. And yet it's so simple, so. . . . Help me, Olga.'

'I don't know what is in your mind.'

'Oh, for Heaven's sake, don't speak like this! Your look of pride is killing me, every word you say chills me like ice. . . .'

She laughed.

'You are mad!' she said, putting her hand on his head.

'That's right, now I have regained the gift of thought and speech! Olga,' he said, kneeling before her, 'be my wife!'

She said nothing and turned her face away.

'Olga, give me your hand!' he continued. She did not give it. He took it himself and put it to his lips. She did not draw it away. Her hand was soft, warm, and slightly moist. He tried to peep into her face, but she turned away more and more.

'Silence?' he asked anxiously, kissing her hand.

'Is a sign of consent,' she said in a low voice, still not looking at him.

'What are you feeling now? What are you thinking?' he asked, recalling his mental picture of the shy consent and the tears.

'The same as you,' she answered, still looking at the forest; only her heaving bosom showed that she was controlling her emotion.

'Has she tears in her eyes?' Oblomov wondered, but she was obstinately looking down.

'You are calm, you are indifferent?' he said, trying to draw her nearer.

'Not indifferent, but calm.'

'Why?'

'Because I foresaw it long ago and have grown used to the thought.'

'Long ago?' he repeated in surprise.

'Yes, from the moment I gave you the spray of lilac . . . in my mind I called you. . . .'

She broke off.

'From that moment?'

He put out his arms wide to embrace her.

'The abyss is opening, lightning flashing . . . take care!' she said mischievously, cleverly avoiding his embrace and moving his arms away with her parasol.

He recalled the terrible *never* and subsided.

'But you have never said anything and did not show it in the least . . .' he said.

'We do not marry, but are given or taken in marriage.'

'From that moment . . . is it possible?' he repeated thoughtfully.

'Do you imagine that if I hadn't understood your

intentions I would have been here alone with you, would have sat with you in the arbour in the evenings, would have listened to you and trusted you?' she asked proudly.

'Then it's . . .' he began, changing colour and letting go her hand.

A strange thought stirred within him. She was looking at him calmly and proudly, waiting confidently; and what he longed for at that moment was not pride and courage, but tears, passion, intoxicating happiness if only for a moment – and then a lifetime of unruffled peace might follow! But there were no sudden tears of unexpected joy, no shy consent! How was he to understand it? The snake of doubt woke up in his heart. . . . Did she love him or was she simply getting married?

'But there is another path to happiness,' he said.

'Which?' she asked.

'Sometimes love does not wait and endure and reckon. . . . A woman is all fire, all tremor, and feels at once such ecstatic pain and joy, that. . . .'

'I don't know what path you mean.'

'The path upon which a woman sacrifices everything: her peace of mind, respect, public opinion, and finds her reward in love – it takes the place of it all.'

'Need we take this path?'

'No.'

'Would you wish to find happiness at the cost of my peace of mind and self-respect?'

'Oh no, no! I swear to God I never would!' he said warmly.

'Then why did you speak of it?'

'I don't know, I am sure. . . .'

'But I know: you wanted to find out if I would have sacrificed to you my peace of mind and followed this path with you – isn't it so?'

'Yes, I believe you are right. . . . Well?'

'Never, not for anything!' she said firmly.

He pondered and heaved a sigh.

'Yes, it's a terrible path and a woman must love a

great deal if she is to follow it – to perish and still go on
loving.'

He looked at her questioningly: he could read nothing
in her face; it was calm and only the fold over her
eyebrow moved a little.

'Imagine Sonitchka, who isn't worth your little finger,
cutting you dead!' he went on.

Olga smiled, and her eyes were as serene as ever. Oblomov's vanity was urging him to obtain some sacrifice from
Olga and to revel in her admissions.

'Imagine that men did not lower their eyes with timid
respect as they approached you, but looked at you with a
bold and meaning smile. . . .'

He looked at her: she was carefully pushing a pebble
along the sand with her parasol.

'You would come into the room and several bonnets
would stir with indignation; one of the ladies would go
and sit farther away from you . . . and your pride would
be the same as ever, and you would know perfectly well
that you were higher and better than they. . . .'

'Why are you telling me these horrors?' she said calmly.
'I will never follow that path.'

'Never?' Oblomov asked dejectedly.

'Never!' she repeated.

'No,' he said thoughtfully, 'you would not have the
strength to face shame. You might not fear death; it's not
the execution itself, but the preparations for it, the hourly
tortures, that are so awful; you couldn't stand it, you
would pine away, wouldn't you?'

He kept looking into her eyes to see what she felt.

She looked cheerful: the horrors he had drawn had not
disturbed her; a slight smile was playing on her lips.

'I don't want either to pine away or die! It's all wrong,'
she said, 'one may not follow that path and yet love all the
more. . . .'

'But why wouldn't you follow it,' he asked insistently,
almost with vexation, 'if you are not afraid?'

'Because on that path . . . people always end . . .

by parting,' she said, 'but that I . . . should part from you. . . .'

She paused, put her hand on his shoulder, and looked long and intently at him; then she suddenly flung aside her parasol, threw her arms round his neck, quickly and ardently kissed him, and flushing crimson pressed her face to his breast, adding softly:

'Never!'

He uttered a cry of joy and sank on the grass at her feet.

PART III

I

OBLOMOV walked home radiant. He was glowing with excitement, his eyes were shining. He felt as though his hair was on fire. He came into his room – and the radiance suddenly disappeared; his eyes fixed with unpleasant surprise on his chair, in which Tarantyev was sitting.

'You do keep one waiting! Where have you been gadding about?' Tarantyev asked sternly, giving him his shaggy hand. 'And your old devil has got out of hand altogether: I asked for food – there isn't any; for vodka – he wouldn't give me any either.'

'I've been for a walk in the wood,' Oblomov said carelessly, still unable to recover from the shock Tarantyev had given him, and at such a moment too!

He had lost the habit of the gloomy surroundings in which he had lived for years and forgotten the stuffy atmosphere he had once breathed. Tarantyev had instantly brought him down, as it were, from heaven into the mire. Oblomov asked himself painfully why had Tarantyev come, how long would he stay, and suffered agonies at the thought that he might stay to dinner, and then Oblomov could not go to the Ilyinskys'. Oblomov's only concern was to get rid of him at any price. He waited in gloomy silence for Tarantyev to speak.

'Well, neighbour, why don't you go and have a look at your flat?' Tarantyev asked.

'I don't need it any more,' Oblomov answered, trying not to look at Tarantyev. 'I . . . am not going to live there.'

'What! Not going to live there?' Tarantyev retorted menacingly. 'You have hired it and you are not going to move? And the contract?'

'What contract?'

'You have forgotten, have you? You have signed the contract for a year. Give me eight hundred paper roubles and then go where you like. Four people were after that flat and they were all refused. One of them would have taken it for three years.'

Oblomov only just remembered that on the very day of his moving to the summer villa Tarantyev brought him a paper which, in his hurry, he signed without reading.

'Oh, my goodness, what have I done?' he thought.

'But I don't need the flat,' Oblomov said, 'I am going abroad.'

'Abroad!' Tarantyev interrupted. 'With that German! Not you! You will never go.'

'Why shouldn't I go? My passport is all ready; I can show it you. And I have bought a portmanteau.'

'You won't go,' Tarantyev repeated indifferently. 'You had better give me the six months' rent in advance.'

'I haven't any money.'

'You must get it somehow; the landlady's brother, Ivan Matveyitch, will stand no nonsense. He will go to law at once and it will be the worse for you. But I have paid him with my own money, so you can pay me.'

'How is it you had so much cash?' Oblomov asked.

'It's none of your business! I collected an old debt. Give me the money! That's what I've come for.'

'Very well; I will call one day soon and sub-let the flat, and now I am in a hurry. . . .'

He began buttoning his coat.

'And what sort of flat do you want? You won't find a better. You haven't seen it, you know.'

'I don't want to see it; why should I move there? It's too far. . . .'

'What from?' Tarantyev asked rudely.

But Oblomov did not answer.

'From the centre,' he added presently.

'What centre? What do you want it for? To lie in bed?'

'No, I don't lie in bed now.'

'How is that?'

'Oh, I don't, that's all. To-day . . .' Oblomov began.

'What?' Tarantyev interrupted him.

'I am not dining at home.'

'Give me the money and then you may go to the devil!'

'What money?' Oblomov repeated impatiently. 'I will call at the flat one of these days and talk to the landlady.'

'What landlady? You mean my friend? What does she know about it? She is a woman! No, talk to her brother – then you will see.'

'Very well, I will call and talk to him.'

'Yes, and when may that be? Give me the money and have done with it.'

'I haven't any; I shall have to borrow.'

'Well, pay at any rate for my cab,' Tarantyev pestered him. 'Three silver roubles.'

'Where is your driver? And why so much as three roubles?'

'I have dismissed him. Why so much? He didn't want to drive me even so – "The road is all sand," he said; and it will be another three roubles from here – that means twenty-two paper roubles.'

'You can go by bus from here for half a rouble,' Oblomov said. 'Here you are.'

He gave him four silver roubles. Tarantyev put them in his pocket.

'You will owe me seven paper roubles,' he added. 'And give me something for my dinner!'

'What dinner?'

'I shall be too late for dinner in town – I'll have to call at some pot-house on the way and it's all so expensive here, they'll be sure to charge me five roubles or more.'

Without speaking, Oblomov pulled out a silver rouble from his pocket and threw it to Tarantyev. He did not sit down so that his visitor should go the sooner; but Tarantyev made no move.

'Do tell them to give me something to eat,' he said.

'But you are going to have dinner at a restaurant, aren't you?' Oblomov remarked.

'Dinner, yes! But now it's only one o'clock.'

Oblomov told Zahar to bring in some lunch.

'There isn't any, nothing has been cooked,' Zahar answered dryly, looking sullenly at Tarantyev. 'And when are you going to return my master's shirt and waistcoat, Mihey Andreyitch?'

'What shirt and waistcoat?' Tarantyev protested. 'I gave it back ages ago.'

'When was that?' Zahar asked.

'Why, I put the things into your hands when you were moving! You shoved them into some bundle, and now you ask me for them!'

Zahar was dumbfoundered.

'Heavens above us! The shame of it, just think, Ilya Ilyitch!' he exclaimed, turning to Oblomov.

'Yes, yes, we know that song!' Tarantyev retorted. 'I expect you sold them for drink and now you ask me. . . .'

'I have never in my life sold my master's things for drink!' hissed Zahar. 'It's you. . . .'

'That will do, Zahar!' Oblomov interrupted him sternly.

'Was it you who took our broom and two cups?' Zahar asked.

'What broom?' Tarantyev roared. 'Ah, you old rascal! You'd better give me some lunch!'

'Do you hear how he reviles me, Ilya Ilyitch!' Zahar said. 'There is no food in the house – not any bread even – and Anissya has gone out,' he concluded, going out of the room.

'Where do you have dinner then?' Tarantyev asked. 'It's very queer – Oblomov goes for walks in the forest, doesn't dine at home. . . . When are you going to move? It will be autumn soon. Come and have a look at the flat.'

'Yes, yes; I will, one of these days.'

'And don't forget to bring the money.'

'Yes, yes, yes,' Oblomov said impatiently.

'Well, do you want anything from the flat? You know,

brother, they've painted the floors and ceilings and windows and doors – everything, for you: it has cost more than a hundred roubles.'

'Yes, yes; very well. . . . Oh, I know what I wanted to tell you,' Oblomov remembered suddenly. 'Will you please go to the courts for me, I have to have a deed of trust witnessed. . . .'

'Why should I do errands for you?'

'I'll give you more for your dinner.'

'The wear and tear of my boots will cost more than what you'll give me.'

'Take a cab, I will pay.'

'I can't go to the courts,' Tarantyev said gloomily.

'Why not?'

'I have enemies: they bear me malice and are planning to ruin me.'

'Very well, I will go myself,' said Oblomov, taking up his cap.

'When you move to the flat, Ivan Matveyitch will do it all for you. He's a priceless man, brother, not like some German upstart! He is a true Russian, an official who has sat on the same chair for thirty years; he runs the whole show at his office and has money too, but he would never think of hiring a cab, and his coat is no better than mine; he looks as though butter would not melt in his mouth, speaks almost in a whisper, doesn't go gadding about in foreign parts like your. . . .'

'Tarantyev,' Oblomov shouted, bringing his fist down on the table, 'don't you dare to talk of what's beyond you!'

Tarantyev opened his eyes wide at such unheard-of behaviour on Oblomov's part and actually forgot to be offended at being put below Stolz.

'So that's how you go on nowadays, brother . . .' he muttered, picking up his hat. 'Very sprightly!'

He stroked his hat with his sleeve, then looked at it and at Oblomov's hat that lay on the chiffonier.

'You don't wear your hat, I see you have a cap,' he

said, taking Oblomov's hat and trying it on. 'Lend it me
for the summer, brother. . . .'

Without saying a word Oblomov took his hat off
Tarantyev's head and put it back on the chiffonier; then
he crossed his arms on his breast, waiting for Tarantyev
to go.

'Well, keep it and be damned!' Tarantyev said, pushing
his way clumsily through the door. 'You are a bit . . .
queer to-day, brother. . . . You have a talk to Ivan Matveyitch and see what happens if you don't bring the
money. . . .'

II

HE went away and Oblomov, feeling thoroughly annoyed, sat down in the arm-chair; it was some time before he could recover from the crude impression. At last he remembered the morning, and the hideous vision of Tarantyev faded out of his mind; he smiled once more. He stopped before the mirror and spent some minutes straightening his tie, smiling, and looking to see if his cheek bore any trace of Olga's ardent kiss.

'Two *nevers*,' he said softly and happily. 'But what a difference between them! One has already withered and the other is flowering so beautifully. . . .'

Then he sank deeper and deeper into thought. He felt that the light, cloudless festival of love had gone, that love was, indeed, becoming a duty, that it was mingling with his life as a whole, forming part of its everyday functions, and gradually losing its rainbow colouring. Perhaps that morning he had seen its last rosy ray and henceforth it would no longer shine brilliantly, but warm his life imperceptibly; life would swallow it up and love would be its mainspring, powerful but hidden. All its expressions would now be so simple, so ordinary. Poetry was over and stern history was beginning: going to the courts, then to Oblomovka; building the house; mortgaging the estate; making the road; endless bother with the peasants; the rotation of work – reaping, threshing; accounts; the bailiff's anxious face; the elections; the sessions of the court. Now and again Olga's eyes would shine, the strains of *Casta diva* would reach him, he would snatch a hasty kiss and then again he would have to go to the fields, to the town, again there would be the bailiff, the accounts. If visitors came it would not be much comfort either: they would talk of how much spirit they had distilled, how many yards of cloth they had sold to the

Government. . . . How was this? Was this what he had promised himself? Was this life? And yet people did live so all their lives – and Andrey liked it!

But the marriage, the wedding – that, anyway, was part of the poetry of life, a fully opened-out flower. He pictured himself leading Olga to the altar: she was wearing a long veil and orange-blossom on her head. There were whispers of admiration in the crowd. Her breast was heaving gently, her head was bowed in her usual proud and graceful way; she shyly gave him her hand, not knowing how to meet the eyes of the crowd. Now she smiled, now tears came into her eyes, the wrinkle over her eyebrow stirred thoughtfully. At home, after the visitors had gone, she would throw herself on his neck as she had to-day, still wearing her wedding-dress. . . .

'No, I must run to Olga, I cannot be thinking and feeling by myself,' he decided. 'I'll tell everyone, the whole world . . . no, first her aunt, then the baron; I will write to Stolz – won't he be surprised! Then I will tell Zahar: he will fall at my feet and howl with joy. I will give him twenty-five roubles. Anissya will come and try to kiss my hand, I'll give her ten roubles; then . . . then I will shout with joy so that the whole world will hear me and say: "Oblomov is happy, Oblomov is getting married!" Now I must run to Olga; we shall whisper together and make our secret pact to merge our lives into one!'

He ran to Olga. She listened to his dreams with a smile, but as soon as he jumped from his chair to run and tell her aunt she frowned in a way that alarmed him.

'Not a word to anyone!' she said, putting her finger to her lips to make him speak lower so that her aunt should not hear in the next room. 'It isn't time yet!'

'It isn't time when everything has been decided between us?' he asked impatiently. 'What are we to do then? How are we to begin? We can't sit with our arms folded! New duties lie before us; serious life is beginning. . . .'

'Yes, it is,' she said, looking at him attentively.

'Well, so I want to take the first step – to go to your aunt. . . .'

'That's the last step!'

'Which is the first?'

'The first is to go to the courts: you have to write some document, haven't you?'

'Yes . . . to-morrow.'

'Why not to-day?'

'To-day . . . fancy leaving you on so great a day, Olga!'

'Very well, to-morrow. And then?'

'Then to tell your aunt and write to Stolz.'

'No, then you must go to Oblomovka. . . . You know, Andrey Ivanitch wrote to you what you had to do in the country; I don't know what business you have there, building, isn't it?' she said, looking straight into his face.

'Oh dear, but if we listen to Stolz,' Oblomov said, 'we shall never get as far as telling your aunt! He says I must first have the house built, then make a road, then open schools. . . . It's enough work for a lifetime. We would go there together, Olga, and then. . . .'

'And where shall we go to? Is there a house there?'

'No – the old house isn't fit to live in; the front porch must be quite rickety by now, I expect.'

'Where are we to live then?' she asked.

'We must find a flat in town.'

'For this you must go to town too,' she said, 'that's the second step. . . .'

'Then . . .' he began.

'Take the two first steps, and then. . . .'

'What's this?' Oblomov thought sadly. 'No whispers, no secret pact to merge two lives into one! It's all quite different, somehow. How strange that Olga is! She never stands still; she doesn't dwell in sweet reverie on a poetic moment, as though she had no imagination, no craving to abandon herself to dreaming! Go at once to the courts, look for a flat – just like Andrey! They all seem to be bent on living in a hurry!'

Next day he reluctantly went to town, taking a piece of stamped paper with him; he yawned and looked about him on the way. He did not know where exactly the courts were, and called first on Ivan Gerasimovitch to ask to which Department he ought to go with his paper. The old man was delighted to see Oblomov and would not let him go without lunch. Then Ivan Gerasimovitch sent for a friend who could tell them how the business was to be done, for he himself had long dropped out of things. The lunch and the consultation were not over till three o'clock and then it was too late to go to the courts; the following day was Saturday and the courts would be closed, so it all had to wait till Monday.

Oblomov went to his new flat on the Vyborg side. He spent a long time driving along quiet streets with long wooden fences on either side. At last he found a policeman, who said the house was in the next street – and he pointed to another street where only fences and no houses were visible, grass grew in the middle of the road and wheel marks were visible in the dry mud. Oblomov drove on, admiring the nettles by the fences and rowan berries growing above them. At last the policeman pointed to an old little house in the yard, adding: 'That's the one.' 'The house of the Collegiate Assessor Pshenitsyn's widow,' Oblomov read on the gate, and told the driver to drive into the yard. The yard was the size of a room, so that the pole of the carriage struck the corner and scared a number of hens that scattered away in all directions, cackling and some of them trying to fly; a big black dog on a chain dashed to left and to right, barking desperately and trying to reach the horses' heads. Oblomov sat in the carriage on a level with the windows wondering how he could step out. In the window, crowded with pots of mignonette, pinks, and marigolds, several heads could be seen peeping out. Oblomov managed to step out of the carriage; the dog barked more desperately than ever. He walked up to the front-door steps and was met by a wrinkled old woman wearing a *sarafan* tucked up at the waist.

'Whom do you wish to see?' she asked.

'The owner of the house, Madame Pshenitsyn.'

The old woman bent her head in perplexity.

'Perhaps it is Ivan Matveyitch you want?' she asked. 'He is not at home; he hasn't returned from the office yet.'

'I want the owner,' Oblomov said.

Meanwhile, the excitement in the house continued; heads looked out of the windows, the door behind the old woman kept shutting and opening slightly and different people peeped out. Oblomov turned round: in the yard two children, a boy and a girl, stood looking at him with interest. A sleepy-looking peasant in a sheepskin appeared from somewhere, and sheltering his eyes with his hand from the sun lazily watched Oblomov and the carriage. The dog kept giving short, deep barks, and as soon as Oblomov moved or a horse stamped it broke into continuous barking and jumped about on its chain. On the other side of the fence, on the right, Oblomov saw an endless kitchen-garden planted with cabbages, and on the left several trees and a green wooden summer-house.

'Do you want Agafya Matveyevna?' the old woman asked. 'What for?'

'Tell the lady of the house,' Oblomov said, 'that I want to see her. I have taken rooms here. . . .'

'So you are the new lodger, Mihey Andreyitch's friend? Wait, I will tell her.'

She opened the door, and several people rushed away from the door, running to the inner rooms. He caught a glimpse of a fair-skinned, rather plump woman with a bare neck and elbows and no bonnet on; she smiled at having been seen by a stranger and also rushed away from the door.

'Come in,' said the old woman, coming back, and led Oblomov across a small entry into a good-sized room where she asked him to wait. 'Agafya Matveyevna will not be a minute.'

'The dog is still barking,' Oblomov thought, looking round. Familiar objects suddenly arrested his eye: the whole room was littered with his belongings; the tables were covered with dust; the chairs were heaped on the bed; mattresses, cupboards, crockery, were stacked together.

'Why, nothing has been sorted out or seen to!' he said. 'How disgusting!'

Suddenly the door behind him creaked slightly and the woman whom he had seen with a bare neck and elbows came into the room. She was about thirty; her skin was very fair and her face so plump that it seemed as though the colour could not find its way to her cheeks. In the place of eyebrows she had two slightly raised shiny patches with scanty, fair hair growing on them. Her greyish eyes were as simple and candid as the whole expression of her face; her hands were white but coarse, with knotted blue veins standing out. Her dress clung to her figure: one could see she used no artifice, not even that of wearing an extra petticoat to increase the size of her hips and make the waist look smaller. And so, even when she was fully clothed but had no shawl on, she could without detriment to her modesty have provided a sculptor with the model of a fine, well-developed bosom. Her dress looked old and worn in comparison with her smart shawl and best bonnet. She had not been expecting visitors, and when Oblomov asked to see her she threw her Sunday shawl over her workaday dress and covered her head with a bonnet. She came in timidly and stopped, looking shyly at Oblomov.

He got up and bowed.

'Have I the pleasure of seeing Madame Pshenitsyn?' he asked.

'Yes, sir,' she answered. 'Perhaps you wish to speak to my brother?' she asked irresolutely. 'He is at the office: he does not come home before five.'

'No, it was you I wanted to see,' Oblomov began when she had sat down on the sofa as far from him as possible, looking at the ends of her shawl which covered her down to her feet like a horse-cloth. She kept hiding her hands under the shawl too.

'I have hired lodgings here, but now my circumstances have changed and I must look for a flat in another part of the town, so I have come to talk to you. . . .'

She listened dully and pondered with a blank expression.

'My brother is not at home,' she said after a pause.

'But the house is yours, isn't it?' Oblomov asked.

'Yes,' she answered briefly.

'So I thought you could decide for yourself.'

'But my brother isn't at home; he sees to it all,' she said monotonously, glancing straight at Oblomov for the first time, and then looking down at her shawl again.

'She has a simple but pleasant face,' Oblomov decided, condescendingly; 'a good woman, I should think.' At that moment a little girl's head peeped through the door. Agafya Matveyevna nodded to her threateningly, unseen by Oblomov, and the child disappeared.

'What does your brother do?'

'He is in a Government office.'

'Which one?'

'Where they register peasants. . . . I keep forgetting the name of it.'

She smiled good-naturedly and then her face immediately assumed its usual expression.

'You don't live alone with your brother, do you?' Oblomov asked.

'No, I have two children by my late husband: a boy of seven and a girl of five,' Agafya Matveyevna began readily, and her face grew more animated, 'and there is our grandmother too, an invalid, she can hardly walk and only goes to church; she used to go marketing with Akulina, but she has given it up since last spring: her legs swell. And even in church she has to sit down most of the time. That's all. Sometimes my sister-in-law stays with us and Mihey Andreyitch.'

'And does Mihey Andreyitch come to you often?'

'He stays for a month at a time: he is a great friend of my brother, they are always together.'

She stopped, having exhausted all her supply of ideas and words.

'How still it is here!' Oblomov said. 'Were it not for the dog barking one might think there wasn't a soul living here.'

She smiled in answer.

'Do you go out much?'

'Sometimes, in the summer. The other day we went to the Gunpowder Works.'

'Do many people go there?' Oblomov asked, looking through an opening in the shawl at her high bosom, firm as a sofa cushion and never stirred by emotion.

'No, this year there weren't many: it rained in the morning, though it turned out fine later. But usually lots of people go.'

'And where else do you go?'

'Hardly anywhere; my brother and Mihey Andreyitch go angling and make fish soup on the river, but we are always at home.'

'Are you really?'

'Yes, indeed. Last year we went to Kolpino, and sometimes we go to the copse near here. It is my brother's name-day on June 24th, then we have all the men from his office to dinner.'

'And do you go out visiting?'

'My brother does, but the children and I only go on Christmas and Easter Day to dinner with my husband's relations.'

There were no more subjects for conversation.

'You have flowers; are you fond of them?' he asked.

She smiled.

'No,' she said, 'I have no time for flowers. The children have been with Akulina to the Count's garden and the gardener has given them these; and the geraniums and aloe were here in my husband's time.'

At this moment Akulina suddenly burst into the room; a big cock was shrieking and fighting desperately in her hands.

'Is it this cock I am to give to the dealer, Agafya Mat-veyevna?' she asked.

'There now! Go,' the lady of the house said shyly, 'you see I have a visitor.'

'I merely came to ask,' Akulina said, taking the cock by the feet and letting its head hang down; 'he will give seventy copecks.'

'Go now, go to the kitchen,' Agafya Matveyevna said. 'The grey, speckled cock, not this one!' she added hastily, and all at once she felt shy, hid her hands under her shawl, and looked down.

'Household cares!' Oblomov said.

'We have a lot of hens; we sell eggs and chickens. The people in the summer villas here and in the Count's house buy everything from us,' she answered, looking at Oblo-mov much more confidently.

Her face assumed a sensible and thoughtful expression; the dull look disappeared when she spoke about a subject she was familiar with. But if a question was not about anything concrete and well known to her she answered it with a smile and silence.

'This ought to be sorted out,' Oblomov remarked, pointing to the heap of his belongings.

'We wanted to, but my brother did not allow us,' she interrupted briskly, looking at Oblomov without any shy-ness this time. ' "Heaven only knows what he has in his table drawers and cupboards . . ." he said, "if anything is lost he will blame us for it. . . ." ' She stopped and smiled.

'What a cautious man your brother is!' Oblomov added.

She smiled slightly again and assumed once more her usual expression. Her smile generally meant that she did not know what to say or do.

'I cannot wait for him,' Oblomov said, 'perhaps you will tell him that my circumstances have changed and I no longer need the flat and so ask you to let it to somebody else; and I, too, will try and find a tenant for it.'

She listened dully, blinking from time to time.

'But he is not at home now,' she repeated, 'you had better come again to-morrow: to-morrow is Saturday and he does not go to the office.'

'I am awfully busy, I haven't a moment to spare,' Oblomov protested. 'If you would just kindly tell him that as the deposit I paid would be yours and I would find another tenant. . . .'

'My brother is not at home, you see,' she said monotonously. 'He isn't coming yet . . .' she looked out into the street. 'He walks here, past the windows: one can see him as he comes along, but he isn't here!'

'Well, I must be going . . .' Oblomov said.

'And what am I to tell him when he comes? When are you going to move in?' she asked, getting up from the sofa.

'Tell him what I have told you,' Oblomov said, 'that my circumstances. . . .'

'You had better come to-morrow and talk to him yourself . . .' she repeated.

'I can't to-morrow.'

'Well, then the day after, on Sunday: we have vodka and lunch after Mass. Mihey Andreyitch comes too.'

'Does he really?'

'Yes, indeed.'

'No, the day after to-morrow I can't come either,' Oblomov refused impatiently.

'Then next week perhaps . . .' she remarked. 'And when are you going to move in? I would have the floors scrubbed and the rooms dusted.'

'I am not going to move in.'

'But how? What shall we do with your things?'

'Please will you kindly tell your brother,' Oblomov began deliberately, fixing his eyes on her bosom, 'that my circumstances. . . .'

'He seems to be late to-day, he is nowhere in sight,' she repeated monotonously, looking at the fence that separated the yard from the street. 'I know his footstep too: one can hear anyone walking along a wooden pavement. There aren't many passers-by. . . .'

'So you will give him my message?' Oblomov said as he bowed himself out of the room.

'He will be here in half an hour . . .' the lady of the house said with an anxiety unusual for her, trying to detain Oblomov with her voice as it were.

'I can't wait any longer,' he decided, opening the door.

Seeing him on the steps the dog began barking and trying to break its chain again. The driver, who had been asleep leaning on his elbow, backed the horses out of the yard; the hens once more scattered away in alarm and several heads peeped out of the windows.

'Then I'll tell my brother that you have called,' Agafya Matveyevna added anxiously, when Oblomov had sat down in the carriage.

'Yes, tell him that my circumstances make it impossible for me to keep the flat and that I will pass it on to somebody else or perhaps he would look out for a tenant.'

'He always does come in about this time . . .' she said, listening to him absentmindedly. 'I will tell him that you mean to call.'

'Yes, I will call one of these days.'

To the accompaniment of desperate barking the carriage left the yard and rocked along the dried mud of the unpaved street.

A middle-aged man in a shabby overcoat appeared at the end of it, with a big paper parcel under his arm, a thick stick in his hands, and goloshes on his feet in spite of the fine hot day. He walked quickly, looking from side to side, and stepped as heavily as though he meant to crush the wooden pavement. Oblomov turned to look at him and saw him turn in at Madame Pshenitsyn's gate.

'That must be her brother,' he concluded; 'but hang it all, I might spend another hour talking to him and I am hungry and it's so hot! And Olga is waiting for me. . . . Another time!'

'Go faster!' he said to the driver.

'What about looking for another flat?' he remembered

suddenly, looking at the fences on either side of the street.
'I must go back to Morskaya or Konyushenny Street. . . .
Another time!' he decided.

He urged the driver on.

III

AT the end of August it began to rain and smoke poured from the chimneys of summer villas that had stoves; the inhabitants of those that were not heated went about with swollen faces and kerchiefs round their heads; gradually all the summer villas were deserted. Oblomov had not been to town any more. One morning he saw the Ilyinskys' furniture being carted past his windows. Although he no longer thought it an heroic feat to leave his lodgings, to dine in a restaurant and not to lie down all day, he was at a loss where to spend the night. To remain alone at the summer villa when the park and the copse were deserted and Olga's shutters were closed seemed to him utterly impossible. He walked through her empty rooms, walked round the park, came down the hill, and his heart was oppressed with sadness. He told Zahar and Anissya to go to the Vyborg side, where he had decided to put up until he could find another flat and himself went to town, had a hasty dinner at a restaurant, and spent the evening at Olga's.

But autumn evenings in town were very different from the long sunny days and evenings in the park and the copse. In town he could not see her three times a day; Katya did not run in and he could not send Zahar three miles with a note. And all the flowering summer poem of their love seemed moving at a slower pace, as though the subject-matter were giving out. Sometimes they were silent for half an hour on end. Olga would be absorbed in her work and be counting to herself the squares of the pattern with her needle while he sank into a chaos of thoughts and lived in a far-distant future. Only at times a passionate shudder passed through him as he gazed at her, or she smiled as she glanced at him, catching a glimpse of tender submissiveness and speechless happiness in his eyes. He went to town and dined at Olga's three days in succession under the pretext that his flat was in a muddle, and as he was going to leave it during the week it was not worth while his settling in. But on the fourth day he thought it would be awkward to go to her, and after pacing up and down the street by the Ilyinskys' house he sighed and drove home. On the fifth day they were dining out. On the sixth Olga told him to go to a certain shop where she would be and then walk home with her while the carriage followed them. All this was awkward: both he and she kept meeting people they knew, who bowed and sometimes stopped to talk. 'Oh my goodness, how awful!' he repeated, hot all over with apprehension and the falsity of the position. Olga's aunt looked at him with her big languid eyes, sniffing her salts thoughtfully, as though she had a headache. And what a long journey it was! Driving from the Vyborg side and back again in the evening took him three hours.

'Let us tell your aunt,' Oblomov insisted, 'then I can be with you all day long and no one will say anything. . . .'

'And have you been to the courts?' Olga asked.

Oblomov felt sorely tempted to say 'Yes, and I have done it all,' but he knew that Olga's intent look would at once detect the lie in his face. He sighed in answer.

'Ah, if you only knew how difficult it is!' he said.

'And have you spoken to your landlady's brother? Have you found a flat?' she asked, without raising her eyes.

'He is never at home in the morning and in the evening I am here,' Oblomov replied, glad to have found a good excuse.

Olga sighed but said nothing.

'I will certainly speak to him to-morrow,' Oblomov reassured her; 'to-morrow is Sunday and he won't go to the office.'

'Until it is all settled,' Olga said thoughtfully, 'we cannot tell *ma tante* and we must see less of each other.'

'Yes, yes . . . it's true,' Oblomov agreed in alarm.

'Dine with us on Sundays, our reception day, and then,

say, on Wednesdays when there are no other visitors,' she
decided. 'And we can meet at the theatre too: you will
know when we are going and come also.'

'Yes, that's true,' he said, pleased that she took upon
herself to arrange their meetings.

'And if it's a fine day,' she concluded, 'I will go to
the Summer Gardens and you can come there; it will
remind us of the park . . . the park!' she repeated with
emotion.

He kissed her hand in silence and took leave of her till
Sunday. She sadly watched him go, then sat down to the
piano and abandoned herself to music. Her heart was
weeping, she hardly knew why, and the notes wept too.
She wanted to sing and could not.

When Oblomov got up the following morning he put
on the light coat he used to wear in the summer. He had
parted with his dressing-gown long ago, and gave orders
that it should be put away in the wardrobe. Zahar clumsily walked to the table, the tray with the coffee and rolls
wobbling in his hands as usual, and Anissya, also as usual,
was peeping through the door behind Zahar to see if he
would carry the cups safely to the table; she noiselessly
hid herself the moment he put the tray on the table, or if
he dropped something instantly rushed up to him to save
the other things from falling. On such occasions Zahar
began to swear first at the things, then at his wife, and
made as though he would give her a poke in the chest
with his elbow.

'What excellent coffee! Who makes it?' Oblomov asked.

'The landlady,' Zahar answered; 'she has been making
it for the last five days. "You add too much chicory and
don't boil it enough. Let me do it," she said.'

'Excellent!' Oblomov repeated, pouring himself out
another cup. 'Thank her.'

'Here she is herself,' said Zahar, pointing to the half-
open door of a side room. 'It's a sort of pantry, I fancy,
and she works there; she keeps tea, sugar, and coffee there
and the crockery.'

Oblomov could only see the landlady's back, her hair, her white neck, and bare elbows.

'What is she doing there, moving her elbows so quickly?' Oblomov asked.

'I don't know; ironing lace, I believe.'

Oblomov watched her moving elbows and her back bending down and straightening out again.

When she bent down he could see a clean petticoat, clean stockings, and firm, well-rounded legs.

'She is only a clerk's widow, but she has elbows good enough for a countess, and with dimples too!' Oblomov thought.

At midday Zahar came in to ask if he would like to taste their pie: the landlady had sent him.

'It's Sunday: they are baking a pie to-day.'

'Not much of a pie, I expect,' Oblomov said casually, 'with carrots and onion. . . .'

'A pie no worse than ours at Oblomovka,' Zahar observed, 'with chicken and fresh mushrooms.'

'Ah, that sounds nice: bring me some! Who does the baking? That dirty peasant?'

'Not she!' Zahar answered scornfully. 'If it weren't for her mistress she wouldn't know how to mix the dough. Agafya Matveyevna is always in the kitchen. She and Anissya baked the pie.'

Five minutes later a bare arm, hardly covered with the shawl he had already seen, was thrust through the door of the side room holding a plate with a huge piece of steaming-hot pie.

'Thank you very much,' Oblomov said amiably, taking the plate, and peeping through the door fixed his eyes on the full bosom and the bare shoulders. The door was hastily closed.

'Won't you have some vodka?' the voice asked.

'I don't take vodka, thank you very much,' Oblomov answered, still more amiably. 'What kind have you?'

'Home-made, we distil it from currant leaves,' the voice said.

'I have never tasted that kind; please let me try it!'

The bare arm was thrust through the door once more with a glass of vodka on a plate. Oblomov drank the vodka; he liked it very much.

'Very much obliged to you,' he said, trying to peep through the door, but it was tightly shut.

'Why don't you let me have a look at you and wish you good morning?' Oblomov said reproachfully.

The landlady smiled behind the door.

'I am still in my working dress: I've been in the kitchen all the time. I will dress directly, my brother will soon be coming home from Mass,' she answered shyly.

'Oh, *à propos* of your brother,' Oblomov remarked, 'I want to speak to him. Please ask him to look in.'

'Very well, I will tell him when he comes.'

'And who is it coughing so? Such a dry cough.'

'That's grandmother; she has had a cough for seven years.'

And the door was banged to.

'How . . . simple she is!' Oblomov thought. 'But there is something about her. . . . And she is so clean!'

He had not met the landlady's brother yet. Once or twice in the early morning, while he was still in bed, he caught a glimpse of a man with a big paper parcel under his arm walking on the other side of the fence and disappearing in the street; and then at five o'clock the same man with the parcel again flitted past the windows on his way home and disappeared behind the front door. He was not heard in the house. And yet one could tell, especially in the mornings, that the house was inhabited: knives were clattering in the kitchen; through the window one could hear the servant washing something in the corner, the porter chopping wood or bringing the barrel of water on two wheels; the sound of the children crying, or of the old woman's dry, obstinate cough, came from behind the wall.

Oblomov had the four best rooms in the house. The landlady and her family occupied the two back rooms, and the brother lived upstairs. Oblomov's bedroom and study looked into the yard, the drawing-room faced the garden, and the parlour the big kitchen-garden with the cabbages and potatoes. The curtains in the drawing-room windows were of faded cotton; plain chairs in imitation walnut stood along the walls; a card-table stood under the mirror; the window-sills were crowded with pots of geraniums and pinks; four cages with canaries and greenfinches hung in the room.

The landlady's brother walked in on tiptoe and bowed three times in answer to Oblomov's greeting. His uniform was buttoned to the throat, so that one could not tell whether he had any linen on; his tie was done in a simple knot and the ends tucked in. He was a man of about forty with a straight lock of hair on his forehead and two similar locks at the sides carelessly waving in the wind, uncommonly like a dog's ears. His grey little eyes did not look at an object at once, but first peeped at it stealthily and only then fixed themselves upon it. He seemed to be ashamed of his hands, and as he talked he tried to hide them behind his back or to put one behind his back and the other in the breast of his coat. When he had to give some paper to his chief at the office and to explain something in it, he held one hand behind his back and with the bent middle finger of the other hand carefully pointed to some line or word and then immediately drew his hand away, perhaps because his fingers were rather thick and red and shook a little, and he thought, with good reason, that it was not quite seemly to display them often.

'It was your pleasure that I should call upon you,' he said, casting his ambiguous glance at Oblomov.

'Yes, I wanted to speak to you about my lodgings. Please sit down,' Oblomov answered politely.

After a second invitation Ivan Matveyitch ventured to sit down, bending his body forward and thrusting his hands in his pockets.

'Circumstances compel me to look for another flat,' Oblomov said, 'and so I would like to sub-let this one.'

'It is difficult to do so now,' Ivan Matveyitch answered, coughing into his hand, which he quickly hid
again in his sleeve, 'you should have favoured me with a
call at the end of the summer, many people were after it
then.'

'I did call, but you weren't in.'

'My sister told me,' Ivan Matveyitch added. 'But don't
trouble about the flat: you will be comfortable here. Perhaps the birds disturb you?'

'What birds?'

'The hens.'

Although Oblomov constantly heard from early morning the deep clucking of a broody hen and the chirrup of
chickens under his window he gave no thought to it.
Olga's image was before his mind and he hardly noticed
his surroundings.

'No, that doesn't matter,' he said, 'I thought you were
speaking of the canaries: they begin twittering as soon as
it's light.'

'We will take them out,' Ivan Matveyitch answered.

'That doesn't matter either,' Oblomov remarked, 'but
my circumstances make it impossible for me to stay.'

'Just as you please,' Ivan Matveyitch answered. 'But if
you don't find another tenant, how shall we manage about
the contract? Will you pay compensation? . . . You will
lose money on it.'

'What does it come to?' Oblomov asked.

'I will bring the account.'

He brought the contract and a frame with counting-
beads.

'The flat is eight hundred paper roubles; you have paid
a hundred roubles deposit, that leaves seven hundred,' he
said.

'Do you mean to say you want a year's rent when I
haven't been here a fortnight?' Oblomov asked.

'But what would you have?' Ivan Matveyitch retorted
gently and modestly. 'It would be unfair if my sister were
to suffer loss. She is a poor widow: she lives by letting the

house and perhaps just makes enough on her chickens and eggs to buy some of the children's clothes.'

'It's all very well, but I really cannot,' Oblomov began, 'just think, I haven't been here a fortnight. It's too much, why should I pay all that?'

'But look what it says in the contract,' Ivan Matveyitch said, pointing with his middle finger to two lines in the document and then hiding the finger in his sleeve. 'Should I, Oblomov, wish to leave the flat before the expiration of the lease I undertake to find another tenant on the same terms, or to pay Madame Pshenitsyn a year's rent up to the first of June next year.'

'But how is that?' Oblomov said. 'That's unfair.'

'It's quite legal,' Ivan Matveyitch remarked. 'You have signed it yourself: here is your signature!'

The finger pointed to the signature and disappeared again.

'How much is it?' Oblomov asked.

'Seven hundred roubles,' Ivan Matveyitch began reckoning on the counting-frame with the same finger, sticking it out and hurriedly withdrawing it again, 'and another hundred and fifty for the stables and the shed.'

He moved some more beads.

'But I have no horses, I don't keep any, what do I want with the stables and the shed?' Oblomov retorted briskly.

'It's mentioned in the contract,' Ivan Matveyitch remarked, pointing to the line in question. 'Mihey Andreyitch said you would keep horses.'

'Mihey Andreyitch told a lie!' Oblomov said in vexation. 'Give me the contract!'

'Here is a copy of it, the contract belongs to my sister,' Ivan Matveyitch responded blandly, holding the document with both hands. 'Besides, if we reckon the kitchen-garden produce – cabbage, turnips, and other vegetables – for one person at two hundred and fifty roubles. . . .'

And he was about to move some more beads.

'What kitchen-garden? What cabbage? I don't know what you are talking about!' Oblomov protested, almost menacingly.

'Here it is, in the contract: Mihey Andreyitch said you wanted the garden produce. . . .'

'What next! The idea of your settling without me what I want for my table! I don't want your cabbages and turnips . . .' said Oblomov, getting up.

Ivan Matveyitch jumped up from his chair too.

'How could we do it without you? – here is your signature!' he retorted.

And again his fat finger shook against the signature and the paper shook in his hand.

'How much do you make it altogether?' Oblomov asked impatiently.

'For painting the doors and the windows, for altering the windows in the kitchen and making new frames for doors, a hundred and fifty-four paper roubles twenty-eight copecks.'

'What! Am I to pay for that too?' Oblomov asked in surprise. 'The landlord always pays for it, and no one moves into a flat that hasn't been done up!'

'Here, it says in the contract you are to pay for it,' Ivan Matveyitch said, pointing from a distance to the lines in question. 'One thousand three hundred and fifty-four paper roubles twenty-eight copecks altogether,' he concluded, gently putting both hands and the contract behind his back.

'But where am I to get it? I haven't the money,' Oblomov retorted, pacing up and down the room. 'Much I care about your cabbages and turnips!'

'Just as you like,' Ivan Matveyitch added softly. 'But don't worry: you will be comfortable here. And as to the money . . . my sister can wait.'

'I can't stay, I can't because of my circumstances, do you hear?'

'Yes, sir. Just as you like,' Ivan Matveyitch answered obediently, taking one step back.

'Very well, I will think it over and try to find another tenant!' Oblomov said, nodding to him.

'It's difficult; but just as you please!' Ivan Matveyitch concluded, and bowing three times left the room.

Oblomov took out his pocket-book and counted his money: there were only three hundred and five roubles. He was dumbfounded.

'What have I done with my money?' he asked himself in surprise, almost in terror. 'Early in the summer they sent me from the country twelve hundred and now there's only three hundred left!'

He began reckoning, trying to remember all he had spent, but could only account for two hundred and fifty roubles. 'Where has the money gone?' he said.

'Zahar, Zahar!'

'Yes, sir?'

'What have we done with all our money? There isn't any left!'

Zahar began fumbling in his pockets, pulled out half a rouble and a ten-copeck piece and put them on the table.

'Here, I've forgotten to give you this, it's been left over from the moving.'

'What's the good of your giving me small coin? I want you to tell me what I've done with eight hundred.'

'How can I tell? I don't know what you spend money on or what you pay for hiring a carriage.'

'Yes, the carriage has cost a good deal,' Oblomov recalled, looking at Zahar. 'You don't remember what we paid the driver in the summer?'

'How can I remember? One day you told me to give him thirty roubles, so I remember that.'

'If you could have written it down, now!' Oblomov said reproachfully. 'It's a bad thing you can't read or write!'

'I've lived all my life without it, and thank Heaven I am no worse than other people!' Zahar responded, looking sideways.

'Stolz is quite right, I ought to open a school in the country!' Oblomov thought.

'The Ilyinskys had a man who could read and write, the servants told me, and he stole all the silver out of the sideboard,' Zahar continued.

'Just fancy!' Oblomov thought in alarm. 'Yes really, men who have had some schooling are so immoral – they do nothing but sit in public-houses, play the accordion, and drink tea. . . . No, it's too soon to open schools!'

'Well, what other expenses were there?' he asked.

'How do I know? You gave Mihey Andreyitch something when he came in the summer. . . .'

'So I did!' Oblomov said joyfully, recalling the incident. 'And so thirty to the driver; twenty-five, I believe, to Tarantyev. . . . What else?'

He looked thoughtfully and inquiringly at Zahar, and Zahar looked at him sideways with a sullen air.

'I wonder if Anissya would remember?' Oblomov asked.

'How is the fool to remember? What does a woman know?' Zahar said contemptuously.

'I can't account for it!' Oblomov concluded dejectedly. 'Could burglars have broken in?'

'If it had been burglars they would have taken everything,' said Zahar, going out of the room.

Oblomov sat down in the arm-chair and sank into thought. 'Where am I to get the money?' he thought, till he was bathed in cold sweat. 'When will they send from the country, and how much?'

He glanced at the clock: it was two; time to go to Olga's. This was the day he was to dine there. He cheered up gradually, ordered a cab and drove to Morskaya Street.

IV

He told Olga that he had spoken to his landlady's brother, and added hurriedly that there was a chance of sub-letting the flat in the course of the week. Olga drove with her aunt to make a call before dinner and he went to look at flats near by. He called at two houses; in one there was a four-roomed flat for four thousand paper roubles, and in another one of five rooms for six thousand.

'Horrible! Horrible!' he repeated, stopping his ears and running away from the astounded porters. Adding to these sums the thousand odd roubles he had to pay to Madame Pshenitsyn he was so terrified that he could not reckon the amount and made haste to join Olga. There were visitors there. Olga was in high spirits, talked, sang, and made quite a sensation. Only Oblomov listened absentmindedly; and yet it was for him that she talked and sang, so that he should not sit looking down dejectedly, but that everything in him should be singing and talking too.

'Come to the theatre to-morrow: we have a box,' she said.

'In the evening, through the mud, all that way!' Oblomov thought, but glancing into her eyes answered her smile with a smile of consent.

'Book a stall for every week,' she added. 'The Maevskys are coming next week, *ma tante* has invited them to our box.'

And she looked into his eyes to see how glad he was.

'My goodness,' he thought in horror, 'and I have only three hundred roubles left!'

'Ask the baron, he knows everybody there and will book a seat for you to-morrow.'

She smiled again, he, too, smiled as he looked at her, and applied to the baron, who, also with a smile, said he would send for a ticket.

'Now you will be in the stalls, and afterwards when you have finished your business,' Olga added, 'you will take your place in our box by right.'

And she smiled as she did when she was perfectly happy. Oh, what a thrill of happiness went through him when Olga slightly lifted the curtain over the enchanting vista wreathed in smiles as in flowers! Oblomov actually forgot about money; but next morning when he saw Ivan Matveyitch with his parcel flit past the windows he remembered about the deed of trust and asked him to have it witnessed at the courts. Ivan Matveyitch read it, said there was one obscure point in it, and offered to put it right. The paper was copied out once more, witnessed, and at last sent to the post. Oblomov triumphantly informed Olga of the fact and felt he could take a long rest. He rejoiced that there was no need to look for a flat till he received an answer from the country, and that meanwhile he was making use of the lodgings for which he had to pay a year's rent in any case. 'One could really live here, if it weren't so far from everything,' he reflected; 'the place is in very good order and admirably managed. . . .'

Agafya Matveyevna really was an excellent house-keeper. Although Oblomov boarded himself, she watched over his table too. Coming into the kitchen one day Ilya Ilyitch found Agafya Matveyevna and Anissya almost in each other's arms. If there is such a thing as spiritual affinity, if kindred souls really do recognize each other from afar, there has never been a clearer proof of this than the sympathy between Agafya Matveyevna and Anissya. They understood and appreciated each other at the first glance, word, and movement. The way Anissya, rolling up her sleeves and armed with a rag and a poker, put into order a kitchen that had not been used for six months, and at one go brushed the dust from the shelves, the walls, and the table; the wide sweep of her broom along the floor and the benches; the rapidity with which she removed the ashes from the stove – all this made Agafya

Matveyevna see what Anissya was, and what a splendid
help she could be to her. From that moment she gave her
a place in her heart. Anissya, in her turn, having once
seen how Agafya Matveyevna reigned in her kitchen; how
with her falcon eyes without eyebrows she saw every
clumsy movement of the slow Akulina; how she rapped
out orders to take a dish out of the oven, to put it in, to
warm it up, to add some salt; how at the market she could
tell at a single glance, or at most by a touch of her finger,
the exact age of a fowl, the length of time that fish had
been out of water or parsley or lettuce had been cut –
having seen all this, Anissya gazed at her in admiration
and respectful fear, deciding that she, Anissya, had missed
her vocation, and that the true field of her activity was
not Oblomov's kitchen, where the restless, feverish, nervous quickness of her movements served no other purpose
than catching in the air a plate or a glass dropped by
Zahar, and where her experience and subtlety were wasted
through her husband's sullen jealousy and disdainful
churlishness. The two women understood each other and
became inseparable. When Oblomov dined out Anissya
spent her time in the landlady's kitchen, and from pure
love of work darted hither and thither, put pots in the
oven and took them out again, opened the cupboard, got
out what was required, and shut it again almost in one
instant, before Akulina had had time to grasp what was
required. Anissya's reward was dinner, six or more cups
of coffee in the morning and as many in the evening, a
long friendly conversation with the mistress of the house,
and sometimes whispered confidences from her. When
Oblomov dined at home Agafya Matveyevna helped Anissya – that is, indicated with her finger or a word if it was
time to take out the meat, if red wine or sour cream
should be added to the sauce, if the fish was being boiled
in the right way. . . . What a wealth of household knowledge they imparted to each other, not only about cooking,
but about linen, yarn, sewing, washing clothes, cleaning
lace and gloves, taking out stains from various materials,

using various home-made medicines and herbs – about all that observant mind and lifelong experience have contributed to that sphere of life!

Ilya Ilyitch got up about nine o'clock in the morning, sometimes catching a glimpse, on the other side of the fence, of the landlady's brother going to his office with a paper parcel under his arm; then he had coffee. The coffee was excellent, the cream thick, the rolls rich and crisp. Then he smoked his cigar, listening to the deep clucking of the broody hen, the squeak of the chickens, and the twitter of the canaries and greenfinches. He said they were not to be taken out, 'They make me think of the country, of Oblomovka,' he said. Then he sat down to finish the books he had begun in the summer, and sometimes casually lay down on the sofa to read. There was perfect stillness around; only some soldier or a group of peasants with axes in their belts passed sometimes down the street. Very seldom a pedlar penetrated to these wilds, and stopping in front of the fence shouted for half an hour: 'Apples! Astrakhan! Water-melons!' so that one could not help buying something. Sometimes Masha, the landlady's daughter, came in, sent by her mother, to say there were pickled mushrooms for sale and ask if he would like to order a cask for himself; or Oblomov called in Vanya, her brother, asked him what he had been learning and made him read and write to see how well he could do it. If the children did not shut the door after them he saw their mother's bare neck and her rapidly moving back and elbows. She was always at work, ironing, rubbing through a sieve, or pounding something in a mortar on the big table; she no longer stood on ceremony with him, and did not hasten to put her shawl on when she noticed him looking at her through the half-open door, but merely smiled and went on with her work. Sometimes he walked to the door with his book in his hands, peeped in, and talked to her.

'You are always at work!' he said to her once.

She smiled and began attentively turning the handle of

the coffee-mill; her elbow was circling round so rapidly that it made Oblomov dizzy.

'You will be tired,' he went on.

'No, I am used to it,' she answered, rattling the coffee-mill.

'And when you have no work, what do you do?'

'How do you mean, no work? There is always something to do: in the morning there's dinner to be cooked, after dinner I do needlework, and in the evening there's supper.'

'Do you have supper?'

'Of course; one can't do without supper. On the eve of holy-days we go to Vespers.'

'That's right,' Oblomov praised her. 'Which church do you go to?'

'The Church of the Nativity; it's our parish church.'

'And do you read anything?'

She looked at him dully and said nothing.

'Have you any books?' he asked.

'My brother has some, but he never reads. We take newspapers from the tavern and he sometimes reads them aloud. . . . Vanya has a lot of books.'

'Don't you ever have a rest?'

'I don't, really.'

'Don't you go to the theatre?'

'My brother goes at Christmas-time.'

'And you?'

'I haven't time: who would see to the supper?' she asked, throwing a sidelong glance at him.

'The cook could do it without you. . . .'

'Akulina!' she protested in surprise. 'How could she? What could she do without me? The supper wouldn't be ready by the morning. I have all the keys.'

There was a pause. Oblomov was admiring her plump, round elbows.

'What lovely arms you have,' he said suddenly, 'one could paint them straight away!'

She smiled a little shyly.

'Sleeves are so awkward,' she said apologetically, 'the dresses nowadays are made so that one can't help getting the sleeves dirty.'

She said nothing more. Oblomov, too, was silent.

'When I have ground the coffee,' the landlady whispered to herself, 'I must chop the sugar-loaf, and I mustn't forget to send for some cinnamon.'

'You ought to get married,' Oblomov said, 'you look after the house so splendidly!'

She smiled and began pouring the coffee into a big glass jar.

'Really!' Oblomov added.

'Who would marry me with my two children?' she answered, and began counting something in her mind.

'A score . . .' she said thoughtfully, 'is she going to put it all in?' And putting the jar into the cupboard she ran to the kitchen. Oblomov returned to his room and began reading.

'Such a fresh, strong woman, and so good at house-keeping. She really ought to be married . . .' he said to himself, and fell to thinking . . . of Olga.

On fine days Oblomov put on his cap and walked about the neighbourhood; he would get stuck in the mud in one place, have an unpleasant encounter with the dogs in another, and return home. And at home the table would be already set for dinner, and the food was so good and so well served. Sometimes a bare arm would be thrust through the door offering some of the landlady's pie on a plate. 'It's nice and quiet in these parts, only rather dull!' Oblomov would say as he drove off to the opera.

One night, returning late from the theatre, he and the driver spent nearly an hour knocking at the gate; the dog lost its voice jumping on the chain and barking. He got chilled and angry and said he would leave the very next day. But the next day and the day after and a whole week passed and he did not leave.

He missed Olga very much on the days when he could not see her, could not hear her voice and read in her eyes the same unchanging love, tenderness, happiness. On the days they met he lived as he had done in the summer, losing himself in her singing or gazing into her eyes; and if there were other people there it was enough for him that her look, indifferent to all, should be deep and significant for him. But with the approach of winter they saw less and less of each other alone. The Ilyinskys now always had visitors, and for days together Oblomov did not succeed in saying two words to her. They exchanged glances; hers expressed at times weariness and impatience. She looked at all the other visitors with a frown. Once or twice Oblomov felt distinctly bored, and one day after dinner he picked up his hat.

'Where are you off to?' Olga asked, coming upon him suddenly and seizing his hat.

'Allow me to go home. . . .'

'Why?' she asked. One of her eyebrows lay higher than the other. 'What are you going to do?'

'Nothing special . . .' he said, hardly able to keep his eyes open.

'As though you would be allowed to! Are you thinking of having a nap, I wonder?' she asked, looking sternly into his eyes.

'Of course not!' Oblomov retorted briskly. 'The idea of sleeping in the day-time! I was simply bored.'

And he gave up the hat to her.

'We are going to the opera to-day!' she said.

'But we shall not be in the box together!' he added with a sigh.

'What of it? Is it nothing to you that we shall see each other, that you will call in the interval, speak to me at the end, lead me to the carriage? . . . Mind you come!' she added imperiously. 'What next!'

There was nothing for it: he went to the opera, yawned as though he wanted to swallow the stage, scratched the back of his head, and crossed and recrossed his legs.

'Oh, I wish it were all over and I sat beside her instead of dragging myself all the way here!' he thought. 'Fancy snatching chance meetings and playing the part of a boy in love after a summer like that! To tell the truth, I wouldn't have gone to the theatre to-day had we been already married; it's the sixth time I am hearing this opera. . . .'

In the interval he went to Olga's box and could hardly squeeze his way to her between two dandies he did not know. Five minutes later he slipped away and stopped in the crowd at the entrance to the stalls. The next act had begun and people were hurrying to their seats. The dandies from Olga's box were there too, but they did not see Oblomov.

'Who was that gentleman in the Ilyinskys' box just now?' one of them asked the other.

'Oh, somebody called Oblomov!' the other answered carelessly.

'What is he?'

'A landowner, a friend of Stolz's.'

'Ah,' the other pronounced significantly, 'a friend of Stolz's! What is he doing here?'

'*Dieu sait!*' the other one answered, and they went to their places. But Oblomov was completely overwhelmed by this trifling conversation.

'Who was that gentleman? . . . Somebody called Oblomov. . . . What is he doing here? . . . *Dieu sait*,' it was all hammering in his head. 'Somebody called Oblomov!' 'What am I doing here? Why, I am loving Olga, I am hers. . . . But there, people are already asking the question – they have noticed me. . . . Oh dear, what am I to do? I must think of something. . . .'

He no longer saw what was happening on the stage, what knights and ladies appeared there; the orchestra thundered away, but he never heard it. He looked about him and counted the number of acquaintances he had in the theatre: they were here, there, everywhere, all asking 'Who was that gentleman in Olga's box? . . .' 'Somebody called Oblomov,' they all said. 'Yes, that's all I am,' he thought in timid dejection, 'people know me because I am a friend of Stolz's! Why am I with Olga? "*Dieu sait.* . . ."

There, those dandies are looking at me and then at Olga's box!' Olga's opera glasses were fixed on him. 'Oh my goodness,' he thought, 'she doesn't take her eyes off me! What can she have found in me? A fine treasure indeed! Now she is nodding to me and pointing to the stage! . . . and those dandies, I believe, are looking at me and laughing. . . . Oh my God!'

Again in his agitation he violently scratched his head and recrossed his legs. Olga had invited the two dandies to tea after the theatre, promised to sing the *Cavatina*, and told him to come too.

'No, I am not going there any more to-day; we must settle the thing as soon as possible and then. . . . Why doesn't that man send me an answer from the country? I would have gone there long ago and announced my engagement to Olga before going. . . . Oh, she is still looking at me! It's simply dreadful!'

He went home without waiting for the end of the opera. Gradually he got over the unpleasant impression of that evening; he again looked at Olga with a tremor of happiness when they were alone, suppressed tears of ecstasy when he listened to her singing in the presence of others, and arriving home lay down on the sofa – unbeknown to Olga – but not to sleep, not to lie like a log, but to dream of her, to play at happiness, to be thrilled by the thoughts of his future peaceful life at home where Olga would shine – and everything around her would shine too. Peeping into the future he sometimes unconsciously and sometimes deliberately peeped through the half-open door at the landlady's rapidly moving elbows.

One day the stillness, both in and out of doors, was perfect: no carriages rattled past, no doors banged; only the clock in the hall ticked regularly and the canaries were singing; but such sounds do not disturb the stillness – they merely make it more alive. Ilya Ilyitch lay in a careless attitude on the sofa playing with his slipper: he dropped it on the floor, threw it up, turned it over in the air, and when it fell he picked it up with his foot. . . . Zahar walked in and stopped in the doorway.

'What is it?' Oblomov asked lightly.

Zahar said nothing and looked at him, not sideways as usual, but almost straight.

'Yes?' Oblomov asked, glancing at him with surprise. 'Is the pie ready or what?'

'Have you found a flat?' Zahar asked in his turn.

'Not yet. Why?'

'I haven't sorted everything out yet: crockery, clothes, and boxes are still all in a heap in the store-room. Shall I sort them out?'

'Wait,' Oblomov said absentmindedly. 'I am waiting for a letter from the country.'

'Then the wedding will be after Christmas?' Zahar added.

'What wedding?' Oblomov asked, getting up suddenly.

'Why, yours, of course!' Zahar answered confidently, as though the whole thing had long been settled. 'You are going to be married.'

'Married! To whom?' Oblomov asked with horror, staring at Zahar in amazement.

'The Ilyinsky young lady . . .' before Zahar had uttered the words Oblomov fairly pounced on him.

'What are you talking of? Who has put the idea into your head, you luckless fellow?' Oblomov exclaimed in a restrained, dramatic voice, coming closer and closer to Zahar.

'Why luckless? There's nothing wrong with me, thank God!' Zahar answered, retreating to the door. 'Who has told me? Why the Ilyinskys' servants spoke of it in the summer.'

'Sh-sh-sh!' Oblomov hissed, raising his finger and shaking it menacingly. 'Not another word!'

'I didn't invent it,' Zahar said.

'Not a word!' Oblomov repeated, looking at him sternly and pointing to the door. Zahar went out and his sigh could be heard all over the house.

Oblomov could not recover from the shock: he remained in the same position, looking with horror at the spot where Zahar had stood, then clutched his head in despair, and sank into an arm-chair.

'The servants know!' he kept thinking. 'There's gossip in the kitchens and the servants' halls! This is what it has come to! He dared to ask me when the wedding would be! And the aunt still suspects nothing, or if she does, it may be something different, something wrong. . . . Aïe-aïe-aïe, what may she think! And I? And Olga? What have I done, wretched man that I am!' he said, throwing himself on the sofa and hiding his face in the cushion. 'Wedding! That poetical moment in the lovers' life, that crown of happiness, is being discussed by valets and coachmen when nothing has been decided yet, when there is no answer from the country, and I have no money and haven't found new lodgings. . . .'

He began analysing the 'poetical moment,' which suddenly lost all its glamour as soon as Zahar had spoken of it. Oblomov began to see the reverse side of the medal and painfully turned from side to side, lay on his back, jumped up suddenly, took three steps across the room and lay down again.

'It's a bad look out!' Zahar thought with apprehension as he sat in the hall. 'I wish to goodness I hadn't said anything!'

'How do they know?' Oblomov kept asking himself. 'Olga has said nothing, I haven't ventured even to think of it aloud, and in the servants' hall they've settled it all! This is what *tête-à-tête* meetings, poetical dawns and sunsets, enchanting singing and passionate glances have come to! Ah, these romances never lead to any good! One must be married first and then float in the rosy mists of love. . . . Oh dear, oh dear! I must run to Olga's aunt, take Olga by the hand and say: "Here is my betrothed," but nothing is ready: there is no answer from the country, no money, no flat! No, I must first of all knock the idea out of Zahar's head, stifle the rumour as one puts out a flame, so that there should be no fire and smoke. . . . Wedding! What is a wedding?'

He smiled, recalling his former poetical ideal of the wedding: a long veil, orange-blossom, whispers among the crowd. . . . But the colours were no longer the same, he saw in the crowd the rude, dirty Zahar and all the Ilyin-skys' servants, a number of carriages, strange faces full of cold curiosity. And then such depressing, such alarming pictures rose before his mind. . . .

'I must knock the idea out of Zahar's head and make him believe it was absurd!' he decided, feverishly excited one moment and painfully thoughtful the next. An hour later he called Zahar. Zahar pretended not to hear and began quietly making his way to the kitchen. He had opened one half of the door noiselessly, but as he was going through it sideways he caught his shoulder in the other half and the doors flew open with a bang.

'Zahar!' Oblomov cried peremptorily.

'What is it?' Zahar answered from the hall.

'Come here!'

'Do you want me to bring you something? Tell me what it is and I'll bring it,' he said.

'Come here!' Oblomov uttered slowly and impressively.

'Ah, what a life!' Zahar hissed, squeezing himself into the room.

'Well, what do you want?' he asked, sticking in the doorway.

'Come here!' Oblomov said in a solemn and mysterious voice, pointing to a place so close to himself that Zahar would have had almost to sit on his lap.

'I can't go there, there isn't room, I can hear from here just as well,' Zahar protested, obstinately remaining in the doorway.

'Come here, I tell you!' Oblomov said menacingly. Zahar took a step and stood still like a monument, looking out of the window at the hens and turning a brush-like whisker to his master. The agitation Ilya Ilyitch had been through had wrought a change in him within a single hour; he looked thinner in the face and his eyes wandered uneasily.

'I am in for it now!' thought Zahar, growing more and more gloomy.

'How could you have asked your master such an absurd question?' Oblomov asked.

'Now he is at it!' Zahar thought, blinking in an agonized expectation of 'heart-rending' words.

'I ask you: how could you have thought of anything so ridiculous?' Oblomov repeated.

Zahar said nothing.

'Do you hear, Zahar? How can you presume to think such things, let alone say them?'

'I'd better call Anissya, Ilya Ilyitch, if you'll let me . . .' Zahar answered, and took a step towards the door.

'I want to speak to you and not to Anissya. Why did you invent such a ridiculous story?'

'I didn't invent it, the Ilyinskys' servants told me.'

'And who told them?'

'How do I know? Katya told Semyon, Semyon told Nikita, Nikita told Vassilissa, Vassilissa told Anissya, and Anissya told me. . . .'

'Oh my God! All of them!' exclaimed Oblomov, horrified. 'It is all nonsense, absurdity, lies, slander – do you hear?' he said, banging his fist on the table. 'It cannot be!'

'Why not?' Zahar retorted indifferently. 'There's nothing extraordinary about a wedding. You are not the only one, everybody gets married.'

'Everybody!' Oblomov repeated. 'You are a hand at comparing me to other people! This cannot be, it is and always has been impossible! Nothing extraordinary about a wedding – do you hear that? Why, do you know what a wedding is?'

Zahar glanced at Oblomov, but meeting his furious stare immediately shifted his eyes and looked at a corner on the right.

'Listen, I'll explain to you what it means. "A wedding, a wedding!" idle people, women and children, will begin saying in the servants' quarters, in shops, in the market-place. A man ceases to be Ilya Ilyitch or Pyotr Petrovitch

and is called "the bridegroom." The day before nobody
would look at him, and the next day all will be staring at
him as though he were a scoundrel! They won't let him
alone in the street or in the theatre, "There he goes, that's
him," they will all whisper. And the number of people
that come up to him in the course of the day and say
something absurd, each trying to look as stupid as possible
– as you do just now' (Zahar quickly shifted his gaze again
and looked at the yard) – 'that's how the news is received!
And you've got to present yourself at your betrothed's
first thing in the morning, without peace or rest, and
must always wear light gloves and brand-new clothes, and
look cheerful, and never have a square meal, but live on
air and bouquets! And that's for three or four months on
end! Do you see? So how could I do that?'

Oblomov stopped to see if Zahar was affected by this
description of the drawbacks of marriage.

'Shall I go now?' Zahar asked, turning to the door.

'No, you wait! You are good at spreading false
rumours, and you may as well know why they are false.'

'What is there for me to know?' said Zahar, examining
the walls.

'You have forgotten what a lot of fussing and running
about the engaged couple have to do: and who is going to
run for me to the tailor, to the bootmaker, to the furniture
shop? You, by any chance? I can't be everywhere at once.
Everyone in the town will know. "Oblomov is getting
married – have you heard?" – "Indeed, to whom? Who is
she? When is the wedding?"' Oblomov said in different
voices. 'They will do nothing but talk about it. Why, that
alone would make me take to my bed – and you talk of a
wedding!'

He looked at Zahar again.

'Shall I call Anissya?' Zahar asked.

'What for? It was you and not Anissya who made this
wild suggestion.'

'Why has the Lord sent this infliction upon me
to-day?' whispered Zahar, heaving a sigh that made him

raise his shoulders.

'And the expense of it!' Oblomov went on. 'Where is the money to come from? You saw how little money I have?' Oblomov asked almost menacingly. 'And the flat? I have to pay a thousand roubles here and pay three thousand for another and as much again to have it done up! And then there's the carriage, the cook, the everyday expenses! Where am I to get the money from?'

'But how do other people with three hundred serfs manage to marry?' asked Zahar, and at once regretted it because his master nearly jumped out of his chair at the remark.

'You are talking of "other people" again? Take care!' he said, shaking his finger. ' "Other people" live in two, or at most in three, rooms: the dining-room and the drawing-room are all in one, and some people sleep there as well; the children are in the next room, and one maid does the work of the whole place. The lady herself goes marketing! And do you imagine Olga Sergeyevna would go to the market?'

'Oh, I could do that,' Zahar observed.

'Do you know how much we receive from Oblomovka?' Oblomov asked. 'Have you heard what the bailiff wrote: "some two thousand less"? And there's the road to be made, schools to be built, I have to go to Oblomovka: there is nowhere to live there, the house isn't built. . . . Wedding indeed! How could you think of it?'

Oblomov stopped. He was himself terrified at the comfortless, menacing picture he had drawn. The roses, the orange-blossom, the festive brilliance, the whispers of admiration in the crowd – all had faded suddenly. He changed colour and sank into thought. Then gradually he came to himself again, looked round and saw Zahar.

'What is it?' he asked morosely.

'Why, you told me to stand here.'

'Go!' said Oblomov with an impatient wave of his hand.

Zahar rapidly moved towards the door.

'No, wait!' Oblomov stopped him.

'One minute it's "go," another "stay"!' Zahar grumbled, holding on to the door.

'How did you dare to spread such absurd rumours about me?' Oblomov asked in an anxious whisper.

'But when did I spread them, Ilya Ilyitch? It wasn't I but the Ilyinskys' servants said that you had made an offer. . . .'

'Sh-sh . . .' Oblomov hissed, waving his hands menacingly, 'not a word, never! Do you hear?'

'Yes,' Zahar answered timidly.

'You will not broadcast this absurdity any more?'

'I won't,' Zahar answered softly, not grasping half the words, but aware that they were 'heart-rending.'

'Mind now, if you hear any talk about it, or if anyone asks you, say it's nonsense, there has been nothing of the sort and there cannot be!' Oblomov added in a whisper.

'Yes, sir,' Zahar whispered almost inaudibly.

Oblomov turned round and shook his finger at him. Zahar was blinking in alarm and retreating towards the door on tiptoe.

'Who was the first to speak of it?' Oblomov asked, catching him up.

'Katya told Semyon, Semyon told Nikita, Nikita told Vassilissa . . .' Zahar whispered.

'And you blurted it out to everyone! I'll give it you!' Oblomov hissed menacingly. 'Spreading slander about your master, eh?'

'Why do you go on at me with such upsetting talk?' Zahar said. 'I'll call Anissya: she knows it all. . . .'

'What does she know? Tell me, tell me at once!'

Zahar instantly scrambled out of the room and walked into the kitchen with extraordinary rapidity.

'Put down the frying-pan, go to the master!' he said to Anissya, pointing with his thumb to the door. Anissya passed the frying-pan to Akulina, straightened her skirt that had been tucked in at the waist, patted herself on the hips, and wiping her nose with her finger went in to the master. She calmed Ilya Ilyitch in five minutes, assuring him that no one had said anything about a wedding: she wouldn't scruple to say on oath and to take the ikon down from the wall, this was the first time she had heard of it; she had heard something quite different, people said that the baron had made the young lady an offer. . . .

'The baron?' Ilya Ilyitch asked, jumping up from his chair, and not only his heart but his hands and feet turned cold.

'That's all nonsense too!' Anissya hastened to say, seeing that she had fallen from the frying-pan into the fire. 'It was merely Katya said this to Semyon, Semyon told Marfa, and Marfa told it Nikita all wrong, and Nikita said "it would be a good thing if your master, Ilya Ilyitch, would propose to our young lady. . . ." '

'What a fool that Nikita is!' Oblomov observed.

'He is indeed,' Anissya acquiesced, 'he looks half asleep when he goes out with the carriage. And Vassilissa did not believe him either,' she rattled on. 'She told me on Assumption Day what the nurse had said to her, that the young lady was not thinking of marrying and that sure enough your master would have looked out someone long ago had he meant to marry, and the nurse had seen Samoilo some time before and he quite laughed at it: a wedding indeed! It looks more like a funeral than a wedding: the auntie keeps having headaches and the young lady cries and doesn't talk, and no trousseau is being made; the young lady has no end of stockings that need darning and they can't see to that even; and last week they pawned their silver. . . .'

'Pawned their silver? Then they haven't any money either!' Oblomov thought, looking round the walls in horror and then fixing his gaze on Anissya's nose because there was nothing else in her that one's eyes could dwell upon. It seemed, indeed, as though she had been saying all this with her nose and not with her mouth.

'Mind, then, you don't talk nonsense!' Oblomov remarked, shaking his finger at her.

'Talk, not likely! I don't even think it, let alone talk!' Anissya rattled on. 'And there is nothing in it, this is the first I have heard of it, God strike me dead! I was surprised when you mentioned it, frightened, I simply trembled! How can it be? What wedding? No one has dreamed of it. I am always in the kitchen and never speak to anyone. I haven't seen the Ilyinskys' servants for the last month, I have forgotten what they are called. And who is there here to talk to? With the mistress we talk of nothing but housekeeping; with the granny one can't talk at all, she coughs and is deaf; Akulina is a fool and the porter a drunkard; there's only the children, but what's the use of talking to them? I have forgotten, indeed, what the young lady looks like. . . .'

'Very well, very well!' Oblomov said impatiently, dismissing her with a gesture.

'How can one say what is not?' Anissya finished up as she walked out of the room. 'And if Nikita did talk it's simply because a fool may say anything! But I could never have thought of such a thing: why, slaving away all day long I haven't time to think! Is it likely? The ikon is my witness . . .' with these words the speaking nose disappeared, but the voice could be heard for another minute behind the door.

'So that's it! Even Anissya says "is it likely?" ' Oblomov whispered, clasping his hands. 'O Happiness,' he added bitterly, 'how frail, how uncertain you are! The veil, the orange-blossom, love! But where is the money? What are we to live on? Even you have to be bought, pure, lawful bliss of love!'

From that moment Oblomov lost his peace of mind and no longer indulged in dreams. He slept badly, ate little, and looked at everything morosely without interest. He had wanted to frighten Zahar, but had frightened himself more when he went into the practical aspect of marriage and saw that in spite of its poetical character a wedding was a concrete, official step towards important and serious realities and stern duties. He had imagined his conversation with Zahar very differently: he recalled how he had intended to break the news to him, how Zahar would cry out with delight and fall at his feet; he would give him twenty-five roubles and Anissya ten. . . . He remembered it all, the thrill of happiness he had felt, the touch of Olga's hand, her passionate kiss . . . and he went cold all over: 'It has gone, faded away,' said a voice within him. What was to happen now?

V

Oblomov did not know with what eyes to look at Olga, what to say to her, what she would say, and decided not to go to her on Wednesday, but to put off their meeting till Sunday, when there would be many visitors at the house and they would have no chance of talking alone. He did not want to tell her about the servants' stupid gossip so as not to worry her with what could not be remedied, but it was very difficult not to tell; he could not pretend to her and she would be sure to extract from him all that was hidden in the deepest recesses of his heart.

Arriving at this decision he calmed down somewhat and wrote a fresh letter to the neighbour who was looking after his affairs in the country, begging him to do his best and to answer promptly. Then he began thinking how he could fill up the long, unendurable day which would have been so full with Olga's presence, her singing, the invisible intercourse of their minds. It was too bad of Zahar to have upset him at the wrong moment! He decided to dine at Ivan Gerasimovitch's on Wednesday so as to notice that unendurable day as little as possible. And then by Sunday he would think of something, and perhaps the letter from the country would come by then.

The next day came. He was wakened by the desperate barking and jumping of the dog on the chain. Someone had come into the yard and was asking something. The porter called Zahar: Zahar brought Oblomov a letter with the town postmark.

'From the Ilyinsky young lady,' Zahar said.

'How do you know?' Oblomov asked angrily. 'It isn't.'

'In the summer she always sent you letters like that.'

'Is she well? What can it mean?' Oblomov thought, opening the letter.

'I don't want to wait till Wednesday [Olga wrote]: I

miss you so much after all these days that I will expect you to-morrow for certain at three o'clock in the Summer Garden.'

That was all. Anxiety again rose up in his mind and he grew restless with the thought of how he would talk to Olga, how he would look at her. 'I can't, I don't know how to,' he said. 'Go and ask Stolz!'

But he comforted himself by reflecting that she would probably come with her aunt or with some other lady – Marya Semyonovna, for instance, who was so fond of her and could not admire her enough. In their presence he hoped to conceal his confusion and be gallant and talkative. 'And just at dinner-time too: a nice hour to choose!' he thought as he set out, none too briskly, towards the Summer Garden.

As soon as he entered the long avenue he saw a lady with a veil over her face get up from a seat and walk towards him. He did not think it was Olga: 'Alone! Impossible! she wouldn't venture, and there could be no pretext for her to leave home. And yet . . . it seems to be her walk: her feet move so quickly and lightly that they seem to glide; her neck and head bend forward as though she were looking for something on the ground at her feet.' Another man would have recognized her by her dress or her hat, but Oblomov, after spending a whole morning with Olga, could never tell what she was wearing. There was hardly anyone in the garden: an elderly gentleman walking briskly, evidently taking his constitutional, two . . . women, not ladies, and a nurse with two children blue in the face with the cold. The leaves had fallen and one could see right through the branches; the crows on the trees cawed unpleasantly. The day, however, was clear and bright, and if one were wrapped up properly it was warm. The woman with the veil drew nearer and nearer. . . . 'It's she!' Oblomov said, and stopped in terror, unable to believe his eyes.

'How are you? What's happening?' he asked, taking her hand.

'How glad I am you have come!' she said, not answering his questions. 'I thought you wouldn't and was beginning to be uneasy!'

'How did you come here? How did you manage?' he asked in confusion.

'Now, don't question me, what does it matter? Why ask, it's such a bore! I wanted to see you and I came – that's all!'

She pressed his hand warmly and looked at him gaily and happily, so obviously enjoying the moment stolen from Fate that he envied her her playful mood and wished he could share it. And yet, troubled as he was, he could not help forgetting himself for a moment when he saw her face bearing no trace of the concentrated thought that found expression in the play of her eyebrows and the wrinkle on her forehead; this time her features had none of the wonderful maturity that so often disturbed him. Her face breathed such childlike confidence in life, in happiness, in him. . . . She was very charming.

'Oh, how glad I am! How glad!' she repeated, smiling and looking at him. 'I thought I should not see you to-day. I suddenly felt so depressed yesterday, I don't know why, so I wrote to you. Are you glad?'

She glanced into his face.

'Why are you so gloomy to-day? You don't speak? You aren't glad? I thought you'd go mad with joy, but you seem to be asleep. Wake up, sir, Olga is with you!'

Reproachfully she slightly pushed him away.

'Aren't you well? What is it?' she insisted.

'Yes, I am well and happy,' he hastened to say, to prevent her probing into his secret heart. 'I am merely anxious at your coming alone. . . .'

'That's my business,' she said impatiently. 'Would it have been better if I had come with my aunt?'

'Better, Olga. . . .'

'Had I known I would have asked her,' Olga interrupted him in an injured voice, letting go his hand. 'I thought there was no greater happiness for you than being with me.'

'There isn't and there cannot be! But how did you manage? . . .'

'It's not worth bothering about; let's talk of something else. Listen . . . Ah, what was I going to say? I have forgotten. . . .'

'Perhaps to tell me how you came here alone?' he asked, looking anxiously about him.

'Oh no! How you do keep on! I wonder you aren't tired of it. What was I going to say? . . . Never mind, I'll think of it presently. Oh, how nice it is here! The leaves have fallen, *feuilles d'automne* – do you remember Hugo? There's sunshine on the Neva. . . . Let's go to the river and have a row in a boat. . . .'

'Mercy on us, what are you talking about? It's fearfully cold and I have only a quilted coat on. . . .'

'I, too, have a quilted dress. What does it matter? Come along.'

She ran and dragged him along. He grumbled and lagged behind, but he had to step into a boat and go.

'However did you come here alone?' Oblomov repeated anxiously.

'Shall I tell you?' she teased him roguishly when they were in the middle of the river. 'Now I can: you won't run away from here, and you would have done so there. . . .'

'Why?' he asked in alarm.

'Are you coming to-morrow?' she asked, instead of answering.

'Oh dear, she seems to have read in my thoughts that I meant not to come,' Oblomov thought. 'Yes,' he said aloud.

'In the morning, and staying all day?'

He hesitated.

'Then I won't tell you.'

'I'll come for the day.'

'You see . . .' she began seriously, 'I asked you to come

here to-day because I wanted to tell you. . . .'

'What?'

'That you . . . should come to us to-morrow.'

'Oh my goodness!' he interrupted impatiently. 'But how did you come here?'

'Here?' she repeated absentmindedly. 'How did I come here? Oh, I just came. . . . Wait a minute . . . but what's the good of talking about it?'

She took a handful of water and threw it in his face. He started, and shut his eyes, and she laughed.

'How cold the water is! My hand feels quite numb. Oh dear, how jolly it all is, how happy I am!' she went on, looking about her. 'Let us come again to-morrow, but straight from home. . . .'

'Haven't you come straight from home now? Where have you been?' he asked hurriedly.

'To a shop.'

'What shop?'

'What shop? Why, I told you in the garden. . . .'

'No, you didn't,' he said impatiently.

'Didn't I? How strange! I have forgotten! I went with the footman to the jeweller's. . . .'

'Yes?'

'Well, that's all. . . . What church is this?' she asked the boatman, pointing to the distance.

'Which? The one over there?' the boatman asked.

'The Smolny,' Oblomov said impatiently. 'Well, you went into the shop and then?'

'Then . . . there were lovely things there. . . . Ah, what a lovely bracelet I saw!'

'We aren't talking of bracelets!' Oblomov interrupted. 'What happened next?'

'Oh, nothing . . .' she said absentmindedly, looking keenly about her.

'Where is the footman?' Oblomov asked.

'He went home,' she answered, watching the buildings on the opposite bank.

'And you?'

'How nice it looks over there! Couldn't we go there?' she asked, pointing with her parasol to the other bank. 'You live there, don't you?'

'Yes.'

'In which street? Show me!'

'What about the footman?' Oblomov asked.

'Nothing,' she answered carelessly. 'I sent him to fetch my bracelet. He went home and I came here.'

'How was that?' said Oblomov, staring at her. He looked alarmed. She made an alarmed face too.

'Speak seriously, Olga, we have had enough joking.'

'I am not joking, it's quite true! I left the bracelet at home on purpose and *ma tante* had asked me to go to the jeweller's. You could never have thought of anything like that!' she added proudly, as though she had done something fine.

'And if the footman comes back?'

'I left word that he was to wait for me, that I had gone to another shop – and really I went to meet you.'

'And if Marya Mihailovna asks which other shop you went to?'

'I shall say I was at my dressmaker's.'

'And if she asks the dressmaker?'

'And if the Neva flows away into the sea, and if the boat turns over, and if Morskaya and our house sink through the ground, and if you suddenly fall out of love with me . . .' she said, and threw some more water in his face.

'The footman must have returned already and is waiting . . . ' he said, wiping his face. 'Hey, boatman, go back to the shore!'

'No, don't!' she said to the boatman.

'Go back! The footman has returned,' Oblomov repeated.

'Let him! Never mind!'

But Oblomov insisted and hurriedly took her through the Garden, while she, on the contrary, walked slowly, leaning on his arm.

'Why are you hurrying?' she said. 'Wait; I want to stay with you a little longer.'

She walked still more slowly, pressing herself to his side and glancing up at him, her face close to his; and he spoke to her dully and heavily about duty and obligations. She listened absentmindedly, with a languid smile, bending her head and looking down, or again glancing closely into his face and thinking of something else.

'Listen, Olga,' he began solemnly at last, 'at the risk of annoying you and bringing your reproaches on myself I must tell you definitely that we have gone too far. I ought to tell you this, it is my duty to do so.'

'To tell me what?' she asked, waking up from her thoughts.

'That it's very wrong of us to meet by stealth.'

'You said so in the summer.'

'Yes, but I was carried away then; I pushed you away with one hand and held you back with the other. You trusted me and I . . . deceived you, as it were. The feeling was still new then. . . .'

'And now it is no longer new and you are beginning to be bored. . . .'

'Oh, no, Olga! You are unjust. I say it was new and so we had not had time to come to reason, we could not do it. My conscience tortures me: you are young, you don't know the world and human nature, and besides, you are so pure, your love is so holy that it never enters your head what severe censure we are incurring by what we are doing – especially I.'

'But what are we doing?' she asked, stopping short.

'What are we doing? Why, you are deceiving your aunt, secretly leaving the house, meeting a man alone. . . . Try to say all this on Sunday before your visitors.'

'Why not?' she said calmly. 'I think I will. . . .'

'And you will see,' he went on, 'that your aunt will faint, the ladies rush out of the room, and the men look at you boldly and provocatively. . . .'

She pondered.

'But we are engaged!' she protested.

'Yes, yes, dear Olga,' he said, pressing both her hands, 'and that is all the more reason for us to be careful and consider our every step. I want to lead you down this very avenue proudly in the presence of all and not by stealth, I want people respectfully to lower their eyes before you, and not glance at you boldly and meaningly! No one should dare to harbour a suspicion that a proud girl like you could lose her head and, forgetting shame and good breeding, stray from the path of duty. . . .'

'I haven't forgotten shame or duty or good breeding!' she answered proudly, taking her hand away from him.

'I know, I know, my innocent angel, it isn't I who say it, but it's what the world will say, and what it will never forgive you. Do, for God's sake, understand what I want: I want you to be as pure and blameless in the eyes of the world as you are in reality.'

She walked on thoughtfully.

'Do understand why I am telling you this: you will be unhappy and I alone shall be responsible for it. People will say that I lured you on and concealed the abyss from you on purpose. You are pure and you can trust me, but can you make other people think so? Who would believe you?'

'That's true,' she said shuddering. 'Listen, then,' she added resolutely, 'let us tell everything to *ma tante* and ask her to give us her blessing to-morrow. . . .'

Oblomov turned pale.

'What's the matter?' she asked.

'Wait, Olga: why be in such a hurry?' he hastened to say.

His lips were trembling.

'Didn't you hurry me yourself a fortnight ago?' she was looking dryly and attentively at him.

'I hadn't thought of the preliminaries then, and they are so many!' he said with a sigh. 'Let us wait for a letter from the country.'

'But why wait for it? Can this or that answer alter your intentions?' she asked, looking at him still more attentively.

'What an idea! No, but I must take it into account: I would have to tell your aunt when the wedding is to be. I would have to talk to her not of love, but of business matters, and I am not yet prepared to do it.'

'We will talk to her about it when the letter comes, and meanwhile everyone will know that we are engaged and we shall see each other every day. I miss you,' she added, 'the days seem endless; everybody notices it, they keep asking me questions and slyly hinting at you. . . . I am tired of it all!'

'Hinting at me?' Oblomov could hardly say the words.

'Yes, thanks to Sonitchka.'

'You see, you see? You wouldn't listen to me then and were angry with me!'

'What is there to see? I don't see anything except that you are a coward. . . . I am not afraid of their hints.'

'I am not a coward, I am only cautious. . . . But for Heaven's sake come away from here, Olga: see, there's a carriage driving up. I wonder if it's someone we know? Ough, it makes me hot all over! Come away, come along . . .' he said fearfully, infecting her with his fear.

'Yes, come quick!' she said in a hurried whisper, and they almost ran down the avenue out of the Garden. They did not speak; Oblomov kept glancing uneasily about him, and she bent her head quite low and covered her face with the veil.

'To-morrow, then,' she said, when they reached the shop where the footman was waiting for her.

'No, better the day after to-morrow . . . or, no . . . Friday or Saturday.'

'But why?'

'Well . . . you see, Olga . . . I keep thinking, perhaps the letter will come.'

'It might. But to-morrow come just simply to dinner, do you hear?'

'Yes, yes, very well!' he muttered hastily, and she went into the shop.

'Oh dear, what have we come to! What a weight has dropped upon me all of a sudden! What shall I do now? Sonitchka! Zahar! Those dandies!'

VI

HE did not notice that the dinner Zahar brought him was
perfectly cold, and after dinner he somehow found himself in bed and dropped into a heavy sleep. The following
day he shuddered at the thought of going to Olga's, vividly
imagining how significantly everyone would look at
him. The hall porter, as it was, always met him in a particularly friendly way; Semyon dashed headlong to fetch
him a glass of water if he asked for one; Katya and the
nurse greeted him with a genial smile. 'He is going to
marry her' was written on all their faces, but he had not
yet asked her aunt's consent, he hadn't a penny of cash,
and he did not know when he would have any, he did not
even know what income he would receive that year from
his estate; there was no house in the country – fine prospects for marriage! He decided that until he received definite news from the country he would only see Olga on
Sundays in other people's presence. And so, when the
next morning came, he did not think of making ready to
go to Olga's; he did not shave or dress, but lazily looked
over some French papers he had borrowed from the Ilyinskys the week before, without glancing constantly at his
watch or frowning because the hand did not seem to move
forward. Zahar and Anissya, thinking that he would be
dining out as usual, did not ask him what he would like
for dinner. He scolded them, declaring that he certainly
did not dine at the Ilyinskys' every Wednesday, that it
was 'slander,' that he had dined at Ivan Gerasimovitch's
and that in future he would always have dinner at home
except for occasional Sundays. Anissya ran headlong to
the market to buy giblets for Oblomov's favourite soup.
The landlady's children came in to him: he corrected
Vanya's sums and found two mistakes. He ruled a copy-
book for Masha and wrote out big A's, then listened to

the canaries singing and looked through the half-open door at the landlady's fast-moving elbows.

About one o'clock the landlady asked him from behind the door if he would like something to eat: she had been baking curd cakes. Curd cakes and a wine-glass of currant vodka were brought in. Ilya Ilyitch's agitation subsided gradually and he only felt a kind of mental torpor in which he remained till nearly dinner-time. After dinner, when he lay down on the sofa and had just begun nodding with sleepiness, the landlady's door opened and Agafya Matveyevna appeared holding a pyramid of stockings in each hand. She placed them on two chairs; Oblomov jumped up and offered her the third one, but she did not sit down; it was not her habit: she was always on her feet, always busy and on the go.

'I have sorted out your stockings to-day,' she said; 'fifty-five pairs, but almost all are in holes. . . .'

'How kind you are!' Oblomov said, going up to her and jokingly taking hold of her elbows.

She smiled.

'Why should you trouble? Really, it makes me quite ashamed.'

'Oh, it's nothing, it's my job to look after things: you have no one to see to it and I like doing it,' she went on. 'Twenty pairs here are no good at all: it isn't worth while darning them.'

'Please don't trouble, throw them all away! Why should you spend your time over this rubbish! I can buy new ones. . . .'

'Throw them away! But why? These can all be refooted.' She began quickly sorting out the stockings.

'But do sit down, please; why do you stand?' he begged her.

'No, thank you very much, I haven't time,' she answered, refusing the chair again. 'It is my washing day, I must get the clothes ready.'

'You are a marvel of a housekeeper!' he said, looking at her throat and bosom.

She smiled.

'Well, then,' she asked, 'shall I refoot the stockings? I will order some yarn. An old woman brings it to us from the country; it isn't worth while buying it here, they sell such poor stuff.'

'Please do, since you are so kind . . . only really I am ashamed at your taking all this trouble.'

'Not at all, it's for me to do it. These I will refoot myself, these I'll give to Granny; to-morrow my sister-in-law is coming to stay with us: we'll have nothing to do in the evenings and we'll refoot them. My Masha, too, is learning to knit, only she keeps pulling out the needles: they are too big for her to handle.'

'Is Masha really taking to knitting?'

'Yes, indeed.'

'I don't know how to thank you,' said Oblomov, looking at her with the same pleasure with which he had looked at the hot curd cake that morning. 'I am very, very much obliged to you and will not remain in your debt, especially not in Masha's: I will buy her silk frocks and dress her up like a little doll.'

'Dear me, no! Why should you thank me? What does she want with silk frocks? It's a job to provide her with cotton ones: she wears her things out in no time, especially her shoes – we can't buy them fast enough.'

She picked up the stockings and moved to go.

'Why do you hurry away?' he said. 'Do stay; I am not busy.'

'Some other time, on a holiday; and you, too, please come to take coffee with us. And now there's the washing; I must go and see if Akulina has begun.'

'Well, so be it, I daren't detain you,' Oblomov said, looking at her back and elbows as she turned to go.

'Oh, and I took your dressing-gown from the store-room,' she continued, 'it can be washed and mended; the stuff is very good! It will serve you for years.'

'There's no need! I don't wear it any more, I have lost the habit of it and don't want it.'

'Well, never mind, it may as well be washed; perhaps you will wear it some day . . . when you are married!' she concluded, smiling, and shut the door after her.

His drowsiness suddenly left him; he pricked up his ears and opened his eyes wide.

'She knows it, too – everyone does!' he said, sinking on to the chair he had offered to her. 'Oh, Zahar, Zahar!'

Again 'heart-rending' words were showered on Zahar, again Anissya protested that she had never heard the land-lady speak about the wedding, it had never been men-tioned when they talked together, there was no marriage in sight, and was it likely to happen? It must have been invented by the common enemy, might she sink through the ground this very minute, and the landlady would be ready to take down the ikon from the wall and swear she had never heard about the Ilyinsky young lady, but meant somebody else. . . . Anissya said so much that Ilya Ilyitch waved his hand to stop her. The following day Zahar asked if he might go to see his friends at the old house in Gorohovy Street, but Oblomov gave him such a talking to that he thought he would never hear the last of it. 'They don't know about it yet, so you want to spread the slander there! Stay at home!' he added menacingly.

Wednesday passed. On Thursday Oblomov received another letter from Olga asking what had happened and why he had not come. She wrote that she had cried the whole evening and hardly slept the night.

'She cries, she doesn't sleep, my angel!' Oblomov exclaimed. 'Oh dear, why does she love me? Why do I love her? Why did we meet? It was all Andrey's doing: he inoculated us with love as with a vaccine. And what sort of life is it? Nothing but anxiety and agitation! When will rest and peaceful happiness come at last?'

Sighing aloud, he lay down, got up and even went out of doors, absorbed in discovering what an ideal life should be – an existence both full and placid that would pass slowly, day after day, in mute contemplation of nature and of the quiet, hardly moving events of a peacefully busy family life. He did not want to picture it as a broad river noisily rushing along with seething waves, as Stolz imagined it.

'It's a disease, a fever,' Oblomov said, 'this rushing over rapids, flooding and breaking down the dams!'

He wrote to Olga that he had caught a slight chill in the Summer Garden, had to drink a hot decoction and stay at home for a couple of days, but that now he was well again and hoped to see her on Sunday. She wrote back praising him for having been careful and advising him to stay in on Sunday, too, if necessary; she added that she did not mind being wretched a whole week so long as he took care of himself. This letter was brought by Nikita, the very man who, according to Anissya, was responsible for the gossip. He brought some new books from Olga, who was asking Oblomov to read them and tell her when they met whether they were worth reading. She was inquiring after his health. Oblomov wrote an answer, gave it to Nikita, and, letting him out of the front door, watched him as far as the gate, fearing that he might call in at the kitchen and repeat 'the slander' there or that Zahar might see him off into the street. He was glad of Olga's suggestion that he should take care of himself and not come on Sunday and wrote to say that for complete recovery it really was necessary for him to stay in a few more days.

On Sunday he called on his landlady, drank coffee, ate hot pie, and sent Zahar across the river to buy some ice cream for dinner and sweets for the children.

Zahar had difficulty in finding a boatman to row him back: the bridges had been removed and the Neva was on the point of freezing. It was out of the question for Oblomov to go to Olga's on Wednesday. Of course, he could have rushed across immediately, settled down for a few days at Ivan Gerasimovitch's and visited Olga every day, even dining there. It was a legitimate pretext: he happened to be on the other side when the river froze and had not had time to cross. Oblomov's first impulse was to do this, and he sat up quickly; but after a little thought he sighed and, with a preoccupied expression, slowly lay down again on his sofa. 'No, let the gossip die down, let the people who come to Olga's house forget me a little and see me there every day only when our engagement has been announced. It's dull to wait, but there's nothing for it,' he added with a sigh, opening one of the books that Olga had sent him. He read some fifteen pages. Masha came to ask him if he would like to go and see the river freezing: everyone was going. He went and returned in time for tea. So the days passed. Ilya Ilyitch was bored; he read, walked about the street, and when he was at home peeped into the landlady's door to exchange a word with her to pass the time. One day he actually ground three pounds of coffee for her with such zeal that his forehead was bathed in perspiration. He tried giving her a book to read. Slowly moving her lips, she read the title to herself and returned the book, saying she would borrow it from him at Christmas-time and make Vanya read it aloud, and then Granny could listen too; and now she had not time. Meanwhile, temporary plank bridges were laid over the Neva and one day the dog's desperate barking and jumping on the chain announced Nikita arriving with a note, inquiries about Oblomov's health, and a book. Oblomov was afraid that he, too, might have to cross the river, walking on planks, and he hid from Nikita, writing to Olga that his throat was swollen and he could not venture out as yet and that 'cruel fate denied him for several more days the happiness of seeing his precious Olga.' He gave strict orders to Zahar not to chatter with Nikita, whom he once more watched going to the gate; and when Anissya poked her nose out of the kitchen, wanting to ask Nikita a question, he menacingly shook his finger at her.

VII

A WEEK passed. Waking up in the morning, Oblomov
first of all anxiously inquired if the bridges had been
fixed. 'Not yet,' he was told, and he spent a peaceful day
listening to the ticking of the clock, the rattle of the
coffee-mill, and the singing of the canaries. The chickens
did not squeak any more: they had long ago turned into
middle-aged hens and were hiding in their coops. He had
not had time to read the books Olga had sent him: he had
read as far as page hundred and five of one book, put it
down, cover uppermost, and so it lay for several days on
end. But he spent more time with the landlady's children.
Vanya was an intelligent boy and after three lessons
learned the chief cities of Europe; Ilya Ilyitch promised to
bring him a present of a small globe next time he went to
the other side of the river. Mashenka hemmed three
handkerchiefs for him – badly, it is true, but the way she
toiled with her plump little hands and ran to show him
every inch of her work was most amusing. He talked to
his landlady whenever he saw her elbows through the
half-open door. He learned to recognize, from the way
her elbows moved, whether she was rubbing something
through a sieve, grinding coffee, or ironing.

He even tried talking to the grandmother, but she
could not carry on a conversation: she stopped half-way
through a word, propped her fist against the wall, bent
double and began coughing as though she were doing
some hard work; then she groaned – and that was the end
of it. The landlady's brother was the only member of the
household whom he did not see at all; he saw his big parcel flit past the window, but the man himself could hardly
be heard in the house. One day Oblomov accidentally
came into the room where they were all huddled together
over their dinner, and the brother hastily wiped his mouth
with his fingers and slipped away to his attic.

One morning, just as Oblomov woke up in a light-
hearted mood and was drinking his coffee, Zahar suddenly
announced that the bridges had been fixed. Oblomov's
heart sank. 'And to-morrow is Sunday!' he thought. 'I
must go to Olga's, manfully endure all day people's significant and inquisitive glances, then tell her when I
intend talking to her aunt – and I am still in the same
impasse.' He clearly pictured to himself how their engagement would be announced, how various ladies and
gentlemen would come to call the next day and the day
after, how he would suddenly become an object of interest, how his health would be drunk at the gala dinner-
party. Then . . . then, as a part of his new rights and
duties, he would bring a present to Olga. 'A present!' he
said to himself in horror, and laughed bitterly. 'A present!' and he had only two hundred roubles in his pocket!
Even if they did send him some money from the country
it would not be until Christmas, and perhaps later, after
the corn had been sold; the letter was to tell him when
that would be, how much corn there was and what it
would fetch – but the letter never came. What was he to
do? Good-bye, fortnight of peace! In the midst of these
worries he pictured Olga's beautiful face, her fluffy,
expressive eyebrows, her intelligent, light-blue eyes, her
head and her plait of hair, which she let down low over
her neck so that it completed the mobility of her figure,
continuing the line of her head down to her shoulders and
waist. But as soon as he felt a thrill of love he was crushed
by the dead weight of the thought: what he was to do,
how to tackle the question of marriage, where to get the
money, what to live on afterwards. . . .

'I will wait a little longer, perhaps the letter will come
to-morrow or the day after.' He began reckoning when his
letter could have been received in the country, how long
his neighbour was likely to delay in answering it, and
what time it would take the answer to reach him. 'It must
come in another three or at most four days; I won't go to

Olga's just yet,' he decided, 'she probably does not know about the bridges being put up. . . .'

'Katya, are the bridges put up?' Olga asked her maid as soon as she woke that morning.

This question had been asked every morning. Oblomov never suspected this.

'I don't know, miss; I haven't seen the coachman or the porter this morning, and Nikita does not know.'

'You never know what I want!' Olga said in vexation, examining the chain round her neck as she lay in bed.

'I'll just go and find out, miss. I didn't dare to go away thinking you might wake, or I would have run round long ago,' and Katya slipped out of the room.

Olga opened a table-drawer and took out Oblomov's last note. 'He is ill, poor dear,' she thought anxiously. 'He is alone there, he is depressed. How much longer will it. . . .'

She had not finished her thought when Katya, with flushed cheeks, dashed into the room.

'Yes, they are, they were put up last night!' she said joyfully.

Olga instantly jumped out of bed, Katya caught her in her arms, threw a dressing-gown over her, and handed her the tiny slippers. Olga quickly opened the drawer, took something out and gave it to Katya, who kissed her hand. It all happened in one minute. 'Oh, it's Sunday to-morrow! How lucky, he will come!' Olga thought. She dressed quickly, hurried through her breakfast, and went shopping with her aunt.

'Let us go to Mass at Smolny to-morrow, *ma tante*,' she begged.

Marya Mihailovna screwed up her eyes, pondered, and said: 'Very well; but such a distance, *ma chère*! What's the idea of going there in winter?'

And Olga had only thought of it because Oblomov had pointed out this church to her from the river and she wanted to pray there . . . for him, that he should be well, that he should love her and be happy in her, that . . . this uncertainty and indecision should end. . . . Poor Olga!

Sunday came. Olga artfully arranged the whole dinner to Oblomov's taste. She put on a white dress, concealed under the lace the bracelet he had given her, did her hair in the way he liked; she had had the piano tuned the day before and in the morning tried singing the *Casta diva*. Her voice had not sounded so well since the summer. Then she waited. Meanwhile the baron arrived and told her she had again grown prettier, as in the summer, but was a little thinner.

'The lack of country air and our irregular habits have obviously affected you,' he said. 'You need the country and the air of the fields, dear Olga Sergeyevna.'

He kissed her hand several times so that his dyed moustache slightly stained her fingers.

'Yes, the country!' she said thoughtfully, speaking not to him but into space.

'*A propos* of the country,' he added, 'next month your lawsuit will be finished and in April you can go to your estate. It isn't big, but the situation is simply delightful. You will be pleased with it. The house and the garden are charming. There's a pavilion at the top of the hill – you will love it. The view of the river . . . you don't remember, you were only five when your papa left the place and took you away.'

'Oh, how glad I shall be!' she said, and pondered. 'It's settled,' she thought; 'we will go there, but he shall not learn this until. . . .'

'Next month, Baron?' she asked quickly. 'Is this certain?'

'As certain as the fact that you are beautiful and to-day particularly so,' he said, and went to her aunt.

Olga remained seated, dreaming of the happiness before her, but she decided not to tell her news and her plans of the future to Oblomov. She wanted to watch to the end the transformation love was working in his lazy soul, to see him finally released from the burden of his past; she pictured him receiving a favourable reply from the country and, radiant at the prospect of near happiness, running to lay it at her feet; then they would both rush to her aunt, and then . . . then she would suddenly tell him that she, too, had an estate with a garden, a pavilion, a view of the river and a house ready to live in and that they would go there first and to Oblomovka afterwards. 'No, I don't want a favourable answer,' she thought, 'he would feel proud then and wouldn't be even glad that I have an estate of my own, a house and a garden. . . . No, it will be better if he comes distressed at the news that his place is in a bad way and he must go there himself. He will rush headlong to Oblomovka, hasten to make the necessary arrangements, forget a great deal, not know how to manage, do everything just anyhow and gallop back – and suddenly learn there had been no need for him to rush, that is a house, a garden and a pavilion with a view, that they have a home apart from his Oblomovka. . . . No, no, she would certainly not tell him, she would hold out to the end; let him go there, let him take trouble and be alive – for her sake, in the name of their future happiness! Or, no: why send him to the country and part from him? No, when he comes to her dressed for the journey, pale and sad, to take leave of her for a month, she will suddenly tell him he need not go till summer: they will go together then. . . . ' Such were her dreams, and, running to the baron, she artfully warned him not to tell the news to anyone at all for the present. By *anyone* she only meant Oblomov.

'No, certainly, why should I?' he agreed. 'Only, perhaps, to Mr. Oblomov, if the subject crops up. . . . '

Olga controlled herself and said indifferently, 'No, don't tell him either.'

'Your will is law, you know that,' the baron added gallantly.

She was not altogether guileless. If she very much wanted to look at Oblomov in the presence of others, she first looked at two or three other people in turn and then at him.

What subtleties – all for Oblomov! How many times her cheeks began to burn! How often she touched this or that key of the piano to see if it had not been tuned too high and shifted the music from one place to another – and he did not come! What could it mean? Three o'clock, four o'clock – he wasn't there! At half-past four her beauty and bloom began to fade: she was visibly drooping and sat down to dinner quite pale. But the others did not care: they never noticed his absence; they were eating the dishes that had been meant for him and talking cheerfully and indifferently. He never came after dinner or in the evening. Till ten o'clock she was agitated with hope and fear; at ten she went to her room. At first she poured on to his head all the bitterness that had accumulated in her heart; all the venomous sarcasms and indignant words in her vocabulary were flung at him. Then she felt as though her whole body were on fire and then turned cold as ice. 'He is ill; he is alone; he cannot even write . . . ' flashed through her mind. The idea gained complete possession of her and kept her awake all night. She drowsed feverishly for a couple of hours, talked in her sleep, but in the morning she got up calm and resolute, though pale.

On Monday morning Agafya Matveyevna peeped into Oblomov's study and said:

'Some girl is asking for you.'

'For me? Impossible!' Oblomov answered. 'Where is she?'

'She is here: she came to our door by mistake. Shall I show her in?'

Oblomov had not yet made up his mind what to do when Katya appeared before him. The landlady went out.

'Katya!' Oblomov said in surprise. 'How is this? What are you doing here?'

'My young lady is here,' she answered in a whisper. 'She has sent me to ask. . . .'

Oblomov changed colour.

'Olga Sergeyevna!' he whispered in horror. 'It isn't true, Katya, you are joking? Don't torment me!'

'I swear it's true: she is in a hired carriage, waiting by the tea-shop, and wants to come here. She asks you to send Zahar out of the way. She will be here in half an hour.'

'I had better go out to her. How can she come here?'

'You won't have time: she may come in any moment; she thinks you are ill. Good-bye, I must run: she is alone, waiting for me.'

She went away.

With extraordinary rapidity Oblomov put on his boots, tie, and waistcoat and called Zahar.

'Zahar, you asked leave the other day to go and see your friends in Gorohovy Street, wasn't it? Well, you may go now!' he said to him with feverish agitation.

'I won't go,' Zahar answered decisively.

'Yes, you go!' Oblomov said insistently.

'Whoever goes visiting on weekdays? I won't go,' Zahar repeated obstinately.

'Do go and enjoy yourself, don't be obstinate when your master does you a favour and lets you off . . . go and see your friends!'

'Friends go hang!'

'Don't you want to see them?'

'They are all such scoundrels that I can't bear the sight of them.'

'But do go out!' Oblomov repeated insistently, flushing heavily.

'No, I will stay all day at home to-day, but I might go on Sunday,' Zahar replied indifferently.

'Go now, at once!' Oblomov hurried him anxiously.

'But why should I go all that way for nothing?'

'Well, go and walk about for a couple of hours – see what a sight you are: your face looks silly with sleep!' Oblomov suggested.

'My face is right enough – my sort always looks like that,' said Zahar, looking lazily out of the window.

'Oh my goodness! She may come in any moment!' Oblomov thought, wiping the perspiration off his forehead.

'There, do go for a walk, I ask you! Here is twenty copecks for you: have a drink of beer with a friend!'

'I would rather sit on the steps – it's not much fun walking about in the frost. I don't mind sitting by the gate, I can do that. . . .'

'No, go farther than the gate,' Oblomov said quickly, 'go into another street, over there, to the left, towards the garden . . . across the river!'

'That's queer,' Zahar thought, 'sending me out for a walk; it has never happened before!'

'I'd rather go on Sunday, Ilya Ilyitch. . . .'

'Will you go?' Oblomov said through his teeth, coming close up to Zahar. Zahar disappeared and Oblomov called Anissya.

'Go to the market,' he said to her, 'and buy for dinner. . . .'

'I've bought everything, dinner will soon be ready,' Anissya began.

'Be quiet and listen!' Oblomov shouted so that Anissya was intimidated.

'Buy . . . well, some asparagus,' he added, trying to think of something to send her for.

'Why, sir, it's not the season for asparagus! And I am not likely to find any here. . . .'

'Off with you!' he shouted, and she ran away. 'Run as fast as you can and don't look round,' he shouted after her; 'but coming back walk your slowest, and don't show yourself here before two hours.'

'What marvel is this?' Zahar said to Anissya, meeting her at the gate. 'He has sent me for a walk and given me twenty copecks. Where am I to go?'

'The master knows what he is about,' observed Anissya, who was a quick-witted woman. 'Go to Artemy, the count's coachman, and treat him to some tea: he is always treating you. And I will run to the market.'

'It's a queer thing, Artemy,' Zahar said to him. 'My master has sent me for a walk and given me twenty copecks. . . .'

'I expect he wants to go on the booze himself and has given you something that you shouldn't envy him. Come along!'

He winked at Zahar and nodded towards a certain street.

'Come along!' Zahar repeated, nodding in the same direction.

'It is a queer thing – his sending me for a walk!' he hissed to himself, with a grin.

They went away, but Anissya ran to the first crossroads, sat down in a ditch behind a fence, and waited to see what would happen.

Oblomov listened expectantly: someone took hold of the gate-latch and at the same moment the dog began barking desperately and jumping on the chain.

'Damn the dog!' Oblomov cursed through his teeth, and, seizing his cap, rushed to the gate, opened it and brought Olga to the steps almost in his arms.

She was alone. Katya was waiting for her in the carriage not far from the gate.

'You are well? You are not in bed? What is the matter with you?' she asked quickly, without taking off her coat or hat and looking him up and down when they came into his study.

'I am better now, my throat is practically well,' he said, touching his throat and coughing slightly.

'Why didn't you come yesterday?' she asked, looking at him so searchingly that he could not utter a word.

'How could you venture to do such a dreadful thing, Olga?' he said in horror. 'Do you know what you are doing? . . .'

'We'll talk of that later!' she interrupted him impatiently. 'I ask you, what is the meaning of your staying away?'

He made no answer.

'Did you have a stye?'

He said nothing.

'You haven't been ill; you haven't had a sore throat?' she said, frowning.

'No, I haven't,' Oblomov answered in the voice of a schoolboy.

'You have deceived me!' She looked at him in amazement. 'Why?'

'I will explain it all to you, Olga,' he said apologetically. 'An important reason has kept me away from you for a fortnight. . . . I was afraid. . . .'

'What of?' she asked, sitting down and taking off her hat and coat.

He took both and put them on the sofa.

'Talk, gossip. . . .'

'And you weren't afraid of my not sleeping the night, imagining all sorts of horrors and almost falling ill?' she said, looking at him searchingly.

'You don't know what is going on in me,' he said, pointing to his heart and his head. 'I am simply consumed with anxiety. You don't know what has happened.'

'What is it now?' she asked coldly.

'How far the rumours about you and me have spread! I didn't want to disturb you and was afraid to show myself before you.'

He told her all he had heard from Zahar and Anissya, recalled the conversation of the dandies at the theatre, and concluded by saying that he had not been able to sleep ever since and in every glance read a question, a reproach, or a sly hint at their meetings.

'But we have decided to tell *ma tante* this week,' she replied, 'and then these rumours will be silenced.'

'Yes, but I did not want to speak to your aunt till this week, till I received the letter. I know she will ask me, not about my love, but about my estate, and will go into details, which I cannot give her till I have received an answer from the country.'

She sighed.

'If I didn't know you,' she said thoughtfully, 'Heaven only knows what I might think. You were afraid of disturbing me by the servants' gossip, but you weren't afraid of causing me all this anxiety! I cease to understand you.'

'I thought their talk would upset you. Katya, Marfa, Semyon, and that fool Nikita are saying all sorts of things. . . .'

'I have known it all along,' she said indifferently.

'What? You knew?'

'Of course. Katya and nurse told me about it months ago, questioned me about you, congratulated me. . . .'

'Congratulated you? Really?' he asked in horror. 'And what did you say?'

'Nothing, I thanked them. I gave nurse a shawl and she vowed to make a pilgrimage to St. Sergius's shrine. I promised Katya to arrange her marriage with the confectioner: she, too, has a love affair. . . .'

He gazed at her with frightened and astonished eyes.

'You come to the house every day: it's perfectly natural that the servants should talk,' she added. 'They are always the first to talk. It was the same with Sonitchka; why does it alarm you so?'

'So that is where the rumours come from!' he said slowly.

'But they are not without foundation – it is all true, isn't it?'

'True!' Oblomov repeated, in a tone that was neither one of question nor of denial. 'Yes,' he added afterwards, 'you are quite right: only I don't want them to know about our meetings, and that's why I am afraid. . . .'

'You are afraid, you tremble like a boy . . . I can't understand it! You aren't stealing me, are you?'

He felt awkward; she was looking at him attentively.

'Listen,' she said, 'there is something wrong about it, something false. . . . Come here and tell me all you have on your mind. You might have stayed away a day, two days – perhaps a week – by way of precaution, but you should have warned me, written to me. You know, I am not a child and am not easily upset by trifles. What does it all mean?'

He pondered, then kissed her hand and sighed.

'I'll tell you what I think, Olga,' he said. 'All this time

I have been so scared on your behalf by these horrors, my mind has been so tortured by cares, my heart so sore with hopes and expectations coming and going, that my whole being is shaken: it turns numb, it needs a rest, if only for a time. . . .'

'Why is it that mine doesn't turn numb and I seek rest only beside you?'

'You are young and vigorous, you love me serenely and peacefully, while I . . . but you know how I love you!' he said, sliding down to the floor and kissing her hands.

'I can hardly say that I do – you are so strange that I am bewildered; my mind fails me and I lose hope . . . we shall soon cease to understand each other: it will go badly with us then!'

They were both silent.

'What have you been doing these days?' she asked, glancing for the first time round the room. 'It isn't nice here: such low ceilings! The windows are small, the wall-paper old. . . . What other rooms have you?'

He rushed to show her the flat so as not to answer the question as to what he had been doing. Then she sat down on the sofa and he settled on the rug at her feet.

'Well, what have you been doing this fortnight?' she questioned him.

'Reading, writing, thinking about you. . . .'

'Have you finished my books? What do you think of them? I will take them home.'

She picked up a book from the table and glanced at the open page: the page was covered with dust.

'You haven't been reading it?' she asked.

'No,' he answered.

She looked at the crumpled embroidered cushions, at the dusty windows, at the writing-table, shifted several dust-covered papers, moved the pen in the dry inkstand, and looked at him in amazement.

'What have you been doing?' she repeated. 'You haven't been either reading or writing!'

'I had so little time,' he began, stumblingly. 'When I

get up in the morning they are tidying the rooms and disturbing me, then conversations about dinner begin, the landlady's children come asking me to correct their sums, and then there's dinner. And after dinner . . . when is there time to read?'

'You slept after dinner,' she said so positively that, after a moment's hesitation, he answered softly:

'Yes.'

'Why?'

'So as not to notice the time: you weren't with me, Olga, and without you life is dull, unendurable. . . .'

He broke off. She was looking at him sternly.

'Ilya,' she began earnestly, 'do you remember that day in the park when you told me that life was kindled in you, assured me that I was the aim of your life, your ideal, took me by the hand and said it was yours – do you remember how I gave you my consent?'

'How could I forget it? Hasn't it transformed my whole life? Don't you see how happy I am?'

'No, I don't,' she said coldly. 'You have deceived me: you are growing lazy once more. . . .'

'Deceived you? How wicked of you! I swear I would throw myself into an abyss this very moment. . . .'

'Yes, if the abyss were here, right at your feet, this instant,' she interrupted, 'but if it were put off for three days you would be frightened and change your mind, especially if Zahar or Anissya began talking about it . . . this isn't love.'

'You doubt my love?' he said hotly. 'You think I delay out of fear for myself and not for you? I guard your good name, I watch like a mother that gossip should not dare to touch you. . . . Ach, Olga, ask for proofs! I repeat, if you could be happier with another man I would give up my rights to him ungrudgingly; if you needed my life, I would be happy to die for you!' he finished, with tears in his eyes.

'There is no need for any of that, nobody asks it of you! Why should I want your life? I want you to do what you ought to. It's the trick of dishonest people to offer sacrifices that are not needed or cannot be made so as to avoid making those that are required. You are honest, I know, but. . . .'

'You can't think how much health I have wasted on these passions and anxieties!' he went on. 'I have had no other thought since I met you. . . . Yes, I repeat again, you are my aim, you alone. I shall die, I shall go out of my mind if I lose you. It is only through you that I breathe, look, think, and feel. How can you wonder that on the days when I don't see you I sink and go to sleep? Everything disgusts me, bores me; I am like a machine; I walk about and do things without noticing what I am doing. You are the fire and the moving power of that machine!' he said, kneeling before her and straightening his back.

His eyes were shining, as in the old days in the park. Once more they glowed with self-confidence and determination.

'I am ready to go now where you tell me, to do what you wish. When you are looking at me, speaking, singing, I feel that I am alive. . . .'

Gravely and thoughtfully Olga listened to his passionate speeches.

'Listen, Ilya,' she said. 'I believe in your love and in my power over you. Why, then, do you frighten me by your indecision, why do you drive me to doubt you? You say I am your aim – and you advance towards it slowly and timidly; but you have yet far to go: you must rise above me, I expect it of you! I have seen happy people, seen how they love,' she added with a sigh. 'They are active and full of life, their rest is different from yours; they don't hang their heads; their eyes are wide open; they hardly sleep, they act! And you . . . no, it does not look as though love and I were your life's aim. . . .'

She shook her head doubtfully.

'Yes, you are, you alone!' he said, kissing her hands again with deep emotion as he lay at her feet. 'Heavens, what happiness!' he repeated, almost deliriously. 'And you imagine one could deceive you, drop asleep after such an awakening, fail to become a hero! You will see, you and Andrey,' he went on, looking like one inspired, 'to what heights the love of a woman like you can lift a man! Look, look at me: haven't I risen from the dead, am I not alive at this moment? Let us come away from here! Out of this place! I can't stay here another minute, I am stifled here, I hate it!' he said, looking round with unfeigned disgust. 'Let me go on feeling like this all to-day.... Oh, if only the same fire that burns in me now would burn to-morrow and always! But if you are not here it fades and I sink! Now I am alive once more, I have risen from the dead! I believe I... Olga, Olga, you are the most beautiful creature in the world, you are higher than all other women, you ... you....'

He pressed his face to her hand and sank into silence. He could not utter another word. He clutched at his heart to still its beating, fixed moist, passionate eyes upon Olga and remained motionless.

'He is tender enough!' Olga said to herself, but with a sigh and not as she had said it in the park.

She sank into profound thought.

'It's time I were going,' she said kindly.

He suddenly came to himself.

'You are here, good heavens! In my room!' he said. The look of inspiration was gone and instead he glanced about him timidly; his tongue could utter no more ardent speeches.

He hastily picked up her hat and coat and in his hurry tried to put the coat on her head.

She laughed.

'Don't be anxious about me,' she reassured him, '*ma tante* has gone out for the day; only my nurse and Katya know I am out. Come and see me off.'

She took his arm and, perfectly self-possessed in the proud consciousness of her innocence, calmly crossed the yard, while the dog barked desperately, jumping on its chain, stepped into her carriage and drove away. Heads were peeping out of the landlady's windows; Anissya's head looked out of the ditch behind the fence round the corner. When the carriage had turned into another street, Anissya came home and said she had been all over the market and could not find any asparagus. Zahar returned after three hours and slept for the next twenty-four.

Oblomov paced up and down the room for some minutes, and did not feel the floor under his feet, did not hear his own footsteps: he might be treading on air. When the wheels of the carriage that had taken away his life, his happinesss, could no longer be heard creaking on the snow, his anxiety left him, his back straightened, his face had once more the glow of inspiration, and his eyes were moist with happiness and emotion. He had a sensation of warmth, vigour, freshness all over his body. Once more he suddenly wanted to go everywhere at once, far away from here: to join Stolz abroad with Olga; to go to the country, to the fields and woods; to shut himself up in his study and bury himself in work; to go to the Rybinsk harbour and make the new road; to read the new book that had just appeared and was being talked of by everyone; to go to the opera – to-night. . . . Yes, to-day she had been to see him, and he would go to her and then to the opera. How full the day was! How easy it was to breathe in this atmosphere, within Olga's orbit, in the rays of her virginal brilliance, her vigour, her young but subtle, deep, and sound intelligence! He felt as though he were being wafted about the room, not walking, but flying. 'Forward! Forward!' Olga had said: higher and higher towards that boundary where grace and tenderness lose their rights and man's kingdom begins! How clearly she saw life! How well she found the right path in that perplexing maze and instinctively guessed his way too! Their two lives, like two rivers, must merge into one: he is to be her guide, her leader! She saw his powers, his gifts; she knew how much he could do and humbly waited to submit to him. Wonderful Olga! Serene and simple, but full of courage and determination, and natural as life itself!

'How nasty this place really is!' he said, looking round. 'And that angel has descended into this squalor and hallowed it with her presence!'

He looked with love at the chair where she had been sitting, and suddenly his eyes sparkled: beside the chair, on the floor, he saw a tiny glove.

'A token! Her hand: it's a prophetic sign! Oh!' he groaned passionately, pressing the glove to his lips.

The landlady peeped in at the door, asking if he would like to see some linen: they had brought it for sale and perhaps he would buy some. But he thanked her dryly, never thought of glancing at her elbows, and excused himself, saying that he was very busy. Then he began recalling the summer, went over all the details, remembered every tree, bush, garden seat, every word that had been said, and found it all more charming than it had been when he was enjoying it. He could not control himself; he sang, addressed friendly remarks to Anissya, joked about her having no children, and promised to stand godfather to her first baby. He played such a noisy game with Masha that the landlady peeped out and sent Masha away so that she should not disturb him 'working.' The rest of the day added to his madness: Olga was gay and sang, then there was more singing at the opera, then he had tea with them, and at tea Olga, her aunt, the baron, and Oblomov talked together so sincerely, so intimately, that he felt truly a member of this small family. His solitary existence was over: he now had a home, he had a firm hold on life; he had warmth and light – and how good life was then!

He slept little that night: he was finishing the books Olga had sent him and read a volume and a half.

'To-morrow there is sure to be a letter from the country,' he thought, with a beating heart. . . . 'At last!'

VIII

NEXT day, when Zahar was tidying the room, he found a small glove on the writing-table; he scrutinized it for some time and then gave it to Oblomov with a grin.

'The Ilyinsky young lady must have left it behind,' he said.

'Devil!' Ilya Ilyitch thundered, snatching the glove out of his hands. 'Nothing of the sort! What are you talking of? It was a dressmaker from a shop who came to fit my shirts. How dare you invent such stories!'

'Why devil? What am I inventing? They are saying at the landlady's. . . .'

'What?'

'Why, that the Ilyinsky young lady and her maid have been here. . . .'

'My God!' Oblomov uttered in horror. 'And how should they know about the Ilyinsky young lady? You and Anissya must have gossiped. . . .'

Suddenly Anissya half thrust herself through the hall door.

'Aren't you ashamed of talking such nonsense, Zahar Trofimitch? Don't listen to him, sir,' she said. 'No one has said anything or knows anything about it, Christ our God is my witness. . . .'

'Now there,' Zahar hissed at her, aiming his elbow at her breast, 'don't you poke your nose where you aren't wanted!'

Anissya disappeared. Oblomov brandished both fists at Zahar, then quickly opened the door into the landlady's part of the house. Agafya Matveyevna was sitting on the floor sorting out the contents of an old box; she was surrounded by heaps of rags, wadding, old clothes, buttons, and bits of fur.

'I say,' Oblomov began kindly, but with agitation, 'my servants talk all sort of rubbish, don't you believe them, for Heaven's sake.'

'I haven't heard anything,' the landlady replied. 'What are they saying?'

'About yesterday's visit,' Oblomov went on. 'They say it was some young lady. . . .'

'It is none of our business what guests our tenants may have,' the landlady said.

'But please don't you believe it, it is an absolute slander! It wasn't a young lady at all, merely the dressmaker, who is making some shirts for me. She came to fit me. . . .'

'And where have you ordered the shirts? Who is making them for you?' the landlady asked with interest.

'In the French shop. . . .'

'Show me when they are ready: I know two girls who sew beautifully and stitch better than any Frenchwoman. I have seen their work, they brought it to show me when they were sewing for Count Metlinsky: no one could sew better. Your shirts, those that you are wearing now, are nothing like so well made. . . .'

'Very good, I will remember. Only for Heaven's sake, don't think it was a young lady. . . .'

'It is none of my business who your visitors are. Even if it were a young lady. . . .'

'No, no!' Oblomov protested. 'Why, the young lady whom Zahar means is a huge creature with a bass voice, and this one, the dressmaker, speaks in a treble; she has a beautiful voice. Please, don't think. . . .'

'It is none of my business,' the landlady said as he turned to go. 'Then don't forget to tell me when you want some shirts made: my friends can stitch wonderfully . . . they are called Lizaveta Nikolavna and Marya Nikolavna.'

'Very well, I certainly won't forget: only, please, you mustn't think. . . .'

He left her, then dressed and drove to Olga's.

When he came home in the evening he found on his table a letter from his neighbour in the country who had

been looking after Oblomovka for him. He rushed to the
lamp, read the letter – and his hands dropped.

'I earnestly beg you to entrust the care of your estate to
someone else [the neighbour wrote]. I have so much to do
that in all conscience I cannot look after Oblomovka as I
should. It would be best for you to come here yourself,
and better still to settle on your estate. It is a fine estate,
but badly neglected. First of all, you must distribute the
work and the taxes more carefully; this cannot be done
without you: the peasants are out of hand, they don't obey
the new bailiff, and the old one is a rogue and wants looking after. It is impossible to tell what your income is. In
the present state of things you are not likely to receive
more than three thousand, and that only if you are on the
spot. I am reckoning on the profits from corn, for you
can't rely on the peasants who are supposed to pay a
yearly tax: they must be taken in hand and their arrears
seen to – it will take three months or so. The harvest was
good and corn prices are high, and if you look after the
sale yourself you will receive the money in March or
April. But at present there isn't a penny in cash. As to the
bridge and the road through Verhlyovo, you were so long
answering my letter that I decided to make the road with
Odontsov and Belovodov from my place to Nelki, so that
it will pass at a considerable distance from Oblomovka. In
conclusion, I beg you once more to come as soon as
possible: in three months you will be able to see what you
can reckon on next year. By the way, it is election-time
now: wouldn't you like to try for the post of a district
magistrate? Make haste and come. Your house is very bad
[was added in the postscript]. I told the dairymaid, the
old coachman, and the two maids to move out of it into
the servants' quarters: it is dangerous to stay in it longer.'

Enclosed with the letter was the statement of the number of bushels harvested, stored away and intended for
sale, and other business details.

'Not a penny in cash, three months, going to the country, looking into the peasants' affairs, determining the income, standing for elections' – it all surrounded Oblomov like a crowd of phantoms. He felt as though he were in a forest at night when one seems to see robbers, corpses, and wild beasts in every tree and bush. 'But it's a disgrace, I am not going to give in,' he repeated, trying to consider the situation just as the coward tries to glance at the phantoms through closed eyelids, feeling a chill at the heart and weakness in the arms and legs. What had Oblomov been hoping for? He had thought the letter would say definitely what income he would have that year, and that, of course, it would be a good deal – for instance, six or seven thousand; that the house was still good so that, if need be, one could live in it while the new one was being built; that he would receive three or four thousand at once – in short, that he would find in the letter the same laughter, playful liveliness and love as in Olga's notes. He was no longer treading on air, joking with Anissya, or being elated with hopes of happiness – they had to be deferred for three months; no, longer than that, in three months he would only put his affairs into order, learn all about his estate, and the wedding. . . . 'It's no use thinking of the wedding before a year,' he said timidly, 'no, not before a year!' He would have first to finish writing his plan, then settle matters with the architect, then . . . then . . . he sighed. 'A loan!' flashed through his mind, but he banished the thought. 'Impossible! What if I don't repay it in time? If things go badly, the creditors will go to law and the name of Oblomov, so far pure and untarnished. . . .' Heaven forbid! Then good-bye to his peace of mind and self-respect. . . . No, no! Other people borrowed money and then worked and worried, had no rest or sleep, as though possessed by a demon. Yes, a debt was a demon, a fiend that could only be exorcized by money! There were, of course, fine fellows who lived all their lives at other people's expense, snatched money right and left and never turned a hair! How they could sleep in

peace and eat their dinner was inconceivable! A debt! Its
consequence was either the endless labour of a galley-slave
or dishonour. To mortgage Oblomovka? But that was the
same as a debt, only a debt that could not be postponed or
cancelled. It would mean paying so much a year – and
perhaps there wouldn't be enough left for him to live on.
His happiness had receded by another year! With a painful groan Oblomov sank on his bed, but suddenly thought
better of it and got up. What had Olga said? She had
appealed to him as a man, had trusted to his strength! She
expected him to go forward and reach the height from
which he could hold out his hand to her and lead her after
him, show her the way. Yes, yes! But how was he to
begin? He thought for a time, then slapped his forehead
and went to his landlady's.

'Is your brother at home?' he asked her.

'Yes, but he has gone to bed.'

'Then please ask him to come in to me to-morrow,'
Oblomov said. 'I want to see him.'

IX

THE landlady's brother came in in the same manner as before, sat down on a chair as carefully, tucked his hands into his sleeves, and waited for Ilya Ilyitch to speak.

'I have received a very unpleasant letter from the country in answer to the one I sent with the deed of trust, you remember?' Oblomov said. 'Here, will you read it, please?'

Ivan Matveyitch took the letter, which slightly trembled in his fingers, as his eyes, accustomed to reading, ran along the lines. When he had finished he put the letter on the table and hid his hands behind his back.

'What do you think ought to be done now?' Oblomov asked.

'Your friend advises you to go there,' Ivan Matveyitch said. 'Well – twelve hundred miles isn't anything very dreadful. In another week the roads will be fit for sleighing, and you had better go.'

'I have quite lost the habit of travelling, not being used to it; and in winter too, I confess I should find it difficult and would rather not go. . . . Besides, it's very dull to be by oneself in the country.'

'Have you many peasants paying you a tax?' Ivan Matveyitch asked.

'I . . . don't know: it's so long since I've been to my estate.'

'You ought to know: how else can you manage? You can't find out what your income is.'

'Yes, I ought,' Oblomov acquiesced. 'My neighbour writes so too, but now winter is upon us. . . .'

'And how much tax do they pay?'

'How much? I believe . . . let me see, I had a list somewhere, Stolz made it for me, but I can't find it: Zahar must have put it away somewhere. I'll show it you later. . . . I believe it is thirty roubles per family.'

'What are your peasants like? How do they live?' Ivan Matveyitch asked. 'Are they rich or poor? How many of them work for you?'

'Listen,' Oblomov said, going up to him and taking him confidentially by both lapels of his uniform. Ivan Matveyitch got up instantly, but Oblomov made him sit down again. 'Listen,' he repeated slowly, almost in a whisper. 'I don't know anything about peasants' work, or agricultural labour. I don't know when peasants are considered rich and when poor; I don't know what a quarter of rye or oats means, what it costs, in which month they sow and reap and which crops, how and when they sell corn; I don't know if I am rich or poor, if in a year's time I shall have enough to eat or be a beggar – I know nothing!' he concluded despondently, letting go Ivan Matveyitch's coat lapels and stepping back from him, 'so you must talk to me and advise me as a child. . . .'

'Why, you ought to know: if you don't you can't reckon things out,' Ivan Matveyitch said with a subservient smile, getting up and putting one hand in the breast of his coat and another behind his back. 'A landowner should know his estate and what to do with it . . .' he said instructively.

'Well, I don't. Teach me if you can.'

'I haven't studied the subject; I must consult those who have. But here, they tell you in the letter,' Ivan Matveyitch continued, pointing with his bent middle finger to the page of the letter, 'to stand for the elections: that would be a good thing! You would live there, hold office in the district court, and meanwhile learn something about farming.'

'I don't know what a district court is, what is done there, what office one can hold in it!' Oblomov said in an impressive undertone again, going right up to Ivan Matveyitch's face.

'You will get used to it. Why, you have been in the service here: the work is everywhere the same, only the forms differ slightly. Everywhere there are instructions, references, protocols. . . . If you have a good secretary, you needn't trouble; all you have to do is to sign your name. . . . If you know how the work is done in a Government Department. . . .'

'I don't know how the work is done in a Government Department,' Oblomov answered monotonously.

Ivan Matveyitch cast his ambiguous glance at Oblomov and said nothing.

'I expect you spent your time reading books?' he observed with the same subservient smile.

'Books!' Oblomov retorted bitterly, and stopped short. He had not the courage to bare his soul before the man and there was no need for him to do so. 'I know nothing about books either,' was on the tip of his tongue, but he did not say it, and only sighed mournfully.

'But you must have done something,' Ivan Matveyitch added humbly, as though having read in Oblomov's mind his answer about books, 'it's impossible not to. . . .'

'No, it isn't, Ivan Matveyitch, and I am the living proof of it! Who am I? What am I? Go and ask Zahar and he will say, "a gentleman"! Yes, I am a gentleman, and I don't know how to do anything. You must do things for me, if you know how to, and help me if you can, and take what you like for your labours – knowledge is worth something!'

He began pacing up and down the room while Ivan Matveyitch stood where he was, slightly turning his body in Oblomov's direction.

'Where have you been educated?' Oblomov asked, stopping in front of him again.

'I began at a gymnasium, but my father took me away from the sixth form and put me into an office. What does our education come to! Reading, writing, grammar, and arithmetic – I never went beyond that. I have picked up the routine of my work after a fashion and make a living in a small way. You case is different: you have learned real sciences. . . .'

'Yes,' Oblomov acquiesced with a sigh, 'it's true, I have learned higher mathematics and political economy and law, but I have never picked up the routine of any work. You see, in spite of higher mathematics I don't know what my income is. I went to the country, I listened and watched how things were done at our house and on the estate and in the neighbourhood – it was all very different from the law I learned. I came here, thinking, perhaps, political economy would help me along. . . . But I was told that learning might perhaps be of use to me later on, in my old age, but first I ought to obtain a rank, and for that only one science was necessary – writing official papers. And so I never fitted myself for any work and simply remained a gentleman; you have – so tell me now how I am to manage. . . .'

'It can be done, don't you trouble,' Ivan Matveyitch said at last.

Oblomov stopped in front of him and waited for him to say more.

'It can all be handed over to a man who understands farming, and the deed of trust can be transferred to him,' Ivan Matveyitch added.

'And where am I to find such a man?'

'I have a colleague, Isay Fomitch Zatyorty; he stammers slightly, but is an experienced and business-like man. He managed a big estate for three years, but the owner dismissed him because of his stammer. So he came to our office.'

'But could I rely on him?'

'He is the soul of honour – don't you worry! He would spend his own substance to please his employer. He has been in our office for eleven years.'

'But how could he go to the country if he is at the office?'

'That's nothing, he would take a four months' leave. If you decide, I will bring him here. I suppose he wouldn't be going for nothing. . . .'

'Of course not,' Oblomov agreed.

'Perhaps you will give him so much for travelling expenses and his keep per day, and then, when the business is over, pay him a definite sum by arrangement. He could go right enough.'

'I am very much obliged to you: you will save me a great deal of trouble,' said Oblomov, holding out his hand. 'What is his name?'

'Isay Fomitch Zatyorty,' Ivan Matveyitch repeated, hastily wiping his hand on the cuff of his other sleeve, giving it for a moment to Oblomov and immediately hiding it inside the sleeve. 'I will talk to him to-morrow and bring him to see you.'

'Yes, come to dinner and we'll talk. I am very, very much obliged to you!' Oblomov said, seeing Ivan Matveyitch to the door.

X

ON the evening of the same day, Ivan Matveyitch and
Tarantyev were sitting in one of the top-floor rooms of a
two-storeyed house that stood in the street where Oblomov
lived and faced with its other side on to the quay. It was
the so-called restaurant; two or three empty droshki could
always be seen outside, while the drivers sat on the
ground-floor drinking tea out of their saucers. The top-
floor was reserved for the 'gentry' of the Vyborg side.
Ivan Matveyitch and Tarantyev had tea and a bottle of
rum before them.

'Real Jamaica rum,' Ivan Matveyitch said, pouring out
some rum into his glass with a trembling hand, 'don't des-
pise a good offer, brother.'

'You must admit I deserve a treat,' Tarantyev
answered, 'the house might have rotted and never seen a
lodger like that.'

'That's so, that's so,' Ivan Matveyitch interrupted.

'And if the thing comes off and Zatyorty goes to the
country, there will be some profit!'

'But you are stingy, brother, I have to bargain with
you,' Tarantyev said. 'Just fancy, fifty roubles for such a
lodger!'

'I am afraid he may be leaving – he threatens to go,'
Ivan Matveyitch remarked.

'A man like you ought to have more sense! Where will
he go? You won't drive him away by force now.'

'And the wedding? They say he is going to marry.'

Tarantyev laughed.

'Marry! I will bet he won't,' he replied. 'Why, he can't
go to sleep without Zahar's help – how could he marry?
Till now I've been his benefactor: if it hadn't been for me
he would have starved or been clapped into prison. If the
police inspector came or the landlord asked about some-

thing, he was completely at sea – I always had to come to the rescue. He doesn't know a thing. . . .'

'No, indeed: he says he doesn't know what is done in the district court or a Government Department, has no idea what his peasants are like. What a fool! I could have laughed.'

'And the contract, the contract we drew up!' Tarantyev boasted. 'You are jolly clever at writing documents, brother, you really are! You make me think of my father! I, too, used to be good at it, but I've lost the habit, I really have. If I sit down to write my eyes begin to water something dreadful. He signed it without reading, and it mentioned store-rooms, and stables, and kitchen-gardens! . . .'

'Yes, brother, so long as there are fools left in Russia who sign documents without reading them, people like us can manage to exist. Or else it would be a bad look out! If one listens to the old men, things used to be very different! What capital have I made after twenty-five years of service? I can live, stowed away on the Vyborg side, and have plenty to eat – no need to complain of that – I can have more bread than I can get through; but a flat in the Liteiny, a rich wife, and children who make their way in the world – that's a thing of the past! It seems my face isn't what it should be, and my fingers are red, if you please; and why do I drink vodka? And how can one help drinking it? You try! They say I am worse than a servant: even servants nowadays change their shirts every day and don't wear boots like mine. I haven't been brought up properly – those greenhorns have cut me out: they give themselves airs, read, and talk French. . . .'

'And don't know their work,' Tarantyev added.

'Oh yes, they do: the work is not what it used to be; they all want it as simple as possible and spoil everything for us. That's not the way to write, they say: it's unnecessary trouble, a waste of time; it can be done quicker . . . they spoil things!'

'But the contract is signed: they haven't spoiled that!' Tarantyev said.

'That, of course, is unalterable. Let's drink, brother! When Zatyorty is sent to Oblomovka he will bleed him a bit: let the heirs make the best of it afterwards. . . .'

'Let them!' Tarantyev observed. 'And there are no direct heirs either: third cousins, hardly any relations at all.'

'All I am afraid of is his marriage!' Ivan Matveyitch said.

'Don't you fear, I tell you. Believe me, it will come to nothing.'

'Really?' Ivan Matveyitch responded gaily. 'And do you know, he is casting sheep's-eyes at my sister,' he added in a whisper.

'You don't say so!'

'Upon my word he is! Only don't you let on.'

'Well, brother,' said Tarantyev, nearly stunned with surprise. 'I wouldn't have dreamed of it! And how does she take it?'

'She? Why, you know her, that's what she is!'

He tapped his fist on the table.

'As though she could look after her interests! She is a cow, a real cow: you may hit her or hug her, she will go on grinning like a horse with oats before it. Another woman in her place . . . oïe-oïe! But I will keep my eye on them – just think what it may lead to!'

XI

'FOUR months – another four months of constraint, of secret meetings, suspicious faces and smiles!' Oblomov thought, as he was climbing the stairs of the Ilyinskys' house. 'Oh dear, when will it end? And Olga will hurry me: to-day, to-morrow. She is so determined, so insistent!'

Oblomov reached Olga's rooms without meeting anyone. Olga was sitting in her small drawing-room, next to her bedroom, engrossed in a book. He appeared before her so suddenly that she started; then she smiled and held out her hand to him affectionately, but her eyes seemed to be still reading the book: she looked absentminded.

'You are alone?' he asked her.

'Yes, *ma tante* has gone to Tsarskoe Selo; she invited me to go too. We shall be almost alone for dinner: only Marya Semyonovna is coming, or I could not have received you. You cannot talk to my aunt to-day. What a bore it all is! But to-morrow . . .' she added with a smile. 'And what if I had gone to Tsarskoe Selo?' she asked jokingly.

He said nothing.

'Is anything troubling you?' she went on.

'I had a letter from the country,' he said dully.

'Where is it? Have you brought it?'

He gave her the letter.

'I can make nothing out,' she said, looking at it.

He took it from her and read it aloud. She was thoughtful.

'What is going to happen now?' she asked, after a pause.

'I consulted my landlady's brother this morning,' Oblomov answered, 'and he recommends a certain Isay Fomitch Zatyorty for the job; I am going to ask him to settle it all for me. . . .'

'A perfect stranger,' Olga protested in surprise, 'to collect the peasants' tax, to settle their disputes, to look after the sale of corn!'

'He says Zatyorty is the soul of honour, they've been in the same office for twelve years. . . . He only stammers a little.'

'And what is your landlady's brother like? Do you know him?'

'No, but he seems such a practical, business-like man, and besides, I am living in his house – he would be ashamed to cheat me!'

Olga sat looking at the ground and said nothing.

'You see, if I don't send that man I should have to go myself,' Oblomov went on, 'and I confess I shouldn't care to do that. I have quite lost the habit of travelling, especially in winter . . . in fact, I have never done it.'

She was still looking down, moving the tip of her shoe to and fro.

'Even if I did go,' Oblomov went on, 'it wouldn't be the slightest use: I couldn't put things right; the peasants would deceive me; the bailiff would tell me anything he liked and I should have to believe him; he'd give me as much money as he thought fit. Oh, what a pity Andrey isn't here: he would have settled it all!' he added sadly.

Olga smiled – that is, smiled only with her lips, not with her heart – her heart was bitter. She began looking out of the window, slightly screwing up one eye and watching every carriage that passed.

'It appears this Zatyorty managed once a big estate,' Oblomov went on, 'but the owner dismissed him because of his stammer. I will give him a deed of trust and pass the plans on to him: he will see to buying the materials for building the house, will collect the tax, sell the corn, bring the money, and then. . . . How glad I am, dear Olga,' he said, kissing her hand, 'that I need not leave you! I couldn't bear to part from you, to be in the country without you, by myself . . . it would be dreadful! Only now we must be very careful. . . .'

She looked at him with wide-open eyes and waited.

'Yes,' he began slowly, almost stammering, 'we must see very little of each other; yesterday they began again talking about us at the landlady's . . . and I don't want that. . . . As soon as things are settled and my agent arranges about the building and brings the money . . . it will all be done in about a year's time . . . we shall part no more, tell everything to your aunt and . . . and. . . .'

He glanced at Olga: she had fainted. Her head was bent to one side and her teeth showed through her bluish lips. He was lost in joyful dreams and never noticed that at the words 'When things are settled and my agent . . .' Olga had turned pale and missed the end of his sentence.

'Olga! . . . good heavens, she has fainted!' he said, and pulled at the bell.

'Olga Sergeyevna has fainted,' he said to Katya, when she ran into the room. 'Make haste and bring some water . . . and the smelling-salts! . . .'

'Dear me! She has been so cheerful all the morning . . . what has come over her?' Katya whispered, bringing the smelling-salts from Olga's aunt's table and fussing round Olga with a glass of water.

Olga came to herself, got up from her chair with Katya's and Oblomov's help, and unsteadily walked to her bedroom.

'It's nothing,' she said weakly, 'it's just my nerves; I slept badly. Shut the door, Katya, and you wait for me: I shall be better directly and come back.'

Oblomov was left alone. He put his ear to the door, peeped through the keyhole, but heard and saw nothing. After half an hour he walked down the corridor to the maids' room and asked Katya how Olga was.

'She is better,' Katya said, 'she lay down and sent me away; I looked in later and she was sitting in the arm-chair.'

Oblomov went back to the drawing-room, peeped through the keyhole again – he heard nothing. He tapped on the door with his finger – there was no answer. He sat down and pondered. A great deal passed through his mind during this hour and a half; much had changed in his thoughts, many new decisions had ripened. At last he decided that he would go to the country together with his agent, but would first obtain the consent of Olga's aunt to their marriage, have their engagement announced, commission Ivan Gerasimovitch to find a flat for him, and would even borrow some money ... a little, just for the wedding. He could pay the debt out of the money he would receive for the corn. Why was he so down-hearted then? To think that everything could look so different in one moment! And in the country he and his agent would have the tax collected; then in the last resort he could write to Stolz: he would give him some money and then come and arrange Oblomovka splendidly for him; he would make roads everywhere and build bridges and open schools. ... And he would be there with Olga! ... Why, this was the happiness he wanted! How was it he had failed to think of it all before?

He suddenly felt so gay, so light-hearted, he began pacing across the room, slightly snapping his fingers and almost shouting with joy; he went up to Olga's door and called to her quietly in a cheerful voice: 'Olga, Olga! I have something to tell you!' he said, pressing his lips to the keyhole. 'You can't think what!'

He actually decided not to leave her that day till her aunt returned. 'We will tell her to-day and I will go home betrothed to Olga!'

The door opened quietly and Olga appeared. He glanced at her, and suddenly his spirits dropped; his joy vanished utterly: Olga seemed to have grown older. She was pale, but her eyes glittered; her closed lips and every feature of her face revealed the presence of an intense inner life, bound as with ice by her enforced calm and immobility. In her eyes he read a decision; he did not yet know what it was, but his heart thumped as it had never done before. He had not experienced a moment like this in his life.

'Oh, Olga, don't look at me like that: it frightens me!' he said. 'I have changed my mind. I ought to have arranged it all quite differently . . .' he went on, gradually lowering his voice, pausing, and trying to grasp this new expression of her eyes, her lips, her speaking eyebrows. 'I have decided to go to the country myself, together with my agent . . . so as to . . .' he finished almost inaudibly.

She was silent and looked at him intently, like a phantom. He vaguely guessed what verdict awaited him and took his hat, but he was afraid to ask: he dreaded hearing the fateful verdict against which there might be no appeal. At last he mastered himself.

'Have I understood you aright?' he asked in a changed voice.

She gently bowed her head in assent. Although he had already guessed her meaning, he turned pale and did not move. She was a little languid, but looked as calm and still as a marble statue. It was the unnatural calm that comes when intense concentration or wounded feeling gives one the power of complete self-control, though only for a moment. She was like a wounded man who presses the wound with his hand, so that he can say all that has to be said and then die.

'You will not hate me?' he asked.

'What for?' she said in a faint voice.

'For everything! For what I have done to you?'

'What have you done?'

'I have loved you: it's an insult!'

She smiled piteously.

'For your mistake . . .' he said, bowing his head. 'Perhaps you will forgive me if you recall that I warned you how ashamed you would be, how you would repent. . . .'

'I don't repent. I only feel wretched, so wretched . . .' she said, and stopped to take breath.

'It's worse for me,' Oblomov answered, 'but I deserve it: why should *you* suffer?'

'For my pride,' she said. 'I am punished, I had relied too much on my own powers – that was my mistake, and not what you feared: it wasn't of youth and beauty I had been dreaming; I had thought that I could revive you, that you could still live for my sake, but you died long ago. I didn't foresee this mistake, I kept hoping and watching . . . and now!' she concluded with a sigh, hardly able to speak.

She paused and sat down.

'I cannot stand, my legs tremble. A stone would have come to life after what I have done,' she went on in a breaking voice. 'Now I will do nothing, will not take a step, not even go to the Summer Garden: it's all useless – you are dead! You do agree with me, Ilya?' she added, after a silence. 'You will never reproach me for parting from you out of pride or caprice, will you?'

He shook his head negatively.

'Are you convinced that there is nothing left us, no hope at all?'

'Yes, that's true . . .' he said. 'But perhaps,' he added irresolutely, 'in a year's time. . . .' He had not the heart to deal a final blow to his happiness.

'Do you really believe that in a year's time you would have put your affairs and your life in order?' she asked. 'Think!'

He sighed and pondered, struggling with himself. She read the struggle in his face.

'Listen,' she said. 'I have been looking at my mother's portrait as I sat in my room and I believe her eyes have given me courage and advice. If, like an honourable man, you will. . . . Remember, Ilya, we are not children, and it isn't a joke: our whole life is at stake! Ask your own conscience earnestly and tell me – I will believe you, I know you: will you be able to live up to my standard all your life? Will you be for me what I want you to be? You know me, so you understand what I mean. If boldly and deliberately you say *yes*, I take back my decision: here is my hand, and let us go where you will – abroad, to the country, even to the Vyborg side!'

He was silent.

'If you only knew how I love you. . . .'

'It isn't protestations of love I want, but a brief answer,' she interrupted him, almost dryly.

'Don't torment me, Olga!' he begged despondently.

'Well, Ilya, am I right or no?'

'Yes,' he said, clearly and decisively, 'you are right.'

'Then we ought to part,' she decided, 'before anyone has found you here and seen how upset I am.'

He did not go.

'Even if we did marry, what would come of it?' she asked.

He said nothing.

'You would sink into deeper and deeper sleep every day – isn't that so? And I? You see what I am. I shall never grow old or be tired of life. And with you I should be living from day to day, waiting for Christmas, then to the Carnival, paying calls, dancing, and not thinking of anything; going to bed in the evening, we would thank God that the day had passed so quickly and wake up in the morning wishing that the coming day would be like the one before . . . that would be our future, wouldn't it? Do you call that life? I should pine away, I should die. . . . What for, Ilya? Would you be happy? . . .'

He painfully looked at the ceiling, wanted to move, to run away, but his legs would not obey him. He wanted to say something, but his mouth was dry, his tongue would not move, he could not command his voice. He put out his hand to her.

'Well, then . . .' he began faintly, but he broke off and his eyes completed the sentence: 'good-bye!'

She, too, tried to speak, but could not; she stretched out her hand to him, but the hand dropped before it had touched his; she, too, wanted to say 'good-bye,' but her voice failed her and broke on a false note; her face worked, she put her hand and her head on his shoulder and broke into sobs. It was as though her weapons had been suddenly snatched away from her. All her good sense had vanished – she was left simply a woman powerless against grief.

'Good-bye, good-bye . . .' she brought out between her sobs.

He said nothing and listened in horror to her weeping, not daring to interrupt it. He was not feeling pity either for her or for himself: he was a pitiful figure. She sank into a chair and, leaning against the table, pressed her handkerchief to her face and wept bitterly. Her tears flowed, not like a hot, impetuous stream, released by a sudden and transitory pain as on that day in the park, but were cold and comfortless, like autumn rain pitilessly wetting the empty fields.

'Olga,' he said at last, 'why do you torture yourself? I may not deserve happiness, but have pity on yourself! You love me, you won't be able to bear the parting. Take me as I am, love what is good in me!'

She shook her head without raising it.

'No . . . no . . .' she brought out with difficulty, 'don't be afraid for me and for my grief. I know myself: I will cry it all out now and then will not cry any more. And now, don't try to stop my tears . . . go away. . . . Oh, no, stay! . . . God is punishing me! . . . It hurts me so, oh, how it hurts me . . . here, in my heart! . . .'

She began sobbing again.

'And what if the pain doesn't stop?' he said, 'and your health suffers? Such tears are poisonous. Olga, my angel, don't cry . . . forget it all. . . .'

'No, let me cry! I am crying, not about the future, but about the past . . .' she articulated with difficulty; 'it's gone, faded away. . . . It isn't I who am crying, but my memories! The summer . . . the park . . . you remember? I am sad thinking of our avenue, the lilac. . . . It has all grown into my heart: it hurts me to tear it out! . . .'

She shook her head in despair and sobbed, repeating:

'Oh, how it hurts, how it hurts!'

'What if you die?' he suddenly said in horror. 'Think, Olga. . . .'

'No,' she interrupted him, lifting her head and trying to look at him through her tears. 'I have only lately understood that I loved in you what I wanted to find in

you, what Stolz had pointed out to me, what we had both
invented. I loved the Oblomov that was to be! You are
gentle, you are honourable, Ilya; you are tender . . . like a
dove; you hide your head under your wing – and want
nothing more; you are ready to spend all your life cooing
under the roof . . . but I am not like that: this isn't enough
for me, I want something else, and what that something else is – I don't know! You cannot teach me, you
cannot tell me what it is I miss, you cannot give it me,
so that I. . . . And as for tenderness . . . anyone can give
it! . . .'

Oblomov's legs gave way under him; he sank into an
arm-chair and passed a handkerchief over his forehead
and his hands.

It was a cruel thing to say and it deeply wounded
Oblomov: it seemed to have scorched him inwardly, while
outwardly it was like a breath of icy air. He met it with
a pitiful, painfully shamefaced smile, like a beggar
reproached for his nakedness. He sat, smiling helplessly,
spent with agitation and wounded feeling; his eyes, from
which all light had faded, clearly said: 'Yes, I am a poor,
pitiful creature, a beggar . . . strike me, put me to shame!'

Olga grasped suddenly how venomous her words were;
she rushed to him impetuously.

'Forgive me, darling!' she said tenderly, with tears in
her voice. 'I don't know what I am saying, I am mad!
Forget it all; let us be as before, let everything remain as
it was. . . .'

'No,' he said, getting up suddenly and warding her off
with a decisive gesture, 'it cannot be! Don't distress yourself because you've spoken the truth: I deserve it . . .' he
added despondently.

'I have such wild, extravagant ideas,' she said, 'it's
wretched to be like that. Why are other women, why is
Sonitchka so happy? . . .'

She burst into tears again.

'Go away!' she decided, twisting her wet handkerchief.
'I shall break down, the past is still dear to me. . . .'

She buried her face in her handkerchief, trying to choke her sobs.

'Why has it all been wrecked?' she asked suddenly, raising her head. 'Who laid a curse on you, Ilya? What have you done? You are kind, intelligent, affectionate, noble . . . and . . . you are . . . doomed! What has ruined you? There is no name for that evil. . . .'

'Yes, there is,' he whispered, almost inaudibly.

She looked at him questioningly, with her eyes full of tears.

'Oblomovism!' he whispered; then he took her hand, wanted to kiss it and could not; he merely pressed it close to his lips and hot tears fell on her fingers. Without raising his head or showing her his face, he turned and walked out of the room.

XII

HEAVEN only knows where he wandered, what he did the rest of the day, but he returned home late at night. The landlady was the first to hear him knocking at the gate and the dog barking, and she roused Zahar and Anissya, telling them that their master had come back.

Ilya Ilyitch hardly noticed how Zahar undressed him, took off his boots, and threw over his shoulders his dressing-gown.

'What is it?' was all he asked, looking at the dressing-gown.

'The landlady brought it to-day; it has been washed and mended,' Zahar said.

Oblomov had sunk into an arm-chair as he came in and he never stirred from it. All around him was plunged in sleep and darkness. He sat leaning his head on his hand, not noticing the darkness, not hearing the clock strike. His mind was lost in a chaos of vague, shapeless thoughts; they raced like clouds in the sky without aim or connection – he did not catch one of them. His heart was dead – all life had ceased in it for a time. The return to life, to order, to the regular flow of vital forces took place slowly. The blow had been very cruel and Oblomov was unconscious of his body, of being tired, of having any needs. He could have lain like a stone for twenty-four hours, or walked, driven, moved along like a machine. Man either grows resigned to his fate slowly and painfully – and then his organism gradually resumes its functions – or he breaks down under the weight of grief without hope of recovery – it depends upon the intensity of grief and on the man's character. Oblomov did not remember where he was sitting or know that he was sitting down; he looked without seeing that the morning had dawned; he heard without noticing it the old woman's dry cough, the porter chopping wood in the yard, the noise and clatter in the house; with unseeing eyes he saw the landlady and Akulina go to the market and Ivan Matveyitch with his paper parcel flit past the fence. Neither the cocks nor the barking of the dog nor the creaking of the gate could rouse him from his stupor. There was a rattle of crockery and the hissing of the *samovar*.

At last, after nine o'clock, Zahar, with the tray, opened the door into the study, kicked the door, as usual, in order to shut it, and, as usual, missed his aim; he did, however, retain the tray – he had grown used to it with long practice, and, besides, he knew that Anissya was peeping in at the door behind him and that if he dropped anything she would instantly skip up to him and put him to shame. He safely arrived at the bed tightly hugging the tray and pressing his beard against it, and was just going to put the cups on the table by the bedside when he suddenly saw that the bed had not been touched and his master was not there! He started, and a cup flew on to the floor, followed by a sugar-basin. He tried to catch them in the air, tilted the tray, and the other things fell too. He succeeded in keeping only a spoon on the tray.

'What infliction is this?' he said, watching Anissya pick off the floor the bread, lumps of sugar, and bits of the cup. 'Where can the master be?'

And his master was sitting in the chair, not looking himself at all. Zahar gaped at him.

'Why did you sit all night in the chair, Ilya Ilyitch, instead of lying down?' he asked.

Oblomov slowly turned his head to him, looked absently at Zahar, at the spilt coffee, at the sugar scattered about on the carpet.

'And why did you break the cup?' he said, and walked up to the window.

Snow was falling in big flakes, thickly covering the ground.

'Snow, snow, snow,' he repeated senselessly, gazing at the snow that lay in a deep layer over the fence, the hurdle, and the kitchen-garden. 'It has buried everything,' he whispered in despair. He lay down on the bed and dropped into a leaden, comfortless sleep. It was past mid-day when he was wakened by the creak of the landlady's door; a bare arm holding a plate was thrust through the door; a piece of steaming pie lay on the plate.

'It's Sunday to-day,' said a friendly voice. 'We have been baking a pie; won't you have some?'

But he made no answer; he was in a high fever.

PART IV

I

A YEAR had passed since Ilya Ilyitch's illness. That year had brought many changes in different parts of the world. One country was in turmoil and another had settled down; some shining lights of the world had set and others had risen; here a new mystery of nature was being mastered, and there homes and whole generations were wiped out. Where the old life lay in ruins the new, like young verdure, sprang up afresh. . . . Although on the Vyborg side, in the widow Pshenitsyn's house, the days and nights passed peacefully, bringing no sudden and violent changes into its monotonous existence, and the four seasons in no way differed from those of the previous year, yet life did not stand still; its forms varied perpetually, but the changes were as slow and gradual as the geological changes on our planet – such as a mountain slowly crumbling away, or the sea receding or washing up silt for centuries and forming new land.

Ilya Ilyitch had recovered. His agent, Zatyorty, had gone to the country and sent the full amount received for the sale of corn; his fares, his keep, and his fee were paid out of it. As to the peasant tax, Zatyorty wrote that it could not be gathered because the peasants were either destitute or had gone away to places unknown and that he was actively collecting information about them. With regard to the high road and the bridges he wrote that there was no hurry, and that the peasants would rather go over the hill and through the ravine to the next village than work at making a new road and bridges. In short, both the report and the amount of money received were satisfactory; Ilya Ilyitch found no urgent necessity to go to his estate himself and felt reassured on that score for the present. The agent had done something too about the building of the house: with the help of the provincial architect he estimated the quantity of materials required and told the bailiff to start carting timber in the spring and to build a shed for bricks, so that it was merely left to Oblomov to arrive in the spring and, with God's blessing, begin building. It was proposed by that time to have the peasant tax collected and the estate mortgaged, so that there would be enough cash to cover expenses. For a long time after his illness Ilya Ilyitch was gloomy, spent hours in melancholy brooding, failed sometimes to answer Zahar's questions or to notice his dropping cups on the floor or forgetting to dust the table; the landlady coming in with the pie on feast-days sometimes found him in tears. Then gradually dumb indifference took the place of acute grief. Ilya Ilyitch gazed for hours at the snow falling and making drifts in the yard and the street, covering the stacks of logs, the hen-houses, the kennel, the garden, the kitchen-garden, forming pyramids out of the posts in the fence – all was dead and wrapped in a winding-sheet. He listened for hours to the rattling of the coffee-mill, to the dog barking and jumping on its chain, to Zahar polishing boots, and the measured ticking of the clock. The landlady came in to him as before, asking if he would like to buy something or if he would have something to eat; the landlady's children ran in; he spoke to her with kindly indifference, set lessons for the children, listened to their reading, and listlessly and reluctantly smiled at their childish prattle.

But the mountain was crumbling away little by little, the sea was receding from the shore or gaining upon it, and Oblomov was gradually resuming his normal life. Summer, autumn, and winter passed dully and quietly, but Oblomov was waiting for the spring once more and planning to go to the country. In March cakes were baked in the shape of larks according to custom, in April the double windows were taken out, and he was told that the Neva had thawed and spring had come. He walked about the garden. Vegetables were planted out in the kitchen-garden; the spring holidays came, Whitsuntide, the first of

May, and were celebrated with the traditional birches and wreaths; there was a picnic in the copse. Early in the summer conversation began about the two great festivals to come: St. John's Day – Ivan Matveyitch's name-day, and St. Ilya's Day – Oblomov's name-day; these were important events to look forward to. When the landlady happened to buy or to see in the market an excellent quarter of veal or to bake a particularly good pie, she said: 'Ah, if I only could buy such veal or bake such a pie for the name-days!' They talked of St. Ilya's Friday and the annual walk to the Powder Works, and of the feast at the Smolensky Cemetery at Kolpino. The deep cluck of the broody hen and the chirrup of a new generation of chicks were heard under the windows; pies with chicken and fresh mushrooms, freshly salted cucumbers, and then strawberries and raspberries appeared on the table. 'Giblets aren't good now,' the landlady said to Oblomov. 'Yesterday they asked seventy copecks for two lots of quite small ones; but there is fresh salmon – we can have cold fish soup every day if you like.'

The meals in Madame Pshenitsyn's house were excellent, not only because Agafya Matveyevna was an ideal manager – it was her vocation – but also because her brother was a great epicure with regard to food. He was more than careless about his clothes and linen: he wore the same suit for years and was vexed and disgusted at having to spend money on a new one; he never hung it up carefully, but flung it in a heap in the corner. He changed his underclothes only on Saturdays, like a navvy; but he spared no expense on food. In this he was guided to some extent by the logic he had worked out for himself when he entered the service: 'No one can see what's in one's stomach and they won't gossip about it; but a heavy watch-chain, a new frock-coat, patent boots, all give rise to unnecessary gossip.' This was the reason why the Pshenitsyns had the best veal, amber-coloured sturgeon, white woodcocks. Sometimes he went himself to the market, walked all round it sniffing the air like a setter, and brought home under his coat the best capon; he did not grudge four roubles for a turkey. He bought wine at the Exchange and kept it under lock and key; but no one ever saw anything on the table except a decanter of vodka distilled from blackcurrant leaves – he drank the wine in his room upstairs. When he went fishing with Tarantyev he always had hidden in his coat a bottle of excellent Madeira, and when they had tea at the restaurant he brought his own rum.

The gradual deposition of silt, the raising of the bottom of the sea, and the crumbling away of mountains was going on everywhere and in Anissya's case too: the mutual sympathy between her and the landlady had developed into an indissoluble bond, a complete unity of life. Seeing the landlady's kind interest in his affairs Oblomov asked her once, by way of a joke, to take entire charge of his board and save him from all trouble. Her face lit up with joy; her smile was positively intelligent. Her field of activity broadened out: she would run two households now instead of one, or rather it would be one big household! Besides, she acquired Anissya. She talked it over with her brother and the following day everything from Oblomov's kitchen was removed to Agafya Matveyevna's; his silver and crockery were put into her sideboard, and Akulina was degraded from being a cook to looking after the poultry and the vegetable-garden. Everything was done on a big scale now: tea, sugar, and provisions were bought in large quantities, jam-making and the pickling of cucumbers, apples, and cherries assumed imposing proportions. Agafya Matveyevna seemed to have grown in stature, Anissya straightened her arms like an eagle stretching its wings, and a busy and active life flowed on like a river. Oblomov dined at three o'clock with the family, only the landlady's brother had his dinner by himself, later on, for the most part in the kitchen, as he returned very late from the office. Tea and coffee were brought in to Oblomov by the landlady herself and not by Zahar. The latter dusted the room if he felt inclined, and if he did not

Anissya flew in like a whirlwind and, partly with her apron, partly with her bare hands and, one almost fancied, with her nose, instantly whisked off the dust, pulled everything straight, set the room in order, and disappeared. Or, when Oblomov went out in the garden, the landlady herself looked into his room and, finding it in disorder, shook her head and, muttering something to herself, beat the pillows till they stood up like a mountain, glanced at the pillow-cases, whispered to herself that they needed changing, and took them off, dusted the windows, and before going out peeped behind the sofa.

Changes as gradual as the silting up of the sea and the crumbling away of the earth had taken place chiefly in Agafya Matveyevna's life, but no one, and herself least of all, had noticed them. They only became noticeable through their numerous, unexpected, and endless consequences.

Why was it that she had not been herself for the last year or so? In the old days, if the roast was overdone, the fish overboiled, the vegetables had not been put in the soup, she upbraided Akulina sternly, but with calm and dignity, and forgot all about it; but if something of the kind happened now she jumped up from the table, rushed to the kitchen, heaped bitter reproaches on Akulina, sulked even with Anissya, and the next day herself saw to it that the vegetables were put in the soup and the fish not overboiled. Why was that? It will be said, perhaps, that she was ashamed in the presence of a stranger to have anything amiss in her housekeeping, on which all her pride and activity was centred. Very well. But why was it that in the old days she could hardly keep her eyes open after eight in the evening, and at nine, when she had put the children to bed and seen that the lights were out in the kitchen, the flues closed, and everything in order, she went to bed and no cannon could have waked her till six o'clock in the morning? But now, if Oblomov went to the theatre or stayed on at Ivan Gerasimovitch's and was late coming home she could not go to sleep; she turned over

from side to side, crossed herself, sighed, closed her eyes
– but no sleep came to her! As soon as there was a knocking in the street she raised her head, sometimes jumped
out of bed, opened the window-pane and listened whether
it was he. If there was a knock at the gate she threw on
her skirt and ran to the kitchen to rouse Zahar or Anissya
and send them to open the gate. It may be said that this
merely proved her to be a conscientious housewife who
did not like to have any disorder in her house and to have
her lodger waiting in the street at night till the drunken
porter heard him and let him in, that continued knocking
might wake the children. . . . Very well. But why did she,
when Oblomov fell ill, allow no one into his room, cover
the floor in it with rugs and carpets, darken the windows
and fly into a rage – she, so gentle and kind-hearted! – if
Masha or Vanya gave the least scream or laughed aloud;
why did she, not trusting Zahar and Anissya, sit by his
bedside all night, never taking her eyes off him? When the
bells rang for early Mass she threw on her coat, wrote in
big letters on a piece of paper 'Ilya,' ran to the church,
and, giving the paper to the priest to pray for the sick
man's health, sank on her knees in a dark corner and lay
for a long time with her face on the ground; then she
hastened to the market, and, anxiously returning home,
glanced at the door and asked Anissya in a whisper: 'How
is he?' It will be said this was merely the pity and sympathy that are the predominant features of feminine character. Very well. Why was it, then, that while Oblomov,
recovering from his illness, was gloomy all the winter,
hardly spoke to her, never looked into her room, took no
interest in what she was doing, did not laugh or joke with
her – she grew thinner, she suddenly felt so cold, so indifferent to everything: she would be grinding coffee and not
know what she was doing, or would put such a lot of
chicory in that one could not drink it, and never notice it,
as though she had no taste. Akulina might serve the fish
half cooked, Ivan Matveyitch might grumble and leave the
table – she was like one turned to stone and did not seem

to see it. In the old days no one had ever seen her thoughtful, and, indeed, it was not in her character: she was always busy and on the go, keeping a keen eye on everything; but now she sometimes sat motionless with the mortar on her lap as though she had fallen asleep, and then suddenly would begin pounding with the pestle so violently that the dog barked, thinking someone was knocking at the gate. But as soon as Oblomov revived, as soon as he began to smile kindly, to look at her in the old friendly way, to peep in at her door and joke – she grew stouter again, her work went on as actively, briskly, and gaily as ever, with one little difference: in the old days she moved all day long smoothly and regularly, like a well-constructed machine; she walked slowly; she spoke in a voice that was neither low nor loud; she ground coffee, chopped up a sugar-loaf, rubbed something through the sieve, then sat down to her sewing, and her needle moved as regularly as a pendulum; she rose from her seat without haste; half-way to the kitchen she stopped, opened the cupboard, took something out, carried it away – and did it all mechanically, as it were. But now that Ilya Ilyitch had become a member of her family, the very way she pounded things in a mortar or rubbed them through a sieve was different. She had almost forgotten her lace. She would sit down to sew, and just as she settled down comfortably Oblomov would shout to Zahar for his coffee – in three skips she was in the kitchen, looked round her as keenly as though she were taking aim, seized a spoon, poured three spoonfuls of coffee out against the light to see it was ready and there were no dregs in it, and looked to see that the cream was thick and foaming. If Oblomov's favourite dish was being cooked she looked at the sauce-pan, lifted the lid, sniffed the contents, tasted them, then seized the saucepan and held it over the fire. If she grated almonds or pounded something for him in a mortar she did it with such vigour and eagerness that she was all in a perspiration. All her household occupations – ironing, sieving, pounding, etc., acquired a new living significance:

Ilya Ilyitch's comfort and well-being. In the old days she regarded it as a duty, now it became a delight. In her own way she began to live a rich and varied life. But she did not know what was happening to her; she never asked herself the question, but accepted the sweet yoke completely, without resisting it or being carried away, without tremor, passion, vague forebodings, or longings, without the play and the music of the nerves. It was as though she had suddenly been converted to another religion and followed it without reasoning what kind of faith it was or what its dogmas were, blindly obeying its laws. It somehow came upon her of itself and covered her like a cloud which she had neither avoided nor run to meet; she fell in love with Oblomov as simply as though she had caught a cold or contracted an incurable fever. She did not suspect anything of this: if she had been told, it would have been news to her – she would have smiled and felt shy. She silently accepted her duties towards Oblomov, learned the individual look of every shirt of his, counted the holes in his stockings, knew with which foot he got out of bed, noticed when he was going to have a stye on his eye, what dishes he liked and what helpings he took; she knew whether he was cheerful or depressed, whether he slept much or little, as though she had studied him all her life; but she never wondered why she did all this, what Oblomov was to her, why she took so much trouble. If she had been asked did she love him, she would have smiled and said yes, but she would have made the same answer when Oblomov had not been with her more than one week.

Why had she fallen in love with him of all people? Why had she married without love and lived without love till she was thirty, and now it had suddenly come upon her? Although love is said to be a capricious, unaccountable feeling that attacks one like an illness, it, too, like everything else, has causes and laws of its own. These laws have been but little studied so far, because a man stricken with love has no thoughts to spare for watching with the eye of a scientist how an impression steals into his soul and casts a spell over his senses, causing him to lose his sight; how and at which moment his pulse and his heart begin to beat faster; how he suddenly develops a lifelong devotion and a longing for self-sacrifice; how his self gradually disappears and passes into the beloved and his intellect grows either extraordinarily dull or extremely subtle; how his will is surrendered to that of another, his head bends, his knees tremble; how the fever and the tears come. . . .

Agafya Matveyevna had not seen many people like Oblomov before, and if she had it was only from a distance; she may have liked them, but they lived in a different sphere and she had no opportunity to come near them. Ilya Ilyitch did not walk with quick, busy little steps like her husband, the late collegiate secretary Pshenitsyn; he did not copy endless documents or shake with fear at being late at the office; he did not look at people as though expecting them to obey him. His face was not rough and reddish, but soft and fair-skinned; his hands were not like her brother's hands – they were not red and shaking, but small and white. Whether he sat down, crossed his legs, or leaned his head on his hand, he did it all so calmly, easily, and gracefully; he spoke differently from her brother and Tarantyev, and from the way her husband used to speak; a great deal of what he said she did not understand, but she felt that it was clever, wonderful, beautiful, and even the things she did understand he said differently from other people. He wore fine linen, he changed it every day, he washed with scented soap, he cleaned his nails – he was all so clean, so lovely, there was no need for him to work, and, in fact, he did nothing, other people did everything for him: he had Zahar and three hundred other Zahars. . . . He was a gentleman, he was resplendent, brilliant! And he was so kind too; he walked and moved so softly, the touch of his hand was like velvet – her husband's touch had been as bad as a blow. He looked and talked so gently, with such kindness. . . . She did not think these things, she was not consciously aware of them, but if anyone had tried to trace and to explain the impression which Oblomov's coming into her life made upon her mind, this was the explanation he would have to give.

Ilya Ilyitch understood what his settling in the house meant for all of them, from the landlady's brother down to the watch-dog, which now received three times as many bones as before; but he did not understand how deep it all went and what an unexpected conquest he had made of his landlady's heart. He regarded her anxious solicitude about his food, linen, and rooms merely as an expression of the main trait of her character, which he had noticed at their first meeting when Akulina suddenly brought into the room a struggling cock and Agafya Matveyevna, put out as she was by the cook's misplaced zeal, managed to tell her that not this cock but the grey speckled one was for sale. Agafya Matveyevna was utterly incapable of any coquetry with Oblomov or of giving him the least hint of what was passing in her, and, indeed, as has already been said, she never understood it or was aware of it herself; she had actually forgotten that only a short time ago none of these things had been happening to her. Her love found expression only in a boundless and lifelong devotion. Oblomov was blind to the true nature of her attitude to him and put it down to her temperament. Agafya Matveyevna's feeling, so normal, so natural and disinterested, remained a secret for Oblomov, for the people around her, and for herself. It was, indeed, disinterested because she put up candles in the church and had prayers said for Oblomov's health simply because she wanted him to recover, and he never knew of it. She had sat by his bedside at night and left it at dawn, and nothing was said about it afterwards. His attitude to her was much simpler. Agafya Matveyevna, with her perpetually moving elbows, her solicitous, all-seeing eyes, her perpetual journeys from the sideboard to the kitchen, from the kitchen to the store-room and the cellar, her thorough knowledge of housekeeping and of all home comforts, was for him the incarnate ideal of a life of boundless and unruffled repose, the picture of which had been indelibly stamped on his mind in childhood, under the parental roof. His father, his grandfather, the children, the grand-children, the visitors, sat or lay about in restful idleness, knowing that there were in the house unsleeping eyes that watched over them and never-weary hands that sewed their clothes, gave them food and drink, dressed them, put them to bed, and closed their eyes when they were dead; and now Oblomov, sitting still on the sofa, saw something quick and lively moving for his benefit, and knew that the sun might not rise to-morrow, whirlwinds might hide the sky, a storm might sweep the world, but his soup and roast would be on the table, his linen would be fresh and clean, the cobwebs would be taken off the wall, and he would not know how it was all done; that before he had taken the trouble to think of what he wanted it would be guessed and placed before him – not rudely and lazily by Zahar's dirty hands, but by clean, white hands and arms bare to the elbow, with a cheerful and gentle glance and a smile of profound devotion.

He made friends with his landlady more and more every day; the thought of love never entered his head – that is, of the kind of love he had just gone through as through an attack of smallpox, measles, or fever; he shuddered at the memory of it. He came closer to Agafya Mat-veyevna as one does to a fire which makes one warmer and warmer, but which cannot be loved. After dinner he readily remained in her room to smoke his pipe, watching her put away the silver and the dinner-service in the dresser, take out the cups, and pour out coffee; after washing and wiping one cup with special care she poured out his coffee first of all, handed it to him, and looked to see if he liked it. His eyes liked to dwell on her plump neck and rounded elbows when the door into her room was open, and if it had remained shut too long he gently pushed it open with his foot and joked with her or played with her children. But he did not miss her if the morning passed without his seeing her; after dinner, instead of remaining with her, he often retired to have a couple of hours' sleep; but he knew that the moment he woke his tea would be ready for him. And the great thing was that everything went on peacefully: he had no lump at his heart, he never once wondered anxiously whether he would see his landlady or not, or worried as to what she would think, what he would say to her, how he would answer her question, how she would look at him – there was nothing of the kind. He had no yearnings, no sleepless nights, no sweet or bitter tears. He sat smoking and looked at her sewing, sometimes he said something and sometimes he said nothing, and all the time he felt at peace, not needing anything, not wanting to go anywhere, as though all he needed were here. Agafya Matveyevna incited him to nothing, made no demands upon him. And he had no ambitious impulses or desires, no longing to do something heroic, no agonizing regrets that time was passing and his powers were being wasted, that he had done nothing, either good or bad, that he was idly vegetating instead of living. It was as though some unseen hand had placed him as a precious plant in a spot where he was sheltered from the heat and the rain and nurtured him tenderly.

'How fast you move your needle past your nose, Agafya Matveyevna!' Oblomov said. 'You raise it so quickly that I am really afraid you might stitch your nose to your skirt.'

She smiled.

'I'll just finish stitching this seam,' she said, almost to herself, 'and we'll have supper.'

'What is there for supper?'

'Pickled cabbage and salmon,' she said. 'There isn't any sturgeon to be had: I've been to all the shops and my brother asked for it, but there isn't any. Only, perhaps, if a live sturgeon is caught – a merchant from the Karetny Ryad has ordered one – the fishmonger promised to cut us some of it. Then there is veal and fried cornmeal. . . .'

'That's splendid! How nice of you to have thought of it, Agafya Matveyevna! I hope Anissya won't forget.'

'But I am here to see to it. Do you hear it sizzling?' she answered, slightly opening the kitchen door. 'It's being fried already.'

She finished her seam, bit off the thread, folded her work, and carried it to her bedroom.

And so he kept drawing closer to her as to a glowing fire, and one day he drew so near that there was very nearly an accident or, at any rate, a little flare-up.

He was walking up and down his room, and when he turned to the landlady's door he saw that her elbows were moving with extraordinary rapidity.

'Always busy!' he said, going in to her. 'What's this?'

'I am pounding cinnamon,' she said, looking into the mortar as though it were an abyss and making a merciless clatter with the pestle.

'And what if I disturb you?' he asked, taking her by the elbows and preventing her going on with her work.

'Let me go! I must pound some sugar too, and pour out some wine for the pudding.'

He was still holding her by the elbows and his face was close to the back of her neck.

'Tell me, what if I . . . loved you?'

She smiled.

'Would you love me?' he asked again.

'Why not? God commanded us to love everyone.'

'And what if I kissed you?' he whispered, bending down so that she felt his hot breath on her cheek.

'It isn't Easter week,' she said with a smile.

'Now, do kiss me!'

'If, God willing, we live till Easter, we'll kiss each other then!' she said, without any surprise, alarm, or confusion, standing straight and still like a horse when it has its collar put on. He slightly kissed her on the neck.

'Take care, or I'll spill the cinnamon and there will be none to put in your pudding!' she remarked.

'Never mind!' he answered.

'What is this on your dressing-gown, another stain?' she asked solicitously, taking hold of the skirt of his dressing-gown. 'I believe it's oil.' She sniffed the stain. 'Where did you pick it up? Could it have dropped off the ikon lamp?'

'I don't know how I got it.'

'You must have caught it in the doorway!' Agafya Matveyevna guessed. 'We had the hinges greased yesterday – they creaked so. Take it off and give it me quick, I will take the stain out and wash the place – there will be nothing left of it to-morrow.'

'Kind Agafya Matveyevna!' Oblomov said, lazily throwing the dressing-gown off his shoulders. 'Do you know what? Let us go and live in the country: housekeeping is a different thing there! There's something of everything there: mushrooms, fruit, jam, the poultry yard, the dairy. . . .'

'No, why should I go?' she concluded with a sigh. 'We've been born here, we've lived here, and here we ought to die.'

He looked at her with slight agitation, but his eyes did not shine or fill with tears, his spirit did not yearn for the heights, for heroic deeds. All he wanted was to sit on the sofa and watch her elbows.

II

St. John's Day was a great festival. On the day before, Ivan Matveyitch did not go to the office but dashed about the town, bringing home each time a sack or a basket. Agafya Matveyevna had lived on nothing but coffee for three days and the whole family was fed on scraps; only Ilya Ilyitch had a three-course dinner. Anissya did not go to bed at all the night before. Zahar alone slept enough for two and looked down upon all these preparations with something like contempt.

'With us at Oblomovka, dinners like this were cooked every holiday,' he said to the two chefs who had been invited from the count's kitchen; 'we used to have five kinds of sweets and more sauces than one could count. The family and visitors would be eating all day and the next day too, and we had the remains for the next five days. And just as we would finish, visitors would come and it would all begin again – and here it's only once a year!'

At dinner he served Oblomov first and would not hear of serving some gentleman with a big cross round his neck.

'Our master is a gentleman born,' he said proudly, 'and these visitors aren't anything!'

Tarantyev, who sat at the end of the table, he did not serve at all, or just shoved as much food on to his plate as the fancy took him. All Ivan Matveyitch's colleagues, about thirty of them, were present. The huge trout, stuffed chickens, partridges, ice cream, and excellent wine were worthy of the annual feast. At the end the visitors embraced one another, praised up to the skies their host's good taste, and sat down to play cards. Ivan Matveyitch bowed and thanked them, saying that he had gladly sacrificed a third of his yearly salary for the pleasure of giving a dinner to his dear guests. The guests left towards morning, hardly able to walk straight, and the house was quiet once more till Oblomov's name-day.

On that day, the only visitors Oblomov had were Ivan Gerasimovitch and Alexeyev, the silent, inoffensive man who had, at the beginning of our story, invited Ilya Ilyitch to Ekaterinhof on the first of May. Oblomov was anxious to do no worse than Ivan Matveyitch, and, indeed, to outshine him by a choiceness and delicacy unknown in those parts.

Instead of the rich pie there were tiny pasties light as air; oysters were served before the soup; there were chickens in *papillotes* with truffles, the best of meat, the finest vegetables, English soup. In the middle of the table there was a huge pineapple surrounded with peaches, apricots, cherries. There were flowers on the table. They had just started on the soup and Tarantyev had sworn at the pasties and the cook for the silly notion of having no stuffing in them, when the dog began barking desperately and jumping on the chain. A carriage drove into the yard, the pole struck against the fence, and someone asked for Oblomov. Everyone stared in astonishment.

'Some one of my last year's friends must have remembered my name-day,' Oblomov said. 'I am not at home – say I am not at home,' he said in a loud whisper to Zahar.

They were having dinner in the arbour in the garden. Zahar rushed off to turn the visitor away and ran straight into Stolz.

'Andrey Ivanitch!' he hissed joyfully.

'Andrey!' Oblomov cried aloud, and flung himself on his neck.

'You are having dinner, that's lucky!' Stolz said. 'Give me something to eat, I am hungry. I thought I would never find you!'

'Come along, come along, sit down!' Oblomov said, fussily making Stolz sit down next to him.

When Stolz appeared Tarantyev rapidly stepped over the fence and rushed into the kitchen-garden; Ivan Matveyitch followed him and retired to his attic. The hostess also got up from her seat.

'I have disturbed you . . .' Stolz said, jumping up.

'Where are you off to? What for? Ivan Matveyitch! Mihey Andreyitch!' Oblomov shouted.

He made Agafya Matveyevna sit down again, but the others could not be recalled.

'Where do you come from? How did you find me? How long are you staying?' he bombarded Stolz with questions.

Stolz had come for a fortnight, on business, and was then going to the country, to Kiev, and several other places. At table he spoke little, but ate a great deal; he evidently was really hungry. The others, of course, ate in silence. After dinner, when everything had been cleared away, Oblomov asked for champagne and seltzer water to be left in the arbour and remained alone with Stolz.

They sat in silence for a time. Stolz looked at him long and intently.

'Well, Ilya?' he asked at last, so sternly that Oblomov looked down and said nothing.

'Then it's "never"?'

'What do you mean, "never"?' Oblomov asked, as though not understanding.

'You have forgotten: "now or never"!'

'I am not the same now . . . as I was then, Andrey,' he said at last. 'My affairs, thank Heaven, are in order, I don't lie idle, my plan is nearly finished, I subscribe to two magazines; I have read almost all the books you had left me. . . .'

'Why, then, didn't you go abroad?' Stolz asked.

'I was prevented by. . . .'

He stopped in confusion.

'Olga?' Stolz asked, looking at him significantly.

Oblomov flushed crimson.

'What? Can you have heard? . . . Where is she now?' he asked quickly with a glance at Stolz.

Stolz made no answer, but went on looking at him with a gaze that penetrated his soul.

'I heard she had gone abroad with her aunt,' Oblomov said, 'soon after. . . .'

'Soon after she had learned her mistake,' Stolz finished for him.

'Why, do you know? . . .' Oblomov asked, overcome with confusion.

'Everything,' Stolz said, 'even about the lilac branch. And aren't you ashamed, aren't you unhappy, Ilya? Aren't you tortured by remorse and regret?'

'Don't speak of it, don't recall it!' Oblomov interrupted him hastily. 'I had brain-fever as it was, when I saw what an abyss lay between her and me, when I grasped that I wasn't worthy of her. . . . Ach, Andrey, if you love me, don't remind me of her: I long ago pointed out her mistake to her, but she would not believe me. . . . I really am not very much to blame. . . .'

'I don't blame you, Ilya,' Stolz said gently and affectionately; 'I have read your letter. I am to blame most of all, then she and you only in the third place, and very little at that.'

'How is she now?' Oblomov asked timidly.

'How? She is inconsolable, sheds tears, and curses you. . . .'

Alarm, sympathy, terror, remorse, appeared on Oblomov's face at every word Stolz uttered.

'What are you saying, Andrey!' he said, getting up. 'Let us, for God's sake, go to her at once, this minute; I will go down on my knees to beg her forgiveness. . . .'

'Sit still!' Stolz interrupted him, laughing. 'She is gay and happy, she sends you her greetings and was going to write to you, but I advised her not to, for fear it would upset you.'

'Well, thank God!' Oblomov said almost with tears. 'How glad I am, Andrey! Let me kiss you and we will drink her health.'

They each drank a glass of champagne.

'Where is she now?'

'In Switzerland. At the end of the summer she and her

aunt are going to her estate. This is why I am here now: there are still some legal points to settle. The baron did not finish the business; he took it into his head to propose to Olga. . . .'

'Indeed? It was true then: well, and what did she do?' Oblomov asked.

'Refused him, of course; he was vexed and left them, and now I have to wind up the business! It will all be settled next week. Well, and how are you? Why have you buried yourself in this wilderness?'

'It's quiet and restful here, Andrey, no one disturbs me. . . .'

'Disturbs you in what?'

'In my work. . . .'

'But, my dear, this is simply another Oblomovka, only worse,' said Stolz, looking about him. 'Let us go to the country, Ilya.'

'To the country . . . yes, perhaps: they will be soon beginning to build there. Only not at once, Andrey, let me consider it. . . .'

'Again! I know you: you will consider it as you considered going abroad two years ago. Let us go next week.'

'Why, how can I go so suddenly – next week?' Oblomov defended himself. 'You are on the go, but I have to make ready. . . . All my belongings are here: how can I leave it all? I have nothing for the journey.'

'But you don't need anything. What can you want?'

Oblomov did not answer.

'I am far from well, Andrey,' he said. 'I am so short of breath. I have been having styes again, first on one eye then on the other, and my legs swell. And sometimes when I am sound asleep someone seems to strike me suddenly on the head or on the back so that I jump up. . . .'

'Look here, Ilya, I tell you quite seriously, you must change your manner of life or you will develop dropsy or have a stroke. I have no more hope for your future: if an angel like Olga couldn't carry you on her wings out of your stagnation, I can do nothing. But you can and must choose for yourself a small field of activity, put your estate in order, keep in touch with your peasants, and enter into their affairs, build, plant trees. . . . I will give you no peace. I am obeying not only my own desire now, but Olga's will: she is anxious – do you hear? – that you should not die altogether, should not bury your-self alive, and I have promised to dig you out of your grave. . . .'

'She has not forgotten me yet! I don't deserve it!' Oblomov said with feeling.

'No, she hasn't forgotten you and I don't think she ever will: she is not that sort of woman. You will have to pay her a visit at her estate.'

'Only not now, for God's sake, not now, Andrey! Let me forget. Oh, I still have here. . . .'

He pointed to his heart.

'What? Love, perhaps?'

'No, shame and grief!' Oblomov answered with a sigh.

'Very well! Let us go to your place; you must be build-ing now: it's summer, precious time is being wasted. . . .'

'No, I have an agent. He is at Oblomovka now and I can come later when I am ready and have thought things over.'

He began boasting to Stolz how excellently he had arranged his affairs without stirring from the spot; his agent was making inquiries about the runaway peasants and selling corn at a profit; he had already sent him fif-teen hundred roubles and this year would probably collect and send him the peasant tax.

Stolz clasped his hands in dismay at this tale.

'You have been simply robbed!' he said. 'Fifteen hun-dred from three hundred serfs! Who is your agent? What sort of man is he?'

'It was more than fifteen hundred,' Oblomov corrected himself; 'he took a fee for his labours out of the money received for the sale of corn. . . .'

'How much?'

'I really don't remember, but I will show you: I have put it down somewhere.'

'Well, Ilya, you really are dead and done for!' Stolz concluded. 'Dress and come along with me!'

Oblomov began to argue, but Stolz took him away almost by force, wrote out a deed of trust in his own name, made Oblomov sign it, and told him that he would rent Oblomovka from him until Oblomov himself came to the country and grew accustomed to farming.

'You will receive three times as much,' he said, 'only I will not rent Oblomovka for long – I have business of my own to see to. Let us go to the country now, or you can come after me. I shall be on Olga's estate: it's two hundred miles from you, so I will call at your place, too, dismiss your agent and arrange matters, and then you must come yourself. I will not leave you in peace.'

Oblomov sighed.

'Life!' he said.

'What about it?'

'It disturbs one, gives one no peace! I wish I could lie down and go to sleep . . . for ever. . . .'

'That is, you would like to put the light out and remain in darkness! Fine sort of life, indeed! Ah, Ilya, you might at least philosophize a little! Life will flit by like an instant, and you say you would like to lie down and sleep! Let it be one continual flame! Oh, I wish I could live two or three hundred years! How much one could do then!'

'You are different, Andrey,' Oblomov retorted, 'you have wings; you don't live, you fly; you have gifts, ambition; you see, you are not fat, you are not bothered with styes, the back of your head doesn't keep itching. . . . You are differently made, somehow. . . .'

'Oh, nonsense! Man has been created to arrange his life himself and to change his very nature, but here he grows a belly and believes nature has sent him this burden! You had wings once, but you took them off.'

'Where are they, those wings?' Oblomov said dejectedly. 'I don't know how to do anything.'

'That is, you don't want to know,' Stolz interrupted him. 'There isn't a man living who can't do something; I assure you there isn't.'

'But I can't,' Oblomov protested.

'To listen to you one would think you couldn't write a petition to the Board or a letter to your landlord, but you did manage to write a letter to Olga, didn't you? You didn't mix up *who* and *which* in it? You found good note-paper and ink from the English shop, and you wrote it quickly enough, didn't you?'

Oblomov blushed.

'When you wanted it, you found both ideas and style good enough for a novel. And when you don't want to, you don't know how to do a thing, and your eyes do not see and your hands feel shaky! You lost your ability for doing things when still a child, at Oblomovka, among your aunts and nurses. It began with your not knowing how to put your stockings on and ended by your not knowing how to live.'

'All this may be true, Andrey, but there is nothing for it, there is no retrieving it!' Ilya Ilyitch said decisively, with a sigh.

'Why no retrieving?' Stolz retorted angrily. 'What non-sense! Listen and do what I tell you and you will retrieve it right enough!'

But Stolz went to the country alone, and Oblomov remained in town, promising to go to his estate in the autumn.

'What shall I tell Olga?' Stolz asked, before going away.

Oblomov bowed his head and paused sadly; then he sighed.

'Don't mention me to her!' he said at last in confusion. 'Tell her you haven't seen me or heard of me. . . .'

'She won't believe it.'

'Well, tell her that I am lost, dead, done for. . . .'

'She will cry and for a long while be inconsolable: why grieve her?'

Oblomov pondered, deeply moved; his eyes were moist.

'Very well, I will tell her a lie and say you are living on memories of her,' Stolz decided, 'and are seeking for a true and serious aim in life. Observe that not woman but life itself with its work is the aim of life: that was the mistake you both made. How glad she will be!'

They said good-bye.

III

The day after St. Ilya's feast Tarantyev and Ivan Matveyitch met again at the restaurant in the evening.

'Tea!' Ivan Matveyitch ordered gloomily, and when the waiter had served tea and rum he shoved the rum bottle back to him testily. 'This tastes more of iron than rum!' he said, and pulling a bottle out of his pocket uncorked it and let the waiter sniff it.

'Don't you produce any of your stuff in the future!' he observed.

'I say, brother, it's a bad look out!' he said, when the waiter had gone.

'Yes, the devil brought him!' Tarantyev replied furiously. 'What a rascal that German is! He has destroyed the deed of trust and is renting the estate! It's simply unheard of! He will fleece the sheep, I bet.'

'If he knows his business, brother, I am afraid there may be trouble. When he hears that the tax has been collected but it was we who received it, he may go to law about it. . . .'

'To law, indeed! You are too easily scared, brother! It's not the first time Zatyorty puts his paw into the gentry's pocket, he knows how to cover up his tracks. Do you imagine he gives a receipt to the peasants? He takes the money from them without witnesses, you may be sure. The German may be angry and shout, and that's all he can do. Going to law, indeed!'

'Is that so?' said Ivan Matveyitch, brightening up. 'Well, let's have a drink.'

He poured out some rum for himself and Tarantyev.

'Sometimes life seems too much of a bad job altogether, but after a drink you feel you can go on with it!' he said, taking comfort.

'And, meanwhile, I'll tell you what you must do,' Tarantyev went on. 'Make out some bills – anything you like – for firewood or cabbage or whatever you please and put them on the debit side – since Oblomov lets your sister look after his keep. And when Zatyorty comes we shall say that he collected so much peasants' tax, but it went to meet the expenses.'

'And what if he takes the accounts and shows them to the German, who will cast them up and then. . . .'

'What next! He will shove them away and the devil himself won't find them. The German won't come for some time and by then he will have forgotten. . . .'

'Is that so? Let's have a drink, brother,' Ivan Matveyitch said, pouring out a glass. 'It's a pity to weaken the good stuff with tea. Just sniff it: three silver roubles! Shall we have some salt fish and cabbage?'

'Let us.'

'Hey, waiter!'

'No, just think of the rascal! "Let me rent it," he says.' Tarantyev began furiously again. 'Russian people like you and me would never have thought of such a thing! It's so German. They are always renting farms and doing that sort of thing. Wait a bit, he will make him go in for shares!'

'What are those shares? I can never quite make out,' Ivan Matveyitch asked.

'A German invention!' Tarantyev said malignantly. 'For instance, some scoundrel may invent fire-proof houses and will undertake to build a town: he needs money for it, so he begins to sell papers, let us say at five hundred roubles each, and a crowd of fools buy them and sell them to each other. If the rumour is that the business is going well, the papers go up in price, if it's going ill the whole thing is burst up. You will have the papers, but they won't be worth anything. Where is the town? you will ask: it's burnt down, they'll tell you, and the inventor has run off with your money. That's what shares are! You may be sure the German will drag him into it! I wonder he hasn't done it yet! I've been in the way, doing all I could for my old neighbour!'

'Yes, that's over and done with; the case has been settled and put in the archives – we are to collect no more peasant tax from Oblomovka . . .' said Ivan Matveyitch, slightly drunk.

'But after all, Oblomovka be damned! You shovel money as it is!' replied Tarantyev, also slightly befogged. 'You have a secure source to draw from if you don't slacken. Let's have a drink!'

'It's not much of a source, brother! One has to collect miserable rouble and three-rouble notes all one's life. . . .'

'But you have been collecting them for twenty years, brother: it's a sin for you to complain!'

'Twenty, indeed!' Ivan Matveyitch answered, speaking thickly. 'You have forgotten that this is only my tenth year as secretary. Before that I used to have only ten- and twenty-copeck pieces in my pocket, and sometimes, I am ashamed to say, I had to take coppers. What sort of life is this, eh, brother? There are lucky people in the world who need only whisper a word in someone's ear or dictate a line or simply write their name on a piece of paper and their pocket suddenly swells out like a pillow so that they could sleep on it! If one could do things like that,' he said dreamily, getting more and more drunk, 'one's clients would practically never see one or dare to come near. A man of that sort steps into his carriage and shouts, "To the club!" and at the club men wearing a star shake hands with him; he plays, not for five-copeck stakes! and his dinners, his dinners – ah! He would scorn to mention salt fish: he would turn up his nose at it in disgust. Those people make a point of having spring chicken in winter, strawberries in April! At home his wife would be dressed in real lace, the children have a governess, their hair well brushed, their clothes smart! Ah, brother, there is a paradise, but our sins keep us out! Let's have a drink! Here they are bringing our salt fish.'

'Don't complain, brother, it's too bad of you: you have a fortune and a good one at that . . .' said Tarantyev, quite drunk by now, his eyes red and bloodshot. 'Thirty-five thousand silver roubles is no joke!'

'Hush, hush, brother!' Ivan Matveyitch interrupted. 'It's still thirty-five, and shall I ever make it up to fifty? And even fifty isn't enough for paradise. If I marry I shall have to live carefully, count every rouble, give up all thought of Jamaica rum – do you call that life?'

'But it's peaceful, brother; one man gives you a rouble, another two, and you can stow away seven roubles or so each day. There's nothing to find fault with, nothing to trip you up, no stains, no smoke. And if you put your name to some big piece of business you sometimes have to smart for it the rest of your life. No, brother, it would be a sin for you to grumble!'

Ivan Matveyitch was not listening; he had been thinking of something else for some time.

'I say, listen,' he began, suddenly staring in front of him and so pleased about something that he had grown almost sober; 'but, no, I am afraid, I won't tell you, I won't let such a precious thought out of my head. It's a real treasure of a thought. . . . Let's have a drink, brother, quick!'

'I won't until you tell me,' Tarantyev said, pushing his glass away.

'It's a serious matter, brother,' Ivan Matveyitch whispered, glancing at the door.

'Yes?' Tarantyev asked impatiently.

'I've hit on something really good. You know, it's the same as signing one's name to a big piece of business, upon my word it is!'

'But what is it? Will you tell me?'

'What profits, I say!'

'Well?' Tarantyev urged him.

'Wait, let me think a bit. Yes, there's nothing to spoil it, it's legal. So be it, brother, I'll tell you, but only because I need you; I couldn't manage without you. If it weren't for that, God is my witness, I wouldn't tell you; it's not the kind of business to let another man into the know.'

'But surely I am not "another man" for you? I should have thought I've done you a good turn, more than once, acted as your witness and copied out things ... you remember? What a pig you are!'

'Hold your tongue, mate. Why, you shoot everything out like a cannon!'

'What devil could hear us here? I haven't lost my senses,' Tarantyev said with annoyance; 'don't keep me in suspense! Speak.'

'Listen: Ilya Ilyitch is easily frightened and knows nothing about things: he quite lost his head over that contract then, and when his neighbour returned the deed of trust to him he did not know what to do; he doesn't even know what his income is, he says himself: "I know nothing. . . ." '

'Well?' Tarantyev asked impatiently.

'Well, he goes to my sister's rooms much too often. The other day he sat there till twelve o'clock, and when he ran up against me in the entry he pretended not to see me. So we shall see how things are going on and then. . . . You speak to him and say it isn't right to bring disgrace upon a family, she is a widow; tell him that people are talking about it and she has no chance of finding a husband now; that she had a suitor, a rich merchant, but now that he has heard about Oblomov spending his evenings with her he has backed out.'

'Well, what then? He will be frightened, get into bed and sigh, turning from side to side like a pig – that's all!' Tarantyev said. 'What's the advantage? Where's the profit?'

'What a man you are! Why, you must say that I want to lodge a complaint against him, that he has been watched and there are witnesses. . . .'

'Well?'

'Well, if he is very much alarmed you can tell him the matter can be settled amicably by his sacrificing a small sum.'

'But he has no money!' Tarantyev said. 'He may promise anything in his fright, ten thousand if you like, but what's the good?'

'You just wink to me then, I shall have an IOU ready . . . in my sister's name, saying, "I, Oblomov, have borrowed from widow so and so ten thousand roubles to be repaid within . . ." and so on.'

'What's the use, brother? I don't understand: the money will go to your sister and her children. Where's the profit?'

'And my sister will give an IOU to me for the same amount: I'll make her sign it.'

'But what if she doesn't? She may refuse.'

'Who, my sister?'

Ivan Matveyitch broke into a shrill laugh.

'She will sign, my dear, she will sign her own death-warrant without asking what it is and merely smile. She will write "Agafya Pshenitsyn" all crookedly and never know what it is she has signed. You see, you and I will not come into it: my sister will have a claim against Oblomov and I against her. The German may be as angry as he likes – it's all perfectly legal!' he said, raising his trembling hands. 'Let's have a drink, brother!'

'Perfectly legal!' Tarantyev said delightedly. 'Let's have a drink.'

'And if it is a success, we can play the same trick in two years' time: we are within the law!'

'Quite!' Tarantyev declared with a nod of approval. 'Let's have another drink!'

'Let us!'

They drank.

'But what if Oblomov refuses and writes to the German?' Ivan Matveyitch remarked apprehensively. 'It's a bad look out then! We can't bring any complaint against him: she is a widow, not a spinster!'

'The idea of his writing! In two years' time, perhaps!' Tarantyev said. 'And if he refuses, I'll give it him. . . .'

'No, no, Heaven forbid! You would spoil it all; he would say we forced him into it, he might speak of blows – it would be a criminal charge. No, that won't do! But I'll tell you what: have something to eat and drink with him first; he likes the currant vodka. When he is a bit dizzy, you just wink to me and I will bring in the IOU. He will never look at the sum, but sign it as he did the contract then, and afterwards, when it has been witnessed at a stockbroker's, it won't be any use his protesting. A gentleman like him will be ashamed to confess he signed it when he was drunk; it will all be perfectly legal!'

'Perfectly!' Tarantyev repeated.

'Let his heirs have Oblomovka when the time comes!'

'Let them! Have a drink, brother.'

'The health of all fools!' Ivan Matveyitch said.

They drank.

IV

WE must now go a little way back to a time before Stolz's
visit on Oblomov's name-day and to a different place, far
from the Vyborg side. The reader will meet there people
he knows, about whom Stolz had not told Oblomov all
there was to tell, either for some reasons of his own or
because Oblomov did not ask all there was to ask – also
probably for reasons of *his* own.

One day Stolz was walking down a boulevard in Paris,
glancing absentmindedly at the passers-by and the shop
signboards, without resting his eyes on anything. He had
not had any letters from Russia for some time, neither
from Kiev, nor from Odessa, nor from Petersburg. He felt
dull and was on his way home after posting three more
letters. Suddenly his eyes fixed on something with amazement and then assumed their ordinary expression once
more. Two ladies left the boulevard to go into a shop.
'No, impossible; what an idea! I should have recognized
them! It can't be they.' He went up, however, to the shop
window and examined the ladies through the glass. 'I
can't make out anything, they are standing with their
backs to the window.' Stolz went into the shop and asked
for something. One of the ladies turned to the light; he
recognized Olga Ilyinsky – and did not know her! He
wanted to rush to her, but stopped to scrutinize her.
Good heavens, what a change! It was she and not she.
The features were hers, but she was pale, her eyes seemed
to have sunk a little, there was no childish smile on her
lips, no care-free *naïveté*. Some earnest or sorrowful
thought was hovering over her brows; her eyes said a
great deal that they had not known, had not said before.
She had not the old candid, calm, and serene expression;
a cloud of sorrow or uncertainty lay over her face.

He went up to her. She frowned slightly and looked at him in perplexity for a moment, then recognized him: her brows straightened and lay evenly, her eyes shone with the light of joy, not impulsive, but quiet and profound. A brother would be happy if a sister he loved had been as glad to see him.

'Good heavens! Is it really you?' she said in a voice that penetrated to his very soul and was joyful to the point of tenderness.

Her aunt turned round quickly and all three spoke at once. He reproached them for not having written to him; they made excuses. They had only come two days before and had been looking for him everywhere. At one address they were told that he had gone to Lyons and they did not know what to do.

'But how is it you came? And not a word to me!' he reproached them.

'We made up our minds so quickly that we didn't want to write to you: Olga meant to give you a surprise.'

He glanced at Olga: her face did not bear out her aunt's words. He looked at her still more closely, but she was impenetrable, inaccessible to his observation.

'What is the matter with her?' Stolz thought. 'I used to see through her at once, but now . . . what a change!'

'How you have developed, Olga Sergeyevna! You have matured, grown up,' he said aloud. 'I don't recognize you. And it's not a year since we met. What have you been doing? What's been happening to you? Do tell me!'

'Oh . . . nothing special,' she said, examining some material.

'How is your singing?' Stolz asked, studying this new Olga and trying to read the play of expression he had never seen before in her face; but it flashed and disappeared like lightning.

'I haven't sung for a long time, two months or more,' she said carelessly.

'And how is Oblomov?' he asked suddenly. 'Is he alive? Does he write to you?'

At this point Olga might have given her secret away in spite of herself had not her aunt come to the rescue.

'Would you believe it,' she said, walking out of the shop, 'he used to come and see us every day and then suddenly disappeared! We prepared to go abroad; I sent a message to him, but was told he was ill and received no one; so we did not meet again.'

'You know nothing either?' Stolz asked Olga with concern.

Olga was examining through her lorgnette a carriage that was driving past.

'He really had fallen ill,' she said, looking with feigned attention at the carriage. 'Look, *ma tante*, I believe it's our travelling companions that have driven by!'

'No, you must account to me for my Ilya,' Stolz insisted. 'What have you done to him? Why haven't you brought him with you?'

'*Mais ma tante vient de dire*,' she replied.

'He is fearfully lazy,' her aunt observed, 'and so unsociable that as soon as three or four other guests arrived he went home. Just think, he booked a weekly seat at the opera for the season and did not hear half the operas!'

'He did not hear Rubini,' Olga added.

Stolz shook his head and sighed.

'How is it you decided to come? Is it for long? What made you do it so suddenly?' he asked.

'It's for her, on the doctor's advice,' the aunt said, nodding towards Olga. 'Petersburg was proving distinctly bad for her and we went away for the winter, only we haven't decided yet whether to spend it at Nice or in Switzerland.'

'Yes, you have changed a great deal,' Stolz said thoughtfully, looking into Olga's eyes.

The Ilyinskys spent six months in Paris; Stolz was their daily and only guide and companion. Olga was obviously recovering: her brooding gave way to calm and indifference, at any rate on the surface; what happened in her inner life, Heaven only knew. She gradually became as friendly with Stolz as before, though she no longer burst into a peal of childish, silvery laughter when he amused her, but merely smiled with restraint. Sometimes she seemed annoyed at not being able to refrain from laughter. He perceived at once that she was not to be amused any more: she often listened to some amusing sally on his part with a frown between her unevenly-lying eyebrows, looking at him in silence without a smile, as though she were impatient with him or reproached him for his lightness; or instead of answering his joke she would suddenly put him some serious question with a look of such insistence that he felt ashamed of his frivolous, empty talk. At times she seemed so weary of the empty chatter and scurry of everyday life that Stolz had suddenly to pass into a sphere which he seldom and reluctantly entered with women. How much thought, subtlety, intelligence, he had to spend simply so that Olga's deep, questioning eyes should grow serene and bright and cease from eagerly seeking something far away, apart from him! How uneasy he was when, because of a careless explanation on his part, her expression grew stern and dry, her eyebrows contracted, and a shadow of silent but profound vexation overspread her face! For the next two or three days he had need of the greatest intellectual subtlety, brilliance, and even slyness, of all his skill in managing women in order, little by little, to bring the dawn of serenity into Olga's face and the gentleness of reconciliation into her eyes and smile. Sometimes he returned home at night worn out by this struggle, and he was happy when he came out victorious.

'Good heavens, how she has matured! How this child has developed! Who was her teacher? Where did she take her lessons of life? From the baron? But he is so glib, there is nothing to be learned from his neat sentences! It couldn't have been from Ilya!'

He could not understand Olga, and when he ran to her again the next day he read her looks cautiously and with fear; he was often in difficulties and only his intelligence and knowledge of life helped him to deal with the questions, doubts, and demands that Olga's features expressed. With the lamp of experience in his hand he ventured into the labyrinth of her mind and character, discovering each day new facts, new qualities; he could not fathom what was in her heart and watched in wonder and alarm the way her mind asked for daily bread, and her soul never ceased begging for life and experience.

Olga's life was becoming part and parcel of Stolz's existence and activity: having surrounded Olga with flowers, books, music, and albums, Stolz, with the comfortable feeling that he had provided plenty of occupations for his friend, went to work or to examine some mines or some model farm, or into society to meet new or remarkable people; then he returned to her exhausted, to sit by her piano, resting at the sound of her voice. And suddenly he found in her face questions ready, in her eyes an obstinate request for an answer. And unconsciously, in spite of himself, he gradually began to lay before her what he had seen and why. Sometimes she expressed a wish to see and learn for herself what he had learned and seen. And he went over the same thing again: he went with her to examine a building or some place or a machine, to reconstruct some old event inscribed on stones or walls. He gradually and imperceptibly acquired the habit of thinking and feeling aloud in her presence; and one day he suddenly discovered, after a stern self-examination, that he was no longer alone in his life, and that this had begun on the very day he met Olga. Almost unconsciously, as though talking to himself, he discussed aloud in her presence the value of the treasure he had acquired and wondered both at her and at himself; then he carefully looked to see if there was still a question left in her eyes, if the glow of satisfied thought was reflected in her face, if her eyes followed him as a conqueror. If this was the case he went home with pride, with tremulous emotion, and secretly spent a large part of the night preparing for the next day. The dullest work he had to do did not seem to him dry, but merely inevitable: it entered deeper into the texture of his life; thoughts, observations, and events were not carelessly put away in silence into the archives of memory, but gave a brilliant colouring to every day that passed. What a warm glow spread over Olga's pale face when, without waiting for her eager, questioning look, he hastened, with fervour and energy, to throw out to her new supplies, new material! He was completely happy when her mind, with charming obedience, anxiously caught his every word, every glance; both looked keenly at each other – he at her to see if there were still a question left in her eyes and she at him to see if he had left anything unsaid or forgotten something, or, worst of all, if he had – Heaven forbid! – failed fully to develop his thought and kept from her some dark corner where she could not follow him. The more important and complicated the subject, the more thoroughly he introduced her to it, and the longer and more attentively her grateful gaze dwelt on him, growing warmer, deeper, and more affectionate.

'That child, Olga,' he thought in amazement, 'she is outgrowing me!'

He pondered over Olga as he had never pondered over anything.

In the spring they all went to Switzerland. While still in Paris Stolz had decided that he could no longer live without Olga. Having settled this question he began asking himself if Olga could live without him. This question was not so easy to answer. He approached it slowly, warily, carefully, now fumbling his way, now advancing boldly, and often thought he had nearly achieved his end: one unmistakable sign, a look, a word, boredom or joy, one more detail – a hardly perceptible movement of Olga's eyebrows, a sigh – and the mystery would be solved to-morrow: he was loved! He read in her face that she had childish confidence in him; she sometimes looked at him as she never looked at anyone, as she might have looked at her mother if she had one. She regarded the fact that he gave her all his leisure and spent days trying to please her, not as a favour, as a flattering gift of love or affectionate kindness, but simply as a duty, as though he were her brother, her father, or her husband: and that is a great deal, it is everything. Her every word and gesture, when she was with him, was so free and candid that it revealed his unquestionable authority over her. He knew he had such authority: she confirmed it every moment, she said she believed him alone and could blindly trust him in life as she could trust no one else. He was proud of it, of course, but then this kind of pride might be felt by an elderly, intelligent, and experienced uncle, or even by the baron had he been a man of intelligence and character. Was it the authority of love – that was the question! Was there the seductive deception of love about it, that flattering blindness through which a woman may be so cruelly mistaken and yet be happy in her mistake?

No, she submitted to him so consciously. It is true her eyes shone when he developed some idea or laid bare his soul to her; she bathed him in the radiance of her gaze, but one could always see why she did it, and sometimes she herself told him the reason. But in love merit is acquired so blindly, so unconsciously, and it is precisely in this blindness and unconsciousness that happiness lies. If she was offended, one could see at once what offended her. He had never surprised a sudden flush, a joy bordering on fear, a languishing or an ardent glance; the only thing that was in the least like it was the look of pain in her face when he said he would soon be going to Italy; but no sooner had the rare and precious moment set his heart throbbing than everything was shrouded in a mist once more: she said naïvely and openly, 'What a pity I can't go there with you, I should simply love to! But you will tell me all about it and do it so well that I shall feel as though I had been there myself!'

The charm was destroyed by this clearly expressed desire concealed from no one, and by this commonplace, conventional praise of his skill in narrative. He would be collecting the tiniest details, weaving a fine network as of

lace, and when just a finishing touch was needed to complete it. . . . Suddenly she would, again all at once, be
calm, even simple, sometimes actually cold. She would be
sitting at her needlework, listening to him in silence, raising her head from time to time and glancing at him in
such a questioning, interested, matter-of-fact way that
more than once he threw down the book in vexation or
stopped in the middle of explaining something, jumped
up and walked away. If he turned round he saw her eyes
following him with surprise: he would feel ashamed, come
back and invent some excuse. She listened to it so simply
and believed it. She had no doubts, no mischievous smile.
'Does she love me or not?' he kept asking himself. 'If she
does, why is she so reserved, so cautious? If she does not,
why is she so obedient, so anxious to please me?' He went
from Paris for a week to London and came to tell her
about it on the very day he was leaving, without any
warning. If she were suddenly alarmed, changed colour, it
would be the end of it, the secret would be solved, he
would be happy! But she pressed his hand warmly and
was grieved: he was in despair.

'I shall be awfully dull without you,' she said. 'I could
cry, I feel like an orphan. *Ma tante*, look, Andrey Ivanitch
is going away!' she added plaintively.

He was utterly defeated.

'Turning to her aunt! That's the last straw,' he
thought. 'I see that she is sorry I am going, that she loves
me, perhaps . . . but that kind of love can be bought like
goods on the market at the cost of so much time, attention, and courtesy. . . . I won't come back,' he thought
sullenly. 'Olga, that child, if you please! She used to be at
my beck and call. What is the matter with her?'

He sank into deep thought.

What was the matter with her? There was a trifle he
did not know – that she had loved and had, so far as she
was capable of it, passed through the period of girlish lack of
self-control, sudden blushes, badly-concealed heartache,
and the first ardour of love with its feverish symptoms.

Had he known this he could, perhaps, have solved the secret of whether she loved him, or would, at any rate, have understood why it was so difficult to guess what was passing within her.

In Switzerland they went to every place where tourists go, but they preferred to stay in quiet, little-frequented spots. They, or, at any rate, Stolz, were so occupied with their own affairs that they wearied of travelling, and it was of secondary importance to them. He followed her up the mountains, looked at precipices and waterfalls, and she was in the foreground of every picture. He would walk after her up some narrow path while her aunt remained in the carriage below; he keenly watched in secret how she would stop and draw breath when she had reached the top of the hill and how she would look at him – at him, certainly, and first of all: he was certain of that by now. It would have all been very nice: his heart felt warm and light, but then she would suddenly glance around her and, spell-bound, lose herself in dreamy contemplation – and he would not exist for her any longer. If he stirred or said a word, and reminded her of himself, she was frightened and sometimes cried out: it was obvious she had forgotten whether he were far or near or, indeed, whether he were in the world at all. But afterwards, at home, at the window, or on the balcony, she would speak to him alone at length, sorting out her impressions until she had put them all into words; she spoke warmly and excitedly, stopping sometimes in search of a word, rapidly seizing some expression he suggested, and giving him a quick, grateful look for his help. Or she would sink into a big arm-chair, pale and tired, and only her eager, never-weary eyes would tell him that she wanted to listen to him.

She listened, without moving or saying a word, and never missed a single point. He stopped, but she still listened, her eyes still questioned him, and in answer to this mute challenge he went on talking with fresh force, fresh inspiration. It would have all been very nice: it was warm

and light, and his heart was beating; that meant her life
was here, she needed nothing more: he was her light, her
fire, her reason. But she would suddenly get up, tired,
and the eyes that had just been so questioning would ask
him to go away, or she would grow hungry and eat with
such an appetite. . . .

All this would have been excellent: he was not a
dreamer; he wanted violent passion no more than Oblomov, though for different reasons. And yet he did wish
that before flowing quietly into its even stream their feeling should surge up hotly at the source, and they should
drink their fill of it and so know all the rest of their lives
where this spring of happiness flowed from. . . . 'Does she
love me or not?' he asked himself anxiously, almost in
bloody sweat, almost in tears. This question absorbed him
more and more, spreading like flame, paralysing his intentions: it was the one essential question, no longer of love,
but of life. There was no room in his soul for anything
else now. It seemed as though during these six months he
had fallen prey to all the agonies and tortures of love from
which he had so skilfully preserved himself in his relations with women. He felt that even his strong constitution would give way if this strain on his mind, his will, his
nerves went on for many months more. He understood
something to which so far he had been a stranger – how
one's powers are wasted by this secret struggle of the soul
with passion and how bloodless but incurable wounds are
dealt to the heart, making one cry out with pain and lose
one's hold on life. He lost some of his proud confidence
in his own powers; he no longer joked lightly when he
heard of people going out of their mind or pining away
for various reasons . . . for love, among other things. He
felt frightened. 'No, I will put an end to it,' he said. 'I
will look into her soul as I used to and to-morrow I shall
either be happy or go away! I can't stand it,' he added,
looking at himself in the glass. 'I am not fit to be seen.
Enough!' He went straight to his purpose – that is, to
Olga.

And what about Olga? Had she not noticed his state or had she no feeling for him? She could not have failed to notice it: women less subtle than she was can feel the difference between friendly devotion and kindliness and the tender expression of another feeling. One could not suspect her of coquetry, for she had a correct instinctive sense of true, genuine morality. She was above that vulgar weakness. The only possible alternative is to suppose that apart from any practical design she liked the continual, ardent, and intelligent devotion of a man like Stolz; of course she liked it; this devotion healed her wounded pride and gradually reinstated her on the pedestal from which she had fallen; her self-respect gradually revived. But did she think what the end of this devotion was bound to be? It could not for ever take the form of a continual combat between Stolz's searching mind and her obstinate silence. Did she foresee that his struggle would not be in vain, that he would win the battle on which he had spent so much will and determination? Was he spending this fire and brilliance for nothing? Would the image of Oblomov and her early love fade in its rays? She understood nothing of this, it was all vague to her, and she struggled desperately with these questions and with herself, not knowing how to escape from this confusion. She could not remain in a state of indecision: some day this mute conflict of hidden feelings would give way to words – what answer would she then make about her past, what name would she give to it and to her feeling for Stolz? If she loved Stolz, what was that first love? Coquetry, frivolity . . . or worse? She flushed crimson and turned hot with shame at this thought. She could not accuse herself of that. But if that was her first pure love, what was her attitude to Stolz? Was it play, deception, subtle calculation to entice him into marriage and thus cover up all traces of her frivolous conduct? . . . She turned cold and pale at the thought. And if it was not play or deception or calculation, then . . . was it love again? She felt completely puzzled: a second love – seven or eight months after the

first! Who would believe her? How could she mention it
without causing surprise . . . perhaps contempt! She dared
not think of it, she had no right! She ransacked her memory, but found no information about a second love. She
appealed to the opinion of various aunts, old maids, persons of intelligence, writers, 'authorities on love' – and on
all sides she heard the implacable verdict: 'A woman loves
truly but once.' Oblomov, too, gave that verdict. She
recalled Sonitchka and wondered what she would have
said of a second love, but visitors from Russia had said
that her friend was already at her third. . . . No, she had
no love for Stolz and could not have! She had loved
Oblomov and that love had died, the flower of life had
faded for ever! She had only friendship for Stolz, based
upon his brilliant qualities and his friendship for her, his
attention, his confidence. . . . Thus she banished the
thought of love, or even of the possibility of love for her
old friend.

This was the reason why Stolz could not catch in her
face and words either any sign of positive indifference or
a momentary glimpse of any feeling which in the least
exceeded warm, affectionate, but ordinary friendship.
There was only one way in which she could have ended it:
as soon as she noticed that Stolz was beginning to love her
she ought to have made haste to go away and so left his
love with nothing to feed upon and grow. But she had lost
the moment: it had passed long ago; she ought to have
foreseen that his feeling would develop into passion;
though, indeed, he was not an Oblomov, and she could
not have escaped from him. And even had it been physically possible, it would have been morally impossible for
her to go away. At first she merely enjoyed the privileges
of their old friendship and found in Stolz, as before,
either a playful, witty, and ironical companion or a deep
and profound observer of life – of all that happened, that
occupied them or merely flitted by. But the oftener they
met, the more intimate they grew spiritually and the more
active his part became: from observing events he imper-

ceptibly passed to explaining them to her and being her
guide.

Imperceptibly he had become her reason and conscience, and this gave rise to new rights, to new secret
bonds that bound the whole of Olga's life, except one
sacred corner which she carefully hid from his judgment
and observation. She had accepted his moral guardianship
of her heart and mind and saw that she had in her turn
acquired an influence over him. They had exchanged
rights; somehow, silently and without observing it, she
had allowed this to happen. How could she now suddenly
take it all back? . . . And, besides, there was in it all so
much . . . interest . . . pleasure, variety . . . life. . . . What
would she do if she were suddenly deprived of it? And
when the idea of running away occurred to her, it was too
late, she no longer had the strength. Each day she passed
away from him, every thought she failed to confide in him
and share with him, lost its colour and significance. 'Oh
dear! If I could only be his sister!' she thought. 'What
happiness it would be to have permanent rights over a
man like that, not only over his mind but his heart as
well, to enjoy his presence openly and legitimately, without having to pay for it by heavy sacrifices, misery, and
confessions of a wretched past! And now, what am I? If he
goes away I have no right to keep him and ought, indeed,
to wish for our parting; and if I do retain him, what shall
I say to him? What right have I to wish to see him and
hear him every minute? . . . Because I am dull, because I
feel wretched, because he teaches me, amuses me, is useful to me, and I like being with him. . . . This is a reason,
of course, but not a right. And what do I give him in
exchange? The right to admire me disinterestedly without
daring to think of his love being returned when so many
other women would have been only too happy. . . .' She
suffered, trying to find a way out of these dilemmas, and
saw no end before her, no decision. The future held only
the fear of his disappointment and of parting from him
for ever. Sometimes she thought of telling him everything

so as to end at one blow both his struggle and her own, but her breath failed her at the very idea. She felt pained, ashamed. The strange thing was that since she had been inseparable from Stolz and he had taken possession of her life she had ceased to respect her past and began, indeed, to be ashamed of it. Had the baron or somebody else heard about it she would, of course, have been confused, and felt awkward, but she would not have suffered so much as she was suffering now at the thought that Stolz would learn of it. She pictured with horror what his expression would be, how he would look at her, what he would say, what he would think afterwards. She would suddenly seem to him so shallow, weak, insignificant. No, no, not for anything! She began watching herself and discovered with horror that she was ashamed not only of her love affair, but also of its hero. She was consumed with remorse for her ingratitude to her former lover for his profound devotion. She might, perhaps, have grown used to her shame, have put up with it – one can grow used to anything! – had her friendship for Stolz been free from any interested desires and thoughts. But even if she stifled the sly and insidious whisper of her heart she could not control the flights of her imagination: the radiant image of this new love often appeared before her eyes against her will; the dream of splendid happiness on the wide arena of a many-sided life with all its depths, sorrows, and delights – of happiness with Stolz and not in drowsy indolence with Oblomov – grew more and more seductive. It was then she shed tears over her past and could not wash it away. She recovered from her dreams and ensconced herself more carefully than ever behind that impenetrable wall of silence and friendly indifference which so tortured Stolz. Then she would forget herself, and once more, disinterestedly delighted with her friend's company, be charming, trustful, and sweet until the illicit dream of happiness to which she had forfeited the right would again remind her that the future was lost for her, that rosy dreams were over and the flower of life had withered.

Probably with years, she would have grown reconciled to her position and, like all old maids, hoped for nothing in the future; she would have sunk into cold apathy or gone in for 'philanthropy'; but suddenly her illicit dream assumed a more menacing shape when, from some words which had escaped Stolz, she clearly saw she had lost him as a friend and won him as a passionate lover. Friendship was sunk in love. She was pale on the morning when she discovered it, she did not go out all day; she was agitated, both with fear and joy; she struggled with herself, thought of what she was to do now, what her duty was – and could arrive at no conclusion. She merely cursed herself for not having overcome her shame at first and told Stolz earlier of her past: now she had to overcome terror as well. She had desperate moments when her heart felt so sore, so full of tears, that she wanted to rush to him and tell him of her past love, not in words, but so that he could see from her sobs, her faintness, her despair, the price she was paying for it. But she had not the strength: what was she to do? Or should she act as other women did in such cases? Sonitchka, for instance, told her betrothed about the lieutenant, that she had made fun of him, that he was a mere boy, that she purposely kept him waiting out in the frost till she came out to go to her carriage, and so on.

Sonitchka would not have hesitated to say about Oblomov that she had merely played with him for a joke, he was so ridiculous, one could not possibly love 'such a sack of flour' – it was quite incredible. But although Sonitchka's husband and many others might justify such conduct, Stolz would not. Olga might put it in a better light by saying that she merely wanted to draw Oblomov 'out of the abyss' and so had recourse to friendly coquetry . . . so as to revive a dying man and then leave him. But this would have been too forced, too elaborate, and, in any case, false. . . . No, no, there was no salvation! 'Oh dear, what an *impasse* I am in!' she said to herself in agony. 'To tell him! . . . Oh, no! I don't want him ever to know about

it, not for years! But not to tell him is as bad as stealing.
It's like deceiving him, trying to make up to him. Help
me, O God! . . .' But there was no help. Much as she
enjoyed Stolz's presence she would have preferred at
times not to meet him again, not to darken his serene and
rational existence by a passion which she could not return,
but to pass through his life as a hardly perceptible shadow. She would grieve for her unhappy love, weep over
her past, bury her soul, her memory of him, and then. . . .
Then, perhaps, she would make 'a decent match,' as many
do, and become a good, wise, and solicitous wife and
mother, dismiss her past as a girlish dream, and, instead
of living, would merely endure life. That is what all
women do! But then it was not a question of her alone,
another person was concerned and that other rested his
best and ultimate hopes in life upon her. 'Why did I . . .
love?' she asked herself miserably, recalling that morning
in the park when Oblomov wanted to run away and she
had thought that her book of life would close for ever if
he did. She had so boldly and easily solved the problem of
love, of life, everything had seemed so clear to her – and
now all was entangled in a hopeless knot! She had been
too clever, she had thought it was enough to look at things
simply, to go straight forward, and life would obediently
spread itself out like a carpet at her feet – and here she
was! She could not even put the blame on anyone: she
alone was the criminal!

Without suspecting what Stolz had come for, Olga
light-heartedly rose from the sofa, put down her book,
and walked to meet him.

'I am not disturbing you?' he asked, sitting down by
the window of her room that overlooked the lake. 'You
have been reading?'

'No, I had stopped: it is getting dark. I was expecting
you!' she said with gentle and trustful friendliness.

'So much the better: I want to speak to you!' he
remarked seriously, drawing up another chair to the window for her.

She started and turned numb. Then she mechanically sank into the chair, and sat in misery with her head bent and her eyes cast down. She wanted to be a hundred miles away. At that moment her past flashed through her mind like lightning. 'It's a judgment! One cannot play with life as one plays with dolls,' some voice seemed to be saying; 'don't trifle with it: you will have to pay for it!' Both were silent for a few minutes. He was evidently collecting his thoughts. Olga glanced fearfully into his face that had grown thinner, his frowning brows, and compressed, resolute lips. 'Nemesis!' she thought with a shudder. Both seemed to be preparing for a duel.

'You guess, of course, what I want to speak of, Olga Sergeyevna?' he asked, looking at her questioningly.

He was sitting with his back to the wall so that his face was in shadow, while the light from the window fell straight upon her and he could read all that was in her mind.

'How can I know?' she answered softly.

Before this dangerous adversary she had none of the penetration, self-control, strength of will and character which she had always displayed with Oblomov. She understood that if she had so far succeeded in hiding from Stolz's keen gaze and fighting him successfully, she owed it not to her own power, as in her struggle with Oblomov, but solely to Stolz's reticence and obstinate silence. In the open field she was at a disadvantage and asked the question: 'How can I know?' merely to gain an inch of space and a moment of time so that the enemy could divulge more of his plan.

'You don't know?' he said ingenuously. 'Very well, I'll tell you. . . .'

'Oh, don't!' suddenly escaped her.

She seized his hand and looked at him as though begging for mercy.

'You see, I guessed that you knew!' he said. 'But why "don't"?' he added sadly afterwards.

She said nothing.

'If you had foreseen that I should declare myself some day, you must have known, of course, what answer you would give me?'

'I have foreseen it and have been wretched!' she said, leaning back in her chair and turning away from the light; she was calling the dusk to her aid so that he could not read the struggle of confusion and misery in her face.

'Wretched! It's a dreadful word,' he said, almost in a whisper. 'It is Dante's "abandon all hope!" I have nothing more to say: it's the end. But I thank you for it, anyway,' he added with a deep sigh. 'I have come out of the chaos and the dark and know, at any rate, what I am to do. My one salvation is to make haste and run away!'

He got up.

'No, for God's sake, no!' she said with alarm and entreaty, rushing to him and seizing him by the hand again. 'Have pity on me: what will become of me?'

He sat down and so did she.

'But I love you, Olga Sergeyevna!' he said, almost sternly. 'You have seen what has been happening to me in the last six months! What do you want, then: complete triumph? That I should waste away or go off my head? I humbly thank you!'

She changed colour.

'Go away, then!' she said with the dignity of suppressed sorrow and a profound injury she was unable to conceal.

'Forgive me, I am sorry!' he apologized. 'Here we have already quarrelled for nothing. I know you cannot wish it, but you cannot enter into my position and so you think it strange that my impulse should be to escape. A man sometimes unconsciously becomes an egoist.'

She shifted her position in the arm-chair as though she were uncomfortable, but said nothing.

'Well, suppose I did stay: what would come of it?' he went on. 'You will, of course, offer me your friendship, but then I have that as it is. I will go away, and in a year or two years' time I shall still have it. Friendship, Olga

Sergeyevna, is a good thing when it is love between a young man and a young woman or the remembrance of love between old people. But Heaven forbid that it should be friendship on one side and love on the other. I know you are not dull with me, but what is it like for me?'

'Yes, if so, go away, I won't keep you!' she whispered, hardly audibly.

'To stay,' he reflected aloud, 'to walk on a knife edge – nice sort of friendship!'

'And do you suppose it's better for me?' she retorted unexpectedly.

'And why should you mind?' he asked quickly. 'You . . . you don't love. . . .'

'I don't know, I swear I don't know! But if you . . . if my present life is in any way changed, what will become of me?' she added despondently, almost to herself.

'How am I to understand this? Explain, for Heaven's sake!' he said, drawing his chair nearer to her, puzzled by her words and by the heartfelt, genuine tone in which she uttered them.

He tried to make out her expression. She was silent. She was longing to reassure him, to take back the word 'wretched,' or to explain it differently from the way he had understood it, but she did not know how; she merely felt vaguely that they were both in a false position, oppressed by a fatal misunderstanding, which made them both miserable and that only he, or she with his help, could bring order and clarity into the past and the present. But to do so she would have to take the plunge, to tell him what had happened to her. How she longed for his verdict and how she feared it!

'I don't understand anything myself; I am more confused, more in the dark than you are!' she said.

'Look here, do you trust me?' he asked, taking her hand.

'Utterly, as a mother – you know it,' she answered weakly.

'Tell me, then, what has happened to you since we

parted. I cannot make you out, and in the old days I could read your thoughts from your face; it seems that is the only way for us to understand each other. Do you agree?'

'Yes, there is nothing for it . . . we must end it some-how . . .' she said, wretched at the inevitable confession. 'Nemesis! Nemesis!' she thought, bowing her head.

She looked down and said nothing. A wave of terror passed through him at her simple words, and still more at her silence.

'She is suffering! Good God, what could have hap-pened to her?' he thought, turning cold and feeling that his arms and legs were trembling. He imagined something very dreadful. She was still silent, evidently struggling with herself.

'And so . . . Olga Sergeyevna . . .' he urged her.

She said nothing and made a nervous movement he could not make out in the dark; he only heard the sudden rustle of her silk dress.

'I am plucking up my courage,' she said at last. 'If you only knew how hard it is!' she added, turning away and trying to control herself.

She wished Stolz could learn it all, not from her but by some miracle. Fortunately it had grown darker and her face was now in the shadow; her voice alone could betray her, and she could not bring herself to speak, as though unable to decide on which note to begin.

'Oh dear, how guilty I must be if I feel so ashamed, so wretched!' she thought miserably.

And such a short time ago she had managed her own life and another's so confidently and was so strong, so intelligent! And now it was her turn to tremble like a little girl! Shame for her past, wounded vanity, and her false position in the present tortured her. . . . It was unendur-able!

'I will help you . . . you . . . have loved?' Stolz could hardly bring himself to say it – his own words hurt him so much.

She confirmed it by her silence. He felt a breath of terror again.

'Who was it? It isn't a secret?' he asked, trying to speak firmly, but feeling that his lips were trembling.

But it was still worse for her. She would have liked to mention some other name, to invent some other story. She hesitated for a moment, but there was nothing for it: like a person jumping off a steep bank or rushing into the flames at a moment of extreme danger, she suddenly said: 'Oblomov!'

He was dumbfounded. There was a two minutes' silence.

'Oblomov!' he repeated in amazement. 'It's impossible!' he added confidently. 'There's some mistake: you could not have understood your own feelings or Oblomov or love.'

She said nothing.

'It was not love, it was something else, I tell you!' he insisted.

'Yes, I flirted with him, led him by the nose, made him miserable . . . and then, in your opinion, I started upon you!' she said, controlling herself; tears of resentment trembled in her voice once more.

'Dear Olga Sergeyevna, don't be angry, don't speak like that: it isn't like you. You know I don't think anything of the sort. But I can't get it into my head, I can't understand how Oblomov. . . .'

'But he is worthy of your friendship; you can't speak highly enough of him; why shouldn't he be worthy of love?' she said in self-defence.

'I know that love is less exacting than friendship,' he said, 'that it is often blind; people are loved not for their merits – all that is true. But something else is needed for love, a trifle, maybe, that one cannot name or define – and this is precisely what is lacking in my incomparable but clumsy Ilya. That is why I am surprised. Look here,' he went on eagerly, 'we shall never get to the bottom of it or understand each other like this. Don't be ashamed of details, don't spare yourself for half an hour, tell me everything and I will tell you what happened to you and perhaps what is going to happen. . . . I keep fancying that there is . . . some mistake about it. . . . Oh, if only it were true,' he added with animation, 'if it were Oblomov and no one else! Oblomov! Don't you see that means that you don't belong to the past, to love, that you are free. . . . Tell me, tell me quick!' he concluded calmly, almost cheerfully.

'Yes, for Heaven's sake!' she answered trustfully, glad that some of her chains had been taken off her. 'Left to myself, I am simply going mad. If you only knew how wretched I am! I don't know if I am to blame, if I ought to be ashamed of the past or regret it, to hope for the future or to despair. . . . You have been talking of your sufferings, but you did not suspect mine. Hear me out, only not with your intellect – I am afraid of it: better with your heart; it will remember, perhaps, that I have no mother, that I was like one lost in the wood . . .' she added in a low and toneless voice. 'No,' she hastily corrected herself a moment later, 'don't spare me. If it was love, you'd better . . . go away . . .' she stopped for a moment, 'and come back later, when you will again feel nothing but friendship for me. But if it was coquetry, frivolousness, punish me, flee from me, and forget me! Listen.'

In answer, he warmly pressed both her hands.

Olga began her confession, long and detailed. Carefully, word for word, she transferred from her mind to his all that had so long been torturing her and causing her to blush, although it had once made her happy and been tenderly remembered by her until she fell into the depths of doubt and sorrow.

She told of their walks, of the park, of her hopes, of Oblomov's regeneration and fall, of the lilac branch and even of the kiss. She only passed in silence over the sultry evening in the garden – probably because she had not yet decided what had come over her then.

At first only her confused whisper could be heard, but as she went on her voice grew clearer and less restrained; from a whisper it rose to an undertone and then to full, deep notes. She finished as calmly as though she were telling somebody else's story. It was as though a curtain were being raised and the past, which so far she had been afraid to consider, were unfolding itself before her. A great deal became clear to her as she spoke, and she would have looked boldly at her listener if it had not been dark. She finished and waited for his verdict. But dead silence was his answer. 'What is he thinking?' She could not hear a word, not a movement, not even his breath, as though there were no one in the room. This dumbness made her doubtful again. The silence lasted. What did it mean? What verdict was the kindest, the wisest judge in the whole world preparing for her? All the rest would condemn her without pity, she would have chosen him alone to be her counsel for defence . . . he would understand it all, weigh it, and settle the case in her favour better than she herself could have done! But he was silent: could she have lost her case? She felt frightened once more. . . .

The door was opened and two candles brought in by the maid lighted up their corner.

She threw a timid but eager, questioning glance at him. He had crossed his arms and was looking at her so kindly, so frankly, enjoying her confusion. She sighed with relief and nearly cried. Pity for herself and confidence in him instantly returned to her. She was happy as a child that has been forgiven, reassured, and petted.

'Is that all?' he asked softly.

'Yes!' she answered.

'And his letter?'

She took the letter out of her case and gave it him. He moved nearer to the candle, read the letter and put it down on the table. His eyes were again turned to her with an expression she had not seen in them for a long time. The old self-confident, slightly ironical and infinitely kind friend who used to spoil her was standing before her.

There was not a shadow of doubt or suffering in his face. He took both her hands, kissed them in turn, and then pondered deeply. She also grew still and watched, open-eyed, the movement of thought in his face.

Suddenly he got up.

'Oh dear, had I known it was a question of Oblomov, I shouldn't have suffered so!' he said, looking at her kindly and trustfully as though she had not had that dreadful past. Her heart felt so light, so festive. She saw clearly that she had been ashamed for him to know, and he did not condemn her, did not run away! What did she care for the judgment of the world!

He was once more cheerful and self-possessed; but this was not enough for her. She saw she was acquitted, but, as the accused, she wanted to hear the verdict. He picked up his hat.

'Where are you off to?' she asked.

'You are excited – rest,' he said. 'We'll talk to-morrow.'

'You want me not to sleep all night!' she interrupted, pulling him back by the hand and making him sit down. 'You want to go without telling me what it . . . was, what I am now, what . . . is to become of me? Have pity on me, Andrey Ivanitch: who can tell me if you don't? Who will punish me if I deserve it, or . . . who will forgive me?' she added, giving him a glance of such tender affection that he threw down his hat and very nearly threw himself at her feet.

'Angel – allow me to say *my* angel,' he said – 'don't torment yourself for nothing: there is no occasion to con-demn or to acquit you. Indeed, I have nothing to add to your story. What doubts can you have? You want to know what it was, what name to give it? You have known it long ago. . . . Where is Oblomov's letter?' He picked up the letter from the table.

'Listen then!' and he read: ' "What you feel now is not real love, but only an expectation of it; it is merely an unconscious need of love which, for lack of proper fuel, burns with a false flame and, with women, finds expression in caressing a child, in loving another woman, or simply in tears and attacks of hysteria. . . . You have *made a mistake*," ' Stolz read, emphasizing the words, ' "the man before you is not the one you have been expecting and dreaming of. Wait, he will appear, and then you will come to yourself and will be vexed and ashamed of your mistake. . . ." You see how true it is!' he said. 'You really were vexed and ashamed of . . . your mistake. There is nothing to add to this. He was right and you did not believe him – this is all the wrong you have done. You ought to have parted at the time, but your beauty was too much for him . . . and you were touched by . . . his dove-like tenderness!' he added, with the faintest tinge of mockery.

'I did not believe him, I thought one's heart cannot be mistaken. . . .'

'Yes, it can: and fatally so sometimes! But with you it never went so far as the heart: it was vanity and imagination on one side and weakness on the other. . . . And you were afraid that there would be no other joy in your life, that that pale ray would light your existence and be followed by an eternal night. . . .'

'But my tears,' she asked, 'did they come from the heart when I wept? I did not deceive him, I was sincere. . . .'

'Good heavens, a woman will shed tears about anything. You say yourself you grieved for your bunch of lilac, your favourite seat in the park. . . . Add to that disappointed vanity, failure in the rôle of his saviour, a certain amount of habit . . . plenty of reasons for tears!'

'And our meetings, our walks, were a mistake too? You remember I have . . . been to his rooms,' she finished in confusion, and seemed anxious to efface her words herself. She was trying to accuse herself merely so that he should defend her the more warmly and she should be more fully justified in his eyes.

'One can see from what you have told me that during your last meetings you had nothing to talk about even.

Your so-called love hadn't enough material, it couldn't have gone on any farther. You had really parted before your separation and were faithful not to love but to the phantom of it, which you had yourself invented – that's the whole secret.'

'And the kiss?' she whispered, so low that he guessed rather than heard it.

'Oh, that's important,' he said with comic severity, 'for that you ought to go . . . without your pudding at dinner.' He was looking at her with more and more tenderness and affection.

'A joke is not a justification of such a "mistake"!' she replied severely, offended by his indifference and his careless tone. 'I would rather you had punished me by some harsh word, called my misdeed by its proper name. . . .'

'I should not have joked had it been somebody else instead of Ilya,' he said, defending himself, 'then your mistake might have ended in . . . disaster: but I know Oblomov. . . .'

'Another, never!' she interrupted him, flaring up. 'I've come to know him better than you do. . . .'

'There, you see!' he agreed.

'But if he had . . . changed, come to life, done what I wanted him to and . . . wouldn't I have loved him then? Would it have still been mistaken and false?' she said, so as to see the position from every point of view and not to have anything left dark and unexplained.

'That is, if another man had been in his place,' Stolz interrupted her, 'your relations would, no doubt, have grown into love, taken root, and then. . . . But that's another story and another hero, and it's nothing to do with us.'

She heaved a sigh as though she had thrown the last burden off her mind. Both were silent.

'Ah, what joy it is . . . to recover!' she said slowly, opening out as it were like a flower, and turned on him a look of such profound gratitude, such new, ardent affection that he fancied he saw in her glance the spark he had been vainly seeking for nearly a year. A tremor of joy ran through him.

'No, it is I who am recovering!' he said, pondering. 'Ah, if I could only have known that the hero of that love affair was Ilya! So much time has been lost, so much strength wasted! And why? What for?' he repeated, almost with vexation.

But he suddenly shook it off and came to himself after his painful brooding. His frown disappeared and his eyes were bright once more.

'But evidently it all had to be; and how reassured I feel now and . . . how happy!' he added delightedly.

'It's like a dream, as though nothing had happened!' she said thoughtfully, almost to herself, surprised at her sudden recovery. 'You have taken away not only the shame and remorse, but the pain and bitterness too, all of it. . . . How have you done it?' she asked softly. 'And will it all pass, this . . . mistake?'

'I should think it has passed already!' he said, looking at her for the first time with eyes of passion and not concealing it. 'All that has been, I mean.'

'And that which . . . will be . . . not the mistake . . . but the real thing?' she asked, without forming her sentence.

'It is written here,' he concluded, taking the letter again: ' "The man before you is not the one you have been expecting and dreaming of. Wait, he will appear and then you will come to yourself. . . ." And will fall in love, I will add, so much in love that not merely a year but a whole life will be too short for that love – only I do not know . . . with whom?' he finished, fixing his eyes on her.

She looked down and pursed up her lips, but her radiant gaze could not be hidden by the eyelids and her lips could not retain a smile. She glanced at him and laughed so whole-heartedly that tears came into her eyes.

'I have told you what has happened to you and even what is going to happen, Olga Sergeyevna,' he concluded, 'but you say nothing in reply to my question, which you did not let me finish.'

'But what can I say?' she said in confusion. 'And if I could, should I have the right to say what you so want me to and what . . . you deserve so much?' she added in a whisper, with a shy glance at him.

He fancied he saw again a spark of a new feeling in her glance and again he felt a thrill of happiness.

'Don't hurry,' he added, 'tell me what I deserve when your heart's mourning, the mourning of decorum, is over. This year has told me a thing or two already. But now decide only one question: am I to go or . . . to stay?'

'I say, you are flirting with me!' she said, with sudden gaiety.

'Oh, no!' he remarked. 'This is not the question I had asked before, it has another meaning now: if I stay . . . in what capacity will that be?'

She was suddenly confused.

'You see, I am not flirting!' he laughed, glad to have caught her. 'After to-night's conversation we shall have to treat each other differently: we are neither of us the same as yesterday.'

'I don't know . . .' she whispered, still more confused.

'Will you allow me to give you advice?'

'Tell me . . . I'll follow it blindly!' she said with almost passionate submissiveness.

'Marry me while you are waiting for *him* to come!'

'I daren't yet . . .' she whispered, burying her face in her hands, with happy emotion.

'Why don't you dare?' he asked, also in a whisper, drawing her head down towards him.

'But this past?' she whispered again, putting her head on his breast as though he were her mother.

He gently drew her hands away from her face, kissed her hair and enjoyed her confusion, looking with delight at the tears that came into her eyes and were absorbed by them again.

'It will wither like your lilac!' he concluded. 'You have learned your lesson: it is time to put it into practice. Life is beginning: give your future to me and don't think of anything – I answer for it all. Let us go to your aunt.'

Stolz went home late that night. 'I have found what I wanted!' he thought, looking with enraptured eyes at the trees, the sky, the lake, and even at the mist rising from the water. 'I've gained it at last! So many years of patience, of saving up my spiritual powers, of thirsting for love! How long I have waited – but now I have my reward: here it is, a man's utmost happiness!'

Happiness blotted out all the business side of his life – the office, his father's trap, the chamois-leather gloves, the greasy accounts. All that rose in his memory was his mother's fragrant room, Herz's *Variations*, the prince's gallery, the blue eyes, the powdered auburn hair; and a tender voice – Olga's voice – resounded through it all: in his mind he heard her singing. . . . 'Olga – my wife,' he whispered with a shudder of passion, 'everything is found, there is nothing more to seek, nowhere further to go!' And he walked home, not noticing his way in the dreamy intoxication of happiness.

Olga followed him for some time with her eyes, then she opened the window and for several minutes breathed the freshness of night; her agitation gradually subsided, her breast rose and fell evenly. She gazed at the lake, into the far distance, and sank into such deep and peaceful brooding that she might have been asleep. She wanted to catch what she was thinking and feeling, but she could not. Her thoughts flowed on evenly, like waves, her blood pulsed gently in her veins. She felt happy, but she could not say where her happiness began or ended and what it was. She wondered why she felt so calm, so peaceful, so serenely happy when . . . 'I am betrothed to him,' she whispered.

'I am betrothed,' a girl thinks with a happy tremor, when the moment that sheds a light over the whole of her life comes at last, lifting her to a height from which she looks down upon the dark path which but yesterday she trod alone and unnoticed.

Why, then, did Olga feel no tremor? She, too, had been treading a lonely, humble path, and had met at the cross-roads *him* who took her hand and brought her out, not into a brilliant, dazzling light, but, as it were, to a broad, overflowing river, a wide expanse of fields and friendly, smiling hills. Her eyes were not blinded by the brilliance, her heart did not stand still, her imagination did not catch fire. Her gaze rested with quiet joy on this overflow of life, on its green hills and boundless plains. A shudder did not run down her shoulders, her eyes did not glow with pride; only, when she moved her gaze from the fields and hills to him who gave her his hand, she felt a tear slowly gliding down her cheek.

She still sat there as though asleep – so peaceful was the dream of her happiness; she did not move, she hardly breathed. Sunk into forgetfulness, she seemed to be gaz-ing into the blue, gentle glimmer of a still, warm, and fragrant night. A vision of happiness spreading out its broad wings slowly floated over her like a cloud in the sky. . . . In that vision she did not see herself swathed in gauze and lace for a couple of hours and in everyday rags for the rest of her life. She did not dream of a festive board, of lights and merry shouts; she dreamed of a hap-piness so simple, so unadorned, that once more, without a tremor of pride, but with a deep and tender emotion, she whispered, 'I am betrothed to him!'

V

GOOD heavens, how dull and gloomy everything in Oblomov's flat seemed some eighteen months after his name-
day, when Stolz had unexpectedly come to dinner with
him! Ilya Ilyitch himself looked older; boredom seemed to
have eaten its way into his eyes like a kind of disease. He
would walk up and down the room, then lie down and
gaze at the ceiling; he would pick up a book from the
chiffonier, open it, read a few lines, yawn, and start
drumming his fingers on the table. Zahar had grown still
more clumsy and untidy; he had patches on his elbows; he
looked starved and miserable, as though he had not
enough food and sleep and had the work of three to do.
Oblomov's dressing-gown was worn out, and, carefully as
the holes in it were darned, it was giving way everywhere,
not only along the seams: it was high time he had a new
one. The blanket on the bed was also worn out and
patched in places; the window-curtains were faded and,
though clean, they looked like rags. Zahar brought an old
table-cloth, spread it over half the table near Oblomov,
then carefully, with his tongue between his teeth, brought
the tray with the dinner-things and a decanter of vodka,
put some bread on the table, and went away. The landlady's door opened and Agafya Matveyevna came in carrying a frying-pan with a sizzling omelette.

She, too, had changed terribly, not to her advantage.
She had grown thinner. She no longer had the smooth
round cheeks that turned neither red nor pale; her scanty
eyebrows were not shiny; her eyes were sunken. She was
dressed in an old cotton dress; her hands were sunburnt
or rough with work, with the heat or the water, or both.
Akulina was no longer in the house. Anissya worked in
the garden and the kitchen, and looked after the poultry,
scrubbed floors, and washed clothes; she could not

manage alone, and Agafya Matveyevna had no choice but
to work in the kitchen; she did but little pounding, gra-
ting, and sieving because coffee, cinnamon, and almonds
were bought in very small quantities, and she never even
thought about lace. She had more often nowadays to chop
onions, to grate horse-radish, and such-like relishes.
There was a look of profound dejection in her face. But it
was not about herself and the coffee she used to drink that
she sighed; she was sad, not because she had no opportunity to use her energy and do things on a big scale, to
pound cinnamon, to put vanilla in the sauce or boil thick
cream, but because it was a year since Ilya Ilyitch had
tasted these things, because his coffee was not bought in
many pounds at a time from the best grocers, but in ten
copecks' worth from the general shop close by; because
his cream came, not from the Finnish dairy, but from the
same general shop; because, instead of a juicy chop, she
was bringing him for lunch an omelette flavoured with
tough ham that had grown stale in that same shop.

What did it all mean? Why, this – that for over a year
the income from Oblomovka, duly sent by Stolz, went in
payment of the IOU given by Oblomov to his landlady.
Her brother's 'perfectly legal' piece of business had succeeded beyond expectation. At the first hint from Tarantyev about the scandal, Ilya Ilyitch flushed crimson and
was thrown into confusion; then they made peace, then all
three of them had a drink and Oblomov signed an IOU
dated four years hence; a month later Agafya Matveyevna
gave a similar IOU to her brother, not suspecting what
she was signing and why. Her brother said it was a document he needed for the house and told her to write:
'So-and-so (rank, name, and surname) has signed this
IOU in her own hand.'

She was only troubled at having so much to write and
asked her brother to make Vanya write instead: 'He writes
quite nicely now,' and she might muddle something. But
her brother insisted, and she signed in a big, slanting, and
uneven hand. Nothing was said any more about it. When

signing the IOU Oblomov partly comforted himself by the thought that Agafya Matveyevna's fatherless children would benefit by the money, and the next day, when he was sober, he recalled the whole incident with shame and tried to forget it; he avoided the landlady's brother, and if Tarantyev referred to the subject he threatened to leave the house at once and go to the country. Afterwards, when he received the money from the country, Ivan Matveyitch came to him and said that it would be better for him to start paying straight away out of his income, for then in three years the debt would be paid, while if he waited for the IOU to expire his estate would have to be sold by auction, since Oblomov had not the necessary cash and was not likely to have it. Oblomov realized what a tight corner he was in when everything that Stolz sent him went in payment of the debt and he had only a small sum left to live on. Ivan Matveyitch was in a hurry to complete the transaction with his debtor in a couple of years for fear some hitch might arise suddenly, and so Oblomov found himself in difficulties. At first he did not notice it very much owing to his habit of never knowing how much money he had in his pocket; but Ivan Matveyitch took it into his head to propose to a shopkeeper's daughter, hired a flat, and moved there! Agafya Matveyevna's housekeeping was suddenly curtailed: the sturgeon, the snow-white veal, the turkeys began to appear in another kitchen, in her brother's new flat. In the evenings it was lit up and her brother's future relatives, his colleagues, and Tarantyev assembled there; everything was transferred to it. Agafya Matveyevna and Anissya suddenly found themselves, to their surprise, with nothing to do and all their pots and pans empty. Agafya Matveyevna learned, for the first time, that all she had was the house, the kitchen-garden, and the chickens, and that neither cinnamon nor vanilla grew in her kitchen-garden; she saw that the shopkeepers gradually stopped smiling and bowing low to her and that the bows and smiles were now all for the fat, well-dressed new cook of her brother's.

Oblomov had given his landlady all the money her brother had left him to live on, and for three or four months she went on as before, desperately grinding pounds and pounds of coffee, pounding cinnamon, roasting veal and turkeys, and did it right up to the day on which she spent her last seventy copecks and came to tell him she had no money left. He turned over three times on the sofa at the news, then looked into his drawer: he had not any either. He began recalling what he had done with it and could remember nothing; he fumbled on the table for some coppers, asked Zahar, but Zahar had not the faintest notion. Agafya Matveyevna went to her brother and naïvely told him there was no money in the house.

'And what have you and your grand gentleman done with the thousand roubles I gave him to live on?' he asked. 'How am I to provide the money? You know I am going to be married: I can't keep two families and you and your gentleman must cut your coat according to your cloth.'

'Why do you throw him up at me?' she said. 'What has he done to you? There's no harm in him, he is a quiet gentleman. It wasn't I who beguiled him to my house, but you and Mihey Andreyitch.'

He gave her ten roubles and said he had nothing more. But after talking matters over with Tarantyev at the 'restaurant' he decided that it would not do to abandon his sister and Oblomov in this way; Stolz might hear of it and pounce upon them, see into the matter, and very likely upset their plans, so that they would not have time to collect the debt in spite of its all being 'perfectly legal': 'he is a German, so he must be a rogue!' He gave them an additional fifty roubles a month, intending to deduct that money from Oblomov's income three years hence; but he made it plain to his sister, calling God to witness, that he would not give another penny; he reckoned out what food they must buy, how to reduce their expenses, told her what dishes she was to cook and when, calculated what she could get for her chickens and cabbage, and decided that with all she had they could live in comfort and plenty.

For the first time in her life Agafya Matveyevna thought of something other than household matters, and wept, not because she was vexed with Akulina for breaking crockery, not because her brother had scolded her for underdone fish; for the first time she was faced with dire privation, terrible not to her but to Ilya Ilyitch. 'How can he, a gentleman,' she reflected, 'eat buttered turnips instead of asparagus, mutton instead of woodcock, salted cod or brawn from the shop instead of the best trout and amber-coloured sturgeon? . . .' Horrible! She did not think it out to the end but dressed hurriedly, hired a cab, and went to her husband's relatives – not as at Easter or Christmas to a family dinner, but in the early morning, in trouble, to tell them a strange tale, to ask what she was to do and to get some money from them. They had a lot: they would be sure to give her some when they knew it was for Ilya Ilyitch. Had it been for her own tea or coffee, for her children's clothes or shoes or such-like luxuries, she would not have breathed a word about it, but this was an urgent, a desperate need: to buy game and asparagus for Ilya Ilyitch, the French peas that he liked. . . . But her relatives were surprised and did not give her any money; they said, however, that if Ilya Ilyitch had any gold or even silver things or furs they could be pawned, and that there existed benefactors who would give him a third of their value, to be repaid when he received his money from the country. At any other time this practical lesson would have been lost upon Agafya Matveyevna and nothing could have made it plain to her brilliant mind, but now she understood it with the wisdom of the heart, considered it all, and weighed . . . the pearls she had received as a dowry. The following day Ilya Ilyitch, who suspected nothing, drank the currant vodka, followed by excellent smoked salmon, ate the giblets he liked and a fresh white woodcock. Agafya Matveyevna and the children had the servants' cabbage-soup and porridge, and it was only to keep Ilya Ilyitch company that she drank two cups of coffee. Soon after the pearls she took out of her chest her diamond brooch, then her silver, then her fur coat. . . . At last the money from the country came: Oblomov gave it all to her. She redeemed the pearls and paid the interest on the diamonds, the silver, and the fur, and once more cooked asparagus and game for him, and drank coffee with him for the sake of appearances. The pearls were pawned once more. From week to week, from day to day she struggled hard to make both ends meet, sold her shawl, sent her best dress to be sold and remained in a workaday, short-sleeved cotton dress, covering her neck on Sundays with an old worn-out kerchief.

This was why she had grown thin, why her eyes looked hollow, and why she brought Ilya Ilyitch his lunch herself. She actually had the courage to look cheerful when Oblomov told her that Tarantyev, Alexeyev, or Ivan Gerasimovitch would be coming to dinner the following day. The dinner was good and well served; she did not disgrace the host. But how much agitation, running about, begging the shopkeepers, sleepless nights and tears it cost her! How deeply she suddenly found herself plunged into life's anxieties! How well she came to know its happy and unhappy days! But she loved this life: in spite of all the bitterness of her tears and anxieties she would not have exchanged it for her former placid existence, when she had not known Oblomov and reigned with dignity among full saucepans, frying-pans, and pots hissing and bubbling on the fire and ruled over Akulina and the porter. She shuddered with horror if she suddenly thought of death, although death would put a speedy end to her never-drying tears, her strenuous days and sleepless nights.

After lunch Ilya Ilyitch heard Masha read French and sat in Agafya Matveyevna's room watching her mend Vanya's coat, which she turned a good ten times this way and that, constantly running, meanwhile, to the kitchen to have a look at the mutton roasting for dinner and to see if it was not time to make the fish soup.

'Why do you take so much trouble?' Oblomov said. 'Don't you bother!'

'But who is to see after things if I don't?' she said. 'I'll just put two patches here and we'll make the soup. What a naughty boy that Vanya is! Last week I mended his coat right through – and here he has torn it again! What are you laughing at?' She turned to Vanya, who was sitting by the table with only his shirt and knickers held up by one brace. 'Here, I will not mend it till the morning, and then you won't be able to run out of the gate. The boys must have torn it: you've been fighting – confess!'

'No, mother, it has torn itself,' Vanya said.

'Wipe your nose, can't you?' she observed, throwing a handkerchief to him.

Vanya snorted, but did not use the handkerchief.

'Wait till I get the money from the country, I will have two coats made for him,' Oblomov intervened. 'A blue jacket and a school uniform next year when he goes to the High School.'

'Oh, his old one will do yet,' Agafya Matveyevna said, 'the money will be needed for housekeeping. We'll lay in a store of salted meat, I'll make a lot of jam for you. . . . I must go and see if Anissya has brought the sour cream.' She got up to go.

'What have we for dinner to-day?' Oblomov said.

'Fish soup, roast mutton, and curd dumplings.'

Oblomov said nothing. Suddenly a carriage drove up, there was a knock at the gate, the dog began jumping and barking. Oblomov went to his room thinking someone had come to see the landlady: the butcher, the greengrocer, or some such person. Such visits were generally accompanied by requests for money, the landlady refused, the trades-men threatened her, she asked them to wait, they swore, doors banged, the gate banged, the dog barked and jumped desperately – in short, it was not pleasant. But this time a carriage had driven up. Butchers and green-grocers did not drive in carriages. Suddenly the landlady ran in to him in alarm.

'A visitor for you!' she said.

'Who is it? Tarantyev or Alexeyev?'

'No, no, the one who came to dinner on your name-day.'

'Stolz!' Oblomov said anxiously, looking round for means of escape. 'Good heavens! What will he say when he sees? . . . Tell him I have gone out!' he added hastily, and went to the landlady's room.

Anissya was running to meet the guest. Agafya Matveyevna had time to give her Oblomov's order. Stolz believed her and was merely surprised at his not being at home.

'Well, tell him I will be back in two hours and have dinner with him,' he said, and went to the public garden close by.

'He will come to dinner!' Anissya repeated in alarm.

'He will come to dinner!' Agafya Matveyevna repeated in dismay to Oblomov.

'You must cook another dinner,' he decided, after a pause.

She looked at him in terror. She had only fifty copecks left and it was still ten days to the first of the month, when her brother gave her the money. She could have nothing on credit.

'We shan't have time, Ilya Ilyitch,' she observed, timidly, 'let him have what there is. . . .'

'He can't eat it, Agafya Matveyevna: he can't bear fish soup, not even made of sturgeon, and he never touches mutton.'

'I might fetch some tongue from the sausage shop,' she said with sudden inspiration, 'it's close by.'

'Yes, that's good, you can do that; and order some vegetables, say, fresh beans. . . .'

'Beans are eighty copecks a pound.' She had on the tip of her tongue to say it, but she did not.

'Very well, I will,' she said, deciding to have cabbage instead of beans.

'Order a pound of Gruyère cheese,' he commanded, knowing nothing about Agafya Matveyevna's means, 'and that's all. I'll apologize and say we had not expected him.'

He walked to the door.

'And the wine?' he remembered suddenly.

She answered with another look of horror.

'You must send for some Laffitte,' he concluded coolly.

VI

Stolz arrived a couple of hours later.

'What is the matter with you? How changed you are! You look pale and puffy. Are you well?' Stolz asked.

'I am in a bad way, Andrey,' Oblomov said, embracing him, 'my left leg keeps getting numb.'

'How nasty your room looks!' Stolz said, looking round. 'And why don't you give up this dressing-gown? Why, it's all in patches!'

'Habit, Andrey; I am sorry to part from it.'

'And the bedspread, the curtains . . .' Stolz began, 'is that also habit? Are you loath to change these rags? My dear, can you really sleep in this bed? But what is the matter with you?'

Stolz looked intently at Oblomov, then again at the curtains and the bed.

'Nothing,' said Oblomov in confusion. 'You know I have never troubled much about my rooms. . . . Let's have dinner. Hey, Zahar, make haste and set the table! Well, and how are you? Are you here for long, and where do you come from?'

'Guess what I am doing and where I come from?' Stolz asked. 'I expect news from the world of the living does not reach you here?'

Oblomov looked at him with interest, waiting for him to speak.

'How is Olga?' he asked.

'Ah, you haven't forgotten! I thought you would forget.'

'No, Andrey, how could I forget her? That would be like forgetting that I had lived once, had been in paradise. . . . And now!' he sighed. 'But where is she?'

'On her estate, looking after it.'

'With her aunt?' Oblomov asked.

'And her husband.'

'She is married?' Oblomov asked, staring at Stolz.

'Why are you alarmed? Is it your memories?' Stolz asked softly, almost tenderly.

'Oh dear me, no!' Oblomov protested, coming to himself. 'I wasn't alarmed, but surprised; I don't know why it struck me so. Has she been married long? Is she happy? Tell me, for Heaven's sake! I feel you have taken a great weight off my mind! Though you assured me she had forgiven me . . . I felt uneasy, you know! Something seemed to be gnawing at me. . . . Dear Andrey, how grateful I am to you!'

He was so genuinely delighted that he could not sit still on his sofa and was almost jumping up. Stolz looked at him with pleasure and was rather touched.

'How good you are, Ilya!' he said. 'Your heart is worthy of her! I'll tell her everything.'

'No, no, don't tell,' Oblomov interrupted, 'she will think me unfeeling if she knows I was overjoyed to hear of her marriage.'

'But isn't joy a feeling, and an unselfish one too? You are only rejoicing at her happiness.'

'That's true, that's true!' Oblomov interrupted him. 'I don't know what I am talking about. . . . And who is he – who is the happy man? I forgot to ask.'

'Who?' Stolz repeated. 'How slow you are, Ilya!'

Oblomov suddenly stared open-eyed at his friend: his features seemed turned to stone for a moment and the colour left his face.

'Is it . . . you?' he asked.

'Alarmed again! What of?' Stolz asked, laughing.

'Don't joke, Andrey, tell me the truth!' Oblomov said with emotion.

'Honour bright, I am not joking. I have been married to Olga for over a year.'

Alarm gradually disappeared from Oblomov's face, giving room to peaceful thought; he did not raise his eyes, but presently his thoughtfulness was changed to a deep and quiet joy, and when at last he looked at Stolz his eyes were tender and full of tears.

'Dear Andrey!' Oblomov said, embracing him. 'Dear Olga . . . Sergeyevna,' he added, controlling his enthusiasm. 'God Himself has blessed you! Heavens, how happy I am! Tell her. . . .'

'I'll tell her that I know of no other Oblomov!' Stolz interrupted him, deeply moved.

'No, tell her, remind her that I came into her life to bring her out into the right path, that I bless our meeting and bless her in her new life! What if it had been some other man! . . .' he added in terror. 'And now,' he concluded gaily, 'I don't blush at the part I played, I don't feel guilty; a load has fallen off my soul; it's all clear now, and I am happy. Thanks be to God!'

He was once more almost jumping off the sofa in his delight, both laughing and crying.

'Zahar, champagne for dinner!' he called, forgetting he had not a penny.

'I'll tell Olga everything, everything!' Stolz said. 'It's no wonder she can't forget you. No, you were worthy of her: your heart is as deep as a well!'

Zahar's head peeped out of the door.

'Come here, sir!' he said, winking to his master.

'What is it?' Oblomov said impatiently. 'Go away!'

'Give me some money, please!' Zahar whispered.

Oblomov subsided suddenly.

'Well, never mind!' he whispered into the door. 'Say you had forgotten, that you hadn't time! Go! . . . No, come here!' he said aloud. 'Have you heard the news, Zahar? Congratulate Andrey Ivanitch: he is married!'

'Dear me! To think I should live to hear such good news! I congratulate you, Andrey Ivanitch, sir. God grant you years without number and children in plenty. This is a joy indeed!'

Zahar bowed, smiled, hissed and wheezed. Stolz took out a note and gave it him.

'Here, take it and buy yourself a coat,' Stolz said, 'you look like a beggar!'

'Whom have you married, sir?' asked Zahar, trying to catch Stolz's hands to kiss.

'Olga Sergeyevna – do you remember?' Oblomov said.

'The Ilyinsky young lady! Dear me! Such a nice young lady! I deserved the scolding you gave me then, Ilya Ilyitch, old dog that I am! I am sorry, I was to blame: I put it all down to you. It was I who told the Ilyinskys' servants about it and not Nikita! And it has, indeed, turned out to be a slander. Dear me! Heavens above us! . . .' he kept repeating, as he went out of the room.

'Olga invites you to the country, to stay at her estate; your love has cooled down, so there's no danger of your being jealous. Come with me!'

Oblomov sighed.

'No, Andrey,' he said, 'it isn't love or jealousy I am afraid of, but I will not go to you all the same.'

'What are you afraid of, then?'

'I am afraid of envying you: your happiness will be like a mirror in which I shall see all my bitter and wasted life; and you know I am not going to live any differently, I cannot.'

'Come, come, dear Ilya! You will, in spite of yourself, begin living the same life as those around you. You will keep accounts, look after your estate, read, listen to music. How her voice has improved! Do you remember *Casta diva*?'

Oblomov waved his hand to stop Stolz from reminding him.

'Do come!' Stolz insisted. 'It is her wish: she will not leave you alone. I may slacken, but not she. There is so much fire in her, so much vitality that she gives me a bad time now and again. The past will rise in your soul once more. You will recall the park, the lilac, and bestir yourself. . . .'

'No, Andrey, no, don't recall it, don't stir it up, for God's sake!' Oblomov interrupted him earnestly. 'It doesn't comfort me, it hurts me. Memories are a thing of the greatest beauty when they are memories of living happiness, but a bitter pain when they remind one of scarcely healed wounds. . . . Let us change the subject. Oh, I haven't thanked you for all the trouble you are taking about my affairs and Oblomovka. My friend, I cannot, it's beyond me; you must find my gratitude in your own heart, in your happiness – in Olga . . . Sergeyevna, and I . . . I . . . cannot! Forgive me for not having taken the work off your hands yet. But now it will soon be spring and I will certainly go to Oblomovka. . . .'

'And do you know what is happening at Oblomovka? You won't recognize it!' Stolz said. 'I haven't written to you because you don't answer letters. The bridge is built, the house last summer was ready but for the roof. But you must see about furnishing it to your own taste – I can't undertake that. A new steward, a man I know, is looking after the place! You have seen the accounts, haven't you?'

Oblomov said nothing.

'You haven't?' Stolz asked, looking at him. 'Where are they?'

'Wait, I'll find them after dinner; I must ask Zahar. . . .'

'Ach, Ilya, Ilya! One doesn't know whether to laugh or to cry.'

'We'll look for them after dinner. Let's have dinner!'

Stolz frowned as he sat down to the table. He remembered Oblomov's name-day: the oysters, the snipe, the pineapples; and now he saw a coarse table-cloth, cruet bottles stopped with paper instead of corks, forks with broken handles; two large pieces of black bread were put on their plates. Oblomov had fish soup and he had pearl barley broth and boiled chicken, followed by tough tongue and mutton. Red wine was served. Stolz poured himself out half a glass, tasted it, put the glass back on the table and did not touch it again. Ilya Ilyitch drank two glasses of currant vodka and greedily attacked the mutton.

'The wine is no good at all!' Stolz said.

'I am sorry, in the rush they haven't had time to go over to the other side,' Oblomov said. 'Here, would you like some currant vodka? It's excellent, try it, Andrey!' He poured out another glass for himself and drank it.

Stolz looked at him in amazement, but said nothing.

'Agafya Matveyevna distils it herself; she is an excellent woman!' said Oblomov, slightly drunk. 'I confess I don't know how I could live in the country without her: there's no one like her for housekeeping!'

Stolz listened to him with a slight frown.

'You think it's Anissya who does the cooking? No!' Oblomov went on. 'Anissya looks after the chickens, weeds the kitchen-garden, and sweeps the floors; Agafya Matveyevna does all this.'

Stolz did not eat either the mutton or the curd dumplings; he put down his fork and watched with what appetite Oblomov ate it all.

'You won't find me now wearing a shirt inside out,' Oblomov continued, sucking a bone with relish, 'she examines it all, sees everything – I haven't a single hole in my stockings. She does everything herself too. And how she makes coffee! You must have some after dinner.'

Stolz listened in silence with a disturbed expression.

'Now her brother has left us – he is getting married, so we have to keep house on a smaller scale now. But in the old days she had her hands full. She used to be flying all over the place from morning till night, to the market, to the shops. . . . I'll tell you what,' concluded Oblomov, whose tongue was not obeying him very well, 'if you gave me two or three thousand I wouldn't offer you tongue and mutton; I would give you a whole sturgeon, trout, the best fillet of beef. And Agafya Matveyevna would do wonders without any *chef* – yes!'

He drank another glass of vodka.

'Do have a drink, Andrey, please: it's splendid vodka! Olga Sergeyevna won't make any vodka like this for you,' he said, speaking thickly; 'she will sing *Casta diva*, but she can't make such vodka, or the chicken and mushroom pie! Such pies used to be baked only at Oblomovka in the old days, and now here! And it's a good thing it isn't a *chef*: there's no knowing what his hands would be like when he kneaded the pastry, and Agafya Matveyevna is neatness itself!'

Stolz listened attentively, not missing a word.

'And her hands used to be so white,' Oblomov went on, rather befogged with vodka. 'One might well have kissed them! Now they are rough because she does everything herself! She starches my shirts!' Oblomov said with feeling, almost tearfully. 'She does, indeed, I've seen it myself. Some men's wives don't look after them so well as she does after me, honour bright! An excellent woman, Agafya Matveyevna! Ah, Andrey, you had better move here with Olga Sergeyevna and hire a summer villa here: it would be so jolly! We would have tea in the wood, go to the Gunpowder Works on St. Ilya's Friday, and a cart with provisions and a *samovar* would follow us. We would spread a carpet on the grass there and lie down! Agafya Matveyevna would teach Olga Sergeyevna housekeeping, she really would. It's only now things have gone badly with us: her brother has moved; but if *we* had three or four thousand I would produce such turkeys for you. . . .'

'You receive five thousand from me!' Stolz said. 'What do you do with it?'

'And the debt?' Oblomov blurted out suddenly.

Stolz jumped up from his chair.

'Debt?' he repeated. 'What debt?'

And he looked at Oblomov like a stern teacher at a child trying to hide from him.

Oblomov subsided suddenly. Stolz sat down beside him on the sofa.

'To whom are you in debt?' he asked.

Oblomov sobered slightly and came to his senses.

'To no one, it wasn't true.'

'No, it's now you are lying, and clumsily too. What is it? What is the matter with you, Ilya? Ah, so that's the meaning of mutton and of sour wine! You have no money! But what do you spend it on?'

'It's true, I am in debt . . . a little, to my landlady for my board . . .' Oblomov said.

'For mutton and tongue! Ilya, tell me what is happening to you? What story is this – the landlady's brother has moved, things have gone badly in the house. . . . There's something queer about it. How much do you owe her?'

'Ten thousand on an IOU . . .' Oblomov whispered.

Stolz jumped up and sat down again.

'Ten thousand to your landlady for your board?' he repeated in horror.

'Yes, we used to spend a lot; I lived in very good style. . . . You remember, pineapples and peaches . . . so I got into debt,' Oblomov muttered. 'But what's the use of discussing it!'

Stolz did not answer. He was thinking. 'The landlady's brother has left, things have gone badly – and so they have: everything looks bare, dirty, poor! What sort of woman is his landlady? Oblomov praises her: she looks after him; he speaks of her warmly. . . .'

Suddenly Stolz changed colour, having caught a glimpse of the truth. He turned cold.

'Ilya! This woman. . . . What is she to you?' he asked. But Oblomov was dozing, with his head on the table.

'She robs him, she takes everything from him . . . it's the usual story, but he hasn't tumbled to it yet,' Stolz thought.

He got up and opened the door into the landlady's rooms so quickly that, seeing him, she dropped in alarm the spoon with which she had been stirring coffee.

'I should like to speak to you,' he said politely.

'Please step into the drawing-room, I'll come at once,' she said timidly.

Throwing the kerchief round her neck, she followed him into the drawing-room and sat down on the end of the sofa. She no longer possessed a shawl and tried to hide her arms under the kerchief.

'Has Ilya Ilyitch given you an IOU?' he asked.

'No . . .' she answered, with a dull look of surprise, 'he hasn't given me anything.'

'How is that?'

'I haven't seen any IOU,' she insisted, with the same dull surprise.

'An IOU!' Stolz repeated.

She thought a little.

'You had better speak to my brother,' she said. 'I haven't seen any IOU.'

'Is she a fool or a rogue?' Stolz wondered.

'But he owes you money, doesn't he?' he asked.

She looked at him dully, but suddenly a look of understanding and even anxiety came into her face. She recalled the pearls, the silver, and the fur coat she had pawned, and imagined that Stolz was referring to this debt, only she could not think how anyone could have found it out: she had not dropped a word about her secret, not only to Oblomov but even to Anissya, to whom she generally accounted for every penny.

'How much does he owe you?' Stolz asked anxiously.

'He doesn't owe me anything, not a penny!'

'She is hiding it from me, she is ashamed, the greedy creature, the shark,' he thought; 'but I'll track her out!'

'And the ten thousand?' he said.

'What ten thousand?' she asked in anxious surprise.

'Ilya Ilyitch owes you ten thousand on an IOU – yes or no?' he asked.

'He doesn't owe me anything. He did owe in Lent twelve and a half roubles to the butcher, but we paid it three weeks ago, and paid the dairywoman for the cream too – he has no debts.'

'Haven't you a document from him?'

She looked at him dully.

'You had better speak to my brother,' she answered. 'He lives in the next street, in Zamykalov's house, just along here; there's a beer-shop in the house.'

'No, please allow me to speak to you,' he said decisively. 'Ilya Ilyitch considers that he is in debt to you and not to your brother. . . .'

'He doesn't owe me anything,' she answered; 'and if I pawned silver, pearls, and fur, I did it for myself. I bought shoes for Masha and myself, stuff for Vanya's shirts, and I paid the greengrocer. But not a penny of it was spent on Ilya Ilyitch.'

He listened and, as he watched her, tried to grasp the meaning of her words. He alone, it seems, came near guessing Agafya Matveyevna's secret, and the look of superiority, almost of contempt, he cast at her during their conversation was involuntarily replaced by a look of interest and even of sympathy. In the pawning of the pearls and silver he read, vaguely and imperfectly, the secret of her sacrifices, but he could not make out whether they were made in a pure spirit of devotion or in the expectation of blessings to come. He did not know whether he ought to grieve or to rejoice for Ilya. It was obvious that he did not owe anything to her, and the debt was some fraudulent trick of her brother's, but a great deal more was coming to light. . . . What did this pawning her pearls and silver mean?

'So you have no claim against Ilya Ilyitch?' he asked.

'Please would you mind speaking to my brother,' she answered monotonously, 'he must be at home by now.'

'You say Ilya Ilyitch doesn't owe you anything?'

'Not a penny, God is my witness!' she swore, looking at the ikon and crossing herself.

'Will you confirm this before witnesses?'

'Before everyone! I would say it at confession. And if I pawned the pearls and the silver it was for my own expenses. . . .'

'Very good!' Stolz interrupted her. 'I will call on you to-morrow with two of my friends, and I hope you will not refuse to say the same thing in their presence.'

'You had better speak to my brother,' she repeated. 'I am not dressed as I should be. . . . I am always in the kitchen; it wouldn't be nice for strangers to see me: they would think ill of me. . . .'

'Don't you trouble about that; and I shall see your brother to-morrow after you have signed a paper. . . .'

'I have quite got out of the way of writing.'

'But there will be very little to write, just a couple of lines.'

'No, please spare me; let Vanya write it instead; he writes very well. . . .'

'No, don't refuse,' he insisted, 'if you don't sign the paper it will mean that Ilya Ilyitch owes you ten thousand.'

'No, he doesn't owe me anything, not a penny,' she repeated, 'as before God.'

'In that case you must sign the paper. Good-bye till to-morrow.'

'You had better call on my brother to-morrow . . .' she said, seeing him off, 'it's just here at the corner, in the next street.'

'No, and I beg you to say nothing to your brother till I come, or it will be very unpleasant for Ilya Ilyitch. . . .'

'Then I won't say anything,' she said obediently.

VII

ON the following day Agafya Matveyevna gave a written statement to Stolz saying that she had no claim of any kind against Oblomov. Stolz suddenly appeared before her brother with this paper. It was truly a thunderbolt for Ivan Matveyitch. He produced the IOU and pointed with the bent and shaking finger of his right hand to Oblomov's signature witnessed by a broker.

'It's the law!' he said. 'It's nothing to do with me: I merely watch over my sister's interests and I don't know what money Ilya Ilyitch had borrowed from her.'

'This will not be the end of it!' Stolz threatened him as he went away.

'It's a perfectly legal business and nothing to do with me,' Ivan Matveyitch said in self-defence, hiding his hands in his sleeves.

Next morning, as soon as he arrived at the office, a messenger came to say that the General requested his presence at once.

'The General?' all the clerks repeated in terror. 'What for? What is it? Does he want some case? Which one? Make haste, make haste! Arrange the papers in order, draw up the lists! What can it be?'

In the evening Ivan Matveyitch came to the 'restaurant' very much upset. Tarantyev had long been waiting for him.

'What is it, brother?' he asked impatiently.

'What!' Ivan Matveyitch said in a dull voice. 'What do you think?'

'Did he swear at you?'

'Swear!' Ivan Matveyitch mimicked him. 'I'd rather he had beaten me! And you are a nice one!' he reproached him. 'You never told me what that German was!'

'I did tell you he was a rogue!'

'Why, that's nothing – a rogue! We have seen plenty of them. Why didn't you tell me he had influence? He and the General are as intimate as you and I. As though I would have had anything to do with him had I known!'

'But it's perfectly legal!' Tarantyev remarked.

'Perfectly legal!' Ivan Matveyitch mimicked him again. 'You try and say it there: your tongue will stick to the roof of your mouth. Do you know what the General asked me?'

'What?' Tarantyev asked with interest.

' "Is it true that you and some scoundrel made Mr. Oblomov drunk and forced him to sign an IOU in your sister's name?" '

'He actually said, "and some scoundrel"?' Tarantyev asked.

'Yes, he did.'

'Who can that scoundrel be?' Tarantyev asked again.

Ivan Matveyitch looked at him.

'I suppose you don't know?' he said bitterly. 'Isn't it you?'

'How did you get me mixed up in it?'

'You must thank the German and your Oblomov. The German has sniffed it all out. . . .'

'Why, brother, you ought to have mentioned somebody else and said I wasn't there.'

'Indeed! And what sort of saint are you?'

'What did you answer, then, when the General asked: "Is it true that you and some scoundrel"? . . . Here was your chance to outwit him.'

'Outwit him, indeed. You try! His eyes are as green as green! I tried hard to say, "It's not true, Your Excellency, it's a slander, I know nothing about any Oblomov; it's all Tarantyev's doing . . ." but the words wouldn't come off my tongue; I merely fell at his feet.'

'Why, are they going to prosecute you, or what?' Tarantyev asked hoarsely. 'It has nothing to do with me, you know; you, of course. . . .'

'Nothing to do with you! What next! No, brother, if we have to pay for it, you will be the first: who was it persuaded Oblomov to drink? Who reviled and threatened him?'

'But you put me up to it!' Tarantyev said.

'Are you under age, may I ask? As for me, I know nothing whatever about the whole business.'

'That's disgraceful, brother! Think of all the money you have had through me, and I have only received three hundred roubles. . . .'

'Oh, you would like me to take the whole responsibility? You are too clever, my dear! No, I know nothing about it. My sister asked me to witness the IOU at a broker's, for she doesn't understand these things, being a woman – that's all. You and Zatyorty were the witnesses, so you are responsible.'

'You'd better go for your sister: she had no business to act against her brother,' Tarantyev said.

'My sister is a fool – what can I do with her?'

'What does she say?'

'What! She cries, but insists that Ilya Ilyitch doesn't owe her anything, and that's all about it – she hadn't given him any money.'

'But you have an IOU from her?' Tarantyev said. 'You won't lose your money.'

Ivan Matveyitch pulled out of his pocket his sister's IOU, tore it up and handed it to Tarantyev.

'Here, I'll make you a present of it, if you like,' he added. 'What can I take from her? The house and the kitchen-garden? It isn't worth a thousand: it's all falling to pieces. And, after all, I am not an infidel, I can't let her go begging with the children!'

'So they'll prosecute us?' Tarantyev asked timidly. 'We must try and get off lightly: I hope you will help me, brother!'

'Prosecute? Nothing of the kind! The General threatened to send us out of town, but the German interceded, he doesn't want to disgrace Oblomov.'

'Is that so, brother? Well, that is a relief! Let's have a drink!'

'Drink? Out of whose income? Yours, perhaps?'

'What about yours? I expect you've raked in some seven roubles to-day?'

'Wha-at! It's all up with my income. I haven't finished telling you what the General said.'

'Why, what was it?' Tarantyev asked, suddenly alarmed again.

'He told me to send in my resignation.'

'You don't say so!' Tarantyev brought out, staring at him. 'Well,' he concluded furiously, 'now I'll swear at Oblomov for all he is worth!'

'All you care for is abusing people!'

'Yes, I'll go for him, say what you like!' Tarantyev said. 'Though perhaps you are right and I had better wait; I'll tell you what I have thought of: listen, brother!'

'What is it now?' Ivan Matveyitch asked doubtfully.

'One can do a fine piece of business. Only it's a pity you aren't living there now. . . .'

'Why?'

'Why,' he said, looking at Ivan Matveyitch, 'you might keep an eye on your sister and Oblomov and see what pies they are baking there . . . and then produce witnesses! The German himself won't be able to do anything. You are a free-lance now: if you bring in a case against him, the law is on your side! I expect the German, too, will be in a funk and come to an agreement with you.'

'Well, perhaps I might!' Ivan Matveyitch answered thoughtfully. 'You are not bad at inventions, but you are no good for business, nor Zatyorty either. But I'll find a way. Wait a bit!' he said, banging his fist on the table. 'I'll give it them! I'll send my cook round to my sister's kitchen: she will make friends with Anissya and find things out, and then. . . . Let's have a drink, brother!'

'Let us!' Tarantyev repeated. 'And then I'll go for Oblomov!'

Stolz tried to take Oblomov with him to the country,

but Oblomov begged so earnestly to be left behind for only a month that Stolz had pity on him. Oblomov said he needed that month to settle his affairs, to give up the flat, and finish everything he had to do in Petersburg, so that he need not return there. Besides, he had to buy all the things he needed for his country house; finally, he wanted to find a good housekeeper, someone like Agafya Matveyevna; he did not despair, indeed, of persuading her to sell her house and move to the country, to a field of activity worthy of her – complicated housekeeping on a big scale.

'By the way, about your landlady,' Stolz interrupted him. 'I wanted to ask you, Ilya, what are your relations with her. . . .'

Oblomov flushed suddenly.

'What do you mean?' he asked hurriedly.

'You know very well,' Stolz remarked, 'or there would have been no reason for you to blush. Look here, Ilya, if warning can be of any use, I beg you in the name of our friendship to be careful. . . .'

'What of? What are you talking about?' Oblomov protested in confusion.

'You spoke of her with such heat that I am really beginning to think you. . . .'

'Love her, do you mean? What next!' Oblomov said, with a forced laugh.

'Well, it's still worse if there is nothing spiritual about it and it's only. . . .'

'Andrey! Have you ever known me for an immoral man?'

'Then why did you blush?'

'That you could have thought of such a thing.'

Stolz shook his head doubtfully.

'Mind you don't fall into the pit, Ilya. An uncultured woman, coarse life, a stifling atmosphere of crudeness and stupidity – ugh!'

Oblomov said nothing.

'Well, good-bye,' Stolz concluded. 'So I will tell Olga

we shall see you either at our house or at Oblomovka. Remember: she will not leave you in peace!'

'Certainly, certainly,' Oblomov answered confidently, 'and you may add that, if she allows me, I'll spend the winter with you.'

'That would be delightful!'

Stolz left the same day, and in the evening Tarantyev came to see Oblomov. He could not resist swearing at him thoroughly on Ivan Matveyitch's behalf. He had not considered, however, that in the Ilyinskys' society Oblomov had lost the habit of associating with people like himself and that his apathetic indulgence for rudeness and impudence had been replaced by disgust. This had been apparent when they met at Oblomov's summer villa, and would have shown itself again, but Tarantyev had visited him less often and came when other people were present, so that there had been no unpleasant encounters between them.

'How do you do, neighbour?' Tarantyev said malignantly, not giving Oblomov his hand.

'How do you do?' Oblomov answered coldly, looking out of the window.

'Well, have you said good-bye to your benefactor?'

'I have. What of it?'

'A fine sort of benefactor!' Tarantyev continued venomously.

'Oh, don't you like him?'

'I would like to hang him!' Tarantyev hissed with hatred.

'Indeed!'

'And you, too, on the same tree!'

'What for?'

'Because you should be honest: if you are in debt, you must pay and not try to wriggle out of it. What have you done now?'

'Look here, Mihey Andreyitch, please spare me your humbug; through laziness and carelessness I have listened to you for years: I thought you had just a little conscience, but you haven't. You and that rascal wanted to deceive me: which of you is the worse, I don't know, but you are both loathsome to me. My friend has saved me from my stupid predicament. . . .'

'A fine friend!' Tarantyev said. 'I have heard he has robbed you of your betrothed: a nice sort of benefactor! And you are a prize fool, neighbour. . . .'

'Please refrain from such compliments,' Oblomov pulled him up.

'No, I won't! You wouldn't have anything to do with me, you ungrateful man! I have settled you here, have found a perfect treasure of a woman for you! I have secured peace and comfort for you, have simply showered benefits on you, and you turn your back on me! You take a German for your benefactor! He rents your estate! You wait a bit, he'll fleece you yet and make you buy some shares! Remember my word, he'll make a beggar of you! You are a fool, I tell you, and more than that, you are a brute, an ungrateful brute!'

'Tarantyev!' Oblomov cried menacingly.

'What's the use of your shouting? I'll shout myself for all the world to hear that you are a fool and a beast!' Tarantyev bawled. 'Ivan Matveyitch and I took care of you, looked after you, served you as though we were your serfs, walked on tiptoe, tried to guess your every wish, and you have slandered him before his superiors: now he has lost his job and can't earn his living! It is a base, vile thing to do! You must now give him half your property; give me an IOU in his name: you are not drunk now and in full possession of your faculties, give it me, I tell you, or I won't go. . . .'

'Why do you shout so, Mihey Andreyitch?' the land-lady and Anissya said, peeping in at the door. 'Two people in the street have stopped to listen.'

'I will shout!' Tarantyev roared. 'I will bring disgrace on this idiot! Let that rogue of a German fleece you now that he has joined forces with your mistress. . . .'

A loud slap resounded in the room. Struck by Oblomov

on the cheek, Tarantyev instantly subsided, sank on to a chair and rolled his eyes in stupid amazement.

'What's this? What's this – eh? What's this?' he said, pale and breathless, holding his cheek. 'Insulting me? You shall pay for this! I'll complain to the Governor-General at once! Have you seen it?'

'We haven't seen anything,' the two women said at once.

'Ah, so this is a conspiracy, it's a robbers' den! A band of brigands robbing and murdering. . . .'

'Out with you, you scoundrel!' cried Oblomov, pale and trembling with rage. 'Clear out this instant or I'll kill you like a dog!'

He was looking round for a stick.

'Murder! Help, good people!' Tarantyev shouted.

'Zahar! Throw out this blackguard and don't let him dare show himself here again!' Oblomov called.

'Come along! Here's the holy ikon, there's the door!' said Zahar, pointing first to one, then to the other.

'I haven't come to you, but to my friend!' Tarantyev bawled.

'Mercy on us, I don't want you, Mihey Andreyitch!' Agafya Matveyevna said. 'It was to my brother you used to come, not to me! You are worse than a bitter radish to me. You eat and drink all we have and abuse us into the bargain!'

'Ah, so that's the way you talk, madam! Very well, your brother will let you know what's what! And you will pay me for your insult! Where is my hat? Damnation take you! Brigands, bloodsuckers!' he shouted as he walked across the yard. 'I'll make you pay for the insult!'

The dog jumped on the chain, barking desperately.

After this Tarantyev and Oblomov did not meet again.

VIII

SEVERAL years had passed before Stolz came to Petersburg. He paid only one short visit to Olga's estate and to Oblomov's. Ilya Ilyitch received a letter from him in which he begged him to go to the country and take up the management of Oblomovka, which was in good order now; he and Olga Sergeyevna were moving to the south coast of the Crimea, because Stolz had business at Odessa and for the sake of Olga, who had been in delicate health since her confinement.

They settled in a quiet little place on the seashore. Their house was small and modest. The architecture, both inside and out, had a style of its own, and all the decoration bore the imprint of the owner's personal taste and thought. They had brought many things with them and had many packages, cases, and cartloads sent them from Russia and from abroad. A lover of comfort might perhaps shrug his shoulders at the apparently incongruous furniture, old pictures, statues with broken arms and legs, prints and knick-knacks, sometimes worthless but dear because of associations. Only a connoisseur's eyes would sparkle eagerly at the sight of this or that picture, at some book yellow with age, at old china, cameos, or coins. And yet the furniture of various epochs, the pictures, the trifles of no significance to anyone, but reminding them of a happy hour, a memorable moment, the masses of books and music, had a warm breath of life about them and stirred the mind and the æsthetic sense; it was all permeated by living thought or radiant with the beauty of human achievement, while all around it was radiant with the eternal beauty of nature. The tall desk that had belonged to Stolz's father was in the house too, and the chamois-leather gloves; the mackintosh hung in the corner next to a cupboard with minerals, shells, stuffed birds, samples of different kinds of clay, of various specimens, and so on. The place of honour was occupied by an Erard's grand piano, shining with gold and inlaid work. The house was covered from top to bottom with a network of vines, creepers, and myrtles. From one side of the balcony one could see the sea, from the other the road to the town. From that end Olga watched for Andrey to return when he had been away from home on business; as she caught sight of him she came down, and, running through the magnificent flower-garden and a long avenue of poplars, fell on her husband's neck, always with the same ardour of impatient happiness, her cheeks flushed with joy and her eyes glowing – though it was not the first or the second year of their marriage.

Stolz's ideas about love and marriage may have been odd and exaggerated, but in any case they were original. In this respect, too, he followed the free and, he thought, simple road; but what a difficult school of observation, labour, and patience he went through before learning to take these 'simple steps'!

Stolz had his father's way of looking earnestly at everything in life, trifles not excepted; he might, perhaps, have copied also the pedantic severity which Germans carry into everything they do, marriage included. Like a stone tablet, old Stolz's life was there for all to read, and there were no hidden implications in it. But the mother, with her songs and tender whispers, the many-sided activities of the prince's household, and later the university, books, and society, had led Andrey away from the straight path marked for him by his father. Russian life was drawing its own invisible patterns and transforming the colourless tablet into a broad and vivid picture. Andrey did not pedantically fetter his feelings and even indulged in day-dreams, within reason, trying merely not to lose 'the ground under his feet,' though, owing to his German nature or perhaps for some other reason, when he returned to sober reality he could not resist drawing some conclusion that had a practical bearing on life. He was vigorous in body because his mind was vigorous. He had been lively and full of mischief as a boy, and when he was not in mischief he was at work under his father's supervision. He had not had time to lose himself in dreams. His imagination was not corrupted, his heart was not spoiled: his mother carefully watched over the virginal purity of both. As a youth he instinctively preserved his powers intact and early in life he began to understand that this freshness gives rise to vigour and gaiety and lies at the basis of the manliness in which the soul must be steeped if it is not to blanch before life, whatever it may be, but to wage the battle with it worthily, regarding it not as a cross or a heavy yoke but merely as a duty. He devoted much careful thought to the heart and its mysterious laws. As he grew older, and looked around him, watching, both consciously and unconsciously, the effect of beauty upon imagination, the transition of impressions into feeling, its symptoms, its play and its outcome, he became convinced that it is love that moves the world with the power of Archimedes' lever, and that there is as much universal and incontrovertible goodness and truth in it as there is falsity and ugliness in its misuse and misinterpretation. What, then, was good? What was evil? What was the dividing line between them?

At the question, 'Where was the falsity?' a motley array of masks, belonging both to the past and to the present, rose before his imagination. With a smile, a blush, or a frown he watched the endless procession of love's heroes and heroines: the Don Quixotes in steel gauntlets and the ladies of their dreams, faithful to one another through fifty years of separation; the rosy shepherds with naïve, wide-open eyes and their Chloes with lambs. Ladies in powdered wigs and lace, with eyes sparkling with intelligence and a dissolute smile, appeared before his mind; then the Werthers who had shot, hanged, or strangled themselves; then faded maidens shedding endless tears for love and retiring into convents, and their heroes with long moustache and unbridled ardour in their eyes; the naïve

and the deliberate Don Juans, the clever coxcombs terrified lest they should be suspected of love, but secretly
adoring their housekeepers . . . a whole army of them!

At the question, 'Where was the real thing?' he sought
far and near, in his mind and with his eyes, instances of
simple, honest, yet deep and indissoluble intimacy with a
woman, but could not find them; or, if he did, it proved
to be only an illusion followed by disappointment, and he
sank into melancholy reflections and at times despaired.
'Evidently this blessing is not to be found in all its fullness,' he thought, 'or perhaps all those that live in the
light of such a love are shy: they are timid and hide, not
trying to argue with clever people; perhaps they pity them
and forgive them, in the name of their own happiness, for
trampling on the flower that cannot take root in such shallow soil and grow into a tree, spreading its branches over
the whole of life.'

He looked at marriages, at husbands, and always saw in
their attitude to their wives the riddle of the sphinx,
something not understood, not fully expressed; and yet
those husbands did not puzzle over knotty problems and
walked along the path of matrimony with even and
deliberate step, as though they had nothing to solve or to
discover. 'Perhaps they are right? Perhaps there really is
no need for anything else?' he wondered, distrusting himself, as he looked at men who quickly go through love as
the A B C of marriage or a form of politeness – like
making a bow on entering a drawing-room – and hurry on
to things of more importance. They are impatient to leave
the spring-time of life behind; many of them look askance
at their wives for the rest of their lives as though vexed at
having once been foolish enough to love them. Others
cling to love for years, sometimes till old age, but there
always is a satyr's smile on their lips. . . . Finally, most
men enter upon marriage as though they were buying an
estate and enjoy its substantial advantages: a wife brings
order into the home, she is the housekeeper, the mother,
the governess; and they look upon love as a good manager

looks upon the situation of his estate – that is, he grows used to it at once and does not notice it any more.

'What does it mean: is it an innate incapacity decreed by nature or the fault of our education and training?' he wondered. 'Where is the sympathy that never loses its natural charm nor wears a ridiculous guise, that changes without being extinguished? What is the natural colour and shade of this all-pervading blessing, of this vital force?' He looked prophetically into distance and there rose before him, as in a mist, the image of love and with it of a woman clothed in its colours and resplendent with its light, an image so simple but pure and radiant. 'A dream, a dream!' he said with a smile, throwing off the idle excitement of imagination. But in spite of himself the outline of the dream lived in his memory. At first that dream image meant for him the woman of the future; but when Olga had grown up and developed and he saw in her not only a fully opened flower of beauty but a force ready to fight the battle of life and eager for understanding – all the elements of his dream – there rose before him that old, half-forgotten image of love and assumed the shape of Olga; and it seemed to him that in the far-off future their feeling for each other might be 'the real thing,' with no affectation, no ridiculous trappings.

Stolz did not toy with the question of love and marriage or complicate it by extraneous consideration of money, connections, position, but he did wonder how his external indefatigable activity could be reconciled with his inner family life, how he could abandon travel and business and turn into a stay-at-home husband. If he gave up this scurrying to and fro, how would he fill up his home life? Bringing up children, educating them and directing their life was, of course, no easy or unimportant task, but it was still a long way off, and what was he going to do meanwhile?

These questions had often troubled him, and he did not find his bachelor life a burden; it had not occurred to him to put on the shackles of matrimony as soon as his heart began beating fast in the presence of beauty. This was why he seemed to overlook Olga as a girl and admired her merely as a charming and very promising child; incidentally, in joke, he would throw some new bold idea, some acute observation about life, into her eager and receptive mind, creating in it, unknown to himself, a lively understanding of events, a correct view of things; and then he would forget both Olga and his casual lessons. And if at times he saw that she had rather unusual opinions and mental characteristics; that there was nothing false in her; that she did not seek general admiration; that her feelings came and went simply and spontaneously; that there was nothing second-hand in her, but everything was her own, and it was so bold, so fresh and so stable, he wondered how she had come to be like this and did not recognize his own fleeting lessons and remarks. Had he considered her attentively then, he would have grasped that she was going her own way almost alone, guarded from extremes by her aunt's superficial surveillance, but not oppressed by the authority of nurses, grandmothers, aunts, with the traditions of the family, the clan, the caste, of outworn manners, customs, and rules; that she was not being forcibly led by a beaten track but walking along a new path which she had to make by her own intelligence, intuition, and feeling. Nature had given her all this in plenty; her aunt did not despotically rule over her mind and will, and Olga guessed and understood a great deal of herself, carefully watching life and listening . . . among other things, to her friend's words and his advice. . . . He had not grasped this and merely expected a great deal of her in the future, a very distant future, without ever thinking of her as his companion for life.

From pride and shyness she would not for a long time allow him to guess what she was, and it was only abroad and after his agonizing struggle that he saw with amazement what a model of simplicity, strength, and naturalness this promising child, forgotten by him, had grown to be. It was there that the depth of her soul, which it was his task to satisfy, was gradually revealed to him.

At first he had to struggle with the vivacity of her nature, to check the fever of youth, to confine her impetuosity to definite limits, to set their life at an even pace if only for a time; but he no sooner closed his eyes, reassured, than she was disturbed again, the stream of life ran fast, new questions came from her eager mind and restless heart; he had to soothe her excited imagination, to calm or to rouse her pride. If she pondered over something, he hastened to give her the key to it.

Mists, hallucinations, belief in chance were gradually disappearing from her life. The distance lay before her sunlit and boundless, and she could see in it, as in limpid water, every stone, every depression, and then the firm river-bed.

'I am happy,' she whispered, looking back with gratitude at her life in the past; thinking of the future she recalled the girlish dream of happiness she had once dreamed in Switzerland on that still, blue night, and she saw that that dream was present in her life like a shadow. 'Why should such happiness have fallen to my lot?' she thought humbly. She pondered and pondered, fearing sometimes that the happiness would end.

Years passed, but they did not grow tired of living. Peace came at last, the emotional upheavals were over; the ups and downs of life no longer perplexed them; they endured them bravely and patiently and yet life never flagged.

Olga reached at last a true understanding of life, though as yet it was only of a happy life. Andrey's existence and hers had been merged into one, there could be no room for the play of wild passions – all was peace and harmony between them. One might think they would go to sleep in this well-earned repose and live in the state of beatitude of those inhabitants of the backwoods who meet together three times a day, yawn over their usual conversations, sink into a dull slumber, and languish from morning till night because everything has been decided, said, and done over and over again, and there is nothing more to think over, to talk about or to do, and because 'such is life in this world.'

To an outside observer their life was the same as other people's. They rose early, though not at dawn; they liked to take their time over breakfast and sometimes seemed to be lazily silent; then they went to their rooms or worked together, dined, drove to the fields, had music . . . like everybody else, as Oblomov had dreamed. Only there was no drowsiness or depression about them; they were not bored or apathetic; not one dull look or word passed between them; their conversations never ended and were often heated. Their ringing voices resounded in the rooms and reached the garden; at other times, tracing as it were the pattern of their dreams, they murmured to each other the first stirrings of thought so impossible to interpret in words, the almost inaudible whisperings of the soul. . . . And their silence was sometimes the dreamy happiness of which Oblomov had dreamed and at other times it was the solitary work of thought over the endless material they provided for each other. They often sank into silent wonder before the ever new and radiant beauty of nature. Their sensitive minds were never tired of this beauty: the earth, the sky, the sea – all roused their feelings, and they sat side by side in silence, looking with one heart at the glory of creation, understanding each other without words. They did not meet the morning with indifference, they could not dully sink into the darkness of a warm, starry southern night. They were kept awake by the constant movement of thought, the constant agitation of the soul and the need to think together, to feel together, to talk!

What was the subject of their heated arguments, quiet conversations, of the books they read? What was the aim of their long walks? Why, everything. While they were still abroad Stolz had lost the habit of working and reading by himself; here, alone with Olga, he shared with her

his very thoughts. It was all he could do to keep pace with
the tempestuous quickness of her thought and will. The
question of what he was going to do as a family man was
settled; it had solved itself. He had to initiate her even
into his workaday business life, for she felt stifled without
activity. He did nothing without her knowledge and help,
whether it was building, looking after his own or Oblomov's estate, or the company's business. He did not post
a single letter without first reading it to her, did not with-
hold from her a single thought, and still less its realization; she knew all, and it interested her because it
interested him. At first it was because he could hide nothing from her: letters were written and conversations with
agents or contractors were held in her presence; then he
continued this from habit and at last it became a necessity
for his own sake. He needed her remarks, advice, appro-
bation or disapprobation to check him: he saw that she
understood, thought, and reasoned as well as he did. . . .
Zahar resented such ability in his wife, and many men
resent it, but Stolz was happy! And then there was reading and learning – the everlasting feast of thought and its
endless development! Olga was jealous of every book and
article he had not shown her, and was seriously angry and
offended if he did not think fit to show her something he
thought would be too serious, dull, and incomprehensible
to her; she called that pedantic, vulgar, retrograde,
and said he was an old German Whig. They had lively
encounters on such occasions. She was angry and he
laughed, she grew angrier still, and they only made peace
when he stopped joking and shared with her his thought,
knowledge, or book. The end of it was that she wanted to
read and to know all that he wanted. He did not force the
technique of learning upon her in order to boast of a
'learned wife' with the silliest of fatuities. Had she said a
single word or even hinted at such an ambition he would
have blushed more violently than if she had answered
with a blank look of ignorance a question that was quite
simple to an educated man but did not as yet form part of

a woman's education. He merely wanted, and she doubly so, that there should be nothing closed to her understanding – if not to her knowledge. He did not draw diagrams and figures for her, but spoke to her about everything and read a great deal without pedantically avoiding economic theories, social or philosophical problems; he spoke with passion, with enthusiasm, as though drawing for her an endless, living picture of knowledge; later on the details escaped her memory, but the pattern was never deleted from her impressionable mind, the colours did not fade, and the fire with which he lighted the world he created for her was never quenched. He felt a tremor of pride and happiness when he noticed a spark of this fire shining in her eyes, an echo of a thought he had imparted to her sounding in her words, when he saw that it had entered her consciousness and understanding, had been transformed in her mind and appeared in her words no longer dry and stern but sparkling with womanly grace, and especially when some fruitful drop out of all that he had said, read, or drawn for her, sank like a pearl into the clear depths of her being. Like an artist and a thinker he was fashioning a rational existence for her, and never in his life – not in his years of study, not in the hard days when he struggled with life, disentangling himself from its coils, and grew strong, strengthening his soul in the ordeals of manhood – never had he been so absorbed as now, tending this unceasing, volcanic work of his wife's spirit!

'How happy I am!' Stolz said to himself, and dreamed in his own way of what the future held for them after the honey years of marriage. A new image smiled to him in the distance, not of a selfish Olga, not of a passionately loving wife, of a mother-nurse fading out in the end in a colourless existence needed by no one, but of something different, lofty, almost unheard of. . . . He dreamed of a mother who created and took part in the moral and social life of a whole happy generation. . . . He questioned himself fearfully whether she would have sufficient strength and will . . . and hastened to help her in conquering life, in acquiring a reserve of courage for battling with it; this had to be done while they were both young and strong, while life spared them or its blows did not seem heavy and grief was drowned in love. Their days had been darkened, but not for long. Business failures, considerable loss of money – it all hardly affected them. It only meant extra journeys and trouble and was soon forgotten. The death of her aunt caused Olga genuine and bitter tears and cast a shadow on her life for the next six months. The children's illnesses were a source of lively anxiety and worry; but as soon as the danger had passed, happiness returned. Stolz was anxious about Olga's health: she was long recovering from her confinements, and though she recovered his anxiety remained: he could think of no misfortune more terrible.

'How happy I am!' Olga repeated to herself softly as she looked upon her life with delight; and sometimes when she did so she pondered . . . especially three or four years after her marriage.

Human beings are strange creatures! The more complete was her happiness, the more thoughtful and even . . . fearful she became. She began watching herself carefully and noticed that what troubled her was this serenity of her life, the way the moments of happiness persisted. With an effort she shook herself free from brooding, and quickened the pace of life; she feverishly sought noise, movement, cares, asked her husband to take her to the town, tried going into society, but not for long. The turmoil of society affected her but little and she hurried back to her quiet home to get rid of some painful, unusual impression and was absorbed once more in the small cares of the home life, not leaving the nursery for days together and acting the part of mother-nurse, or gave herself up to reading with Andrey, to talking of 'dull and serious things,' or read the poets and talked of a journey to Italy. She was afraid of sinking into an apathy like Oblomov's. But though she did her best to banish these moments of occasional numbness and slumber of the soul, she was waylaid now and again, first by the dream of happiness; the blue night surrounded her once more, binding her with a drowsy spell, then again came an interval of brooding, like a rest from life, and then . . . confusion, fear, yearning, a kind of dull melancholy, vague and obscure questions rising in her restless head. Olga listened to them intently, analysed herself, but with no result; she could not find out what her soul was seeking, and yet it was seeking and longing for something, dreadful to say; she was depressed as though the life of happiness were not enough and she had grown tired of it and were demanding new, fresh happenings, peeping into a more distant future. . . . 'What is it?' she thought in terror. 'Is it necessary, is it possible to wish for something else? Where am I to go? Nowhere! The road does not lead any farther. . . . Doesn't it? Have I, then, completed the circle of life? Is this all . . . all?' her heart asked, and left the question unfinished . . . and Olga looked round anxiously lest someone should overhear this whisper of her heart. . . . Her eyes questioned the sky, the sea, the forest . . . there was no answer anywhere: distance, depth, and darkness lay before her. Nature said the same things over and over again; she saw in it the endless and monotonous flow of life without beginning or end. She knew whom she could ask about her troubles and from whom she could have an answer; but what answer? What if he said it was the repining of a barren intellect or worse still the thirst of an unresponsive, unwomanly heart? My God, to think that she, his idol, should be heartless, with a hard, never contented mind! What was she becoming? Surely not a bluestocking? How she would fall in his eyes when she told him of these new, fresh sufferings that no doubt he knew quite well! She hid from him or pretended to be ill when, in spite of herself, her eyes lost their velvety softness and looked hot and dry, a cloud of depression lay on her face and, though she tried her best, she could not force herself to smile or speak but listened indifferently to the most exciting news of the political world, the most interesting explanations of a new step in science or new creative work in art. And yet she did not want to cry, she had no sudden tremors as when her nerves were strained and her virginal powers were awakening and finding expression. No, that was not it! 'What is it, then?' she asked herself in despair when she suddenly felt bored, indifferent to everything on a beautiful peaceful evening, sitting beside her baby's cot or listening to her husband's words of endearment. . . . She suddenly turned stony and grew silent, then bustled about with a feigned liveliness to conceal her strange discomfort, or said she had a headache and went to bed.

But it was not easy for her to hide from Stolz's keen eye: she knew it and prepared herself for the conversation that was to come with as much inward anxiety as she had once felt at the thought of confessing her past. The time for this conversation came.

One evening they were walking in the poplar avenue. She almost hung on his shoulder, plunged in deep silence. She was suffering from one of her mysterious attacks and answered shortly to everything he said.

'The nurse says Olenka was coughing in the night. Hadn't we better send for the doctor to-morrow?' he asked.

'I've given her a warm drink and will keep her indoors to-morrow, and then we shall see,' she answered dully.

They walked in silence to the end of the avenue.

'Why haven't you answered your friend Sonitchka's letter?' he asked. 'I waited and nearly missed the post. This is her third letter you have left unanswered.'

'Yes, I want to make haste and forget her . . .' she said, and broke off.

'I gave your greetings to Bichurin,' Andrey began again, 'he is in love with you, you know, so I thought it might comfort him a little for his wheat arriving too late.'

She smiled dryly.

'What is it, are you sleepy?' he asked.

Her heart gave a jump, as it did every time that he began questioning her closely.

'Not yet,' she answered with assumed brightness. 'What makes you think so?'

'Are you unwell?' he asked again.

'No. Why do you ask?'

'Well, then you are bored.'

She pressed his shoulder lightly with both hands.

'No, no!' she denied in an artificially cheerful voice in which there certainly was a note of something like boredom.

He took her out of the avenue and turned her face to the moonlight.

'Look at me!' he said, gazing intently into her eyes. 'One might think you were . . . unhappy! Your eyes are so strange to-day, and not only to-day. . . . What is it, Olga?'

He put his arm round her waist and took her back into the avenue.

'You know what: I am . . . hungry!' she said, trying to laugh.

'Now, don't tell fibs! I don't like it!' he added with feigned severity.

'Unhappy!' she said reproachfully, stopping him in the avenue. 'Yes, the only thing to make me unhappy is . . . too much happiness!' she added, with such a soft, tender note in her voice that he kissed her.

She grew bolder. The suggestion that she was unhappy, though offered lightly and in joke, suddenly made her want to confess.

'I am not bored and couldn't be – you know that yourself and you don't really mean it, of course; and I am not ill, but . . . I feel sad . . . sometimes . . . there, you insufferable man – since there's no hiding it from you! Yes, sad and I don't know why!' She put her head on his shoulder.

'So that's it! But why?' he asked softly, bending over her.

'I don't know,' she repeated.

'And yet there must be a reason, if not in me or in your

surroundings, then in yourself. Sometimes such sadness is simply the germ of disease. . . . Are you well?'

'Yes, it may be something of the kind,' she said seriously, 'though I feel perfectly well. You see I eat and sleep and work and go for walks. And suddenly a mood seems to come over me, a sort of depression . . . and life seems . . . as though it were lacking in something . . . But no, don't listen to me, it's all nonsense. . . .'

'Do go on!' he begged her earnestly. 'Yes, life is lacking in something; what else?'

'Sometimes I seem to fear that things might change or come to an end. . . . I don't know myself, or I am tormented by the silly thought: What more is there going to happen? . . . What does this happiness . . . and all life . . . mean?' she said, speaking still lower, ashamed of her questions. 'All these joys and sorrows . . . and nature,' she whispered, 'it all seems to make me yearn for something more; I grow discontented with everything. . . . Oh dear, I am really ashamed of all this foolishness . . . it's just my imagination. . . . Don't take any notice, don't see it. . . .' she added in an imploring voice, snuggling herself up to him. 'This sadness soon passes and then I feel gay and light-hearted again, as I do just now!'

She pressed herself close to him timidly and affectionately, genuinely ashamed, and, as it were, begging forgiveness for her 'foolishness.'

Her husband went on questioning her and it took her a long time to tell him, as a patient tells a doctor, the symptoms of her sadness, the vague questions that arose in her, to describe the confusion in her mind and the way the mirage disappeared – all, all that she had observed and remembered.

Anxious and perplexed, Stolz walked on in silence, his head bowed, completely absorbed by Olga's vague avowal.

She peeped into his eyes, but saw nothing; and when they reached the end of the avenue for the third time, she did not let him turn back, but, in her turn, took him out into the moonlight and looked questioningly into his eyes.

'What are you thinking?' she asked shyly. 'Are you laughing at my foolishness – yes? It is very foolish, this sadness, isn't it?'

He said nothing.

'Why are you silent?'

'You have been silent for a long time, though, of course, you have known all along that I was watching you, so you must let me, too, be silent for a bit and think. You've set me a difficult task. . . .'

'There, now you will be thinking and I shall be wretched, trying to guess what you are devising all by yourself. I wish I hadn't told you!' she added. 'You had much better say something. . . .'

'What am I to say to you?' he brought out thoughtfully. 'Perhaps it is your nerves again, and in that case it's the doctor and not I who is to decide what is the matter with you. We must send for him to-morrow. . . . But if it isn't . . .' he began, and stopped to think.

'What "if it isn't"? Speak!'

He walked on, still lost in thought.

'Yes, well?' she said, shaking him by the arm.

'It may be an excess of imagination: you are much too lively . . . or perhaps you have reached the age when . . .' he finished in an undertone, speaking almost to himself.

'Please speak up, Andrey! I can't bear your habit of muttering to yourself!' she complained. 'I have told him a lot of silly nonsense and now he has hung his head and is whispering under his breath! I feel positively nervous with you here in the dark. . . .'

'I don't know what to say . . . "sadness comes over you, you are troubled by thoughts" – what is one to make of it? We will talk of it again and we shall see: it looks as though you needed sea bathing again. . . .'

'You have just said to yourself, "If . . . perhaps . . . reached the age." What was in your mind?' she asked.

'I was thinking . . .' he said slowly and thoughtfully, distrusting his own thoughts and, like Olga, ashamed, as it were, of his words. 'You see . . . there come moments . . .

I mean, if this isn't a sign of a breakdown, if you are in perfect health, it may be that you have reached maturity, the time of life when one stops growing . . . when there are no riddles left and the whole of life is seen plainly. . . .'

'I believe you want to say that I have grown old?' she interrupted him quickly. 'Don't you dare!' she shook her finger at him. 'I am still young and vigorous . . .' she added, drawing herself up.

He laughed.

'Don't be afraid!' he said. 'I don't think you intend to grow old at all! No, that's not it . . . in old age one's powers fail and cease to struggle with life. No, your sadness and yearning – if it is what I think – is rather a sign of strength. . . . A lively, active mind strives sometimes to go beyond the boundaries of life, finds, of course, no response to its questionings, and the result is sadness, temporary dissatisfaction with life. . . . It's the sadness of the soul questioning life about its mysteries. . . . Maybe this is what's . . . the matter with you. . . . If so – it isn't silly nonsense.'

She sighed, but it seemed more like a sigh of joy that her apprehensions were over and that instead of falling she rose in her husband's esteem. . . .

'But I am happy; my mind is not idle; I don't indulge in day-dreams; my life is full – what more do I want? What's the use of these questionings?' she said. 'It's a disease, an oppression!'

'Yes, perhaps it is for a weak, untrained, unenlightened mind. This sadness and questioning may have driven many men crazy; others regard it as a hideous nightmare or a mental delirium. . . .

'My life is brimming over with happiness, I so want to live . . . and all of a sudden there is bitterness in it all. . . .'

'Ah, that is what one has to pay for Prometheus's fire! You must not merely endure but love this sadness and respect your doubts and questions: they are the overflow, the luxury of life, and appear for the most part on the summits of happiness, when no coarse desires are left; they do not spring up in ordinary life; people in need and sorrow cannot be bothered with them; the crowd knows nothing about this mist of doubt, this yearning to understand. . . . But to those who have faced them in time they are not a burden, but welcome guests.'

'But there is no managing them: they make one wretched and indifferent . . . to almost everything,' she added irresolutely.

'Not for long though – afterwards life seems all the fresher. They bring us to an abyss from which no answer is to be had and make us look upon life again all the more lovingly. . . . They call out forces to struggle with them that have been tried already, as though on purpose not to let them go to sleep. . . .'

'To suffer from a mist, from phantoms!' she complained. 'All is so sunny and suddenly a sinister shadow falls upon life! Is there no defence against it?'

'Of course there is: you must find strength in life! And if you cannot, life is wretched enough even without these questions.'

'What is one to do then? To give in and be miserable?'

'Nothing,' he said. 'Arm yourself with fortitude and follow your path patiently and perseveringly. You and I are not Titans,' he went on, putting his arm round her, 'we are not like Manfred and Faust, going to struggle defiantly with insoluble questions, we shall not take up their challenge, but humbly bowing our heads will live through the difficult time and then again life and happiness will smile upon us and. . . .'

'But what if they never leave us alone and the sadness goes on tormenting us more and more?' she asked.

'Well, what of it? We will accept it as a new element in life. . . . But no, that does not happen, it cannot be so with us! It isn't your sadness, it's the general disease of mankind. One drop of it has fallen upon you. . . . All this is terrible when one is out of touch with life . . . when there is nothing to sustain one. But with us . . . God grant that your sadness should be what I think and not a symptom of some illness . . . that would be worse. It would be a misfortune that would leave me utterly helpless and defenceless. . . . But how can vague sadness, doubts, or questionings take away our happiness, our. . . .'

He broke off and she threw herself into his arms like one possessed, clasping her arms round his neck in passionate self-abandonment.

'Neither sadness, nor doubts, nor illness, nor . . . death itself!' she whispered ecstatically, once more happy, calm, and gay. It seemed to her she had never loved him more passionately than at that moment.

'Mind that Fate doesn't overhear your repining and take it for ingratitude,' he concluded, superstitiously, moved by tender solicitude; 'it doesn't like people not to value its gifts. So far you have been merely studying life, but you will have to test it by experience. . . . Wait till you are in the thick of it, till trouble and sorrow come, as come they must, then . . . you will have no time to spare for these questions. . . . Husband your strength!' he added softly, almost to himself, in answer to her passionate outburst. There was a note of sorrow in his words as though he already saw 'the trouble and sorrow' in the distance.

She said nothing, struck by the sadness in his voice. She had boundless confidence in him, and trusted the very sound of his voice. She was infected by his thoughtfulness and grew absorbed in her own musings. Leaning on his arm she slowly and unconsciously walked up and down the avenue, plunged in deep silence. Like her husband, she looked fearfully into life's distance, where, he said, trials, trouble, and sorrow were awaiting them. She was now dreaming of something other than the blue night, seeing another aspect of life, no longer clear and festive, amidst stillness and plenty, alone with *him*. . . . No, she saw a succession of privations and losses bewailed with tears, inevitable sacrifices, fasting and forcible renunciation of luxurious desires born in idleness, groans and lamentations caused by feelings they had not known as yet; she dreamed of illnesses, business losses, her husband's death. . . . She shuddered, her heart sank, but she looked with courage and interest at this new picture of life, inspected it with horror and measured her strength against it. . . . Love alone did not fail her in this dream, but watched faithfully over the new life as over the old; and yet it, too, was different! There were no ardent sighs, no silvery rays, no blue nights; after the passage of years all that seemed child's play in comparison with the far-off love fashioned by the grave and menacing life of the future. There were in it no sounds of kisses and laughter, no tremulously thoughtful conversations in the arbour among the flowers, at the festival of nature and life – all 'had withered and gone.' But that unfading and indestructible love could be seen, strong as life itself, in their faces at the time of common sorrow, in the silent glance they exchanged when in pain, and was felt in the infinite patience with which they endured life's torture, in their restrained tears and stifled sobs. . . . Olga's vague sadness and doubts imperceptibly merged into other dreams, distant but clear, definite and menacing. . . .

Under the influence of the firm and reassuring words of her husband, in whom she had boundless confidence, Olga found relief both from that mysterious sadness, not known to all, and from the menacing and prophetic dreams of the future, and went boldly forward. The 'mist' was followed by a sunny morning, with the cares of a mother and a housewife; she felt drawn now to the flower-garden and the fields and now to her husband's study. But she did not play at life with care-free and selfish delight; secret courage and thought inspired her as she prepared herself and waited. . . . She grew nobler and nobler. . . . Andrey saw that his old ideal of woman and wife was unattainable, but he was happy even at the pale reflection of it in Olga; he had never expected as much.

Meanwhile he was faced for years, for almost his whole life, with the hard task of maintaining, on the same high

level, his dignity as a man in the eyes of the proud, ambitious Olga – not from vulgar jealousy, but so that her
crystal-clear life should not be dimmed; and this might
happen if her faith in him were in the least shaken.

Many women need nothing of the kind: once married,
they submissively accept their husband's good and bad
qualities, are completely resigned to the position and
environment in which they find themselves, or as submissively succumb to the first casual infatuation, deciding at
once that it is impossible or unnecessary to resist it,
saying: 'It's fate; passion; woman is a weak creature,' and
so on. Even if the husband is superior to the crowd in
intelligence, which gives a man such charm and power,
women of that type pride themselves on their husband's
superiority as though it were an expensive necklace, and
then only if his intellect remains blind to their pitiful
feminine trickery. But if he dares to see through the petty
comedy of their sly, insignificant, and sometimes vicious
existence, they find his intelligence hard and oppressive.

Olga did not know this logic of obedience to blind fate
and could not understand women's petty passions and
infatuations. Having once recognized the worth of the
man she had chosen and his claims upon herself, she
believed in him, and when she ceased to believe she
ceased to love, as had happened with Oblomov. But at
that time her steps were uncertain, her will wavered. She
was only just beginning to observe life and to think about
it, to be conscious of the elements of her mind and character; she was only collecting her materials, as it were;
creative work had not yet begun, she had not yet found
her path in life. She believed in Andrey, however, not
blindly, but with the consciousness that he was her ideal
of masculine perfection. The more deeply and more consciously she believed in him the more difficult it was for
him to remain on the same height, to be the hero, not
only of her heart and mind, but of her imagination as
well. She believed in him so much that she acknowledged
no intermediary except God between herself and him.

This was why she could not have endured the least falling off in the qualities she admired in him; a single false note in his mind or character would have produced a shattering discord. The crash of her happiness would have buried her under its ruins, or had her strength remained unimpaired, she would have sought. . . . But no, women like her do not make mistakes twice over. If such faith, such love had failed, it would have been impossible for her to begin life again.

Stolz was deeply happy in his full and agitated life, in which an unfading spring was flowering, and he jealously, keenly, and actively tended, cherished, and fostered it. Terror only stirred in him when he recalled that Olga had been within a hair's-breadth of perdition; that they might have missed their true path in life and their two lives, now merged into one, might have diverged; that ignorance of the ways of life might have brought about a disastrous mistake; that Oblomov . . . he shuddered. What! Olga in the life which Oblomov had been preparing for her! To think of her dragging out her existence from day to day, living in the country, nursing her children, looking after the house – and nothing more! All her questionings, doubts, feverish energy would have gone into housekeeping, preparing for the feast-days, visitors, family gatherings, birthdays, christenings, and her husband's sloth and apathy! Marriage would have been a mere form without meaning, a means and not an end; it would have been the permanent frame for visits, guests, dinners, evening-parties, empty chatter. . . . How would she have endured such a life? At first she would have struggled, trying to find and guess the secret of existence, wept and suffered, then she would have accepted it, spent her time eating and sleeping, grown fat and stupid. . . . No, it would not have been so with her: she would have wept, suffered, pined away and died in the arms of a loving, kind, and helpless husband. . . . Poor Olga!

And if the fire had not gone out, if life had not failed, if her powers had resisted and demanded freedom, if she had stretched her wings like a strong and keen-eyed eagle, caught captive for a moment by feeble hands, and had rushed to the high cliff where she had seen an eagle who was still stronger and keener-sighted than she? . . . Poor Ilya!

'Poor Ilya!' Andrey said aloud one day, recalling the past.

At the sound of that name Olga suddenly dropped her hands with the embroidery on to her knees, threw back her head and sank into deep thought. His exclamation called up memories.

'How is he?' she asked presently. 'Can't we really find out?'

Andrey shrugged his shoulders.

'One might think,' he said, 'we were living in the days when there was no post and on parting people gave up each other for lost and really lost all trace of each other.'

'You might write to some of your friends again; we should learn something, at any rate. . . .'

'We should learn nothing except what we know already – that he is alive and well and is living in the same place. I know it without troubling my friends. But what is happening to him, how he is enduring his life, whether he is morally dead or there is still a spark of life glowing in him – a stranger could not find that out. . . .'

'Don't speak like that, Andrey: it frightens me, it hurts me to hear you! I should like to know and yet I am afraid. . . .'

She was ready to cry.

'We'll be in Petersburg in the spring, then we shall see for ourselves.'

'It's not enough that we should see, we must do all we can. . . .'

'Haven't I done it? The time I have spent persuading him, doing things for him, arranging his affairs – and he hasn't made the slightest response! While I am with him he is ready to do anything, but as soon as I am out of sight, it's all over: he goes to sleep again. It's like trying to reform a drunkard!'

'Well, you mustn't let him out of your sight!' Olga said impatiently. 'With him one has to act decisively: put him in the carriage with you and take him away. Now we are going to move to our estate, he will be near us . . . we'll take him with us.'

'That's a pleasant job for us,' Andrey said meditatively, pacing up and down the room; 'and there seems to be no end to it!'

'Do you find it a burden?' Olga asked. 'That's something new! It's the first time I've heard you complain of it.'

'I don't complain,' he answered, 'I reflect.'

'And why should you do that? You have confessed to yourself it's a bore and a worry, is that it?'

She looked at him searchingly. He shook his head. 'No, but I do sometimes think it's no use.'

'Don't, don't say it,' she stopped him, 'or I shall again think of it all day, as I did last week, and be wretched. If your friendship for him is dead, you ought to look after him simply from human feeling. If you grow tired, I shall go alone and not leave the house without him: he will be touched by my entreaties; I feel that I shall cry bitterly if I find him done for, dead! Maybe, tears. . . .'

'Will bring him back to life, you think?' Andrey asked.

'No, not bring him back to active life, but, at any rate, will make him look around him and change his way of living for something better. He will not be in squalor but near his equals, with us. The moment I appeared that time he instantly came to himself and was ashamed. . . .'

'Perhaps you love him as before?' Andrey asked jokingly.

'No,' Olga said thoughtfully, without joking and looking, as it were, into the past, 'I don't love him as before, but there is something in him that I do love and have remained faithful to – and I shall not change, like other people. . . .'

'Who are those other people, please? Say it, bite me,

you poisonous snake: you are thinking of me? You are wrong there; and if you want to know the truth, it was I who taught you to love him and very nearly brought you into trouble. If it hadn't been for me you would have passed him by without noticing him. It was I made you understand that he had no less intelligence than other people, only it was sleeping idly, hidden, covered over by all sorts of rubbish. Would you like me to tell you why he is dear to you, what it is in him that you still love?'

She nodded assent.

'You love that in him which is worth more than any amount of intelligence: his honest, faithful heart! It is like pure gold in him from nature; he has preserved it throughout his life unharmed. He sank under difficulties, grew cold, dropped asleep, and finally, crushed and disappointed, lost the strength to live, but he has not lost his faith and honesty. His heart has never struck a single false note and nothing has sullied it. The most alluring sham cannot deceive him and nothing will make him go wrong; a regular ocean of evil and meanness may be storming around him, the whole world may be poisoned and turn upside down – Oblomov will never worship false idols and his soul will always be pure, honest, good. . . . His soul is clear as crystal; there aren't many men like him, they are rare; they are like pearls among the crowd. His heart cannot be bribed; one can rely on it at all times and in all places. It's to this you have remained faithful and this will always prevent me from feeling him a burden. I have known many people of great merit, but never have I met a purer, better, and simpler heart. I have loved many people, but none so warmly and deeply as Oblomov. Once you know him, you cannot cease loving him. Isn't that so? Have I guessed right?'

Olga said nothing and kept her eyes on her work. Andrey pondered.

'Isn't that all? What else? Ah,' he added gaily, 'I had quite forgotten his "dove-like" tenderness! . . .'

Olga laughed, quickly put down her sewing, and, running

up to Andrey, put her arms round his neck. For a few moments she gazed with shining eyes right into his, then put her head on his shoulder and sank into thought. There rose in her memory Oblomov's gentle, dreamy face, his tender eyes, his submissiveness, then the pitiful smile of shame with which he answered her reproach at parting, and she felt so wretched, so sorry for him. . . .

'You won't leave him, you won't give him up?' she said, with her arms still round her husband's neck.

'Never! Not unless an abyss opens suddenly, or a wall rises between us. . . .'

She kissed her husband.

'You will take me to see him in Petersburg, won't you?'

He hesitated and said nothing.

'Yes? Yes?' she insisted.

'Listen, Olga,' he said, trying to disentangle himself from the circle of her arms, 'we must first. . . .'

'No, say "yes," promise, or I won't give you any peace.'

'Very well,' he answered, 'only not the first, but the second time: I know what you will feel like if . . .'

'Don't say it, don't say it!' she interrupted. 'Yes, you will take me: together we can do it all. Alone you won't be able to, you will not want to do it!'

'Oh, very well, but you will be upset and perhaps for long!' he said, not altogether pleased at Olga having wrung a consent from him.

'Remember, then,' she concluded, settling down in her place once more, 'you will only give him up if "an abyss opens or a wall rises between you." I will not forget these words.'

IX

PEACE and quiet reigned over the Vyborg side, with its unpaved streets, wooden side-walks, sickly gardens, and ditches overgrown with nettles; a goat with a bedraggled rope round its neck was busily grazing near a fence or drowsing dully; at midday a clerk's smart high heels rattled along the planks, a muslin curtain in some window moved and a woman peeped from behind the geraniums; or a girl's fresh, jolly face appeared above the fence in some garden and instantly disappeared again, then another girlish face also appeared and disappeared, then the first again, and again the second, and the girls on the swing could be heard shrieking and laughing.

All was quiet in Madame Pshenitsyn's house too. If you walked into the small courtyard you found yourself in the midst of a living idyll: cocks and hens rushed away in a flurry to hide in the corners; the dog jumped on its chain and barked desperately; Akulina left off milking the cow and the porter chopping wood, and both stared at the visitor with interest. 'Whom do you want?' the porter asked, and, hearing Ilya Ilyitch's or the landlady's name, pointed silently to the front steps and began chopping wood once more; the visitor walked down a clean, sand-strewn path to the steps covered with a plain, clean carpet, pulled the brightly polished brass handle of the bell and the door was opened by Anissya, the children, sometimes the landlady herself, or Zahar – Zahar being the last.

Everything in Madame Pshenitsyn's house bore witness to a prosperity and abundance not to be seen there even in the days when Agafya Matveyevna kept house for her brother. The kitchen, the sideboard, the pantries were full of crockery, of big and small, round and oval dishes, sauce-boats, cups, piles of plates, iron, brass, and earthenware pots. Agafya Matveyevna's silver, redeemed long ago and never pawned since, was kept in the cupboards, together with Oblomov's. There were rows of tiny and of huge round teapots and china cups, plain and gilded, and painted with mottoes, flaming hearts, and Chinamen. There were huge glass jars of coffee, cinnamon, vanilla, crystal tea-caddies, cruets of oil and vinegar. Whole shelves were taken up with packets, bottles, and boxes of household remedies, herbs, lotions, plasters, decoctions, camphor, fumigating powders; there was also soap, material for cleaning lace, taking out stains, and so on, and so on – all that every good housewife in a country house keeps by her. When Agafya Matveyevna suddenly opened the door of the cupboard full of all these goods, she herself was overcome by the combined scent of the strong-smelling materials and had to turn her face away for a moment.

In the store-room, hams, cheeses, loaves of sugar, dried fish, bags of dried mushrooms and nuts bought from pedlars, were strung up to the ceiling so that mice could not touch them. On the floor there were barrels of butter, big covered jars of sour cream, baskets of eggs and all sorts of good things! Another Homer would be needed to describe in full detail all that had been accumulated in the corners and shelves of this small ark of domesticity. The kitchen was the true arena of Agafya Matveyevna's and her worthy helper Anissya's activity. Everything in the house was in its proper place and easy to find; everywhere there was order and, one might say, cleanliness, had it not been for one corner into which not a ray of light, not a breath of fresh air, ever penetrated; neither Agafya Matveyevna's eye nor Anissya's quick, all-sweeping hand had access to it. This was Zahar's den. His room had no window and perpetual darkness helped to turn a human habitation into a dark hole. If Zahar sometimes found there the mistress of the house, bent upon improving and cleaning the place, he firmly stated that it was not a woman's business to settle where and how brushes, blacking, and boots should

be kept; that it was no one's affair why he kept his clothes
in a heap on the floor and had his bed in a dusty corner
behind the stove; that it was *he* and not she who wore the
clothes and slept on the bed. As to the broom, some
planks, two bricks, the bottom of a barrel, and two logs of
wood which he kept in his room, he could not do without
them in his work – though he did not explain why; then
he said that dust and cobwebs did not disturb him, that,
in short, he did not poke his nose into their kitchen and
did not wish to be disturbed either. When one day he
found Anissya in his room, he poured such contempt
upon her, threatened her so seriously with his elbow, that
she was afraid to look in any more. When the case was
transferred to a higher court and submitted to his master's
decision, Ilya Ilyitch went to have a look and to settle
matters then and there, with all severity; but, thrusting
his head through Zahar's door and contemplating for a
moment all that was there, he merely spat on the ground
and did not say a word. 'Much good it has done you!'
Zahar said to Agafya Matveyevna and Anissya, who had
come together with Ilya Ilyitch in the hope that his inter-
vention might lead to some reform. Then Zahar smiled
his usual broad smile so that his eyebrows and whiskers
moved apart.

All the other rooms were bright, clean, and fresh. The
old faded curtains had gone and the windows and doors of
the drawing-room and the study were hung with blue and
green blinds and muslin curtains with red festoons – all
Agafya Matveyevna's handiwork. The pillows were white
as snow and rose in a mountain almost up to the ceilings;
the quilted eiderdowns were of silk. For weeks the landlady's room was lumbered with several card-tables opened
out and put close together so that the eiderdowns and Ilya
Ilyitch's new dressing-gown could be spread on them.
Agafya Matveyevna did the cutting-out and the quilting,
pressing her firm bosom to the work, riveting her gaze
and even her teeth upon it when she had to bite the
thread off; she worked with love, with indefatigable zeal,

having for her modest reward the thought that the dressing-gown and the eiderdowns would clothe, warm, caress, and comfort the magnificent Ilya Ilyitch. As he lay on his sofa he admired for days the way her bare elbows moved to and fro following the needle and cotton. More than once, as in the old days at Oblomovka, he dozed to the sound of the thread rustling through the material and snapping when it was bitten off.

'There, that's enough working, you will be tired!' he tried to stop her.

'God likes us to work,' she answered, never taking her eyes and hands off her sewing.

His coffee was as well made and served as nicely and carefully as at the beginning, when he had moved into the house several years before. Giblet soup, macaroni, and Parmesan cheese, pies, cold fish soup, home-grown chickens – all this alternated in strict succession and introduced pleasant variety into the monotonous life at the little house. Bright sunshine streamed in at the windows all day, first on one side of the house and then on the other; with kitchen-gardens all round, there was nothing to impede it. Canaries trilled gaily; geraniums and occasionally hyacinths that the children brought from the count's garden gave out a strong scent in the small room, mixing pleasantly with the smoke of a pure Havana cigar or with cinnamon or vanilla that Agafya Matveyevna pounded, energetically moving her elbows. Ilya Ilyitch's life was, as it were, put in a golden frame in which, as in a diorama, nothing changed except the usual phases of the day and night and the seasons; there were no other changes, no serious accidents that stir up one's whole life, often raising a muddy and bitter sediment. Since Stolz had saved Oblomovka from Ivan Matveyitch's fraudulent debts and both the latter and Tarantyev had disappeared, everything hostile disappeared from Ilya Ilyitch's life. He was now surrounded by simple, kind, loving people who had all agreed to devote their lives to his welfare, to help him not to notice life, not to feel. Agafya Matveyevna was at the zenith of her existence; she lived, feeling that her life was full as it had never been before; only, as before, she could never have expressed it or, rather, the thought of it never entered her head. She merely prayed that God would prolong Ilya Ilyitch's days and save him from 'all sorrow, need, and wrath,' committing herself, her children, and her household to God's will. Her face always wore the same expression of complete and perfect happiness, without any desires and therefore rare, and impossible for a person of a different temperament. She had grown stouter. There was the same comfortable look about her ample bosom and shoulders; her eyes were alight with kindness and housewifely solicitude. She regained the calm and dignity with which she had ruled her house in the old days, when she had the obedient Anissya, Akulina, and the porter under her. As before, she seemed to float rather than walk from the cupboard to the kitchen, from the kitchen to the store-room, and gave her orders in slow and measured tones, fully conscious of what she was doing.

Anissya had grown still livelier because there was more to do: she was always on the run, racing about in a flurry and working at Agafya Matveyevna's bidding. Her eyes had positively grown brighter and her nose – that expressive nose – was more prominent than ever; it glowed with thoughts, intentions, cares, and seemed to speak even though her tongue was silent. Both women were dressed in accordance with their dignity and station in life. Agafya Matveyevna now possessed a big wardrobe with a row of silk dresses, mantillas, and pelisses; she ordered her bonnets on the other side of the river, in the Liteiny; her shoes were bought, not in the market, but in the arcade, and her hat actually came from Morskaya Street! Anissya, when she had finished in the kitchen, and especially on Sundays, put on a woollen dress. Only Akulina still had her skirt always tucked up at the waist, and the porter could not bring himself to part with his sheepskin, even in the summer. Zahar, of course, was hopeless: he had his grey frock-coat turned into a jacket, and one could not tell what colour his trousers were or of what material his tie was made. He cleaned boots, slept, sat at the gate, looking dully at the few passers-by, or went to sit at the nearest general shop and did exactly the same things and in the same way as he had done before, first at Oblomovka and then in Gorohovy Street.

And Oblomov himself? Oblomov was the complete and natural embodiment and expression of the unruffled peace, quiet, and plenty around him. Thinking about his way of living and growing more and more used to it, he decided at last that there was nothing further for him to aim at, nothing further to seek, that he had attained his ideal of life, though it had not the poetic setting and radiance with which his imagination had once clothed his ideas of an easy and care-free existence in his native village among the peasants and house serfs. He considered his present life a continuation of that same Oblomovka existence, though the setting was different because of the place and the time. Here, too, as at Oblomovka, he succeeded in getting off cheaply, in making a good bargain with life and ensuring for himself undisturbed peace. He triumphed inwardly at having escaped life's persistent, painful claims and storms raging under the wide expanse of sky lit up by the lightnings of great joys and resounding with the thunder of great sorrows; where false hopes and magnificent phantoms of happiness are at play and man's own thought consumes and devours him; where passion destroys him and intellect triumphs or is defeated; where man is engaged in a continuous combat and leaves the battlefield wounded and exhausted, but still insatiate and discontented. Not having experienced the delights won by struggle, Oblomov mentally renounced them and felt at peace only in his out-of-the-way corner where there was no movement, struggle, or life. And if his imagination caught fire once more, if forgotten memories and unfulfilled dreams rose before him, if his conscience suddenly reproached him for the way he had spent his life – he slept badly, woke up in the night, jumped out of bed, and sometimes wept hopeless tears for his bright ideal of life, now gone for ever, as one weeps for the beloved dead with the bitter consciousness of not having done enough for them while they lived. Then he looked at his surroundings, tasted the transitory sweets of life, calmed down, watching dreamily the evening sun melt in the fiery afterglow; finally, he came to the conclusion that his life had not merely happened to be so simple and uneventful, but had been created and designed to be such, in order to demonstrate the ideally restful aspect of human existence. It was other people's lot, he thought, to express its tempestuous aspects, to set in motion the creative and destructive forces; everyone had his own appointed task! Such was the philosophy that the Plato from Oblomovka had arrived at and that lulled him to rest in the midst of the stern demands of duty and problems of human destiny! He had been born and brought up, not as a gladiator for the arena, but as a peaceful spectator of the battle; his timid and indolent soul would not have stood either the anxieties of happiness or the blows of Fate – therefore he was the expression just of one particular aspect of life, and it was no use struggling for something else, changing anything, or repenting. With years, agitation and remorse visited him less and less often, and he settled down slowly and gradually in the plain and wide coffin he had made of his existence, like ancient hermits who, turning away from life, dig their own graves. He gave up dreaming about arranging his estate and moving there with all his household. The steward put there by Stolz regularly sent him a very considerable income, before Christmas the peasants brought corn and provisions; abundance and gaiety reigned in the house. Ilya Ilyitch actually acquired a pair of horses, but, with characteristic caution, had selected slow, quiet ones that started only at the third blow of the whip; at the first and second blows, first one horse and then the other moved and took a step aside and only then, straining their necks, backs, and tails, they moved together and trotted along, nodding their heads. They took Vanya to the High School on the other side of the Neva and Agafya Matveyevna to do her shopping. During Carnival and Easter Week the whole family, including Ilya Ilyitch, went for a drive and to the fair; sometimes they took a box at the theatre and went there also all together. In the summer they drove out into the country, on St. Ilya's Friday they went to the Gunpowder Works, and life went on punctuated by the usual events and, one would like to say, bringing with it no destructive changes – were it true that its blows did not reach quiet little corners. Unfortunately, however, a thunder-clap that shakes the foundations of mountains and vast aerial spaces is also heard in the mouse-hole, less loudly and strongly, it is true, but yet very perceptibly.

Ilya Ilyitch enjoyed his food and ate good meals, as at Oblomovka, he walked and worked little and lazily, also as at Oblomovka. In spite of his growing years he drank wine and currant vodka without giving the matter a thought, and indulged in long after-dinner sleep. Suddenly all this was changed. One day, when he had had his midday rest, he wanted to get up from the sofa and could not, wanted to speak and his tongue would not obey him. Terrified, he merely waved his hand, signalling for help. Had he been living alone with Zahar he might have gone on signalling till the morning and died at last – which would not have been discovered till the following day; but Agafya Matveyevna's eye watched over him like Providence: she did not need intelligence, but only an intuition of the heart to tell her that Ilya Ilyitch was not well. No sooner had it dawned on her than Anissya was dispatched in a cab to fetch a doctor and Agafya Matveyevna put ice round his head and immediately produced from the special cupboard all the lotions and decoctions – all that habit and hearsay prompted her to use in the emergency. Even Zahar had succeeded meanwhile in putting on one of his boots and, not troubling about the other, helped the doctor, the landlady, and Anissya to wait on his master. The doctor bled Ilya Ilyitch, brought him to his senses, and then told him that he had had a stroke and must change his manner of life. Vodka, wine, beer, and coffee were forbidden him, except on few rare occasions, as well as meat and all rich and highly spiced dishes; he was to take exercise every day and sleep in moderation only at night. None of this would have been carried out without Agafya Matveyevna, but she managed to introduce the regime by making the whole household follow it, and by cunning and affection distracted Oblomov from being tempted by wine, rich pastry, and after-dinner sleep. The moment he dozed a chair fell in the room, just of itself, or old, good-for-nothing crockery was smashed noisily in the next room, or the children made such an uproar that one could not stand it! If this did not help, her gentle voice was heard: she called Ilya Ilyitch and asked him some question. The garden path was continued into the kitchen-garden and Ilya Ilyitch walked down it for two hours in the morning and in the evening. She walked with him, or if she could not, Vanya or Masha or our old friend Alexeyev, always ready to fall in with what was suggested to him.

Here was Ilya Ilyitch slowly walking down the path, leaning on Vanya's shoulder; Vanya, almost a youth by now, wearing a High-School uniform, could hardly control his quick, lively steps, trying to keep up with Ilya Ilyitch's walk. Oblomov had a slight difficulty in moving one of his legs after the stroke.

'Well, let's go in, Vanya!' he said. They set off towards the door. Agafya Matveyevna appeared in the doorway.

'Where are you going so soon?' she asked, not letting them in.

'So soon, indeed! We have walked twenty times up and down, and you know it is three hundred and fifty feet from here to the fence, so we have done over a mile.'

'How many times have you done?' she asked Vanya. He hesitated.

'None of your stories, mind you!' she threatened him,

looking into his eyes. 'I can tell at once! Remember, I won't let you go out on Sunday.'

'No, mother, we really did walk . . . some twelve times.'

'Ah, you rascal,' Oblomov said, 'you kept picking acacia pods, but I counted every time!'

'No, you had better walk a little longer; and besides, the fish soup isn't ready yet,' Agafya Matveyevna decided, shutting the door in their faces.

And so, willy-nilly, Oblomov counted another eight times and only then went indoors.

The fish soup was steaming on a big round table. Oblomov sat down in his usual place on the sofa by himself; to the right of him sat Agafya Matveyevna on a chair, and to the left a child of three on a high baby-chair. Next to the child was Masha, a girl of about thirteen by now, then Vanya and then, on this occasion, Alexeyev, who sat facing Oblomov.

'Wait a minute, I'll give you a carp, I have found such a fat one!' said Agafya Matveyevna, putting a carp on Oblomov's plate.

'A pie would go well with this!' Oblomov said.

'I forgot, I really forgot all about it! I had meant to last night, but it went completely out of my mind!' said Agafya Matveyevna artfully.

'And I forgot to cook any cabbage for your cutlets, Ivan Alexeyitch,' she added, turning to Alexeyev. 'Please forgive me.'

This was a ruse too.

'It's of no consequence; I can eat anything,' Alexeyev said.

'Why, indeed, don't you have some ham with green peas or a beefsteak cooked for him?' Oblomov asked. 'He likes it.'

'I've been to the shops myself, Ilya Ilyitch, I could find no good beef! But I had some cherry juice mould made for you: I know you like it,' she added, turning to Alexeyev.

The cherry mould could do no harm to Ilya Ilyitch, and so the obliging Alexeyev had to like it and eat it.

After dinner nothing and no one could prevent Oblomov from lying down. He generally lay down on his back on the sofa, where he had been sitting, not to sleep but merely to rest for an hour. To keep him awake Agafya Matveyevna poured out coffee in his presence, the children played on the rug, and Ilya Ilyitch could not help taking part in it all.

'Don't you tease Andryusha: he is going to cry in a minute!' he chid Vanya, who had been teasing the little boy.

'Mashenka, mind Andryusha does not knock himself against the chair!' he said solicitously, when the child crawled under a chair.

And Masha rushed to rescue her 'little brother,' as she called him.

All was quiet for a moment; Agafya Matveyevna went to the kitchen to see if the coffee was ready. The children were quiet. A sound of snoring was heard in the room, at first gentle and as it were muffled, then louder, and when she appeared with a steaming coffee-pot it was as loud as in a cabman's shelter. She shook her head reproachfully at Alexeyev. 'I did try to wake him, but he took no notice,' he said apologetically. She quickly put the coffee-pot down on the table, picked up Andryusha from the floor and quietly put him on Ilya Ilyitch's sofa. The child crawled along, reached Oblomov's face and seized him by the nose. 'Eh! What? Who is that?' said Ilya Ilyitch, waking up in alarm.

'You dozed off and Andryusha climbed on the sofa and wakened you,' Agafya Matveyevna said gently.

'When could I have dozed?' Oblomov protested, taking Andryusha in his arms. 'I heard him perfectly well crawling up to me on his little arms. I hear everything! Ah, you rogue: catching me by the nose! I'll give it you! You wait a bit!' he said, fondling and caressing the child. Then he put him down on the floor and gave a loud sigh.

'Tell me something, Ivan Alexeyitch!' he said.

'We have talked over everything, Ilya Ilyitch; there is nothing to tell,' he answered.

'Come, how can that be? You go to see people: perhaps there is some news? I suppose you read?'

'Yes, I do sometimes, or other people read and talk and I listen. Yesterday I was at Alexey Spiridonitch's and his son, a university student, read aloud. . . .'

'What did he read?'

'About the English, that they had brought rifles and gunpowder somewhere. Alexey Spiridonitch said there was going to be a war.'

'Where did they bring it to?'

'It was to Spain or to India, I don't remember, only the ambassador was very much displeased.'

'What ambassador?'

'That I have forgotten!' said Alexeyev, looking at the ceiling and trying to remember.

'But with whom is the war to be?'

'With a Turkish pasha, I believe.'

'Well, what other news is there in politics?' Ilya Ilyitch asked after a pause.

'They write that the earth is cooling down: one day it will freeze altogether.'

'That isn't politics, is it?' Oblomov said.

Alexeyev was taken aback.

'He first mentioned politics,' he said in self-defence, 'and then read straight on and didn't say when he had come to the end of it. I know that was literature, not politics.'

'And what did he read about literature?' Oblomov asked.

'Oh, he read that our very best writers were Dmitriev, Karamzin, Batyushkov, and Zhukovsky. . . .'

'What about Pushkin?'

'Pushkin wasn't mentioned. I, too, wondered why he wasn't. Surely he was a genius!' said Alexeyev, mispronouncing the word 'genius.'

There was a silence. Agafya Matveyevna brought her needlework and began plying the needle, glancing now and again at Ilya Ilyitch and Alexeyev and listening with

her keen ears if there was any noise or disorder anywhere, if Zahar was not quarrelling with Anissya in the
kitchen, if Akulina was washing up, if the yard gate had
creaked – that is, if the porter had gone out to have a
drink.

Oblomov slowly sank into silence and thoughtfulness.
He was neither asleep nor awake: he let his thoughts wander pleasantly at will without concentrating them on anything and calmly listened to the measured beating of his
heart, blinking occasionally like a man who is not looking
at anything in particular. He fell into a vague, mysterious
state, a kind of hallucination. There are rare and brief
moments when man seems to be living over again what he
has already lived through once at a different time and
place. He may have dreamed what is happening to him
now, or have lived through it before and forgotten it, but
he recognizes the same people sitting beside him once
more, hears words that have been spoken already;
imagination is powerless to re-create the scene, memory
does not bring up the past and merely makes one wonder.
This was how Oblomov felt at that moment. He was
wrapped in a stillness that he seemed to have experienced
before; the familiar pendulum was ticking, there was the
snapping of the thread bitten off; the familiar words were
repeated once more, and the whisper: 'I simply cannot
thread the needle; you come and do it for me, Masha,
your eyes are sharper!' Lazily, absentmindedly, almost
unconsciously, he looked into Agafya Matveyevna's face
and a familiar image he had seen somewhere arose from
the depths of his memory. He was trying to think where
he had heard all this. . . . He saw before him a big dark
drawing-room in his parents' house, lighted by a tallow
candle; his mother and her visitors sitting at the round
table; they were sewing in silence; his father paced up and
down the room in silence too. The past and the present
merged together. He was dreaming he had reached the
promised land flowing with milk and honey, where people
ate bread they had not earned and went clothed in gold

and silver. . . . He seemed to hear the tales of dreams and tokens, the rattle of crockery and the clatter of knives; he clung to his nurse, listening to her old shaky voice: 'Militrissa Kirbityevna,' she said, pointing to his landlady. It seemed to him that the same cloud as then was floating in the blue sky, the same wind was blowing in at the window and playing with his hair; the Oblomovka turkeycock was strutting by the windows and making a noise. Now a dog was barking: a visitor must have come. Perhaps it was Andrey and his father come from Verhlyovo? It was a day of joy for him. It must indeed be Andrey: the steps came nearer and nearer, the door opened. . . . 'Andrey!' he said. And indeed Andrey was before him, though no longer a boy, but a middle-aged man. Oblomov came to himself: Stolz real and actual was standing before him, not an hallucination, but a fact.

Agafya Matveyevna seized the baby, picked up her work from the table, and took the children away; Alexeyev disappeared too. Stolz and Oblomov were left alone, looking at each other without moving or speaking. Stolz seemed to pierce him with his eyes.

'Is it you, Andrey?' Oblomov asked in a voice stifled with emotion, as only a lover, after a long parting, can ask his sweetheart.

'It's me,' Andrey said softly. 'Are you alive and well?'

Oblomov threw his arms round him and pressed himself closely to him.

'Ah!' he brought out in answer, expressing in that long drawn-out '*Ah!*' all the intensity of the sorrow and gladness that had lain hidden in his heart from the time of their parting and never, perhaps, been roused by anyone or anything.

They sat down and once more looked intently at each other.

'Are you well?' Andrey asked.

'Yes, I am now, thank God.'

'Why, have you been ill?'

'Yes, Andrey, I have had a stroke. . . .'

'You don't mean it? How dreadful!' Andrey said with alarm and sympathy. 'But it has left no trace?'

'No, except that I can't freely use my left leg,' Oblomov answered.

'Ah, Ilya, Ilya! What has come over you? You have simply run to seed! What have you been doing all this time? It's no joke, we haven't seen each other for five years!'

Oblomov heaved a sigh.

'Why didn't you come to Oblomovka? Why haven't you written?'

'What am I to tell you, Andrey? You know me, and you mustn't ask!' Oblomov said sadly.

'And all the time here, in this flat?' Stolz said, looking round the room. 'You never moved?'

'No, I've lived here all the time. . . . I will never move now!'

'What, do you really mean it?'

'Yes, Andrey . . . I do.'

Stolz looked at him attentively and began thoughtfully pacing up and down the room.

'And Olga Sergeyevna, is she well? Where is she? Does she remember? . . .'

He broke off.

'She is well and remembers you as though you had parted only yesterday. I will tell you directly where she is.'

'And your children?'

'They are well too. . . . But I say, Ilya, you don't seriously mean that you are going to stay here? I have come for you, you know, to take you to us, to the country. . . .'

'No, no!' Oblomov replied, obviously alarmed, lowering his voice and glancing at the door. 'No, please don't say anything about it, don't talk of it!'

'Why? What is the matter with you?' Stolz began. 'You know me: I have set myself this task long ago and I won't give it up. Till now all sorts of business has kept me from it, but now I am free. You must live with us, near us:

Olga and I have made up our minds and so it shall be.
Thank Heaven that I have found you as you are and not
worse. I hadn't hoped. . . . Well, come along! . . . I am
ready to take you away by force: you must live differently,
you know how. . . .'

Oblomov listened impatiently to this tirade.

'Please don't shout, speak low!' he begged Stolz. 'They
may. . . .'

'What?'

'Hear you . . . my landlady may think that I really mean
to go away. . . .'

'Well, what of it? Let her!'

'Oh, no, that would never do! Listen, Andrey!' he
added suddenly, in a decisive tone Stolz had never heard
from him. 'It's useless your trying to persuade me: I shall
stay here.'

Stolz looked at his friend in surprise. Oblomov looked
at him calmly and decidedly.

'You are done for, Ilya!' he said. 'This house, this
woman . . . all this way of living. . . . It's impossible! Come
along, let's go!'

He seized him by the sleeve and pulled him towards
the door.

'Why do you want to take me away? Where to?' Oblomov asked, holding back.

'Out of this hole, this stagnation, into the world, into
the open, to normal healthy life!' Stolz insisted sternly,
almost imperatively. 'Where are you? What has become of
you? Come to your senses! Is this the kind of life you had
dreamed of, this sleeping like a mole in its burrow? Recall
everything. . . .'

'Don't remind me, don't disturb the past: you won't
bring it back!' Oblomov said, his face animated by
thought and decision, his mind perfectly clear. 'What do
you want to do with me? I have broken for ever with the
world into which you are dragging me; you cannot weld
together two separate halves. I have grown into this hole
bodily: if you try to pull me away – it will be my death.'

'But look about you: where are you, in what company?'

'I know, I feel it. . . . Ah, Andrey, I feel and understand it all: I have been for years ashamed to live in the world! But I cannot go the road you are going, even if I wanted to. . . . It might, perhaps, have been possible last time you were here. Now . . .' (he lowered his eyes and paused for a moment) 'it's too late . . . go and don't linger over me. God knows I deserve your friendship – but I am not worth your trouble.'

'No, Ilya, there's something you are keeping from me. But I certainly will carry you away, just because I suspect you. . . . Look here,' he said, 'put on some clothes and let us go to my place, spend the evening with me. I have a very great deal to tell you: you don't know what is on foot now. You haven't heard?'

Oblomov looked at him questioningly.

'I forgot, you never see people: come along, I'll tell you all about it. . . . Do you know who is waiting for me in the carriage at the gate? . . . I'll call her!'

'Olga!' Oblomov suddenly cried in alarm. He actually changed colour. 'For Heaven's sake don't let her come here, go away. Good-bye, good-bye, for God's sake!'

He was almost pushing his friend out, but Stolz did not stir.

'I cannot go to her without you: I've given her my word, do you hear, Ilya? If not to-day, then to-morrow – you will merely put me off, but not drive me away. . . . To-morrow or the day after we'll meet again!'

Oblomov bowed his head and said nothing, not daring to look at Stolz.

'When is it to be? Olga will ask me.'

'Oh, Andrey,' Oblomov said, in a tender, imploring voice, putting his head on Stolz's shoulder and embracing him, 'leave me altogether . . . forget me. . . .'

'What, for ever?' Stolz asked in surprise, disengaging himself from Oblomov's arms and looking him straight in the face.

'Yes!' Oblomov whispered.

Stolz stepped back from him.

'Is this you, Ilya?' he reproached him. 'You repulse me! And it's because of her, of that woman. . . . My God!' he almost shouted, as with sudden pain. 'The child that I saw here just now. . . . Ilya, Ilya! Escape from here, make haste, come away! How low you have fallen! This woman . . . what is she to you?'

'She is my wife!' Oblomov said calmly.

Stolz was dumbfounded.

'And this child is my son! He is called Andrey in memory of you!' Oblomov made an end of it and breathed freely, having unburdened himself of his secret.

Now it was Stolz who changed colour and looked round with bewildered, almost senseless eyes. 'The abyss' suddenly opened before him, 'the wall of stone' rose up and Oblomov seemed to be no longer there, he had disappeared, sunk through the ground, and Stolz was only conscious of the burning anguish a man feels when he hastens in excitement to see a friend from whom he had been parted and learns that the friend had long been dead.

'He is done for!' he whispered mechanically. 'What shall I say to Olga?'

Oblomov heard the last words, tried to say something and could not. He stretched out both arms to Andrey and they clasped each other closely in silence, as men do before a battle, before death. This embrace stifled their words, their tears, their feelings. . . .

'Don't forget my Andrey when I am gone!' Oblomov said brokenly as they parted.

Without speaking Stolz walked slowly out of the room, slowly and thoughtfully crossed the yard and stepped into the carriage, while Oblomov sat down on the sofa, leaned his elbows on the table and buried his face in his hands.

'No, I won't forget your Andrey!' Stolz was thinking sadly as he walked across the yard. 'You are done for, Ilya! It is no use telling you that your Oblomovka is no longer in the backwoods, that its turn has come and rays of sunshine have fallen upon it too! I won't tell you that in another four years there will be a station there, that your peasants will be working on the line and your corn will be carried by train to the river. . . . And then . . . schools, education . . . and beyond that. . . . No, you will be alarmed at the dawn of the new happiness, it will hurt your eyes used to darkness. But I will lead your Andrey to where you could not go . . . and with him I will carry out our youthful dreams. Good-bye, old Oblomovka,' he said, looking round for the last time at the windows of the little house, 'your day is passed!'

'What is it?' Olga asked with a beating heart.

'Nothing!' Andrey answered, abruptly and dryly.

'Is he alive and well?'

'Yes,' Andrey answered reluctantly.

'Why have you come back so soon? Why haven't you called me there or brought him? Let me go to him!'

'I can't!'

'What's happening there?' Olga asked anxiously. 'Has "the abyss" opened before you? Will you tell me?'

He said nothing.

'But what is going on there?'

'Oblomovism!' Andrey answered gloomily, and in spite of Olga's further questions he preserved a morose silence till they reached home.

X

FIVE years had passed. There had been many changes on the Vyborg side, as in the rest of the world: the empty street leading to Madame Pshenitsyn's house had summer villas built on either side of it, and among them was a long brick, official-looking building that kept sunshine from gaily pouring in at the windows of the quiet abode of peace and indolence. And the house itself had grown a little shabby and looked untidy and unkempt, like a man who has not washed and shaved. The paint had come off, some of the gutters were broken, and consequently there were pools of mud in the yard across which, as in the old days, a narrow plank was laid. When someone came in at the gate the dog did not jump vigorously on its chain, but barked hoarsely and lazily without coming out of its kennel. And the changes inside the house! Another woman was ruling over it, other children were at play. The red, battered face of the rowdy Tarantyev appeared there again from time to time, but the mild, gentle Alexeyev never came now. Neither Zahar nor Anissya was to be seen. A fat new cook was at work in the kitchen, rudely and reluctantly carrying out Agafya Matveyevna's quiet directions, and the same Akulina, her skirt tucked in at the waist, was washing troughs and milk-pans; the same sleepy porter in the same sheepskin was idly spending the remainder of his life in his little room. In the early morning and at dinner-time Ivan Matveyitch's figure again flitted past the lattice-worked fence with a big parcel under his arm and goloshes on his feet, summer and winter.

What had become of Oblomov? Where was he? Where? His body is resting under a modest urn with shrubs round it, in the quiet of the nearest churchyard. Branches of lilac, planted by a friendly hand, slumber over his grave, and the scent of wormwood rises in the still air. The angel of peace itself seems to be guarding his sleep. In spite of the keen watch that his loving wife kept over every moment of his existence, continual stillness, rest, and indolence slowly brought the mechanism of life to a halt. Ilya Ilyitch passed away apparently without pain, without agony, like a clock that stops because it hasn't been wound up. No one saw his last moments or heard his last groan. He had another apoplectic stroke a year after the first and again it left no trace: only Ilya Ilyitch grew weak and pale, ate little, seldom went into the garden, and became more and more silent and dreamy; at times he shed tears. He felt that death was near and was afraid of it. He had several fainting fits, but they passed off. One morning Agafya Matveyevna brought him his coffee as usual – and found him resting in death as gently as he had rested in sleep. Only his head had slightly moved off the pillow and his hand was convulsively pressed to his heart, where apparently the pain had centred and the circulation stopped.

Agafya Matveyevna had been a widow for three years; during that time everything had reverted to what it had been in the old days. Her brother had gone in for Government contracts, but lost his money, and succeeded, by means of various stratagems and entreaties, in obtaining his old job of secretary 'in the office where they registered peasants'; once more he walked to his office and brought home half-roubles, twenty- and twenty-five-copeck pieces, to put them away in a secret box. They had once more the plain and coarse but rich and plentiful fare, as in the days before Oblomov. The person of most importance in the house was Ivan Matveyitch's wife, Irina Panteleyevna – that is, she reserved for herself the right to get up late, to drink coffee three times a day and to change her dress as often, and to see to one thing only – that her petticoats should be starched as stiffly as possible. She did not go into anything else and Agafya Matveyevna was, as before, the living pendulum of the house: she saw to the cooking and the catering, poured out tea and coffee for the whole family, made their clothes, supervised the washing, looked after the children, Akulina, and the porter. But why did she do all this? She was Madame Oblomov, a landowner; she might have lived by herself, independently and in plenty. What could have made her take upon herself the burden of other people's housekeeping, of looking after other people's children and all those trifles to which a woman sacrifices herself either for love and the sacred duty of family ties or for the sake of a livelihood? Where are Zahar and Anissya, her servants by every right? Where is the living token left her by her husband, little Andryusha? Where are her children by her first marriage?

Her children are settled in life – that is, Vanya has finished his course of studies and is in a Government office, Masha has married the superintendent of some orphanage; and Andryusha has been given to Stolz and his wife to bring up, at their earnest request. Agafya Matveyevna had never thought of Andryusha's future as on the same level as her other children's, though in her heart she perhaps unconsciously gave an equal place to them all. There was for her all the difference in the world between Andryusha's education, manner of living and future, and the lives of Vanya and Masha.

'Those two are no more gentry than I am,' she said carelessly, 'they were born to rough it; and this one,' she added, almost with respect, caressing Andryusha cautiously if not timidly, 'this one is a little gentleman! See how fair his skin is, he is like a peach; what small hands and feet he has, and hair like silk! The image of his father!'

And so she agreed whole-heartedly and even with a certain joy when Stolz offered to adopt Andryusha; she believed his real place was there and not here, 'in low life,' with her dirty nephews, her brother's children.

For some six months after Oblomov's death she lived with Zahar and Anissya in the house, abandoning herself to grief. She trod a path to her husband's grave and wept her eyes out; took hardly any food and lived chiefly on tea; had sleepless nights and was completely worn out.

She never complained to anyone, and as time passed she seemed to concentrate in herself and her sorrow, confiding in no one, not even in Anissya. No one knew what was passing in her soul.

'Your mistress is still weeping for her husband!' the shopman from whom they bought provisions said to the cook. 'She is still sorrowing for her husband,' said the churchwarden, pointing her out to a crony in the cemetery church, where the inconsolable widow came every Sunday to weep and pray. 'She is still grieving,' they said in her brother's house.

One day the whole of her brother's family, the children, and even Tarantyev suddenly descended upon her, apparently on a visit of condolence. Commonplace consolations and admonitions 'to spare herself for the children's sake' were lavished upon her – all that had been said to her fifteen years ago when her first husband had died, and that had then produced the desired effect, but now, for some reason, made her feel disgusted and miserable. She was relieved when they changed the subject and told her that now they could all live together again, that it would be better for her 'to bear her sorrow among her own people,' and it would be very good for them, since no one could look after the house so well as she. She asked for time to think it over, then spent another two months grieving, and at last agreed to their proposal. At that time the Stolzes took Andryusha to live with them and she was left alone.

Dressed in a dark-coloured dress, with a black cashmere shawl round her neck, she walked from her room to the kitchen like a shadow, opened and closed cupboards as before, did needlework, ironed lace, but slowly, without energy; she spoke, as it were, reluctantly, in a low voice, and instead of glancing about her, as in the old days, with unconcern, her eyes shifting from object to object, she had a look of concentration and there was a hidden thought in her eyes. This thought seemed to have imperceptibly settled on her face at the moment when she gazed intently and with full understanding at her husband's dead face, and since then it never left her. She moved about the house, did with her hands all that needed doing; but her mind had no part in it. Over her husband's dead body she seemed suddenly to have grasped the meaning of her life and pondered over it – and ever since the thought had remained like a shadow on her face. When the acute sorrow had spent itself in tears she concentrated on the sense of her loss: everything else was dead for her – except little Andryusha. It was only when she saw him that she showed signs of life; her features revived, her eyes filled with the light of joy and then with the tears of remembrance. She was a stranger to all that happened around her: if her brother was angry because an extra rouble had been spent, or the meat was overdone or the fish not quite fresh; if her sister-in-law sulked because her skirts had not been starched enough or her tea was cold and weak; if the fat cook was rude – Agafya Matveyevna noticed nothing, as though they were not talking of her and never heard their sarcastic whisper, 'A lady, a land-owner!' She met it all with the dignity of her grief and a proud silence. But at Christmas-time, or on Easter Sunday or on a gay carnival evening, when everyone in the house was eating and drinking, singing, and making merry, she would suddenly burst into tears among the general rejoicing and hide herself in her corner. Then she would withdraw into herself again and sometimes, indeed, look at her brother and his wife with compassion and, as it were, with pride. She felt that her life had had its music and radiance; that God had breathed a soul into it and taken it away; that the sun had brought light into it and was darkened for ever. . . . For ever, it is true; but her life had gained a meaning for ever too: she knew now why she had lived and knew that she had not lived in vain.

She had loved so much and so completely: she had loved Oblomov as lover, as husband, as a superior being; but, as before, she could never tell this to anyone. And no one around her would have understood her. Where would

she have found the language? There were no such words
in her brother's or her sister-in-law's or Tarantyev's vocabulary, because there were no ideas of the sort; Ilya
Ilyitch alone would have understood her, but she had
never told him because at that time she did not understand it herself and did not know how to say it. As the
years went by she understood her past better and better
and hid it more deeply, growing more and more silent and
reserved. Her whole life was bathed in the gentle radiance
of the seven years that had flown by like a moment, and
there was nothing more for her to desire, nowhere further
to go. Only when Stolz came to Petersburg for the winter
she ran to his house and looked greedily at Andryusha,
caressing him with timid tenderness; she wanted to say
something to Andrey Ivanitch, to thank him, to lay before
him all that was pent up in her heart and lived there
always: he would have understood, but she did not know
how to say it; she merely rushed to Olga, pressed her
hands to her lips and burst into such a flood of scalding
tears that Olga could not help weeping with her too, and
Andrey, deeply moved, made haste to leave the room.
They were all bound by the same feeling, by the same
memory of the pure soul of their dead friend. They tried
to persuade her to go to the country with them and live
together, to be near Andryusha, but she always answered,
'Where one has been born and lived, there one must die.'
It was in vain Stolz accounted to her for the estate management and sent to her the income due to her: she
returned it all, asking him to keep it for Andryusha: 'It
isn't mine, it's his,' she repeated obstinately. 'He will
need it, he is a gentleman, and I can get on without.'

XI

TWO gentlemen were walking along a street on the Vyborg side one midday; a carriage slowly followed them. One of them was Stolz and the other a friend of his, a writer, a stout, apathetic-looking man with dreamy and, as it were, sleepy eyes. They reached a church; Mass was over and people were pouring into the street; beggars had come out first.

'I should like to know, where do beggars come from?' said the writer, looking at the beggars.

'Where from? Why, they crawl out of all sorts of nooks and crevices. . . .'

'I don't mean that,' the writer answered. 'I want to know, how does one become a beggar, how does one come to that position? Does it happen suddenly or gradually, is it false or genuine?'

'Why do you want to know? Are you thinking of writing *Mystères de Pétersbourg*?'

'Perhaps . . .' the writer answered, yawning lazily.

'Well, here's your opportunity: ask any one of them. For a silver rouble he will sell you all his history and you can write it down and resell it at a profit. Here's an old man that looks the most usual type of beggar. Hey, old man! Come here!'

The old man turned in answer to the call, took off his cap and walked up to them.

'Kind gentleman,' he hissed, 'help a poor old soldier wounded in thirty battles! . . .'

'Zahar!' Stolz said in surprise. 'Is that you?'

Zahar stopped suddenly and, screening his eyes from the sun with his hand, looked attentively at Stolz.

'Excuse me, Your Excellency, I don't recognize you . . . I am almost blind!'

'You've forgotten Stolz, your master's friend!' Stolz said reproachfully.

'Goodness me! Andrey Ivanitch, sir! I must be blind indeed! Dear father, kind sir!'

He tried in a flurry to catch Stolz's hand, and, not succeeding, kissed the skirt of his coat.

'To think the Lord has sent such a joy to a miserable cur like me!' he shouted, and one could not tell if he was weeping or laughing. All his face, from forehead to chin, seemed to have been branded with purple and the nose had a bluish tint as well. He was quite bald; his whiskers were as big as before, but tangled into a mat and looked as though a lump of snow had been put into each. He wore an ancient and completely faded overcoat torn on one side, old broken-down goloshes on his bare feet, and he held a worn fur cap in his hands.

'Well, well! The Lord has indeed done me a favour this morning, as though on purpose for the feast-day. . . .'

'How is it you are in such a state? Why, aren't you ashamed?' Stolz asked sternly.

'Ah, Andrey Ivanitch, sir! What was I to do?' Zahar began with a heavy sigh. 'I had to live. While Anissya was alive I wasn't a vagabond and had enough to eat, but when she died during the cholera – God rest her soul! – the mistress's brother wouldn't keep me any longer, said I ate the bread of idleness, and Mihey Andreyitch Tarantyev always tried to kick me from behind, if I walked past him: my life wasn't worth living! The abuse I had to bear! Would you believe it, sir, I was quite off my food! Had it not been for the mistress – God bless her!' – Zahar added, 'I should have perished in the frost long ago. She gives me clothes for the winter and as much bread as I want, and in her kindness she gave me a corner on the stove, but they began nagging at her, too, because of me, so I simply walked out of the house! I've been homeless for the last two years. . . .'

'Why didn't you take a job?' Stolz asked.

'Where can one get a job nowadays, Andrey Ivanitch, sir? I did try two posts, but I didn't suit. It's all different now, not as it used to be; it's much worse. A footman must be able to read and write, and fine gentlemen don't have their halls crammed full of servants as in the old days. They keep one, or at most two, valets. They take off their boots themselves: some sort of machine has been invented!' Zahar went on despondently. 'It's a shame and disgrace, there will soon be no gentry left!'

He heaved a sigh.

'I had a job with a German merchant, to sit in the hall; all went well, but he sent me to wait at the table – as though it were my business! One day I carried some crockery, Bohemian ware, I believe it was called, and the floors were smooth and slippery, damnation take them! My feet suddenly slided apart and the whole of the crockery and the tray went bang on the floor, so they dismissed me. Another time an old countess liked the look of me. "He seems respectable," she said, and engaged me as hall porter. It's a good old-fashioned sort of job: all you have to do is to look important as you sit there, your legs crossed and swinging one foot, and if anyone comes you mustn't answer them at once, but first give a growl and then let them in or kick them out, as the case may be; and if nice visitors come, you must, of course, salute them with your staff, like this.' Zahar showed it with his arm. 'It's a pleasant job, there's no denying! But the lady was so difficult to please, bless her! One day she looked into my room, saw a bug, and made such a to-do – as though it was I who invented bugs! You can't have a house without bugs. Another time she walked past me and fancied that I smelt of drink . . . a very trying lady! And so she dismissed me.'

'You certainly do smell of it and very much so!' Stolz remarked.

'It's through trouble, Andrey Ivanitch, sir, that's all it is!' Zahar hissed, wrinkling up his face bitterly. 'I did try, too, being a cab-driver and hired myself out for it, but I had my feet frozen: I haven't much strength left, I am old! My horse was a regular devil; once it threw itself under a carriage and very nearly did for me, and another time I ran over an old woman and was taken to the police station. . . .'

'There, now, don't drink and be a tramp; come to me, I will give you a home and we'll go to the country together – do you hear?'

'I hear, Andrey Ivanitch, sir, but. . . .'

He sighed.

'I don't want to go away from here, from his grave, I mean! Our dear master, Ilya Ilyitch, you know . . .' he cried. 'I've been praying for him again to-day, the King-dom of Heaven be his! To think that the Lord should have taken such a man from us! He was a joy to all, he ought to have lived a hundred years . . .' said Zahar, sob-bing and wrinkling up his face. 'I've been to his grave to-day; whenever I come to these parts I go there; I sit down and cry and cry. . . . Sometimes I lose myself think-ing, it is so still around, and suddenly I fancy he is calling me, "Zahar, Zahar!" and a shudder runs down my back! We shall never have another such master! And how fond he was of you – may the Lord remember his dear soul in His kingdom!'

'Well, come and have a look at Andryusha; I'll tell them to give you some dinner and decent clothes and then you can do as you like!' said Stolz, giving him some money.

'I'll come: I must come and look at Andrey Ilyitch! I expect he is quite grown up now! Goodness me! What a joy the Lord has sent me! I'll come, my dear, God give you health and years without number . . .' Zahar muttered, as the carriage drove away.

'Well, have you heard this beggar's story?' Stolz asked his friend.

'And who is this Ilya Ilyitch he mentioned?' the writer asked.

'Oblomov: I have often spoken to you about him.'

'Yes, I remember the name: he was your friend and school-fellow. What became of him?'

'He is dead, and how he was wasted!'

Stolz sighed and sank into thought.

'And he was as intelligent as other people, his soul was pure and clear as crystal; he was noble and affectionate – and yet he did nothing!'

'But why? What was the reason?'

'The reason . . . what reason was there? Oblomovism!' Stolz said.

'Oblomovism?' the writer repeated in perplexity. 'What's that?'

'I'll tell you directly: let me collect my thoughts and memories. And you write it down: it may be of use to someone.'

And he told him what is written here.